HISTORIES

To the Reader.

This Figure, that thou here seest put,
It was for gentle Shakespeare cut;
Wherein the Grauer had a strife
with Nature, to out-doo the life:
O, could he but haue drawne his wit
As well in brasse, as he hath hit
His face; the Print would then surpasse
All, that vvas euer vvrit in brasse.
But, since he cannot, Reader, looke
Not on his Picture, but his Booke.

B. I.

Mr. WILLIAM

SHAKESPEARES

COMEDIES, HISTORIES, & TRAGEDIES.

Publiſhed according to the True Originall Copies.

LONDON

Printed by Iſaac Iaggard, and Ed. Blount. 1623.

ISBN 978-0-557-01164-3

TO THE MOST NOBLE AND INCOMPARABLE PAIRE OF BRETHREN.

WILLIAM
Earle of Pembroke, &c. Lord Chamberlaine to the *Kings moſt Excellent Maieſty.*

AND

PHILIP
Earle of Montgomery, &c. Gentleman of his Maieſties Bed-Chamber. Both Knights of the moſt Noble Order of the Garter, and our ſingular good
LORDS.

Right Honourable,

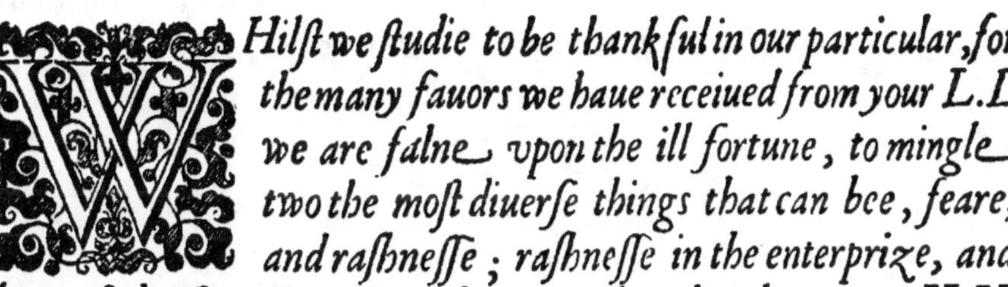

Hilſt we ſtudie to be thankful in our particular, for the many fauors we haue receiued from your L.L. we are falne vpon the ill fortune, to mingle two the moſt diuerſe things that can bee, feare, and raſhneſſe; raſhneſſe in the enterprize, and feare of the ſucceſſe. For, when we valew the places your H.H. ſuſtaine, we cannot but know their dignity greater, then to deſcend to the reading of theſe trifles: and, while we name them trifles, we haue depriu'd our ſelues of the defence of our Dedication. But ſince your L.L. haue beene pleas'd to thinke theſe trifles ſome-thing, heeretofore; and haue proſequuted both them, and their Authour liuing, with ſo much fauour: we hope, that (they out-liuing him, and he not hauing the fate, common with ſome, to be exequutor to his owne writings) you will vſe the like indulgence toward them, you haue done

vnto their parent. There is a great difference, whether any Booke choose his Patrones, or finde them: This hath done both. For, so much were your L L. likings of the seuerall parts, when they were acted, as before they were published, the Volume ask'd to be yours. We haue but collected them, and done an office to the dead, to procure his Orphanes, Guardians; without ambition either of selfe-profit, or fame: onely to keepe the memory of so worthy a Friend, & Fellow aliue, as was our SHAKESPEARE, *by humble offer of his playes, to your most noble patronage. Wherein, as we haue iustly obserued, no man to come neere your L.L. but with a kind of religious addresse; it hath bin the height of our care, who are the Presenters, to make the present worthy of your H.H. by the perfection. But, there we must also craue our abilities to be considerd, my Lords. We cannot go beyond our owne powers. Country hands reach foorth milke, creame, fruites, or what they haue: and many Nations (we haue heard) that had not gummes & incense, obtained their requests with a leauened Cake. It was no fault to approch their Gods, by what meanes they could: And the most, though meanest, of things are made more precious, when they are dedicated to Temples. In that name therefore, we most humbly consecrate to your H.H. these remaines of your seruant* Shakespeare; *that what delight is in them, may be euer your L.L. the reputation his, & the faults ours, if any be committed, by a payre so carefull to shew their gratitude both to the liuing, and the dead, as is*

Your Lordshippes most bounden,

IOHN HEMINGE.
HENRY CONDELL.

To the great Variety of Readers.

Rom the most able, to him that can but spell: There you are number'd. We had rather you were weighd. Especially, when the fate of all Bookes depends vp on your capacities: and not of your heads alone, but of your purses. Well! It is now publique, & you wil stand for your priuiledges wee know: to read, and censure. Do so, but buy it first. That doth best commend a Booke, the Stationer saies. Then, how odde soeuer your braines be, or your wisedomes, make your licence the same, and spare not. Iudge your sixe-pen'orth, your shillings worth, your fiue shillings worth at a time, or higher, so you rise to the iust rates, and welcome. But, what euer you do, Buy. Censure will not driue a Trade, or make the Iacke go. And though you be a Magistrate of wit, and sit on the Stage at *Black-Friers*, or the *Cock-pit*, to arraigne Playes dailie, know, these Playes haue had their triall alreadie, and stood out all Appeales; and do now come forth quitted rather by a Decree of Court, then any purchas'd Letters of commendation.

It had bene a thing, we confesse, worthie to haue bene wished, that the Author himselfe had liu'd to haue set forth, and ouerseen his owne writings; But since it hath bin ordain'd otherwise, and he by death departed from that right, we pray you do not envie his Friends, the office of their care, and paine, to haue collected & publish'd them; and so to haue publish'd them, as where (before) you were abus'd with diuerse stolne, and surreptitious copies, maimed, and deformed by the frauds and stealthes of iniurious impostors, that expos'd them: euen those, are now offer'd to your view cur'd, and perfect of their limbes; and all the rest, absolute in their numbers, as he conceiued the. Who, as he was a happie imitator of Nature, was a most gentle expresser of it. His mind and hand went together: And what he thought, he vttered with that easinesse, that wee haue scarse receiued from him a blot in his papers. But it is not our prouince, who onely gather his works, and giue them you, to praise him. It is yours that reade him. And there we hope, to your diuers capacities, you will finde enough, both to draw, and hold you: for his wit can no more lie hid, then it could be lost. Reade him, therefore; and againe, and againe: And if then you doe not like him, surely you are in some manifest danger, not to vnderstand him. And so we leaue you to other of his Friends, whom if you need, can bee your guides: if you neede them not, you can leade your selues, and others. And such Readers we wish him.

John Heminge.
Henrie Condell.

To the memory of my beloued, The AVTHOR Mr. William Shakespeare: And what he hath left vs.

*To draw no enuy (*Shakespeare*) on thy name,*
Am I thus ample to thy Booke, and Fame:
While I confesse thy writings to be such,
As neither Man, *nor* Muse, *can praise too much.*
'Tis true, and all mens suffrage. But these wayes
Were not the paths I meant vnto thy praise:
For seeliest Ignorance on these may light,
Which, when it sounds at best, but eccho's right;
Or blinde Affection, which doth ne're aduance
The truth, but gropes, and vrgeth all by chance;
Or crafty Malice, might pretend this praise,
And thinke to ruine, where it seem'd to raise.
These are, as some infamous Baud, or Whore,
Should praise a Matron. What could hurt her more?
But thou art proofe against them, and indeed
Aboue th'ill fortune of them, or the need.
I, therefore will begin. Soule of the Age!
The applause! delight! the wonder of our Stage!
My Shakespeare, *rise; I will not lodge thee by*
Chaucer, *or* Spenser, *or bid* Beaumont *lye*
A little further, to make thee a roome:
Thou art a Moniment, without a tombe,
And art aliue still, while thy Booke doth liue,
And we haue wits to read, and praise to giue.
That I not mixe thee so, my braine excuses;
I meane with great, but disproportion'd Muses:
For, if I thought my iudgement were of yeeres,
I should commit thee surely with thy peeres,
And tell, how farre thou didstst our Lily *out-shine,*
Or sporting Kid, *or* Marlowes *mighty line.*
And though thou hadst small Latine, *and lesse* Greeke,
From thence to honour thee, I would not seeke
For names; but call forth thund'ring Æschilus,
Euripides, *and* Sophocles *to vs,*
Paccuuius, Accius, *him of* Cordoua *dead,*
To life againe, to heare thy Buskin tread,
And shake a Stage: Or, when thy Sockes were on,
Leaue thee alone, for the comparison

of

Of all, that insolent Greece, *or haughtie* Rome
sent forth, or since did from their ashes come.
Triumph, my Britaine, *thou hast one to showe,*
To whom all Scenes of Europe *homage owe.*
He was not of an age, but for all time!
And all the Muses *still were in their prime,*
when like Apollo *he came forth to warme*
Our eares, or like a Mercury *to charme!*
Nature her selfe was proud of his designes,
And ioy'd to weare the dressing of his lines!
Which were so richly spun, and wouen so fit,
As, since, she will vouchsafe no other Wit.
The merry Greeke, *tart* Aristophanes,
Neat Terence, *witty* Plautus, *now not please;*
But antiquated, and deserted lye
As they were not of Natures family.
Yet must I not giue Nature all: Thy Art,
My gentle Shakespeare, *must enioy a part.*
For though the Poets *matter, Nature be,*
His Art doth giue the fashion. And, that he,
Who casts to write a liuing line, must sweat,
(such as thine are) and strike the second heat
Vpon the Muses *anuile: turne the same,*
(And himselfe with it) that he thinkes to frame;
Or for the lawrell, he may gaine a scorne,
For a good Poet's *made, as well as borne.*
And such wert thou. Looke how the fathers face
Liues in his issue, euen so, the race
Of Shakespeares *minde, and manners brightly shines*
In his well torned, and true-filed lines:
In each of which, he seemes to shake a Lance,
As brandish't at the eyes of Ignorance.
Sweet Swan of Auon! *what a sight it were*
To see thee in our waters yet appeare,
And make those flights vpon the bankes of Thames,
That so did take Eliza, *and our* Iames!
But stay, I see thee in the Hemisphere
Aduanc'd, and made a Constellation there!
Shine forth, thou Starre of Poets, *and with rage,*
Or influence, chide, or cheere the drooping Stage;
Which, since thy flight frō hence, hath mourn'd like night,
And despaires day, but for thy Volumes light.

BEN: IONSON.

Vpon the Lines and Life of the Famous Scenicke Poet, Master VVilliam Shakespeare.

THose hands, which you ſo clapt, go now, and wring
You *Britaines* braue; for done are *Shakeſpeares* dayes:
His dayes are done, that made the dainty Playes,
Which made the Globe of heau'n and earth to ring.
Dry'de is that veine, dry'd is the *Theſpian* Spring,
Turn'd all to teares, and *Phœbus* clouds his rayes:
That corp's, that coffin now beſticke thoſe bayes,
Which crown'd him *Poet* firſt, then *Poets* King.
If *Tragedies* might any *Prologue* haue,
All thoſe he made, would ſcarſe make one to this:
Where *Fame*, now that he gone is to the graue
(Deaths publique tyring-houſe) the *Nuncius* is.
For though his line of life went ſoone about,
The life yet of his lines ſhall neuer out.

HVGH HOLLAND.

A CATALOGVE

of the seuerall Comedies, Histories, and Tragedies contained in this Volume.

COMEDIES.

HISTORIES.

TRAGEDIES.

TO THE MEMORIE

of the deceaſed Authour Maiſter W. SHAKESPEARE.

SHake-ſpeare, *at length thy pious fellowes giue*
The world thy Workes: thy Workes, by which, out-liue
Thy Tombe, thy name muſt · when that ſtone is rent,
And Time diſſolues thy Stratford *Moniment,*
Here we aliue ſhall view thee ſtill. This Booke,
When Braſſe and Marble fade, ſhall make thee looke
Freſh to all Ages: when Poſteritie
Shall loath what's new, thinke all is prodegie
That is not Shake-ſpeares; *eu'ry Line, each Verſe*
Here ſhall reuiue, redeeme thee from thy Herſe.
Nor Fire, nor cankring Age, as Naſo *ſaid,*
Of his, thy wit-fraught Booke ſhall once inuade.
Nor ſhall I e're beleeue, or thinke thee dead
(Though miſt) vntill our bankrout Stage be ſped
(Impoſsible) with ſome new ſtraine t'out-do
Paſsions of Iuliet, *and her* Romeo;
Or till I heare a Scene more nobly take,
Then when thy half-Sword parlying Romans *ſpake.*
Till theſe, till any of thy Volumes reſt
Shall with more fire, more feeling be expreſt,
Be ſure, our Shake-ſpeare, *thou canſt neuer dye,*
But crown'd with Lawrell, liue eternally.

L. Digges.

To the memorie of M. *W. Shake-ſpeare.*

VVEE *wondred* (Shake-ſpeare) *that thou went'ſt ſo ſoone*
From the Worlds-Stage, to the Graues-Tyring-roome.
Wee thought thee dead, but this thy printed worth,
Tels thy Spectators, that thou went'ſt but forth
To enter with applauſe. An Actors Art,
Can dye, and liue, to acte a ſecond part.
That's but an Exit *of Mortalitie;*
This, a Re-entrance to a Plaudite.

I. M.

TO THE MEMORIE
of the deceased Authour Maister
W. SHAKESPEARE.

[illegible]

To the memorie of M. W. Shake-speare.

[illegible]

I. M.

The Workes of William Shakeſpeare, containing all his Comedies, Hiſtories, and Tragedies: Truely ſet forth, according to their firſt ORIGINALL.

The Names of the Principall Actors in all theſe Playes.

*Illiam Shakeſpeare.*

Richard Burbadge.

John Hemmings.

Auguſtine Phillips.

William Kempt.

Thomas Poope.

George Bryan.

Henry Condell.

William Slye.

Richard Cowly.

John Lowine.

Samuell Croſſe.

Alexander Cooke.

Samuel Gilburne.

Robert Armin.

William Oſtler.

Nathan Field.

John Underwood.

Nicholas Tooley.

William Eccleſtone.

Joſeph Taylor.

Robert Benfield.

Robert Goughe.

Richard Robinſon.

Iohn Shancke.

Iohn Rice.

HISTORIES

The life and death of King Iohn.

Actus Primus, Scæna Prima.

Enter King Iohn, Queene Elinor, Pembroke, Essex, and Salisbury, with the Chattylion of France.

King Iohn.
Now say *Chatillion*, what would *France* with vs ?
Chat. Thus (after greeting) speakes the King of France,
In my behauiour to the Maiesty,
The borrowed Maiesty of *England* heere.
Elea. A strange beginning : borrowed Maiesty ?
K.Iohn. Silence (good mother) heare the Embassie.
Chat. *Philip* of *France*, in right and true behalfe
Of thy deceased brother, *Geffreyes* sonne,
Arthur Plantaginet, laies most lawfull claime
To this faire Iland, and the Territories:
To *Ireland*, *Poyctiers*, *Aniowe*, *Torayne*, *Maine*,
Desiring thee to lay aside the sword
Which swaies vsurpingly these seuerall titles,
And put the same into yong *Arthurs* hand,
Thy Nephew, and right royall Soueraigne.
K. Iohn. What followes if we disallow of this ?
Chat. The proud controle of fierce and bloudy warre,
To inforce these rights, so forcibly with-held,
K.Io. Heere haue we war for war, & bloud for bloud,
Controlement for controlement: so answer *France*.
Chat. Then take my Kings defiance from my mouth,
The farthest limit of my Embassie.
K. Iohn. Beare mine to him, and so depart in peace,
Be thou as lightning in the eies of *France* ;
For ere thou canst report, I will be there:
The thunder of my Cannon shall be heard.
So hence : be thou the trumpet of our wrath,
And sullen presage of your owne decay:
An honourable conduct let him haue,
Pembroke looke too't : farewell *Chattillion*.
Exit Chat. and Pem.
Ele. What now my sonne, haue I not euer said
How that ambitious *Constance* would not cease
Till she had kindled *France* and all the world,
Vpon the right and party of her sonne.
This might haue beene preuented, and made whole
With very easie arguments of loue,
Which now the mannage of two kingdomes must
With fearefull bloudy issue arbitrate.
K.Iohn. Our strong possession, and our right for vs.
Eli. Your strong possessiõ much more then your right,
Or else it must go wrong with you and me,
So much my conscience whispers in your eare,
Which none but heauen, and you, and I, shall heare.
Enter a Sheriffe.
Essex. My Liege, here is the strangest controuersie
Come from the Country to be iudg'd by you
That ere I heard : shall I produce the men ?
K.Iohn. Let them approach :
Our Abbies and our Priories shall pay
This expeditious charge : what men are you ?
Enter Robert Faulconbridge, and Philip.
Philip. Your faithfull subiect, I a gentleman,
Borne in *Northamptonshire*, and eldest sonne
As I suppose, to *Robert Faulconbridge*,
A Souldier by the Honor-giuing-hand
Of *Cordelion*, Knighted in the field.
K.Iohn. What art thou ?
Robert. The son and heire to that same *Faulconbridge*.
K.Iohn. Is that the elder, and art thou the heyre ?
You came not of one mother then it seemes.
Philip. Most certain of one mother, mighty King,
That is well knowne, and as I thinke one father :
But for the certaine knowledge of that truth,
I put you o're to heauen, and to my mother ;
Of that I doubt, as all mens children may.
Eli. Out on thee rude man, ŷ dost shame thy mother,
And wound her honor with this diffidence.
Phil. I Madame ? No, I haue no reason for it,
That is my brothers plea, and none of mine,
The which if he can proue, a pops me out,
At least from faire fiue hundred pound a yeere :
Heauen guard my mothers honor, and my Land.
K.Iohn. A good blunt fellow: why being yonger born
Doth he lay claime to thine inheritance ?
Phil. I know not why, except to get the land :
But once he slanderd me with bastardy :
But where I be as true begot or no,
That still I lay vpon my mothers head,
But that I am as well begot my Liege
(Faire fall the bones that tooke the paines for me)
Compare our faces, and be Iudge your selfe
If old Sir *Robert* did beget vs both,
And were our father, and this sonne like him :
O old sir *Robert* Father, on my knee
I giue heauen thankes I was not like to thee.
K.Iohn. Why what a mad-cap hath heauen lent vs here?
Elen. He hath a tricke of *Cordelions* face,
The accent of his tongue affecteth him :
Doe you not read some tokens of my sonne
In the large composition of this man ?

K.Iohn. Mine eye hath well examined his parts,
And findes them perfect *Richard*: sirra speake,
What doth moue you to claime your brothers land.
Philip. Because he hath a half-face like my father?
With halfe that face would he haue all my land,
A halfe-fac'd groat, fiue hundred pound a yeere?
Rob. My gracious Liege, when that my father liu'd,
Your brother did imploy my father much.
Phil. Well sir, by this you cannot get my land,
Your tale must be how he employ'd my mother.
Rob. And once dispatch'd him in an Embassie
To *Germany*, there with the Emperor
To treat of high affaires touching that time:
Th'aduantage of his absence tooke the King,
And in the meane time soiourn'd at my fathers;
Where how he did preuaile, I shame to speake:
But truth is truth, large lengths of seas and shores
Betweene my father, and my mother lay,
As I haue heard my father speake himselfe
When this same lusty gentleman was got:
Vpon his death bed he by will bequeath'd
His lands to me, and tooke it on his death
That this my mothers sonne was none of his;
And if he were, he came into the world
Full fourteene weekes before the course of time:
Then good my Liedge let me haue what is mine,
My fathers land, as was my fathers will.
K.Iohn. Sirra, your brother is Legittimate,
Your fathers wife did after wedlocke beare him:
And if she did play false, the fault was hers,
Which fault lyes on the hazards of all husbands
That marry wiues: tell me, how if my brother
Who as you say, tooke paines to get this sonne,
Had of your father claim'd this sonne for his,
Insooth, good friend, your father might haue kept
This Calfe, bred from his Cow from all the world:
Insooth he might: then if he were my brothers,
My brother might not claime him, nor your father
Being none of his, refuse him: this concludes,
My mothers sonne did get your fathers heyre,
Your fathers heyre must haue your fathers land.
Rob. Shal then my fathers Will be of no force,
To dispossesse that childe which is not his.
Phil. Of no more force to dispossesse me sir,
Then was his will to get me, as I think.
Eli. Whether hadst thou rather be a *Faulconbridge*,
And like thy brother to enioy thy land:
Or the reputed sonne of *Cordelion*,
Lord of thy presence, and no land beside.
Bast. Madam, and if my brother had my shape
And I had his, sir *Roberts* his like him,
And if my legs were two such riding rods,
My armes, such eele skins stuft, my face so thin,
That in mine eare I durst not sticke a rose,
Lest men should say, looke where three farthings goes,
And to his shape were heyre to all this land,
Would I might neuer stirre from off this place,
I would giue it euery foot to haue this face:
It would not be sir nobbe in any case.
Elinor. I like thee well: wilt thou forsake thy fortune,
Bequeath thy land to him, and follow me?
I am a Souldier, and now bound to *France*.
Bast. Brother, take you my land, Ile take my chance;
Your face hath got fiue hundred pound a yeere,
Yet sell your face for fiue pence and 'tis deere:
Madam, Ile follow you vnto the death.
Elinor. Nay, I would haue you go before me thither.
Bast. Our Country manners giue our betters way.
K.Iohn. What is thy name?
Bast. *Philip* my Liege, so is my name begun,
Philip, good old Sir *Roberts* wiues eldest sonne.
K.Iohn. From henceforth beare his name
Whose forme thou bearest:
Kneele thou downe *Philip*, but rise more great,
Arise Sir *Richard*, and *Plantagenet*.
Bast. Brother by th'mothers side, giue me your hand,
My father gaue me honor, yours gaue land:
Now blessed be the houre by night or day
When I was got, Sir *Robert* was away.
Ele. The very spirit of *Plantaginet*:
I am thy grandame *Richard*, call me so.
Bast. Madam by chance, but not by truth, what tho;
Something about a little from the right,
In at the window, or else ore the hatch:
Who dares not stirre by day, must walke by night,
And haue is haue, how euer men doe catch:
Neere or farre off, well wonne is still well shot,
And I am I, how ere I was begot.
K.Iohn. Goe, *Faulconbridge*, now hast thou thy desire,
A landlesse Knight, makes thee a landed Squire:
Come Madam, and come *Richard*, we must speed
For *France*, for *France*, for it is more then need.
Bast. Brother adieu, good fortune come to thee,
For thou wast got i'th way of honesty.
Exeunt all but bastard.

Bast. A foot of Honor better then I was,
But many a many foot of Land the worse.
Well, now can I make any *Ioane* a Lady,
Good den Sir *Richard*, Godamercy fellow,
And if his name be *George*, Ile call him *Peter*;
For new made honor doth forget mens names:
'Tis two respectiue, and too sociable
For your conuersion, now your traueller,
Hee and his tooth-picke at my worships messe,
And when my knightly stomacke is suffis'd,
Why then I sucke my teeth, and catechize
My picked man of Countries: my deare sir,
Thus leaning on mine elbow I begin,
I shall beseech you; that is question now,
And then comes answer like an Absey booke:
O sir, sayes answer, at your best command,
At your employment, at your seruice sir:
No sir, saies question, I sweet sir at yours,
And so ere answer knowes what question would,
Sauing in Dialogue of Complement,
And talking of the Alpes and Appenines,
The Perennean and the riuer *Poe*,
It drawes toward supper in conclusion so.
But this is worshipfull society,
And fits the mounting spirit like my selfe;
For he is but a bastard to the time
That doth not smoake of obseruation,
And so am I whether I smacke or no:
And not alone in habit and deuice,
Exterior forme, outward accoutrement;
But from the inward motion to deliuer
Sweet, sweet, sweet poyson for the ages tooth,
Which though I will not practice to deceiue,
Yet to auoid deceit I meane to learne;
For it shall strew the footsteps of my rising:
But who comes in such haste in riding robes?

What

What woman post is this? hath she no husband
That will take paines to blow a horne before her?
O me, 'tis my mother: how now good Lady,
What brings you heere to Court so hastily?

Enter Lady Faulconbridge and Iames Gurney.

Lady. Where is that slaue thy brother? where is he?
That holds in chase mine honour vp and downe.
Bast. My brother *Robert*, old Sir *Roberts* sonne:
Colbrand the Gyant, that same mighty man,
Is it Sir *Roberts* sonne that you seeke so?
Lady. Sir *Roberts* sonne, I thou vnreuerend boy,
Sir *Roberts* sonne? why scorn'st thou at sir *Robert*?
He is Sir *Roberts* sonne, and so art thou.
Bast. *Iames Gournie*, wilt thou giue vs leaue a while?
Gour. Good leaue good *Philip*.
Bast. *Philip*, sparrow, *Iames*,
There's toyes abroad, anon Ile tell thee more.
Exit Iames.
Madam, I was not old Sir *Roberts* sonne,
Sir *Robert* might haue eat his part in me
Vpon good Friday, and nere broke his fast:
Sir *Robert* could doe well, marrie to confesse
Could get me sir *Robert* could not doe it;
We know his handy-worke, therefore good mother
To whom am I beholding for these limmes?
Sir *Robert* neuer holpe to make this legge.
Lady. Hast thou conspired with thy brother too,
That for thine owne gaine shouldst defend mine honor?
What meanes this scorne, thou most vntoward knaue?
Bast. Knight, knight good mother, Basilisco-like:
What, I am dub'd, I haue it on my shoulder:
But mother, I am not Sir *Roberts* sonne,
I haue disclaim'd Sir *Robert* and my land,
Legitimation, name, and all is gone;
Then good my mother, let me know my father,
Some proper man I hope, who was it mother?
Lady. Hast thou denied thy selfe a *Faulconbridge*?
Bast. As faithfully as I denie the deuill.
Lady. *King Richard Cordelion* was thy father,
By long and vehement suit I was seduc'd
To make roome for him in my husbands bed:
Heauen lay not my transgression to my charge,
That art the issue of my deere offence
Which was so strongly vrg'd past my defence.
Bast. Now by this light were I to get againe,
Madam I would not wish a better father:
Some sinnes doe beare their priuiledge on earth,
And so doth yours: your fault, was not your follie,
Needs must you lay your heart at his dispose,
Subiected tribute to commanding loue,
Against whose furie and vnmatched force,
The awlesse Lion could not wage the fight,
Nor keepe his Princely heart from *Richards* hand:
He that perforce robs Lions of their hearts,
May easily winne a womans: aye my mother,
With all my heart I thanke thee for my father:
Who liues and dares but say, thou didst not well
When I was got, Ile send his soule to hell.
Come Lady I will shew thee to my kinne,
And they shall say, when *Richard* me begot,
If thou hadst sayd him nay, it had beene sinne;
Who sayes it was, he lyes, I say twas not.

Exeunt.

Scæna Secunda.

Enter before Angiers, Philip King of France, Lewis, Dauphin, Austria, Constance, Arthur.

Lewis. Before *Angiers* well met braue *Austria*,
Arthur that great fore-runner of thy bloud,
Richard that rob'd the Lion of his heart,
And fought the holy Warres in *Palestine*,
By this braue Duke came early to his graue:
And for amends to his posteritie,
At our importance hether is he come,
To spread his colours boy, in thy behalfe,
And to rebuke the vsurpation
Of thy vnnaturall Vncle, English *Iohn*,
Embrace him, loue him, giue him welcome hether.
Arth. God shall forgiue you *Cordelions* death
The rather, that you giue his off-spring life,
Shadowing their right vnder your wings of warre:
I giue you welcome with a powerlesse hand,
But with a heart full of vnstained loue,
Welcome before the gates of *Angiers* Duke.
Lewis. A noble boy, who would not doe thee right?
Aust. Vpon thy cheeke lay I this zelous kisse,
As seale to this indenture of my loue:
That to my home I will no more returne
Till *Angiers*, and the right thou hast in *France*,
Together with that pale, that white-fac'd shore,
Whose foot spurnes backe the Oceans roaring tides,
And coopes from other lands her Ilanders,
Euen till that *England* hedg'd in with the maine,
That Water-walled Bulwarke, still secure
And confident from forreine purposes,
Euen till that vtmost corner of the West
Salute thee for her King, till then faire boy
Will I not thinke of home, but follow Armes.
Const. O take his mothers thanks, a widdows thanks,
Till your strong hand shall helpe to giue him strength,
To make a more requitall to your loue.
Aust. The peace of heauen is theirs y lift their swords
In such a iust and charitable warre.
King. Well, then to worke our Cannon shall be bent
Against the browes of this resisting towne,
Call for our cheefest men of discipline,
To cull the plots of best aduantages:
Wee'll lay before this towne our Royal bones,
Wade to the market-place in *French*-mens bloud,
But we will make it subiect to this boy.
Con. Stay for an answer to your Embassie,
Lest vnaduis'd you staine your swords with bloud,
My Lord *Chattilion* may from *England* bring
That right in peace which heere we vrge in warre,
And then we shall repent each drop of bloud;
That hot rash haste so indirectly shedde.

Enter Chattilion.

King. A wonder Lady: lo vpon thy wish
Our Messenger *Chattilion* is arriu'd,
What *England* saies, say breefely gentle Lord,
We coldly pause for thee, *Chatilion* speake,
Chat. Then turne your forces from this paltry siege,
And stirre them vp against a mightier taske:
England impatient of your iust demands,
Hath put himselfe in Armes, the aduerse windes

Whose leisure I haue staid, haue giuen him time
To land his Legions all as soone as I:
His marches are expedient to this towne,
His forces strong, his Souldiers confident:
With him along is come the Mother Queene,
An Ace stirring him to bloud and strife,
With her her Neece, the Lady *Blanch of Spaine*,
With them a Bastard of the Kings deceast,
And all th'vnsetled humors of the Land,
Rash, inconsiderate, fiery voluntaries,
With Ladies faces, and fierce Dragons spleenes,
Haue sold their fortunes at their natiue homes,
Bearing their birth-rights proudly on their backs,
To make a hazard of new fortunes heere:
In briefe, a brauer choyse of dauntlesse spirits
Then now the *English* bottomes haue waft o're,
Did neuer flote vpon the swelling tide,
To doe offence and scathe in Christendome:
The interruption of their churlish drums
Cuts off more circumstance, they are at hand,
Drum beats.
To parlie or to fight, therefore prepare.

Kin. How much vnlook'd for, is this expedition.

Aust. By how much vnexpected, by so much
We must awake indeuor for defence,
For courage mounteth with occasion,
Let them be welcome then, we are prepar'd.

Enter K. of England, Bastard, Queene, Blanch, Pembroke, and others.

K. Iohn. Peace be to *France*: If France in peace permit
Our iust and lineall entrance to our owne;
If not, bleede *France*, and peace ascend to heauen.
Whiles we Gods wrathfull agent doe correct
Their proud contempt that beats his peace to heauen.

Fran. Peace be to *England*, if that warre returne
From *France* to *England*, there to liue in peace:
England we loue, and for that *Englands* sake,
With burden of our armor heere we sweat:
This toyle of ours should be a worke of thine;
But thou from louing *England* art so farre,
That thou hast vnder-wrought his lawfull King,
Cut off the sequence of posterity,
Out-faced Infant State, and done a rape
Vpon the maiden vertue of the Crowne:
Looke heere vpon thy brother *Geffreyes* face,
These eyes, these browes, were moulded out of his;
This little abstract doth containe that large,
Which died in *Geffrey*: and the hand of time,
Shall draw this breefe into as huge a volume:
That *Geffrey* was thy elder brother borne,
And this his sonne, *England* was *Geffreys* right,
And this is *Geffreyes* in the name of God:
How comes it then that thou art call'd a King,
When liuing blood doth in these temples beat
Which owe the crowne, that thou ore-masterest?

K. Iohn. From whom hast thou this great commission *France*,
To draw my answer from thy Articles?

Fra. Fro that supernal Iudge that stirs good thoughts
In any beast of strong authoritie,
To looke into the blots and staines of right,
That Iudge hath made me guardian to this boy,
Vnder whose warrant I impeach thy wrong,
And by whose helpe I meane to chastise it.

K. Iohn. Alack thou dost vsurpe authoritie.

Fran. Excuse it is to beat vsurping downe.

Queen. Who is it thou dost call vsurper *France*?

Const. Let me make answer: thy vsurping sonne.

Queen. Out insolent, thy bastard shall be King,
That thou maist be a Queen, and checke the world.

Con. My bed was euer to thy sonne as true
As thine was to thy husband, and this boy
Liker in feature to his father *Geffrey*
Then thou and *Iohn*, in manners being as like,
As raine to water, or deuill to his damme;
My boy a bastard? by my soule I thinke
His father neuer was so true begot,
It cannot be, and if thou wert his mother.

Queen. Theres a good mother boy, that blots thy father

Const. There's a good grandame boy
That would blot thee.

Aust. Peace.

Bast. Heare the Cryer.

Aust. What the deuill art thou?

Bast. One that wil play the deuill sir with you,
And a may catch your hide and you alone:
You are the Hare of whom the Prouerb goes
Whose valour plucks dead Lyons by the beard;
Ile smoake your skin-coat and I catch you right,
Sirra looke too't, yfaith I will, yfaith.

Blan. O well did he become that Lyons robe,
That did disrobe the Lion of that robe.

Bast. It lies as sightly on the backe of him
As great *Alcides* shooes vpon an Asse:
But Asse, Ile take that burthen from your backe,
Or lay on that shall make your shoulders cracke.

Aust. What cracker is this same that deafes our eares
With this abundance of superfluous breath?
King *Lewis*, determine what we shall doe strait.

Lew. Women & fooles, breake off your conference.
King *Iohn*, this is the very summe of all:
England and *Ireland*, *Angiers*, *Toraine*, *Maine*,
In right of *Arthur* doe I claime of thee:
Wilt thou resigne them, and lay downe thy Armes?

Iohn. My life as soone: I doe defie thee *France*,
Arthur of *Britaine*, yeeld thee to my hand,
And out of my deere loue Ile giue thee more,
Then ere the coward hand of *France* can win;
Submit thee boy.

Queen. Come to thy grandame child.

Cons. Doe childe, goe to yt grandame childe,
Giue grandame kingdome, and it grandame will
Giue yt a plum, a cherry, and a figge,
There's a good grandame.

Arthur. Good my mother peace,
I would that I were low laid in my graue,
I am not worth this coyle that's made for me. (*weepes.*

Qu. Mo. His mother shames him so, poore boy hee

Con. Now shame vpon you where she does or no,
His grandames wrongs, and not his mothers shames
Drawes those heauen-mouing pearles frō his poor eies,
Which heauen shall take in nature of a fee:
I, with these Christall beads heauen shall be brib'd
To doe him Iustice, and reuenge on you.

Qu. Thou monstrous slanderer of heauen and earth.

Con. Thou monstrous Iniurer of heauen and earth
Call not me slanderer, thou and thine vsurpe
The Dominations, Royalties, and rights
Of this oppressed boy; this is thy eldest sonnes sonne,
Infortunate in nothing but in thee:

Thy

Thy sinnes are visited in this poore childe,
The Canon of the Law is laide on him,
Being but the second generation
Remoued from thy sinne-conceiuing wombe.
Iohn. Bedlam haue done.
Con. I haue but this to say,
That he is not onely plagued for her sin,
But God hath made her sinne and her, the plague
On this remoued issue, plagued for her,
And with her plague her sinne: his iniury
Her iniurie the Beadle to her sinne,
All punish'd in the person of this childe,
And all for her, a plague vpon her.
Que. Thou vnaduised scold, I can produce
A Will, that barres the title of thy sonne.
Con. I who doubts that, a Will: a wicked will,
A womans will, a cankred Grandams will.
Fra. Peace Lady, pause, or be more temperate,
It ill beseemes this presence to cry ayme
To these ill-tuned repetitions:
Some Trumpet summon hither to the walles
These men of Angiers, let vs heare them speake,
Whose title they admit, *Arthurs* or *Iohns*.

Trumpet sounds.
Enter a Citizen vpon the walles.

Cit. Who is it that hath warn'd vs to the walles?
Fra. 'Tis France, for England.
Iohn. England for it selfe:
You men of Angiers, and my louing subiects.
Fra. You louing men of Angiers, *Arthurs* subiects,
Our Trumpet call'd you to this gentle parle.
Iohn. For our aduantage, therefore heare vs first:
These flagges of France that are aduanced heere
Before the eye and prospect of your Towne,
Haue hither march'd to your endamagement.
The Canons haue their bowels full of wrath,
And ready mounted are they to spit forth
Their Iron indignation 'gainst your walles:
All preparation for a bloody siedge
And merciles proceeding, by these French.
Comfort yours Citties eies, your winking gates:
And but for our approch, those sleeping stones,
That as a waste doth girdle you about
By the compulsion of their Ordinance,
By this time from their fixed beds of lime
Had bin dishabited, and wide hauocke made
For bloody power to rush vppon your peace.
But on the sight of vs your lawfull King,
Who painefully with much expedient march
Haue brought a counter-checke before your gates,
To saue vnscratch'd your Citties threatned cheekes:
Behold the French amaz'd vouchsafe a parle,
And now insteed of bulletts wrapt in fire
To make a shaking feuer in your walles,
They shoote but calme words, folded vp in smoake,
To make a faithlesse errour in your eares,
Which trust accordingly kinde Cittizens,
And let vs in. Your King, whose labour'd spirits
Fore-wearied in this action of swift speede,
Craues harbourage within your Citie walles.
France. When I haue saide, make answer to vs both.
Loe in this right hand, whose protection
Is most diuinely vow'd vpon the right
Of him it holds, stands yong *Plantagenet*,
Sonne to the elder brother of this man,
And King ore him, and all that he enioyes:
For this downe-troden equity, we tread
In warlike march, these greenes before your Towne,
Being no further enemy to you
Then the constraint of hospitable zeale,
In the releefe of this oppressed childe,
Religiously prouokes. Be pleased then
To pay that dutie which you truly owe,
To him that owes it, namely, this yong Prince,
And then our Armes, like to a muzled Beare,
Saue in aspect, hath all offence seal'd vp:
Our Cannons malice vainly shall be spent
Against th' involuerable clouds of heauen,
And with a blessed and vn-vext retyre,
With vnhack'd swords, and Helmets all vnbruis'd,
We will beare home that lustie blood againe,
Which heere we came to spout against your Towne,
And leaue your children, wiues, and you in peace.
But if you fondly passe our proffer'd offer,
'Tis not the rounder of your old-fac'd walles,
Can hide you from our messengers of Warre,
Though all these English, and their discipline
Were harbour'd in their rude circumference:
Then tell vs, Shall your Citie call vs Lord,
In that behalfe which we haue challeng'd it?
Or shall we giue the signall to our rage,
And stalke in blood to our possession?
Cit. In breefe, we are the King of Englands subiects
For him, and in his right, we hold this Towne.
Iohn. Acknowledge then the King, and let me in.
Cit. That can we not: but he that proues the King
To him will we proue loyall, till that time
Haue we ramm'd vp our gates against the world.
Iohn. Doth not the Crowne of England, prooue the King?
And if not that, I bring you Witnesses
Twice fifteene thousand hearts of Englands breed.
Bast. Bastards and else.
Iohn. To verifie our title with their liues.
Fran. As many and as well-borne bloods as those.
Bast. Some Bastards too.
Fran. Stand in his face to contradict his claime.
Cit. Till you compound whose right is worthiest,
We for the worthiest hold the right from both.
Iohn. Then God forgiue the sinne of all those soules,
That to their euerlasting residence,
Before the dew of euening fall, shall fleete
In dreadfull triall of our kingdomes King.
Fran. Amen, Amen, mount Cheualiers to Armes.
Bast. Saint George that swindg'd the Dragon,
And ere since sit's on's horsebacke at mine Hostesse dore
Teach vs some fence. Sirrah, were I at home
At your den sirrah, with your Lionnesse,
I would set an Oxe-head to your Lyons hide:
And make a monster of you
Aust. Peace, no more.
Bast. O tremble: for you heare the Lyon rore.
Iohn. Vp higher to the plaine, where we'l set forth
In best appointment all our Regiments.
Bast. Speed then to take aduantage of the field.
Fra. It shall be so, and at the other hill
Command the rest to stand, God and our right. *Exeunt*

Heere after excursions, Enter the Herald of France with Trumpets to the gates.

F. Her. You men of Angiers open wide your gates,
And let yong *Arthur* Duke of Britaine in,

Who by the hand of France, this day hath made
Much worke for teares in many an English mother,
Whose sonnes lye scattered on the bleeding ground:
Many a widdowes husband groueling lies,
Coldly embracing the discoloured earth,
And victorie with little losse doth play
Vpon the dancing banners of the French,
Who are at hand triumphantly displayed
To enter Conquerors, and to proclaime
Arthur of Britaine, Englands King, and yours.

Enter English Herald with Trumpet.

E.Har. Reioyce you men of Angiers, ring your bels,
King *Iohn*, your king and Englands, doth approach,
Commander of this hot malicious day,
Their Armours that march'd hence so siluer bright,
Hither returne all gilt with Frenchmens blood:
There stucke no plume in any English Crest,
That is remoued by a staffe of France.
Our colours do returne in those same hands
That did display them when we first marcht forth:
And like a iolly troope of Huntsmen come
Our lustie English, all with purpled hands,
Dide in the dying slaughter of their foes,
Open your gates, and giue the Victors way.

Hubert. Heralds, from off our towres we might behold
From first to last, the on-set and retyre;
Of both yonr Armies, whose equality
By our best eyes cannot be censured: (blowes:
Blood hath bought blood, and blowes haue answerd
Strength matcht with strength, and power confronted
power,
Both are alike, and both alike we like:
One must proue greatest. While they weigh so euen,
We hold our Towne for neither: yet for both.

Enter the two Kings with their powers, at seuerall doores.

Iohn. France, hast thou yet more blood to cast away?
Say, shall the currant of our right rome on,
Whose passage vext with thy impediment,
Shall leaue his natiue channell, and ore-swell
with course disturb'd euen thy confining shores,
Vnlesse thou let his siluer Water, keepe
A peacefull progresse to the Ocean.

Fra. England thou hast not sau'd one drop of blood
In this hot triall more then we of France,
Rather lost more. And by this hand I sweare
That swayes the earth this Climate ouer-lookes,
Before we will lay downe our iust-borne Armes,
Wee'l put thee downe,'gainst whom these Armes we
Or adde a royall number to the dead: (beare,
Gracing the scroule that tels of this warres losse,
With slaughter coupled to the name of kings.

Bast. Ha Maiesty: how high thy glory towres,
When the rich blood of kings is set on fire:
Oh now doth death line his dead chaps with steele,
The swords of souldiers are his teeth, his phangs,
And now he feasts, mousing the flesh of men
In vndetermin'd differences of kings.
Why stand these royall fronts amazed thus:
Cry hauocke kings, backe to the stained field
You equall Potents, fierie kindled spirits,
Then let confusion of one part confirm
The others peace: till then, blowes, blood, and death.

Iohn. Whose party do the Townesmen yet admit?

Fra. Speake Citizens for England, whose your king.

Hub. The king of England, when we know the king.

Fra. Know him in vs, that heere hold vp his right.

Iohn. In Vs, that are our owne great Deputie,
And beare possession of our Person heere,
Lord of our presence Angiers, and of you.

Fra. A greater powre then We denies all this,
And till it be vndoubted, we do locke
Our former scruple in our strong barr'd gates:
Kings of our feare, vntill our feares resolu'd
Be by some certaine king, purg'd and depos'd.

Bast. By heauen, these scroyles of Angiers flout you
And stand securely on their battelments, (kings,
As in a Theater, whence they gape and point
At your industrious Scenes and acts of death.
Your Royall presences be rul'd by mee,
Do like the Mutines of Ierusalem,
Be friends a-while, and both conioyntly bend
Your sharpest Deeds of malice on this Towne.
By East and West let France and England mount.
Their battering Canon charged to the mouthes,
Till their soule-fearing clamours haue braul'd downe
The flintie ribbes of this contemptuous Citie,
I'de play incessantly vpon these Iades,
Euen till vnfenced desolation
Leaue them as naked as the vulgar ayre:
That done, disseuer your vnited strengths,
And part your mingled colours once againe,
Turne face to face, and bloody point to point:
Then in a moment Fortune shall cull forth
Out of one side her happy Minion,
To whom in fauour she shall giue the day,
And kisse him with a glorious victory:
How like you this wilde counsell mighty States,
Smackes it not something of the policie.

Iohn. Now by the sky that hangs aboue our heads,
I like it well. France, shall we knit our powres,
And lay this Angiers euen with the ground,
Then after fight who shall be king of it?

Bast. And if thou hast the mettle of a king,
Being wrong'd as we are by this peeuish Towne:
Turne thou the mouth of thy Artillerie,
As we will ours, against these sawcie walles,
And when that we haue dash'd them to the ground,
Why then defie each other, and pell-mell,
Make worke vpon our selues, for heauen or hell.

Fra. Let it be so: say, where will you assault?

Iohn. We from the West will send destruction
Into this Cities bosome.

Aust. I from the North.

Fran. Our Thunder from the South,
Shall raine their drift of bullets on this Towne.

Bast. O prudent discipline! From North to South:
Austria and France shoot in each others mouth.
Ile stirre them to it: Come, away, away.

Hub. Heare vs great kings, vouchsafe awhile to stay
And I shall shew you peace, and faire-fac'd league:
Win you this Citie without stroke, or wound,
Rescue those breathing liues to dye in beds,
That heere come sacrifices for the field.
Perseuer not, but heare me mighty kings.

Iohn. Speake on with fauour, we are bent to heare.

Hub. That daughter there of Spaine, the Lady *Blanch*
Is neere to England, looke vpon the yeeres
Of *Lewes* the Dolphin, and that louely maid.
If lustie loue should go in quest of beautie,

Where should he finde it fairer, then in *Blanch*:
If zealous loue should go in search of vertue,
Where should he finde it purer then in *Blanch*?
If loue ambitious, sought a match of birth,
Whose veines bound richer blood then Lady *Blanch*?
Such as she is, in beautie, vertue, birth,
Is the yong Dolphin euery way compleat,
If not compleat of, say he is not shee,
And she againe wants nothing, to name want,
If want it be not, that she is not hee:
He is the halfe part of a blessed man,
Left to be finished by such as shee,
And she a faire diuided excellence,
Whose fulnesse of perfection lyes in him.
O two such siluer currents when they ioyne
Do glorifie the bankes that bound them in:
And two such shores, to two such streames made one,
Two such controlling bounds shall you be, kings,
To these two Princes, if you marrie them:
This Vnion shall do more then batterie can
To our fast closed gates: for at this match,
With swifter spleene then powder can enforce
The mouth of passage shall we fling wide ope,
And giue you entrance: but without this match,
The sea enraged is not halfe so deafe,
Lyons more confident, Mountaines and rockes
More free from motion, no not death himselfe
In mortall furie halfe so peremptorie,
As we to keepe this Citie.

Bast. Heeres a stay,
That shakes the rotten carkasse of old death
Out of his ragges. Here's a large mouth indeede,
That spits forth death, and mountaines, rockes, and seas,
Talkes as familiarly of roaring Lyons,
As maids of thirteene do of puppi-dogges.
What Cannoneere begot this lustie blood,
He speakes plaine Cannon fire, and smoake, and bounce,
He giues the bastinado with his tongue:
Our eares are cudgel'd, not a word of his
But buffets better then a fist of France:
Zounds, I was neuer so bethumpt with words,
Since I first cal'd my brothers father Dad.

Old Qu. Son, list to this coniunction, make this match
Giue with our Neece a dowrie large enough,
For by this knot, thou shalt so surely tye
Thy now vnsur'd assurance to the Crowne,
That yon greene boy shall haue no Sunne to ripe
The bloome that promiseth a mightie fruite.
I see a yeelding in the lookes of France:
Marke how they whisper, vrge them while their soules
Are capeable of this ambition,
Least zeale now melted by the windie breath
Of soft petitions, pittie and remorse,
Coole and congeale againe to what it was.

Hub. Why answer not the double Maiesties,
This friendly treatie of our threatned Towne.

Fra. Speake England first, that hath bin forward first
To speake vnto this Cittie: what say you?

Iohn. If that the Dolphin there thy Princely sonne,
Can in this booke of beautie read, I loue:
Her Dowrie shall weigh equall with a Queene:
For *Angiers*, and faire *Toraine Maine*, *Poyctiers*,
And all that we vpon this side the Sea,
(Except this Cittie now by vs besiedg'd)
Finde liable to our Crowne and Dignitie,
Shall gild her bridall bed and make her rich
In titles, honors, and promotions,
As she in beautie, education, blood,
Holdes hand with any Princesse of the world.

Fra. What sai'st thou boy? looke in the Ladies face.

Dol. I do my Lord, and in her eie I find
A wonder, or a wondrous miracle,
The shadow of my selfe form'd in her eye,
Which being but the shadow of your sonne,
Becomes a sonne and makes your sonne a shadow:
I do protest I neuer lou'd my selfe
Till now, infixed I beheld my selfe,
Drawne in the flattering table of her eie.

Whispers with Blanch.

Bast. Drawne in the flattering table of her eie,
Hang'd in the frowning wrinkle of her brow,
And quarter'd in her heart, hee doth espie
Himselfe loues traytor, this is pittie now;
That hang'd, and drawne, and quarter'd there should be
In such a loue, so vile a Lout as he.

Blan. My vnckles will in this respect is mine,
If he see ought in you that makes him like,
That any thing he see's which moues his liking,
I can with ease translate it to my will:
Or if you will, to speake more properly,
I will enforce it easlie to my loue.
Further I will not flatter you, my Lord,
That all I see in you is worthie loue,
Then this, that nothing do I see in you,
Though churlish thoughts themselues should bee your Iudge,
That I can finde, should merit any hate.

Iohn. What saie these yong-ones? What say you my Neece?

Blan. That she is bound in honor still to do
What you in wisedome still vouchsafe to say.

Iohn. Speake then Prince Dolphin, can you loue this Ladie?

Dol. Nay aske me if I can refraine from loue,
For I doe loue her most vnfainedly.

Iohn. Then do I giue *Volquessen*, *Toraine*, *Maine*,
Poyctiers, and *Aniow*, these fiue Prouinces
With her to thee, and this addition more,
Full thirty thousand Markes of English coyne:
Phillip of France, if thou be pleas'd withall,
Command thy sonne and daughter to ioyne hands.

Fra. It likes vs well young Princes: close your hands

Aust. And your lippes too, for I am well assur'd,
That I did so when I was first assur'd.

Fra. Now Citizens of Angires ope your gates,
Let in that amitie which you haue made,
For at Saint Maries Chappell presently,
The rights of marriage shallbe solemniz'd.
Is not the Ladie *Constance* in this troope?
I know she is not for this match made vp,
Her presence would haue interrupted much.
Where is she and her sonne, tell me, who knowes?

Dol. She is sad and passionate at your highnes Tent.

Fra. And by my faith, this league that we haue made
Will giue her sadnesse very little cure:
Brother of England, how may we content
This widdow Lady? In her right we came,
Which we God knowes, haue turn'd another way,
To our owne vantage.

Iohn. We will heale vp all,
For wee'l create yong *Arthur* Duke of Britaine
And Earle of Richmond, and this rich faire Towne

We

We make him Lord of. Call the Lady *Constance*,
Some speedy Messenger bid her repaire
To our solemnity: I trust we shall,
(If not fill vp the measure of her will)
Yet in some measure satisfie her so,
That we shall stop her exclamation,
Go we as well as hast will suffer vs,
To this vnlook'd for vnprepared pompe. *Exeunt.*

Bast. Mad world, mad kings, mad composition:
Iohn to stop *Arthurs* Title in the whole,
Hath willingly departed with a part,
And France, whose armour Conscience buckled on,
Whom zeale and charitie brought to the field,
As Gods owne souldier, rounded in the eare,
With that same purpose-changer, that slye diuel,
That Broker, that still breakes the pate of faith,
That dayly breake-vow, he that winnes of all,
Of kings, of beggers, old men, yong men, maids,
Who hauing no externall thing to loose,
But the word Maid, cheats the poore Maide of that.
That smooth-fac'd Gentleman, tickling commoditie,
Commoditie, the byas of the world,
The world, who of it selfe is peysed well,
Made to run euen, vpon euen ground;
Till this aduantage, this vile drawing byas,
This sway of motion, this commoditie,
Makes it take head from all indifferency,
From all direction, purpose, course, intent.
And this same byas, this Commoditie,
This Bawd, this Broker, this all-changing-word,
Clap'd on the outward eye of fickle France,
Hath drawne him from his owne determin'd ayd,
From a resolu'd and honourable warre,
To a most base and vile-concluded peace.
And why rayle I on this Commoditie?
But for because he hath not wooed me yet:
Not that I haue the power to clutch my hand,
When his faire Angels would salute my palme,
But for my hand, as vnattempted yet,
Like a poore begger, raileth on the rich.
Well, whiles I am a begger, I will raile,
And say there is no sin but to be rich:
And being rich, my vertue then shall be,
To say there is no vice, but beggerie:
Since Kings breake faith vpon commoditie,
Gaine be my Lord, for I will worship thee. *Exit.*

Actus Secundus

Enter Constance, Arthur, and Salisbury.

Con. Gone to be married? Gone to sweare a peace?
False blood to false blood ioyn'd. Gone to be freinds?
Shall *Lewis* haue *Blaunch*, and *Blaunch* those Prouinces?
It is not so, thou hast mispoke, misheard,
Be well aduis'd, tell ore thy tale againe.
It cannot be, thou do'st but say 'tis so.
I trust I may not trust thee, for thy word
Is but the vaine breath of a common man:
Beleeue me, I doe not beleeue thee man,
I haue a Kings oath to the contrarie.
Thou shalt be punish'd for thus frighting me,
For I am sicke, and capeable of feares,
Opprest with wrongs, and therefore full of feares,
A widdow, husbandles, subiect to feares,
A woman naturally borne to feares;
And though thou now confesse thou didst but iest
With my vext spirits, I cannot take a Truce,
But they will quake and tremble all this day.
What dost thou meane by shaking of thy head?
Why dost thou looke so sadly on my sonne?
What meanes that hand vpon that breast of thine?
Why holdes thine eie that lamentable rhewme,
Like a proud riuer peering ore his bounds?
Be these sad signes confirmers of thy words?
Then speake againe, not all thy former tale,
But this one word, whether thy tale be true.

Sal. As true as I beleeue you thinke them false,
That giue you cause to proue my saying true.

Con. Oh if thou teach me to beleeue this sorrow,
Teach thou this sorrow, how to make me dye,
And let beleefe, and life encounter so,
As doth the furie of two desperate men,
Which in the very meeting fall, and dye.
Lewes marry *Blaunch*? O boy, then where art thou?
France friend with *England*, what becomes of me?
Fellow be gone: I cannot brooke thy sight,
This newes hath made thee a most vgly man.

Sal. What other harme haue I good Lady done,
But spoke the harme, that is by others done?

Con. Which harme within it selfe so heynous is,
As it makes harmefull all that speake of it.

Ar. I do beseech you Madam be content.

Con. If thou that bidst me be content, wert grim
Vgly, and slandrous to thy Mothers wombe,
Full of vnpleasing blots, and sightlesse staines,
Lame, foolish, crooked, swart, prodigious,
Patch'd with foule Moles, and eye-offending markes,
I would not care, I then would be content,
For then I should not loue thee: no, nor thou
Become thy great birth, nor deserue a Crowne.
But thou art faire, and at thy birth (deere boy)
Nature and Fortune ioyn'd to make thee great.
Of Natures guifts, thou mayst with Lillies boast,
And with the halfe-blowne Rose. But Fortune, oh,
She is corrupted, chang'd, and wonne from thee,
Sh'adulterates hourely with thine Vnckle *Iohn*,
And with her golden hand hath pluckt on France
To tread downe faire respect of Soueraigntie,
And made his Maiestie the bawd to theirs.
France is a Bawd to Fortune, and king *Iohn*,
That strumpet Fortune, that vsurping *Iohn*:
Tell me thou fellow, is not France forsworne?
Euvenom him with words, or get thee gone,
And leaue those woes alone, which I alone
Am bound to vnder-beare.

Sal. Pardon me Madam,
I may not goe without you to the kings.

Con. Thou maist, thou shalt, I will not go with thee,
I will instruct my sorrowes to bee proud,
For greefe is proud, and makes his owner stoope,
To me and to the state of my great greefe,
Let kings assemble: for my greefe's so great,
That no supporter but the huge firme earth
Can hold it vp: here I and sorrowes sit,
Heere is my Throne, bid kings come bow to it.

Actus

Actus Tertius, Scæna prima.

Enter King Iohn, France, Dolphin, Blanch, Elianor, Philip, Austria, Constance.

Fran. 'Tis true (faire daughter) and this blessed day,
Euer in *France* shall be kept festiuall:
To solemnize this day the glorious sunne
Stayes in his course, and playes the Alchymist,
Turning with splendor of his precious eye
The meager cloddy earth to glittering gold:
The yearely course that brings this day about,
Shall neuer see it, but a holy day.

Const. A wicked day, and not a holy day.
What hath this day deseru'd? what hath it done,
That it in golden letters should be set
Among the high tides in the Kalender?
Nay, rather turne this day out of the weeke,
This day of shame, oppression, periury.
Or if it must stand still, let wiues with childe
Pray that their burthens may not fall this day,
Least that their hopes prodigiously be crost:
But (on this day) let Sea-men feare no wracke,
No bargaines breake that are not this day made;
This day all things begun, come to ill end,
Yea, faith it selfe to hollow falshood change.

Fra. By heauen Lady, you shall haue no cause
To curse the faire proceedings of this day:
Haue I not pawn'd to you my Maiesty?

Const. You haue beguil'd me with a counterfeit
Resembling Maiesty, which being touch'd and tride,
Proues valuelesse: you are forsworne, forsworne,
You came in Armes to spill mine enemies bloud,
But now in Armes, you strengthen it with yours.
The grapling vigor, and rough frowne of Warre
Is cold in amitie, and painted peace,
And our oppression hath made vp this league:
Arme, arme, you heauens, against these periur'd Kings,
A widdow cries, be husband to me (heauens)
Let not the howres of this vngodly day
Weare out the daies in Peace; but ere Sun-set,
Set armed discord 'twixt these periur'd Kings,
Heare me, Oh, heare me.

Aust. Lady *Constance*, peace.

Const. War, war, no peace, peace is to me a warre:
O *Lymoges*, O *Austria*, thou dost shame
That bloudy spoyle: thou slaue, thou wretch, ŷ coward,
Thou little valiant, great in villanie,
Thou euer strong vpon the stronger side;
Thou Fortunes Champion, that do'st neuer fight
But when her humourous Ladiship is by
To teach thee safety: thou art periur'd too,
And sooth'st vp greatnesse. What a foole art thou,
A ramping foole, to brag, and stamp, and sweare,
Vpon my partie: thou cold blooded slaue,
Hast thou not spoke like thunder on my side?
Beene sworne my Souldier, bidding me depend
Vpon thy starres, thy fortune, and thy strength,
And dost thou now fall ouer to my foes?
Thou weare a Lyons hide, doff it for shame,
And hang a Calues skin on those recreant limbes.

Aus. O that a man should speake those words to me.

Phil. And hang a Calues-skin on those recreant limbs

Aus. Thou dar'st not say so villaine for thy life.

Phil. And hang a Calues-skin on those recreant limbs.

Iohn. We like not this, thou dost forget thy selfe.

Enter Pandulph.

Fra. Heere comes the holy Legat of the Pope.

Pan. Haile you annointed deputies of heauen;
To thee King *Iohn* my holy errand is:
I *Pandulph*, of faire *Millane* Cardinall,
And from Pope *Innocent* the Legate heere,
Doe in his name religiously demand
Why thou against the Church, our holy Mother
So wilfully dost spurne; and force perforce
Keepe *Stephen Langton* chosen Arshbishop
Of *Canterbury* from that holy Sea:
This in our foresaid holy Fathers name
Pope *Innocent*, I doe demand of thee.

Iohn. What earthie name to Interrogatories
Can tast the free breath of a sacred King?
Thou canst not (Cardinall) deuise a name
So slight, vnworthy, and ridiculous
To charge me to an answere, as the Pope:
Tell him this tale, and from the mouth of *England*,
Adde thus much more, that no *Italian* Priest
Shall tythe or toll in our dominions:
But as we, vnder heauen, are supreame head,
So vnder him that great supremacy
Where we doe reigne, we will alone vphold
Without th'assistance of a mortall hand:
So tell the Pope, all reuerence set apart
To him and his vsurp'd authoritie.

Fra. Brother of *England*, you blaspheme in this.

Iohn. Though you, and all the Kings of Christendom
Are led so grossely by this medling Priest,
Dreading the curse that money may buy out,
And by the merit of vilde gold, drosse, dust,
Purchase corrupted pardon of a man,
Who in that sale sels pardon from himselfe:
Though you, and al the rest so grossely led,
This iugling witchcraft with reuennue cherish,
Yet I alone, alone doe me oppose
Against the Pope, and count his friends my foes.

Pand. Then by the lawfull power that I haue,
Thou shalt stand curst, and excommunicate,
And blessed shall he be that doth reuolt
From his Allegeance to an heretique,
And meritorious shall that hand be call'd,
Canonized and worship'd as a Saint,
That takes away by any secret course
Thy hatefull life.

Con. O lawfull let it be
That I haue roome with *Rome* to curse a while,
Good Father Cardinall, cry thou Amen
To my keene curses; for without my wrong
There is no tongue hath power to curse him right.

Pan. There's Law and Warrant (Lady) for my curse.

Cons. And for mine too, when Law can do no right.
Let it be lawfull, that Law barre no wrong:
Law cannot giue my childe his kingdome heere;
For he that holds his Kingdome, holds the Law:
Therefore since Law it selfe is perfect wrong,
How can the Law forbid my tongue to curse?

Pand. *Philip* of *France*, on perill of a curse,
Let goe the hand of that Arch-heretique,
And raise the power of *France* vpon his head,
Vnlesse he doe submit himselfe to *Rome*.

Elea. Look'st thou pale *France*? do not let go thy hand.

Con. Looke to that Deuill, lest that *France* repent,

And by disioyning hands hell lose a soule.
Aust. King *Philip*, listen to the Cardinall.
Bast. And hang a Calues-skin on his recreant limbs.
Aust. Well ruffian, I must pocket vp these wrongs,
Because,
Bast. Your breeches best may carry them.
Iohn. *Philip*, what saist thou to the Cardinall?
Con. What should he say, but as the Cardinall?
Dolph. Bethinke you father, for the difference
Is purchase of a heauy curse from *Rome*,
Or the light losse of *England*, for a friend:
Forgoe the easier.
Bla. That s the curse of *Rome*.
Con. O *Lewis*, stand fast, the deuill tempts thee heere
In likenesse of a new vntrimmed Bride.
Bla. The Lady *Constance* speakes not from her faith,
But from her need.
Con. Oh, if thou grant my need,
Which onely liues but by the death of faith,
That need, must needs inferre this principle,
That faith would liue againe by death of need:
O then tread downe my need, and faith mounts vp,
Keepe my need vp, and faith is trodden downe.
Iohn. The king is moud, and answers not to this.
Con. O be remou'd from him, and answere well.
Aust. Doe so king *Philip*, hang no more in doubt.
Bast. Hang nothing but a Calues skin most sweet lout.
Fra. I am perplext, and know not what to say.
Pan. What canst thou say, but wil perplex thee more?
If thou stand excommunicate, and curst?
Fra. Good reuerend father, make my person yours,
And tell me how you would bestow your selfe?
This royall hand and mine are newly knit,
And the coniunction of our inward soules
Married in league, coupled, and link'd together
With all religous strength of sacred vowes,
The latest breath that gaue the sound of words
Was deepe-sworne faith, peace, amity, true loue
Betweene our kingdomes and our royall selues,
And euen before this truce, but new before,
No longer then we well could wash our hands,
To clap this royall bargaine vp of peace,
Heauen knowes they were besmear'd and ouer-staind
With slaughters pencill; where reuenge did paint
The fearefull difference of incensed kings:
And shall these hands so lately purg'd of bloud?
So newly ioyn'd in loue? so strong in both,
Vnyoke this seysure, and this kinde regreete?
Play fast and loose with faith? so iest with heauen,
Make such vnconstant children of onr selues
As now againe to snatch our palme from palme:
Vn-sweare faith sworne, and on the marriage bed
Of smiling peace to march a bloody hoast,
And make a ryot on the gentle brow
Of true sincerity? O holy Sir
My reuerend father, let it not be so;
Out of your grace, deuise, ordaine, impose
Some gentle order, and then we shall be blest
To doe your pleasure, and continue friends.
Pand. All forme is formelesse, Order orderlesse,
Saue what is opposite to *Englands* loue.
Therefore to Armes, be Champion of our Church,
Or let the Church our mother breathe her curse,
A mothers curse, on her reuolting sonne:
France, thou maist hold a serpent by the tongue,
A cased Lion by the mortall paw,
A fasting Tyger safer by the tooth,
Then keepe in peace that hand which thou dost hold.
Fra. I may dis-ioyne my hand, but not my faith.
Pand. So mak'st thou faith an enemy to faith,
And like a ciuill warre setst oath to oath,
Thy tongue against thy tongue. O let thy vow
First made to heauen, first be to heauen perform'd,
That is, to be the Champion of our Church,
What since thou sworst, is sworne against thy selfe,
And may not be performed by thy selfe,
For that which thou hast sworne to doe amisse,
Is not amisse when it is truely done:
And being not done, where doing tends to ill,
The truth is then most done not doing it:
The better Act of purposes mistooke,
Is to mistake again, though indirect,
Yet indirection thereby growes direct,
And falshood, falshood cures, as fire cooles fire
Within the scorched veines of one new burn'd:
It is religion that doth make vowes kept,
But thou hast sworne against religion:
By what thou swear'st against the thing thou swear'st,
And mak'st an oath the suretie for thy truth,
Against an oath the truth, thou art vnsure
To sweare, sweares onely not to be forsworne,
Else what a mockerie should it be to sweare?
But thou dost sweare, onely to be forsworne,
And most forsworne, to keepe what thou dost sweare,
Therefore thy later vowes, against thy first,
Is in thy selfe rebellion to thy selfe:
And better conquest neuer canst thou make,
Then arme thy constant and thy nobler parts
Against these giddy loose suggestions:
Vpon which better part, our prayrs come in,
If thou vouchsafe them. But if not, then know
The perill of our curses light on thee
So heauy, as thou shalt not shake them off
But in despaire, dye vnder their blacke weight.
Aust. Rebellion, flat rebellion.
Bast. Wil't not be?
Will not a Calues-skin stop that mouth of thine?
Daul. Father, to Armes.
Blanch. Vpon thy wedding day?
Against the blood that thou hast married?
What, shall our feast be kept with slaughtered men?
Shall braying trumpets, and loud churlish drums
Clamors of hell, be measures to our pomp?
O husband heare me: aye, alacke, how new
Is husband in my mouth? euen for that name
Which till this time my tongue did nere pronounce;
Vpon my knee I beg, goe not to Armes
Against mine Vncle.
Const. O, vpon my knee made hard with kneeling,
I doe pray to thee, thou vertuous *Daulphin*,
Alter not the doome fore-thought by heauen.
Blan. Now shall I see thy loue, what motiue may
Be stronger with thee, then the name of wife?
Con. That which vpholdeth him, that thee vpholds,
His Honor, Oh thine Honor, *Lewis* thine Honor.
Dolph. I muse your Maiesty doth seeme so cold,
When such profound respects doe pull you on?
Pand. I will denounce a curse vpon his head.
Fra. Thou shalt not need. *England*, I will fall fro thee.
Const. O faire returne of banish'd Maiestie.
Elea. O foule reuolt of French inconstancy.
Eng. *France*, ŷ shalt rue this houre within this houre.

Bast.

Bast. Old Time the clocke setter, ȳ bald sexton Time:
Is it as he will? well then, *France* shall rue.
Bla. The Sun's orecast with bloud: faire day adieu,
Which is the side that I must goe withall?
I am with both, each Army hath a hand,
And in their rage, I hauing hold of both,
They whurle a-sunder, and dismember mee.
Husband, I cannot pray that thou maist winne:
Vncle, I needs must pray that thou maist lose:
Father, I may not wish the fortune thine:
Grandam, I will not wish thy wishes thriue:
Who-euer wins on that side shall I lose:
Assured losse, before the match be plaid.
Dolph. Lady, with me, with me thy fortune lies.
Bla. There where my fortune liues, there my life dies.
Iohn. *Cosen*, goe draw our puisance together,
France, I am burn'd vp with inflaming wrath,
A rage, whose heat hath this condition;
That nothing can allay, nothing but blood,
The blood and deerest valued bloud of *France*.
Fra. Thy rage shall burne thee vp, & thou shalt turne
To ashes, ere our blood shall quench that fire:
Looke to thy selfe, thou art in ieopardie.
Iohn. No more then he that threats. To Arms le'ts hie.
Exeunt.

Scœna Secunda.

Allarums, Excursions: Enter Bastard with Austria's head.

Bast. Now by my life, this day grows wondrous hot,
Some ayery Deuill houers in the skie,
And pour's downe mischiefe. *Austrias* head lye there,
Enter Iohn, Arthur, Hubert
While *Philip* breathes.
Iohn. *Hubert*, keepe this boy: *Philip* make vp,
My Mother is assayled in our Tent,
And tane I feare.
Bast. My Lord I rescued her,
Her Highnesse is in safety, feare you not:
But on my Liege, for very little paines
Will bring this labor to an happy end. *Exit.*

Alarums, excursions, Retreat. Enter Iohn, Eleanor, Arthur Bastard, Hubert, Lords.

Iohn. So shall it be: your Grace shall stay behinde
So strongly guarded: Cosen, looke not sad,
Thy Grandame loues thee, and thy Vnkle will
As deere be to thee, as thy father was.
Arth. O this will make my mother die with griefe.
Iohn. Cosen away for *England*, haste before,
And ere our comming see thou shake the bags
Of hoording Abbots, imprisoned angells
Set at libertie: the fat ribs of peace
Must by the hungry now be fed vpon:
Vse our Commission in his vtmost force.
Bast. Bell, Booke, & Candle, shall not driue me back,
When gold and siluer becks me to come on.
I leaue your highnesse: Grandame, I will pray
(If euer I remember to be holy)
For your faire safety: so I kisse your hand
Ele. Farewell gentle Cosen
Iohn. Coz, farewell.
Ele. Come hether little kinsman, harke, a worde.
Iohn. Come hether *Hubert*. O my gentle *Hubert*,
We owe thee much: within this wall of flesh
There is a soule counts thee her Creditor,
And with aduantage meanes to pay thy loue:
And my good friend, thy voluntary oath
Liues in this bosome, deerely cherished
Giue me thy hand, I had a thing to say,
But I will fit it with some better tune.
By heauen *Hubert*, I am almost asham'd
To say what good respect I haue of thee.
Hub. I am much bounden to your Maiesty
Iohn. Good friend, thou hast no cause to say so yet,
But thou shalt haue: and creepe time nere so slow,
Yet it shall come, for me to doe thee good.
I had a thing to say, but let it goe:
The Sunne is in the heauen, and the proud day,
Attended with the pleasures of the world,
Is all too wanton, and too full of gawdes
To giue me audience: If the mid-night bell
Did with his yron tongue, and brazen mouth
Sound on into the drowzie race of night:
If this same were a Church-yard where we stand,
And thou possessed with a thousand wrongs:
Or if that surly spirit melancholy
Had bak'd thy bloud, and made it heauy, thicke,
Which else runnes tickling vp and downe the veines,
Making that idiot laughter keepe mens eyes,
And straine their cheekes to idle merriment,
A passion hatefull to my purposes:
Or if that thou couldst see me without eyes,
Heare me without thine eares, and make reply
Without a tongue, vsing conceit alone,
Without eyes, eares, and harmefull sound of words
Then, in despight of brooded watchfull day,
I would into thy bosome poure my thoughts
But (ah) I will not, yet I loue thee well,
And by my troth I thinke thou lou'st me well.
Hub. So well, that what you bid me vndertake,
Though that my death were adiunct to my Act,
By heauen I would doe it.
Iohn. Doe not I know thou wouldst?
Good *Hubert*, *Hubert*, *Hubert* throw thine eye
On yon young boy: Ile tell thee what my friend,
He is a very serpent in my way,
And wheresoere this foot of mine doth tread,
He lies before me: dost thou vnderstand me?
Thou art his keeper.
Hub And Ile keepe him so,
That he shall not offend your Maiesty.
Iohn. Death.
Hub. My Lord.
Iohn. A Graue.
Hub. He shall not liue.
Iohn. Enough.
I could be merry now, *Hubert*, I loue thee.
Well, Ile not say what I intend for thee:
Remember: Madam, Fare you well,
Ile send those powers o're to your Maiesty.
Ele. My blessing goe with thee.
Iohn. For *England* Cosen, goe.
Hubert shall be your man, attend on you
With al true duetie: On toward *Callice*, hoa.
Exeunt.

Scæna Tertia.

Enter France, Dolphin, Pandulpho, Attendants.

Fra. So by a roaring Tempest on the flood,
A whole Armado of conuicted saile
Is scattered and dis-ioyn'd from fellowship.
Pand. Courage and comfort, all shall yet goe well.
Fra. What can goe well, when we haue runne so ill?
Are we not beaten? Is not *Angiers* lost?
Arthur tane prisoner? diuers deere friends slaine?
And bloudy *England* into *England* gone,
Ore-bearing interruption spight of *France*?
Dol. What he hath won, that hath he fortified:
So hot a speed, with such aduice dispos'd,
Such temperate order in so fierce a cause,
Doth want example: who hath read, or heard
Of any kindred-action like to this?
Fra. Well could I beare that *England* had this praise,
So we could finde some patterne of our shame:
Enter Constance.
Looke who comes heere? a graue vnto a soule,
Holding th eternall spirit against her will,
In the vilde prison of afflicted breath:
I prethee Lady goe away with me.
Con. Lo; now: now see the issue of your peace.
Fra. Patience good Lady, comfort gentle *Constance.*
Con. No, I defie all Counsell, all redresse,
But that which ends all counsell, true Redresse:
Death, death, O amiable, louely death,
Thou odoriferous stench: sound rottennesse,
Arise forth from the couch of lasting night,
Thou hate and terror to prosperitie,
And I will kisse thy detestable bones,
And put my eye-balls in thy vaultie browes,
And ring these fingers with thy houshold wormes,
And stop this gap of breath with fulsome dust,
And be a Carrion Monster like thy selfe;
Come, grin on me, and I will thinke thou smil'st,
And busse thee as thy wife: Miseries Loue,
O come to me.
Fra. O faire affliction, peace.
Con. No, no, I will not, hauing breath to cry:
O that my tongue were in the thunders mouth,
Then with a passion would I shake the world,
And rowze from sleepe that fell Anatomy
Which cannot heare a Ladies feeble voyce,
Which scornes a moderne Inuocation.
Pand.. Lady, you vtter madnesse, and not sorrow.
Con. Thou art holy to belye me so,
I am not mad: this haire I teare is mine,
My name is *Constance*, I was *Geffreyes* wife,
Yong *Arthur* is my sonne, and he is lost:
I am not mad, I would to heauen I were,
For then 'tis like I should forget my selfe:
O, if I could, what griefe should I forget?
Preach some Philosophy to make me mad,
And thou shalt be Canoniz'd (Cardinall.)
For, being not mad, but sensible of greefe,
My reasonable part produces reason
How I may be deliuer'd of these woes,
And teaches mee to kill or hang my selfe:
If I were mad, I should forget my sonne,
Or madly thinke a babe of clowts were he;
I am not mad: too well, too well I feele
The different plague of each calamitie.
Fra. Binde vp those tresses: O what loue I note
In the faire multitude of those her haires;
Where but by chance a siluer drop hath falne,
Euen to that drop ten thousand wiery fiends
Doe glew themselues in sociable griefe,
Like true, inseparable, faithfull loues,
Sticking together in calamitie.
Con. To *England*, if you will.
Fra. Binde vp your haires.
Con. Yes that I will: and wherefore will I do it?
I tore them from their bonds, and cride aloud,
O, that these hands could so redeeme my sonne,
As they haue giuen these hayres their libertie:
But now I enuie at their libertie,
And will againe commit them to their bonds,
Because my poore childe is a prisoner.
And Father Cardinall, I haue heard you say
That we shall see and know our friends in heauen:
If that be true, I shall see my boy againe;
For since the birth of *Caine*, the first male-childe
To him that did but yesterday suspire,
There was not such a gracious creature borne:
But now will Canker-sorrow eat my bud,
And chase the natiue beauty from his cheeke,
And he will looke as hollow as a Ghost,
As dim and meager as an Agues fitte,
And so hee'll dye: and rising so againe,
When I shall meet him in the Court of heauen
I shall not know him: therefore neuer, neuer
Must I behold my pretty *Arthur* more.
Pand. You hold too heynous a respect of greefe.
Const. He talkes to me, that neuer had a sonne.
Fra. You are as fond of greefe, as of your childe.
Con. Greefe fils the roome vp of my absent childe:
Lies in his bed, walkes vp and downe with me,
Puts on his pretty lookes, repeats his words,
Remembers me of all his gracious parts,
Stuffes out his vacant garments with his forme;
Then, haue I reason to be fond of griefe?
Fareyouwell: had you such a losse as I,
I could giue better comfort then you doe.
I will not keepe this forme vpon my head,
When there is such disorder in my witte:
O Lord, my boy, my *Arthur*, my faire sonne,
My life, my ioy, my food, my all the world:
My widow-comfort, and my sorrowes cure. *Exit.*
Fra. I feare some out-rage, and Ile follow her. *Exit.*
Dol. There's nothing in this world can make me ioy
Life is as tedious as a twice-told tale,
Vexing the dull eare of a drowsie man;
And bitter shame hath spoyl'd the sweet words taste,
That it yeelds nought but shame and bitternesse.
Pand. Before the curing of a strong disease,
Euen in the instant of repaire and health,
The fit is strongest: Euils that take leaue
On their departure, most of all shew euill:
What haue you lost by losing of this day?
Dol. All daies of glory, ioy, and happinesse.
Pan. If you had won it, certainely you had.
No, no: when Fortune meanes to men most good,
Shee lookes vpon them with a threatning eye:
'Tis strange to thinke how much King *Iohn* hath lost
In this which he accounts so clearely wonne:

Are

Are not you grieu'd that *Arthur* is his prisoner?
Dol. As heartily as he is glad he hath him.
Pan. Your minde is all as youthfull as your blood.
Now heare me speake with a propheticke spirit:
For euen the breath of what I meane to speake,
Shall blow each dust, each straw, each little rub
Out of the path which shall directly lead
Thy foote to Englands Throne. And therefore marke:
Iohn hath seiz'd *Arthur*, and it cannot be,
That whiles warme life playes in that infants veines,
The mis-plac'd *Iohn* should entertaine an houre,
One minute, nay one quiet breath of rest.
A Scepter snatch'd with an vnruly hand,
Must be as boysterously maintain'd as gain'd.
And he that stands vpon a slipp'ry place,
Makes nice of no vilde hold to stay him vp:
That *Iohn* may stand, then *Arthur* needs must fall,
So be it, for it cannot be but so.
Dol. But what shall I gaine by yong *Arthurs* fall?
Pan. You, in the right of Lady *Blanch* your wife,
May then make all the claime that *Arthur* did.
Dol. And loose it, life and all, as *Arthur* did.
Pan. How green you are, and fresh in this old world?
Iohn layes you plots: the times conspire with you,
For he that steepes his safetie in true blood,
Shall finde but bloodie safety, and vntrue.
This Act so euilly borne shall coole the hearts
Of all his people, and freeze vp their zeale,
That none so small aduantage shall step forth
To checke his reigne, but they will cherish it.
No naturall exhalation in the skie,
No scope of Nature, no distemper'd day,
No common winde, no customed euent,
But they will plucke away his naturall cause,
And call them Meteors, prodigies, and signes,
Abbortiues, presages, and tongues of heauen,
Plainly denouncing vengeance vpon *Iohn*.
Dol. May be he will not touch yong *Arthurs* life,
But hold himselfe safe in his prisonment.
Pan. O Sir, when he shall heare of your approach,
If that yong *Arthur* be not gone alreadie,
Euen at that newes he dies: and then the hearts
Of all his people shall reuolt from him,
And kisse the lippes of vnacquainted change,
And picke strong matter of reuolt, and wrath
Out of the bloody fingers ends of *Iohn*.
Me thinkes I see this hurley all on foot;
And O, what better matter breeds for you,
Then I haue nam'd. The Bastard *Falconbridge*
Is now in England ransacking the Church,
Offending Charity: If but a dozen French
Were there in Armes, they would be as a Call
To traine ten thousand English to their side;
Or, as a little snow, tumbled about,
Anon becomes a Mountaine. O noble Dolphine,
Go with me to the King, 'tis wonderfull,
What may be wrought out of their discontent,
Now that their soules are topfull of offence,
For England go; I will whet on the King.
Dol. Strong reasons makes strange actions: let vs go,
If you say I, the King will not say no. *Exeunt.*

Actus Quartus, Scæna prima.

Enter Hubert and Executioners.

Hub. Heate me these Irons hot, and looke thou stand
Within the Arras: when I strike my foot
Vpon the bosome of the ground, rush forth
And binde the boy, which you shall finde with me
Fast to the chaire: be heedfull: hence, and watch.
Exec. I hope your warrant will beare out the deed.
Hub. Vncleanly scruples feare not you: looke too't.
Yong Lad come forth; I haue to say with you.

Enter Arthur.

Ar. Good morrow *Hubert*.
Hub. Good morrow, little Prince.
Ar. As little Prince, hauing so great a Title
To be more Prince, as may be: you are sad.
Hub. Indeed I haue beene merrier.
Art. 'Mercie on me:
Me thinkes no body should be sad but I:
Yet I remember, when I was in France,
Yong Gentlemen would be as sad as night
Onely for wantonnesse: by my Christendome,
So I were out of prison, and kept Sheepe
I should be as merry as the day is long:
And so I would be heere, but that I doubt
My Vnckle practises more harme to me:
He is affraid of me, and I of him:
Is it my fault, that I was *Geffreyes* sonne?
No in deede is't not: and I would to heauen
I were your sonne, so you would loue me, Hubert:
Hub. If I talke to him, with his innocent prate
He will awake my mercie, which lies dead:
Therefore I will be sodaine, and dispatch.
Ar Are you sicke Hubert? you looke pale to day,
Insooth I would you were a little sicke,
That I might sit all night, and watch with you.
I warrant I loue you more then you do me.
Hub. His words do take possession of my bosome.
Reade heere yong *Arthur*. How now foolish rheume?
Turning dispitious torture out of doore?
I must be breefe, least resolution drop
Out at mine eyes, in tender womanish teares.
Can you not reade it? Is it not faire writ?
Ar. Too fairely *Hubert*, for so foule effect,
Must you with hot Irons, burne out both mine eyes?
Hub. Yong Boy, I must.
Art. And will you?
Hub. And I will.
Art. Haue you the heart? When your head did but ake,
I knit my hand-kercher about your browes
(The best I had, a Princesse wrought it me)
And I did neuer aske it you againe:
And with my hand, at midnight held your head;
And like the watchfull minutes, to the houre,
Still and anon cheer'd vp the heauy time;
Saying, what lacke you? and where lies your greefe?
Or what good loue may I performe for you?
Many a poore mans sonne would haue lyen still,
And nere haue spoke a louing word to you:
But you, at your sicke seruice had a Prince:
Nay, you may thinke my loue was craftie loue,
And call it cunning. Do, and if you will,

If heauen be pleas'd that you must vse me ill,
Why then you must. Will you put out mine eyes?
These eyes, that neuer did, nor neuer shall
So much as frowne on you.
Hub. I haue sworne to do it:
And with hot Irons must I burne them out.
Ar. Ah, none but in this Iron Age, would do it:
The Iron of it selfe, though heate red hot,
Approaching neere these eyes, would drinke my teares,
And quench this fierie indignation,
Euen in the matter of mine innocence:
Nay, after that, consume away in rust,
But for containing fire to harme mine eye:
Are you more stubborne hard, then hammer'd Iron?
And if an Angell should haue come to me,
And told me *Hubert* should put out mine eyes,
I would not haue beleeu'd him: no tongue but *Huberts.*
Hub. Come forth: Do as I bid you do.
Art. O saue me *Hubert*, saue me: my eyes are out
Euen with the fierce lookes of these bloody men.
Hub. Giue me the Iron I say, and binde him heere
Art. Alas, what neede you be so boistrous rough?
I will not struggle, I will stand stone still:
For heauen sake *Hubert* let me not be bound:
Nay heare me *Hubert*, driue these men away,
And I will sit as quiet as a Lambe.
I will not stirre, nor winch, nor speake a word,
Nor looke vpon the Iron angerly:
Thrust but these men away, and Ile forgiue you,
What euer torment you do put me too.
Hub. Go stand within: let me alone with him.
Exec. I am best pleas'd to be from such a deede.
Art. Alas, I then haue chid away my friend,
He hath a sterne looke, but a gentle heart:
Let him come backe, that his compassion may
Giue life to yours.
Hub. Come (Boy) prepare your selfe.
Art. Is there no remedie?
Hub. None, but to lose your eyes.
Art. O heauen: that there were but a moth in yours,
A graine, a dust, a gnat, a wandering haire,
Any annoyance in that precious sense:
Then feeling what small things are boysterous there,
Your vilde intent must needs seeme horrible.
Hub. Is this your promise? Go too, hold your toong
Art. *Hubert*, the vtterance of a brace of tongues,
Must needes want pleading for a paire of eyes:
Let me not hold my tongue: let me not *Hubert*,
Or *Hubert*, if you will cut out my tongue,
So I may keepe mine eyes. O spare mine eyes,
Though to no vse, but still to looke on you.
Loe, by my troth, the Instrument is cold,
And would not harme me.
Hub. I can heate it, Boy.
Art. No, in good sooth: the fire is dead with griefe,
Being create for comfort, to be vs'd
In vndeserued extreames: See else your selfe,
There is no malice in this burning cole,
The breath of heauen, hath blowne his spirit out,
And strew'd repentant ashes on his head.
Hub. But with my breath I can reuiue it Boy.
Art. And if you do, you will but make it blush,
And glow with shame of your proceedings, *Hubert:*
Nay, it perchance will sparkle in your eyes:
And, like a dogge that is compell'd to fight,
Snatch at his Master that doth tarre him on.
All things that you should vse to do me wrong
Deny their office: onely you do lacke
That mercie, which fierce fire, and Iron extends,
Creatures of note for mercy, lacking vses.
Hub. Well, see to liue: I will not touch thine eye,
For all the Treasure that thine Vnckle owes,
Yet am I sworne, and I did purpose, Boy,
With this same very Iron, to burne them out.
Art. O now you looke like *Hubert*. All this while
You were disguis'd.
Hub. Peace: no more. Adieu,
Your Vnckle must not know but you are dead.
Ile fill these dogged Spies with false reports:
And, pretty childe, sleepe doubtlesse, and secure,
That *Hubert* for the wealth of all the world,
Will not offend thee.
Art. O heauen! I thanke you *Hubert*.
Hub. Silence, no more; go closely in with mee,
Much danger do I vndergo for thee. *Exeunt*

Scena Secunda.

Enter Iohn, Pembroke, Salisbury, and other Lordes.
Iohn. Heere once againe we sit: once against crown'd
And look'd vpon, I hope, with cheerefull eyes.
Pem This once again (but that your Highnes pleas'd)
Was once superfluous: you were Crown'd before,
And that high Royalty was nere pluck'd off:
The faiths of men, nere stained with reuolt:
Fresh expectation troubled not the Land
With any long'd-for-change, or better State.
Sal. Therefore, to be possess'd with double pompe,
To guard a Title, that was rich before;
To gilde refined Gold, to paint the Lilly;
To throw a perfume on the Violet,
To smooth the yce, or adde another hew
Vnto the Raine-bow; or with Taper-light
To seeke the beauteous eye of heauen to garnish,
Is wastefull, and ridiculous excesse.
Pem. But that your Royall pleasure must be done,
This acte, is as an ancient tale new told,
And, in the last repeating, troublesome,
Being vrged at a time vnseasonable.
Sal. In this the Anticke, and well noted face
Of plaine old forme, is much disfigured,
And like a shifted winde vnto a saile,
It makes the course of thoughts to fetch about,
Startles, and frights consideration:
Makes sound opinion sicke, and truth suspected,
For putting on so new a fashion'd robe.
Pem. When Workemen striue to do better then wel,
They do confound their skill in couetousnesse,
And oftentimes excusing of a fault,
Doth make the fault the worse by th'excuse:
As patches set vpon a little breach,
Discredite more in hiding of the fault,
Then did the fault before it was so patch'd.
Sal. To this effect, before you were new crown'd
We breath'd our Councell: but it pleas'd your Highnes
To ouer-beare it, and we are all well pleas'd,
Since all, and euery part of what we would
Doth make a stand, at what your Highnesse will.

Ioh. Some reasons of this double Corronation
I haue possest you with, and thinke them strong.
And more, more strong, then lesser is my feare
I shall indue you with: Meane time, but aske
What you would haue reform'd that is not well,
And well shall you perceiue, how willingly
I will both heare, and grant you your requests.

Pem. Then I, as one that am the tongue of these
To sound the purposes of all their hearts,
Both for my selfe, and them: but chiefe of all
Your safety: for the which, my selfe and them
Bend their best studies, heartily request
Th'infranchisement of *Arthur*, whose restraint
Doth moue the murmuring lips of discontent
To breake into this dangerous argument.
If what in rest you haue, in right you hold,
Why then your feares, which (as they say) attend
The steppes of wrong, should moue you to mew vp
Your tender kinsman, and to choake his dayes
With barbarous ignorance, and deny his youth
The rich aduantage of good exercise,
That the times enemies may not haue this
To grace occasions: let it be our suite,
That you haue bid vs aske his libertie,
Which for our goods, we do no further aske,
Then, whereupon our weale on you depending,
Counts it your weale: he haue his liberty

Enter Hubert.

Iohn. Let it be so: I do commit his youth
To your direction: *Hubert*, what newes with you?

Pem. This is the man should do the bloody deed:
He shew'd his warrant to a friend of mine,
The image of a wicked heynous fault
Liues in his eye: that close aspect of his,
Do shew the mood of a much troubled brest,
And I do fearefully beleeue 'tis done,
What we so fear'd he had a charge to do.

Sal. The colour of the King doth come, and go
Betweene his purpose and his conscience,
Like Heralds 'twixt two dreadfull battailes set·
His passion is so ripe, it needs must breake.

Pem. And when it breakes, I feare will issue thence
The foule corruption of a sweet childes death.

Iohn. We cannot hold mortalities strong hand.
Good Lords, although my will to giue, is liuing,
The suite which you demand is gone, and dead.
He tels vs *Arthur* is deceas'd to night.

Sal. Indeed we fear'd his sicknesse was past cure.

Pem. Indeed we heard how neere his death he was,
Before the childe himselfe felt he was sicke :
This must be answer'd either heere, or hence.

Ioh. Why do you bend such solemne browes on me?
Thinke you I beare the Sheeres of destiny ?
Haue I commandement on the pulse of life?

Sal. It is apparant foule-play, and 'tis shame
That Greatnesse should so grossely offer it;
So thriue it in your game, and so farewell.

Pem. Stay yet (Lord Salisbury) Ile go with thee,
And finde th'inheritance of this poore childe,
His little kingdome of a forced graue.
That blood which ow'd the bredth of all this Ile,
Three foot of it doth hold; bad world the while:
This must not be thus borne, this will breake out
To all our sorrowes, and ere long I doubt. *Exeunt*

Io. They burn in indignation: I repent: *Enter Mes.*
There is no sure foundation set on blood:
No certaine life atchieu'd by others death:
A fearefull eye thou hast. Where is that blood,
That I haue seene inhabite in those cheekes?
So foule a skie, cleeres not without a storme,
Poure downe thy weather: how goes all in France?

Mes. From France to England, neuer such a powre
For any forraigne preparation,
Was leuied in the body of a land.
The Copie of your speede is learn'd by them:
For when you should be told they do prepare,
The tydings comes, that they are all arriu'd

Ioh. Oh where hath our Intelligence bin drunke?
Where hath it slept? Where is my Mothers care?
That such an Army could be drawne in France,
And she not heare of it?

Mes. My Liege, her eare
Is stopt with dust: the first of Aprill di'de
Your noble mother; and as I heare, my Lord,
The Lady *Constance* in a frenzie di'de
Three dayes before: but this from Rumors tongue
I idely heard: if true, or false I know not.

Iohn. With-hold thy speed, dreadfull Occasion.
O make a league with me, 'till I haue pleas'd
My discontented Peeres. What? Mother dead?
How wildely then walkes my Estate in France?
Vnder whose conduct came those powres of France,
That thou for truth giu'st out are landed heere?

Mes. Vnder the Dolphin.

Enter Bastard and Peter of Pomfret.

Ioh. Thou hast made me giddy
With these ill tydings: Now? What sayes the world
To your proceedings? Do not seeke to stuffe
My head with more ill newes: for it is full.

Bast. But if you be a-feard to heare the worst,
Then let the worst vn-heard, fall on your head.

Iohn. Beare with me Cosen, for I was amaz'd
Vnder the tide; but now I breath againe
Aloft the flood, and can giue audience
To any tongue, speake it of what it will.

Bast. How I haue sped among the Clergy men,
The summes I haue collected shall expresse:
But as I trauail'd hither through the land,
I finde the people strangely fantasied,
Possest with rumors, full of idle dreames,
Not knowing what they feare, but full of feare.
And here's a Prophet that I brought with me
From forth the streets of Pomfret, whom I found
With many hundreds treading on his heeles:
To whom he sung in rude harsh sounding rimes,
That ere the next Ascension day at noone,
Your Highnes should deliuer vp your Crowne.

Iohn Thou idle Dreamer, wherefore didst thou so?

Pet. Fore-knowing that the truth will fall out so.

Iohn *Hubert*, away with him: imprison him,
And on that day at noone, whereon he sayes
I shall yeeld vp my Crowne, let him be hang'd.
Deliuer him to safety, and returne,
For I must vse thee. O my gentle Cosen,
Hear'st thou the newes abroad, who are arriu'd?

Bast. The *French* (my Lord) mens mouths are ful of it:
Besides I met Lord *Bigot*, and Lord *Salisburie*
With eyes as red as new enkindled fire,
And others more, going to seeke the graue
Of *Arthur*, whom they say is kill'd to night, on your (suggestion.

Iohn. Gentle kinsman, go
And thrust thy selfe into their Companies,

I haue a way to winne their loues againe:
Bring them before me.

Bast. I will seeke them out.

John. Nay, but make haste: the better foote before.
O, let me haue no subiect enemies,
When aduerse Forreyners affright my Townes
With dreadfull pompe of stout inuasion.
Be Mercurie, set feathers to thy heeles,
And flye (like thought) from them, to me againe.

Bast. The spirit of the time shall teach me speed. *Exit*

Iohn. Spoke like a sprightfull Noble Gentleman.
Go after him: for he perhaps shall neede
Some Messenger betwixt me, and the Peeres,
And be thou hee.

Mes. With all my heart, my Liege.

Iohn. My mother dead?

Enter Hubert.

Hub. My Lord, they say fiue Moones were seene to (night:
Foure fixed, and the fift did whirle about
The other foure, in wondrous motion.

Ioh. Fiue Moones?

Hub. Old men, and Beldames, in the streets
Do prophesie vpon it dangerously:
Yong *Arthurs* death is common in their mouths,
And when they talke of him, they shake their heads,
And whisper one another in the eare.
And he that speakes, doth gripe the hearers wrist,
Whilst he that heares, makes fearefull action
With wrinkled browes, with nods, with rolling eyes.
I saw a Smith stand with his hammer (thus)
The whilst his Iron did on the Anuile coole,
With open mouth swallowing a Taylors newes,
Who with his Sheeres, and Measure in his hand,
Standing on slippers, which his nimble haste
Had falsely thrust vpon contrary feete,
Told of a many thousand warlike French,
That were embattailed, and rank'd in Kent.
Another leane, vnwash'd Artificer,
Cuts off his tale, and talkes of *Arthurs* death.

Io. Why seek'st thou to possesse me with these feares?
Why vrgest thou so oft yong *Arthurs* death?
Thy hand hath murdred him: I had a mighty cause
To wish him dead, but thou hadst none to kill him.

H. No had (my Lord?) why, did you not prouoke me?

Iohn. It is the curse of Kings, to be attended
By slaues, that take their humors for a warrant,
To breake within the bloody house of life,
And on the winking of Authoritie
To vnderstand a Law; to know the meaning
Of dangerous Maiesty, when perchance it frownes
More vpon humor, then aduis'd respect.

Hub. Heere is your hand and Seale for what I did.

Ioh. Oh, when the last accompt twixt heauen & earth
Is to be made, then shall this hand and Seale
Witnesse against vs to damnation.
How oft the sight of meanes to do ill deeds,
Make deeds ill done? Had'st not thou beene by,
A fellow by the hand of Nature mark'd,
Quoted, and sign'd to do a deede of shame,
This murther had not come into my minde.
But taking note of thy abhorr'd Aspect,
Finding thee fit for bloody villanie:
Apt, liable to be employ'd in danger,
I faintly broke with thee of *Arthurs* death:
And thou, to be endeered to a King,
Made it no conscience to destroy a Prince.

Hub. My Lord.

Ioh. Had'st thou but shooke thy head, or made a pause
When I spake darkely, what I purposed:
Or turn'd an eye of doubt vpon my face;
As bid me tell my tale in expresse words:
Deepe shame had struck me dumbe, made me break off,
And those thy feares, might haue wrought feares in me.
But, thou didst vnderstand me by my signes,
And didst in signes againe parley with sinne,
Yea, without stop, didst let thy heart consent,
And consequently, thy rude hand to acte
The deed, which both our tongues held vilde to name.
Out of my sight, and neuer see me more:
My Nobles leaue me, and my State is braued,
Euen at my gates, with rankes of forraigne powres;
Nay, in the body of this fleshly Land,
This kingdome, this Confine of blood, and breathe
Hostilitie, and ciuill tumult reignes
Betweene my conscience, and my Cosins death.

Hub. Arme you against your other enemies.
Ile make a peace betweene your soule, and you.
Yong *Arthur* is aliue: This hand of mine
Is yet a maiden, and an innocent hand.
Not painted with the Crimson spots of blood,
Within this bosome, neuer entred yet
The dreadfull motion of a murderous thought,
And you haue slander'd Nature in my forme,
Which howsoeuer rude exteriorly,
Is yet the couer of a fayrer minde,
Then to be butcher of an innocent childe.

Iohn. Doth *Arthur* liue? O hast thee to the Peeres,
Throw this report on their incens'd rage,
And make them tame to their obedience.
Forgiue the Comment that my passion made
Vpon thy feature, for my rage was blinde,
And foule immaginarie eyes of blood
Presented thee more hideous then thou art.
Oh, answer not; but to my Closset bring
The angry Lords, with all expedient hast,
I coniure thee but slowly: run more fast. *Exeunt.*

Scœna Tertia.

Enter Arthur on the walles.

Ar. The Wall is high, and yet will I leape downe.
Good ground be pittifull, and hurt me not:
There's few or none do know me, if they did,
This Ship-boyes semblance hath disguis'd me quite.
I am afraide, and yet Ile venture it.
If I get downe, and do not breake my limbes,
Ile finde a thousand shifts to get away;
As good to dye, and go; as dye, and stay.
Oh me, my Vnckles spirit is in these stones,
Heauen take my soule, and England keep my bones. *Dies*

Enter Pembroke, Salisbury, & Bigot.

Sal. Lords, I will meet him at S. *Edmondsbury*,
It is our safetie, and we must embrace
This gentle offer of the perillous time.

Pem. Who brought that Letter from the Cardinall?

Sal. The Count *Meloone*, a Noble Lord of France,
Whose priuate with me of the Dolphines loue,
Is much more generall, then these lines import.

Big.

Big. To morrow morning let vs meete him then.
Sal. Or rather then set forward, for 'twill be
Two long dayes iourney (Lords)or ere we meete.
Enter Bastard.
*Bast.*Once more to day well met, distemper'd Lords,
The King by me requests your presence straight.
Sal. The king hath dispossest himselfe of vs,
We will not lyne his thin-bestained cloake
With our pure Honors : nor attend the foote
That leaues the print of blood where ere it walkes.
Returne,and tell him so : we know the worst.
Bast. What ere you thinke,good words I thinke were best.
Sal. Our greefes, and not our manners reason now.
Bast. But there is little reason in your greefe.
Therefore 'twere reason you had manners now.
Pem. Sir, sir, impatience hath his priuiledge.
Bast. 'Tis true, to hurt his master, no mans else.
Sal. This is the prison : What is he lyes heere?
*P.*Oh death,made proud with pure & princely beuty,
The earth had not a hole to hide this deede.
Sal. Murther, as hating what himselfe hath done,
Doth lay it open to vrge on reuenge.
Big. Or when he doom'd this Beautie to a graue,
Found it too precious Princely, for a graue.
Sal. Sir *Richard*, what thinke you? you haue beheld,
Or haue you read, or heard, or could you thinke?
Or do you almost thinke, although you see,
That you do see? Could thought, without this obiect
Forme such another? This is the very top,
The heighth, the Crest : or Crest vnto the Crest
Of murthers Armes : This is the bloodiest shame,
The wildest Sauagery, the vildest stroke
That euer wall-ey'd wrath, or staring rage
Presented to the teares of soft remorse.
Pem. All murthers past, do stand excus'd in this :
And this so sole, and so vnmatcheable,
Shall giue a holinesse, a puritie,
To the yet vnbegotten sinne of times;
And proue a deadly blood-shed, but a iest,
Exampled by this heynous spectacle.
Bast. It is a damned,and a bloody worke,
The gracelesse action of a heauy hand,
If that it be the worke of any hand.
Sal. If that it be the worke of any hand?
We had a kinde of light, what would ensue:
It is the shamefull worke of *Huberts* hand,
The practice, and the purpose of the king :
From whose obedience I forbid my soule,
Kneeling before this ruine of sweete life,
And breathing to his breathlesse Excellence
The Incense of a Vow,a holy Vow :
Neuer to taste the pleasures of the world,
Neuer to be infected with delight,
Nor conuersant with Ease, and Idlenesse,
Till I haue set a glory to this hand,
By giuing it the worship of Reuenge.
Pem. Big. Our soules religiously confirme thy words.
Enter Hubert.
Hub. Lords, I am hot with haste, in seeking you,
Arthur doth liue, the king hath sent for you.
Sal. Oh he is bold, and blushes not at death,
Auant thou hatefull villain,get thee gone.
Hu. I am no villaine. *Sal.* Must I rob (the Law?
Bast. Your sword is bright sir, put it vp againe.
Sal. Not till I sheath it in a murtherers skin.
Hub. Stand backe Lord Salsbury,stand backe I say :
By heauen, I thinke my sword's as sharpe as yours.
I would not haue you (Lord) forget your selfe,
Nor tempt the danger of my true defence;
Least I, by marking of your rage, forget
your Worth, your Greatnesse, and Nobility.
Big. Out dunghill : dar'st thou braue a Nobleman?
Hub. Not for my life : But yet I dare defend
My innocent life against an Emperor.
Sal. Thou art a Murtherer.
Hub. Do not proue me so :
Yet I am none. Whose tongue so ere speakes false,
Not truely speakes : who speakes not truly, Lies.
Pem. Cut him to peeces.
Bast. Keepe the peace, I say.
Sal. Stand by, or I shall gaul you *Faulconbridge*.
Bast. Thou wer't better gaul the diuell Salsbury.
If thou but frowne on me, or stirre thy foote,
Or teach thy hastie spleene to do me shame,
Ile strike thee dead. Put vp thy sword betime,
Or Ile so maule you, and your tosting-Iron,
That you shall thinke the diuell is come from hell.
Big. What wilt thou do, renowned *Faulconbridge*?
Second a Villaine, and a Murtherer?
Hub. Lord *Bigot*, I am none.
Big. Who kill'd this Prince?
Hub. 'Tis not an houre since I left him well :
I honour'd him, I lou'd him, and will weepe
My date of life out, for his sweete liues losse.
Sal. Trust not those cunning waters of his eyes,
For villanie is not without such rheume,
And he, long traded in it, makes it seeme
Like Riuers of remorse and innocencie.
Away with me, all you whose soules abhorre
Th'vncleanly sauours of a Slaughter-house,
For I am stifled with this smell of sinne.
Big. Away, toward *Burie*, to the Dolphin there.
*P.*There tel the king,he may inquire vs out. *Ex. Lords.*
*Ba.*Here's a good world:knew you of this faire work?
Beyond the infinite and boundlesse reach of mercie,
(If thou didst this deed of death) art ÿ damn'd *Hubert*.
Hub Do but heare me sir.
Bast. Ha? Ile tell thee what.
Thou'rt damn'd as blacke, nay nothing is so blacke,
Thou art more deepe damn'd then Prince Lucifer :
There is not yet so vgly a fiend of hell
As thou shalt be, if thou didst kill this childe.
Hub. Vpon my soule.
Bast. If thou didst but consent
To this most cruell Act : do but dispaire,
And if thou want'st a Cord, the smallest thred
That euer Spider twisted from her wombe
Will serue to strangle thee : A rush will be a beame
To hang thee on. Or wouldst thou drowne thy selfe,
Put but a little water in a spoone,
And it shall be as all the Ocean,
Enough to stifle such a villaine vp.
I do suspect thee very greeuously.
Hub. If I in act, consent, or sinne of thought,
Be guiltie of the stealing that sweete breath
Which was embounded in this beauteous clay,
Let hell want paines enough to torture me :
I left him well.
Bast. Go, beare him in thine armes:
I am amaz'd me thinkes, and loose my way
Among the thornes,and dangers of this world.

How easie dost thou take all *England* vp,
From forth this morcell of dead Royaltie?
The life, the right, and truth of all this Realme
Is fled to heauen: and *England* now is left
To tug and scamble, and to part by th'teeth
The vn-owed interest of proud swelling State:
Now for the bare-pickt bone of Maiesty,
Doth dogged warre bristle his angry crest,
And snarleth in the gentle eyes of peace:
Now Powers from home, and discontents at home
Meet in one line: and vast confusion waites
As doth a Rauen on a sicke-falne beast,
The iminent decay of wrested pompe.
Now happy he, whose cloake and center can
Hold out this tempest. Beare away that childe,
And follow me with speed: Ile to the King:
A thousand businesses are briefe in hand,
And heauen it selfe doth frowne vpon the Land. *Exit.*

Actus Quartus, Scæna prima.

Enter King Iohn and Pandolph, attendants.

K.Iohn. Thus haue I yeelded vp into your hand
The Circle of my glory.
Pan. Take againe
From this my hand, as holding of the Pope
Your Soueraigne greatnesse and authoritie.
Iohn. Now keep your holy word, go meet the *French,*
And from his holinesse vse all your power
To stop their marches 'fore we are enflam'd:
Our discontented Counties doe reuolt:
Our people quarrell with obedience,
Swearing Allegiance, and the loue of soule
To stranger-bloud, to forren Royalty;
This inundation of mistempred humor,
Rests by you onely to be qualified.
Then pause not: for the present time's so sicke,
That present medcine must be ministred,
Or ouerthrow incureable ensues.
Pand. It was my breath that blew this Tempest vp,
Vpon your stubborne vsage of the Pope:
But since you are a gentle conuertite,
My tongue shall hush againe this storme of warre,
And make faire weather in your blustring land:
On this Ascention day, remember well,
Vpon your oath of seruice to the Pope,
Goe I to make the *French* lay downe their Armes. *Exit.*
Iohn. Is this Ascension day? did not the Prophet
Say, that before Ascension day at noone,
My Crowne I should giue off? euen so I haue:
I did suppose it should be on constraint,
But (heau'n be thank'd) it is but voluntary.

Enter Bastard.

Bast. All Kent hath yeelded: nothing there holds out
But Douer Castle: London hath receiu'd
Like a kinde Host, the Dolphin and his powers.
Your Nobles will not heare you, but are gone
To offer seruice to your enemy:
And wilde amazement hurries vp and downe
The little number of your doubtfull friends.
Iohn. Would not my Lords returne to me againe
After they heard yong *Arthur* was aliue?
Bast. They found him dead, and cast into the streets,
An empty Casket, where the Iewell of life
By some damn'd hand was rob'd, and tane away.
Iohn. That villaine *Hubert* told me he did liue.
Bast. So on my soule he did, for ought he knew:
But wherefore doe you droope? why looke you sad?
Be great in act, as you haue beene in thought:
Let not the world see feare and sad distrust
Gouerne the motion of a kinglye eye:
Be stirring as the time, be fire with fire,
Threaten the threatner, and out-face the brow
Of bragging horror: So shall inferior eyes
That borrow their behauiours from the great,
Grow great by your example, and put on
The dauntlesse spirit of resolution.
Away, and glister like the god of warre
When he intendeth to become the field:
Shew boldnesse and aspiring confidence:
What, shall they seeke the Lion in his denne,
And fright him there? and make him tremble there?
Oh let it not be said: forrage, and runne
To meet displeasure farther from the dores,
And grapple with him ere he come so nye.
Iohn. The Legat of the Pope hath beene with mee,
And I haue made a happy peace with him,
And he hath promis'd to dismisse the Powers
Led by the Dolphin.
Bast. Oh inglorious league:
Shall we vpon the footing of our land,
Send fayre-play-orders, and make comprimise,
Insinuation, parley, and base truce
To Armes Inuasiue? Shall a beardlesse boy,
A cockred-silken wanton braue our fields,
And flesh his spirit in a warre-like soyle,
Mocking the ayre with colours idlely spred,
And finde no checke? Let vs my Liege to Armes:
Perchance the Cardinall cannot make your peace;
Or if he doe, let it at least be said
They saw we had a purpose of defence.
Iohn. Haue thou the ordering of this present time.
Bast. Away then with good courage: yet I know
Our Partie may well meet a prowder foe. *Exeunt.*

Scœna Secunda.

Enter (in Armes) Dolphin, Salisbury, Meloone, Pembroke, Bigot, Souldiers.

Dol. My Lord *Melloone*, let this be coppied out,
And keepe it safe for our remembrance:
Returne the president to these Lords againe,
That hauing our faire order written downe,
Both they and we, perusing ore these notes
May know wherefore we tooke the Sacrament,
And keepe our faithes firme and inuiolable.
Sal. Vpon our sides it neuer shall be broken.
And Noble Dolphin, albeit we sweare
A voluntary zeale, and an vn-urg'd Faith
To your proceedings; yet beleeue me Prince,
I am not glad that such a sore of Time
Should seeke a plaster by contemn'd reuolt,
And heale the inueterate Canker of one wound,

By making many: Oh it grieues my soule,
That I must draw this mettle from my side
To be a widdow-maker: oh, and there
Where honourable rescue, and defence
Cries out vpon the name of *Salisbury*.
But such is the infection of the time,
That for the health and Physicke of our right,
We cannot deale but with the very hand
Of sterne Iniustice, and confused wrong:
And is't not pitty, (oh my grieued friends)
That we, the sonnes and children of this Isle,
Was borne to see so sad an houre as this,
Wherein we step after a stranger, march
Vpon her gentle bosom, and fill vp
Her Enemies rankes? I must withdraw, and weepe
Vpon the spot of this inforced cause,
To grace the Gentry of a Land remote,
And follow vnacquainted colours heere:
What heere? O Nation that thou couldst remoue,
That *Neptunes* Armes who clippeth thee about,
Would beare thee from the knowledge of thy selfe,
And cripple thee vnto a Pagan shore,
Where these two Christian Armies might combine
The bloud of malice, in a vaine of league,
And not to spend it so vn-neighbourly.

Dolph. A noble temper dost thou shew in this,
And great affections wrastling in thy bosome
Doth make an earth-quake of Nobility:
Oh, what a noble combat hast fought
Between compulsion, and a braue respect:
Let me wipe off this honourable dewe,
That siluerly doth progresse on thy cheekes:
My heart hath melted at a Ladies teares,
Being an ordinary Inundation:
But this effusion of such manly drops,
This showre, blowne vp by tempest of the soule,
Startles mine eyes, and makes me more amaz'd
Then had I seene the vaultie top of heauen
Figur'd quite ore with burning Meteors.
Lift vp thy brow (renowned *Salisburie*)
And with a great heart heaue away this storme:
Commend these waters to those baby-eyes
That neuer saw the giant-world enrag'd,
Nor met with Fortune, other then at feasts,
Full warm of blood, of mirth, of gossipping:
Come, come; for thou shalt thrust thy hand as deepe
Into the purse of rich prosperity
As *Lewis* himselfe: so (Nobles) shall you all,
That knit your sinewes to the strength of mine.

Enter Pandulpho.

And euen there, methinkes an Angell spake,
Looke where the holy Legate comes apace,
To giue vs warrant from the hand of heauen,
And on our actions set the name of right
With holy breath.

Pand. Haile noble Prince of *France*:
The next is this: King *Iohn* hath reconcil'd
Himselfe to *Rome*, his spirit is come in,
That so stood out against the holy Church,
The great Metropolis and Sea of Rome:
Therefore thy threatning Colours now winde vp,
And tame the sauage spirit of wilde warre,
That like a Lion fostered vp at hand,
It may lie gently at the foot of peace,
And be no further harmefull then in shewe.

Dol. Your Grace shall pardon me, I will not backe:
I am too high-borne to be proportied
To be a secondary at controll,
Or vsefull seruing-man, and Instrument
To any Soueraigne State throughout the world.
Your breath first kindled the dead coale of warres,
Betweene this chastiz'd kingdome and my selfe,
And brought in matter that should feed this fire;
And now 'tis farre too huge to be blowne out
With that same weake winde, which enkindled it:
You taught me how to know the face of right,
Acquainted me with interest to this Land,
Yea, thrust this enterprize into my heart,
And come ye now to tell me *Iohn* hath made
His peace with *Rome*? what is that peace to me?
I (by the honour of my marriage bed)
After yong *Arthur*, claime this Land for mine,
And now it is halfe conquer'd, must I backe,
Because that *Iohn* hath made his peace with *Rome*?
Am I *Romes* slaue? What penny hath *Rome* borne?
What men prouided? What munition sent
To vnder-prop this Action? Is't not I
That vnder-goe this charge? Who else but I,
And such as to my claime are liable,
Sweat in this businesse, and maintaine this warre?
Haue I not heard these Islanders shout out
Viue le Roy, as I haue bank'd their Townes?
Haue I not heere the best Cards for the game
To winne this easie match, plaid for a Crowne?
And shall I now giue ore the yeelded Set?
No, no, on my soule it neuer shall be said.

Pand. You looke but on the out-side of this worke.

Dol. Out-side or in-side I will not returne
Till my attempt so much be glorified,
As to my ample hope was promised,
Before I drew this gallant head of warre,
And cull'd these fiery spirits from the world
To out looke Conquest, and to winne renowne
Euen in the iawes of danger, and of death:
What lusty Trumpet thus doth summon vs?

Enter Bastard.

Bast. According to the faire-play of the world,
Let me haue audience: I am sent to speake:
My holy Lord of Millane, from the King
I come to learne how you haue dealt for him:
And, as you answer, I doe know the scope
And warrant limited vnto my tongue.

Pand. The *Dolphin* is too wilfull opposite
And will not temporize with my intreaties:
He flatly saies, hee ll not lay downe his Armes.

Bast. By all the bloud that euer fury breath'd,
The youth saies well. Now heare our *English* King,
For thus his Royaltie doth speake in me:
He is prepar'd, and reason to he should,
This apish and vnmannerly approach,
This harness'd Maske, and vnaduised Reuell,
This vn-heard sawcinesse and boyish Troopes,
The King doth smile at, and is well prepar'd
To whip this dwarfish warre, this Pigmy Armes
From out the circle of his Territories.
That hand which had the strength, euen at your dore,
To cudgell you, and make you take the hatch,
To diue like Buckets in concealed Welles,
To crowch in litter of your stable plankes,
To lye like pawnes, lock'd vp in chests and truncks,
To hug with swine, to seeke sweet safety out
In vaults and prisons, and to thrill and shake,

Euen at the crying of your Nations crow,
Thinking this voyce an armed Englishman.
Shall that victorious hand be feebled heere,
That in your Chambers gaue you chasticement?
No: know the gallant Monarch is in Armes,
And like an Eagle, o're his ayerie towres,
To sowsse annoyance that comes neere his Nest;
And you degenerate, you ingrate Reuolts,
you bloudy Nero's, ripping vp the wombe
Of your deere Mother-England: blush for shame:
For your owne Ladies, and pale-visag'd Maides,
Like *Amazons*, come tripping after drummes:
Their thimbles into armed Gantlets change,
Their Needl's to Lances, and their gentle hearts
To fierce and bloody inclination.
Dol. There end thy braue, and turn thy face in peace,
We grant thou canst out-scold vs: Far thee well,
We hold our time too precious to be spent
With such a brabler.
Pan. Giue me leaue to speake.
Bast. No, I will speake.
Dol. We will attend to neyther:
Strike vp the drummes, and let the tongue of warre
Pleade for our interest, and our being heere.
Bast. Indeede your drums being beaten, wil cry out;
And so shall you, being beaten: Do but start
An eccho with the clamor of thy drumme,
And euen at hand, a drumme is readie brac'd,
That shall reuerberate all, as lowd as thine.
Sound but another, and another shall
(As lowd as thine) rattle the Welkins eare,
And mocke the deepe mouth'd Thunder: for at hand
(Not trusting to this halting Legate heere,
Whom he hath vs'd rather for sport, then neede)
Is warlike *Iohn*: and in his fore-head sits
A bare-rib'd death, whose office is this day
To feast vpon whole thousands of the French.
Dol. Strike vp our drummes, to finde this danger out.
Bast. And thou shalt finde it (Dolphin) do not doubt
Exeunt.

Scæna Tertia.

Alarums. Enter Iohn and Hubert.

Iohn. How goes the day with vs? oh tell me *Hubert.*
Hub. Badly I feare; how fares your Maiesty?
Iohn. This Feauer that hath troubled me so long,
Lyes heauie on me: oh, my heart is sicke.
Enter a Messenger.
Mes. My Lord: your valiant kinsman *Falconbridge,*
Desires your Maiestie to leaue the field,
And send him word by me, which way you go.
Iohn. Tell him toward *Swinsted*, to the Abbey there.
Mes. Be of good comfort: for the great supply
That was expected by the Dolphin heere,
Are wrack'd three nights ago on *Goodwin* sands.
This newes was brought to *Richard* but euen now,
The French fight coldly, and retyre themselues.
Iohn. Aye me, this tyrant Feauer burnes mee vp,
And will not let me welcome this good newes.
Set on toward *Swinsted*: to my Litter straight,
Weaknesse possesseth me, and I am faint. *Exeunt.*

Scena Quarta.

Enter Salisbury, Pembroke, and Bigot.

Sal. I did not thinke the King so stor'd with friends.
Pem. Vp once againe: put spirit in the French,
If they miscarry: we miscarry too.
Sal. That misbegotten diuell *Falconbridge,*
In spight of spight, alone vpholds the day.
Pem. They say King *Iohn* sore sick, hath left the field.
Enter Meloon wounded.
Mel. Lead me to the Reuolts of England heere.
Sal. When we were happie, we had other names.
Pem. It is the Count *Meloone.*
Sal. Wounded to death.
Mel. Fly Noble English, you are bought and sold,
Vnthred the rude eye of Rebellion,
And welcome home againe discarded faith,
Seeke out King *Iohn*, and fall before his feete:
For if the French be Lords of this loud day,
He meanes to recompence the paines you take,
By cutting off your heads: Thus hath he sworne,
And I with him, and many moe with mee,
Vpon the Altar at S. *Edmondsbury,*
Euen on that Altar, where we swore to you
Deere Amity, and euerlasting loue.
Sal. May this be possible? May this be true?
Mel. Haue I not hideous death within my view,
Retaining but a quantity of life,
Which bleeds away, euen as a forme of waxe
Resolueth from his figure 'gainst the fire?
What in the world should make me now deceiue,
Since I must loose the vse of all deceite?
Why should I then be false, since it is true
That I must dye heere, and liue hence, by Truth?
I say againe, if *Lewis* do win the day,
He is forsworne, if ere those eyes of yours
Behold another day breake in the East:
But euen this night, whose blacke contagious breath
Already smoakes about the burning Crest
Of the old, feeble, and day-wearied Sunne,
Euen this ill night, your breathing shall expire,
Paying the fine of rated Treachery,
Euen with a treacherous fine of all your liues:
If *Lewis*, by your assistance win the day.
Commend me to one *Hubert*, with your King;
The loue of him, and this respect besides
(For that my Grandsire was an Englishman)
Awakes my Conscience to confesse all this.
In lieu whereof, I pray you beare me hence
From forth the noise and rumour of the Field;
Where I may thinke the remnant of my thoughts
In peace: and part this bodie and my soule
With contemplation, and deuout desires.
Sal. We do beleeue thee, and beshrew my soule,
But I do loue the fauour, and the forme
Of this most faire occasion, by the which
We will vntread the steps of damned flight,
And like a bated and retired Flood,
Leauing our ranknesse and irregular course,
Stoope lowe within those bounds we haue ore-look'd,
And calmely run on in obedience
Euen to our Ocean, to our great King *Iohn.*
My arme shall giue thee helpe to beare thee hence,
For

For I do see the cruell pangs of death
Right in thine eye. Away, my friends, new flight,
And happie newnesse, that intends old right. *Exeunt*

Scena Quinta.

Enter Dolphin, and his Traine.

Dol. The Sun of heauen (me thought) was loth to set;
But staid, and made the Westerne Welkin blush,
When English measure backward their owne ground
In faint Retire: Oh brauely came we off,
When with a volley of our needlesse shot,
After such bloody toile, we bid good night,
And woon'd our tott'ring colours clearly vp,
Last in the field, and almost Lords of it.

Enter a Messenger.

Mes. Where is my Prince, the Dolphin?
Dol. Heere: what newes?
Mes. The Count *Meloone* is slaine: The English Lords
By his perswasion, are againe falne off,
And your supply, which you haue wish'd so long,
Are cast away, and sunke on *Goodwin* sands.
Dol. Ah fowle, shrew'd newes. Beshrew thy very (hart:
I did not thinke to be so sad to night
As this hath made me. Who was he that said
King *Iohn* did flie an houre or two before
The stumbling night did part our wearie powres?
Mes. Who euer spoke it, it is true my Lord.
Dol. Well: keepe good quarter, & good care to night,
The day shall not be vp so soone as I,
To try the faire aduenture of to morrow. *Exeunt*

Scena Sexta.

Enter Bastard and Hubert, seuerally.

Hub. Whose there? Speake hoa, speake quickely, or I shoote.
Bast. A Friend. What art thou?
Hub. Of the part of England.
Bast. Whether doest thou go?
Hub. What's that to thee?
Why may not I demand of thine affaires,
As well as thou of mine?
Bast. *Hubert*, I thinke.
Hub. Thou hast a perfect thought:
I will vpon all hazards well beleeue
Thou art my friend, that know'st my tongue so well:
Who art thou?
Bast. Who thou wilt: and if thou please
Thou maist be-friend me so much, as to thinke
I come one way of the *Plantagenets*.
Hub. Vnkinde remembrance: thou, & endles night,
Haue done me shame: Braue Soldier, pardon me,
That any accent breaking from thy tongue,
Should scape the true acquaintance of mine eare.
Bast. Come, come: sans complement, What newes abroad?
Hub. Why heere walke I, in the black brow of night
To finde you out.
Bast. Breefe then: and what's the newes?
Hub. O my sweet sir, newes fitting to the night,
Blacke, fearefull, comfortlesse, and horrible.
Bast. Shew me the very wound of this ill newes,
I am no woman, Ile not swound at it.
Hub. The King I feare is poyson'd by a Monke,
I left him almost speechlesse, and broke out
To acquaint you with this euill, that you might
The better arme you to the sodaine time,
Then if you had at leisure knowne of this.
Bast. How did he take it? Who did taste to him?
Hub. A Monke I tell you, a resolued villaine
Whose Bowels sodainly burst out: The King
Yet speakes, and peraduenture may recouer.
Bast Who didst thou leaue to tend his Maiesty?
Hub. Why know you not? The Lords are all come backe,
And brought Prince *Henry* in their companie,
At whose request the king hath pardon'd them,
And they are all about his Maiestie.
Bast. With-hold thine indignation, mighty heauen,
And tempt vs not to beare aboue our power.
Ile tell thee *Hubert*, halfe my power this night
Passing these Flats, are taken by the Tide,
These Lincolne-Washes haue deuoured them,
My selfe, well mounted, hardly haue escap'd.
Away before: Conduct me to the king,
I doubt he will be dead, or ere I come. *Exeunt*

Scena Septima.

Enter Prince Henry, Salisburie, and Bigot.

Hen. It is too late, the life of all his blood
Is touch'd, corruptibly: and his pure braine
(Which some suppose the soules fraile dwelling house)
Doth by the idle Comments that it makes,
Fore-tell the ending of mortality.

Enter Pembroke.

Pem. His Highnesse yet doth speak, & holds beleefe,
That being brought into the open ayre,
It would allay the burning qualitie
Of that fell poison which assayleth him.
Hen. Let him be brought into the Orchard heere:
Doth he still rage?
Pem. He is more patient
Then when you left him; euen now he sung.
Hen. Oh vanity of sicknesse: fierce extreames
In their continuance, will not feele themselues.
Death hauing praide vpon the outward parts
Leaues them inuisible, and his seige is now
Against the winde, the which he prickes and wounds
With many legions of strange fantasies,
Which in their throng, and presse to that last hold,
Counfound themselues. 'Tis strange y^t death shold sing:
I am the Symet to this pale faint Swan,
Who chaunts a dolefull hymne to his owne death,
And from the organ-pipe of frailety sings
His soule and body to their lasting rest.
Sal. Be of good comfort (Prince) for you are borne
To set a forme vpon that indigest
Which he hath left so shapelesse, and so rude.

Iohn brought in.

Iohn. I marrie, now my soule hath elbow roome,

It would not out at windowes, nor at doores,
There is so hot a summer in my bosome,
That all my bowels crumble vp to dust:
I am a scribled forme drawne with a pen
Vpon a Parchment, and against this fire
Do I shrinke vp.

Hen. How fares your Maiesty?

Ioh. Poyson'd, ill fare: dead, forsooke, cast off,
And none of you will bid the winter come
To thrust his ycie fingers in my maw;
Nor let my kingdomes Riuers take their course
Through my burn'd bosome: nor intreat the North
To make his bleake windes kisse my parched lips,
And comfort me with cold. I do not aske you much,
I begge cold comfort: and you are so straight
And so ingratefull, you deny me that.

Hen. Oh that there were some vertue in my teares,
That might releeue you.

Iohn. The salt in them is hot.
Within me is a hell, and there the poyson
Is, as a fiend, confin'd to tyrannize,
On vnrepreeuable condemned blood.

Enter Bastard.

Bast. Oh, I am scalded with my violent motion
And spleene of speede, to see your Maiesty.

Iohn. Oh Cozen, thou art come to set mine eye:
The tackle of my heart, is crack'd and burnt,
And all the shrowds wherewith my life should saile,
Are turned to one thred, one little haire:
My heart hath one poore string to stay it by,
Which holds but till thy newes be vttered,
And then all this thou seest, is but a clod,
And module of confounded royalty.

Bast. The Dolphin is preparing hither-ward,
Where heauen he knowes how we shall answer him.
For in a night the best part of my powre,
As I vpon aduantage did remoue,
Were in the *Washes* all vnwarily,
Deuoured by the vnexpected flood.

Sal. You breath these dead newes in as dead an eare
My Liege, my Lord: but now a King, now thus.

Hen. Euen so must I run on, and euen so stop.
What surety of the world, what hope, what stay,
When this was now a King, and now is clay?

Bast. Art thou gone so? I do but stay behinde,
To do the office for thee, of reuenge,
And then my soule shall waite on thee to heauen,
As it on earth hath bene thy seruant still.
Now, now you Starres, that moue in your right spheres,
Where be your powres? Shew now your mended faiths,
And instantly returne with me againe.
To push destruction, and perpetuall shame
Out of the weake doore of our fainting Land:
Straight let vs seeke, or straight we shall be sought,
The Dolphine rages at our verie heeles.

Sal. It seemes you know not then so much as we,
The Cardinall *Pandulph* is within at rest,
Who halfe an houre since came from the Dolphin,
And brings from him such offers of our peace,
As we with honor and respect may take,
With purpose presently to leaue this warre.

Bast. He will the rather do it, when he sees
Our selues well sinew'd to our defence.

Sal. Nay, 'tis in a manner done already,
For many carriages hee hath dispatch'd
To the sea side, and put his cause and qearrell
To the disposing of the Cardinall,
With whom your selfe, my selfe, and other Lords,
If you thinke meete, this afternoone will poast
To consummate this businesse happily.

Bast. Let it be so, and you my noble Prince,
With other Princes that may best be spar'd,
Shall waite vpon your Fathers Funerall.

Hen. At Worster must his bodie be interr'd,
For so he will'd it.

Bast. Thither shall it then,
And happily may your sweet selfe put on
The lineall state, and glorie of the Land,
To whom with all submission on my knee,
I do bequeath my faithfull seruices
And true subiection euerlastingly.

Sal. And the like tender of our loue wee make
To rest without a spot for euermore.

Hen. I haue a kinde soule, that would giue thankes,
And knowes not how to do it, but with teares.

Bast. Oh let vs pay the time: but needfull woe,
Since it hath beene before hand with our greefes.
This England neuer did, nor neuer shall
Lye at the proud foote of a Conqueror,
But when it first did helpe to wound it selfe.
Now, these her Princes are come home againe,
Come the three corners of the world in Armes,
And we shall shocke them: Naught shall make vs rue,
If England to it selfe, do rest but true. *Exeunt.*

The life and death of King Richard the Second.

Actus Primus, Scæna Prima.

Enter King Richard, Iohn of Gaunt, with other Nobles and Attendants.

King Richard.
Old *Iohn of Gaunt*, time-honoured Lancaster,
Hast thou according to thy oath and band
Brought hither *Henry* Herford thy bold son:
Heere to make good ye boistrous late appeale,
Which then our leysure would not let vs heare,
Against the Duke of Norfolke, *Thomas Mowbray*?
Gaunt. I haue my Liege.
King. Tell me moreouer, hast thou sounded him,
If he appeale the Duke on ancient malice,
Or worthily as a good subiect should
On some knowne ground of treacherie in him.
Gaunt. As neere as I could sift him on that argument,
On some apparant danger seene in him,
Aym'd at your Highnesse, no inueterate malice.
Kin. Then call them to our presence face to face,
And frowning brow to brow, our selues will heare
Th'accuser, and the accused, freely speake;
High stomack d are they both, and full of ire,
In rage, deafe as the sea; hastie as fire.

Enter Bullingbrooke and Mowbray.

Bul. Many yeares of happy dayes befall
My gracious Soueraigne, my most louing Liege.
Mow. Each day still better others happinesse,
Vntill the heauens enuying earths good hap,
Adde an immortall title to your Crowne.
King. We thanke you both, yet one but flatters vs,
As well appeareth by the cause you come,
Namely, to appeale each other of high treason.
Coosin of Hereford, what dost thou obiect
Against the Duke of Norfolke, *Thomas Mowbray*?
Bul. First, heauen be the record to my speech,
In the deuotion of a subiects loue,
Tendering the precious safetie of my Prince,
And free from other misbegotten hate,
Come I appealant to this Princely presence.
Now *Thomas Mowbray* do I turne to thee,
And marke my greeting well: for what I speake,
My body shall make good vpon this earth,
Or my diuine soule answer it in heauen.
Thou art a Traitor, and a Miscreant;
Too good to be so, and too bad to liue,
Since the more faire and christall is the skie,
The vglier seeme the cloudes that in it flye:
Once more, the more to aggrauate the note,
With a foule Traitors name stuffe I thy throte,
And wish (so please my Soueraigne) ere I moue,
What my tong speaks, my right drawn sword may proue
Mow. Let not my cold words heere accuse my zeale:
'Tis not the triall of a Womans warre,
The bitter clamour of two eager tongues,
Can arbitrate this cause betwixt vs twaine:
The blood is hot that must be cool'd for this.
Yet can I not of such tame patience boast,
As to be husht, and nought at all to say.
First the faire reuerence of your Highnesse curbes mee,
From giuing reines and spurres to my free speech,
Which else would post, vntill it had return'd
These tearmes of treason, doubly downe his throat.
Setting aside his high bloods royalty,
And let him be no Kinsman to my Liege,
I do defie him, and I spit at him,
Call him a slanderous Coward, and a Villaine:
Which to maintaine, I would allow him oddes,
And meete him, were I tide to runne afoote,
Euen to the frozen ridges of the Alpes,
Or any other ground inhabitable,
Where euer Englishman durst set his foote.
Meane time, let this defend my loyaltie,
By all my hopes most falsely doth he lie.
Bul. Pale trembling Coward, there I throw my gage,
Disclaiming heere the kindred of a King,
And lay aside my high bloods Royalty,
Which feare, not reuerence makes thee to except.
If guilty dread hath left thee so much strength,
As to take vp mine Honors pawne, then stoope.
By that, and all the rites of Knight-hood else,
Will I make good against thee arme to arme,
What I haue spoken, or thou canst deuise.
Mow. I take it vp, and by that sword I sweare,
Which gently laid my Knight-hood on my shoulder,
Ile answer thee in any faire degree,
Or Chiualrous designe of knightly triall:
And when I mount, aliue may I not light,
If I be Traitor, or vniustly fight.
King. What doth our Cosin lay to *Mowbraies* charge?
It must be great that can inherite vs,
So much as of a thought of ill in him.
Bul. Looke what I said, my life shall proue it true,
That *Mowbray* hath receiu'd eight thousand Nobles,
In

In name of lendings for your Highnesse Soldiers,
The which he hath detain'd for lewd employments,
Like a false Traitor, and iniurious Villaine.
Besides I say, and will in battaile proue,
Or heere, or elsewhere to the furthest Verge
That euer was suruey'd by English eye,
That all the Treasons for these eighteene yeeres
Complotted, and contriued in this Land,
Fetch'd from false *Mowbray* their first head and spring.
Further I say, and further will maintaine
Vpon his bad life, to make all this good.
That he did plot the Duke of Glousters death,
Suggest his soone beleeuing aduersaries,
And consequently, like a Traitor Coward,
Sluc'd out his innocent soule through streames of blood:
Which blood, like sacrificing *Abels* cries,
(Euen from the toonglesse cauernes of the earth)
To me for iustice, and rough chasticement:
And by the glorious worth of my discent,
This arme shall do it, or this life be spent.

King. How high a pitch his resolution soares:
Thomas of Norfolke, what sayest thou to this?

Mow. Oh let my Soueraigne turne away his face,
And bid his eares a little while be deafe,
Till I haue told this slander of his blood,
How God, and good men, hate so foule a lyar.

King. Mowbray, impartiall are our eyes and eares,
Were he my brother, nay our kingdomes heyre,
As he is but my fathers brothers sonne;
Now by my Scepters awe, I make a vow,
Such neighbour-neerenesse to our sacred blood,
Should nothing priuiledge him, nor partialize
The vn-stooping firmenesse of my vpright soule.
He is our subiect (*Mowbray*) so art thou,
Free speech, and fearelesse, I to thee allow.

Mow. Then *Bullingbrooke*, as low as to thy heart,
Through the false passage of thy throat; thou lyest:
Three parts of that receipt I had for Callice,
Disburst I to his Highnesse souldiers;
The other part reseru'd I by consent,
For that my Soueraigne Liege was in my debt,
Vpon remainder of a deere Accompt,
Since last I went to France to fetch his Queene:
Now swallow downe that Lye. For Glousters death,
I slew him not; but (to mine owne disgrace)
Neglected my sworne duty in that case:
For you my noble Lord of *Lancaster*,
The honourable Father to my foe,
Once I did lay an ambush for your life,
A trespasse that doth vex my greeued soule:
But ere I last receiu'd the Sacrament,
I did confesse it, and exactly begg'd
Your Graces pardon, and I hope I had it.
This is my fault: as for the rest appeal'd,
It issues from the rancour of a Villaine,
A recreant, and most degenerate Traitor,
Which in my selfe I boldly will defend,
And interchangeably hurle downe my gage
Vpon this ouer-weening Traitors foote,
To proue my selfe a loyall Gentleman,
Euen in the best blood chamber'd in his bosome.
In hast whereof, most heartily I pray
Your Highnesse to assigne our Triall day.

King. Wrath-kindled Gentlemen be rul'd by me:
Let's purge this choller without letting blood:
This we prescribe, though no Physition,
Deepe malice makes too deepe incision.
Forget, forgiue, conclude, and be agreed,
Our Doctors say, This is no time to bleed.
Good Vnckle, let this end where it begun,
Wee'l calme the Duke of Norfolke; you, your son.

Gaunt. To be a make-peace shall become my age,
Throw downe (my sonne) the Duke of Norfolkes gage.

King. And Norfolke, throw downe his.

Gaunt. When *Harrie* when? Obedience bids,
Obedience bids I should not bid agen.

King. Norfolke, throw downe, we bidde; there is no boote.

Mow. My selfe I throw (dread Soueraigne) at thy foot.
My life thou shalt command, but not my shame,
The one my dutie owes, but my faire name
Despight of death, that liues vpon my graue
To darke dishonours vse, thou shalt not haue.
I am disgrac'd, impeach'd, and baffel'd heere,
Pierc'd to the soule with slanders venom'd speare:
The which no balme can cure, but his heart blood
Which breath'd this poyson.

King. Rage must be withstood:
Giue me his gage: Lyons make Leopards tame.

Mo. Yea, but not change his spots: take but my shame,
And I resigne my gage. My deere, deere Lord,
The purest treasure mortall times afford
Is spotlesse reputation: that away,
Men are but gilded loame, or painted clay.
A Iewell in a ten times barr'd vp Chest,
Is a bold spirit, in a loyall brest.
Mine Honor is my life; both grow in one:
Take Honor from me, and my life is done.
Then (deere my Liege) mine Honor let me trie,
In that I liue; and for that will I die.

King. Coosin, throw downe your gage,
Do you begin.

Bul. Oh heauen defend my soule from such foule sin.
Shall I seeme Crest-falne in my fathers sight,
Or with pale beggar-feare impeach my hight
Before this out-dar'd dastard? Ere my toong,
Shall wound mine honor with such feeble wrong;
Or sound so base a parle: my teeth shall teare
The slauish motiue of recanting feare,
And spit it bleeding in his high disgrace,
Where shame doth harbour, euen in *Mowbrayes* face.

Exit Gaunt.

King. We were not borne to sue, but to command,
Which since we cannot do to make you friends,
Be readie, (as your liues shall answer it)
At Couentree, vpon S. *Lamberts* day:
There shall your swords and Lances arbitrate
The swelling difference of your setled hate:
Since we cannot attone you, you shall see
Iustice designe the Victors Chiualrie.
Lord Marshall, command our Officers at Armes,
Be readie to direct these home Alarmes. *Exeunt.*

Scæna Secunda.

Enter Gaunt, and Dutchesse of Gloucester.

Gaunt. Alas, the part I had in Glousters blood,
Doth more solicite me then your exclaimes,
To stirre against the Butchers of his life.

But

But since correction lyeth in those hands
Which made the fault that we cannot correct,
Put we our quarrell to the will of heauen,
Who when they see the houres ripe on earth,
Will raigne hot vengeance on offenders heads.

Dut. Findes brotherhood in thee no sharper spurre?
Hath loue in thy old blood no liuing fire?
Edwards seuen sonnes (whereof thy selfe art one)
Were as seuen violles of his Sacred blood,
Or seuen faire branches springing from one roote:
Some of those seuen are dride by natures course,
Some of those branches by the destinies cut:
But *Thomas*, my deere Lord, my life, my Glouster,
One Violl full of *Edwards* Sacred blood,
One flourishing branch of his most Royall roote
Is crack'd, and all the precious liquor spilt;
Is hackt downe, and his summer leafes all vaded
By Enuies hand, and Murders bloody Axe.
Ah *Gaunt*! His blood was thine, that bed, that wombe,
That mettle, that selfe-mould that fashion'd thee,
Made him a man: and though thou liu'st, and breath'st,
Yet art thou slaine in him: thou dost consent
In some large measure to thy Fathers death,
In that thou seest thy wretched brother dye,
Who was the modell of thy Fathers life.
Call it not patience (*Gaunt*) it is dispaire,
In suff'ring thus thy brother to be slaughter'd,
Thou shew'st the naked pathway to thy life,
Teaching sterne murther how to butcher thee:
That which in meane men we intitle patience
Is pale cold cowardice in noble brests:
What shall I say, to safegard thine owne life,
The best way is to venge my Glousters death.

Gaunt. Heauens is the quarrell: for heauens substitute
His Deputy annointed in his sight,
Hath caus'd his death, the which if wrongfully
Let heauen reuenge: for I may neuer lift
An angry arme against his Minister.

Dut. Where then (alas may I) complaint my selfe?

Gau. To heauen, the widdowes Champion to defence

Dut. Why then I will: farewell old *Gaunt*.
Thou go'st to Couentrie, there to behold
Our Cosine Herford, and fell Mowbray fight:
O sit my husbands wrongs on Herfords speare,
That it may enter butcher Mowbrayes brest:
Or if misfortune misse the first carreere,
Be Mowbrayes sinnes so heauy in his bosome,
That they may breake his foaming Coursers backe,
And throw the Rider headlong in the Lists,
A Caytiffe recreant to my Cosine Herford:
Farewell old *Gaunt*, thy sometimes brothers wife
With her companion Greefe, must end her life.

Gau. Sister farewell: I must to Couentree,
As much good stay with thee, as go with mee.

Dut. Yet one word more: Greefe boundeth where it (falls,
Not with the emptie hollownes, but weight:
I take my leaue, before I haue begun,
For sorrow ends not, when it seemeth done.
Commend me to my brother *Edmund Yorke*.
Loe, this is all: nay, yet depart not so,
Though this be all, do not so quickly go,
I shall remember more. Bid him, Oh, what?
With all good speed at Plashie visit mee.
Alacke, and what shall good old Yorke there see
But empty lodgings, and vnfurnish'd walles,
Vn-peopel'd Offices, vntroden stones?
And what heare there for welcome, but my grones?
Therefore commend me, let him not come there,
To seeke out sorrow, that dwels euery where:
Desolate, desolate will I hence, and dye,
The last leaue of thee, takes my weeping eye. *Exeunt*

Scena Tertia.

Enter Marshall, and Aumerle.

Mar. My L. *Aumerle*, is *Harry Herford* arm'd.

Aum. Yea, at all points, and longs to enter in.

Mar. The Duke of Norfolke, sprightfully and bold,
Stayes but the summons of the Appealants Trumpet.

Au. Why then the Champions, are prepar'd, and stay
For nothing but his Maiesties approach. *Flourish.*

Enter King, Gaunt, Bushy, Bagot, Greene, & others: Then Mowbray in Armor, and Harrold.

Rich. Marshall, demand of yonder Champion
The cause of his arriuall heere in Armes,
Aske him his name, and orderly proceed
To sweare him in the iustice of his cause.

Mar. In Gods name, and the Kings, say who ý art,
And why thou com'st thus knightly clad in Armes?
Against what man thou com'st, and what's thy quarrell,
Speake truly on thy knighthood, and thine oath,
As so defend thee heauen, and thy valour.

Mow. My name is *Tho. Mowbray*, Duke of Norfolk,
Who hither comes engaged by my oath
(Which heauen defend a knight should violate)
Both to defend my loyalty and truth,
To God, my King, and his succeeding issue,
Against the Duke of Herford, that appeales me:
And by the grace of God, and this mine arme,
To proue him (in defending of my selfe)
A Traitor to my God, my King, and me,
And as I truly fight, defend me heauen.

Tucket. Enter Hereford, and Harold.

Rich. Marshall: Aske yonder Knight in Armes,
Both who he is, and why he commeth hither,
Thus placed in habiliments of warre:
And formerly according to our Law
Depose him in the iustice of his cause.

Mar. What is thy name? and wherfore com'st ý hither
Before King *Richard* in his Royall Lists?
Against whom com'st thou? and what's thy quarrell?
Speake like a true Knight, so defend thee heauen.

Bul. *Harry* of Herford, Lancaster, and Derbie,
Am I: who ready heere do stand in Armes,
To proue by heauens grace, and my bodies valour,
In Lists, on *Thomas Mowbray* Duke of Norfolke,
That he's a Traitor foule, and dangerous,
To God of heauen, King *Richard*, and to me,
And as I truly fight, defend me heauen.

Mar. On paine of death, no person be so bold,
Or daring hardie as to touch the Listes,
Except the Marshall, and such Officers
Appointed to direct these faire designes.

Bul. Lord Marshall, let me kisse my Soueraigns hand,
And bow my knee before his Maiestie:
For *Mowbray* and my selfe are like two men,
That vow a long and weary pilgrimage,

Then let vs take a ceremonious leaue
And louing farwell of our seuerall friends.
Mar. The Appealant in all duty greets your Highnes,
And craues to kisse your hand, and take his leaue.
Rich. We will descend, and fold him in our armes.
Cosin of Herford, as thy cause is iust,
So be thy fortune in this Royall fight:
Farewell, my blood, which if to day thou shead,
Lament we may, but not reuenge thee dead.
Bull. Oh let no noble eye prophane a teare
For me, if I be gor'd with *Mowbrayes* speare:
As confident, as is the Falcons flight
Against a bird, do I with *Mowbray* fight.
My louing Lord, I take my leaue of you,
Of you (my Noble Cosin) Lord *Aumerle*;
Not sicke, although I haue to do with death,
But lustie, yong, and cheerely drawing breath.
Loe, as at English Feasts, so I regreete
The daintiest last, to make the end most sweet.
Oh thou the earthy author of my blood,
Whose youthfull spirit in me regenerate,
Doth with a two-fold rigor lift mee vp
To reach at victory aboue my head,
Adde proofe vnto mine Armour with thy prayres,
And with thy blessings steele my Lances point,
That it may enter *Mowbrayes* waxen Coate,
And furnish new the name of *Iohn a Gaunt*,
Euen in the lusty hauiour of his sonne.
Gaunt. Heauen in thy good cause make thee prosp'rous
Be swift like lightning in the execution,
And let thy blowes doubly redoubled,
Fall like amazing thunder on the Caske
Of thy amaz'd pernicious enemy.
Rouze vp thy youthfull blood, be valiant, and liue.
Bul. Mine innocence, and S. *George* to thriue.
Mow. How euer heauen or fortune cast my lot,
There liues, or dies, true to Kings *Richards* Throne,
A loyall, iust, and vpright Gentleman:
Neuer did Captiue with a freer heart,
Cast off his chaines of bondage, and embrace
His golden vncontroul'd enfranchisement,
More then my dancing soule doth celebrate
This Feast of Battell, with mine Aduersarie.
Most mighty Liege, and my companion Peeres,
Take from my mouth, the wish of happy yeares,
As gentle, and as iocond, as to iest,
Go I to fight: Truth, hath a quiet brest.
Rich. Farewell, my Lord, securely I espy
Vertue with Valour, couched in thine eye:
Order the triall Marshall, and begin.
Mar. *Harrie* of *Herford*, *Lancaster*, and *Derby*,
Receiue thy Launce, and heauen defend thy right.
Bul. Strong as a towre in hope, I cry Amen.
Mar. Go beare this Lance to *Thomas* D. of Norfolke.
1. *Har.* *Harry* of *Herford*, *Lancaster*, and *Derbie*,
Stands heere for God, his Soueraigne, and himselfe,
On paine to be found false, and recreant,
To proue the Duke of Norfolke, *Thomas Mowbray*,
A Traitor to his God, his King, and him,
And dares him to set forwards to the fight.
2. *Har.* Here standeth *Tho: Mowbray* Duke of Norfolk
On paine to be found false and recreant,
Both to defend himselfe, and to approue
Henry of *Herford*, *Lancaster*, and *Derby*,
To God, his Soueraigne, and to him disloyall:
Couragiously, and with a free desire
Attending but the signall to begin. *A charge sounded*
Mar. Sound Trumpets, and set forward Combatants:
Stay, the King hath throwne his Warder downe.
Rich. Let them lay by their Helmets & their Speares,
And both returne backe to their Chaires againe:
Withdraw with vs, and let the Trumpets sound,
While we returne these Dukes what we decree.
A long Flourish.
Draw neere and list
What with our Councell we haue done.
For that our kingdomes earth should not be soyld
With that deere blood which it hath fostered,
And for our eyes do hate the dire aspect
Of ciuill wounds plowgh'd vp with neighbors swords,
Which so rouz'd vp with boystrous vntun'd drummes,
With harsh resounding Trumpets dreadfull bray,
And grating shocke of wrathfull yron Armes,
Might from our quiet Confines fright faire peace,
And make vs wade euen in our kindreds blood:
Therefore, we banish you our Territories.
You Cosin Herford, vpon paine of death,
Till twice fiue Summers haue enrich'd our fields,
Shall not regreet our faire dominions,
But treade the stranger pathes of banishment.
Bul. Your will be done: This must my comfort be,
That Sun that warmes you heere, shall shine on me:
And those his golden beames to you heere lent,
Shall point on me, and gild my banishment.
Rich. Norfolke: for thee remaines a heauier dombe,
Which I with some vnwillingnesse pronounce,
The slye slow houres shall not determinate
The datelesse limit of thy deere exile:
The hopelesse word, of Neuer to returne,
Breath I against thee, vpon paine of life.
Mow. A heauy sentence, my most Soueraigne Liege,
And all vnlook'd for from your Highnesse mouth:
A deerer merit, not so deepe a maime,
As to be cast forth in the common ayre
Haue I deserued at your Highnesse hands.
The Language I haue learn'd these forty yeares
(My natiue English) now I must forgo,
And now my tongues vse is to me no more,
Then an vnstringed Vyall, or a Harpe,
Or like a cunning Instrument cas'd vp,
Or being open, put into his hands
That knowes no touch to tune the harmony.
Within my mouth you haue engaol'd my tongue,
Doubly percullist with my teeth and lippes,
And dull, vnfeeling, barren ignorance,
Is made my Gaoler to attend on me:
I am too old to fawne vpon a Nurse,
Too farre in yeeres to be a pupill now:
What is thy sentence then, but speechlesse death,
Which robs my tongue from breathing natiue breath?
Rich, It boots thee not to be compassionate,
After our sentence, plaining comes too late.
Mow. Then thus I turne me from my countries light
To dwell in solemne shades of endlesse night.
Ric. Returne againe, and take an oath with thee,
Lay on our Royall sword, your banisht hands;
Sweare by the duty that you owe to heauen
(Our part therein we banish with your selues)
To keepe the Oath that we administer:
You neuer shall (so helpe you Truth, and Heauen)
Embrace each others loue in banishment,
Nor euer looke vpon each others face,

Nor euer write, regreete, or reconcile
This lowring tempest of your home-bred hate,
Nor euer by aduised purpose meete,
To plot, contriue, or complot any ill,
'Gainst Vs, our State, our Subiects, or our Land.
Bull. I sweare.
Mow. And I, to keepe all this.
Bul. Norfolke, so fare, as to mine enemie,
By this time (had the King permitted vs)
One of our soules had wandred in the ayre,
Banish'd this fraile sepulchre of our flesh,
As now our flesh is banish'd from this Land.
Confesse thy Treasons, ere thou flye this Realme,
Since thou hast farre to go, beare not along
The clogging burthen of a guilty soule.
Mow. No *Bullingbroke*: If euer I were Traitor,
My name be blotted from the booke of Life,
And I from heauen banish'd, as from hence:
But what thou art, heauen, thou, and I do know,
And all too soone (I feare) the King shall rue.
Farewell (my Liege) now no way can I stray,
Saue backe to England, all the worlds my way. *Exit.*
Rich. Vncle, euen in the glasses of thine eyes
I see thy greeued heart: thy sad aspect,
Hath from the number of his banish'd yeares
Pluck'd foure away: Six frozen Winters spent,
Returne with welcome home, from banishment.
Bul. How long a time lyes in one little word:
Foure lagging Winters, and foure wanton springs
End in a word, such is the breath of Kings.
Gaunt. I thanke my Liege, that in regard of me
He shortens foure yeares of my sonnes exile:
But little vantage shall I reape thereby.
For ere the sixe yeares that he hath to spend
Can change their Moones, and bring their times about,
My oyle-dride Lampe, and time-bewasted light
Shall be extinct with age, and endlesse night:
My inch of Taper, will be burnt, and done,
And blindfold death, not let me see my sonne.
Rich. Why Vncle, thou hast many yeeres to liue.
Gaunt. But not a minute (King) that thou canst giue;
Shorten my dayes thou canst with sudden sorow,
And plucke nights from me, but not lend a morrow:
Thou canst helpe time to furrow me with age,
But stop no wrinkle in his pilgrimage:
Thy word is currant with him, for my death,
But dead, thy kingdome cannot buy my breath.
Ric. Thy sonne is banish'd vpon good aduice,
Whereto thy tongue a party-verdict gaue,
Why at our Iustice seem'st thou then to lowre?
Gau. Things sweet to tast, proue in digestion sowre:
You vrg'd me as a Iudge, but I had rather
you would haue bid me argue like a Father.
Alas, I look'd when some of you should say,
I was too strict to make mine owne away:
But you gaue leaue to my vnwilling tong,
Against my will, to do my selfe this wrong.
Rich. Cosine farewell: and Vncle bid him so:
Six yeares we banish him, and he shall go. *Exit.*
Flourish.
Au. Cosine farewell: what presence must not know
From where you do remaine, let paper show.
Mar. My Lord, no leaue take I, for I will ride
As farre as land will let me, by your side.
Gaunt. Oh to what purpose dost thou hord thy words,
That thou returnst no greeting to thy friends?
Bull. I haue too few to take my leaue of you,
When the tongues office should be prodigall,
To breath th'abundant dolour of the heart.
Gau. Thy greefe is but thy absence for a time.
Bull. Ioy absent, greefe is present for that time.
Gau. What is sixe Winters, they are quickely gone?
Bul. To men in ioy, but greefe makes one houre ten.
Gau. Call it a trauell that thou tak'st for pleasure.
Bul. My heart will sigh, when I miscall it so,
Which findes it an inforced Pilgrimage.
Gau. The sullen passage of thy weary steppes
Esteeme a soyle, wherein thou art to set
The precious Iewell of thy home returne.
Bul. Oh who can hold a fire in his hand
By thinking on the frostie *Caucasus*?
Or cloy the hungry edge of appetite,
by bare imagination of a Feast?
Or Wallow naked in December snow
by thinking on fantasticke summers heate?
Oh no, the apprehension of the good
Giues but the greater feeling to the worse:
Fell sorrowes tooth, doth euer ranckle more
Then when it bites, but lanceth not the sore.
Gau. Come, come (my son) Ile bring thee on thy way
Had I thy youth, and cause, I would not stay.
Bul. Then Englands ground farewell: sweet soil adieu,
My Mother, and my Nurse, which beares me yet:
Where ere I wander, boast of this I can,
Though banish'd, yet a true-borne English man.

Scœna Quarta.

Enter King, Aumerle, Greene, and Bagot.
Rich. We did obserue. Cosine *Aumerle*,
How far brought you high Herford on his way?
Aum. I brought high Herford (if you call him so)
but to the next high way, and there I left him.
Rich. And say, what store of parting tears were shed?
Aum. Faith none for me: except the Northeast wind
Which then grew bitterly against our face,
Awak'd the sleepie rhewme, and so by chance
Did grace our hollow parting with a teare.
Rich. What said our Cosin when you parted with him?
Au. Farewell: and for my hart disdained ỳ my tongue
Should so prophane the word, that taught me craft
To counterfeit oppression of such greefe,
That word seem'd buried in my sorrowes graue.
Marry, would the word Farwell, haue lengthen'd houres,
And added yeeres to his short banishment,
He should haue had a volume of Farwels,
but since it would not, he had none of me.
Rich. He is our Cosin (Cosin) but 'tis doubt,
When time shall call him home from banishment,
Whether our kinsman come to see his friends,
Our selfe, and *Bushy*: heere *Bagot* and *Greene*
Obseru'd his Courtship to the common people:
How he did seeme to diue into their hearts,
With humble, and familiar courtesie,
What reuerence he did throw away on slaues;
Wooing poore Craftes-men, with the craft of soules.
And patient vnder-bearing of his Fortune,
As 'twere to banish their effects with him.
Off goes his bonnet to an Oyster-wench,

A brace of Dray-men bid God speed him well,
And had the tribute of his supple knee,
With thankes my Countrimen, my louing friends,
As were our England in reuersion his,
And he our subiects next degree in hope.

Gr. Well, he is gone, & with him go these thoughts:
Now for the Rebels, which stand out in Ireland,
Expedient manage must be made my Liege
Ere further leysure, yeeld them further meanes
For their aduantage, and your Highnesse losse.

Ric. We will our selfe in person to this warre,
And for our Coffers, with too great a Court,
And liberall Largesse, are growne somewhat light,
We are inforc'd to farme our royall Realme,
The Reuennew whereof shall furnish vs
For our affayres in hand: if that come short
Our Substitutes at home shall haue Blanke-charters:
Whereto, when they shall know what men are rich,
They shall subscribe them for large summes of Gold,
And send them after to supply our wants:
For we will make for Ireland presently.

Enter Bushy.

Bushy, what newes?

Bu. Old *Iohn of Gaunt* is verie sicke my Lord,
Sodainly taken, and hath sent post haste
To entreat your Maiesty to visit him.

Ric. Where lyes he?

Bu. At Ely house.

Ric. Now put it (heauen) in his Physitians minde,
To helpe him to his graue immediately:
The lining of his coffers shall make Coates
To decke our souldiers for these Irish warres.
Come Gentlemen, let's all go visit him:
Pray heauen we may make hast, and come too late. *Exit.*

Actus Secundus. Scena Prima.

Enter Gaunt, sicke with Yorke.

Gau. Will the King come, that I may breath my last
In wholsome counsell to his vnstaid youth?

Yor. Vex not your selfe, nor striue not with your breth,
For all in vaine comes counsell to his eare.

Gau. Oh but (they say) the tongues of dying men
Inforce attention like deepe harmony;
Where words are scarse, they are seldome spent in vaine,
For they breath truth, that breath their words in paine.
He that no more must say, is listen'd more,
Then they whom youth and ease haue taught to glose,
More are mens ends markt, then their liues before,
The setting Sun, and Musicke is the close
As the last taste of sweetes, is sweetest last,
Writ in remembrance, more then things long past;
Though *Richard* my liues counsell would not heare,
My deaths sad tale, may yet vndeafe his eare.

Yor. No, it is stopt with other flatt'ring sounds
As praises of his state: then there are sound
Lasciuious Meeters, to whose venom sound
The open eare of youth doth alwayes listen,
Report of fashions in proud Italy,
Whose manners still our tardie apish Nation
Limpes after in base imitation.
Where doth the world thrust forth a vanity,
So it be new, there's no respect how vile,
That is not quickly buz'd into his eares?
That all too late comes counsell to be heard,
Where will doth mutiny with wits regard:
Direct not him, whose way himselfe will choose,
Tis breath thou lackst, and that breath wilt thou loose.

Gaunt. Me thinkes I am a Prophet new inspir'd,
And thus expiring, do foretell of him,
His rash fierce blaze of Ryot cannot last,
For violent fires soone burne out themselues,
Small showres last long, but sodaine stormes are short,
He tyres betimes, that spurs too fast betimes;
With eager feeding, food doth choake the feeder:
Light vanity, insatiate cormorant,
Consuming meanes soone preyes vpon it selfe.
This royall Throne of Kings, this sceptred Isle,
This earth of Maiesty, this seate of Mars,
This other Eden, demy paradise,
This Fortresse built by Nature for her selfe,
Against infection, and the hand of warre:
This happy breed of men, this little world,
This precious stone, set in the siluer sea,
Which serues it in the office of a wall,
Or as a Moate defensiue to a house,
Against the enuy of lesse happier Lands,
This blessed plot, this earth, this Realme, this England,
This Nurse, this teeming wombe of Royall Kings,
Fear'd by their breed, and famous for their birth,
Renowned for their deeds, as farre from home,
For Christian seruice, and true Chiualrie,
As is the sepulcher in stubborne *Iury*
Of the Worlds ransome, blessed *Maries* Sonne.
This Land of such deere soules, this deere-deere Land,
Deere for her reputation through the world,
Is now Leas'd out (I dye pronouncing it)
Like to a Tenement or pelting Farme.
England bound in with the triumphant sea,
Whose rocky shore beates backe the enuious siedge
Of watery Neptune, is now bound in with shame,
With Inky blottes, and rotten Parchment bonds.
That England, that was wont to conquer others,
Hath made a shamefull conquest of it selfe.
Ah! would the scandall vanish with my life,
How happy then were my ensuing death?

Enter King, Queene, Aumerle, Bushy, Greene, Bagot, Ros, and Willoughby.

Yor. The King is come, deale mildly with his youth,
For young hot Colts, being rag'd, do rage the more.

Qu. How fares our noble Vncle Lancaster?

Ri. What comfort man? How ist with aged *Gaunt*?

Ga. Oh how that name befits my composition:
Old *Gaunt* indeed, and gaunt in being old:
Within me greefe hath kept a tedious fast,
And who abstaynes from meate, that is not gaunt?
For sleeping England long time haue I watcht,
Watching breeds leannesse, leannesse is all gaunt.
The pleasure that some Fathers feede vpon,
Is my strict fast, I meane my Childrens lookes,
And therein fasting, hast thou made me gaunt:
Gaunt am I for the graue, gaunt as a graue,
Whose hollow wombe inherits naught but bones.

Ric. Can sicke men play so nicely with their names?

Gau. No, misery makes sport to mocke it selfe:
Since thou dost seeke to kill my name in mee,

I mocke my name (great King) to flatter thee.
Ric. Should dying men flatter those that liue?
Gau. No, no, men liuing flatter those that dye.
Rich. Thou now a dying, sayst thou flatter'st me.
Gau. Oh no, thou dyest, though I the sicker be.
Rich. I am in health, I breath, I see thee ill.
Gau. Now he that made me, knowes I see thee ill:
Ill in my selfe to see, and in thee, seeing ill,
Thy death-bed is no lesser then the Land,
Wherein thou lyest in reputation sicke,
And thou too care-lesse patient as thou art,
Commit'st thy'anointed body to the cure
Of those Physitians, that first wounded thee.
A thousand flatterers sit within thy Crowne,
Whose compasse is no bigger then thy head,
And yet incaged in so small a Verge,
The waste is no whit lesser then thy Land:
Oh had thy Grandsire with a Prophets eye,
Seene how his sonnes sonne, should destroy his sonnes,
From forth thy reach he would haue laid thy shame,
Deposing thee before thou wert possest,
Which art possest now to depose thy selfe.
Why (Cosine) were thou Regent of the world,
It were a shame to let his Land by lease:
But for thy world enioying but this Land,
Is it not more then shame, to shame it so?
Landlord of England art thou, and not King:
Thy state of Law, is bondslaue to the law,
And———
Rich. And thou, a lunaticke leane-witted foole,
Presuming on an Agues priuiledge,
Dar'st with thy frozen admonition
Make pale our cheeke, chafing the Royall blood
With fury, from his natiue residence?
Now by my Seates right Royall Maiestie,
Wer't thou not Brother to great *Edwards* sonne,
This tongue that runs so roundly in thy head,
Should run thy head from thy vnreuerent shoulders.
Gau. Oh spare me not, my brothers *Edwards* sonne,
For that I was his Father *Edwards* sonne:
That blood already (like the Pellican)
Thou hast tapt out, and drunkenly carows'd.
My brother Gloucester, plaine well meaning soule
(Whom faire befall in heauen 'mongst happy soules)
May be a president, and witnesse good,
That thou respect'st not spilling *Edwards* blood:
Ioyne with the present sicknesse that I haue,
And thy vnkindnesse be like crooked age,
To crop at once a too-long wither'd flowre.
Liue in thy shame, but dye not shame with thee,
These words heereafter, thy tormentors bee.
Conuey me to my bed, then to my graue,
Loue they to liue, that loue and honor haue. *Exit*
Rich. And let them dye, that age and sullens haue,
For both hast thou, and both become the graue.
Yor. I do beseech your Maiestie impute his words
To wayward sicklinesse, and age in him:
He loues you on my life, and holds you deere
As *Harry* Duke of *Herford*, were he heere.
Rich. Right, you say true: as *Herfords* loue, so his;
As theirs, so mine: and all be as it is.

Enter Northumberland.

Nor. My Liege, olde *Gaunt* commends him to your Maiestie.
Rich. What sayes he?
Nor. Nay nothing, all is said:
His tongue is now a stringlesse instrument,
Words, life, and all, old Lancaster hath spent.
Yor. Be Yorke the next, that must be bankrupt so,
Though death be poore, it ends a mortall wo.
Rich. The ripest fruit first fals, and so doth he,
His time is spent, our pilgrimage must be:
So much for that. Now for our Irish warres,
We must supplant those rough rug-headed Kernes,
Which liue like venom, where no venom else
But onely they, haue priuiledge to liue.
And for these great affayres do aske some charge
Towards our assistance, we do seize to vs
The plate, coine, reuennewes, and moueables,
Whereof our Vncle *Gaunt* did stand possest.
Yor. How long shall I be patient? Oh how long
Shall tender dutie make me suffer wrong?
Not *Glousters* death, nor *Herfords* banishment,
Nor *Gauntes* rebukes, nor Englands priuate wrongs,
Nor the preuention of poore *Bullingbrooke*,
About his marriage, nor my owne disgrace
Haue euer made me sowre my patient cheeke,
Or bend one wrinckle on my Soueraignes face:
I am the last of noble *Edwards* sonnes,
Of whom thy Father Prince of Wales was first,
In warre was neuer Lyon rag'd more fierce:
In peace, was neuer gentle Lambe more milde,
Then was that yong and Princely Gentleman,
His face thou hast, for euen so look'd he
Accomplish'd with the number of thy he wers:
But when he frown'd, it was against the French,
And not against his friends: his noble hand
Did win what he did spend: and spent not that
Which his triumphant fathers hand had won:
His hands were guilty of no kindreds blood,
But bloody with the enemies of his kinne:
Oh *Richard*, *Yorke* is too farre gone with greefe,
Or else he neuer would compare betweene.
Rich. Why Vncle,
What's the matter?
Yor. Oh my Liege, pardon me if you please, if not
I pleas'd not to be pardon'd, am content with all:
Seeke you to seize, and gripe into your hands
The Royalties and Rights of banish'd Herford?
Is not *Gaunt* dead? and doth not Herford liue?
Was not *Gaunt* iust? and is not *Harry* true?
Did not the one deserue to haue an heyre?
Is not his heyre a well-deseruing sonne?
Take Herfords rights away, and take from time
His Charters, and his customarie rights:
Let not to morrow then insue to day,
Be not thy selfe. For how art thou a King
But by faire sequence and succession?
Now afore God, God forbid I say true,
If you do wrongfully seize Herfords right,
Call in his Letters Patents that he hath
By his Atturneyes generall, to sue
His Liuerie, and denie his offer'd homage,
You plucke a thousand dangers on your head,
You loose a thousand well-disposed hearts,
And pricke my tender patience to those thoughts
Which honor and allegeance cannot thinke.
Ric. Thinke what you will: we seise into our hands,
His plate, his goods, his money, and his lands.
Yor. Ile not be by the while: My Liege farewell,

What will ensue heereof, there's none can tell.
But by bad cou ses may be vnderstood,
That their euents can neuer fall out good. *Exit.*

Rich. Go *Bushie* to the Earle of *Wiltshire* streight,
Bid him repaire to vs to *Ely* house,
To see this businesse: to morrow next
We will for *Ireland*, and 'tis time, I trow:
And we create in absence of our selfe
Our Vncle Yorke, Lord Gouernor of England:
For he is iust, and alwayes lou'd vs well.
Come on our Queene, to morrow must we part,
Be merry, for our time of stay is short. *Flourish.*

Manet North. Willoughby, & Ross.

Nor. Well Lords, the Duke of Lancaster is dead.

Ross. And liuing too, for now his sonne is Duke.

Wil. Barely in title, not in reuennew.

Nor. Richly in both, if iustice had her right.

Ross. My heart is great: but it must break with silence,
Er't be disburthen'd with a liberall tongue.

Nor. Nay speake thy mind: & let him ne'r speak more
That speakes thy words againe to do thee harme.

Wil. Tends that thou'dst speake to th'Du. of Hereford,
If it be so, out with it boldly man,
Quicke is mine eare to heare of good towards him.

Ross. No good at all that I can do for him,
Vnlesse you call it good to pitie him,
Bereft and gelded of his patrimonie.

Nor. Now afore heauen, 'tis shame such wrongs are borne,
In him a royall Prince, and many moe
Of noble blood in this declining Land;
The King is not himselfe, but basely led
By Flatterers, and what they will informe
Meerely in hate 'gainst any of vs all,
That will the King seuerely prosecute
'Gainst vs, our liues, our children, and our heires.

Ros. The Commons hath he pil'd with greeuous taxes
And quite lost their hearts: the Nobles hath he finde
For ancient quarrels, and quite lost their hearts.

Wil. And daily new exactions are deuis'd,
As blankes, beneuolences, and I wot not what:
But what o'Gods name doth become of this?

Nor. Wars hath not wasted it, for war'd he hath not.
But basely yeelded vpon comprimize,
That which his Ancestors atchieu'd with blowes:
More hath he spent in peace, then they in warres.

Ros. The Earle of Wiltshire hath the realme in Farme.

Wil. The Kings growne bankrupt like a broken man.

Nor. Reproach, and dissolution hangeth ouer him.

Ros. He hath not monie for these Irish warres:
(His burthenous taxations notwithstanding)
But by the robbing of the banish'd Duke.

Nor. His noble Kinsman, most degenerate King:
But Lords, we heare this fearefull tempest sing,
Yet seeke no shelter to auoid the storme:
We see the winde sit sore vpon our salles,
And yet we strike not, but securely perish

Ros. We see the very wracke that we must suffer,
And vnauoyded is the danger now
For suffering so the causes of our wracke.

Nor. Not so: euen through the hollow eyes of death,
I spie life peering: but I dare not say
How neere the tidings of our comfort is.

Wil. Nay let vs share thy thoughts, as thou dost ours

Ros. Be confident to speake Northumberland,
We three, are but thy selfe, and speaking so,
Thy words are but as thoughts, therefore be bold.

Nor. Then thus: I haue from Port *le Blan*
A Bay in *Britaine*, receiu'd intelligence,
That *Harry* Duke of *Herford*, *Rainald* Lord *Cobham*,
That late broke from the Duke of *Exeter*,
His brother Archbishop, late of *Canterbury*,
Sir *Thomas Erpingham*, Sir *Iohn Rainston*,
Sir *Iohn Norberie*, Sir *Robert Waterton*, & *Francis Quoint*,
All these well furnish'd by the Duke of *Britaine*,
With eight tall ships, three thousand men of warre
Are making hither with all due expedience,
And shortly meane to touch our Northerne shore:
Perhaps they had ere this, but that they stay
The first departing of the King for Ireland.
If then we shall shake off our slauish yoake,
Impe out our drooping Countries broken wing,
Redeeme from broaking pawne the blemish'd Crowne,
Wipe off the dust that hides our Scepters gilt,
And make high Maiestie looke like it selfe,
Away with me in poste to *Rauenspurgh*,
But if you faint, as fearing to do so,
Stay, and be secret, and my selfe will go.

Ros. To horse, to horse, vrge doubts to them ӱ feare.

Wil. Hold out my horse, and I will first be there.

Exeunt.

Scena Secunda.

Enter Queene, Bushy, and Bagot.

Bush. Madam, your Maiesty is too much sad,
You promis'd when you parted with the King,
To lay aside selfe-harming heauinesse,
And entertaine a cheerefull disposition.

Qu. To please the King, I did: to please my selfe
I cannot do it; yet I know no cause
Why I should welcome such a guest as greefe,
Saue bidding farewell to so sweet a guest
As my sweet *Richard*; yet againe me thinkes,
Some vnborne sorrow, ripe in fortunes wombe
Is comming towards me, and my inward soule
With nothing trembles, at something it greeues,
More then with parting from my Lord the King.

Bush. Each substance of a greefe hath twenty shadows
Which shewes like greefe it selfe, but is not so:
For sorrowes eye, glazed with blinding teares,
Diuides one thing intire, to many obiects,
Like perspectiues, which rightly gaz'd vpon
Shew nothing but confusion, ey'd awry,
Distinguish forme: so your sweet Maiestie
Looking awry vpon your Lords departure,
Finde shapes of greefe, more then himselfe to waile,
Which look'd on as it is, is naught but shadowes
Of what it is not: then thrice-gracious Queene,
More then your Lords departure weep not, more's not
Or if it be, 'tis with false sorrowes eie, (seene;
Which for things true, weepe things imaginary.

Qu. It may be so: but yet my inward soule
Perswades me it is otherwise: how ere it be,
I cannot but be sad: so heauy sad,
As though on thinking on no thought I thinke,
Makes me with heauy nothing faint and shrinke.

Bush. 'Tis nothing but conceit (my gracious Lady.)

Queene.

Qu. 'Tis nothing lesse: conceit is still deriu'd
From some fore father greefe, mine is not so,
For nothing hath begot my something greefe,
Or something, hath the nothing that I greeue,
'Tis in reuersion that I do possesse,
But what it is, that is not yet knowne, what
I cannot name, 'tis namelesse woe I wot.

Enter Greene.

Gree. Heauen saue your Maiesty, and wel met Gentle-
I hope the King is not yet shipt for Ireland. (men:
Qu. Why hop'st thou so? Tis better hope he is:
For his designes craue hast, his hast good hope,
Then wherefore dost thou hope he is not shipt?
Gre. That he our hope, might haue retyr'd his power,
and driuen into dispaire an enemies hope,
Who strongly hath set footing in this Land.
The banish'd *Bullingbrooke* repeales himselfe,
And with vp-lifted Armes is safe arriu'd
At *Rauenspurg*.
Qu. Now God in heauen forbid.
Gr. O Madam 'tis too true: and that is worse,
The L.Northumberland, his yong sonne *Henrie Percie*,
The Lords of *Rosse, Beaumond*, and *Willoughby*,
With all their powrefull friends are fled to him.
Bush. Why haue you not proclaim'd Northumberland
And the rest of the reuolted faction, Traitors?
Gre. We haue: whereupon the Earle of Worcester
Hath broke his staffe, resign'd his Stewardship,
And al the houshold seruants fled with him to *Bullinbrook*
Qu. So *Greene*, thou art the midwife of my woe,
And *Bullinbrooke* my sorrowes dismall heyre:
Now hath my soule brought forth her prodegie,
And I a gasping new deliuered mother,
Haue woe to woe, sorrow to sorrow ioyn'd.
Bush. Dispaire not Madam.
Qu. Who shall hinder me?
I will dispaire, and be at enmitie
With couzening hope; he is a Flatterer,
A Parasite, a keeper backe of death,
Who gently would dissolue the bands of life,
Which falie hopes linger in extremity.

Enter Yorke

Gre. Heere comes the Duke of Yorke.
Qu. With signes of warre about his aged necke,
Oh full of carefull businesse are his lookes:
Vncle, for heauens sake speake comfortable words:
Yor. Comfort's in heauen, and we are on the earth,
Where nothing liues but crosses, care and greefe:
Your husband he is gone to saue farre off,
Whilst others come to make him loose at home;
Heere am I left to vnder-prop his Land,
Who weake with age, cannot support my selfe:
Now comes the sicke houre that his surfet made,
Now shall he try his friends that flattered him.

Enter a seruant.

Ser. My Lord, your sonne was gone before I came.
Yor. He was: why so: go all which way it will:
The Nobles they are fled, the Commons they are cold,
And will I feare reuolt on Herfords side.
Sirra, get thee to Plashie to my sister Gloster,
Bid her send me presently a thousand pound,
Hold, take my Ring
Ser. My Lord, I had forgot
To tell your Lordship, to day I came by, and call'd there,
But I shall greeue you to report the rest.
Yor. What is't knaue?
Ser. An houre before I came, the Dutchesse di'de.
Yor. Heau'n for his mercy, what a tide of woes
Come rushing on this wofull Land at once?
I know not what to do: I would to heauen
(So my vntruth had not prouok'd him to it)
The King had cut off my head with my brothers.
What, are there postes dispatcht for Ireland?
How shall we do for money for these warres?
Come sister (Cozen I would say) pray pardon me.
Go fellow, get thee home, prouide some Carts,
And bring away the Armour that is there.
Gentlemen, will you muster men?
If I know how, or which way to order these affaires
Thus disorderly thrust into my hands,
Neuer beleeue me. Both are my kinsmen,
Th'one is my Soueraigne, whom both my oath
And dutie bids defend: th'other againe
Is my kinsman, whom the King hath wrong'd,
Whom conscience, and my kindred bids to right:
Well, somewhat we must do: Come Cozen,
Ile dispose of you. Gentlemen, go muster vp your men,
And meet me presently at Barkley Castle:
I should to Plashy too: but time will not permit,
All is vneuen, and euery thing is left at six and seuen. *Exit*
Bush. The winde sits faire for newes to go to Ireland,
But none returnes: For vs to leuy power
Proportionable to th'enemy, is all impossible.
Gr. Besides our neerenesse to the King in loue,
Is neere the hate of those loue not the King.
Ba. And that's the wauering Commons, for their loue
Lies in their purses, and who so empties them,
By so much fils their hearts with deadly hate.
Bush. Wherein the king stands generally condemn'd
Bag. If iudgement lye in them, then so do we,
Because we haue beene euer neere the King.
Gr. Well: I will for refuge straight to Bristoll Castle,
The Earle of Wiltshire is alreadie there.
Bush. Thither will I with you, for little office
Will the hatefull Commons performe for vs,
Except like Curres, to teare vs all in peeces:
Will you go along with vs?
Bag. No, I will to Ireland to his Maiestie:
Farewell, if hearts presages be not vaine,
We three here part, that neu'r shall meete againe.
Bu. That's as Yorke thriues to beate back *Bullinbroke*
Gr. Alas poore Duke, the taske he vndertakes
Is numbring sands, and drinking Oceans drie,
Where one on his side fights, thousands will flye.
Bush. Farewell at once, for once, for all, and euer.
Well, we may meete againe.
Bag. I feare me neuer. *Exit.*

Scæna Tertia.

Enter the Duke of Hereford, and Northumberland.

Bul. How farre is it my Lord to Berkley now?
Nor. Beleeue me noble Lord,
I am a stranger heere in Gloustershire,
These high wilde hilles, and rough vneeuen waies,
Drawes out our miles, and makes them wearisome:
And yet our faire discourse hath beene as sugar,

Mak in

Making the hard way sweet and delectable:
But I bethinke me, what a wearie way
From Rauenspurgh to Cottshold will be found,
In *Rosse* and *Willoughby*, wanting your companie,
Which I protest hath very much beguild
The tediousnesse, and processe of my trauell:
But theirs is sweetned with the hope to haue
The present benefit that I possesse;
And hope to ioy, is little lesse in ioy,
Then hope enioy'd: By this, the wearie Lords
Shall make their way seeme short, as mine hath done,
By sight of what I haue, your Noble Companie.

Bull. Of much lesse value is my Companie,
Then your good words: but who comes here?

Enter H. Percie.

North. It is my Sonne, young *Harry Percie*,
Sent from my Brother *Worcester*: Whence soeuer.
Harry, how fares your Vnckle?

Percie. I had thought, my Lord, to haue learn'd his health of you.

North. Why, is he not with the Queene?

Percie. No, my good Lord, he hath forsook the Court,
Broken his Staffe of Office, and disperst
The Houshold of the King.

North. What was his reason?
He was not so resolu'd, when we last spake together.

Percie. Because your Lordship was proclaimed Traitor.
But hee, my Lord, is gone to Rauenspurgh,
To offer seruice to the Duke of Hereford,
And sent me ouer by Barkely, to discouer
What power the Duke of Yorke had leuied there,
Then with direction to repaire to Rauenspurgh.

North. Haue you forgot the Duke of Hereford (Boy.)

Percie. No, my good Lord; for that is not forgot
Which ne're I did remember: to my knowledge,
I neuer in my life did looke on him.

North. Then learne to know him now: this is the Duke.

Percie. My gracious Lord, I tender you my seruice,
Such as it is, being tender, raw, and young,
Which elder dayes shall ripen, and confirme
To more approued seruice, and desert.

Bull. I thanke thee gentle *Percie*, and be sure
I count my selfe in nothing else so happy,
As in a Soule remembring my good Friends:
And as my Fortune ripens with thy Loue,
It shall be still thy true Loues recompence,
My Heart this Couenant makes, my Hand thus seales it.

North. How farre is it to Barkely? and what stirre
Keepes good old *Yorke* there, with his Men of Warre?

Percie. There stands the Castle, by yond tuft of Trees,
Mann'd with three hundred men, as I haue heard,
And in it are the Lords of *Yorke*, *Barkely*, and *Seymor*,
None else of Name, and noble estimate.

Enter Rosse and Willoughby.

North. Here come the Lords of *Rosse* and *Willoughby*,
Bloody with spurring, fierie red with haste.

Bull. Welcome my Lords, I wot your loue pursues
A banisht Traytor; all my Treasurie
Is yet but vnfelt thankes, which more enrich'd,
Shall be your loue, and labours recompence.

Ross. Your presence makes vs rich, most Noble Lord.

Willo. And farre surmounts our labour to attaine it.

Bull. Euermore thankes, th'Exchequer of the poore,
Which till my infant-fortune comes to yeeres,
Stands for my Bountie: but who comes here?

Enter Barkely.

North. It is my Lord of Barkely, as I ghesse.

Bark. My Lord of Hereford, my Message is to you.

Bull. My Lord, my Answere is to *Lancaster*,
And I am come to seeke that Name in England,
And I must finde that Title in your Tongue,
Before I make reply to aught you say.

Bark. Mistake me not, my Lord, 'tis not my meaning
To raze one Title of your Honor out.
To you, my Lord, I come (what Lord you will)
From the most glorious of this Land,
The Duke of Yorke, to know what pricks you on
To take aduantage of the absent time,
And fright our Natiue Peace with selfe-borne Armes.

Enter Yorke.

Bull. I shall not need transport my words by you,
Here comes his Grace in Person. My Noble Vnckle.

York. Shew me thy humble heart, and not thy knee,
Whose dutie is deceiuable, and false.

Bull. My gracious Vnckle.

York. Tut, tut, Grace me no Grace, nor Vnckle me,
I am no Traytors Vnckle; and that word Grace,
In an vngracious mouth, is but prophane.
Why haue these banish'd, and forbidden Legges,
Dar'd once to touch a Dust of Englands Ground?
But more then why, why haue they dar'd to march
So many miles vpon her peacefull Bosome,
Frighting her pale-fac'd Villages with Warre,
And ostentation of despised Armes?
Com'st thou because th'anoynted King is hence?
Why foolish Boy, the King is left behind,
And in my loyall Bosome lyes his power.
Were I but now the Lord of such hot youth,
As when braue *Gaunt*, thy Father, and my selfe
Rescued the *Black Prince* that yong *Mars* of men,
From forth the Rankes of many thousand French:
Oh then, how quickly should this Arme of mine,
Now Prisoner to the Palsie, chastise thee,
And minister correction to thy Fault.

Bull. My gracious Vnckle, let me know my Fault,
On what Condition stands it, and wherein?

York. Euen in Condition of the worst degree,
In grosse Rebellion, and detested Treason:
Thou art a banish'd man, and here art come
Before th'expiration of thy time,
In brauing Armes against thy Soueraigne.

Bull. As I was banish'd, I was banish'd *Hereford*,
But as I come, I come for *Lancaster*.
And Noble Vnckle, I beseech your Grace
Looke on my Wrongs with an indifferent eye:
You are my Father, for me thinkes in you
I see old *Gaunt* aliue. Oh then my Father,
Will you permit, that I shall stand condemn'd
A wandring Vagabond; my Rights and Royalties
Pluckt from my armes perforce, and giuen away
To vpstart Vnthrifts? Wherefore was I borne?
If that my Cousin King, be King of England,
It must be graunted, I am Duke of Lancaster.
You haue a Sonne, *Aumerle*, my Noble Kinsman,
Had you first died, and he beene thus trod downe,
He should haue found his Vnckle *Gaunt* a Father,
To rowze his Wrongs, and chase them to the bay.
I am denyde to sue my Liuerie here,
And yet my Letters Patents giue me leaue:
My Fathers goods are all distraynd, and sold,
And these, and all, are all amisse imployd.

What

What would you haue me doe? I am a Subiect,
And challenge Law: Attorneyes are deny'd me;
And therefore personally I lay my claime
To my Inheritance of free Discent.
North. The Noble Duke hath been too much abus'd.
Ross. It stands your Grace vpon, to doe him right.
Willo. Base men by his endowments are made great.
York. My Lords of England, let me tell you this,
I haue had feeling of my Cosens Wrongs,
And labour'd all I could to doe him right:
But in this kind, to come in brauing Armes,
Be his owne Caruer, and cut out his way,
To find out Right with Wrongs, it may not be;
And you that doe abett him in this kind,
Cherish Rebellion, and are Rebels all.
North. The Noble Duke hath sworne his comming is
But for his owne; and for the right of that,
Wee all haue strongly sworne to giue him ayd,
And let him neu'r see Ioy, that breakes that Oath.
York. Well, well, I see the issue of these Armes,
I cannot mend it, I must needes confesse,
Because my power is weake, and all ill left:
But if I could, by him that gaue me life,
I would attach you all, and make you stoope
Vnto the Soueraigne Mercy of the King.
But since I cannot, be it knowne to you,
I doe remaine as Neuter. So fare you well,
Vnlesse you please to enter in the Castle,
And there repose you for this Night.
Bull. An offer Vnckle, that wee will accept:
But wee must winne your Grace to goe with vs
To Bristow Castle, which they say is held
By *Bushie, Bagot*, and their Complices,
The Caterpillers of the Commonwealth,
Which I haue sworne to weed, and plucke away.
York. It may be I will go with you: but yet Ile pawse,
For I am loth to breake our Countries Lawes:
Nor Friends, nor Foes, to me welcome you are,
Things past redresse, are now with me past care. *Exeunt.*

Scœna Quarta.

Enter Salisbury, and a Captaine.

Capt. My Lord of Salisbury, we haue stayd ten dayes,
And hardly kept our Countreymen together,
And yet we heare no tidings from the King;
Therefore we will disperse our selues: farewell.
Sal. Stay yet another day, thou trustie Welchman,
The King reposeth all his confidence in thee.
Capt. 'Tis thought the King is dead, we will not stay;
The Bay-trees in our Countrey all are wither'd,
And Meteors fright the fixed Starres of Heauen;
The pale-fac'd Moone lookes bloody on the Earth,
And leane-look'd Prophets whisper fearefull change;
Rich men looke sad, and Ruffians dance and leape,
The one in feare, to loose what they enioy,
The other to enioy by Rage, and Warre:
These signes fore-run the death of Kings.
Farewell, our Countreymen are gone and fled,
As well assur'd *Richard* their King is dead. *Exit.*
Sal. Ah *Richard*, with eyes of heauie mind,
I see thy Glory, like a shooting Starre,
Fall to the base Earth, from the Firmament:
Thy Sunne sets weeping in the lowly West,
Witnessing Stormes to come, Woe, and Vnrest:
Thy Friends are fled, to wait vpon thy Foes,
And crossely to thy good, all fortune goes. *Exit.*

Actus Tertius. Scena Prima.

Enter Bullingbrooke, Yorke, Northumberland, Rosse, Percie Willoughby, with Bushie and Greene Prisoners.

Bull. Bring forth these men:
Bushie and *Greene*, I will not vex your soules,
(Since presently your soules must part your bodies)
With too much vrging your pernitious liues,
For 'twere no Charitie: yet to wash your blood
From off my hands, here in the view of men,
I will vnfold some causes of your deaths.
You haue mis-led a Prince, a Royall King,
A happie Gentleman in Blood, and Lineaments,
By you vnhappied, and disfigur'd cleane:
You haue in manner with your sinfull houres
Made a Diuorce betwixt his Queene and him,
Broke the possession of a Royall Bed,
And stayn'd the beautie of a faire Queenes Cheekes,
With teares drawn fro her eyes, with your foule wrongs.
My selfe a Prince, by fortune of my birth,
Neere to the King in blood, and neere in loue,
Till you did make him mis-interprete me,
Haue stoopt my neck vnder your iniuries,
And sigh'd my English breath in forraine Clouds,
Eating the bitter bread of banishment;
While you haue fed vpon my Seignories,
Dis-park'd my Parkes, and fell'd my Forrest Woods;
From mine owne Windowes torne my Household Coat,
Raz'd out my Impresse, leauing me no signe,
Saue mens opinions, and my liuing blood,
To shew the World I am a Gentleman.
This, and much more, much more then twice all this,
Condemnes you to the death: see them deliuered ouer
To execution, and the hand of death.
Bushie. More welcome is the stroake of death to me,
Then *Bullingbrooke* to England.
Greene. My comfort is, that Heauen will take our soules,
And plague Iniustice with the paines of Hell.
Bull. My Lord *Northumberland*, see them dispatch'd:
Vnckle, you say the Queene is at your House,
For Heauens sake fairely let her be entreated,
Tell her I send to her my kind commends;
Take speciall care my Greetings be deliuer'd.
York. A Gentleman of mine I haue dispatch'd
With Letters of your loue, to her at large.
Bull. Thankes gentle Vnckle: come Lords away,
To fight with *Glendoure*, and his Complices;
A while to worke, and after holliday.
Exeunt.

Scœna

Scena Secunda.

Drums: Flourish, and Colours.

Enter Richard, Aumerle, Carlile, and Souldiers.

Rich. Barkloughly Castle call you this at hand?
Au. Yea, my Lord: how brooks your Grace the ayre,
After your late tossing on the breaking Seas?
Rich. Needs must I like it well: I weepe for ioy
To stand vpon my Kingdome once againe.
Deere Earth, I doe salute thee with my hand,
Though Rebels wound thee with their Horses hoofes:
As a long parted Mother with her Child,
Playes fondly with her teares, and smiles in meeting;
So weeping, smiling, greet I thee my Earth,
And doe thee fauor with my Royall hands.
Feed not thy Soueraignes Foe, my gentle Earth,
Nor with thy Sweetes, comfort his rauenous sence:
But let thy Spiders, that suck vp thy Venome.
And heauie-gated Toades lye in their way,
Doing annoyance to the trecherous feete,
Which with vsurping steps doe trample thee.
Yeeld stinging Nettles to mine Enemies;
And when they from thy Bosome pluck a Flower,
Guard it I prethee with a lurking Adder,
Whose double tongue may with a mortall touch
Throw death vpon thy Soueraignes Enemies.
Mock not my fencelesse Coniuration, Lords;
This Earth shall haue a feeling, and these Stones
Proue armed Souldiers, ere her Natiue King
Shall falter vnder foule Rebellious Armes.
Car. Feare not my Lord, that Power that made you King
Hath power to keepe you King, in spight of all.
Aum. He meanes, my Lord, that we are too remisse,
Whilest *Bullingbrooke* through our securitie,
Growes strong and great, in substance and in friends.
Rich. Discomfortable Cousin, knowest thou not,
That when the searching Eye of Heauen is hid
Behind the Globe, that lights the lower World,
Then Theeues and Robbers raunge abroad vnseene,
In Murthers and in Out-rage bloody here:
But when from vnder this Terrestriall Ball
He fires the prowd tops of the Easterne Pines,
And darts his Lightning through eu'ry guiltie hole,
Then Murthers, Treasons, and detested sinnes
(The Cloake of Night being pluckt from off their backs)
Stand bare and naked, trembling at themselues.
So when this Theefe, this Traytor *Bullingbrooke*,
Who all this while hath reuell'd in the Night,
Shall see vs rising in our Throne, the East,
His Treasons will sit blushing in his face,
Not able to endure the sight of Day;
But selfe-affrighted, tremble at his sinne.
Not all the Water in the rough rude Sea
Can wash the Balme from an anoynted King;
The breath of worldly men cannot depose
The Deputie elected by the Lord:
For euery man that *Bullingbrooke* hath prest,
To lift shrewd Steele against our Golden Crowne,
Heauen for his *Richard* hath in heauenly pay
A glorious Angell: then if Angels fight,
Weake men must fall, for Heauen still guards the right.

Enter Salisbury.

Welcome my Lord, how farre off lyes your Power?
Salisb. Nor neere, nor farther off, my gracious Lord,
Then this weake arme; discomfort guides my tongue,
And bids me speake of nothing but despaire.
One day too late, I feare (my Noble Lord)
Hath clouded all thy happie dayes on Earth:
Oh call backe Yesterday, bid Time returne,
And thou shalt haue twelue thousand fighting men:
To day, to day, vnhappie day too late
Orethrowes thy Ioyes, Friends, Fortune, and thy State;
For all the Welchmen hearing thou wert dead,
Are gone to *Bullingbrooke*, disperst, and fled.
Aum. Comfort my Liege, why lookes your Grace so pale?
Rich. But now the blood of twentie thousand men.
Did triumph in my face, and they are fled,
And till so much blood thither come againe,
Haue I not reason to looke pale, and dead?
All Soules that will be safe, flye from my side,
For Time hath set a blot vpon my pride.
Aum. Comfort my Liege, remember who you are.
Rich. I had forgot my selfe. Am I not King?
Awake thou sluggard Maiestie, thou sleepest:
Is not the Kings Name fortie thousand Names?
Arme, arme my Name: a punie subiect strikes
At thy great glory. Looke not to the ground,
Ye Fauorites of a King: are wee not high?
High be our thoughts: I know my Vnckle *Yorke*
Hath Power enough to serue our turne.
But who comes here? *Enter Scroope.*
Scroope. More health and happinesse betide my Liege,
Then can my care-tun'd tongue deliuer him.
Rich. Mine eare is open, and my heart prepar'd:
The worst is worldly losse, thou canst vnfold:
Say, Is my Kingdome lost? why 'twas my Care:
And what losse is it to be rid of Care?
Striues *Bullingbrooke* to be as Great as wee?
Greater he shall not be: If hee serue God,
Wee'l serue him too, and be his Fellow so.
Reuolt our Subiects? That we cannot mend,
They breake their Faith to God, as well as vs:
Cry Woe, Destruction, Ruine, Losse, Decay,
The worst is Death, and Death will haue his day.
Scroope. Glad am I, that your Highnesse is so arm'd
To beare the tidings of Calamitie.
Like an vnseasonable stormie day,
Which make the Siluer Riuers drowne their Shores,
As if the World were all dissolu'd to teares:
So high, aboue his Limits, swells the Rage
Of *Bullingbrooke*, coueting your fearefull Land
With hard bright Steele, and hearts harder then Steele:
White Beares haue arm'd their thin and hairelesse Scalps
Against thy Maiestie, and Boyes with Womens Voyces,
Striue to speake bigge, and clap their female ioints
In stiffe vnwieldie Armes: against thy Crowne
Thy very Beads-men learne to bend their Bowes
Of double fatall Eugh: against thy State
Yea Distaffe-Women manage rustie Bills:
Against thy Seat both young and old rebell,
And all goes worse then I haue power to tell.
Rich. Too well, too well thou tell'st a Tale so ill.
Where is the Earle of Wiltshire? where is *Bagot*?
What is become of *Bushie*? where is *Greene*?

That

That they haue let the dangerous Enemie
Measure our Confines with such peacefull steps?
If we preuaile, their heads shall pay for it.
I warrant they haue made peace with *Bullingbrooke*.

Scroope. Peace haue they made with him indeede (my Lord.)

Rich. Oh Villains, Vipers, damn'd without redemption,
Dogges, easily woon to fawne on any man,
Snakes in my heart blood warm'd, that sting my heart,
Three Iudasses, each one thrice worse then *Iudas*,
Would they make peace? terrible Hell make warre
Vpon their spotted Soules for this Offence.

Scroope. Sweet Loue (I see) changing his propertie,
Turnes to the sowrest, and most deadly hate:
Againe vncurse their Soules; their peace is made
With Heads, and not with Hands: those whom you curse
Haue felt the worst of Deaths destroying hand,
And lye full low, grau'd in the hollow ground.

Aum. Is *Bushie*, *Greene*, and the Earle of Wiltshire dead?

Scroope. Yea all of them at Bristow lost their heads.

Aum. Where is the Duke my Father with his Power?

Rich. No matter where; of comfort no man speake:
Let's talke of Graues, of Wormes, and Epitaphs,
Make Dust our Paper, and with Raynie eyes
Write Sorrow on the Bosome of the Earth.
Let's chuse Executors, and talke of Wills:
And yet not so; for what can we bequeath,
Saue our deposed bodies to the ground?
Our Lands, our Liues, and all are *Bullingbrookes*,
And nothing can we call our owne, but Death,
And that small Modell of the barren Earth,
Which serues as Paste, and Couer to our Bones:
For Heauens sake let vs sit vpon the ground,
And tell sad stories of the death of Kings:
How some haue been depos'd, some slaine in warre,
Some haunted by the Ghosts they haue depos'd,
Some poyson'd by their Wiues, some sleeping kill'd,
All murther'd. For within the hollow Crowne
That rounds the mortall Temples of a King,
Keepes Death his Court, and there the Antique sits
Scoffing his State, and grinning at his Pompe,
Allowing him a breath, a little Scene,
To Monarchize, be fear'd, and kill with lookes,
Infusing him with selfe and vaine conceit,
As if this Flesh, which walls about our Life.
Were Brasse impregnable: and humor'd thus,
Comes at the last, and with a little Pinne
Bores through his Castle Walls, and farwell King.
Couer your heads, and mock not flesh and blood
With solemne Reuerence: throw away Respect,
Tradition, Forme, and Ceremonious dutie,
For you haue but mistooke me all this while:
I liue with Bread like you, feele Want,
Taste Griefe, need Friends: subiected thus,
How can you say to me, I am a King?

Carl. My Lord, wise men ne're waile their present woes,
But presently preuent the wayes to waile:
To feare the Foe, since feare oppresseth strength,
Giues in your weakenesse, strength vnto your Foe;
Feare, and be slaine, no worse can come to fight,
And fight and die, is death destroying death,
Where fearing, dying, payes death seruile breath.

Aum. My Father hath a Power, enquire of him,
And learne to make a Body of a Limbe.

Rich. Thou chid'st me well: proud *Bullingbrooke* I come
To change Blowes with thee, for our day of Doome:
This ague fit of feare is ouer-blowne,
An easie taske it is to winne our owne.
Say *Scroope*, where lyes our Vnckle with his Power?
Speake sweetly man, although thy lookes be sowre.

Scroope. Men iudge by the complexion of the Skie
The state and inclination of the day;
So may you by my dull and heauie Eye:
My Tongue hath but a heauier Tale to say:
I play the Torturer, by small and small
To lengthen out the worst, that must be spoken.
Your Vnckle *Yorke* is ioyn'd with *Bullingbrooke*,
And all your Northerne Castles yeelded vp,
And all your Southerne Gentlemen in Armes
Vpon his Faction.

Rich. Thou hast said enough.
Beshrew thee Cousin, which didst lead me forth
Of that sweet way I was in, to despaire:
What say you now? What comfort haue we now?
By Heauen Ile hate him euerlastingly,
That bids me be of comfort any more.
Goe to Flint Castle, there Ile pine away,
A King, Woes slaue, shall Kingly Woe obey:
That Power I haue, discharge, and let 'em goe
To eare the Land, that hath some hope to grow,
For I haue none. Let no man speake againe
To alter this, for counsaile is but vaine.

Aum. My Liege, one word.

Rich. He does me double wrong,
That wounds me with the flatteries of his tongue.
Discharge my followers: let them hence away,
From *Richards* Night, to *Bullingbrookes* faire Day.

Exeunt.

Scæna Tertia.

Enter with Drum and Colours, Bullingbrooke, Yorke, Northumberland, Attendants.

Bull. So that by this intelligence we learne
The Welchmen are dispers'd, and *Salisbury*
Is gone to meet the King, who lately landed
With some few priuate friends, vpon this Coast.

North. The newes is very faire and good, my Lord,
Richard, not farre from hence, hath hid his head.

York. It would beseeme the Lord Northumberland,
To say King *Richard*: alack the heauie day,
When such a sacred King should hide his head.

North. Your Grace mistakes: onely to be briefe,
Left I his Title out.

York. The time hath beene,
Would you haue beene so briefe with him, he would
Haue beene so briefe with you, to shorten you,
For taking so the Head, your whole heads length.

Bull. Mistake not (Vnckle) farther then you should.

York. Take not (good Cousin) farther then you should.
Least you mistake the Heauens are ore your head.

Bull. I know it (Vnckle) and oppose not my selfe
Against their will. But who comes here?

Enter Percie.

Welcome *Harry*: what, will not this Castle yeeld?

Per. The Castle royally is mann'd, my Lord,
Against thy entrance.

Bull. Roy-

Bull. Royally? Why,it containes no King?
Per. Yes (my good Lord)
It doth containe a King: King *Richard* lyes
Within the limits of yond Lime and Stone,
And with him,the Lord *Aumerle*, Lord *Salisbury*,
Sir *Stephen Scroope*, besides a Clergie man
Of holy reuerence; who,I cannot learne.
North. Oh,belike it is the Bishop of Carlile.
Bull. Noble Lord,
Goe to the rude Ribs of that ancient Castle,
Through Brazen Trumpet send the breath of Parle
Into his ruin'd Eares, and thus deliuer:
Henry Bullingbrooke vpon his knees doth kisse
King *Richards* hand,and sends allegeance
And true faith of heart to his Royall Person: hither come
Euen at his feet,to lay my Armes and Power,
Prouided,that my Banishment repeal'd,
And Lands restor'd againe,be freely graunted:
If not,Ile vse th'aduantage of my Power,
And lay the Summers dust with showers of blood,
Rayn'd from the wounds of slaughter'd Englishmen;
The which,how farre off from the mind of *Bullingbrooke*
It is, such Crimson Tempest should bedrench
The fresh greene Lap of faire King *Richards* Land,
My stooping dutie tenderly shall shew.
Goe signifie as much,while here we march
Vpon the Grassie Carpet of this Plaine:
Let's march without the noyse of threatning Drum,
That from this Castles tatter'd Battlements
Our faire Appointments may be well perus'd.
Me thinkes King *Richard* and my selfe should meet
With no lesse terror then the Elements
Of Fire and Water,when their thundring smoake
At meeting teares the cloudie Cheekes of Heauen:
Be he the fire,Ile be the yeelding Water;
The Rage be his,while on the Earth I raine
My Waters on the Earth, and not on him.
March on,and marke King *Richard* how he lookes.

Parle without, and answere within: then a Flourish. Enter on the Walls, Richard, Carlile, Aumerle, Scroop, Salisbury.

See,see, King *Richard* doth himselfe appeare
As doth the blushing discontented Sunne,
From out the fierie Portall of the East,
When he perceiues the enuious Clouds are bent
To dimme his glory,and to staine the tract
Of his bright passage to the Occident.
Yorke. Yet lookes he like a King: behold his Eye
(As bright as is the Eagles) lightens forth
Controlling Maiestie: alack,alack,for woe,
That any harme should staine so faire a shew.
Rich. Wee are amaz'd,and thus long haue we stood
To watch the fearefull bending of thy knee,
Because we thought our selfe thy lawfull King:
And if we be,how dare thy ioynts forget
To pay their awfull dutie to our presence?
If we be not,shew vs the Hand of God,
That hath dismiss'd vs from our Stewardship,
For well wee know,no Hand of Blood and Bone
Can gripe the sacred Handle of our Scepter,
Vnlesse he doe prophane,steale,or vsurpe.
And though you thinke,that all,as you haue done,
Haue torne their Soules,by turning them from vs,
And we are barren, and bereft of Friends:
Yet know,my Master,God Omnipotent,
Is mustring in his Clouds, on our behalfe,
Armies of Pestilence, and they shall strike
Your Children yet vnborne,and vnbegot,
That lift your Vassall Hands against my Head,
And threat the Glory of my precious Crowne.
Tell *Bullingbrooke*, for yond me thinkes he is,
That euery stride he makes vpon my Land,
Is dangerous Treason: He is come to ope
The purple Testament of bleeding Warre;
But ere the Crowne he lookes for,liue in peace,
Ten thousand bloody crownes of Mothers Sonnes
Shall ill become the flower of Englands face,
Change the complexion of her Maid-pale Peace
To Scarlet Indignation, and bedew
Her Pastors Grasse with faithfull English Blood.
North. The King of Heauen forbid our Lord the King
Should so with ciuill and vnciuill Armes
Be rush'd vpon: Thy thrice-noble Cousin,
Harry Bullingbrooke, doth humbly kisse thy hand,
And by the Honorable Tombe he sweares,
That stands vpon your Royall Grandsires Bones,
And by the Royalties of both your Bloods,
(Currents that spring from one most gracious Head)
And by the buried Hand of Warlike *Gaunt*,
And by the Worth and Honor of himselfe,
Comprising all that may be sworne,or said,
His comming hither hath no further scope,
Then for his Lineall Royalties,and to begge
Infranchisement immediate on his knees:
Which on thy Royall partie graunted once,
His glittering Armes he will commend to Rust,
His barbed Steedes to Stables,and his heart
To faithfull seruice of your Maiestie:
This sweares he,as he is a Prince,is iust,
And as I am a Gentleman, I credit him.
Rich. Northumberland, say thus: The King returnes,
His Noble Cousin is right welcome hither,
And all the number of his faire demands
Shall be accomplish'd without contradiction:
With all the gracious vtterance thou hast,
Speake to his gentle hearing kind commends.
We doe debase our selfe (Cousin) doe we not,
To looke so poorely,and to speake so faire?
Shall we call back *Northumberland*, and send
Defiance to the Traytor,and so die?
Aum. No,good my Lord,let's fight with gentle words,
Till time lend friends,and friends their helpeful Swords.
Rich. Oh God,oh God,that ere this tongue of mine,
That layd the Sentence of dread Banishment
On yond prowd man,should take it off againe
With words of sooth: Oh that I were as great
As is my Griefe,or lesser then my Name,
Or that I could forget what I haue beene,
Or not remember what I must be now:
Swell'st thou prowd heart? Ile giue thee scope to beat,
Since Foes haue scope to beat both thee and me.
Aum. Northumberland comes backe from *Bullingbrooke*.
Rich. What must the King doe now? must he submit?
The King shall doe it: Must he be depos'd?
The King shall be contented: Must he loose
The Name of King? o' Gods Name let it goe.
Ile giue my Iewels for a sett of Beades,
My gorgeous Pallace,for a Hermitage,
My gay Apparrell,for an Almes-mans Gowne,
My figur'd Goblets,for a Dish of Wood,
My Scepter,for a Palmers walking Staffe,

My Subiects,for a payre of carued Saints,
And my large Kingdome,for a little Graue,
A little little Graue,an obscure Graue.
Or Ile be buryed in the Kings high-way,
Some way of common Trade,where Subiects feet
May howrely trample on their Soueraignes Head:
For on my heart they tread now,whilest I liue;
And buryed once,why not vpon my Head?
Aumerle,thou weep'st (my tender-hearted Cousin)
Wee'le make foule Weather with despised Teares:
Our sighes,and they, shall lodge the Summer Corne,
And make a Dearth in this reuolting Land.
Or shall we play the Wantons with our Woes,
And make some prettie Match,with shedding Teares?
As thus: to drop them still vpon one place,
Till they haue fretted vs a payre of Graues,
Within the Earth: and therein lay'd there lyes
Two Kinsmen,digg'd their Graues with weeping Eyes?
Would not this ill,doe well? Well,well,I see
I talke but idly,and you mock at mee.
Most mightie Prince,my Lord *Northumberland*,
What sayes King *Bullingbrooke*? Will his Maiestie
Giue *Richard* leaue to liue,till *Richard* die?
You make a Legge,and *Bullingbrooke* sayes I.
North. My Lord,in the base Court he doth attend
To speake with you, may it please you to come downe.
Rich. Downe,downe I come,like glist'ring *Phaeton*,
Wanting the manage of vnruly Iades.
In the base Court? base Court,where Kings grow base,
To come at Traytors Calls,and doe them Grace.
In the base Court come down: down Court, down King,
For night-Owls shrike,where mouting Larks should sing.
Bull. What sayes his Maiestie?
North. Sorrow,and griefe of heart
Makes him speake fondly,like a frantick man:
Yet he is come.
Bull. Stand all apart,
And shew faire dutie to his Maiestie.
My gracious Lord.
Rich. Faire Cousin,
You debase your Princely Knee,
To make the base Earth prowd with kissing it.
Me rather had,my Heart might feele your Loue,
Then my vnpleas'd Eye see your Courtesie.
Vp Cousin,vp, your Heart is vp I know,
Thus high at least,although your Knee be low.
Bull. My gracious Lord, I come but for mine owne.
Rich. Your owne is yours, and I am yours, and all.
Bull. So farre be mine,my most redoubted Lord,
As my true seruice shall deserue your loue.
Rich. Well you deseru'd:
They well deserue to haue,
That know the strong'st, and surest way to get.
Vnckle giue me your Hand: nay,drie your Eyes,
Teares shew their Loue,but want their Remedies.
Cousin,I am too young to be your Father,
Though you are old enough to be my Heire.
What you will haue,Ile giue,and willing to,
For doe we must,what force will haue vs doe.
Set on towards London:
Cousin, is it so?
Bull. Yea,my good Lord.
Rich. Then I must not say,no.
Flourish. *Exeunt.*

Scena Quarta.

Enter the Queene, and two Ladies.

Qu. What sport shall we deuise here in this Garden,
To driue away the heauie thought of Care?
La. Madame,wee'le play at Bowles.
Qu. 'Twill make me thinke the World is full of Rubs,
And that my fortune runnes against the Byas.
La. Madame,wee'le Dance.
Qu My Legges can keepe no measure in Delight,
When my poore Heart no measure keepes in Griefe.
Therefore no Dancing(Girle) some other sport.
La. Madame,wee'le tell Tales.
Qu. Of Sorrow, or of Griefe?
La. Of eyther,Madame.
Qu. Of neyther,Girle.
For if of Ioy,being altogether wanting,
It doth remember me the more of Sorrow:
Or if of Griefe,being altogether had,
It addes more Sorrow to my want of Ioy:
For what I haue,I need not to repeat;
And what I want,it bootes not to complaine.
La. Madame,Ile sing.
Qu. 'Tis well that thou hast cause:
But thou should'st please me better,would'st thou weepe.
La. I could weepe,Madame, would it doe you good.
Qu. And I could sing,would weeping doe me good,
And neuer borrow any Teare of thee.
Enter a Gardiner,and two Seruants.
But stay,here comes the Gardiners,
Let's step into the shadow of these Trees.
My wretchednesse,vnto a Rowe of Pinnes,
They'le talke of State: for euery one doth so,
Against a Change; Woe is fore-runne with Woe.
Gard. Goe binde thou vp yond dangling Apricocks,
Which like vnruly Children,make their Syre
Stoupe with oppression of their prodigall weight:
Giue some supportance to the bending twigges.
Goe thou,and like an Executioner
Cut off the heads of too fast growing sprayes,
That looke too loftie in our Common-wealth:
All must be euen,in our Gouernment.
You thus imploy'd,I will goe root away
The noysome Weedes,that without profit sucke
The Soyles fertilitie from wholesome flowers
Ser. Why should we,in the compasse of a Pale,
Keepe Law and Forme,and due Proportion,
Shewing as in a Modell our firme Estate?
When our Sea-walled Garden, the whole Land,
Is full of Weedes,her fairest Flowers choakt vp,
Her Fruit-trees all vnpruin'd,her Hedges ruin'd,
Her Knots disorder'd,and her wholesome Hearbes
Swarming with Caterpillers.
Gard. Hold thy peace.
He that hath suffer'd this disorder'd Spring,
Hath now himselfe met with the Fall of Leafe.
The Weeds that his broad-spreading Leaues did shelter,
That seem'd,in eating him,to hold him vp,
Are pull'd vp,Root and all,by *Bullingbrooke*:
I meane,the Earle of Wiltshire,*Bushie*,*Greene*.

Ser. What are they dead?
Gard. They are,
And *Bullingbrooke* hath seiz'd the wastefull King.
Oh, what pitty is it, that he had not so trim'd
And drest his Land, as we this Garden, at time of yeare,
And wound the Barke, the skin of our Fruit-trees,
Least being ouer-proud with Sap and Blood,
With too much riches it confound it selfe?
Had he done so, to great and growing men,
They might haue liu'd to beare, and he to taste
Their fruites of dutie. Superfluous branches
We lop away, that bearing boughes may liue:
Had he done so, himselfe had borne the Crowne,
Which waste and idle houres, hath quite thrown downe.
Ser. What thinke you the King shall be depos'd?
Gar. Deprest he is already, and depos'd
'Tis doubted he will be. Letters came last night
To a deere Friend of the Duke of Yorkes,
That tell blacke tydings.
Qu. Oh I am prest to death through want of speaking:
Thou old *Adams* likenesse, set to dresse this Garden:
How dares thy harsh rude tongue sound this vnpleasing newes
What Eue? what Serpent hath suggested thee,
To make a second fall of cursed man?
Why do'st thou say, King *Richard* is depos'd,
Dar'st thou, thou little better thing then earth,
Diuine his downfall? Say, where, when, and how
Cam'st thou by this ill-tydings? Speake thou wretch.
Gard. Pardon me Madam. Little ioy haue I
To breath these newes; yet what I say, is true;
King *Richard*, he is in the mighty hold
Of *Bullingbrooke*, their Fortunes both are weigh'd:
In your Lords Scale, is nothing but himselfe,
And some few Vanities, that make him light:
But in the Ballance of great *Bullingbrooke*,
Besides himselfe, are all the English Peeres,
And with that oddes he weighes King *Richard* downe.
Poste you to London, and you'l finde it so,
I speake no more, then euery one doth know.
Qu. Nimble mischance, that art so light of foote,
Doth not thy Embassage belong to me?
And am I last that knowes it? Oh thou think'st
To serue me last, that I may longest keepe
Thy sorrow in my breast. Come Ladies goe,
To meet at London, Londons King in woe.
What was I borne to this: that my sad looke,
Should grace the Triumph of great *Bullingbrooke*.
Gard'ner, for telling me this newes of woe,
I would the Plants thou graft'st, may neuer grow. *Exit.*
G. Poore Queen, so that thy State might be no worse,
I would my skill were subiect to thy curse:
Heere did she drop a teare, heere in this place
Ile set a Banke of Rew, sowre Herbe of Grace:
Rue, eu'n for ruth, heere shortly shall be seene,
In the remembrance of a Weeping Queene. *Exit.*

Actus Quartus. Scœna Prima.

Enter as to the Parliament, Bullingbrooke, Aumerle, Northumberland, Percie, Fitz-Water, Surrey, Carlile, Abbot of Westminster. Herauld, Officers, and Bagot.

Bullingbrooke. Call forth *Bagot*.
Now *Bagot*, freely speake thy minde,
What thou do'st know of Noble Glousters death:
Who wrought it with the King, and who perform'd
The bloody Office of his Timelesse end.
Bag. Then set before my face, the Lord *Aumerle*.
Bul. Cosin, stand forth, and looke vpon that man.
Bag. My Lord *Aumerle*, I know your daring tongue
Scornes to vnsay, what it hath once deliuer'd.
In that dead time, when Glousters death was plotted,
I heard you say, Is not my arme of length,
That reacheth from the restfull English Court
As farre as Callis, to my Vnkles head.
Amongst much other talke, that very time,
I heard you say, that you had rather refuse
The offer of an hundred thousand Crownes,
Then *Bullingbrookes* returne to England; adding withall,
How blest this Land would be, in this your Cosins death.
Aum. Princes, and Noble Lords:
What answer shall I make to this base man?
Shall I so much dishonor my faire Starres,
On equall termes to giue him chasticement?
Either I must, or haue mine honor soyl'd
With th'Attaindor of his sland'rous Lippes.
There is my Gage, the manuall Seale of death
That markes thee out for Hell. Thou lyest.
And will maintaine what thou hast said, is false,
In thy heart blood, though being all too base
To staine the temper of my Knightly sword.
Bul. *Bagot* forbeare, thou shalt not take it vp.
Aum. Excepting one, I would he were the best
In all this presence, that hath mou'd me so.
Fitz. If that thy valour stand on sympathize:
There is my Gage, *Aumerle*, in Gage to thine:
By that faire Sunne, that shewes me where thou stand'st,
I heard thee say (and vauntingly thou spak'st it)
That thou wer't cause of Noble Glousters death.
If thou deniest it, twenty times thou lyest,
And I will turne thy falshood to thy hart,
Where it was forged with my Rapiers point.
Aum. Thou dar'st not (Coward) liue to see the day.
Fitz. Now by my Soule, I would it were this houre.
Aum. *Fitzwater* thou art damn'd to hell for this.
Per. *Aumerle*, thou lye'st: his Honor is as true
In this Appeale, as thou art all vniust:
And that thou art so, there I throw my Gage
To proue it on thee, to th'extreamest point
Of mortall breathing. Seize it, if thou dar'st.
Aum. And if I do not, may my hands rot off,
And neuer brandish more reuengefull Steele,
Ouer the glittering Helmet of my Foe.
Surrey. My Lord *Fitz-water*:
I do remember well, the very time
Aumerle, and you did talke.
Fitz. My Lord,
'Tis very true: You were in presence then,
And you can witnesse with me, this is true.
Surrey. As false, by heauen,
As Heauen it selfe is true.
Fitz. Surrey, thou Lyest.
Surrey. Dishonourable Boy;
That Lye, shall lie so heauy on my Sword,
That it shall render Vengeance, and Reuenge,
Till thou the Lye-giuer, and that Lye, doe lye
In earth as quiet, as thy Fathers Scull.
In proofe whereof, there is mine Honors pawne,
Engage it to the Triall, if thou dar'st.

Fitz-

Fitz.w. How fondly do'st thou spurre a forward Horse?
If I dare eate, or drinke, or breathe, or liue,
I dare meete *Surrey* in a Wildernesse,
And spit vpon him, whilest I say he Lyes,
And Lyes, and Lyes: there is my Bond of Faith,
To tye thee to my strong Correction.
As I intend to thriue in this new World,
Aumerle is guiltie of my true Appeale.
Besides, I heard the banish'd *Norfolke* say,
That thou *Aumerle* didst send two of thy men,
To execute the Noble Duke at Callis.

Aum. Some honest Christian trust me with a Gage,
That *Norfolke* lyes: here doe I throw downe this,
If he may be repeal'd, to trie his Honor.

Bull. These differences shall all rest vnder Gage,
Till *Norfolke* be repeal'd: repeal'd he shall be;
And (though mine Enemie) restor'd againe
To all his Lands and Seignories: when hee's return'd,
Against *Aumerle* we will enforce his Tryall.

Carl. That honorable day shall ne're be seene.
Many a time hath banish'd *Norfolke* fought
For Iesu Christ, in glorious Christian field
Streaming the Ensigne of the Christian Crosse,
Against black Pagans, Turkes, and Saracens:
And toyl'd with workes of Warre, retyr'd himselfe
To Italy, and there at Venice gaue
His Body to that pleasant Countries Earth,
And his pure Soule vnto his Captaine Christ,
Vnder whose Colours he had fought so long.

Bull. Why Bishop, is *Norfolke* dead?

Carl. As sure as I liue, my Lord.

Bull. Sweet peace conduct his sweet Soule
To the Bosome of good old *Abraham*.
Lords Appealants your differẽces shal all rest vnder gage,
Till we assigne you to your dayes of Tryall.

Enter Yorke.

Yorke. Great Duke of Lancaster, I come to thee
From plume-pluckt *Richard*, who with willing Soule
Adopts thee Heire, and his high Scepter yeelds
To the possession of thy Royall Hand.
Ascend his Throne, descending now from him,
And long liue *Henry*, of that Name the Fourth.

Bull. In Gods Name, Ile ascend the Regall Throne.

Carl. Mary, Heauen forbid.
Worst in this Royall Presence may I speake,
Yet best beseeming me to speake the truth.
Would God, that any in this Noble Presence
Were enough Noble, to be vpright Iudge
Of Noble *Richard*. then true Noblenesse would
Learne him forbearance from so foule a Wrong.
What Subiect can giue Sentence on his King?
And who sits here, that is not *Richards* Subiect?
Theeues are not iudg'd, but they are by to heare,
Although apparant guilt be seene in them:
And shall the figure of Gods Maiestie,
His Captaine, Steward, Deputie elect,
Anoynted, Crown'd, planted many yeeres,
Be iudg'd by subiect, and inferior breathe,
And he himselfe not present? Oh, forbid it, God,
That in a Christian Climate, Soules refin'de
Should shew so heynous, black, obsceene a deed.
I speake to Subiects, and a Subiect speakes,
Stirr'd vp by Heauen, thus boldly for his King.
My Lord of Hereford here, whom you call King,
Is a foule Traytor to prowd *Herefords* King.
And if you Crowne him, let me prophecie,
The blood of English shall manure the ground,
And future Ages groane for his foule Act.
Peace shall goe sleepe with Turkes and Infidels,
And in this Seat of Peace, tumultuous Warres
Shall Kinne with Kinne, and Kinde with Kinde confound.
Disorder, Horror, Feare, and Mutinie
Shall here inhabite, and this Land be call'd
The field of Golgotha, and dead mens Sculls.
Oh, if you reare this House, against this House
It will the wofullest Diuision proue,
That euer fell vpon this cursed Earth.
Preuent it, resist it, and let it not be so,
Least Child, Childs Children cry against you, Woe.

North. Well haue you argu'd Sir: and for your paines,
Of Capitall Treason we arrest you here.
My Lord of Westminster, be it your charge,
To keepe him safely, till his day of Tryall.
May it please you, Lords, to grant the Commons Suit?

Bull. Fetch hither *Richard*, that in common view
He may surrender: so we shall proceede
Without suspition.

Yorke. I will be his Conduct. *Exit.*

Bull. Lords, you that here are vnder our Arrest,
Procure your Sureties for your Dayes of Answer:
Little are we beholding to your Loue,
And little look'd for at your helping Hands.

Enter Richard and Yorke.

Rich. Alack, why am I sent for to a King,
Before I haue shooke off the Regall thoughts
Wherewith I reign'd? I hardly yet haue learn'd
To insinuate, flatter, bowe, and bend my Knee.
Giue Sorrow leaue a while, to tuture me
To this submission. Yet I well remember
The fauors of these men: were they not mine?
Did they not sometime cry, All hayle to me?
So *Iudas* did to Christ: but he in twelue,
Found truth in all, but one; I, in twelue thousand, none.
God saue the King: will no man say, Amen?
Am I both Priest, and Clarke? well then, Amen.
God saue the King, although I be not hee:
And yet Amen, if Heauen doe thinke him mee.
To doe what seruice, am I sent for hither?

Yorke. To doe that office of thine owne good will,
Which tyred Maiestie did make thee offer:
The Resignation of thy State and Crowne
To *Henry Bullingbrooke*.

Rich. Giue me the Crown. Here Cousin, seize ỹ Crown:
Here Cousin, on this side my Hand, on that side thine.
Now is this Golden Crowne like a deepe Well,
That owes two Buckets, filling one another,
The emptier euer dancing in the ayre,
The other downe, vnseene, and full of Water:
That Bucket downe, and full of Teares am I,
Drinking my Griefes, whil'st you mount vp on high.

Bull. I thought you had been willing to resigne.

Rich. My Crowne I am, but still my Griefes are mine:
You may my Glories and my State depose,
But not my Griefes; still am I King of those.

Bull Part of your Cares you giue me with your Crowne.

Rich. Your Cares set vp, do not pluck my Cares downe.
My Care, is losse of Care, by old Care done,
Your Care, is gaine of Care, by new Care wonne:
The Cares I giue, I haue, though giuen away,
They 'tend the Crowne, yet still with me they stay:

Bull. Are you contented to resigne the Crowne?

Rich. I,no; no,I: for I must nothing bee:
Therefore no,no, for I resigne to thee.
Now, marke me how I will vndoe my selfe.
I giue this heauie Weight from off my Head,
And this vnwieldie Scepter from my Hand,
The pride of Kingly sway from out my Heart.
With mine owne Teares I wash away my Balme,
With mine owne Hands I giue away my Crowne,
With mine owne Tongue denie my Sacred State,
With mine owne Breath release all dutious Oathes;
All Pompe and Maiestie I doe forsweare:
My Manors,Rents,Reuenues,I forgoe;
My Acts,Decrees,and Statutes I denie:
God pardon all Oathes that are broke to mee,
God keepe all Vowes vnbroke are made to thee.
Make me,that nothing haue,with nothing grieu'd,
And thou with all pleas'd,that hast all atchieu'd.
Long may'st thou liue in *Richards* Seat to sit,
And soone lye *Richard* in an Earthie Pit.
God saue King *Henry*,vn-King'd *Richard* sayes,
And send him many yeeres of Sunne-shine dayes.
What more remaines?

North. No more: but that you reade
These Accusations, and these grieuous Crymes,
Committed by your Person, and your followers,
Against the State,and Profit of this Land:
That by confessing them,the Soules of men
May deeme,that you are worthily depos'd.

Rich. Must I doe so? and must I rauell out
My weau'd-vp follyes? Gentle *Northumberland*,
If thy Offences were vpon Record,
Would it not shame thee,in so faire a troupe,
To reade a Lecture of them? If thou would'st,
There should'st thou finde one heynous Article,
Contayning the deposing of a King,
And cracking the strong Warrant of an Oath,
Mark'd with a Blot,damn'd in the Booke of Heauen.
Nay,all of you,that stand and looke vpon me,
Whil'st that my wretchednesse doth bait my selfe,
Though some of you,with *Pilate*,wash your hands,
Shewing an outward pittie: yet you *Pilates*
Haue here deliuer'd me to my sowre Crosse,
And Water cannot wash away your sinne.

North. My Lord dispatch,reade o're these Articles.

Rich. Mine Eyes are full of Teares,I cannot see:
And yet salt-Water blindes them not so much,
But they can see a sort of Traytors here.
Nay,if I turne mine Eyes vpon my selfe,
I finde my selfe a Traytor with the rest:
For I haue giuen here my Soules consent,
T'vndeck the pompous Body of a King;
Made Glory base; a Soueraigntie,a Slaue;
Prowd Maiestie,a Subiect; State,a Pesant.

North. My Lord.

Rich. No Lord of thine,thou haught-insulting man;
No,nor no mans Lord: I haue no Name,no Title;
No,not that Name was giuen me at the Font,
But 'tis vsurpt: alack the heauie day,
That I haue worne so many Winters out,
And know not now,what Name to call my selfe.
Oh,that I were a Mockerie, King of Snow,
Standing before the Sunne of *Bullingbrooke*,
To melt my selfe away in Water-drops.
Good King;great King, and yet not greatly good,
And if my word be Sterling yet in England,
Let it command a Mirror hither straight,
That it may shew me what a Face I haue,
Since it is Bankrupt of his Maiestie.

Bull. Goe some of you,and fetch a Looking-Glasse.

North. Read o're this Paper,while ỳ Glasse doth come.

Rich. Fiend,thou torments me,ere I come to Hell.

Bull. Vrge it no more,my Lord *Northumberland*.

North. The Commons will not then be satisfy'd.

Rich. They shall be satisfy'd: Ile reade enough,
When I doe see the very Booke indeede,
Where all my sinnes are writ,and that's my selfe.

Enter one with a Glasse.

Giue me that Glasse,and therein will I reade.
No deeper wrinckles yet? hath Sorrow strucke
So many Blowes vpon this Face of mine,
And made no deeper Wounds? Oh flatt'ring Glasse,
Like to my followers in prosperitie,
Thou do'st beguile me. Was this Face,the Face
That euery day,vnder his House-hold Roofe,
Did keepe ten thousand men? Was this the Face,
That like the Sunne,did make beholders winke?
Is this the Face,which fac'd so many follyes,
That was at last out-fac'd by *Bullingbrooke*?
A brittle Glory shineth in this Face,
As brittle as the Glory,is the Face,
For there it is, crackt in an hundred shiuers.
Marke silent King,the Morall of this sport,
How soone my Sorrow hath destroy'd my Face.

Bull. The shadow of your Sorrow hath destroy'd
The shadow of your Face.

Rich. Say that againe.
The shadow of my Sorrow: ha,let's see,
'Tis very true,my Griefe lyes all within,
And these externall manner of Laments,
Are meerely shadowes,to the vnseene Griefe,
That swells with silence in the tortur'd Soule.
There lyes the substance: and I thanke thee King
For thy great bountie,that not onely giu'st
Me cause to wayle, but teachest me the way
How to lament the cause. Ile begge one Boone,
And then be gone,and trouble you no more.
Shall I obtaine it?

Bull. Name it,faire Cousin.

Rich. Faire Cousin? I am greater then a King:
For when I was a King,my flatterers
Were then but subiects; being now a subiect,
I haue a King here to my flatterer:
Being so great,I haue no neede to begge.

Bull. Yet aske.

Rich. And shall I haue?

Bull. You shall.

Rich. Then giue me leaue to goe.

Bull. Whither?

Rich. Whither you will,so I were from your sights.

Bull. Goe some of you,conuey him to the Tower.

Rich. Oh good: conuey: Conueyers are you all,
That rise thus nimbly by a true Kings fall.

Bull. On Wednesday next,we solemnly set downe
Our Coronation: Lords,prepare your selues. *Exeunt.*

Abbot. A wofull Pageant haue we here beheld.

Carl. The Woes to come,the Children yet vnborne,
Shall feele this day as sharpe to them as Thorne.

Aum. You holy Clergie-men, is there no Plot
To rid the Realme of this pernicious Blot.

Abbot. Before I freely speake my minde herein,
You shall not onely take the Sacrament,
To bury mine intents,but also to effect

What

What euer I shall happen to deuise.
I see your Browes are full of Discontent,
Your Heart of Sorrow, and your Eyes of Teares.
Come home with me to Supper, Ile lay a Plot
Shall shew vs all a merry day. *Exeunt.*

Actus Quintus. Scena Prima.

Enter Queene, and Ladies.

Qu. This way the King will come: this is the way
To *Iulius Cæsars* ill-erected Tower:
To whose flint Bosome, my condemned Lord
Is doom'd a Prisoner, by prowd *Bullingbrooke.*
Here let vs rest, if this rebellious Earth
Haue any resting for her true Kings Queene.
Enter Richard, and Guard.
But soft, but see, or rather doe not see,
My faire Rose wither: yet looke vp; behold,
That you in pittie may dissolue to dew,
And wash him fresh againe with true-loue Teares.
Ah thou, the Modell where old Troy did stand,
Thou Mappe of Honor, thou King *Richards* Tombe,
And not King *Richard:* thou most beauteous Inne,
Why should hard-fauor'd Griefe be lodg'd in thee,
When Triumph is become an Ale-house Guest.

Rich. Ioyne not with griefe, faire Woman, do not so,
To make my end too sudden: learne good Soule,
To thinke our former State a happie Dreame,
From which awak'd, the truth of what we are,
Shewes vs but this. I am sworne Brother (Sweet)
To grim Necessitie; and hee and I
Will keepe a League till Death. High thee to France,
And Cloyster thee in some Religious House:
Our holy liues must winne a new Worlds Crowne,
Which our prophane houres here haue stricken downe.

Qu. What, is my *Richard* both in shape and minde
Transform'd, and weaken'd? Hath *Bullingbrooke*
Depos'd thine Intellect? hath he beene in thy Heart?
The Lyon dying, thrusteth forth his Paw,
And wounds the Earth, if nothing else, with rage
To be o're-powr'd: and wilt thou, Pupill-like,
Take thy Correction mildly, kisse the Rodde,
And fawne on Rage with base Humilitie,
Which art a Lyon, and a King of Beasts?

Rich. A King of Beasts indeed: if aught but Beasts,
I had beene still a happy King of Men.
Good (sometime Queene) prepare thee hence for France:
Thinke I am dead, and that euen here thou tak'st,
As from my Death-bed, my last liuing leaue.
In Winters tedious Nights sit by the fire
With good old folkes, and let them tell thee Tales
Of wofull Ages, long agoe betide:
And ere thou bid good-night, to quit their griefe,
Tell thou the lamentable fall of me,
And send the hearers weeping to their Beds:
For why? the sencelesse Brands will sympathize
The heauie accent of thy mouing Tongue,
And in compassion, weepe the fire out:
And some will mourne in ashes, some coale-black,
For the deposing of a rightfull King.
Enter Northumberland.

North. My Lord, the mind of *Bullingbrooke* is chang'd.
You must to Pomfret, not vnto the Tower.
And Madame, there is order ta'ne for you:
With all swift speed, you must away to France.

Rich. *Northumberland,* thou Ladder wherewithall
The mounting *Bullingbrooke* ascends my Throne,
The time shall not be many houres of age,
More then it is, ere foule sinne, gathering head,
Shall breake into corruption: thou shalt thinke,
Though he diuide the Realme, and giue thee halfe,
It is too little, helping him to all:
He shall thinke, that thou which know'st the way
To plant vnrightfull Kings, wilt know againe,
Being ne're so little vrg'd another way,
To pluck him headlong from the vsurped Throne.
The Loue of wicked friends conuerts to Feare;
That Feare, to Hate; and Hate turnes one, or both,
To worthie Danger, and deserued Death.

North. My guilt be on my Head, and there an end:
Take leaue, and part, for you must part forthwith.

Rich. Doubly diuorc'd? (bad men) ye violate
A two-fold Marriage; 'twixt my Crowne, and me,
And then betwixt me, and my marryed Wife.
Let me vn-kisse the Oath 'twixt thee, and me;
And yet not so, for with a Kisse 'twas made.
Part vs, *Northumberland:* I, towards the North,
Where shiuering Cold and Sicknesse pines the Clyme:
My Queene to France: from whence, set forth in pompe,
She came adorned hither like sweet May;
Sent back like Hollowmas, or short'st of day.

Qu. And must we be diuided? must we part?

Rich. I, hand from hand (my Loue) and heart fro heart.

Qu. Banish vs both, and send the King with me.

North. That were some Loue, but little Pollicy.

Qu. Then whither he goes, thither let me goe.

Rich. So two together weeping, make one Woe.
Weepe thou for me in France; I, for thee heere:
Better farre off, then neere, be ne're the neere.
Goe, count thy Way with Sighes; I, mine with Groanes.

Qu. So longest Way shall haue the longest Moanes.

Rich. Twice for one step Ile groane, ẏ Way being short,
And peece the Way out with a heauie heart.
Come, come, in wooing Sorrow let's be briefe,
Since wedding it, there is such length in Griefe:
One Kisse shall stop our mouthes, and dumbely part;
Thus giue I mine, and thus take I thy heart.

Qu. Giue me mine owne againe: 'twere no good part,
To take on me to keepe, and kill thy heart.
So, now I haue mine owne againe, be gone,
That I may striue to kill it with a groane.

Rich. We make Woe wanton with this fond delay:
Once more adieu; the rest, let Sorrow say. *Exeunt.*

Scœna Secunda.

Enter Yorke, and his Duchesse.

Duch. My Lord, you told me you would tell the rest,
When weeping made you breake the story off,
Of our two Cousins comming into London.

Yorke. Where did I leaue?

Duch. At that sad stoppe, my Lord,
Where rude mis-gouern'd hands, from Windowes tops,
Threw dust and rubbish on King *Richards* head.

Yorke. Then, as I said, the Duke, great *Bullingbrooke*,
Mounted vpon a hot and fierie Steed,
Which his aspiring Rider seem'd to know,
With slow, but stately pace, kept on his course:
While all tongues cride, God saue thee *Bullingbrooke*.
You would haue thought the very windowes spake,
So many greedy lookes of yong and old,
Through Casements darted their desiring eyes
Vpon his visage: and that all the walles,
With painted Imagery had said at once,
Iesu preserue thee, welcom *Bullingbrooke*.
Whil'st he, from one side to the other turning,
Bare-headed, lower then his proud Steeds necke,
Bespake them thus: I thanke you Countrimen:
And thus still doing, thus he past along.

Dutch. Alas poore *Richard*, where rides he the whilst?

Yorke. As in a Theater, the eyes of men
After a well grac'd Actor leaues the Stage,
Are idlely bent on him that enters next,
Thinking his prattle to be tedious:
Euen so, or with much more contempt, mens eyes
Did scowle on *Richard*: no man cride, God saue him:
No ioyfull tongue gaue him his welcome home,
But dust was throwne vpon his Sacred head,
Which with such gentle sorrow he shooke off,
His face still combating with teares and smiles
(The badges of his greefe and patience)
That had not God (for some strong purpose) steel'd
The hearts of men, they must perforce haue melted,
And Barbarisme it selfe haue pittied him.
But heauen hath a hand in these euents,
To whose high will we bound our calme contents.
To *Bullingbrooke*, are we sworne Subiects now,
Whose State, and Honor, I for aye allow.

Enter Aumerle.

Dut. Heere comes my sonne *Aumerle*.

Yor. *Aumerle* that was,
But that is lost, for being *Richards* Friend.
And Madam, you must call him *Rutland* now:
I am in Parliament pledge for his truth,
And lasting fealtie to the new-made King.

Dut. Welcome my sonne: who are the Violets now,
That strew the greene lap of the new-come Spring?

Aum. Madam, I know not, nor I greatly care not,
God knowes, I had as liefe be none, as one.

Yorke. Well, beare you well in this new-spring of time
Least you be cropt before you come to prime.
What newes from Oxford? Hold those Iusts & Triumphs?

Aum. For ought I know my Lord, they do.

Yorke. You will be there I know.

Aum. If God preuent not, I purpose so.

Yor. What Seale is that that hangs without thy bosom?
Yea, look'st thou pale? Let me see the Writing.

Aum. My Lord, 'tis nothing.

Yorke. No matter then who sees it,
I will be satisfied, let me see the Writing.

Aum. I do beseech your Grace to pardon me,
It is a matter of small consequence,
Which for some reasons I would not haue seene.

Yorke. Which for some reasons sir, I meane to see:
I feare, I feare.

Dut. What should you feare?
Tis nothing but some bond, that he is enter'd into
For gay apparrell, against the Triumph.

Yorke. Bound to himselfe? What doth he with a Bond
That he is bound to? Wife, thou art a foole.
Boy, let me see the Writing.

Aum. I do beseech you pardon me, I may not shew it.

Yor. I will be satisfied: let me see it I say. *Snatches it*
Treason, foule Treason, Villaine, Traitor, Slaue.

Dut. What's the matter, my Lord?

Yorke. Hoa, who's within there? Saddle my horse.
Heauen for his mercy: what treachery is heere?

Dut. Why, what is't my Lord?

Yorke. Giue me my boots, I say: Saddle my horse:
Now by my Honor, my life, my troth,
I will appeach the Villaine.

Dut. What is the matter?

Yorke. Peace foolish Woman.

Dut. I will not peace. What is the matter Sonne?

Aum. Good Mother be content, it is no more
Then my poore life must answer.

Dut. Thy life answer?

Enter Seruant with Boots.

Yor. Bring me my Boots, I will vnto the King.

Dut. Strike him *Aumerle*. Poore boy, ÿ art amaz'd,
Hence Villaine, neuer more come in my sight.

Yor. Giue me my Boots, I say.

Dut. Why Yorke, what wilt thou do?
Wilt thou not hide the Trespasse of thine owne?
Haue we more Sonnes? Or are we like to haue?
Is not my teeming date drunke vp with time?
And wilt thou plucke my faire Sonne from mine Age,
And rob me of a happy Mothers name?
Is he not like thee? Is he not thine owne?

Yor. Thou fond mad woman:
Wilt thou conceale this darke Conspiracy?
A dozen of them heere haue tane the Sacrament,
And interchangeably set downe their hands
To kill the King at Oxford.

Dut. He shall be none:
Wee'l keepe him heere: then what is that to him?

Yor. Away fond woman: were hee twenty times my Son, I would appeach him.

Dut. Hadst thou groan'd for him as I haue done,
Thou wouldest be more pittifull:
But now I know thy minde; thou do'st suspect
That I haue bene disloyall to thy bed,
And that he is a Bastard, not thy Sonne:
Sweet Yorke, sweet husband, be not of that minde:
He is as like thee, as a man may bee,
Not like to me, nor any of my Kin,
And yet I loue him.

Yorke. Make way, vnruly Woman. *Exit*

Dut. After *Aumerle*. Mount thee vpon his horse,
Spurre post, and get before him to the King,
And begge thy pardon, ere he do accuse thee,
Ile not be long behind: though I be old,
I doubt not but to ride as fast as Yorke:
And neuer will I rise vp from the ground,
Till *Bullingbrooke* haue pardon'd thee: Away be gone. *Exit*

Scœna Tertia.

Enter Bullingbrooke, Percie, and other Lords.

Bul. Can no man tell of my vnthriftie Sonne?
'Tis full three monthes since I did see him last,
If any plague hang ouer vs, 'tis he,
I would to heauen (my Lords) he might be found:
Enquire at London, 'mongst the Tauernes there:

For

For there (they say) he dayly doth frequent,
With vnrestrained loose Companions,
Euen such (they say) as stand in narrow Lanes,
And rob our Watch, and beate our passengers,
Which he, yong wanton, and effeminate Boy
Takes on the point of Honor, to support
So dissolute a crew.

Per. My Lord, some two dayes since I saw the Prince,
And told him of these Triumphes held at Oxford.

Bul. And what said the Gallant?

Per. His answer was: he would vnto the Stewes,
And from the common'st creature plucke a Gloue
And weare it as a fauour, and with that
He would vnhorse the lustiest Challenger.

Bul. As dissolute as desp'rate, yet through both,
I see some sparkes of better hope: which elder dayes
May happily bring forth. But who comes heere?

Enter Aumerle.

Aum. Where is the King?

Bul. What meanes our Cosin, that hee stares
And lookes so wildely?

Aum. God saue your Grace. I do beseech your Maiesty
To haue some conference with your Grace alone.

Bul. Withdraw your selues, and leaue vs here alone:
What is the matter with our Cosin now?

Aum. For euer may my knees grow to the earth,
My tongue cleaue to my roofe within my mouth,
Vnlesse a Pardon, ere I rise, or speake.

Bul. Intended, or committed was this fault?
If on the first, how heynous ere it bee,
To win thy after loue, I pardon thee.

Aum. Then giue me leaue, that I may turne the key,
That no man enter, till my tale be done.

Bul. Haue thy desire. *Yorke within.*

Yor. My Liege beware, looke to thy selfe,
Thou hast a Traitor in thy presence there.

Bul. Villaine, Ile make thee safe.

Aum. Stay thy reuengefull hand, thou hast no cause to feare.

Yorke. Open the doore, secure foole-hardy King:
Shall I for loue speake treason to thy face?
Open the doore, or I will breake it open.

Enter Yorke.

Bul. What is the matter (Vnkle) speak, recouer breath,
Tell vs how neere is danger,
That we may arme vs to encounter it.

Yor. Peruse this writing heere, and thou shalt know
The reason that my haste forbids me show.

Aum. Remember as thou read'st, thy promise past:
I do repent me, reade not my name there,
My heart is not confederate with my hand.

Yor. It was (villaine) ere thy hand did set it downe.
I tore it from the Traitors bosome, King.
Feare, and not Loue, begets his penitence;
Forget to pitty him, least thy pitty proue
A Serpent, that will sting thee to the heart.

Bul. Oh heinous, strong, and bold Conspiracie,
O loyall Father of a treacherous Sonne:
Thou sheere, immaculate, and siluer fountaine,
From whence this streame, through muddy passages
Hath had his current, and defil'd himselfe.
Thy ouerflow of good, conuerts to bad,
And thy abundant goodnesse shall excuse
This deadly blot, in thy digressing sonne.

Yorke. So shall my Vertue be his Vices bawd,
And he shall spend mine Honour, with his Shame;
As thriftlesse Sonnes, their scraping Fathers Gold.
Mine honor liues, when his dishonor dies,
Or my sham'd life, in his dishonor lies:
Thou kill'st me in his life, giuing him breath,
The Traitor liues, the true man's put to death.

Dutchesse within.

Dut. What hoa (my Liege) for heauens sake let me in.

Bul. What shrill-voic'd Suppliant, makes this eager cry?

Dut. A woman, and thine Aunt (great King) 'tis I.
Speake with me, pitty me, open the dore,
A Begger begs, that neuer begg'd before.

Bul. Our Scene is alter'd from a serious thing,
And now chang'd to the Begger, and the King.
My dangerous Cosin, let your Mother in,
I know she's come, to pray for your foule sin.

Yorke. If thou do pardon, whosoeuer pray,
More sinnes for this forgiuenesse, prosper may.
This fester'd ioynt cut off, the rest rests sound,
This let alone, will all the rest confound.

Enter Dutchesse.

Dut. O King, beleeue not this hard-hearted man,
Loue, louing not it selfe, none other can.

Yor. Thou franticke woman, what dost ÿ make here,
Shall thy old dugges, once more a Traitor reare?

Dut. Sweet Yorke be patient, heare me gentle Liege.

Bul. Rise vp good Aunt.

Dut. Not yet, I thee beseech.
For euer will I kneele vpon my knees,
And neuer see day, that the happy sees,
Till thou giue ioy: vntill thou bid me ioy,
By pardoning Rutland, my transgressing Boy.

Aum. Vnto my mothers prayres, I bend my knee.

Yorke. Against them both, my true ioynts bended be.

Dut. Pleades he in earnest? Looke vpon his Face,
His eyes do drop no teares: his prayres are in iest:
His words come from his mouth, ours from our brest.
He prayes but faintly, and would be denide,
We pray with heart, and soule, and all beside:
His weary ioynts would gladly rise, I know,
Our knees shall kneele, till to the ground they grow:
His prayers are full of false hypocrisie,
Ours of true zeale, and deepe integritie:
Our prayers do out-pray his, then let them haue
That mercy, which true prayers ought to haue.

Bul. Good Aunt stand vp.

Dut. Nay, do not say stand vp.
But Pardon first, and afterwards stand vp.
And if I were thy Nurse, thy tongue to teach,
Pardon should be the first word of thy speach.
I neuer long'd to heare a word till now:
Say Pardon (King,) let pitty teach thee how.
The word is short: but not so short as sweet,
No word like Pardon, for Kings mouth's so meet.

Yorke. Speake it in French (King) say *Pardon'ne moy.*

Dut. Dost thou teach pardon, Pardon to destroy?
Ah my sowre husband, my hard-hearted Lord,
That set's the word it selfe, against the word.
Speake Pardon, as 'tis currant in our Land,
The chopping French we do not vnderstand.
Thine eye begins to speake, set thy tongue there,
Or in thy pitteous heart, plant thou thine eare,
That hearing how our plaints and prayres do pearce,
Pitty may moue thee, Pardon to rehearse.

Bul. Good Aunt, stand vp.

Dut. I do not sue to stand,
Pardon is all the suite I haue in hand.

Bul. I pardon him, as heauen shall pardon mee.
Dut. O happy vantage of a kneeling knee:
Yet am I sicke for feare: Speake it againe,
Twice saying Pardon, doth not pardon twaine,
But makes one pardon strong.
Bul. I pardon him with all my hart.
Dut. A God on earth thou art.
Bul. But for our trusty brother-in-Law, the Abbot,
With all the rest of that consorted crew,
Destruction straight shall dogge them at the heeles:
Good Vnckle helpe to order seuerall powres
To Oxford, or where ere these Traitors are:
They shall not liue within this world I sweare,
But I will haue them, if I once know where.
Vnckle farewell, and Cosin adieu:
Your mother well hath praid, and proue you true.
Dut. Come my old son, I pray heauen make thee new.
Exeunt.

Enter Exton and Seruants.

Ext. Didst thou not marke the King what words hee spake?
Haue I no friend will rid me of this liuing feare:
Was it not so?
Ser. Those were his very words.
Ex. Haue I no Friend? (quoth he:) he spake it twice,
And vrg'd it twice together, did he not?
Ser. He did.
Ex. And speaking it, he wistly look'd on me,
As who should say, I would thou wer't the man
That would diuorce this terror from my heart,
Meaning the King at Pomfret: Come, let's goe;
I am the Kings Friend, and will rid his Foe. *Exit.*

Scæna Quarta.

Enter Richard.

Rich. I haue bin studying, how to compare
This Prison where I liue, vnto the World:
And for because the world is populous,
And heere is not a Creature, but my selfe,
I cannot do it: yet Ile hammer't out.
My Braine, Ile proue the Female to my Soule,
My Soule, the Father: and these two beget
A generation of still breeding Thoughts;
And these same Thoughts, people this Little World
In humors, like the people of this world,
For no thought is contented. The better sort,
As thoughts of things Diuine, are intermixt
With scruples, and do set the Faith it selfe
Against the Faith: as thus: Come litle ones: & then again,
It is as hard to come, as for a Camell
To thred the posterne of a Needles eye.
Thoughts tending to Ambition, they do plot
Vnlikely wonders; how these vaine weake nailes
May teare a passage through the Flinty ribbes
Of this hard world, my ragged prison walles:
And for they cannot, dye in their owne pride.
Thoughts tending to Content, flatter themselues,
That they are not the first of Fortunes slaues,
Nor shall not be the last. Like silly Beggars,
Who sitting in the Stockes, refuge their shame
That many haue, and others must sit there;
And in this Thought, they finde a kind of ease,
Bearing their owne misfortune on the backe
Of such as haue before indur'd the like.
Thus play I in one Prison, many people,
And none contented. Sometimes am I King;
Then Treason makes me wish my selfe a Beggar,
And so I am. Then crushing penurie,
Perswades me, I was better when a King:
Then am I king'd againe: and by and by,
Thinke that I am vn-king'd by *Bullingbrooke*,
And straight am nothing. But what ere I am, *Musick*
Nor I, nor any man, that but man is,
With nothing shall be pleas'd, till he be eas'd
With being nothing. Musicke do I heare?
Ha, ha? keepe time: How sowre sweet Musicke is,
When Time is broke, and no Proportion kept?
So is it in the Musicke of mens liues:
And heere haue I the daintinesse of eare,
To heare time broke in a disorder'd string:
But for the Concord of my State and Time,
Had not an eare to heare my true Time broke.
I wasted Time, and now doth Time waste me:
For now hath Time made me his numbring clocke;
My Thoughts, are minutes; and with Sighes they iarre,
Their watches on vnto mine eyes, the outward Watch,
Whereto my finger, like a Dialls point,
Is pointing still, in cleansing them from teares.
Now sir, the sound that tels what houre it is,
Are clamorous groanes, that strike vpon my heart,
Which is the bell: so Sighes, and Teares, and Grones,
Shew Minutes, Houres, and Times: but my Time
Runs poasting on, in *Bullingbrookes* proud ioy,
While I stand fooling heere, his iacke o'th'Clocke.
This Musicke mads me, let it sound no more,
For though it haue holpe madmen to their wits,
In me it seemes, it will make wise-men mad:
Yet blessing on his heart that giues it me;
For 'tis a signe of loue, and loue to *Richard*,
Is a strange Brooch, in this all-hating world.

Enter Groome.

Groo. Haile Royall Prince.
Rich. Thankes Noble Peere,
The cheapest of vs, is ten groates too deere.
What art thou? And how com'st thou hither?
Where no man euer comes, but that sad dogge
That brings me food, to make misfortune liue?
Groo. I was a poore Groome of thy Stable (King)
When thou wer't King: who trauelling towards Yorke,
With much adoo, at length haue gotten leaue
To looke vpon my (sometimes Royall) masters face.
O how it yern'd my heart, when I beheld
In London streets, that Coronation day,
When *Bullingbrooke* rode on Roane Barbary,
That horse, that thou so often hast bestrid,
That horse, that I so carefully haue drest.
Rich. Rode he on Barbary? Tell me gentle Friend,
How went he vnder him?
Groo. So proudly, as if he had disdain'd the ground.
Rich. So proud, that *Bullingbrooke* was on his backe;
That Iade hath eate bread from my Royall hand.
This hand hath made him proud with clapping him.
Would he not stumble? Would he not fall downe
(Since Pride must haue a fall) and breake the necke
Of that proud man, that did vsurpe his backe?
Forgiuenesse horse: Why do I raile on thee,
Since thou created to be aw'd by man
Was't borne to beare? I was not made a horse,

And yet I beare a burthen like an Asse.
Spur-gall'd, and tyrd by iauncing *Bullingbrooke*.

Enter Keeper with a Dish.

Keep. Fellow, giue place, heere is no longer stay.
Rich. If thou loue me, 'tis time thou wer't away.
Groo. What my tongue dares not, that my heart shall say. *Exit.*
Keep. My Lord, wilt please you to fall too?
Rich. Taste of it first, as thou wer't wont to doo.
Keep. My Lord I dare not: Sir *Pierce* of Exton,
Who lately came from th'King, commands the contrary.
Rich. The diuell take *Henrie* of Lancaster, and thee;
Patience is stale, and I am weary of it.
Keep. Helpe, helpe, helpe.

Enter Exton and Seruants.

Ri. How now? what meanes Death in this rude assalt?
Villaine, thine owne hand yeelds thy deaths instrument,
Go thou and fill another roome in hell.

Exton strikes him downe.

That hand shall burne in neuer-quenching fire,
That staggers thus my person. *Exton*, thy fierce hand,
Hath with the Kings blood, stain'd the Kings own land.
Mount, mount my soule, thy seate is vp on high,
Whil'st my grosse flesh sinkes downward, heere to dye.
Exton. As full of Valor, as of Royall blood,
Both haue I spilt: Oh would the deed were good.
For now the diuell, that told me I did well,
Sayes, that this deede is chronicled in hell.
This dead King to the liuing King Ile beare,
Take hence the rest, and giue them buriall heere. *Exit.*

Scœna Quinta.

Flourish. Enter Bullingbrooke, Yorke, with other Lords & attendants.

Bul. Kinde Vnkle Yorke, the latest newes we heare,
Is that the Rebels haue consum'd with fire
Our Towne of Ciceter in Gloucestershire,
But whether they be tane or slaine, we heare not.

Enter Northumberland.

Welcome my Lord: What is the newes?
Nor. First to thy Sacred State, wish I all happinesse:
The next newes is, I haue to London sent
The heads of *Salsbury*, *Spencer*, *Blunt*, and *Kent*:
The manner of their taking may appeare
At large discoursed in this paper heere.
Bul. We thank thee gentle *Percy* for thy paines,
And to thy worth will adde right worthy gaines.

Enter Fitz-waters.

Fitz. My Lord, I haue from Oxford sent to London,
The heads of *Broccas*, and Sir *Bennet Seely*,
Two of the dangerous consorted Traitors,
That sought at Oxford, thy dire ouerthrow.
Bul. Thy paines *Fitzwaters* shall not be forgot,
Right Noble is thy merit, well I wot.

Enter Percy and Carlile.

Per. The grand Conspirator, Abbot of Westminster,
With clog of Conscience, and sowre Melancholly,
Hath yeelded vp his body to the graue:
But heere is *Carlile*, liuing to abide
Thy Kingly doome, and sentence of his pride.
Bul. *Carlile*, this is your doome:
Choose out some secret place, some reuerend roome
More then thou hast, and with it ioy thy life:
So as thou liu'st in peace, dye free from strife:
For though mine enemy thou hast euer beene,
High sparkes of Honor in thee haue I seene.

Enter Exton with a Coffin.

Exton. Great King, within this Coffin I present
Thy buried feare. Heerein all breathlesse lies
The mightiest of thy greatest enemies
Richard of Burdeaux, by me hither brought.
Bul. *Exton*, I thanke thee not, for thou hast wrought
A deede of Slaughter, with thy fatall hand,
Vpon my head, and all this famous Land.
Ex. From your owne mouth my Lord, did I this deed.
Bul. They loue not poyson, that do poyson neede,
Nor do I thee: though I did wish him dead,
I hate the Murtherer, loue him murthered.
The guilt of conscience take thou for thy labour,
But neither my good word, nor Princely fauour.
With *Caine* go wander through the shade of night,
And neuer shew thy head by day, nor light.
Lords, I protest my soule is full of woe,
That blood should sprinkle me, to make me grow.
Come mourne with me, for that I do lament,
And put on sullen Blacke incontinent:
Ile make a voyage to the Holy-land,
To wash this blood off from my guilty hand.
March sadly after, grace my mourning heere,
In weeping after this vntimely Beere. *Exeunt.*

FINIS.

The First Part of Henry the Fourth, with the Life and Death of HENRY Sirnamed HOT-SPVRRE.

Actus Primus. Scœna Prima.

Enter the King, Lord Iohn of Lancaster, Earle of Westmerland, with others.

King.

SO shaken as we are, so wan with care,
Finde we a time for frighted Peace to pant,
And breath shortwinded accents of new broils
To be commenc'd in Stronds a-farre remote:
No more the thirsty entrance of this Soile,
Shall daube her lippes with her owne childrens blood:
No more shall trenching Warre channell her fields,
Nor bruise her Flowrets with the Armed hoofes
Of hostile paces. Those opposed eyes,
Which like the Meteors of a troubled Heauen,
All of one Nature, of one Substance bred,
Did lately meete in the intestine shocke,
And furious cloze of ciuill Butchery,
Shall now in mutuall well-beseeming rankes
March all one way, and be no more oppos'd
Against Acquaintance, Kindred, and Allies.
The edge of Warre, like an ill-sheathed knife,
No more shall cut his Master. Therefore Friends,
As farre as to the Sepulcher of Christ,
Whose Souldier now vnder whose blessed Crosse
We are impressed and ingag'd to fight,
Forthwith a power of English shall we leuie,
Whose armes were moulded in their Mothers wombe,
To chace these Pagans in those holy Fields,
Ouer whose Acres walk'd those blessed feete
Which fourteene hundred yeares ago were nail'd
For our aduantage on the bitter Crosse.
But this our purpose is a tweluemonth old,
And bootlesse 'tis to tell you we will go:
Therefore we meete not now. Then let me heare
Of you my gentle Cousin Westmerland,
What yesternight our Councell did decree,
In forwarding this deere expedience.

West. My Liege: This haste was hot in question,
And many limits of the Charge set downe
But yesternight: when all athwart there came
A Post from Wales, loaden with heauy Newes;
Whose worst was, That the Noble *Mortimer*,
Leading the men of Herefordshire to fight
Against the irregular and wilde *Glendower*,
Was by the rude hands of that Welshman taken,
And a thousand of his people butchered:
Vpon whose dead corpes there was such misuse,
Such beastly, shamelesse transformation,
By those Welshwomen done, as may not be
(Without much shame) re-told or spoken of.

King. It seemes then, that the tidings of this broile,
Brake off our businesse for the Holy land.

West. This matcht with other like, my gracious Lord,
Farre more vneuen and vnwelcome Newes
Came from the North, and thus it did report:
On Holy-roode day, the gallant *Hotspurre* there,
Young *Harry Percy*, and braue *Archibald*,
That euer-valiant and approoued Scot,
At *Holmeden* met, where they did spend
A sad and bloody houre:
As by discharge of their Artillerie,
And shape of likely-hood the newes was told:
For he that brought them, in the very heate
And pride of their contention, did take horse,
Vncertaine of the issue any way.

King. Heere is a deere and true industrious friend,
Sir *Walter Blunt*, new lighted from his Horse,
Strain'd with the variation of each soyle,
Betwixt that *Holmedon*, and this Seat of ours:
And he hath brought vs smooth and welcomes newes.
The Earle of *Dowglas* is discomfited,
Ten thousand bold Scots, two and twenty Knights
Balk'd in their owne blood did Sir *Walter* see
On *Holmedons* Plaines. Of Prisoners, *Hotspurre* tooke
Mordake Earle of Fife, and eldest sonne
To beaten *Dowglas*, and the Earle of *Atholl*,
Of *Murry*, *Angus*, and *Menteith*.
And is not this an honourable spoyle?
A gallant prize? Ha Cosin, is it not? Infaith it is.

West. A Conquest for a Prince to boast of.

King. Yea, there thou mak'st me sad, & mak'st me sin,
In enuy, that my Lord Northumberland
Should be the Father of so blest a Sonne:
A Sonne, who is the Theame of Honors tongue;
Among'st a Groue, the very straightest Plant,
Who is sweet Fortunes Minion, and her Pride:
Whil'st I by looking on the praise of him,
See Ryot and Dishonor staine the brow
Of my yong *Harry*. O that it could be prou'd,
That some Night-tripping-Faiery, had exchang'd
In Cradle-clothes, our Children where they lay,
And call'd mine *Percy*, his *Plantagenet*:

The n

Then would I haue his *Harry*, and he mine:
But let him from my thoughts. What thinke you Coze
Of this young *Percies* pride? The Prisoners
Which he in this aduenture hath surpriz'd,
To his owne vse he keepes, and sends me word
I shall haue none but *Mordake* Earle of *Fife*.

West. This is his Vnckles teaching. This is Worcester
Maleuolent to you in all Aspects:
Which makes him prune himselfe, and bristle vp
The crest of Youth against your Dignity.

King. But I haue sent for him to answer this:
And for this cause a-while we must neglect
Our holy purpose to Ierusalem.
Cosin, on Wednesday next, our Councell we will hold
At Windsor, and so informe the Lords:
But come your selfe with speed to vs againe,
For more is to be said, and to be done,
Then out of anger can be vttered.

West. I will my Liege. *Exeunt*

Scæna Secunda.

Enter Henry Prince of Wales, Sir Iohn Falstaffe, and Pointz.

Fal. Now *Hal*, what time of day is it Lad?

Prince. Thou art so fat-witted with drinking of olde Sacke, and vnbuttoning thee after Supper, and sleeping vpon Benches in the afternoone, that thou hast forgotten to demand that truely, which thou wouldest truly know. What a diuell hast thou to do with the time of the day? vnlesse houres were cups of Sacke, and minutes Capons, and clockes the tongues of Bawdes, and dialls the signes of Leaping-houses, and the blessed Sunne himselfe a faire hot Wench in Flame-coloured Taffata; I see no reason, why thou shouldest bee so superfluous, to demaund the time of the day.

Fal. Indeed you come neere me now *Hal*, for we that take Purses, go by the Moone and seuen Starres, and not by Phœbus hee, that wand'ring Knight so faire. And I prythee sweet Wagge, when thou art King, as God saue thy Grace, Maiesty I should say, for Grace thou wilte haue none.

Prin. What, none?

Fal. No, not so much as will serue to be Prologue to an Egge and Butter.

Prin. Well, how then? Come roundly, roundly.

Fal. Marry then, sweet Wagge, when thou art King, let not vs that are Squires of the Nights bodie, bee call'd Theeues of the Dayes beautie. Let vs be *Dianaes* Forresters, Gentlemen of the Shade, Minions of the Moone; and let men say, we be men of good Gouernment, being gouerned as the Sea is, by our noble and chast mistris the Moone, vnder whose countenance we steale.

Prin. Thou say'st well, and it holds well too: for the fortune of vs that are the Moones men, doeth ebbe and flow like the Sea, beeing gouerned as the Sea is, by the Moone: as for proofe. Now a Purse of Gold most resolutely snatch'd on Monday night, and most dissolutely spent on Tuesday Morning; got with swearing, Lay by: and spent with crying, Bring in: now, in as low an ebbe as the foot of the Ladder, and by and by in as high a flow as the ridge of the Gallowes.

Fal Thou say'st true Lad: and is not my Hostesse of the Tauerne a most sweet Wench?

Prin. As is the hony, my old Lad of the Castle: and is not a Buffe Ierkin a most sweet robe of durance?

Fal. How now? how now mad Wagge? What in thy quips and thy quiddities? What a plague haue I to doe with a Buffe-Ierkin?

Prin. Why, what a poxe haue I to doe with my Hostesse of the Tauerne?

Fal. Well, thou hast call'd her to a reck'ning many a time and oft.

Prin. Did I euer call for thee to pay thy part?

Fal. No, Ile giue thee thy due, thou hast paid al there.

Prin. Yea and elsewhere, so farre as my Coine would stretch, and where it would not, I haue vs'd my credit.

Fal. Yea, and so vs'd it, that were it heere apparant, that thou art Heire apparant. But I prythee sweet Wag, shall there be Gallowes standing in England when thou art King? and resolution thus fobb'd as it is, with the rustie curbe of old Father Anticke the Law? Doe not thou when thou art a King, hang a Theefe.

Prin. No, thou shalt.

Fal. Shall I? O rare! Ile be a braue Iudge.

Prin. Thou iudgest false already. I meane, thou shalt haue the hanging of the Theeues, and so become a rare Hangman.

Fal. Well *Hal*, well: and in some sort it iumpes with my humour, as well as waiting in the Court, I can tell you.

Prin. For obtaining of suites?

Fal. Yea, for obtaining of suites, whereof the Hangman hath no leane Wardrobe. I am as Melancholly as a Gyb-Cat, or a lugg'd Beare.

Prin. Or an old Lyon, or a Louers Lute.

Fal. Yea, or the Drone of a Lincolnshire Bagpipe.

Prin. What say'st thou to a Hare, or the Melancholly of Moore Ditch?

Fal. Thou hast the most vnsauoury smiles, and art indeed the most comparatiue rascallest sweet yong Prince. But *Hal*, I prythee trouble me no more with vanity, I wold thou and I knew, where a Commodity of good names were to be bought: an olde Lord of the Councell rated me the other day in the street about you sir; but I mark'd him not, and yet hee talk'd very wisely, but I regarded him not, and yet he talkt wisely, and in the street too.

Prin. Thou didst well: for no man regards it.

Fal. O, thou hast damnable iteration, and art indeede able to corrupt a Saint. Thou hast done much harme vnto me *Hall*, God forgiue thee for it. Before I knew thee *Hal*, I knew nothing: and now I am (if a man shold speake truly) little better then one of the wicked. I must giue ouer this life, and I will giue it ouer: and I do not, I am a Villaine. Ile be damn'd for neuer a Kings sonne in Christendome.

Prin. Where shall we take a purse to morrow, Iacke?

Fal. Where thou wilt Lad, Ile make one: and I doe not, call me Villaine, and baffle me.

Prin. I see a good amendment of life in thee: From Praying, to Purse-taking.

Fal. Why, *Hal*, 'tis my Vocation *Hal*: 'Tis no sin for a man to labour in his Vocation.

Pointz. Now shall wee know if Gads hill haue set a Watch. O, if men were to be saued by merit, what hole in Hell were hot enough for him? This is the most omnipotent Villaine, that euer cryed, Stand, to a true man.

Prin. Good morrow *Ned*.

Pointz.

Poines. Good morrow sweet *Hal.* What saies Monsieur Remorse? What sayes Sir Iohn Sacke and Sugar: Iacke? How agrees the Diuell and thee about thy Soule, that thou soldest him on Good-Friday last, for a Cup of Madera, and a cold Capons legge?

Prin. Sir Iohn stands to his word, the diuel shall haue his bargaine, for he was neuer yet a Breaker of Prouerbs: *He will giue the diuell his due.*

Poin. Then art thou damn'd for keeping thy word with the diuell.

Prin. Else he had damn'd for cozening the diuell.

Poy. But my Lads, my Lads, to morrow morning, by foure a clocke early at Gads hill, there are Pilgrimes going to Canterbury with rich Offerings, and Traders riding to London with fat Purses. I haue vizards for you all; you haue horses for your selues: Gads-hill lyes to night in Rochester, I haue bespoke Supper to morrow in Eastcheape; we may doe it as secure as sleepe: if you will go, I will stuffe your Purses full of Crownes: if you will not, tarry at home and be hang'd.

Fal. Heare ye Yedward, if I tarry at home and go not, Ile hang you for going.

Poy. You will chops.

Fal. *Hal,* wilt thou make one?

Prin. Who, I rob? I a Theefe? Not I.

Fal. There's neither honesty, manhood, nor good fellowship in thee, nor thou cam'st not of the blood-royall, if thou dar'st not stand for ten shillings.

Prin. Well then, once in my dayes Ile be a mad-cap.

Fal. Why, that's well said.

Prin. Well, come what will, Ile tarry at home.

Fal. Ile be a Traitor then, when thou art King.

Prin. I care not.

Poyn. Sir *Iohn,* I prythee leaue the Prince & me alone, I will lay him downe such reasons for this aduenture, that he shall go.

Fal. Well, maist thou haue the Spirit of perswasion; and he the eares of profiting, that what thou speakest, may moue; and what he heares may be beleeued, that the true Prince, may (for recreation sake) proue a false theefe; for the poore abuses of the time, want countenance. Farwell, you shall finde me in Eastcheape.

Prin. Farwell the latter Spring. Farewell Alhollown Summer.

Poy. Now, my good sweet Hony Lord, ride with vs to morrow. I haue a iest to execute, that I cannot mannage alone. *Falstaffe, Haruey, Rossill,* and *Gads-hill,* shall robbe those men that wee haue already way-layde, your selfe and I, wil not be there: and when they haue the booty, if you and I do not rob them, cut this head from my shoulders.

Prin. But how shal we part with them in setting forth?

Poyn. Why, we wil set forth before or after them, and appoint them a place of meeting, wherin it is at our pleasure to faile; and then will they aduenture vppon the exploit themselues, which they shall haue no sooner atchieued, but wee'l set vpon them.

Prin. I, but tis like that they will know vs by our horses, by our habits, and by euery other appointment to be our selues.

Poy. Tut our horses they shall not see, Ile tye them in the wood, our vizards wee will change after wee leaue them: and sirrah, I haue Cases of Buckram for the nonce, to immaske our noted outward garments.

Prin. But I doubt they will be too hard for vs.

Poin. Well, for two of them, I know them to bee as true bred Cowards as euer turn'd backe: and for the third if he fight longer then he sees reason, Ile forswear Armes. The vertue of this Iest will be, the incomprehensible lyes that this fat Rogue will tell vs, when we meete at Supper: how thirty at least he fought with, what Wardes, what blowes, what extremities he endured; and in the reproofe of this, lyes the iest.

Prin. Well, Ile goe with thee, prouide vs all things necessary, and meete me to morrow night in Eastcheape, there Ile sup. Farewell.

Poyn. Farewell, my Lord. *Exit Pointz.*

Prin. I know you all, and will a-while vphold
The vnyoak'd humor of your idlenesse:
Yet heerein will I imitate the Sunne,
Who doth permit the base contagious cloudes
To smother vp his Beauty from the world,
That when he please againe to be himselfe,
Being wanted, he may be more wondred at,
By breaking through the foule and vgly mists
Of vapours, that did seeme to strangle him.
If all the yeare were playing holidaies,
To sport, would be as tedious as to worke;
But when they seldome come, they wisht-for come,
And nothing pleaseth but rare accidents.
So when this loose behauiour I throw off,
And pay the debt I neuer promised;
By how much better then my word I am,
By so much shall I falsifie mens hopes,
And like bright Mettall on a sullen ground:
My reformation glittering o're my fault,
Shall shew more goodly, and attract more eyes,
Then that which hath no foyle to set it off.
Ile so offend, to make offence a skill,
Redeeming time, when men thinke least I will.

Scœna Tertia.

Enter the King, Northumberland, Worcester, Hotspurre, Sir Walter Blunt, and others.

King. My blood hath beene too cold and temperate,
Vnapt to stirre at these indignities,
And you haue found me; for accordingly,
You tread vpon my patience: But be sure,
I will from henceforth rather be my Selfe,
Mighty, and to be fear'd, then my condition
Which hath beene smooth as Oyle, soft as yong Downe,
And therefore lost that Title of respect,
Which the proud soule ne're payes, but to the proud.

Wor. Our house (my Soueraigne Liege) little deserues
The scourge of greatnesse to be vsed on it,
And that same greatnesse too, which our owne hands
Haue holpe to make so portly.

Nor. My Lord.

King. Worcester get thee gone: for I do see
Danger and disobedience in thine eye.
O sir, your presence is too bold and peremptory,
And Maiestie might neuer yet endure
The moody Frontier of a seruant brow,
You haue good leaue to leaue vs. When we need
Your vse and counsell, we shall send for you.
You were about to speake.

North. Yea, my good Lord.

Those

Those Prisoners in your Highnesse demanded,
Which *Harry Percy* heere at *Holmedon* tooke,
Were (as he sayes) not with such strength denied
As was deliuered to your Maiesty:
Who either through enuy, or misprision,
Was guilty of this fault; and not my Sonne.
Hot. My Liege, I did deny no Prisoners.
But, I remember when the fight was done,
When I was dry with Rage, and extreame Toyle,
Breathlesse, and Faint, leaning vpon my Sword,
Came there a certaine Lord, neat and trimly drest;
Fresh as a Bride-groome, and his Chin new reapt,
Shew'd like a stubble Land at Haruest home.
He was perfumed like a Milliner,
And 'twixt his Finger and his Thumbe, he held
A Pouncet-box: which euer and anon
He gaue his Nose, and took't away againe:
Who therewith angry, when it next came there,
Tooke it in Snuffe. And still he smil'd and talk'd
And as the Souldiers bare dead bodies by,
He call'd them vntaught Knaues, Vnmannerly,
To bring a slouenly vnhandsome Coarse
Betwixt the Winde, and his Nobility.
With many Holiday and Lady tearme
He question'd me: Among the rest, demanded
My Prisoners, in your Maiesties behalfe.
I then, all-smarting, with my wounds being cold,
(To be so pestered with a Popingay)
Out of my Greefe, and my Impatience,
Answer'd (neglectingly) I know not what,
He should, or should not: For he made me mad,
To see him shine so briske, and smell so sweet,
And talke so like a Waiting-Gentlewoman,
Of Guns, & Drums, and Wounds: God saue the marke;
And telling me, the Soueraign'st thing on earth
Was Parmacity, for an inward bruise:
And that it was great pitty, so it was,
That villanous Salt-peter should be digg'd
Out of the Bowels of the harmlesse Earth,
Which many a good Tall Fellow had destroy'd
So Cowardly. And but for these vile Gunnes,
He would himselfe haue beene a Souldier.
This bald, vnioynted Chat of his (my Lord)
Made me to answer indirectly (as I said.)
And I beseech you, let not this report
Come currant for an Accusation,
Betwixt my Loue, and your high Maiesty.
Blunt. The circumstance considered, good my Lord,
What euer *Harry Percie* then had said,
To such a person, and in such a place,
At such a time, with all the rest retold,
May reasonably dye, and neuer rise
To do him wrong, or any way impeach
What then he said, so he vnsay it now.
King. Why yet doth deny his Prisoners,
But with Prouiso and Exception,
That we at our owne charge, shall ransome straight
His Brother-in-Law, the foolish *Mortimer*,
Who (in my soule) hath wilfully betraid
The liues of those, that he did leade to Fight,
Against the great Magitian, damn'd *Glendower*:
Whose daughter (as we heare) the Earle of March
Hath lately married. Shall our Coffers then,
Be emptied, to redeeme a Traitor home?
Shall we buy Treason? and indent with Feares,
When they haue lost and forfeyted themselues.
No: on the barren Mountaine let him sterue:
For I shall neuer hold that man my Friend,
Whose tongue shall aske me for one peny cost
To ransome home reuolted *Mortimer*.
Hot. Reuolted *Mortimer*?
He neuer did fall off, my Soueraigne Liege,
But by the chance of Warre: to proue that true,
Needs no more but one tongue. For all those Wounds,
Those mouthed Wounds, which valiantly he tooke,
When on the gentle Seuernes siedgie banke,
In single Opposition hand to hand,
He did confound the best part of an houre
In changing hardiment with great *Glendower*:
Three times they breath'd, and three times did they drink
Vpon agreement, of swift Seuernes flood;
Who then affrighted with their bloody lookes,
Ran fearefully among the trembling Reeds,
And hid his crispe-head in the hollow banke,
Blood-stained with these Valiant Combatants.
Neuer did base and rotten Policy
Colour her working with such deadly wounds;
Nor neuer could the Noble *Mortimer*
Receiue so many, and all willingly:
Then let him not be sland'red with Reuolt.
King. Thou do'st bely him *Percy*, thou dost bely him;
He neuer did encounter with *Glendower*:
I tell thee, he durst as well haue met the diuell alone,
As *Owen Glendower* for an enemy.
Art thou not asham'd? But Sirrah, henceforth
Let me not heare you speake of *Mortimer*.
Send me your Prisoners with the speediest meanes,
Or you shall heare in such a kinde from me
As will displease ye. My Lord *Northumberland*,
We License your departure with your sonne,
Send vs your Prisoners, or you'l heare of it. *Exit King.*
Hot. And if the diuell come and roare for them
I will not send them. I will after straight
And tell him so: for I will ease my heart,
Although it be with hazard of my head.
Nor. What? drunke with choller? stay & pause awhile,
Heere comes your Vnckle. *Enter Worcester.*
Hot. Speake of *Mortimer*?
Yes, I will speake of him, and let my soule
Want mercy, if I do not ioyne with him.
In his behalfe, Ile empty all these Veines,
And shed my deere blood drop by drop i'th dust,
But I will lift the downfall *Mortimer*
As high i'th Ayre, as this Vnthankfull King,
As this Ingrate and Cankred *Bullingbrooke*.
Nor. Brother, the King hath made your Nephew mad
Wor. Who strooke this heate vp after I was gone?
Hot. He will (forsooth) haue all my Prisoners:
And when I vrg'd the ransom once againe
Of my Wiues Brother, then his cheeke look'd pale,
And on my face he turn'd an eye of death,
Trembling euen at the name of *Mortimer*.
Wor. I cannot blame him: was he not proclaim'd
By *Richard* that dead is, the next of blood?
Nor. He was: I heard the Proclamation,
And then it was, when the vnhappy King
(Whose wrongs in vs God pardon) did set forth
Vpon his Irish Expedition:
From whence he intercepted, did returne
To be depos'd, and shortly murthered.
Wor. And for whose death, we in the worlds wide mouth
Liue scandaliz'd, and fouly spoken of.

Hot. But soft I pray you; did King *Richard* then
Proclaime my brother *Mortimer*,
Heyre to the Crowne?
Nor. He did, my selfe did heare it.
Hot. Nay then I cannot blame his Cousin King,
That wish'd him on the barren Mountaines staru'd.
But shall it be, that you that set the Crowne
Vpon the head of this forgetfull man,
And for his sake, wore the detested blot
Of murtherous subornation? Shall it be,
That you a world of curses vndergoe,
Being the Agents, or base second meanes,
The Cords, the Ladder, or the Hangman rather?
O pardon, if that I descend so low,
To shew the Line, and the Predicament
Wherein you range vnder this subtill King.
Shall it for shame, be spoken in these dayes,
Or fill vp Chronicles in time to come,
That men of your Nobility and Power,
Did gage them both in an vniust behalfe
(As Both of you, God pardon it, haue done)
To put downe *Richard*, that sweet louely Rose,
And plant this Thorne, this Canker *Bullingbrooke*?
And shall it in more shame be further spoken,
That you are fool'd, discarded, and shooke off
By him, for whom these shames ye vnderwent?
No: yet time serues, wherein you may redeeme
Your banish'd Honors, and restore your selues
Into the good Thoughts of the world againe.
Reuenge the geering and disdain'd contempt
Of this proud King, who studies day and night
To answer all the Debt he owes vnto you,
Euen with the bloody Payment of your deaths:
Therefore I say———
Wor. Peace Cousin, say no more.
And now I will vnclaspe a Secret booke,
And to your quicke conceyuing Discontents,
Ile reade you Matter, deepe and dangerous,
As full of perill and aduenturous Spirit,
As to o're-walke a Current, roaring loud
On the vnstedfast footing of a Speare.
Hot. If he fall in, good night, or sinke or swimme:
Send danger from the East vnto the West,
So Honor crosse it from the North to South,
And let them grapple: The blood more stirres
To rowze a Lyon, then to start a Hare.
Nor. Imagination of some great exploit,
Driues him beyond the bounds of Patience.
Hot By heauen, me thinkes it were an easie leap,
To plucke bright Honor from the pale-fac'd Moone,
Or diue into the bottome of the deepe,
Where Fadome-line could neuer touch the ground,
And plucke vp drowned Honor by the Lockes:
So he that doth redeeme her thence, might weare
Without Co-riuall, all her Dignities:
But out vpon this halfe-fac'd Fellowship.
Wor. He apprehends a World of Figures here,
Bnt not the forme of what he should attend:
Good Cousin giue me audience for a-while,
And list to me.
Hot. I cry you mercy.
Wor. Those same Noble Scottes
That are your Prisoners.
Hot. Ile keepe them all.
By heauen, he shall not haue a Scot of them:
No, if a Scot would saue his Soule, he shall not.
Ile keepe them, by this Hand.
Wor. You start away,
And lend no eare vnto my purposes.
Those Prisoners you shall keepe.
Hot. Nay, I will; that's flat:
He said, he would not ransome *Mortimer*:
Forbad my tongue to speake of *Mortimer*.
But I will finde him when he lyes asleepe,
And in his eare, Ile holla *Mortimer*.
Nay, Ile haue a Starling shall be taught to speake
Nothing but *Mortimer*, and giue it him,
To keepe his anger still in motion.
Wor. Heare you Cousin: a word.
Hot. All studies heere I solemnly desie,
Saue how to gall and pinch this *Bullingbrooke*,
And that same Sword and Buckler Prince of Wales.
But that I thinke his Father loues him not,
And would be glad he met with some mischance,
I would haue poyson'd him with a pot of Ale.
Wor. Farewell Kinsman: Ile talke to you
When you are better temper'd to attend.
Nor. Why what a Waspe-tongu'd & impatient foole
Art thou, to breake into this Womans mood,
Tying thine eare to no tongue but thine owne?
Hot. Why look you, I am whipt & scourg'd with rods,
Netled, and stung with Pismires, when I heare
Of this vile Politician *Bullingbrooke*.
In *Richards* time: What de'ye call the place?
A plague vpon't, it is in Gloustershire:
'Twas, where the madcap Duke his Vncle kept,
His Vncle Yorke, where I first bow'd my knee
Vnto this King of Smiles, this *Bullingbrooke*:
When you and he came backe from Rauenspurgh.
Nor. At Barkley Castle.
Hot. You say true:
Why what a caudie deale of curtesie,
This fawning Grey-hound then did proffer me.
Looke when his infant Fortune came to age,
And gentle *Harry Percy*, and kinde Cousin:
O, the Diuell take such Couzeners, God forgiue me,
Good Vncle tell your tale, for I haue done.
Wor. Nay, if you haue not, too't againe,
Wee'l stay your leysure.
Hot. I haue done insooth.
Wor. Then once more to your Scottish Prisoners.
Deliuer them vp without their ransome straight,
And make the *Dowglas* sonne your onely meane
For powres in Scotland: which for diuers reasons
Which I shall send you written, be assur'd
Will easily be granted you, my Lord.
Your Sonne in Scotland being thus imply'd,
Shall secretly into the bosome creepe
Of that same noble Prelate, well belou'd,
The Archbishop.
Hot. Of Yorke, is't not?
Wor. True, who beares hard
His Brothers death at *Bristow*, the Lord *Scroope*.
I speake not this in estimation,
As what I thinke might be, but what I know
Is ruminated, plotted, and set downe,
And onely stayes but to behold the face
Of that occasion that shall bring it on.
Hot. I smell it:
Vpon my life, it will do wond'rous well.
Nor. Before the game's a-foot, thou still let'st slip.
Hot. Why it cannot choose but be a Noble plot,

And then the power of Scotland, and of Yorke
To ioyne with *Mortimer*, Ha.

Wor. And so they shall.

Hot. Infaith it is exceedingly well aym'd.

Wor. And tis no little reason bids vs speed,
To saue our heads, by raising of a Head:
For, beare our selues as euen as we can,
The King will alwayes thinke him in our debt,
And thinke, we thinke our selues vnsatisfied,
Till he hath found a time to pay vs home.
And see already, how he doth beginne
To make vs strangers to his lookes of loue.

Hot. He does, he does; wee'l be reueng'd on him.

Wor. Cousin, farewell. No further go in this,
Then I by Letters shall direct your course
When time is ripe, which will be sodainly:
Ile steale to *Glendower*, and loe, *Mortimer*,
Where you, and *Dowglas*, and our powres at once,
As I will fashion it, shall happily meete,
To beare our fortunes in our owne strong armes,
Which now we hold at much vncertainty.

Nor. Farewell good Brother, we shall thriue, I trust.

Hot. Vncle, adieu: O let the houres be short,
Till fields, and blowes, and grones, applaud our sport. *exit*

Actus Secundus. Scena Prima.

Enter a Carrier with a Lanterne in his hand.

1.Car. Heigh-ho, an't be not foure by the day, Ile be hang'd. *Charles waine* is ouer the new Chimney, and yet our horse not packt. What Ostler?

Ost. Anon, anon.

1.Car. I prethee Tom, beate Cuts Saddle, put a few Flockes in the point: the poore Iade is wrung in the withers, out of all cesse.

Enter another Carrier.

2.Car. Pease and Beanes are as danke here as a Dog, and this is the next way to giue poore Iades the Bottes: This house is turned vpside downe since *Robin* the Ostler dyed.

1.Car. Poore fellow neuer ioy'd since the price of oats rose, it was the death of him.

2. Car. I thinke this is the most villanous house in al London rode for Fleas: I am stung like a Tench.

1.Car. Like a Tench? There is ne're a King in Christendome, could be better bit, then I haue beene since the first Cocke.

2.Car. Why, you will allow vs ne're a Iourden, and then we leake in your Chimney: and your Chamber-lye breeds Fleas like a Loach.

1.Car. What Ostler, come away, and be hangd: come away.

2.Car. I haue a Gammon of Bacon, and two razes of Ginger, to be deliuered as farre as Charing-crosse.

1.Car. The Turkies in my Pannier are quite starued. What Ostler? A plague on thee, hast thou neuer an eye in thy head? Can'st not heare? And t'were not as good a deed as drinke, to break the pate of thee, I am a very Villaine. Come and be hang'd, hast no faith in thee?

Enter Gads-hill.

Gad. Good-morrow Carriers. What's a clocke?

Car. I thinke it be two a clocke.

Gad. I prethee lend me thy Lanthorne to see my Gelding in the stable.

1.Car. Nay soft I pray ye, I know a trick worth two of that.

Gad. I prethee lend me thine.

2.Car. I, when, canst tell? Lend mee thy Lanthorne (quoth-a) marry Ile see thee hang'd first.

Gad. Sirra Carrier: What time do you mean to come to London?

2.Car. Time enough to goe to bed with a Candle, I warrant thee. Come neighbour *Mugges*, wee'll call vp the Gentlemen, they will along with company, for they haue great charge. *Exeunt*

Enter Chamberlaine.

Gad. What ho, Chamberlaine?

Cham. At hand quoth Pick-purse.

Gad. That's euen as faire, as at hand quoth the Chamberlaine: For thou variest no more from picking of Purses, then giuing direction, doth from labouring. Thou lay'st the plot, how.

Cham. Good morrow Master *Gads-Hill*, it holds currant that I told you yesternight. There's a Franklin in the wilde of Kent, hath brought three hundred Markes with him in Gold: I heard him tell it to one of his company last night at Supper; a kinde of Auditor, one that hath abundance of charge too (God knowes what) they are vp already, and call for Egges and Butter. They will away presently.

Gad. Sirra, if they meete not with S. Nicholas Clarks, Ile giue thee this necke.

Cham. No, Ile none of it: I prythee keep that for the Hangman, for I know thou worshipst S. Nicholas as truly as a man of falshood may.

Gad. What talkest thou to me of the Hangman? If I hang, Ile make a fat payre of Gallowes. For, if I hang, old Sir *Iohn* hangs with mee, and thou know'st hee's no Starueling. Tut, there are other Troians that ÿ dream'st not of, the which (for sport sake) are content to doe the Profession some grace; that would (if matters should bee look'd into) for their owne Credit sake make all Whole. I am ioyned with no Foot-land-Rakers, no Long-staffe six-penny strikers, none of these mad Mustachio-purple-hu'd-Maltwormes, but with Nobility, and Tranquilitie; Bourgomasters, and great Oneyers, such as can holde in, such as will strike sooner then speake; and speake sooner then drinke, and drinke sooner then pray: and yet I lye, for they pray continually vnto their Saint the Commonwealth; or rather, not to pray to her, but prey on her: for they ride vp & downe on her, and make hit their Boots.

Cham. What, the Commonwealth their Bootes? Will she hold out water in foule way?

Gad. She will, she will; Iustice hath liquor'd her. We steale as in a Castle, cocksure: we haue the receit of Fernseede, we walke inuisible.

Cham. Nay, I thinke rather, you are more beholding to the Night, then to the Fernseed, for your walking inuisible.

Gad. Giue me thy hand.
Thou shalt haue a share in our purpose,
As I am a true man.

Cham. Nay, rather let mee haue it, as you are a false Theefe.

Gad. Goe too: *Homo* is a common name to all men. Bid the Ostler bring the Gelding out of the stable. Farewell, ye muddy Knaue. *Exeunt.*

Scæna Secunda.

Enter Prince, Poynes, and Peto.

Poines. Come shelter, shelter, I haue remoued *Falstafs* Horse, and he frets like a gum'd Veluet.

Prin. Stand close.

Enter Falstaffe.

Fal. *Poines, Poines*, and be hang'd *Poines.*

Prin. Peace ye fat-kidney'd Rascall, what a brawling dost thou keepe.

Fal. What *Poines. Hal?*

Prin. He is walk'd vp to the top of the hill, Ile go seek him.

Fal. I am accurst to rob in that Theefe company: that Rascall hath remoued my Horse, and tied him I know not where. If I trauell but foure foot by the squire further a foote, I shall breake my winde. Well, I doubt not but to dye a faire death for all this, if I scape hanging for killing that Rogue, I haue forsworne his company hourely any time this two and twenty yeare, & yet I am bewitcht with the Rogues company. If the Rascall haue not giuen me medicines to make me loue him, Ile be hang'd; it could not be else: I haue drunke Medicines. *Poines, Hal*, a Plague vpon you both. *Bardolph, Peto*: Ile starue ere I rob a foote further. And 'twere not as good a deede as to drinke, to turne True-man, and to leaue these Rogues, I am the veriest Varlet that euer chewed with a Tooth. Eight yards of vneuen ground, is threescore & ten miles afoot with me: and the stony-hearted Villaines knowe it well enough. A plague vpon't when Theeues cannot be true one to another. *They Whistle.* Whew: a plague light vpon you all. Giue my Horse you Rogues: giue me my Horse, and be hang'd.

Prin. Peace ye fat guttes, lye downe, lay thine eare close to the ground, and list if thou can heare the tread of Trauellers.

Fal. Haue you any Leauers to lift me vp again being downe? Ile not beare mine owne flesh so far afoot again, for all the coine in thy Fathers Exchequer. What a plague meane ye to colt me thus?

Prin. Thou ly'st, thou art not colted, thou art vncolted.

Fal. I prethee good Prince *Hal*, help me to my horse, good Kings sonne.

Prin. Out you Rogue, shall I be your Ostler?

Fal. Go hang thy selfe in thine owne heire-apparant-Garters: If I be tane, Ile peach for this: and I haue not Ballads made on all, and sung to filthy tunes, let a Cup of Sacke be my poyson: when a iest is so forward, & a foote too, I hate it.

Enter Gads-hill.

Gad. Stand.

Fal. So I do against my will.

Poin. O 'tis our Setter, I know his voyce: *Bardolfe*, what newes?

Bar. Case ye, case ye; on with your Vizards, there's mony of the Kings comming downe the hill, 'tis going to the Kings Exchequer.

Fal. You lie you rogue, 'tis going to the Kings Tauern.

Gad. There's enough to make vs all.

Fal. To be hang'd.

Prin. You foure shall front them in the narrow Lane: *Ned* and I, will walke lower; if they scape from your encounter, then they light on vs.

Peto. But how many be of them?

Gad. Some eight or ten.

Fal. Will they not rob vs?

Prin. What, a Coward Sir *Iohn* Paunch?

Fal. Indeed I am not *Iohn of Gaunt* your Grandfather; but yet no Coward, *Hal.*

Prin. Wee'l leaue that to the proofe.

Poin. Sirra Iacke, thy horse stands behinde the hedg, when thou need'st him, there thou shalt finde him. Farewell, and stand fast.

Fal. Now cannot I strike him, if I should be hang'd.

Prin. *Ned*, where are our disguises?

Poin. Heere hard by: Stand close.

Fal. Now my Masters, happy man be his dole, say I: euery man to his businesse.

Enter Trauellers.

Tra. Come Neighbor: the boy shall leade our Horses downe the hill: Wee'l walke a-foot a while, and ease our Legges.

Theeues. Stay.

Tra. Iesu blesse vs.

Fal. Strike: down with them, cut the villains throats; a whorson Caterpillars: Bacon-fed Knaues, they hate vs youth; downe with them, fleece them.

Tra. O, we are vndone, both we and ours for euer.

Fal. Hang ye gorbellied knaues, are you vndone? No ye Fat Chuffes, I would your store were heere. On Bacons, on, what ye knaues? Yong men must liue, you are Grand Iurers, are ye? Wee'l iure ye ifaith.

Heere they rob them, and binde them. Enter the Prince and Poines.

Prin. The Theeues haue bound the True-men: Now could thou and I rob the Theeues, and go merily to London, it would be argument for a Weeke, Laughter for a Moneth, and a good iest for euer.

Poynes. Stand close, I heare them comming.

Enter Theeues againe.

Fal. Come my Masters, let vs share, and then to horsse before day: and the Prince and Poynes bee not two arrand Cowards, there's no equity stirring. There's no moe valour in that Poynes, than in a wilde Ducke.

Prin. Your money.

Poin. Villaines.

As they are sharing, the Prince and Poynes set vpon them. They all run away, leauing the booty behind them.

Prince. Got with much ease. Now merrily to Horse: The Theeues are scattred, and possest with fear so strongly, that they dare not meet each other: each takes his fellow for an Officer. Away good *Ned*, *Falstaffe* sweates to death, and Lards the leane earth as he walkes along: wer't not for laughing, I should pitty him.

Poin. How the Rogue roar'd. *Exeunt.*

Scæna Tertia.

Enter Hotspurre solus, reading a Letter.

But for mine owne part my Lord, I could bee well contented to be there, in respect of the loue I beare your house.

He

He could be contented: Why is he not then? in respect of the loue he beares our house. He shewes in this, he loues his owne Barne better then he loues our house. Let me see some more. *The purpose you vndertake is dangerous.* Why that's certaine: 'Tis dangerous to take a Colde, to sleepe, to drinke: but I tell you (my Lord foole) out of this Nettle, Danger; we plucke this Flower, Safety. *The purpose you vndertake is dangerous, the Friends you haue named vncertaine, the Time it selfe vnsorted, and your whole Plot too light, for the counterpoize of so great an Opposition.* Say you so, say you so: I say vnto you againe, you are a shallow cowardly Hinde, and you Lye. What a lacke-braine is this? I protest, our plot is as good a plot as euer was laid; our Friend true and constant: A good Plotte, good Friends, and full of expectation: An excellent plot, very good Friends. What a Frosty-spirited rogue is this? Why, my Lord of Yorke commends the plot, and the generall course of the action. By this hand, if I were now by this Rascall, I could braine him with his Ladies Fan. Is there not my Father, my Vnckle, and my Selfe, Lord *Edmund Mortimer*, my Lord of *Yorke*, and *Owen Glendour*? Is there not besides, the *Dowglas*? Haue I not all their letters, to meete me in Armes by the ninth of the next Moneth? and are they not some of them set forward already? What a Pagan Rascall is this? An Infidell. Ha, you shall see now in very sincerity of Feare and Cold heart, will he to the King, and lay open all our proceedings. O, I could diuide my selfe, and go to buffets, for mouing such a dish of skim'd Milk with so honourable an Action. Hang him, let him tell the King we are prepared. I will set forwards to night.

Enter his Lady.

How now Kate, I must leaue you within these two hours.

La. O my good Lord, why are you thus alone?
For what offence haue I this fortnight bin
A banish'd woman from my *Harries* bed?
Tell me (sweet Lord) what is't that takes from thee
Thy stomacke, pleasure, and thy golden sleepe?
Why dost thou bend thine eyes vpon the earth?
And start so often when thou sitt'st alone?
Why hast thou lost the fresh blood in thy cheekes?
And giuen my Treasures and my rights of thee,
To thicke-ey'd musing, and curst melancholly?
In my faint-slumbers, I by thee haue watcht,
And heard thee murmore tales of Iron Warres:
Speake tearmes of manage to thy bounding Steed,
Cry courage to the field. And thou hast talk'd
Of Sallies, and Retires; Trenches, Tents,
Of Palizadoes, Frontiers, Parapets,
Of Basiliskes, of Canon, Culuerin,
Of Prisoners ransome, and of Souldiers slaine,
And all the current of a headdy fight.
Thy spirit within thee hath beene so at Warre,
And thus hath so bestirr'd thee in thy sleepe,
That beds of sweate hath stood vpon thy Brow,
Like bubbles in a late-disturbed Streame;
And in thy face strange motions haue appear'd,
Such as we see when men restraine their breath
On some great sodaine hast. O what portents are these?
Some heauie businesse hath my Lord in hand,
And I must know it: else he loues me not.

Hot. What ho; Is *Gilliams* with the Packet gone?

Ser. He is my Lord, an houre agone.

Hot. Hath *Butler* brought those horses frō the Sheriffe?

Ser. One horse, my Lord, he brought euen now.

Hot. What Horse? A Roane, a crop eare, is it not.

Ser. It is my Lord.

Hot. That Roane shall be my Throne. Well, I will backe him straight. *Esperance*, bid *Butler* lead him forth into the Parke.

La. But heare you, my Lord.

Hot. What say'st thou my Lady?

La. What is it carries you away?

Hot. Why, my horse (my Loue) my horse.

La. Out you mad-headed Ape, a Weazell hath not such a deale of Spleene, as you are tost with. In sooth Ile know your businesse *Harry*, that I will. I feare my Brother *Mortimer* doth stirre about his Title, and hath sent for you to line his enterprize. But if you go——

Hot. So farre a foot, I shall be weary, Loue.

La. Come, come, you Paraquito, answer me directly vnto this question, that I shall aske. Indeede Ile breake thy little finger *Harry*, if thou wilt not tel me true.

Hot. Away, away you trifler: Loue, I loue thee not,
I care not for thee *Kate*: this is no world
To play with Mammets, and to tilt with lips.
We must haue bloodie Noses, and crack'd Crownes,
And passe them currant too. Gods me, my horse.
What say'st thou *Kate*? what wo'd'st thou haue with me?

La. Do ye not loue me? Do ye not indeed?
Well, do not then. For since you loue me not,
I will not loue my selfe. Do you not loue me?
Nay, tell me if thou speak'st in iest, or no.

Hot. Come, wilt thou see me ride?
And when I am a horsebacke, I will sweare
I loue thee infinitely. But hearke you *Kate*,
I must not haue you henceforth, question me,
Whether I go: nor reason whereabout.
Whether I must, I must: and to conclude,
This Euening must I leaue thee, gentle *Kate*.
I know you wise, but yet no further wise
Then *Harry Percies* wife. Constant you are,
But yet a woman: and for secrecie,
No Lady closer. For I will beleeue
Thou wilt not vtter what thou do'st not know,
And so farre wilt I trust thee, gentle Kate.

La. How so farre?

Hot. Not an inch further. But harke you *Kate*,
Whither I go, thither shall you go too:
To day will I set forth, to morrow you.
Will this content you *Kate*?

La. It must of force. *Exeunt*

Scena Quarta.

Enter Prince and Poines.

Prin. *Ned*, prethee come out of that fat roome, & lend me thy hand to laugh a little.

Poines. Where hast bene *Hall*?

Prin. With three or foure Logger-heads, amongst 3. or fourescore Hogsheads. I haue sounded the verie base string of humility. Sirra, I am sworn brother to a leash of Drawers, and can call them by their names, as *Tom*, *Dicke*, and *Francis*. They take it already vpon their confidence, that though I be but Prince of Wales, yet I am the King of Curtesie: telling me flatly I am no proud Iack like *Falstaffe*, but a Corinthian, a lad of mettle, a good boy, and when I am King of England, I shall command al the good Laddes in East-cheape. They call drinking deepe, dying Scarlet; and when you breath in your watering, then they

they cry hem, and bid you play it off. To conclude, I am so good a proficient in one quarter of an houre, that I can drinke with any Tinker in his owne Language during my life. I tell thee *Ned*, thou hast lost much honor, that thou wer't not with me in this action: but sweet *Ned*, to sweeten which name of *Ned*, I giue thee this peniworth of Sugar, clapt euen now into my hand by an vnder Skinker, one that neuer spake other English in his life, then *Eight shillings and six pence*, and, *You are welcome*: with this shril addition, *Anon, Anon sir, Score a Pint of Bastard in the Halfe Moone*, or so. But *Ned*, to driue away time till *Falstaffe* come, I prythee doe thou stand in some by-roome, while I question my puny Drawer, to what end hee gaue me the Sugar, and do neuer leaue calling *Francis*, that his Tale to me may be nothing but, Anon: step aside, and Ile shew thee a President.

Poines. *Francis*.

Prin. Thou art perfect.

Poin. *Francis*.

Enter Drawer.

Fran. Anon, anon sir; looke downe into the Pomgarnet, *Ralfe*.

Prince. Come hither *Francis*.

Fran. My Lord.

Prin. How long hast thou to serue, Francis?

Fran. Forsooth fiue yeares, and as much as to——

Poin. Francis.

Fran. Anon, anon sir.

Prin. Fiue yeares: Berlady a long Lease for the clinking of Pewter. But Francis, darest thou be so valiant, as to play the coward with thy Indenture, & shew it a faire paire of heeles, and run from it?

Fran. O Lord sir, Ile be sworne vpon all the Books in England, I could finde in my heart.

Poin. Francis.

Fran. Anon, anon sir.

Prin. How old art thou, *Francis*?

Fran. Let me see, about Michaelmas next I shalbe——

Poin. Francis.

Fran. Anon sir, pray you stay a little, my Lord.

Prin. Nay but harke you Francis, for the Sugar thou gauest me, 'twas a penyworth, was't not?

Fran. O Lord sir, I would it had bene two.

Prin. I will giue thee for it a thousand pound: Aske me when thou wilt, and thou shalt haue it.

Poin. Francis.

Fran. Anon, anon.

Prin. Anon Francis? No Francis, but to morrow Francis: or Francis, on thursday: or indeed Francis when thou wilt. But Francis.

Fran. My Lord.

Prin. Wilt thou rob this Leatherne Ierkin, Christall button, Not-pated, Agat ring, Puke stocking, Caddice garter, Smooth tongue, Spanish pouch.

Fran. O Lord sir, who do you meane?

Prin. Why then your browne Bastard is your onely drinke: for looke you Francis, your white Canuas doublet will sulley. In Barbary sir, it cannot come to so much.

Fran. What sir?

Poin. Francis.

Prin. Away you Rogue, dost thou heare them call?

Heere they both call him, the Drawer stands amazed, not knowing which way to go.

Enter Vintner.

Vint. What, stand'st thou still, and hear'st such a calling? Looke to the Guests within: My Lord, olde Sir *Iohn* with halfe a dozen more, are at the doore: shall I let them in?

Prin. Let them alone awhile, and then open the doore. *Poines*.

Enter Poines.

Poin. Anon, anon sir.

Prin. Sirra, *Falstaffe* and the rest of the Theeues, are at the doore, shall we be merry?

Poin. As merrie as Crickets my Lad. But harke yee, What cunning match haue you made with this iest of the Drawer? Come, what's the issue?

Prin. I am now of all humors, that haue shewed themselues humors, since the old dayes of goodman *Adam*, to the pupill age of this present twelue a clock at midnight. What's a clocke Francis?

Fran. Anon, anon sir.

Prin. That euer this Fellow should haue fewer words then a Parret, and yet the sonne of a Woman. His industry is vp-staires and down-staires, his eloquence the parcell of a reckoning. I am not yet of *Percies* mind, the Hotspurre of the North, he that killes me some sixe or seauen dozen of Scots at a Breakfast, washes his hands, and saies to his wife; Fie vpon this quiet life, I want worke. O my sweet *Harry* sayes she, how many hast thou kill'd to day? Giue my Roane horse a drench (sayes hee) and answeres, some fourteene, an houre after: a trifle, a trifle. I prethee call in *Falstaffe*, Ile play *Percy*, and that damn'd Brawne shall play Dame *Mortimer* his wife. *Rivo*, sayes the drunkard. Call in Ribs, call in Tallow.

Enter Falstaffe.

Poin. Welcome Iacke, where hast thou beene?

Fal. A plague of all Cowards I say, and a Vengeance too, marry and Amen. Giue me a cup of Sacke Boy. Ere I leade this life long, Ile sowe nether stockes, and mend them too. A plague of all cowards. Giue me a Cup of Sacke, Rogue. Is there no Vertue extant?

Prin. Didst thou neuer see Titan kisse a dish of Butter, pittifull hearted Titan that melted at the sweete Tale of the Sunne? If thou didst, then behold that compound.

Fal. You Rogue, heere's Lime in this Sacke too: there is nothing but Roguery to be found in Villanous man; yet a Coward is worse then a Cup of Sack with lime. A villanous Coward, go thy wayes old Iacke, die when thou wilt, if manhood, good manhood be not forgot vpon the face of the earth, then am I a shotten Herring: there liues not three good men vnhang'd in England, & one of them is fat, and growes old, God helpe the while, a bad world I say. I would I were a Weauer, I could sing all manner of songs. A plague of all Cowards, I say still.

Prin. How now Woolsacke, what mutter you?

Fal. A Kings Sonne? If I do not beate thee out of thy Kingdome with a dagger of Lath, and driue all thy Subiects afore thee like a flocke of Wilde-geese, Ile neuer weare haire on my face more. You Prince of Wales?

Prin. Why you horson round man? what's the matter?

Fal. Are you not a Coward? Answer me to that, and *Poines* there?

Prin. Ye fatch paunch, and yee call mee Coward, Ile stab thee.

Fal. I call thee Coward? Ile see thee damn'd ere I call the Coward: but I would giue a thousand pound I could run as fast as thou canst. You are straight enough in the shoulders, you care not who sees your backe: Call you that

that backing of your friends? a plague vpon such backing: giue me them that will face me. Giue me a Cup of Sack, I am a Rogue if I drunke to day.

Prince. O Villaine, thy Lippes are scarce wip'd, since thou drunk'st last.

Falst. All's one for that. *He drinkes.*
A plague of all Cowards still, say I.

Prince. What's the matter?

Falst. What's the matter? here be foure of vs, haue ta'ne a thousand pound this Morning.

Prince. Where is it, *Iack?* where is it?

Falst. Where is it? taken from vs, it is: a hundred vpon poore foure of vs.

Prince. What, a hundred, man?

Falst. I am a Rogue, if I were not at halfe Sword with a dozen of them two houres together. I haue scaped by miracle. I am eight times thrust through the Doublet, foure through the Hose, my Buckler cut through and through, my Sword hackt like a Hand-saw, *ecce signum.* I neuer dealt better since I was a man: all would not doe. A plague of all Cowards: let them speake; if they speake more or lesse then truth, they are villaines, and the sonnes of darknesse.

Prince. Speake sirs, how was it?

Gad. We foure set vpon some dozen.

Falst. Sixteene, at least, my Lord.

Gad. And bound them.

Peto. No, no, they were not bound.

Falst. You Rogue, they were bound, euery man of them, or I am a Iew else, an Ebrew Iew.

Gad. As we were sharing, some sixe or seuen fresh men set vpon vs.

Falst. And vnbound the rest, and then come in the other.

Prince. What, fought yee with them all?

Falst. All? I know not what yee call all: but if I fought not with fiftie of them, I am a bunch of Radish: if there were not two or three and fiftie vpon poore olde *Iack*, then am I no two-legg'd Creature.

Poin. Pray Heauen, you haue not murthered some of them.

Falst. Nay, that's past praying for, I haue pepper'd two of them: Two I am sure I haue payed, two Rogues in Buckrom Sutes. I tell thee what, *Hal*, if I tell thee a Lye, spit in my face, call me Horse: thou knowest my olde word: here I lay, and thus I bore my point; foure Rogues in Buckrom let driue at me.

Prince. What, foure? thou sayd'st but two, euen now.

Falst. Foure *Hal*, I told thee foure.

Poin. I, I, he said foure.

Falst. These foure came all a-front, and mainely thrust at me; I made no more adoe, but tooke all their seuen points in my Targuet, thus.

Prince. Seuen? why there were but foure, euen now.

Falst. In Buckrom.

Poin. I, foure, in Buckrom Sutes.

Falst. Seuen, by these Hilts, or I am a Villaine else.

Prin. Prethee let him alone, we shall haue more anon.

Falst. Doest thou heare me, *Hal?*

Prin. I, and marke thee too, *Iack.*

Falst. Doe so, for it is worth the listning too: these nine in Buckrom, that I told thee of.

Prin. So, two more alreadie.

Falst. Their Points being broken.

Poin. Downe fell his Hose.

Falst. Began to giue me ground: but I followed me close, came in foot and hand; and with a thought, seuen of the eleuen I pay'd.

Prin. O monstrous! eleuen Buckrom men growne out of two?

Falst. But as the Deuill would haue it, three mis-begotten Knaues, in Kendall Greene, came at my Back, and let driue at me; for it was so darke, *Hal*, that thou could'st not see thy Hand.

Prin. These Lyes are like the Father that begets them, grosse as a Mountaine, open, palpable. Why thou Clay-brayn'd Guts, thou Knotty-pated Foole, thou Horson obscene greasie Tallow Catch.

Falst. What, art thou mad? art thou mad? is not the truth, the truth?

Prin. Why, how could'st thou know these men in Kendall Greene, when it was so darke, thou could'st not see thy Hand? Come, tell vs your reason: what say'st thou to this?

Poin. Come, your reason *Iack*, your reason.

Falst. What, vpon compulsion? No: were I at the Strappado, or all the Racks in the World, I would not tell you on compulsion. Giue you a reason on compulsion? If Reasons were as plentie as Black-berries, I would giue no man a Reason vpon compulsion, I.

Prin. Ile be no longer guiltie of this sinne. This sanguine Coward, this Bed-presser, this Horse-back-breaker, this huge Hill of Flesh.

Falst. Away you Starueling, you Elfe-skin, you dried Neats tongue, Bulles-pissell, you stocke fish: O for breth to vtter. What is like thee? You Tailors yard, you sheath you Bow-case you vile standing tucke.

Prin. Well, breath a-while, and then to't againe: and when thou hast tyr'd thy selfe in base comparisons, heare me speake but thus.

Poin. Marke Iacke.

Prin. We two, saw you foure set on foure and bound them, and were Masters of their Wealth: mark now how a plaine Tale shall put you downe. Then did we two, set on you foure, and with a word, outfac'd you from your prize, and haue it: yea, and can shew it you in the House. And *Falstaffe*, you caried your Guts away as nimbly, with as quicke dexteritie, and roared for mercy, and still ranne and roar'd, as euer I heard Bull-Calfe. What a Slaue art thou, to hacke thy sword as thou hast done, and then say it was in fight. What trick? what deuice? what starting hole canst thou now find out, to hide thee from this open and apparant shame?

Poines. Come, let's heare Iacke: What tricke hast thou now?

Fal. I knew ye as well as he that made ye. Why heare ye my Masters, was it for me to kill the Heire apparant? Should I turne vpon the true Prince? Why, thou knowest I am as valiant as *Hercules*: but beware Instinct, the Lion will not touch the true Prince: Instinct is a great matter. I was a Coward on Instinct: I shall thinke the better of my selfe, and thee, during my life: I, for a valiant Lion, and thou for a true Prince. But Lads, I am glad you haue the Mony. Hostesse, clap to the doores: watch to night, pray to morrow. Gallants, Lads, Boyes, Harts of Gold, all the good Titles of Fellowship come to you. What, shall we be merry? shall we haue a Play extempory.

Prin. Content, and the argument shall be, thy runing away.

Fal. A, no more of that *Hall*, and thou louest me.

Enter Hostesse.

Host. My Lord, the Prince?

Prin. How now my Lady the Hostesse, what say'st thou to me?

Hostesse. Marry, my Lord, there is a Noble man of the Court at doore would speake with you. hee sayes, hee comes from your Father.

Prin. Giue him as much as will make him a Royall man, and send him backe againe to my Mother.

Falst. What manner of man is hee?

Hostesse. An old man.

Falst. What doth Grauitie out of his Bed at Midnight? Shall I giue him his answere?

Prin. Prethee doe *Iacke*.

Falst. 'Faith, and Ile send him packing. *Exit.*

Prince. Now Sirs: you fought faire; so did you *Peto*, so did you *Bardol*: you are Lyons too, you ranne away vpon instinct: you will not touch the true Prince; no, fie.

Bard. 'Faith, I ranne when I saw others runne.

Prin. Tell mee now in earnest, how came *Falstaffes* Sword so hackt?

Peto. Why, he hackt it with his Dagger, and said, hee would sweare truth out of England, but hee would make you beleeue it was done in fight, and perswaded vs to doe the like.

Bard Yea, and to tickle our Noses with Spear-grasse, to make them bleed, and then to beslubber our garments with it, and sweare it was the blood of true men. I did that I did not this seuen yeeres before, I blusht to heare his monstrous deuices.

Prin. O Villaine, thou stolest a Cup of Sacke eighteene yeeres agoe, and wert taken with the manner, and euer since thou hast blusht extempore: thou hadst fire and sword on thy side, and yet thou ranst away; what instinct hadst thou for it?

Bard. My Lord, doe you see these Meteors? doe you behold these Exhalations?

Prin. I doe.

Bard. What thinke you they portend?

Prin. Hot Liuers, and cold Purses.

Bard. Choler, my Lord, if rightly taken.

Prin. No, if rightly taken, Halter.

Enter Falstaffe.

Heere comes leane *Iacke*, heere comes bare-bone. How now my sweet Creature of Bombast, how long is't agoe, *Iacke*, since thou saw'st thine owne Knee?

Falst. My owne Knee? When I was about thy yeeres (*Hal*) I was not an Eagles Talent in the Waste, I could haue crept into any Aldermans Thumbe-Ring: a plague of sighing and griefe, it blowes a man vp like a Bladder. There's villanous Newes abroad: heere was Sir *Iohn Braby* from your Father; you must goe to the Court in the Morning. The same mad fellow of the North, *Percy*; and hee of Wales, that gaue *Amamon* the Bastinado, and made *Lucifer* Cuckold, and swore the Deuill his true Liege-man vpon the Crosse of a Welch-hooke; what a plague call you him?

Pain. O, *Glendower*.

Falst. *Owen, Owen*; the same, and his Sonne in Law *Mortimer*, and old *Northumberland*, and the sprightly Scot of Scots, *Dowglas*, that runnes a Horse-backe vp a Hill perpendicular.

Prin. Hee that rides at high speede, and with a Pistoll kills a Sparrow flying.

Falst. You haue hit it.

Prin. So did he neuer the Sparrow.

Falst. Well, that Rascall hath good mettall in him, hee will not runne.

Prin. Why, what a Rascall art thou then, to prayse him so for running?

Falst. A Horse-backe (ye Cuckoe) but a foot hee will not budge a foot.

Prin. Yes *Iacke*, vpon instinct.

Falst. I grant ye, vpon instinct: Well, hee is there too, and one *Mordake*, and a thousand blew-Cappes more. *Worcester* is stolne away by Night: thy Fathers Beard is turn'd white with the Newes; you may buy Land now as cheape as stinking Mackrell.

Prin. Then 'tis like, if there come a hot Sunne, and this ciuill buffetting hold, wee shall buy Maiden-heads as they buy Hob-nayles, by the Hundreds.

Falst. By the Masse Lad, thou say'st true, it is like wee shall haue good trading that way. But tell me *Hal*, art not thou horrible afear'd? thou being Heire apparant, could the World picke thee out three such Enemyes againe, as that Fiend *Dowglas*, that Spirit *Percy*, and that Deuill *Glendower*? Art not thou horrible afraid? Doth not thy blood thrill at it?

Prin. Not a whit: I lacke some of thy instinct.

Falst. Well thou wilt be horrible chidde to morrow, when thou commest to thy Father: if thou doe loue me, practise an answere.

Prin. Doe thou stand for my Father, and examine mee vpon the particulars of my Life.

Falst. Shall I? content: This Chayre shall bee my State, this Dagger my Scepter, and this Cushion my Crowne.

Prin. Thy State is taken for a Ioyn'd-Stoole, thy Golden Scepter for a Leaden Dagger, and thy precious rich Crowne, for a pittifull bald Crowne.

Falst. Well, and the fire of Grace be not quite out of thee now shalt thou be moued. Giue me a Cup of Sacke to make mine eyes looke redde, that it may be thought I haue wept, for I must speake in passion, and I will doe it in King *Cambyses* vaine.

Prin. Well, heere is my Legge.

Falst. And heere is my speech: stand aside Nobilitie.

Hostesse. This is excellent sport, yfaith.

Falst. Weepe not, sweet Queene, for trickling teares are vaine.

Hostesse. O the Father, how hee holdes his countenance?

Falst. For Gods sake Lords, conuey my trustfull Queen,
For teares doe stop the floud-gates of her eyes.

Hostesse. O rare, he doth it as like one of these harlotry Players, as euer I see.

Falst. Peace good Pint-pot, peace good Tickle-braine. *Harry*, I doe not onely maruell where thou spendest thy time; but also, how thou art accompanied: For though the Camomile, the more it is troden, the faster it growes; yet Youth, the more it is wasted, the sooner it weares. Thou art my Sonne: I haue partly thy Mothers Word, partly my Opinion; but chiefely, a villanous tricke of thine Eye, and a foolish hanging of thy nether Lippe, that doth warrant me. If then thou be Sonne to mee, heere lyeth the point: why, being Sonne to me, art thou so poynted at? Shall the blessed Sonne of Heauen proue a Micher, and eate Black-berryes? a question not to bee askt. Shall the Sonne of England proue a Theefe, and take Purses? a question to be askt. There is a thing, *Harry*, which thou hast often heard of, and it is knowne to many

many in our Land, by the Name of Pitch: this Pitch (as ancient Writers doe report) doth defile; so doth the companie thou keepest: for *Harry*, now I doe not speake to thee in Drinke, but in Teares; not in Pleasure, but in Passion; not in Words onely, but in Woes also: and yet there is a vertuous man, whom I haue often noted in thy companie, but I know not his Name.

Prin. What manner of man, and it like your Maiestie?

Falst. A goodly portly man ysaith, and a corpulent, of a chearefull Looke, a pleasing Eye, and a most noble Carriage, and as I thinke, his age some fiftie, or (byrlady) inclining to threescore; and now I remember mee, his Name is *Falstaffe*: if that man should be lewdly giuen, hee deceiues mee; for *Harry*, I see Vertue in his Lookes. If then the Tree may be knowne by the Fruit, as the Fruit by the Tree, then peremptorily I speake it, there is Vertue in that *Falstaffe*: him keepe with, the rest banish. And tell mee now, thou naughtie Varlet, tell mee, where hast thou beene this moneth?

Prin. Do'st thou speake like a King? doe thou stand for mee, and Ile play my Father.

Falst. Depose me: if thou do'st it halfe so grauely, so maiestically, both in word and matter, hang me vp by the heeles for a Rabbet-sucker, or a Poulters Hare.

Prin. Well, heere I am set.

Falst. And heere I stand: iudge my Masters.

Prin. Now *Harry*, whence come you?

Falst. My Noble Lord, from East-cheape.

Prin. The complaints I heare of thee, are grieuous.

Falst. Yfaith, my Lord, they are false: Nay, Ile tickle ye for a young Prince.

Prin. Swearest thou, vngracious Boy? henceforth ne're looke on me: thou art violently carryed away from Grace: there is a Deuill haunts thee, in the likenesse of a fat old Man; a Tunne of Man is thy Companion: Why do'st thou conuerse with that Trunke of Humors, that Boulting-Hutch of Beastlinesse, that swolne Parcell of Dropsies, that huge Bombard of Sacke, that stuft Cloake-bagge of Guts, that rosted Manning Tree Oxe with the Pudding in his Belly, that reuerend Vice, that grey Iniquitie, that Father Ruffian, that Vanitie in yeeres? wherein is he good, but to taste Sacke, and drinke it? wherein neat and cleanly, but to carue a Capon, and eat it? wherein Cunning, but in Craft? wherein Craftie, but in Villanie? wherein Villanous, but in all things? wherein worthy, but in nothing?

Falst. I would your Grace would take me with you: whom meanes your Grace?

Prince. That villanous abhominable mis-leader of Youth, *Falstaffe*, that old white-bearded Sathan.

Falst. My Lord, the man I know.

Prince. I know thou do'st.

Falst. But to say, I know more harme in him then in my selfe, were to say more then I know. That hee is olde (the more the pittie) his white hayres doe witnesse it: but that hee is (sauing your reuerence) a Whore-master, that I vtterly deny. If Sacke and Sugar bee a fault, Heauen helpe the Wicked: if to be olde and merry, be a sinne, then many an olde Hoste that I know, is damn'd: if to be fat, be to be hated, then *Pharaohs* leane Kine are to be loued. No, my good Lord, banish *Peto*, banish *Bardolph*, banish *Poines*: but for sweete *Iacke Falstaffe*, kinde *Iacke Falstaffe* true *Iacke Falstaffe*, valiant *Iacke Falstaffe*, and therefore more valiant, being as hee is olde *Iack Falstaffe*, banish not him thy *Harryes* companie, banish not him thy *Harryes* companie; banish plumpe *Iacke*, and banish all the World.

Prince. I doe, I will.

Enter Bardolph running.

Bard. O, my Lord, my Lord, the Sherife, with a most most monstrous Watch, is at the doore.

Falst. Out you Rogue, play out the Play: I haue much to say in the behalfe of that *Falstaffe*.

Enter the Hostesse.

Hostesse. O, my Lord, my Lord.

Falst. Heigh, heigh, the Deuill rides vpon a Fiddle-sticke: what's the matter?

Hostesse. The Sherife and all the Watch are at the doore: they are come to search the House, shall I let them in?

Falst. Do'st thou heare *Hal*, neuer call a true peece of Gold a Counterfeit: thou art essentially made, without seeming so.

Prince. And thou a naturall Coward, without instinct.

Falst. I deny your *Maior*: if you will deny the Sherife, so: if not, let him enter. If I become not a Cart as well as another man, a plague on my bringing vp: I hope I shall as soone be strangled with a Halter, as another.

Prince. Goe hide thee behinde the Arras, the rest walke vp aboue. Now my Masters, for a true Face and good Conscience.

Falst. Both which I haue had: but their date is out, and therefore Ile hide me. *Exit.*

Prince. Call in the Sherife.

Enter Sherife and the Carrier.

Prince. Now Master Sherife, what is your will with mee?

She. First pardon me, my Lord. A Hue and Cry hath followed certaine men vnto this house.

Prince. What men?

She. One of them is well knowne, my gracious Lord, a grosse fat man.

Car. As fat as Butter.

Prince. The man, I doe assure you, is not heere,
For I my selfe at this time haue imploy'd him:
And Sherife, I will engage my word to thee,
That I will by to morrow Dinner time,
Send him to answere thee, or any man,
For any thing he shall be charg'd withall:
And so let me entreat you, leaue the house.

She. I will, my Lord: there are two Gentlemen
Haue in this Robberie lost three hundred Markes.

Prince. It may be so: if he haue robb'd these men,
He shall be answerable: and so farewell.

She. Good Night, my Noble Lord.

Prince. I thinke it is good Morrow, is it not?

She. Indeede, my Lord, I thinke it be two a Clocke. *Exit.*

Prince. This oyly Rascall is knowne as well as Poules: goe call him forth.

Peto. *Falstaffe*? fast asleepe behinde the Arras, and snorting like a Horse.

Prince. Harke, how hard he fetches breath: search his Pockets. He

He searcheth his Pockets, and findeth certaine Papers.

Prince. What hast thou found?

Peto. Nothing but Papers, my Lord.

Prince. Let's see, what be they? reade them.

Peto. Item, a Capon. ii.s.ii.d.
Item, Sawce. iiii.d.
Item, Sacke, two Gallons. v.s, viii.d.
Item, Anchoues and Sacke after Supper. ii.s.vi.d.
Item, Bread. ob.

Prince. O monstrous, but one halfe penny-worth of Bread to this intollerable deale of Sacke? What there is else, keepe close, wee'le reade it at more aduantage: there let him sleepe till day. Ile to the Court in the Morning: Wee must all to the Warres, and thy place shall be honorable. Ile procure this fat Rogue a Charge of Foot, and I know his death will be a Match of Twelue-score. The Money shall be pay'd backe againe with aduantage. Be with me betimes in the Morning: and so good morrow *Peto*.

Peto. Good morrow, good my Lord. *Exeunt.*

Actus Tertius. Scena Prima.

Enter Hotspurre, Worcester, Lord Mortimer, Owen Glendower.

Mort. These promises are faire, the parties sure,
And our induction full of prosperous hope.

Hotsp. Lord *Mortimer*, and Cousin *Glendower*,
Will you sit downe?
And Vnckle *Worcester*; a plague vpon it,
I haue forgot the Mappe.

Glend. No, here it is:
Sit Cousin *Percy*, sit good Cousin *Hotspurre*:
For by that Name, as oft as *Lancaster* doth speake of you,
His Cheekes looke pale, and with a rising sigh,
He wisheth you in Heauen.

Hotsp. And you in Hell, as oft as he heares *Owen Glendower* spoke of.

Glend. I cannot blame him: At my Natiuitie,
The front of Heauen was full of fierie shapes,
Of burning Cressets: and at my Birth,
The frame and foundation of the Earth
Shak'd like a Coward.

Hotsp. Why so it would haue done at the same season, if your Mothers Cat had but kitten'd, though your selfe had neuer beene borne.

Glend. I say the Earth did shake when I was borne.

Hotsp. And I say the Earth was not of my minde,
If you suppose, as fearing you, it shooke.

Glend. The Heauens were all on fire, the Earth did tremble.

Hotsp. Oh, then the Earth shooke
To see the Heauens on fire,
And not in feare of your Natiuitie.
Diseased Nature oftentimes breakes forth
In strange eruptions; and the teeming Earth
Is with a kinde of Collick pincht and vext,
By the imprisoning of vnruly Winde
Within her Wombe: which for enlargement striuing,
Shakes the old Beldame Earth, and tombles downe
Steeples, and mosse-growne Towers. At your Birth,
Our Grandam Earth, hauing this distemperature,
In passion shooke.

Glend. Cousin: of many men
I doe not beare these Crossings: Giue me leaue
To tell you once againe, that at my Birth
The front of Heauen was full of fierie shapes,
The Goates ranne from the Mountaines, and the Heards
Were strangely clamorous to the frighted fields:
These signes haue markt me extraordinarie,
And all the courses of my Life doe shew,
I am not in the Roll of common men.
Where is the Liuing, clipt in with the Sea,
That chides the Bankes of England, Scotland, and Wales,
Which calls me Pupill, or hath read to me?
And bring him out, that is but Womans Sonne,
Can trace me in the tedious wayes of Art,
And hold me pace in deepe experiments.

Hotsp. I thinke there's no man speakes better Welsh: Ile to Dinner.

Mort. Peace Cousin *Percy*, you will make him mad.

Glend. I can call Spirits from the vastie Deepe.

Hotsp. Why so can I, or so can any man:
But will they come, when you doe call for them?

Glend. Why, I can teach thee, Cousin, to command the Deuill.

Hotsp. And I can teach thee, Cousin, to shame the Deuil,
By telling truth. *Tell truth, and shame the Deuill.*
If thou haue power to rayse him, bring him hither,
And Ile be sworne, I haue power to shame him hence.
Oh, while you liue, tell truth, and shame the Deuill.

Mort. Come, come, no more of this vnprofitable Chat.

Glend. Three times hath *Henry Bullingbrooke* made head
Against my Power: thrice from the Banks of Wye,
And sandy-bottom'd Seuerne, haue I hent him
Bootlesse home, and Weather-beaten backe.

Hotsp. Home without Bootes,
And in foule Weather too,
How scapes he Agues in the Deuils name?

Glend. Come, heere's the Mappe:
Shall wee diuide our Right,
According to our three-fold order ta'ne?

Mort. The Arch-Deacon hath diuided it
Into three Limits, very equally:
England, from Trent, and Seuerne hitherto,
By South and East is to my part assign'd:
All Westward, Wales, beyond the Seuerne shore,
And all the fertile Land within that bound,
To *Owen Glendower*: And deare Couze, to you
The remnant Northward, lying off from Trent.
And our Indentures Tripartite are drawne:
Which being sealed enterchangeably,
(A Businesse that this Night may execute)
To morrow, Cousin *Percy*, you and I,
And my good Lord of Worcester, will set forth,
To meete your Father, and the Scottish Power,
As is appointed vs at Shrewsbury.
My Father *Glendower* is not readie yet,
Nor shall wee neede his helpe these foureteene dayes:
Within that space, you may haue drawne together
Your Tenants, Friends, and neighbouring Gentlemen.

Glend. A shorter time shall send me to you, Lords:
And in my Conduct shall your Ladies come,
From whom you now must steale, and take no leaue,
For there will be a World of Water shed,

Vpon

Vpon the parting of your Wiues and you.

Hotsp. Me thinks my Moity, North from Burton here,
In quantitie equals not one of yours:
See, how this Riuer comes me cranking in,
And cuts me from the best of all my Land,
A huge halfe Moone, a monstrous Cantle out.
Ile haue the Currant in this place damn'd vp,
And here the smug and Siluer Trent shall runne,
In a new Channell, faire and euenly:
It shall not winde with such a deepe indent,
To rob me of so rich a Bottome here.

Glend. Not winde? it shall, it must, you see it doth.

Mort. Yea, but marke how he beares his course,
And runnes me vp, with like aduantage on the other side,
Gelding the opposed Continent as much,
As on the other side it takes from you.

Worc. Yea, but a little Charge will trench him here,
And on this North side winne this Cape of Land,
And then he runnes straight and euen.

Hotsp. Ile haue it so, a little Charge will doe it.

Glend. Ile not haue it alter'd.

Hotsp. Will not you?

Glend. No, nor you shall not.

Hotsp. Who shall say me nay?

Glend. Why, that will I.

Hotsp. Let me not vnderstand you then, speake it in Welsh.

Glend. I can speake English, Lord, as well as you:
For I was trayn'd vp in the English Court;
Where, being but young, I framed to the Harpe
Many an English Dittie, louely well,
And gaue the Tongue a helpefull Ornament;
A Vertue that was neuer seene in you.

Hotsp. Marry, and I am glad of it with all my heart,
I had rather be a Kitten, and cry mew,
Then one of these same Meeter Ballad-mongers:
I had rather heare a Brazen Candlestick turn'd,
Or a dry Wheele grate on the Axle-tree,
And that would set my teeth nothing an edge,
Nothing so much, as mincing Poetrie;
'Tis like the forc't gate of a shuffling Nagge.

Glend. Come, you shall haue Trent turn'd.

Hotsp. I doe not care: Ile giue thrice so much Land
To any well-deseruing friend;
But in the way of Bargaine, marke ye me,
Ile cauill on the ninth part of a hayre.
Are the Indentures drawne? shall we be gone?

Glend. The Moone shines faire,
You may away by Night:
Ile haste the Writer; and withall,
Breake with your Wiues, of your departure hence:
I am afraid my Daughter will runne madde,
So much she doteth on her *Mortimer*. *Exit*

Mort. Fie, Cousin *Percy*, how you crosse my Father.

Hotsp. I cannot chuse: sometime he angers me,
With telling me of the Moldwarpe and the Ant,
Of the Dreamer *Merlin*, and his Prophecies;
And of a Dragon, and a finne-lesse Fish,
A clip-wing'd Griffin, and a moulten Rauen,
A couching Lyon, and a ramping Cat,
And such a deale of skimble-skamble Stuffe,
As puts me from my Faith. I tell you what,
He held me last Night, at least, nine howres,
In reckning vp the seuerall Deuils Names,
That were his Lacqueyes:
I cry'd hum, and well, goe too,
But mark'd him not a word. O, he is as tedious
As a tyred Horse, a rayling Wife,
Worse then a smoakie House. I had rather liue
With Cheese and Garlick in a Windmill farre,
Then feede on Cates, and haue him talke to me,
In any Summer-House in Christendome.

Mort. In faith he was a worthy Gentleman,
Exceeding well read, and profited,
In strange Concealements:
Valiant as a Lyon, and wondrous affable,
And as bountifull, as Mynes of India.
Shall I tell you, Cousin,
He holds your temper in a high respect,
And curbes himselfe, euen of his naturall scope,
When you doe crosse his humor: 'faith he does.
I warrant you, that man is not aliue,
Might so haue tempted him, as you haue done,
Without the taste of danger, and reproofe:
But doe not vse it oft, let me entreat you.

Worc. In faith, my Lord, you are too wilfull blame,
And since your comming hither, haue done enough,
To put him quite besides his patience.
You must needes learne, Lord, to amend this fault:
Though sometimes it shew Greatnesse, Courage, Blood,
And that's the dearest grace it renders you;
Yet oftentimes it doth present harsh Rage,
Defect of Manners, want of Gouernment,
Pride, Haughtinesse, Opinion, and Disdaine:
The least of which, haunting a Nobleman,
Loseth mens hearts, and leaues behinde a stayne
Vpon the beautie of all parts besides,
Beguiling them of commendation.

Hotsp. Well, I am school'd:
Good-manners be your speede;
Heere come your Wiues, and let vs take our leaue.

Enter Glendower, with the Ladies.

Mort. This is the deadly spight, that angers me,
My Wife can speake no English, I no Welsh.

Glend. My Daughter weepes, shee'le not part with you,
Shee'le be a Souldier too, shee'le to the Warres.

Mort. Good Father tell her, that she and my Aunt *Percy*
Shall follow in your Conduct speedily.

Glendower speakes to her in Welsh, and she answeres him in the same.

Glend. Shee is desperate heere:
A peeuish selfe-will'd Harlotry,
One that no perswasion can doe good vpon.

The Lady speakes in Welsh.

Mort. I vnderstand thy Lookes: that pretty Welsh
Which thou powr'st down from these swelling Heauens,
I am too perfect in: and but for shame,
In such a parley should I answere thee.

The Lady againe in Welsh.

Mort. I vnderstand thy Kisses, and thou mine,
And that's a feeling disputation:
But I will neuer be a Truant, Loue,
Till I haue learn'd thy Language: for thy tongue

Makes

Makes Welsh as sweet as Ditties highly penn'd,
Sung by a faire Queene in a Summers Bowre,
With rauishing Diuision to her Lute.
Glend. Nay, if thou melt, then will she runne madde.

The Lady speakes againe in Welsh.

Mort. O, I am Ignorance it selfe in this.
Glend. She bids you,
On the wanton Rushes lay you downe,
And rest your gentle Head vpon her Lappe,
And she will sing the Song that pleaseth you,
And on your Eye-lids Crowne the God of Sleepe,
Charming your blood with pleasing heauinesse;
Making such difference betwixt Wake and Sleepe,
As is the difference betwixt Day and Night,
The houre before the Heauenly Harneis'd Teeme
Begins his Golden Progresse in the East.
Mort. With all my heart Ile sit, and heare her sing:
By that time will our Booke, I thinke, be drawne.
Glend. Doe so:
And those Musitians that shall play to you,
Hang in the Ayre a thousand Leagues from thence;
And straight they shall be here: sit, and attend.
Hotsp. Come *Kate*, thou art perfect in lying downe:
Come, quicke, quicke, that I may lay my Head in thy Lappe.
Lady. Goe, ye giddy-Goose.

The Musicke playes.

Hotsp. Now I perceiue the Deuill vnderstands Welsh,
And 'tis no maruell he is so humorous:
Byrlady hee's a good Musitian.
Lady. Then would you be nothing but Musicall,
For you are altogether gouerned by humors:
Lye still ye Theefe, and heare the Lady sing in Welsh.
Hotsp. I had rather heare (Lady) my Brach howle in Irish.
Lady. Would'st haue thy Head broken?
Hotsp. No.
Lady. Then be still.
Hotsp. Neyther 'tis a Womans fault.
Lady. Now God helpe thee.
Hotsp. To the Welsh Ladies Bed.
Lady. What's that?
Hotsp. Peace, shee sings.

Heere the Lady sings a Welsh Song.

Hotsp. Come, Ile haue your Song too.
Lady. Not mine, in good sooth.
Hotsp. Not yours, in good sooth?
You sweare like a Comfit-makers Wife:
Not you, in good sooth; and, as true as I liue;
And, as God shall mend me; and, as sure as day:
And giuest such Sarcenet suretie for thy Oathes,
As if thou neuer walk'st further then Finsbury.
Sweare me, *Kate*, like a Lady, as thou art,
A good mouth-filling Oath: and leaue in sooth,
And such protest of Pepper Ginger-bread,
To Veluet-Guards, and Sunday-Citizens.
Come, sing.
Lady. I will not sing.
Hotsp. 'Tis the next way to turne Taylor, or be Red-brest teacher: and the Indentures be drawne, Ile away within these two howres: and so come in, when yee will. *Exit.*
Glend. Come, come, Lord *Mortimer*, you are as slow,
As hot Lord *Percy* is on fire to goe.
By this our Booke is drawne: wee'le but seale,
And then to Horse immediately.
Mort. With all my heart. *Exeunt.*

Scæna Secunda.

Enter the King, Prince of Wales, and others.

King. Lords, giue vs leaue:
The Prince of Wales, and I,
Must haue some priuate conference:
But be neere at hand,
For wee shall presently haue neede of you.
Exeunt Lords.
I know not whether Heauen will haue it so,
For some displeasing seruice I haue done;
That in his secret Doome, out of my Blood,
Hee'le breede Reuengement, and a Scourge for me:
But thou do'st in thy passages of Life,
Make me beleeue, that thou art onely mark'd
For the hot vengeance, and the Rod of heauen
To punish my Mistreadings. Tell me else,
Could such inordinate and low desires,
Such poore, such bare, such lewd, such meane attempts,
Such barren pleasures, rude societie,
As thou art matcht withall, and grafted too,
Accompanie the greatnesse of thy blood,
And hold their leuell with thy Princely heart?
Prince. So please your Maiesty, I would I could
Quit all offences with as cleare excuse,
As well as I am doubtlesse I can purge
My selfe of many I am charg'd withall:
Yet such extenuation let me begge,
As in reproofe of many Tales deuis'd,
Which oft the Eare of Greatnesse needes must heare,
By smiling Pick-thankes, and base Newes-mongers;
I may for some things true, wherein my youth
Hath faultie wandred, and irregular,
Finde pardon on my true submission.
King. Heauen pardon thee:
Yet let me wonder, *Harry*,
At thy affections, which doe hold a Wing
Quite from the flight of all thy ancestors.
Thy place in Councell thou hast rudely lost,
Which by thy younger Brother is supply'de;
And art almost an alien to the hearts
Of all the Court and Princes of my blood.
The hope and expectation of thy time
Is ruin'd, and the Soule of euery man
Prophetically doe fore-thinke thy fall.
Had I so lauish of my presence beene,
So common hackney'd in the eyes of men,
So stale and cheape to vulgar Company;
Opinion, that did helpe me to the Crowne,
Had still kept loyall to possession,
And left me in reputelesse banishment,
A fellow of no marke, nor likelyhood.
By being seldome seene, I could not stirre,
But like a Comet, I was wondred at,

That

That men would tell their Children This is hee:
Others would say; Where, Which is *Bullingbrooke*.
And then I stole all Courtesie from Heauen,
And drest my selfe in such Humilitie,
That I did plucke Allegeance from mens hearts,
Lowd Showts and Salutations from their mouthes,
Euen in the presence of the Crowned King.
Thus I did keepe my Person fresh and new,
My Presence like a Robe Pontificall,
Ne're seene, but wondred at: and so my State,
Seldome but sumptuous, shewed like a Feast,
And wonne by rarenesse such Solemnitie.
The skipping King hee ambled vp and downe,
With shallow Iesters, and rash Bauin Wits,
Soone kindled, and soone burnt, carded his State,
Mingled his Royaltie with Carping Fooles,
Had his great Name prophaned with their Scornes,
And gaue his Countenance, against his Name,
To laugh at gybing Boyes, and stand the push
Of euery Beardlesse vaine Comparatiue;
Grew a Companion to the common Streetes,
Enfeoff'd himselfe to Popularitie:
That being dayly swallowed by mens Eyes,
They surfeted with Honey, and began to loathe
The taste of Sweetnesse, whereof a little
More then a little, is by much too much.
So when he had occasion to be seene,
He was but as the Cuckow is in Iune,
Heard, not regarded: seene but with such Eyes,
As sicke and blunted with Communitie,
Affoord no extraordinarie Gaze,
Such as is bent on Sunne-like Maiestie,
When it shines seldome in admiring Eyes:
But rather drowz'd, and hung their eye-lids downe,
Slept in his Face, and rendred such aspect
As Cloudie men vse to doe to their aduersaries,
Being with his presence glutted, gorg'd, and full.
And in that very Line, *Harry*, standest thou:
For thou hast lost thy Princely Priuiledge,
With vile participation. Not an Eye
But is awearie of thy common sight,
Saue mine, which hath desir'd to see thee more:
Which now doth that I would not haue it doe,
Make blinde it selfe with foolish tendernesse.

Prince. I shall hereafter, my thrice gracious Lord,
Be more my selfe.

King. For all the World,
As thou art to this houre, was *Richard* then,
When I from France set foot at Rauenspurgh;
And euen as I was then, is *Percy* now:
Now by my Scepter, and my Soule to boot,
He hath more worthy interest to the State
Then thou, the shadow of Succession;
For of no Right, nor colour like to Right.
He doth fill fields with Harneis in the Realme,
Turnes head against the Lyons armed Iawes;
And being no more in debt to yeeres, then thou,
Leades ancient Lords, and reuerent Bishops on
To bloody Battailes, and to brusing Armes.
What neuer-dying Honor hath he got,
Against renowned *Dowglas*? whose high Deedes,
Whose hot Incursions, and great Name in Armes,
Holds from all Souldiers chiefe Maioritie,
And Militarie Title Capitall.
Through all the Kingdomes that acknowledge Christ,
Thrice hath the *Hotspur Mars*, in swathing Clothes,
This Infant Warrior, in his Enterprises,
Discomfited great *Dowglas*, ta'ne him once,
Enlarged him, and made a friend of him,
To fill the mouth of deepe Defiance vp,
And shake the peace and safetie of our Throne.
And what say you to this? *Percy, Northumberland*,
The Arch-bishops Grace of Yorke, *Dowglas, Mortimer*,
Capitulate against vs, and are vp.
But wherefore doe I tell these Newes to thee?
Why, *Harry*, doe I tell thee of my Foes,
Which art my neer'st and dearest Enemie?
Thou, that art like enough, through vassall Feare,
Base Inclination, and the start of Spleene,
To fight against me vnder *Percies* pay,
To dogge his heeles, and curtsie at his frownes,
To shew how much thou art degenerate.

Prince. Doe not thinke so, you shall not finde it so:
And Heauen forgiue them, that so much haue sway'd
Your Maiesties good thoughts away from me:
I will redeeme all this on *Percies* head,
And in the closing of some glorious day,
Be bold to tell you, that I am your Sonne,
When I will weare a Garment all of Blood,
And staine my fauours in a bloody Maske:
Which washt away, shall scowre my shame with it.
And that shall be the day, when ere it lights,
That this same Child of Honor and Renowne,
This gallant *Hotspur*, this all-praysed Knight,
And your vnthought-of *Harry* chance to meet:
For euery Honor sitting on his Helme,
Would they were multitudes, and on my head
My shames redoubled. For the time will come,
That I shall make this Northerne Youth exchange
His glorious Deedes for my Indignities:
Percy is but my Factor, good my Lord,
To engrosse vp glorious Deedes on my behalfe:
And I will call him to so strict account,
That he shall render euery Glory vp,
Yea, euen the sleightest worship of his time,
Or I will teare the Reckoning from his Heart.
This, in the Name of Heauen, I promise here:
The which, if I performe, and doe suruiue,
I doe beseech your Maiestie, may salue
The long-growne Wounds of my intemperature:
If not, the end of Life cancells all Bands,
And I will dye a hundred thousand Deaths,
Ere breake the smallest parcell of this Vow.

King. A hundred thousand Rebels dye in this:
Thou shalt haue Charge, and soueraigne trust herein.

Enter Blunt.

How now good *Blunt*? thy Lookes are full of speed.

Blunt. So hath the Businesse that I come to speake of.
Lord *Mortimer* of Scotland hath sent word,
That *Dowglas* and the English Rebels met
The eleuenth of this moneth, at Shrewsbury:
A mightie and a fearefull Head they are,
(If Promises be kept on euery hand)
As euer offered foule play in a State.

King. The Earle of Westmerland set forth to day:
With him my sonne, Lord *Iohn* of Lancaster,
For this aduertisement is fiue dayes old.
On Wednesday next, *Harry* thou shalt set forward:
On Thursday, wee our selues will march.
Our meeting is Bridgenorth: and *Harry*, you shall march

Through Glocestershire: by which account,
Our Businesse valued some twelue dayes hence,
Our generall Forces at Bridgenorth shall meete.
Our Hands are full of Businesse: let's away,
Aduantage feedes him fat, while men delay. *Exeunt.*

Scena Tertia.

Enter Falstaffe and Bardolph.

Falst. *Bardolph*, am I not falne away vilely, since this last action? doe I not bate? doe I not dwindle? Why my skinne hangs about me like an olde Ladies loose Gowne: I am withered like an olde Apple *Iohn.* Well, Ile repent, and that suddenly, while I am in some liking: I shall be out of heart shortly, and then I shall haue no strength to repent. And I haue not forgotten what the in-side of a Church is made of, I am a Pepper-Corne, a Brewers Horse, the in-side of a Church. Company, villanous Company hath beene the spoyle of me.

Bard. Sir *Iohn*, you are so fretfull, you cannot liue long.

Falst. Why there is it: Come, sing me a bawdy Song, make me merry: I was as vertuously giuen, as a Gentleman need to be; vertuous enough, swore little, dic'd not aboue seuen times a weeke, went to a Bawdy-house not aboue once in a quarter of an houre, payd Money that I borrowed, three or foure times; liued well, and in good compasse: and now I liue out of all order, out of compasse.

Bard. Why, you are so fat, Sir *Iohn*, that you must needes bee out of all compasse; out of all reasonable compasse Sir *Iohn.*

Falst. Doe thou amend thy Face, and Ile amend thy Life: Thou art our Admirall, thou bearest the Lanterne in the Poope, but 'tis in the Nose of thee; thou art the Knight of the burning Lampe.

Bard. Why, Sir *Iohn*, my Face does you no harme.

Falst. No, Ile be sworne: I make as good vse of it, as many a man doth of a Deaths-Head, or a *Memento Mori.* I neuer see thy Face, but I thinke vpon Hell fire, and *Diues* that liued in Purple; for there he is in his Robes burning, burning. If thou wert any way giuen to vertue, I would sweare by thy Face; my Oath should bee, *By this Fire:* But thou art altogether giuen ouer; and wert indeede, but for the Light in thy Face, the Sunne of vtter Darkenesse. When thou ran'st vp Gads-Hill in the Night, to catch my Horse, if I did not thinke that thou hadst beene an *Ignis fatuus*, or a Ball of Wild-fire, there's no Purchase in Money. O, thou art a perpetuall Triumph, an euerlasting Bone-fire-Light: thou hast saued me a thousand Markes in Linkes and Torches, walking with thee in the Night betwixt Tauerne and Tauerne: But the Sack that thou hast drunke me, would haue bought me Lights as good cheape, as the dearest Chandlers in Europe. I haue maintain'd that Salamander of yours with fire, any time this two and thirtie yeeres, Heauen reward me for it.

Bard. I would my Face were in your Belly.

Falst. So should I be sure to be heart-burn'd.

Enter Hostesse.

How now, Dame *Partlet* the Hen, haue you enquir'd yet who pick'd my Pocket?

Hostesse. Why Sir *Iohn*, what doe you thinke, Sir *Iohn*? doe you thinke I keepe Theeues in my House? I haue search'd, I haue enquired, so has my Husband, Man by Man, Boy by Boy, Seruant by Seruant: the tight of a hayre was neuer lost in my house before.

Falst. Ye lye Hostesse: *Bardolph* was shau'd, and lost many a hayre; and Ile be sworne my Pocket was pick'd: goe to, you are a Woman, goe.

Hostesse. Who I? I defie thee: I was neuer call'd so in mine owne house before.

Falst. Goe to, I know you well enough.

Hostesse. No, Sir *Iohn*, you doe not know me, Sir *Iohn*: I know you, Sir *Iohn*: you owe me Money, Sir *Iohn*, and now you picke a quarrell, to beguile me of it: I bought you a dozen of Shirts to your Backe.

Falst. Doulas, filthy Doulas: I haue giuen them away to Bakers Wiues, and they haue made Boulters of them.

Hostesse. Now as I am a true Woman, Holland of eight shillings an Ell: You owe Money here besides, Sir *Iohn*, for your Dyet, and by-Drinkings, and Money lent you, foure and twentie pounds.

Falst. Hee had his part of it, let him pay.

Hostesse. Hee? alas hee is poore, hee hath nothing.

Falst. How? Poore? Looke vpon his Face: What call you Rich? Let them coyne his Nose, let them coyne his Cheekes, Ile not pay a Denier. What, will you make a Younker of me? Shall I not take mine ease in mine Inne, but I shall haue my Pocket pick'd? I haue lost a Seale-Ring of my Grand-fathers, worth fortie Marke.

Hostesse. I haue heard the Prince tell him, I know not how oft, that that Ring was Copper.

Falst. How? the Prince is a Iacke, a Sneake-Cuppe: and if hee were heere, I would cudgell him like a Dogge, if hee would say so.

Enter the Prince marching, and Falstaffe meets him, playing on his Truncheon like a Fife.

Falst. How now Lad? is the Winde in that Doore? Must we all march?

Bard. Yea, two and two, Newgate fashion.

Hostesse. My Lord, I pray you heare me.

Prince. What say'st thou, Mistresse *Quickly*? How does thy Husband? I loue him well, hee is an honest man.

Hostesse. Good, my Lord, heare mee.

Falst. Prethee let her alone, and list to mee.

Prince. What say'st thou, *Iacke*?

Falst. The other Night I fell asleepe heere behind the Arras, and had my Pocket pickt: this House is turn'd Bawdy-house, they picke Pockets.

Prince. What didst thou lose, *Iacke*?

Falst. Wilt thou beleeue me, *Hal*? Three or foure Bonds of fortie pound apeece, and a Seale-Ring of my Grandfathers.

Prince. A Trifle, some eight-penny matter.

Host. So I told him, my Lord; and I said, I heard your Grace say so: and (my Lord) hee speakes most vilely of you, like a foule-mouth'd man as hee is, and said, hee would cudgell you.

Prince. What hee did not?

Host. There's neyther Faith, Truth, nor Woman-hood in me else.

Falst. There's

Falst. There's no more faith in thee then a stu'de Prune; nor no more truth in thee, then in a drawne Fox: and for Wooman-hood, Maid-marian may be the Deputies wife of the Ward to thee. Go you nothing: go.

Host. Say, what thing? what thing?

Falst. What thing? why a thing to thanke heauen on.

Host. I am no thing to thanke heauen on, I wold thou shouldst know it: I am an honest mans wife: and setting thy Knighthood aside, thou art a knaue to call me so.

Falst. Setting thy woman-hood aside, thou art a beast to say otherwise.

Host. Say, what beast, thou knaue thou?

Fal. What beast? Why an Otter.

Prin. An Otter, sir *Iohn*? Why an Otter?

Fal. Why? She's neither fish nor flesh; a man knowes not where to haue her.

Host. Thou art vniust man in saying so; thou, or anie man knowes where to haue me, thou knaue thou.

Prince. Thou say'st true Hostesse, and he slanders thee most grossely.

Host. So he doth you, my Lord, and sayde this other day, You ought him a thousand pound.

Prince. Sirrah, do I owe you a thousand pound?

Falst. A thousand pound *Hal*? A Million. Thy loue is worth a Million: thou ow'st me thy loue.

Host. Nay my Lord, he call'd you Iacke, and said hee would cudgell you.

Fal. Did I, *Bardolph*?

Bar. Indeed Sir *Iohn*, you said so.

Fal. Yea, if he said my Ring was Copper.

Prince. I say 'tis Copper. Dar'st thou bee as good as thy word now?

Fal. Why *Hal*? thou know'st, as thou art but a man, I dare: but, as thou art a Prince, I feare thee, as I feare the roaring of the Lyons Whelpe.

Prince. And why not as the Lyon?

Fal. The King himselfe is to bee feared as the Lyon: Do'st thou thinke Ile feare thee, as I feare thy Father? nay if I do, let my Girdle breake.

Prin. O, if it should, how would thy guttes fall about thy knees. But sirra: There's no roome for Faith, Truth, nor Honesty, in this bosome of thine: it is all fill'd vppe with Guttes and Midriffe. Charge an honest Woman with picking thy pocket? Why thou horson impudent imbost Rascall, if there were any thing in thy Pocket but Tauerne Reckonings, *Memorandums* of Bawdie-houses, and one poore peny-worth of Sugar-candie to make thee long-winded: if thy pocket were enrich'd with anie other iniuries but these, I am a Villaine: And yet you will stand to it, you will not Pocket vp wrong. Art thou not asham'd?

Fal. Do'st thou heare *Hal*? Thou know'st in the state of Innocency, *Adam* fell: and what should poore *Iacke Falstaffe* do, in the dayes of Villany? Thou seest, I haue more flesh then another man, and therefore more frailty. You confesse then you pickt my Pocket?

Prin. It appeares so by the Story.

Fal. Hostesse, I forgiue thee:
Go make ready Breakfast, loue thy Husband,
Looke to thy Seruants, and cherish thy Guests:
Thou shalt find me tractable to any honest reason:
Thou seest, I am pacified still.
Nay, I prethee be gone.

Exit Hostesse.

Now *Hal*, to the newes at Court for the Robbery, Lad? How is that answered?

Prin. O my sweet Beefe:
I must still be good Angell to thee.
The Monie is paid backe againe.

Fal. O, I do not like that paying backe, 'tis a double Labour.

Prin. I am good Friends with my Father, and may do any thing.

Fal. Rob me the Exchequer the first thing thou do'st and do it with vnwash'd hands too.

Bard. Do my Lord.

Prin. I haue procured thee *Iacke*, a Charge of Foot.

Fal. I would it had beene of Horse. Where shal I finde one that can steale well? O, for a fine theefe of two and twentie, or thereabout: I am heynously vnprouided. Wel God be thanked for these Rebels, they offend none but the Vertuous. I laud them, I praise them.

Prin. *Bardolph*.

Bar. My Lord.

Prin. Go beare this Letter to Lord *Iohn* of Lancaster
To my Brother *Iohn*. This to my Lord of Westmerland,
Go *Peto*, to horse: for thou, and I,
Haue thirtie miles to ride yet ere dinner time.
Iacke, meet me to morrow in the Temple Hall
At two a clocke in the afternoone,
There shalt thou know thy Charge, and there receiue
Money and Order for their Furniture.
The Land is burning, *Percie* stands on hye,
And either they, or we must lower lye.

Fal. Rare words! braue world.
Hostesse, my breakfast, come:
Oh, I could wish this Tauerne were my drumme.

Exeunt omnes.

Actus Quartus. Scœna Prima.

Enter Harrie Hotspurre, Worcester, and Dowglas.

Hot. Well said, my Noble Scot, if speaking truth
In this fine Age, were not thought flatterie,
Such attribution should the *Dowglas* haue,
As not a Souldiour of this seasons stampe,
Should go so generall currant through the world.
By heauen I cannot flatter: I defie
The Tongues of Soothers. But a Brauer place
In my hearts loue, hath no man then your Selfe.
Nay, taske me to my word: approue me Lord.

Dow. Thou art the King of Honor:
No man so potent breathes vpon the ground,
But I will Beard him.

Enter a Messenger.

Hot. Do so, and 'tis well. What Letters hast there?
I can but thanke you.

Mess. These Letters come from your Father.

Hot. Letters from him?
Why comes he not himselfe?

Mes. He cannot come, my Lord,
He is greeuous sicke.

Hot. How? haz he the leysure to be sicke now,
In such a iustling time? Who leades his power?
Vnder whose Gouernment come they along?

Mess. His Letters beares his minde, not I his minde.
Wor I prethee tell me, doth he keepe his Bed?
Mess. He did, my Lord, foure dayes ere I set forth:
And at the time of my departure thence,
He was much fear'd by his Physician.
Wor. I would the state of time had first beene whole,
Ere he by sicknesse had beene visited:
His health was neuer better worth then now.
Hotsp. Sicke now? droope now? this sicknes doth infect
The very Life-blood of our Enterprise,
Tis catching hither, euen to our Campe.
He writes me here, that inward sicknesse,
And that his friends by deputation
Could not so soone be drawne: nor did he thinke it meet,
To lay so dangerous and deare a trust
On any Soule remou'd, but on his owne.
Yet doth he giue vs bold aduertisement,
That with our small coniunction we should on,
To see how Fortune is dispos'd to vs:
For, as he writes, there is no quailing now,
Because the King is certainely possest
Of all our purposes. What say you to it?
Wor. Your Fathers sicknesse is a mayme to vs.
Hotsp. A perillous Gash, a very Limme lopt off:
And yet, in faith, it is not his present want
Seemes more then we shall finde it.
Were it good, to set the exact wealth of all our states
All at one Cast? To set so rich a mayne
On the nice hazard of one doubtfull houre,
It were not good: for therein should we reade
The very Bottome, and the Soule of Hope,
The very List, the very vtmost Bound
Of all our fortunes.
Dowg. Faith, and so wee should,
Where now remaines a sweet reuersion.
We may boldly spend, vpon the hope
Of what is to come in:
A comfort of retyrement liues in this.
Hotsp. A Randeuous, a Home to flye vnto,
If that the Deuill and Mischance looke bigge
Vpon the Maydenhead of our Affaires.
Wor. But yet I would your Father had beene here:
The Qualitie and Heire of our Attempt
Brookes no diuision: It will be thought
By some, that know not why he is away,
That wisedome, loyaltie, and meere dislike
Of our proceedings, kept the Earle from hence.
And thinke, how such an apprehension
May turne the tyde of fearefull Faction,
And breede a kinde of question in our cause:
For well you know, wee of the offring side,
Must keepe aloofe from strict arbitrement,
And stop all sight-holes, euery loope, from whence
The eye of reason may prie in vpon vs.
This absence of your Father drawes a Curtaine,
That shewes the ignorant a kinde of feare,
Before not dreamt of.
Hotsp. You strayne too farre.
I rather of his absence make this vse:
It lends a Lustre, and more great Opinion,
A larger Dare to your great Enterprize,
Then if the Earle were here: for men must thinke,
If we without his helpe, can make a Head
To push against the Kingdome; with his helpe,
We shall o're-turne it topsie-turuy downe:
Yet all goes well, yet all our ioynts are whole.
Dowg. As heart can thinke:
There is not such a word spoke of in Scotland,
At this Dreame of Feare.

Enter Sir Richard Vernon.

Hotsp. My Cousin *Vernon*, welcome by my Soule.
Vern. Pray God my newes be worth a welcome, Lord,
The Earle of Westmerland, seuen thousand strong,
Is marching hither-wards, with Prince *Iohn*.
Hotsp. No harme: what more?
Vern. And further, I haue learn'd,
The King himselfe in person hath set forth,
Or hither-wards intended speedily,
With strong and mightie preparation.
Hotsp. He shall be welcome too.
Where is his Sonne,
The nimble-footed Mad-Cap, Prince of Wales,
And his Cumrades, that daft the World aside,
And bid it passe?
Vern. All furnisht, all in Armes,
All plum'd like Estridges, that with the Winde
Bayted like Eagles, hauing lately bath'd,
Glittering in Golden Coates, like Images,
As full of spirit as the Moneth of May,
And gorgeous as the Sunne at Mid-summer,
Wanton as youthfull Goates, wilde as young Bulls.
I saw young *Harry* with his Beuer on,
His Cushes on his thighes, gallantly arm'd,
Rise from the ground like feathered *Mercury*,
And vaulted with such ease into his Seat,
As if an Angell dropt downe from the Clouds,
To turne and winde a fierie *Pegasus*,
And witch the World with Noble Horsemanship.
Hotsp. No more, no more,
Worse then the Sunne in March:
This prayse doth nourish Agues: let them come.
They come like Sacrifices in their trimme,
And to the fire-ey'd Maid of smoakie Warre,
All hot, and bleeding, will wee offer them:
The mayled *Mars* shall on his Altar sit
Vp to the eares in blood. I am on fire,
To heare this rich reprizall is so nigh,
And yet not ours. Come, let me take my Horse,
Who is to beare me like a Thunder-bolt,
Against the bosome of the Prince of Wales.
Harry to *Harry*, shall not Horse to Horse
Meete, and ne're part, till one drop downe a Coarse?
Oh, that *Glendower* were come.
Ver. There is more newes:
I learned in Worcester, as I rode along,
He cannot draw his Power this foureteene dayes.
Dowg That's the worst Tidings that I heare of yet.
Wor. I by my faith, that beares a frosty sound.
Hotsp. What may the Kings whole Battaile reach vnto?
Ver. To thirty thousand.
Hot. Forty let it be,
My Father and *Glendower* being both away,
The powres of vs, may serue so great a day.
Come, let vs take a muster speedily:
Doomesday is neere; dye all, dye merrily.
Dow. Talke not of dying, I am out of feare
Of death, or deaths hand, for this one halfe yeare.
Exeunt Omnes.

Scena

Scæna Secunda.

Enter Falstaffe and Bardolph.

Falst. *Bardolph*,get thee before to Couentry, fil me a Bottle of Sack,our Souldiers shall march through:wee'le to Sutton-cop-hill to Night.

Bard. Will you giue me Money,Captaine?

Falst. Lay out,lay out.

Bard. This Bottle makes an Angell.

Falst. And if it doe, take it for thy labour: and if it make twentie, take them all, Ile answere the Coynage. Bid my Lieutenant *Peto* meete me at the Townes end.

Bard. I will Captaine: farewell. *Exit.*

Falst. If I be not asham'd of my Souldiers, I am a sowc't-Gurnet: I haue mis-vs'd the Kings Presse damnably. I haue got, in exchange of a hundred and fiftie Souldiers, three hundred and odde Pounds. I presse me none but good House-holders, Yeomens Sonnes:enquire me out contracted Batchelers, such as had beene ask'd twice on the Banes: such a Commoditie of warme slaues, as had as lieue heare the Deuill, as a Drumme; such as feare the report of a Caliuer,worse then a struck-Foole, or a hurt wilde-Ducke. I prest me none but such Tostes and Butter,with Hearts in their Bellyes no bigger then Pinnes heads, and they haue bought out their seruices: And now, my whole Charge consists of Ancients, Corporals, Lieutenants,Gentlemen of Companies, Slaues as ragged as *Lazarus* in the painted Cloth,where the Gluttons Dogges licked his Sores; and such, as indeed were neuer Souldiers, but dis-carded vniust Seruingmen, younger Sonnes to younger Brothers, reuolted Tapsters and Ostlers,Trade-falne, the Cankers of a calme World,and long Peace, tenne times more dis-honorable ragged, then an old-fac'd Ancient; and such haue I to fill vp the roomes of them that haue bought out their seruices: that you would thinke, that I had a hundred and fiftie totter'd Prodigalls,lately come from Swine-keeping,from eating Draffe and Huskes. A mad fellow met me on the way, and told me,I had vnloaded all the Gibbets,and prest the dead bodyes. No eye hath seene such skar-Crowes: Ile not march through Couentry with them,that's flat. Nay, and the Villaines march wide betwixt the Legges, as if they had Gyues on; for indeede, I had the most of them out of Prison. There's not a Shirt and a halfe in all my Company: and the halfe Shirt is two Napkins tackt together, and throwne ouer the shoulders like a Heralds Coat,without sleeues: and the Shirt, to say the truth, stolne from my Host of S. Albones, or the Red-Nose Inne-keeper of Dauintry. But that's all one,they'le finde Linnen enough on euery Hedge.

Enter the Prince,and the Lord of Westmerland.

Prince. How now blowne *Iack*? how now Quilt?

Falst. What *Hal*? How now mad Wag,what a Deuill do'st thou in Warwickshire? My good Lord of Westmerland,I cry you mercy, I thought your Honour had already beene at Shrewsbury.

West. 'Faith,Sir *Iohn*,'tis more then time that I were there, and you too: but my Powers are there alreadie. The King,I can tell you, lookes for vs all: we must away all to Night.

Falst. Tut,neuer feare me,I am as vigilant as a Cat,to steale Creame.

Prince. I thinke to steale Creame indeed,for thy theft hath alreadie made thee Butter: but tell me,*Iack*,whose fellowes are these that come after?

Falst. Mine, *Hal*,mine.

Prince. I did neuer see such pittifull Rascals.

Falst. Tut,tut,good enough to tosse: foode for Powder, foode for Powder: they'le fill a Pit,as well as better: tush man,mortall men,mortall men.

Westm. I, but Sir *Iohn*, me thinkes they are exceeding poore and bare,too beggarly.

Falst. Faith,for their pouertie,I know not where they had that; and for their barenesse, I am sure they neuer learn'd that of me.

Prince. No,Ile be sworne,vnlesse you call three fingers on the Ribbes bare. But sirra,make haste,*Percy* is already in the field.

Falst. What,is the King encamp'd?

Westm. Hee is, Sir *Iohn*, I feare wee shall stay too long.

Falst. Well,to the latter end of a Fray, and the beginning of a Feast, fits a dull fighter, and a keene Guest.

Exeunt.

Scæna Tertia.

Enter Hotspur,Worcester,Dowglas,and Vernon.

Hotsp. Wee'le fight with him to Night.

Worc. It may not be.

Dowg. You giue him then aduantage.

Vern. Not a whit.

Hotsp. Why say you so? lookes he not for supply?

Vern. So doe wee.

Hotsp. His is certaine, ours is doubtfull.

Worc. Good Cousin be aduis'd,stirre not to night.

Vern. Doe not,my Lord.

Dowg. You doe not counsaile well:
You speake it out of feare,and cold heart.

Vern. Doe me no slander, *Dowglas*: by my Life,
And I dare well maintaine it with my Life,
If well-respected Honor bid me on,
I hold as little counsaile with weake feare,
As you,my Lord,or any Scot that this day liues.
Let it be seene to morrow in the Battell,
Which of vs feares.

Dowg. Yea,or to night.

Vern. Content.

Hotsp. To night,say I.

Vern. Come,come,it may not be.
I wonder much,being me of such great leading as you are
That you fore-see not what impediments
Drag backe our expedition: certaine Horse
Of my Cousin *Vernons* are not yet come vp,
Your Vnckle *Worcesters* Horse came but to day,
And now their pride and mettall is asleepe,
Their courage with hard labour tame and dull,
That not a Horse is halfe the halfe of himselfe

Hotsp. So are the Horses of the Enemie
In generall iourney bated,and brought low:
The better part of ours are full of rest.

Worc. The number of the King exceedeth ours:
For Gods sake, Cousin, stay till all come in.

The Trumpet sounds a Parley. Enter Sir Walter Blunt.

Blunt. I come with gracious offers from the King,
If you vouchsafe me hearing, and respect.
Hotsp. Welcome, Sir *Walter Blunt*:
And would to God you were of our determination.
Some of vs loue you well: and euen those some
Enuie your great deseruings, and good name,
Because you are not of our qualitie,
But stand against vs like an Enemie.
Blunt. And Heauen defend, but still I should stand so,
So long as out of Limit, and true Rule,
You stand against anoynted Maiestie.
But to my Charge.
The King hath sent to know
The nature of your Griefes, and whereupon
You coniure from the Brest of Ciuill Peace,
Such bold Hostilitie, teaching his dutious Land
Audacious Crueltie. If that the King
Haue any way your good Deserts forgot,
Which he confesseth to be manifold,
He bids you name your Griefes, and with all speed
You shall haue your desires, with interest;
And Pardon absolute for your selfe, and these,
Herein mis-led, by your suggestion.
Hotsp. The King is kinde:
And well wee know, the King
Knowes at what time to promise, when to pay.
My Father, my Vnckle, and my selfe,
Did giue him that same Royaltie he weares:
And when he was not sixe and twentie strong,
Sicke in the Worlds regard, wretched, and low,
A poore vnminded Out-law, sneaking home,
My Father gaue him welcome to the shore:
And when he heard him sweare, and vow to God,
He came but to be Duke of Lancaster,
To sue his Liuerie, and begge his Peace,
With teares of Innocencie, and tearmes of Zeale;
My Father, in kinde heart and pitty mou'd,
Swore him assistance, and perform'd it too.
Now, when the Lords and Barons of the Realme
Perceiu'd *Northumberland* did leane to him,
The more and lesse came in with Cap and Knee,
Met him in Boroughs, Cities, Villages,
Attended him on Bridges, stood in Lanes,
Layd Gifts before him, proffer'd him their Oathes,
Gaue him their Heires, as Pages followed him,
Euen at the heeles, in golden multitudes.
He presently, as Greatnesse knowes it selfe,
Steps me a little higher then his Vow
Made to my Father, while his blood was poore,
Vpon the naked shore at Rauenspurgh:
And now (forsooth) takes on him to reforme
Some certaine Edicts, and some strait Decrees,
That lay too heauie on the Common-wealth;
Cryes out vpon abuses, seemes to weepe
Ouer his Countries Wrongs: and by this Face,
This seeming Brow of Iustice, did he winne
The hearts of all that hee did angle for.
Proceeded further, cut me off the Heads
Of all the Fauorites, that the absent King
In deputation left behinde him heere,
When hee was personall in the Irish Warre.
Blunt. Tut, I came not to heare this.
Hotsp. Then to the point.
In short time after, hee depos'd the King.
Soone after that, depriu'd him of his Life:
And in the neck of that, task't the whole State.
To make that worse, suffer'd his Kinsman *March*,
Who is, if euery Owner were plac'd,
Indeede his King, to be engag'd in Wales,
There, without Ransome, to lye forfeited:
Disgrac'd me in my happie Victories,
Sought to intrap me by intelligence,
Rated my Vnckle from the Councell-Boord,
In rage dismiss'd my Father from the Court,
Broke Oath on Oath, committed Wrong on Wrong,
And in conclusion, droue vs to seeke out
This Head of safetie; and withall, to prie
Into his Title: the which wee finde
Too indirect, for long continuance.
Blunt. Shall I returne this answer to the King?
Hotsp. Not so, Sir *Walter*.
Wee'le with-draw a while:
Goe to the King, and let there be impawn'd
Some suretie for a safe returne againe,
And in the Morning early shall my Vnckle
Bring him our purpose: and so farewell.
Blunt. I would you would accept of Grace and Loue.
Hotsp. And't may be, so wee shall.
Blunt. Pray Heauen you doe. *Exeunt.*

Scena Quarta.

Enter the Arch-Bishop of Yorke, and Sir Michell.

Arch. Hie, good Sir *Michell*, beare this sealed Briefe
With winged haste to the Lord Marshall,
This to my Cousin *Scroope*, and all the rest
To whom they are directed.
If you knew how much they doe import,
You would make haste.
Sir Mich. My good Lord, I guesse their tenor.
Arch. Like enough you doe.
To morrow, good Sir *Michell*, is a day,
Wherein the fortune of ten thousand men
Must bide the touch. For Sir, at Shrewsbury,
As I am truly giuen to vnderstand,
The King, with mightie and quick-raysed Power,
Meetes with Lord *Harry*: and I feare, Sir *Michell*,
What with the sicknesse of *Northumberland*,
Whose Power was in the first proportion;
And what with *Owen Glendowers* absence thence,
Who with them was rated firmely too,
And comes not in, ouer-rul'd by Prophecies,
I feare the Power of *Percy* is too weake,
To wage an instant tryall with the King.
Sir Mich. Why, my good Lord, you need not feare,
There is *Dowglas*, and Lord *Mortimer*.
Arch. No, *Mortimer* is not there.
Sir Mic. But there is *Mordake*, *Vernon*, Lord *Harry Percy*,
And there is my Lord of Worcester,
And a Head of gallant Warriors,
Noble Gentlemen.

Arch. And so there is, but yet the King hath drawne
The speciall head of all the Land together:
The Prince of Wales, Lord *Iohn* of Lancaster,
The Noble Westmerland, and warlike *Blunt*;
And many moe Corriuals, and deare men
Of estimation, and command in Armes.
Sir M. Doubt not my Lord, he shall be well oppos'd
Arch. I hope no lesse? Yet needfull 'tis to feare,
And to preuent the worst, Sir *Michell* speed;
For if Lord *Percy* thriue not, ere the King
Dismisse his power, he meanes to visit vs:
For he hath heard of our Confederacie,
And, 'tis but Wisedome to make strong against him:
Therefore make hast, I must go write againe
To other Friends: and so farewell, Sir *Michell*. *Exeunt.*

Actus Quintus. Scena Prima.

Enter the King, Prince of Wales, Lord Iohn of Lancaster, Earle of Westmerland, Sir Walter Blunt, and Falstaffe.

King. How bloodily the Sunne begins to peere
Aboue yon busky hill: the day lookes pale
At his distemperature.
Prin. The Southerne winde
Doth play the Trumpet to his purposes,
And by his hollow whistling in the Leaues,
Fortels a Tempest, and a blust'ring day.
King. Then with the losers let it sympathize,
For nothing can seeme foule to those that win.
The Trumpet sounds.
Enter Worcester.

King. How now my Lord of Worster? 'Tis not well
That you and I should meet vpon such tearmes,
As now we meet. You haue deceiu'd our trust,
And made vs doffe our easie Robes of Peace,
To crush our old limbes in vngentle Steele:
This is not well, my Lord, this is not well.
What say you to it? Will you againe vnknit
This churlish knot of all-abhorred Warre?
And moue in that obedient Orbe againe,
Where you did giue a faire and naturall light,
And be no more an exhall'd Meteor,
A prodigie of Feare, and a Portent
Of broached Mischeefe, to the vnborne Times?
Wor. Heare me, my Liege:
For mine owne part, I could be well content
To entertaine the Lagge-end of my life
With quiet houres: For I do protest,
I haue not sought the day of this dislike.
King. You haue not sought it: how comes it then?
Fal. Rebellion lay in his way, and he found it.
Prin. Peace, Chewet, peace.
Wor. It pleas'd your Maiesty, to turne your lookes
Of Fauour, from my Selfe, and all our House;
And yet I must remember you my Lord,
We were the first, and dearest of your Friends:
For you, my staffe of Office did I breake
In *Richards* time, and poasted day and night
To meete you on the way, and kisse your hand,
When yet you were in place, and in account
Nothing so strong and fortunate, as I;
It was my Selfe, my Brother, and his Sonne,
That brought you home, and boldly did out-dare
The danger of the time. You swore to vs,
And you did sweare that Oath at Doncaster,
That you did nothing of purpose 'gainst the State,
Nor claime no further, then your new-falne right,
The seate of *Gaunt*, Dukedome of Lancaster,
To this, we sware our aide: But in short space,
It rain'd downe Fortune showring on your head,
And such a floud of Greatnesse fell on you,
What with our helpe, what with the absent King,
What with the iniuries of wanton time,
The seeming sufferances that you had borne,
And the contrarious Windes that held the King
So long in the vnlucky Irish Warres,
That all in England did repute him dead:
And from this swarme of faire aduantages,
You tooke occasion to be quickly woo'd,
To gripe the generall sway into your hand,
Forgot your Oath to vs at Doncaster,
And being fed by vs, you vs'd vs so,
As that vngentle gull the Cuckowes Bird,
Vseth the Sparrow, did oppresse our Nest,
Grew by our Feeding, to so great a bulke,
That euen our Loue durst not come neere your sight
For feare of swallowing: But with nimble wing
We were inforc'd for safety sake, to flye
Out of your sight, and raise this present Head,
Whereby we stand opposed by such meanes
As you your selfe, haue forg'd against your selfe,
By vnkinde vsage, dangerous countenance,
And violation of all faith and troth
Sworne to vs in yonger enterprize.
Kin. These things indeede you haue articulated,
Proclaim'd at Market Crosses, read in Churches,
To face the Garment of Rebellion
With some fine colour, that may please the eye
Of fickle Changelings, and poore Discontents,
Which gape, and rub the Elbow at the newes
Of hurly burly Innouation:
And neuer yet did Insurrection want
Such water-colours, to impaint his cause:
Nor moody Beggars, staruing for a time
Of pell-mell hauocke, and confusion.
Prin. In both our Armies, there is many a soule
Shall pay full dearely for this encounter,
If once they ioyne in triall. Tell your Nephew,
The Prince of Wales doth ioyne with all the world
In praise of *Henry Percie*: By my Hopes,
This present enterprize set off his head,
I do not thinke a brauer Gentleman,
More actiue, valiant, or more valiant yong,
More daring, or more bold, is now aliue,
To grace this latter Age with Noble deeds.
For my part, I may speake it to my shame,
I haue a Truant beene to Chiualry,
And so I heare, he doth account me too:
Yet this before my Fathers Maiesty,
I am content that he shall take the oddes
Of his great name and estimation,
And will, to saue the blood on either side,
Try fortune with him, in a Single Fight.
King. And Prince of Wales, so dare we venter thee,
Albeit, considerations infinite

Do

Do make against it: No good Worster, no,
We loue our people well; euen those we loue
That are misled vpon your Cousins part:
And will they take the offer of our Grace:
Both he, and they, and you; yea, euery man
Shall be my Friend againe, and Ile be his.
So tell your Cousin, and bring me word,
What he will do. But if he will not yeeld,
Rebuke and dread correction waite on vs,
And they shall do their Office. So bee gone,
We will not now be troubled with reply,
We offer faire, take it aduisedly.

Exit Worcester.

Prin. It will not be accepted, on my life,
The *Dowglas* and the *Hotspurre* both together,
Are confident against the world in Armes.

King. Hence therefore, euery Leader to his charge,
For on their answer will we set on them;
And God befriend vs, as our cause is iust. *Exeunt.*

Manet Prince and Falstaffe.

Fal. *Hal*, if thou see me downe in the battell,
And bestride me, so; 'tis a point of friendship.

Prin. Nothing but a Colossus can do thee that frendship
Say thy prayers, and farewell.

Fal. I would it were bed time *Hal*, and all well.

Prin. Why, thou ow'st heauen a death.

Falst. 'Tis not due yet: I would bee loath to pay him before his day. What neede I bee so forward with him, that call's not on me? Well, 'tis no matter, Honor prickes me on. But how if Honour pricke me off when I come on? How then? Can Honour set too a legge? No: or an arme? No: Or take away the greefe of a wound? No. Honour hath no skill in Surgerie, then? No. What is Honour? A word. What is that word Honour? Ayre: A trim reckoning. Who hath it? He that dy'de a Wednesday. Doth he feele it? No. Doth hee heare it? No. Is it insensible then? yea, to the dead. But wil it not liue with the liuing? No. Why? Detraction wil not suffer it, therfore Ile none of it. Honour is a meere Scutcheon, and so ends my Catechisme. *Exit.*

Scena Secunda.

Enter Worcester, and Sir Richard Vernon.

Wor. O no, my Nephew must not know, Sir *Richard*,
The liberall kinde offer of the King.

Ver. 'Twere best he did.

Wor. Then we are all vndone.
It is not possible, it cannot be,
The King would keepe his word in louing vs,
He will suspect vs still, and finde a time
To punish this offence in others faults:
Supposition, all our liues, shall be stucke full of eyes;
For Treason is but trusted like the Foxe,
Who ne're so tame, so cherisht, and lock'd vp,
Will haue a wilde tricke of his Ancestors:
Looke how he can, or sad or merrily,
Interpretation will misquote our lookes,
And we shall feede like Oxen at a stall,
The better cherisht, still the nearer death.
My Nephewes trespasse may be well forgot,
It hath the excuse of youth, and heate of blood,
And an adopted name of Priuiledge,
A haire-brain'd *Hotspurre*, gouern'd by a Spleene:
All his offences liue vpon my head,
And on his Fathers. We did traine him on,
And his corruption being tane from vs,
We as the Spring of all, shall pay for all:
Therefore good Cousin, let not *Harry* know
In any case, the offer of the King.

Ver. Deliuer what you will, Ile say 'tis so.
Heere comes your Cosin.

Enter Hotspurre.

Hot. My Vnkle is return'd,
Deliuer vp my Lord of Westmerland.
Vnkle, what newes?

Wor. The King will bid you battell presently.

Dow. Defie him by the Lord of Westmerland.

Hot. Lord *Dowglas*: Go you and tell him so.

Dow. Marry and shall, and verie willingly.

Exit Dowglas.

Wor. There is no seeming mercy in the King.

Hot. Did you begge any? God forbid.

Wor. I told him gently of our greeuances,
Of his Oath-breaking: which he mended thus,
By now forswearing that he is forsworne,
He cals vs Rebels, Traitors, and will scourge
With haughty armes, this hatefull name in vs.

Enter Dowglas.

Dow. Arme Gentlemen, to Armes, for I haue thrown
A braue defiance in King *Henries* teeth:
And Westmerland that was ingag'd did beare it,
Which cannot choose but bring him quickly on.

Wor. The Prince of Wales stept forth before the king,
And Nephew, challeng'd you to single fight.

Hot. O, would the quarrell lay vpon our heads,
And that no man might draw short breath to day,
But I and *Harry Monmouth*. Tell me, tell mee,
How shew'd his Talking? Seem'd it in contempt?

Ver. No, by my Soule: I neuer in my life
Did heare a Challenge vrg'd more modestly,
Vnlesse a Brother should a Brother dare
To gentle exercise, and proofe of Armes.
He gaue you all the Duties of a Man,
Trimm'd vp your praises with a Princely tongue,
Spoke your deseruings like a Chronicle,
Making you euer better then his praise,
By still dispraising praise, valew'd with you:
And which became him like a Prince indeed,
He made a blushing citall of himselfe,
And chid his Trewant youth with such a Grace,
As if he mastred there a double spirit
Of teaching, and of learning instantly:
There did he pause. But let me tell the World,
If he out-liue the enuie of this day,
England did neuer owe so sweet a hope,
So much misconstrued in his Wantonnesse.

Hot. Cousin, I thinke thou art enamored
On his Follies: neuer did I heare
Of any Prince so wilde at Liberty.
But be he as he will, yet once ere night,
I will imbrace him with a Souldiers arme,
That he shall shrinke vnder my curtesie.
Arme, arme with speed. And Fellow's, Soldiers, Friends,
Better consider what you haue to do,
That I that haue not well the gift of Tongue,

Can lift your blood vp with perswasion.

Enter a Messenger.

Mes. My Lord, heere are Letters for you.

Hot. I cannot reade them now.
O Gentlemen, the time of life is short;
To spend that shortnesse basely, were too long.
If life did ride vpon a Dials point,
Still ending at the arriuall of an houre,
And if we liue, we liue to treade on Kings:
If dye; braue death, when Princes dye with vs.
Now for our Consciences, the Armes is faire,
When the intent for bearing them is iust.

Enter another Messenger.

Mes. My Lord prepare, the King comes on apace.

Hot. I thanke him, that he cuts me from my tale:
For I professe not talking: Onely this,
Let each man do his best. And heere I draw a Sword,
Whose worthy temper I intend to staine
With the best blood that I can meete withall,
In the aduenture of this perillous day.
Now Esperance *Percy*, and set on:
Sound all the lofty Instruments of Warre,
And by that Musicke, let vs all imbrace:
For heauen to earth, some of vs neuer shall,
A second time do such a curtesie.

They embrace, the Trumpets sound, the King entereth with his power, alarum vnto the battell. Then enter Dowglas, and Sir Walter Blunt.

Blu. What is thy name, that in battel thus ŷ crossest me?
What honor dost thou seeke vpon my head?

Dow. Know then my name is *Dowglas*,
And I do haunt thee in the battell thus,
Because some tell me, that thou art a King.

Blunt. They tell thee true.

Dow. The Lord of Stafford deere to day hath bought
Thy likenesse: for insted of thee King *Harry*,
This Sword hath ended him, so shall it thee,
Vnlesse thou yeeld thee as a Prisoner.

Blu. I was not borne to yeeld, thou haughty Scot,
And thou shalt finde a King that will reuenge
Lords Staffords death.

Fight, Blunt is slaine, then enters Hotspur.

Hot. O *Dowglas*, hadst thou fought at Holmedon thus
I neuer had triumphed o're a Scot.

Dow. All's done, all's won, here breathles lies the king

Hot. Where?

Dow. Heere.

Hot. This *Dowglas*? No I know this face full well:
A gallant Knight he was, his name was *Blunt*,
Semblably furnish'd like the King himselfe.

Dow. Ah foole: go with thy soule whether it goes,
A borrowed Title hast thou bought too deere.
Why didst thou tell me, that thou wer't a King?

Hot. The King hath many marching in his Coats.

Dow. Now by my Sword, I will kill all his Coates,
Ile murder all his Wardrobe peece by peece,
Vntill I meet the King.

Hot. Vp, and away,
Our Souldiers stand full fairely for the day. *Exeunt*

Alarum, and enter Falstaffe solus.

Fal. Though I could scape shot-free at London, I fear the shot heere: here's no scoring, but vpon the pate. Soft who are you? Sir *Walter Blunt*, there's Honour for you: here's no vanity, I am as hot as molten Lead, and as heauy too; heauen keepe Lead out of mee, I neede no more weight then mine owne Bowelles. I haue led my rag of Muffins where they are pepper'd: there's not three of my 150. left aliue, and they for the Townes end, to beg during life. But who comes heere?

Enter the Prince.

Pri. What, stand'st thou idle here? Lend me thy sword,
Many a Nobleman lies starke and stiffe
Vnder the hooues of vaunting enemies,
Whose deaths are vnreueng'd. Prethy lend me thy sword

Fal. O *Hal*, I prethee giue me leaue to breath awhile: Turke *Gregory* neuer did such deeds in Armes, as I haue done this day. I haue paid *Percy*, I haue made him sure.

Prin. He is indeed, and liuing to kill thee:
I prethee lend me thy sword.

Falst. Nay *Hal*, if *Percy* bee aliue, thou getst not my Sword; but take my Pistoll if thou wilt.

Prin. Giue it me: What, is it in the Case?

Fal. I *Hal*, 'tis hot: There's that will Sacke a City.

The Prince drawes out a Bottle of Sacke.

Prin. What, is it a time to iest and dally now. *Exit.*

Throwes it at him.

Fal. If *Percy* be aliue, Ile pierce him: if he do come in my way, so: if he do not, if I come in his (willingly) let him make a Carbonado of me. I like not such grinning honour as Sir *Walter* hath: Giue mee life, which if I can saue, so: if not, honour comes vnlook'd for, and ther's an end. *Exit*

Scena Tertia.

Alarum, excursions, enter the King, the Prince, Lord Iohn of Lancaster, and Earle of Westmerland.

King. I prethee *Harry* withdraw thy selfe, thou bleedest too much: Lord *Iohn of Lancaster*, go you with him.

P. Ioh. Not I, my Lord, vnlesse I did bleed too.

Prin. I beseech your Maiesty make vp,
Least you retirement do amaze your friends.

King. I will do so:
My Lord of Westmerland leade him to his Tent.

West. Come my Lord, Ile leade you to your Tent.

Prin. Lead me my Lord? I do not need your helpe;
And heauen forbid a shallow scratch should driue
The Prince of Wales from such a field as this,
Where stain'd Nobility lyes troden on,
And Rebels Armes triumph in massacres.

Ioh. We breath too long: Come cosin Westmerland
Our duty this way lies, for heauens sake come.

Prin. By heauen thou hast deceiu'd me Lancaster,
I did not thinke thee Lord of such a spirit:
Before, I lou'd thee as a Brother, *Iohn*;
But now, I do respect thee as my Soule.

King. I saw him hold Lord *Percy* at the point
With lustier maintenance then I did looke for
Of such an vngrowne Warriour.

Prin. O this Boy, lends mettall to vs all. *Exit.*

Enter Dowglas.

Dow. Another King? They grow like Hydra's heads:
I am the *Dowglas*, fatall to all those
That weare those colours on them. What art thou
That counterfeit'st the person of a King?

King. The King himselfe: who *Dowglas* grieues at hart

So many of his shadowes thou hast met,
And not the very King. I haue two Boyes
Seeke *Percy* and thy selfe about the Field:
But seeing thou fall'st on me so luckily,
I will assay thee: so defend thy selfe.

Dow. I feare thou art another counterfeit:
And yet infaith thou bear'st thee like a King:
But mine I am sure thou art, whoere thou be,
And thus I win thee. *They fight, the K. being in danger,*

Enter Prince.

Prin. Hold vp they head vile Scot, or thou art like
Neuer to hold it vp againe: the Spirits
Of valiant *Sherly, Stafford, Blunt,* are in my Armes;
It is the Prince of Wales that threatens thee,
Who neuer promiseth, but he meanes to pay.

They Fight, Dowglas flyeth.

Cheerely My Lord: how fare's your Grace?
Sir *Nicholas Gawsey* hath for succour sent,
And so hath *Clifton*: Ile to *Clifton* straight.

King. Stay, and breath awhile.
Thou hast redeem'd thy lost opinion,
And shew'd thou mak'st some tender of my life
In this faire rescue thou hast brought to mee.

Prin. O heauen, they did me too much iniury,
That euer said I hearkned to your death.
If it were so, I might haue let alone
The insulting hand of *Dowglas* ouer you,
Which would haue bene as speedy in your end,
As all the poysonous Potions in the world,
And sau'd the Treacherous labour of your Sonne.

K. Make vp to *Clifton*, Ile to Sir *Nicholas Gausey. Exit*

Enter Hotspur.

Hot. If I mistake not, thou art *Harry Monmouth.*

Prin. Thou speak'st as if I would deny my name.

Hot. My name is *Harrie Percie.*

Prin. Why then I see a very valiant rebel of that name.
I am the Prince of Wales, and thinke not *Percy,*
To share with me in glory any more:
Two Starres keepe not their motion in one Sphere,
Nor can one England brooke a double reigne,
Of *Harry Percy,* and the Prince of Wales.

Hot. Nor shall it *Harry* for the houre is come
To end the one of vs; and would to heauen,
Thy name in Armes, were now as great as mine.

Prin. Ile make it greater, ere I part from thee,
And all the budding Honors on thy Crest,
Ile crop, to make a Garland for my head.

Hot. I can no longer brooke thy Vanities. *Fight.*

Enter Falstaffe.

Fal. Well said *Hal*, to it *Hal*. Nay you shall finde no
Boyes play heere, I can tell you.

Enter Dowglas, he fights with Falstaffe, who fals down as if he were dead. The Prince killeth Percie.

Hot. Oh *Harry*, thou hast rob'd me of my youth:
I better brooke the losse of brittle life,
Then those proud Titles thou hast wonne of me,
They wound my thoghts worse, then the sword my flesh:
But thought's the slaue of Life, and Life, Times foole;
And Time, that takes suruey of all the world,
Must haue a stop. O, I could Prophesie,
But that the Earth, and the cold hand of death,
Lyes on my Tongue: No *Percy*, thou art dust
And food for

Prin. For Wormes, braue *Percy*. Farewell great heart:
Ill-weau'd Ambition, how much art thou shrunke?
When that this bodie did containe a spirit,
A Kingdome for it was too small a bound:
But now two paces of the vilest Earth
Is roome enough. This Earth that beares the dead,
Beares not aliue so stout a Gentleman.
If thou wer't sensible of curtesie,
I should not make so great a shew of Zeale.
But let my fauours hide thy mangled face,
And euen in thy behalfe, Ile thanke my selfe
For doing these fayre Rites of Tendernesse.
Adieu, and take thy praise with thee to heauen,
Thy ignomy sleepe with thee in the graue,
But not remembred in thy Epitaph.
What? Old Acquaintance? Could not all this flesh
Keepe in a little life? Poore Iacke, farewell:
I could haue better spar'd a better man.
O, I should haue a heauy misse of thee,
If I were much in loue with Vanity.
Death hath not strucke so fat a Deere to day,
Though many dearer in this bloody Fray:
Imbowell'd will I see thee by and by,
Till then, in blood, by Noble *Percie* lye. *Exit.*

Falstaffe riseth vp.

Falst. Imbowell'd? If thou imbowell mee to day, Ile giue you leaue to powder me, and eat me too to morow. 'Twas time to counterfet, or that hotte Termagant Scot, had paid me scot and lot too. Counterfeit? I am no counterfeit; to dye, is to be a counterfeit, for hee is but the counterfeit of a man, who hath not the life of a man: But to counterfeit dying, when a man thereby liueth, is to be no counterfeit, but the true and perfect image of life indeede. The better part of Valour, is Discretion; in the which better part, I haue saued my life. I am affraide of this Gun-powder *Percy* though he be dead. How if hee should counterfeit too, and rise? I am afraid hee would proue the better counterfeit: therefore Ile make him sure: yea, and Ile sweare I kill'd him. Why may not hee rise as well as I: Nothing confutes me but eyes, and no-bodie sees me. Therefore sirra, with a new wound in your thigh come you along me. *Takes Hotspurre on his backe.*

Enter Prince and Iohn of Lancaster.

Prin. Come Brother *Iohn*, full brauely hast thou flesht thy Maiden sword.

Iohn. But soft, who haue we heere?
Did you not tell me this Fat man was dead?

Prin. I did, I saw him dead,
Breathlesse and bleeding on the ground: Art thou aliue?
Or is it fantasie that playes vpon our eye-sight?
I prethee speake, we will not trust our eyes
Without our eares. Thou art not what thou seem'st.

Fal. No, that's certaine: I am not a double man: but if I be not *Iacke Falstaffe*, then am I a Iacke: There is *Percy*, if your Father will do me any Honor, so: if not, let him kill the next *Percie* himselfe. I looke to be either Earle or Duke, I can assure you.

Prin. Why, *Percy* I kill'd my selfe, and saw thee dead.

Fal. Did'st thou? Lord, Lord, how the world is giuen to Lying? I graunt you I was downe, and out of Breath, and so was he, but we rose both at an instant, and fought a long houre by Shrewsburie clocke. If I may bee beleeued, so: if not, let them that should reward Valour, beare the sinne vpon their owne heads. Ile take't on my death I gaue him this wound in the Thigh: if the man vvere aliue, and would deny it, I would make him eate a peece of my sword.

Iohn. This is the strangest Tale that e're I heard.

Prin. This is the strangest Fellow, Brother *Iohn.*

Come

Come bring your luggage Nobly on your backe:
For my part, if a lye may do thee grace,
Ile gil'd it with the happiest tearmes I haue.

A Retreat is sounded.

The Trumpets sound Retreat, the day is ours:
Come Brother, let's to the highest of the field,
To see what Friends are liuing, who are dead. *Exeunt*

Fal. Ile follow as they say, for Reward. Hee that rewards me, heauen reward him. If I do grow great again, Ile grow lesse? For Ile purge, and leaue Sacke, and liue cleanly, as a Nobleman should do. *Exit*

Scæna Quarta.

The Trumpets sound.
Enter the King, Prince of Wales, Lord Iohn of Lancaster, Earle of Westmerland, with Worcester & Vernon Prisoners.

King. Thus euer did Rebellion finde Rebuke.
Ill-spirited Worcester, did we not send Grace,
Pardon, and tearmes of Loue to all of you?
And would'st thou turne our offers contrary?
Misuse the tenor of thy Kinsmans trust?
Three Knights vpon our party slaine to day,
A Noble Earle, and many a creature else,
Had beene aliue this houre,
If like a Christian thou had'st truly borne
Betwixt out Armies, true Intelligence.

Wor. What I haue done, my safety vrg'd me to,
And I embrace this fortune patiently,
Since not to be auoyded, it fals on mee.

King. Beare Worcester to death, and *Vernon* too:
Other Offenders we will pause vpon.

Exit Worcester and Vernon.

How goes the Field?

Prin. The Noble Scot Lord *Dowglas*, when hee saw
The fortune of the day quite turn'd from him,
The Noble *Percy* slaine, and all his men,
Vpon the foot of feare, fled with the rest;
And falling from a hill, he was so bruiz'd
That the pursuers tooke him. At my Tent
The *Dowglas* is, and I beseech your Grace,
I may dispose of him.

King. With all my heart.

Prin. Then Brother *Iohn* of Lancaster,
To you this honourable bounty shall belong:
Go to the *Dowglas*, and deliuer him
Vp to his pleasure, ransomlesse and free:
His Valour shewne vpon our Crests to day,
Hath taught vs how to cherish such high deeds,
Euen in the bosome of our Aduersaries.

King. Then this remaines: that we diuide our Power.
You Sonne *Iohn*, and my Cousin Westmerland
Towards Yorke shall bend you, with your deerest speed
To meet Northumberland, and the Prelate *Scroope*,
Who (as we heare) are busily in Armes.
My Selfe, and you Sonne *Harry* will towards Wales,
To fight with *Glendower*, and the Earle of March.
Rebellion in this Land shall lose his way,
Meeting the Checke of such another day:
And since this Businesse so faire is done,
Let vs not leaue till all our owne be wonne. *Exeunt.*

FINIS.

The Second Part of Henry the Fourth, Containing his Death: and the Coronation of King Henry the Fift.

Actus Primus. Scœna Prima.

INDVCTION.

Enter Rumour.

OPen your Eares: For which of you will stop
The vent of Hearing, when loud *Rumor* speakes?
I, from the Orient, to the drooping West
(Making the winde my Post-horse) still vnfold
The Acts commenced on this Ball of Earth.
Vpon my Tongue, continuall Slanders ride,
The which, in euery Language, I pronounce,
Stuffing the Eares of them with false Reports:
I speake of Peace, while couert Enmitie
(Vnder the smile of Safety) wounds the World:
And who but *Rumour*, who but onely I
Make fearfull Musters, and prepar'd Defence,
Whil'st the bigge yeare, swolne with some other griefes,
Is thought with childe, by the sterne Tyrant, Warre,
And no such matter? *Rumour*, is a Pipe
Blowne by Surmises, Ielousies, Coniectures;
And of so easie, and so plaine a stop,
That the blunt Monster, with vncounted heads,
The still discordant, wauering Multitude,
Can play vpon it. But what neede I thus
My well-knowne Body to Anathomize
Among my houshold? Why is *Rumour* heere?
I run before King *Harries* victory,
Who in a bloodie field by Shrewsburie
Hath beaten downe yong *Hotspurre*, aud his Troopes,
Quenching the flame of bold Rebellion,
Euen with the Rebels blood. But what meane I
To speake so true at first? My Office is
To noyse abroad, that *Harry Monmouth* fell
Vnder the Wrath of Noble *Hotspurres* Sword:
And that the King, before the *Dowglas* Rage
Stoop'd his Annointed head, as low as death.
This haue I rumour'd through the peasant-Townes,
Betweene the Royall Field of Shrewsburie,
And this Worme-eaten-Hole of ragged Stone,
Where *Hotspurres* Father, old Northumberland,
Lyes crafty sicke. The Postes come tyring on,
And not a man of them brings other newes
Then they haue learn'd of Me. From *Rumours* Tongues,
They bring smooth-Comforts-false, worse then True-wrongs. *Exit.*

Scena Secunda.

Enter Lord Bardolfe, and the Porter.

L.Bar. Who keepes the Gate heere hoa?
Where is the Earle?
Por. What shall I say you are?
Bar. Tell thou the Earle
That the Lord *Bardolfe* doth attend him heere.
Por. His Lordship is walk'd forth into the Orchard,
Please it your Honor, knocke but at the Gate,
And he himselfe will answer.

Enter Northumberland.

L.Bar. Heere comes the Earle.
Nor. What newes Lord *Bardolfe*? Eu'ry minute now
Should be the Father of some Stratagem;
The Times are wilde: Contention (like a Horse
Full of high Feeding) madly hath broke loose,
And beares downe all before him.
L.Bar. Noble Earle,
I bring you certaine newes from Shrewsbury.
Nor. Good, and heauen will.
L.Bar. As good as heart can wish:
The King is almost wounded to the death:
And in the Fortune of my Lord your Sonne,
Prince *Harrie* slaine out-right: and both the *Blunts*
Kill'd by the hand of *Dowglas*. Yong Prince *Iohn*,
And Westmerland, and Stafford, fled the Field.
And *Harrie Monmouth's* Brawne (the Hulke Sir *Iohn*)
Is prisoner to your Sonne. O, such a Day,
(So fought, so follow'd, and so fairely wonne)
Came not, till now, to dignifie the Times
Since *Cæsars* Fortunes.
Nor. How is this deriu'd?
Saw you the Field? Came you from Shrewsbury?
L.Bar I spake with one (my L.) that came frõ thence,
A Gentleman well bred, and of good name,
That freely render'd me these newes for true.
Nor. Heere comes my Seruant *Trauers*, whom I sent
On Tuesday last, to listen after Newes.

Enter Trauers.

L.Bar. My Lord, I ouer-rod him on the way,
And he is furnish'd with no certainties,
More then he (haply) may retaile from me.
Nor. Now *Trauers*, what good tidings comes frõ you?

Tra.

Tra. My Lord, Sir *Iohn Umfreuill* turn'd me backe
With ioyfull tydings; and (being better hors'd)
Out-rod me. After him, came spurring head
A Gentleman (almost fore-spent with speed)
That stopp'd by me, to breath his bloodied horse.
He ask'd the way to Chester: And of him
I did demand what Newes from Shrewsbury:
He told me, that Rebellion had ill lucke,
And that yong *Harry Percies* Spurre was cold.
With that he gaue his able Horse the head,
And bending forwards strooke his able heeles
Against the panting sides of his poore Iade
Vp to the Rowell head, and starting so,
He seem'd in running, to deuoure the way,
Staying no longer question.

North. Ha? Againe:
Said he yong *Harrie Percyes* Spurre was cold?
(Of *Hot-Spurre*, cold-Spurre?) that Rebellion,
Had met ill lucke?

L.Bar. My Lord: Ile tell you what,
If my yong Lord your Sonne, haue not the day,
Vpon mine Honor, for a silken point
Ile giue my Barony. Neuer talke of it.

Nor. Why should the Gentleman that rode by *Trauers*
Giue then such instances of Losse?

L.Bar. Who, he?
He was some hielding Fellow, that had stolne
The Horse he rode-on: and vpon my life
Speake at aduenture. Looke, here comes more Newes.

Enter Morton.

Nor. Yea, this mans brow, like to a Title-leafe,
Fore-tels the Nature of a Tragicke Volume:
So lookes the Strond, when the Imperious Flood
Hath left a witnest Vsurpation.
Say *Morton*, did'st thou come from Shrewsbury?

Mor. I ran from Shrewsbury (my Noble Lord)
Where hatefull death put on his vgliest Maske
To fright our party.

North. How doth my Sonne, and Brother?
Thou trembl'st; and the whitenesse in thy Cheeke
Is apter then thy Tongue, to tell thy Errand.
Euen such a man, so faint, so spiritlesse,
So dull, so dead in looke, so woe-be-gone,
Drew *Priams* Curtaine, in the dead of night,
And would haue told him, Halfe his Troy was burn'd.
But *Priam* found the Fire, ere he his Tongue:
And I, my *Percies* death, ere thou report'st it.
This, thou would'st say: Your Sonne did thus, and thus:
Your Brother, thus. So fought the Noble *Dowglas*,
Stopping my greedy eare, with their bold deeds.
But in the end (to stop mine Eare indeed)
Thou hast a Sigh, to blow away this Praise,
Ending with Brother, Sonne, and all are dead.

Mor. *Dowglas* is liuing, and your Brother, yet:
But for my Lord, your Sonne.

North. Why he is dead.
See what a ready tongue Suspition hath:
He that but feares the thing, he would not know,
Hath by Instinct, knowledge from others Eyes,
That what he feard, is chanc'd. Yet speake (*Morton*)
Tell thou thy Earle, his Diuination Lies,
And I will take it, as a sweet Disgrace,
And make thee rich, for doing me such wrong.

Mor. You are too great, to be (by me) gainsaid:
Your Spirit is too true, your Feares too certaine.

North. Yet for all this, say not that *Percies* dead.
I see a strange Confession in thine Eye:
Thou shak'st thy head, and hold'st it Feare, or Sinne,
To speake a truth. If he be slaine, say so:
The Tongue offends not, that reports his death:
And he doth sinne that doth belye the dead:
Not he, which sayes the dead is not aliue:
Yet the first bringer of vnwelcome Newes
Hath but a loosing Office: and his Tongue,
Sounds euer after as a sullen Bell
Remembred, knolling a departing Friend.

L.Bar. I cannot thinke (my Lord) your son is dead.

Mor. I am sorry, I should force you to beleeue
That, which I would to heauen, I had not seene.
But these mine eyes, saw him in bloody state,
Rend'ring faint quittance (wearied, and out-breath'd)
To *Henrie Monmouth*, whose swift wrath beate downe
The neuer-daunted *Percie* to the earth,
From whence (with life) he neuer more sprung vp.
In few; his death (whose spirit lent a fire,
Euen to the dullest Peazant in his Campe)
Being bruited once, tooke fire and heate away
From the best temper'd Courage in his Troopes.
For from his Mettle, was his Party steel'd;
Which once, in him abated, all the rest
Turn'd on themselues, like dull and heauy Lead:
And as the Thing, that's heauy in it selfe,
Vpon enforcement, flyes with greatest speede,
So did our Men, heauy in *Hotspurres* losse,
Lend to this weight, such lightnesse with their Feare,
That Arrowes fled not swifter toward their ayme,
Then did our Soldiers (ayming at their safety)
Fly from the field. Then was that Noble Worcester
Too soone ta'ne prisoner: and that furious Scot,
(The bloody *Dowglas*) whose well-labouring sword
Had three times slaine th'appearance of the King,
Gan vaile his stomacke, and did grace the shame
Of those that turn'd their backes: and in his flight,
Stumbling in Feare, was tooke. The summe of all,
Is, that the King hath wonne: and hath sent out
A speedy power, to encounter you my Lord,
Vnder the Conduct of yong Lancaster
And Westmerland. This is the Newes at full.

North. For this, I shall haue time enough to mourne.
In Poyson, there is Physicke: and this newes
(Hauing beene well) that would haue made me sicke,
Being sicke, haue in some measure, made me well.
And as the Wretch, whose Feauer-weakned ioynts,
Like strengthlesse Hindges, buckle vnder life,
Impatient of his Fit, breakes like a fire
Out of his keepers armes: Euen so, my Limbes
(Weak'ned with greefe) being now inrag'd with greefe,
Are thrice themselues. Hence therefore thou nice crutch,
A scalie Gauntlet now, with ioynts of Steele
Must gloue this hand. And hence thou sickly Quoife,
Thou art a guard too wanton for the head,
Which Princes, flesh'd with Conquest, ayme to hit.
Now binde my Browes with Iron, and approach
The ragged'st houre, that Time and Spight dare bring
To frowne vpon th'enrag'd Northumberland.
Let Heauen kisse Earth: now let not Natures hand
Keepe the wilde Flood confin'd: Let Order dye,
And let the world no longer be a stage
To feede Contention in a ling'ring Act:
But let one spirit of the First-borne *Caine*

Reigne in all bosomes, that each heart being set
On bloody Courses, the rude Scene may end,
And darknesse be the burier of the dead.

L.Bar. Sweet Earle, diuorce not wisedom from your (Honor.

Mor. The liues of all your louing Complices
Leane-on your health, the which if you giue o're
To stormy Passion, must perforce decay.
You cast th'euent of Warre (my Noble Lord)
And summ'd the accompt of Chance, before you said
Let vs make head: It was your presurmize,
That in the dole of blowes, your Son might drop.
You knew he walk'd o're perils, on an edge
More likely to fall in, then to get o're:
You were aduis'd his flesh was capeable
Of Wounds, and Scarres; and that his forward Spirit
Would lift him, where most trade of danger rang'd,
Yet did you say go forth: and none of this
(Though strongly apprehended) could restraine
The stiffe-borne Action: What hath then befalne?
Or what hath this bold enterprize bring forth,
More then that Being, which was like to be?

L.Bar. We all that are engaged to this losse,
Knew that we ventur'd on such dangerous Seas,
That if we wrought out life, was ten to one:
And yet we ventur'd for the gaine propos'd,
Choak'd the respect of likely perill fear'd,
And since we are o're-set, venture againe.
Come, we will all put forth; Body, and Goods,

Mor. 'Tis more then time: And (my most Noble Lord)
I heare for certaine, and do speake the truth:
The gentle Arch-bishop of Yorke is vp
With well appointed Powres: he is a man
Who with a double Surety bindes his Followers.
My Lord (your Sonne) had onely but the Corpes,
But shadowes, and the shewes of men to fight.
For that same word (Rebellion) did diuide
The action of their bodies, from their soules,
And they did fight with queasinesse, constrain'd
As men drinke Potions; that their Weapons only
Seem'd on our side: but for their Spirits and Soules,
This word (Rebellion) it had froze them vp,
As Fish are in a Pond. But now the Bishop
Turnes Insurrection to Religion,
Suppos'd sincere, and holy in his Thoughts:
He's follow'd both with Body, and with Minde:
And doth enlarge his Rising, with the blood
Of faire King *Richard*, scrap'd from Pomfret stones,
Deriues from heauen, his Quarrell, and his Cause:
Tels them, he doth bestride a bleeding Land,
Gasping for life, vnder great *Bullingbrooke*,
And more, and lesse, do flocke to follow him.

North. I knew of this before. But to speake truth,
This present greefe had wip'd it from my minde.
Go in with me, and councell euery man
The aptest way for safety, and reuenge:
Get Posts, and Letters, and make Friends with speed,
Neuer so few, nor neuer yet more need. *Exeunt.*

Scena Tertia.

Enter Falstaffe, and Page.

Fal. Sirra, you giant, what saies the Doct. to my water?

Pag. He said sir, the water it selfe was a good healthy water: but for the party that ow'd it, he might haue more diseases then he knew for.

Fal. Men of all sorts take a pride to gird at mee: the braine of this foolish compounded Clay-man, is not able to inuent any thing that tends to laughter, more then I inuent, or is inuented on me. I am not onely witty in my selfe, but the cause that wit is in other men. I doe heere walke before thee, like a Sow, that hath o'rewhelm'd all her Litter, but one. If the Prince put thee into my Seruice for any other reason, then to set mee off, why then I haue no iudgement. Thou horson Mandrake, thou art fitter to be worne in my cap, then to wait at my heeles. I was neuer mann'd with an Agot till now: but I will sette you neyther in Gold, nor Siluer, but in vilde apparell, and send you backe againe to your Master, for a Iewell. The *Iuuenall* (the Prince your Master) whose Chin is not yet fledg'd, I will sooner haue a beard grow in the Palme of my hand, then he shall get one on his cheeke: yet he will not sticke to say, his Face is a Face-Royall. Heauen may finish it when he will, it is not a haire amisse yet: he may keepe it still at a Face-Royall, for a Barber shall neuer earne six pence out of it; and yet he will be crowing, as if he had writ man euer since his Father was a Batchellour. He may keepe his owne Grace, but he is almost out of mine, I can assure him. What said M. *Dombledon*, about the Satten for my short Cloake, and Slops?

Pag. He said sir, you should procure him better Assurance, then *Bardolfe*: he wold not take his Bond & yours, he lik'd not the Security.

Fal. Let him bee damn'd like the Glutton, may his Tongue be hotter, a horson *Achitophel*; a Rascally-yea-forsooth-knaue, to beare a Gentleman in hand, and then stand vpon Security? The horson smooth-pates doe now weare nothing but high shoes, and bunches of Keyes at their girdles: and if a man is through with them in honest Taking-vp, then they must stand vpon Securitie: I had as liefe they would put Rats-bane in my mouth, as offer to stoppe it with Security. I look'd hee should haue sent me two and twenty yards of Satten (as I am true Knight) and he sends me Security. Well, he may sleep in Security, for he hath the horne of Abundance: and the lightnesse of his Wife shines through it, and yet cannot he see, though he haue his owne Lanthorne to light him. Where's *Bardolfe*?

Pag. He's gone into Smithfield to buy your worship a horse.

Fal. I bought him in Paules, and hee'l buy mee a horse in Smithfield. If I could get mee a wife in the Stewes, I were Mann'd, Hors'd, and Wiu'd.

Enter Chiefe Iustice, and Seruant.

Pag. Sir, heere comes the Nobleman that committed the Prince for striking him, about *Bardolfe*.

Fal. Wait close, I will not see him.

Ch.Iust. What's he that goes there?

Ser. *Falstaffe*, and't please your Lordship.

Iust. He that was in question for the Robbery?

Ser. He my Lord, but he hath since done good seruice at Shrewsbury: and (as I heare) is now going with some Charge, to the Lord *Iohn of Lancaster*.

Iust. What to Yorke? Call him backe againe.

Ser. Sir *Iohn Falstaffe*.

Fal. Boy, tell him, I am deafe.

Pag. You must speake lowder, my Master is deafe.

Iust. I am sure he is, to the hearing of any thing good. Go plucke him by the Elbow, I must speake with him.

Ser. Sir *Iohn*.

Fal. What? a yong knaue and beg? Is there not wars? Is there not imployment? Doth not the K. lack subiects? Do not the Rebels want Soldiers? Though it be a shame to be on on any side but one, it is worse shame to begge, then to be on the worst side, were it worse then the name of Rebellion can tell how to make it.

Ser. You mistake me Sir.

Fal. Why sir? Did I say you were an honest man? Setting my Knight-hood, and my Souldiership aside, I had lyed in my throat, if I had said so.

Ser. I pray you (Sir) then set your Knighthood and your Souldier-ship aside, and giue mee leaue to tell you, you lye in your throat, if you say I am any other then an hor-st man.

Fal. I giue thee leaue to tell me so? I lay a-side that which growes to me? If thou get'st any leaue of me, hang me: if thou tak'st leaue, thou wer't better be hang'd: you Hunt-counter, hence: Auant.

Ser. Sir, my Lord would speake with you.

Iust. Sir *Iohn Falstaffe*, a word with you.

Fal. My good Lord: giue your Lordship good time of the day. I am glad to see your Lordship abroad: I heard say your Lordship was sicke. I hope your Lordship goes abroad by aduise. Your Lordship (though not clean past your youth) hath yet some smack of age in you, some rellish of the saltnesse of Time, and I most humbly beseech your Lordship, to haue a reuerend care of your health.

Iust. Sir *Iohn*, I sent you before your Expedition, to Shrewsburie.

Fal. If it please your Lordship, I heare his Maiestie is return'd with some discomfort from Wales.

Iust. I talke not of his Maiesty: you would not come when I sent for you?

Fal. And I heare moreouer, his Highnesse is falne into this same whorson Apoplexie.

Iust. Well, heauen mend him. I pray let me speak with (you.

Fal. This Apoplexie is (as I take it) a kind of Lethargie, a sleeping of the blood, a horson Tingling.

Iust. What tell you me of it? be it as it is.

Fal. It hath it originall from much greefe; from study and perturbation of the braine. I haue read the cause of his effects in *Galen*. It is a kinde of deafenesse.

Iust. I thinke you are falne into the disease: For you heare not what I say to you.

Fal. Very well (my Lord) very well: rather an't please you) it is the disease of not Listning, the malady of not Marking, that I am troubled withall.

Iust. To punish you by the heeles, would amend the attention of your eares, & I care not if I be your Physitian

Fal. I am as poore as *Iob*, my Lord; but not so Patient: your Lordship may minister the Potion of imprisonment to me, in respect of Pouertie: but how I should bee your Patient, to follow your prescriptions, the wise may make some dram of a scruple, or indeede, a scruple it selfe.

Iust. I sent for you (when there were matters against you for your life) to come speake with me.

Fal. As I was then aduised by my learned Councel, in the lawes of this Land-seruice, I did not come.

Iust. Wel, the truth is (sir *Iohn*) you liue in great infamy

Fal. He that buckles him in my belt, cãnot liue in lesse.

Iust. Your Meanes is very slender, and your wast great.

Fal. I would it were otherwise: I would my Meanes were greater, and my waste slenderer.

Iust. You haue misled the youthfull Prince.

Fal. The yong Prince hath misled mee. I am the Fellow with the great belly, and he my Dogge.

Iust. Well, I am loth to gall a new-heal'd wound: your daies seruice at Shrewsbury, hath a little gilded ouer your Nights exploit on Gads-hill. You may thanke the vnquiet time, for your quiet o're-posting that Action.

Fal. My Lord?

Iust. But since all is wel, keep it so: wake not a sleeping (Wolfe.

Fal. To wake a Wolfe, is as bad as to smell a Fox.

Iu. What? you are as a candle, the better part burnt out

Fal. A Wassell-Candle, my Lord; all Tallow: if I did say of wax, my growth would approue the truth.

Iust. There is not a white haire on your face, but shold haue his effect of grauity.

Fal. His effect of grauy, grauy, grauy.

Iust You follow the yong Prince vp and downe, like his euill Angell.

Fal. Not so (my Lord) your ill Angell is light: but I hope, he that lookes vpon mee, will take mee without, weighing: and yet, in some respects I grant, I cannot go: I cannot tell. Vertue is of so little regard in these Costor-mongers, that true valor is turn'd Beare-heard. Pregnancie is made a Tapster, and hath his quicke wit wasted in giuing Recknings: all the other gifts appertinent to man (as the malice of this Age shapes them) are not woorth a Gooseberry. You that are old, consider not the capacities of vs that are yong: you measure the heat of our Liuers, with the bitternes of your gals: & we that are in the vaward of our youth, I must confesse, are wagges too.

Iust. Do you set downe your name in the scrowle of youth, that are written downe old, with all the Charracters of age? Haue you not a moist eye? a dry hand? a yellow cheeke? a white beard? a decreasing leg? an incresing belly? Is not your voice broken? your winde short? your wit single? and euery part about you blasted with Antiquity? and wil you cal your selfe yong? Fy, fy, fy, sir *Iohn*

Fal. My Lord, I was borne with a white head, & somthing a round belly For my voice, I haue lost it with hallowing and singing of Anthemes. To approue my youth farther, I will not: the truth is, I am onely olde in iudgement and vnderstanding: and he that will caper with mee for a thousand Markes, let him lend me the mony, & haue at him. For the boxe of th'eare that the Prince gaue you, he gaue it like a rude Prince, and you tooke it like a sensible Lord. I haue checkt him for it, and the yong Lion repents: Marry not in ashes and sacke-cloath, but in new Silke, and old Sacke.

Iust. Wel, heauen send the Prince a better companion.

Fal. Heauen send the Companion a better Prince: I cannot rid my hands of him.

Iust. Well, the King hath seuer'd you and Prince *Harry*, I heare you are going with Lord *Iohn* of Lancaster, against the Archbishop, and the Earle of Northumberland

Fal. Yes, I thanke your pretty sweet wit for it: but looke you pray, (all you that kisse my Ladie Peace, at home) that our Armies ioyn not in a hot day: for if I take but two shirts out with me, and I meane not to sweat extraordinarily: if it bee a hot day, if I brandish any thing but my Bottle, would I might neuer spit white againe: There is not a daungerous Action can peepe out his head, but I am thrust vpon it. Well, I cannot last euer.

Iust. Well, be honest, be honest, and heauen blesse your Expedition.

Fal. Will your Lordship lend mee a thousand pound, to furnish me forth?

Iust. Not a peny, not a peny: you are too impatient to beare crosses. Fare you well. Commend mee to my Cosin Westmerland.

Fal. If I do fillop me with a three-man-Beetle. A man can no more separate Age and Couetousnesse, then he can part yong limbes and lechery: but the Gowt galles the one,and the pox pinches the other; and so both the Degrees preuent my curses. Boy?

Page. Sir.

Fal. What money is in my purse?

Page. Seuen groats and two pence.

Fal. I can get no remedy against this Consumption of the purse. Borrowing onely lingers, and lingers it out, but the disease is incureable. Go beare this letter to my Lord of Lancaster, this to the Prince, this to the Earle of Westmerland, and this to old Mistris *Vrsula,* whome I haue weekly sworne to marry, since I perceiu'd the first white haire on my chin. About it: you know where to finde me. A pox of this Gowt, or a Gowt of this Poxe: for the one or th'other playes the rogue with my great toe: It is no matter, if I do halt, I haue the warres for my colour, and my Pension shall seeme the more reasonable. A good wit will make vse of any thing: I will turne diseases to commodity. *Exeunt*

Scena Quarta.

Enter Archbishop, Hastings, Mowbray, and Lord Bardolfe.

Ar. Thus haue you heard our causes & kno our Means:
And my most noble Friends, I pray you all
Speake plainly your opinions of our hopes,
And first (Lord Marshall) what say you to it?

Mow. I well allow the occasion of our Armes,
But gladly would be better satisfied,
How (in our Meanes) we should aduance our selues
To looke with forhead bold and big enough
Vpon the Power and puisance of the King.

Hast. Our present Musters grow vpon the File
To fiue and twenty thousand men of choice:
And our Supplies, liue largely in the hope
Of great Northumberland, whose bosome burnes
With an incensed Fire of Iniuries.

L.Bar. The question then (Lord *Hastings*) standeth thus
Whether our present fiue and twenty thousand
May hold-vp-head, without Northumberland:

Hast. With him, we may.

L.Bar. I marry, there's the point:
But if without him we be thought to feeble,
My iudgement is, we should not step too farre
Till we had his Assistance by the hand.
For in a Theame so bloody fac'd, as this,
Coniecture, Expectation, and Surmise
Of Aydes incertaine, should not be admitted.

Arch. 'Tis very true Lord *Bardolfe,* for indeed
It was yong *Hotspurres* case, at Shrewsbury.

L.Bar. It was (my Lord) who lin'd himself with hope,
Eating the ayre, on promise of Supply,
Flatt'ring himselfe with Proiect of a power,
Much smaller, then the smallest of his Thoughts,
And so with great imagination
(Proper to mad men) led his Powers to death,
And (winking) leap'd into destruction.

Hast. But (by your leaue) it neuer yet did hurt,
To lay downe likely-hoods, and formes of hope.

L Bar. Yes, if this present quality of warre,
Indeed the instant action: a cause on foot,
Liues so in hope: As in an early Spring,
We see th'appearing buds, which to proue fruite,
Hope giue not so much warrant, as Dispaire
That Frosts will bite them. When we meane to build,
We first suruey the Plot, then draw the Modell,
And when we see the figure of the house,
Then must we rate the cost of the Erection,
Which if we finde out-weighes Ability,
What do we then, but draw a-new the Modell
In fewer offices? Or at least, desist
To builde at all? Much more, in this great worke,
(Which is (almost) to plucke a Kingdome downe,
And set another vp) should we suruey
The plot of Situation, and the Modell;
Consent vpon a sure Foundation:
Question Surueyors, know our owne estate,
How able such a Worke to vndergo,
To weigh against his Opposite? Or else,
We fortifie in Paper, and in Figures,
Vsing the Names of men, instead of men:
Like one, that drawes the Modell of a house
Beyond his power to builde it; who (halfe through)
Giues o're, and leaues his part-created Cost
A naked subiect to the Weeping Clouds,
And waste, for churlish Winters tyranny.

Hast. Grant that our hopes (yet likely of faire byrth)
Should be still-borne. and that we now possest
The vtmost man of expectation:
I thinke we are a Body strong enough
(Euen as we are) to equall with the King.

L.Bar. What is the King but fiue & twenty thousand?

Hast. To vs no more: nay not so much Lord *Bardolf,*
For his diuisions (as the Times do braul)
Are in three Heads: one Power against the French,
And one against *Glendower:* Perforce a third
Must take vp vs: So is the vnfirme King
In three diuided: and his Coffers sound
With hollow Pouerty, and Emptinesse.

Ar. That he should draw his seuerall strengths togither
And come against vs in full puissance
Need not be dreaded.

Hast. If he should do so,
He leaues his backe vnarm'd, the French, and Welch
Baying him at the heeles: neuer feare that.

L.Bar. Who is it like should lead his Forces hither?

Hast. The Duke of Lancaster, and Westmerland:
Against the Welsh himselfe. and *Harrie Monmouth.*
But who is substituted 'gainst the French,
I haue no certaine notice.

Arch. Let vs on:
And publish the occasion of our Armes.
The Common-wealth is sicke of their owne Choice,
Their ouer-greedy loue hath surfetted:
An habitation giddy, and vnsure
Hath he that buildeth on the vulgar heart.
O thou fond Many, with what loud applause
Did'st thou beate heauen with blessing *Bullingbrooke,*
Before he was, what thou would'st haue him be?
And being now trimm'd in thine owne desires,
Thou (beastly Feeder) art so full of him,
That thou prouok'st thy selfe to cast him vp.
So, so, (thou common Dogge) did'st thou disgorge
Thy glutton-bosome of the Royall *Richard,*
And now thou would'st eate thy dead vomit vp,
And howl'st to finde it. What trust is in these Times?
They, that when *Richard* liu'd, would haue him dye,
Are now become enamour'd on his graue.
Thou that threw'st dust vpon his goodly head
When through proud London he came sighing on,
After th'admired heeles of *Bullingbrooke,*
Cri'st now, O Earth, yeeld vs that King agine,

And

And take thou this (O thoughts of men accurs'd)
"*Past, and to Come, seemes best; things Present, worst.*
Mow. Shall we go draw our numbers, and set on?
Hast. We are Times subiects, and Time bids, be gon.

Actus Secundus. Scœna Prima.

Enter Hostesse, with two Officers. Fang, and Snare.

Hostesse. Mr. *Fang*, haue you entred the Action?

Fang. It is enter'd.

Hostesse. Wher's your Yeoman? Is it a lusty yeoman? Will he stand to it?

Fang. Sirrah, where's *Snare*?

Hostesse. I, I, good M. *Snare*.

Snare. Heere, heere.

Fang. *Snare*, we must Arrest Sir *Iohn Falstaffe.*

Host. I good M. *Snare*, I haue enter'd him, and all.

Sn. It may chance cost some of vs our liues: he wil stab

Hostesse. Alas the day: take heed of him: he stabd me in mine owne house, and that most beastly: he cares not what mischeefe he doth, if his weapon be out. Hee will foyne like any diuell, he will spare neither man, woman, nor childe.

Fang. If I can close with him, I care not for his thrust.

Hostesse. No, nor I neither: Ile be at your elbow.

Fang. If I but fist him once: if he come but within my Vice.

Host. I am vndone with his going: I warrant he is an infinitiue thing vpon my score. Good M. *Fang* hold him sure: good M. *Snare* let him not scape, he comes continuantly to Py-Corner (sauing your manhoods) to buy a saddle, and hee is indited to dinner to the Lubbars head in Lombardstreet, to M. *Smoothes* the Silkman. I pra'ye, since my Exion is enter'd, and my Case so openly known to the world, let him be brought in to his answer: A 100. Marke is a long one, for a poore lone woman to beare: & I haue borne, and borne, and borne, and haue bin fub'd off, and fub'd-off, from this day to that day, that it is a shame to be thought on. There is no honesty in such dealing, vnles a woman should be made an Asse and a Beast, to beare euery Knaues wrong. *Enter Falstaffe and Bardolfe.* Yonder he comes, and that arrant Malmesey-Nose *Bardolfe* with him. Do your Offices, do your offices: M. *Fang*, & M. *Snare*, do me, do me, do me your Offices.

Fal. How now? whose Mare's dead? what's the matter?

Fang. Sir *Iohn*, I arrest you, at the suit of Mist. *Quickly.*

Falst. Away Varlets, draw *Bardolfe*: Cut me off the Villaines head: throw the Queane in the Channel.

Host. Throw me in the channell? Ile throw thee there. Wilt thou? wilt thou? thou bastardly rogue. Murder, murder, O thou Hony-suckle villaine, wilt thou kill Gods officers, and the Kings? O thou hony-seed Rogue, thou art a honyseed, a Man-queller, and a woman-queller.

Falst. Keep them off, *Bardolfe*. *Fang.* A rescu, a rescu.

Host. Good people bring a rescu. Thou wilt not? thou wilt not? Do, do thou Rogue: Do thou Hempseed.

Page. Away you Scullion, you Rampallian, you Fustillirian: Ile tucke your Catastrophe. *Enter. Ch. Iustice.*

Iust. What's the matter? Keepe the Peace here, hoa.

Host. Good my Lord be good to mee. I beseech you stand to me.

Ch. Iust. How now sir *Iohn*? What are you brauling here? Doth this become your place, your time, and businesse? You should haue bene well on your way to Yorke. Stand from him Fellow; wherefore hang'st vpon him?

Host. Oh my most worshipfull Lord, and't please your Grace, I am a poore widdow of Eastcheap, and he is arrested at my suit. *Ch. Iust.* For what summe?

Host. It is more then for some (my Lord) it is for all: all I haue, he hath eaten me out of house and home; hee hath put all my substance into that fat belly of his: but I will haue some of it out againe, or I will ride thee o'Nights, like the Mare.

Falst. I thinke I am as like to ride the Mare, if I haue any vantage of ground, to get vp.

Ch: Iust. How comes this, Sir *Iohn*? Fy, what a man of good temper would endure this tempest of exclamation? Are you not asham'd to inforce a poore Widdowe to so rough a course, to come by her owne?

Falst. What is the grosse summe that I owe thee?

Host. Marry (if thou wer't an honest man) thy selfe, & the mony too. Thou didst sweare to mee vpon a parcell gilt Goblet, sitting in my Dolphin-chamber at the round table, by a sea-cole fire, on Wednesday in Whitson week, when the Prince broke thy head for lik'ning him to a singing man of Windsor; Thou didst sweare to me then (as I was washing thy wound) to marry me, and make mee my Lady thy wife. Canst ý deny it? Did not goodwife *Keech* the Butchers wife come in then, and cal me gossip *Quickly*? comming in to borrow a messe of Vinegar: telling vs, she had a good dish of Prawnes: whereby ý didst desire to eat some: whereby I told thee they were ill for a greene wound? And didst not thou (when she was gone downe staires) desire me to be no more familiar with such poore people, saying, that ere long they should call me Madam? And did'st ý not kisse me, and bid mee fetch thee 30. s? I put thee now to thy Book-oath, deny it if thou canst?

Fal. My Lord, this is a poore mad soule: and she sayes vp & downe the town, that her eldest son is like you. She hath bin in good case, & the truth is, pouerty hath distracted her: but for these foolish Officers, I beseech you, I may haue redresse against them.

Iust. Sir *Iohn*, sir *Iohn*, I am well acquainted with your maner of wrenching the true cause, the false way. It is not a confident brow, nor the throng of wordes, that come with such (more then impudent) sawcines from you, can thrust me from a leuell consideration, I know you ha' practis'd vpon the easie-yeelding spirit of this woman.

Host. Yes in troth my Lord.

Iust. Prethee peace: pay her the debt you owe her, and vnpay the villany you haue done her: the one you may do with sterling mony, & the other with currant repentance.

Fal. My Lord, I will not vndergo this sneape without reply. You call honorable Boldnes, impudent Saweinesse: If a man wil curt'sie, and say nothing, he is vertuous: No, my Lord (your humble duty remẽbred) I will not be your sutor. I say to you, I desire deliu'rance from these Officers being vpon hasty employment in the Kings Affaires.

Iust. You speake, as hauing power to do wrong: But answer in the effect of your Reputation, and satisfie the poore woman.

Falst. Come hither Hostesse. *Enter M. Gower*

Ch. Iust. Now Master *Gower*; What newes?

Gow. The King (my Lord) and *Henrie* Prince of Wales Are neere at hand: The rest the Paper telles.

Falst. As I am a Gentleman.

Host. Nay, you said so before.

Fal. As I am a Gentleman. Come, no more words of it

Host. By this Heauenly ground I tread on, I must be faine to pawne both my Plate, and the Tapistry of my dyning Chambers.

Fal. Glasses, glasses, is the onely drinking: and for thy walles a pretty slight Drollery, or the Storie of the Prodigall, or the Germane hunting in Waterworke, is worth a thousand of these Bed-hangings, and these Fly-bitten Tapistries. Let it be tenne pound (if thou canst.) Come, if it were not for thy humors, there is not a better Wench in England. Go, wash thy face, and draw thy Action: Come, thou must not bee in this humour with me, come, I know thou was't set on to this.

Host. Prethee (Sir *Iohn*) let it be but twenty Nobles, I loath to pawne my Plate, in good earnest la.

Fal. Let it alone, Ile make other shift: you'l be a fool still.

Host. Well, you shall haue it although I pawne my Gowne. I hope you'l come to Supper: You'l pay me altogether?

Fal. Will I liue? Go with her, with her: hooke-on, hooke-on.

Host. Will you haue *Doll Teare-sheet* meet you at supper?

Fal. No more words. Let's haue her.

Ch.Iust. I haue heard bitter newes.

Fal What's the newes (my good Lord?)

Ch.Iu. Where lay the King last night?

Mes. At Basingstoke my Lord.

Fal. I hope (my Lord) all's well. What is the newes my Lord?

Ch.Iust. Come all his Forces backe?

Mes. No: Fifteene hundred Foot, fiue hundred Horse
Are march'd vp to my Lord of Lancaster,
Against Northumberland, and the Archbishop.

Fal. Comes the King backe from Wales, my noble L?

Ch.Iust. You shall haue Letters of me presently.
Come, go along with me, good M. *Gowre.*

Fal. My Lord.

Ch.Iust. What's the matter?

Fal. Master *Gowre*, shall I entreate you with mee to dinner?

Gow. I must waite vpon my good Lord heere.
I thanke you, good Sir *Iohn.*

Ch Iust. Sir *Iohn*, you loyter heere too long, being you are to take Souldiers vp, in Countries as you go.

Fal. Will you sup with me, Master *Gowre*?

Ch.Iust. What foolish Master taught you these manners, Sir *Iohn*?

Fal. Master *Gower*, if they become mee not, hee was a Foole that taught them mee. This is the right Fencing grace (my Lord) tap for tap, and so part faire.

Ch.Iust. Now the Lord lighten thee, thou art a great Foole. *Exeunt*

Scena Secunda.

Enter Prince Henry, Pointz, Bardolfe, and Page.

Prin. Trust me, I am exceeding weary.

Poin. Is it come to that? I had thought wearines durst not haue attach'd one of so high blood.

Prin. It doth me: though it discolours the complexion of my Greatnesse to acknowledge it. Doth it not shew vildely in me, to desire small Beere?

Poin. Why, a Prince should not be so loosely studied, as to remember so weake a Composition.

Prince. Belike then, my Appetite was not Princely got: for (in troth) I do now remember the poore Creature, Small Beere. But indeede these humble considerations make me out of loue with my Greatnesse. What a disgrace is it to me, to remember thy name? Or to know thy face to morrow? Or to take note how many paire of Silk stockings ŷ hast? (Viz. these, and those that were thy peach-colour'd ones:) Or to beare the Inuentorie of thy shirts, as one for superfluity, and one other, for vse. But that the Tennis-Court-keeper knowes better then I, for it is a low ebbe of Linnen with thee, when thou kept'st not Racket there, as thou hast not done a great while, because the rest of thy Low Countries, haue made a shift to eate vp thy Holland.

Poin. How ill it followes, after you haue labour'd so hard, you should talke so idlely? Tell me how many good yong Princes would do so, their Fathers lying so sicke, as yours is?

Prin. Shall I tell thee one thing, *Pointz*?

Poin. Yes: and let it be an excellent good thing.

Prin. It shall serue among wittes of no higher breeding then thine.

Poin. Go to: I stand the push of your one thing, that you'l tell.

Prin. Why, I tell thee, it is not meet, that I should be sad now my Father is sicke: albeit I could tell to thee (as to one it pleases me, for fault of a better, to call my friend) I could be sad, and sad indeed too.

Poin. Very hardly, vpon such a subiect.

Prin. Thou think'st me as farre in the Diuels Booke, as thou, and *Falstaffe*, for obduracie and persistencie. Let the end try the man. But I tell thee, my hart bleeds inwardly, that my Father is so sicke: and keeping such vild company as thou art, hath in reason taken from me, all ostentation of sorrow.

Poin. The reason?

Prin. What would'st thou think of me, if I shold weep?

Poin. I would thinke thee a most Princely hypocrite.

Prin. It would be euery mans thought: and thou art a blessed Fellow, to thinke as euery man thinkes: neuer a mans thought in the world, keepes the Rode-way better then thine: euery man would thinke me an Hypocrite indeede. And what accites your most worshipful thought to thinke so?

Poin. Why, because you haue beene so lewde, and so much ingraffed to *Falstaffe*.

Prin. And to thee.

Pointz. Nay, I am well spoken of, I can heare it with mine owne eares: the worst that they can say of me is, that I am a second Brother, and that I am a proper Fellowe of my hands: and those two things I confesse I canot helpe. Looke, looke, here comes *Bardolfe*.

Prince. And the Boy that I gaue *Falstaffe*, he had him from me Christian, and see if the fat villain haue not transform'd him Ape.

Enter Bardolfe.

Bar. Saue your Grace.

Prin. And yours, most Noble *Bardolfe*.

Poin. Come you pernitious Asse, you bashfull Foole, must you be blushing? Wherefore blush you now? what a Maidenly man at Armes are you become? Is it such a matter to get a Pottle-pots Maiden-head?

Page. He call'd me euen now (my Lord) through a red Lattice, and I could discerne no part of his face from the window:

window: at last I spy'd his eyes, and me thought he had made two holes in the Ale-wiues new Petticoat, & peeped through.

Prin. Hath not the boy profited?

Bar. Away, you horson vpright Rabbet, away.

Page. Away, you rascally *Altheas* dreame, away.

Prin. Instruct vs Boy: what dreame, Boy?

Page. Marry (my Lord) *Althea* dream'd, she was deliuer'd of a Firebrand, and therefore I call him hir dream.

Prince. A Crownes-worth of good Interpretation: There it is, Boy.

Poin. O that this good Blossome could bee kept from Cankers: Well, there is six pence to preserue thee.

Bard. If you do not make him be hang'd among you, the gallowes shall be wrong'd.

Prince. And how doth thy Master, *Bardolph*?

Bar. Well, my good Lord: he heard of your Graces comming to Towne. There's a Letter for you.

Poin. Deliuer'd with good respect: And how doth the Martlemas, your Master?

Bard. In bodily health Sir.

Poin. Marry, the immortall part needes a Physitian: but that moues not him: though that bee sicke, it dyes not.

Prince. I do allow this Wen to bee as familiar with me, as my dogge: and he holds his place, for looke you he writes.

Poin. Letter. *Iohn Falstaffe Knight*: (Euery man must know that, as oft as hee hath occasion to name himselfe:) Euen like those that are kinne to the King, for they neuer pricke their finger, but they say, there is som of the kings blood spilt. How comes that (sayes he) that takes vpon him not to conceiue? the answer is as ready as a borrowed cap: I am the Kings poore Cosin, Sir.

Prince. Nay, they will be kin to vs, but they wil fetch it from *Iaphet*. But to the Letter: —*Sir Iohn Falstaffe, Knight, to the Sonne of the King, neerest his Father, Harrie Prince of Wales, greeting.*

Poin. Why this is a Certificate.

Prin. Peace.

I will imitate the honourable Romaines in breuitie.

Poin. Sure he meanes breuity in breath: short-winded. *I commend me to thee, I commend thee, and I leaue thee. Bee not too familiar with* Pointz, *for hee misuses thy Fauours so much, that he sweares thou art to marrie his Sister* Nell. *Repent at idle times as thou mayst, and so farewell.*

Thine, by yea and no: which is as much as to say, as thou vsest him. Iacke Falstaffe *with my Familiars:* Iohn *with my Brothers and Sister: & Sir* Iohn, *with all Europe.*

My Lord, I will steepe this Letter in Sack, and make him eate it.

Prin. That's to make him eate twenty of his Words. But do you vse me thus *Ned*? Must I marry your Sister?

Poin. May the Wench haue no worse Fortune. But I neuer said so.

Prin. Well, thus we play the Fooles with the time & the spirits of the wise, sit in the clouds, and mocke vs: Is your Master heere in London?

Bard. Yes my Lord.

Prin. Where suppes he? Doth the old Sore, feede in the old Franke?

Bard. At the old place my Lord, in East-cheape.

Prin. What Company?

Page. Ephesians my Lord, of the old Church.

Prin. Sup any women with him?

Page. None my Lord, but old Mistris *Quickly*, and M. *Doll Teare-sheet.*

Prin. What Pagan may that be?

Page. A proper Gentlewoman, Sir, and a Kinswoman of my Masters.

Prin. Euen such Kin, as the Parish Heyfors are to the Towne-Bull? Shall we steale vpon them (*Ned*) at Supper?

Poin. I am your shadow, my Lord, Ile follow you.

Prin. Sirrah, you boy, and *Bardolph*, no word to your Master that I am yet in Towne. There's for your silence.

Bar. I haue no tongue, sir.

Page. And for mine Sir, I will gouerne it.

Prin. Fare ye well: go. This *Doll Teare-sheet* should be some Rode.

Poin. I warrant you, as common as the way betweene S. Albans, and London.

Prin. How might we see *Falstaffe* bestow himselfe to night, in his true colours, and not our selues be seene?

Poin. Put on two Leather Ierkins, and Aprons, and waite vpon him at his Table, like Drawers.

Prin. From a God, to a Bull? A heauie declension: It was Ioues case. From a Prince, to a Prentice, a low transformation, that shall be mine: for in euery thing, the purpose must weigh with the folly. Follow me *Ned*. *Exeunt*

Scena Tertia.

Enter Northumberland, his Ladie, and Harrie Percies Ladie.

North. I prethee louing Wife, and gentle Daughter,
Giue an euen way vnto my rough Affaires:
Put not you on the visage of the Times,
And be like them to Percie, troublesome.

Wife. I haue giuen ouer, I will speak no more,
Do what you will: your Wisedome, be your guide.

North. Alas (sweet Wife) my Honor is at pawne,
And but my going, nothing can redeeme it.

La. Oh yet, for heauens sake, go not to these Warrs;
The Time was (Father) when you broke your word,
When you were more endeer'd to it, then now,
When your owne Percy, when my heart-deere *Harry*,
Threw many a Northward looke, to see his Father
Bring vp his Powres: but he did long in vaine.
Who then perswaded you to stay at home?
There were two Honors lost; Yours, and your Sonnes.
For Yours, may heauenly glory brighten it:
For His, it stucke vpon him, as the Sunne
In the gray vault of Heauen: and by his Light
Did all the Cheualrie of England moue
To do braue Acts. He was (indeed) the Glasse
Wherein the Noble-Youth did dresse themselues.
He had no Legges, that practic'd not his Gate:
And speaking thicke (which Nature made his blemish)
Became the Accents of the Valiant.
For those that could speake low, and tardily,
Would turne their owne Perfection, to Abuse,
To seeme like him. So that in Speech, in Gate,
In Diet, in Affections of delight,
In Militarie Rules, Humors of Blood,

He was the Marke, and Glasse, Coppy, and Booke,
That fashion'd others. And him, O wondrous! him,
O Miracle of Men! Him did you leaue
(Second to none) vn-seconded by you,
To looke vpon the hideous God of Warre,
In dis-aduantage, to abide a field,
Where nothing but the sound of *Hotspurs* Name
Did seeme defensible: so you left him.
Neuer, O neuer doe his Ghost the wrong,
To hold your Honor more precise and nice
With others, then with him. Let them alone:
The Marshall and the Arch-bishop are strong.
Had my sweet *Harry* had but halfe their Numbers,
To day might I (hanging on *Hotspurs* Necke)
Haue talk'd of *Monmouth's* Graue.

North. Beshrew your heart,
(Faire Daughter) you doe draw my Spirits from me,
With new lamenting ancient Ouer-sights.
But I must goe, and meet with Danger there,
Or it will seeke me in another place,
And finde me worse prouided.

Wife. O flye to Scotland,
Till that the Nobles, and the armed Commons,
Haue of their Puissance made a little taste.

Lady. If they get ground, and vantage of the King,
Then ioyne you with them, like a Ribbe of Steele,
To make Strength stronger. But, for all our loues,
First let them trye themselues. So did your Sonne,
He was so suffer'd; so came I a Widow:
And neuer shall haue length of Life enough,
To raine vpon Remembrance with mine Eyes,
That it may grow, and sprowt, as high as Heauen,
For Recordation to my Noble Husband.

North. Come, come, go in with me: 'tis with my Minde
As with the Tyde, swell'd vp vnto his height,
That makes a still-stand, running neyther way.
Faine would I goe to meet the Arch-bishop,
But many thousand Reasons hold me backe.
I will resolue for Scotland: there am I,
Till Time and Vantage craue my company. *Exeunt.*

Scæna Quarta.

Enter two Drawers.

1. *Drawer.* What hast thou brought there? Apple-Iohns? Thou know'st Sir *Iohn* cannot endure an Apple-Iohn.

2. *Draw.* Thou say'st true: the Prince once set a Dish of Apple-Iohns before him, and told him there were fiue more Sir *Iohns*: and, putting off his Hat, said, I will now take my leaue of these sixe drie, round, old-wither'd Knights. It anger'd him to the heart: but hee hath forgot that.

1. *Draw.* Why then couer, and set them downe: and see if thou canst finde out *Sneakes* Noyse; Mistris *Teare-sheet* would faine haue some Musique.

2. *Draw.* Sirrha, heere will be the Prince, and Master *Points*, anon: and they will put on two of our Ierkins, and Aprons, and Sir *Iohn* must not know of it: *Bardolph* hath brought word.

1. *Draw.* Then here will be old *Vtis*: it will be an excellent stratagem.

2. *Draw.* Ile see if I can finde out *Sneake*. *Exit.*

Enter Hostesse, and Dol.

Host. Sweet-heart, me thinkes now you are in an excellent good temperalitie: your Pulsidge beates as extraordinarily, as heart would desire; and your Colour (I warrant you) is as red as any Rose: But you haue drunke too much Canaries, and that's a maruellous searching Wine; and it perfumes the blood, ere wee can say what's this. How doe you now?

Dol. Better then I was: Hem.

Host. Why that was well said: A good heart's worth Gold. Looke, here comes Sir *Iohn*.

Enter Falstaffe.

Falst. When Arthur first in Court--(emptie the Iordan) *and was a worthy King:* How now Mistris *Dol*?

Host. Sick of a Calme: yea, good-sooth.

Falst. So is all her Sect: if they be once in a Calme, they are sick.

Dol. You muddie Rascall, is that all the comfort you giue me?

Falst. You make fat Rascalls, Mistris *Dol*.

Dol. I make them? Gluttonie and Diseases make them, I make them not.

Falst. If the Cooke make the Gluttonie, you helpe to make the Diseases (*Dol*) we catch of you (*Dol*) we catch of you: Grant that, my poore Vertue, grant that.

Dol. I marry, our Chaynes, and our Iewels.

Falst. Your Brooches, Pearles, and Owches: For to serue brauely, is to come halting off: you know, to come off the Breach, with his Pike bent brauely, and to Surgerie brauely; to venture vpon the charg'd-Chambers brauely.

Host. Why this is the olde fashion: you two neuer meete, but you fall to some discord: you are both (in good troth) as Rheumatike as two drie Tostes, you cannot one beare with anothers Confirmities. What the good-yere? One must beare, and that must bee you: you are the weaker Vessell; as they say, the emptier Vessell.

Dol. Can a weake emptie Vessell beare such a huge full Hogs-head? There's a whole Marchants Venture of Burdeux-Stuffe in him: you haue not seene a Hulke better stufft in the Hold. Come, Ile be friends with thee *Iacke*: Thou art going to the Warres, and whether I shall euer see thee againe, or no, there is no body cares.

Enter Drawer.

Drawer. Sir, Ancient *Pistoll* is below, and would speake with you.

Dol. Hang him, swaggering Rascall, let him not come hither: it is the foule-mouth'dst Rogue in England.

Host. If hee swagger, let him not come here: I must liue amongst my Neighbors, Ile no Swaggerers: I am in good name, and fame, with the very best: shut the doore, there comes no Swaggerers heere: I haue not liu'd all this while, to haue swaggering now: shut the doore, I pray you.

Falst. Do'st thou heare, Hostesse?

Host. 'Pray you pacifie your selfe (Sir *Iohn*) there comes no Swaggerers heere.

Falst. Do'st

Falst. Do'st thou heare? it is mine Ancient.

Host. Tilly-fally (Sir *Iohn*) neuer tell me, your ancient Swaggerer comes not in my doores. I was before Master *Tisick* the Deputie, the other day: and as hee said to me, it was no longer agoe then Wednesday last: Neighbour *Quickly* (sayes hee;) Master *Dombe*, our Minister, was by then: Neighbour *Quickly* (sayes hee) receiue those that are Ciuill; for (sayth hee) you are in an ill Name: now hee said so, I can tell whereupon: for (sayes hee) you are an honest Woman, and well thought on; therefore take heede what Guests you receiue: Receiue (sayes hee) no swaggering Companions. There comes none heere. You would blesse you to heare what hee said. No, Ile no Swaggerers.

Falst. Hee's no Swaggerer (Hostesse:) a tame Cheater, hee: you may stroake him as gently, as a Puppie Grey-hound: hee will not swagger with a Barbarie Henne, if her feathers turne backe in any shew of resistance. Call him vp (Drawer.)

Host. Cheater, call you him? I will barre no honest man my house, nor no Cheater: but I doe not loue swaggering; I am the worse when one sayes, swagger: Feele Masters, how I shake: looke you, I warrant you.

Dol. So you doe, Hostesse.

Host. Doe I? yea, in very truth doe I, if it were an Aspen Leafe: I cannot abide Swaggerers.

Enter Pistol, and Bardolph and his Boy.

Pist. 'Saue you, Sir *Iohn*.

Falst. Welcome Ancient *Pistol*. Here (*Pistol*) I charge you with a Cup of Sacke: doe you discharge vpon mine Hostesse.

Pist. I will discharge vpon her (Sir *Iohn*) with two Bullets.

Falst. She is Pistoll-proofe (Sir) you shall hardly offend her.

Host. Come, Ile drinke no Proofes, nor no Bullets: I will drinke no more then will doe me good, for no mans pleasure, I.

Pist. Then to you (Mistris *Dorothie*) I will charge you.

Dol. Charge me? I scorne you (scuruie Companion) what? you poore, base, rascally, cheating, lacke-Linnen-Mate: away you mouldie Rogue, away; I am meat for your Master.

Pist. I know you, Mistris *Dorothie*.

Dol. Away you Cut-purse Rascall, you filthy Bung, away: By this Wine, Ile thrust my Knife in your mouldie Chappes, if you play the sawcie Cuttle with me. Away you Bottle-Ale Rascall, you Basket-hilt stale Iugler, you. Since when, I pray you, Sir? what, with two Points on your shoulder? much.

Pist. I will murther your Ruffe, for this.

Host. No, good Captaine *Pistol*: not heere, sweete Captaine.

Dol. Captaine? thou abhominable damn'd Cheater, art thou not asham'd to be call'd Captaine? If Captaines were of my minde, they would trunchion you out, for taking their Names vpon you, before you haue earn'd them. You a Captaine? you slaue, for what? for tearing a poore Whores Ruffe in a Bawdy-house? Hee a Captaine? hang him Rogue, hee liues vpon mouldie stew'd-Prunes, and dry'de Cakes. A Captaine? These Villaines will make the word Captaine odious: Therefore Captaines had neede looke to it.

Bard. 'Pray thee goe downe, good Ancient.

Falst. Hearke thee hither, Mistris *Dol*.

Pist. Not I: I tell thee what, Corporall *Bardolph*, I could teare her: Ile be reueng'd on her.

Page. 'Pray thee goe downe.

Pist. Ile see her damn'd first: to *Pluto's* damn'd Lake, to the Infernall Deepe, where *Erebus* and Tortures vilde also. Hold Hooke and Line, say I: Downe: downe Dogges, downe Fates: haue wee not *Hiren* here?

Host. Good Captaine *Peesel* be quiet, it is very late: I beseeke you now, aggrauate your Choler.

Pist. These be good Humors indeede. Shall Pack-Horses, and hollow-pamper'd Iades of Asia, which cannot goe but thirtie miles a day, compare with *Cæsar*, and with Caniballs, and Troian Greekes? nay, rather damne them with King *Cerberus*, and let the Welkin roare: shall wee fall foule for Toyes?

Host. By my troth Captaine, these are very bitter words.

Bard. Be gone, good Ancient: this will grow to a Brawle anon.

Pist. Die men, like Dogges; giue Crownes like Pinnes: Haue we not *Hiren* here?

Host. On my word (Captaine) there's none such here. What the good-yere, doe you thinke I would denye her? I pray be quiet.

Pist. Then feed, and be fat (my faire *Calipolis*.) Come, giue me some Sack, *Si fortune me tormente, sperato me contente*. Feare wee broad-sides? No, let the Fiend giue fire: Giue me some Sack: and Sweet-heart lye thou there: Come wee to full Points here, and are *et cetera's* nothing?

Fal. *Pistol*, I would be quiet.

Pist. Sweet Knight, I kisse thy Neaffe: what? wee haue seene the seuen Starres.

Dol. Thrust him downe stayres, I cannot endure such a Fustian Rascall.

Pist. Thrust him downe stayres? know we not Galloway Nagges?

Fal. Quoit him downe (*Bardolph*) like a shoue-groat shilling: nay, if hee doe nothing but speake nothing, hee shall be nothing here.

Bard. Come, get you downe stayres.

Pist. What? shall wee haue Incision? shall wee embrew? then Death rocke me asleepe, abridge my dolefull dayes: why then let grieuous, gastly, gaping Wounds, vntwin'd the Sisters three: Come *Atropos*, I say.

Host. Here's good stuffe toward.

Fal. Giue me my Rapier Boy.

Dol. I prethee *Iack*, I prethee doe not draw.

Fal. Get you downe stayres.

Host. Here's a goodly tumult: Ile forsweare keeping house, before Ile be in these tirrits, and frights. So: Murther I warrant now. Alas, alas, put vp your naked Weapons, put vp your naked Weapons.

Dol. I prethee *Iack* be quiet, the Rascall is gone: ah, you whorson little valiant Villaine, you.

Host. Are you not hurt i'th' Groyne? me thought hee made a shrewd Thrust at your Belly.

Fal. Haue you turn'd him out of doores?

Bard. Yes Sir: the Rascall's drunke: you haue hurt him (Sir) in the shoulder.

Fal. A Rascall to braue me.

Dol. Ah, you sweet little Rogue, you: alas, poore Ape how thou sweat'st? Come, let me wipe thy Face: Come on, you whorson Chops: Ah Rogue, I loue thee: Thou

art

art as valorous as *Hector* of Troy, worth fiue of *Agamemnon*, and tenne times better then the nine Worthies: ah Villaine.

Fal. A rascally Slaue, I will tosse the Rogue in a Blanket.

Dol. Doe, if thou dar'st for thy heart: if thou doo'st, Ile canuas thee betweene a paire of Sheetes.

Enter Musique.

Page. The Musique is come, Sir.

Fal. Let them play: play Sirs. Sit on my Knee, *Dol.* A Rascall, bragging Slaue: the Rogue fled from me like Quick-siluer.

Dol. And thou followd'st him like a Church: thou whorson little tydie Bartholmew Bore-pigge, when wilt thou leaue fighting on dayes, and foyning on nights, and begin to patch vp thine old Body for Heauen?

Enter the Prince and Poines disguis'd.

Fal. Peace (good *Dol*) doe not speake like a Deaths-head: doe not bid me remember mine end.

Dol. Sirrha, what humor is the Prince of?

Fal. A good shallow young fellow: hee would haue made a good Pantler, hee would haue chipp'd Bread well.

Dol. They say *Poines* hath a good Wit.

Fal. Hee a good Wit? hang him Baboone, his Wit is as thicke as Tewksburie Mustard: there is no more conceit in him, then is in a Mallet.

Dol. Why doth the Prince loue him so then?

Fal. Because their Legges are both of a bignesse: and hee playes at Quoits well, and eates Conger and Fennell, and drinkes off Candles ends for Flap-dragons, and rides the wilde-Mare with the Boyes, and iumpes vpon Ioyn'd-stooles, and sweares with a good grace, and weares his Boot very smooth, like vnto the Signe of the Legge; and breedes no bate with telling of discreete stories: and such other Gamboll Faculties hee hath, that shew a weake Minde, and an able Body, for the which the Prince admits him; for the Prince himselfe is such another: the weight of an hayre will turne the Scales betweene their *Haber-de-pois*.

Prince. Would not this Naue of a Wheele haue his Eares cut off?

Poin. Let vs beat him before his Whore.

Prince. Looke, if the wither'd Elder hath not his Poll claw'd like a Parrot.

Poin. Is it not strange, that Desire should so many yeeres out-liue performance?

Fal. Kisse me *Dol.*

Prince. *Saturne* and *Venus* this yeere in Coniunction? What sayes the Almanack to that?

Poin. And looke whether the fierie *Trigon*, his Man, be not lisping to his Masters old Tables, his Note-Booke, his Councell-keeper?

Fal. Thou do'st giue me flatt'ring Busses.

Dol. Nay truely, I kisse thee with a most constant heart.

Fal. I am olde, I am olde.

Dol. I loue thee better, then I loue ere a scuruie young Boy of them all.

Fal. What Stuffe wilt thou haue a Kirtle of? I shall receiue Money on Thursday: thou shalt haue a Cappe to morrow. A merrie Song, come: it growes late, wee will to Bed. Thou wilt forget me, when I am gone.

Dol. Thou wilt set me a weeping, if thou say'st so: proue that euer I dresse my selfe handsome, till thy returne: well, hearken the end.

Fal. Some Sack, *Francis*.

Prin. Poin. Anon, anon, Sir.

Fal. Ha? a Bastard Sonne of the Kings? And art not thou *Poines*, his Brother?

Prince. Why thou Globe of sinfull Continents, what a Life do'st thou lead?

Fal. A better then thou: I am a Gentleman, thou art a Drawer.

Prince. Very true, Sir: and I come to draw you out by the Eares.

Host. Oh, the Lord preserue thy good Grace: Welcome to London. Now Heauen blesse that sweete Face of thine: what, are you come from Wales?

Fal. Thou whorson mad Compound of Maiestie: by this light Flesh, and corrupt Blood, thou art welcome.

Dol. How? you fat Foole, I scorne you.

Poin. My Lord, hee will driue you out of your reuenge, and turne all to a merryment, if you take not the heat.

Prince. You whorson Candle-myne you, how vildly did you speake of me euen now, before this honest, vertuous, ciuill Gentlewoman?

Host. 'Blessing on your good heart, and so shee is by my troth.

Fal Didst thou heare me?

Prince. Yes: and you knew me, as you did when you ranne away by Gads-hill: you knew I was at your back, and spoke it on purpose, to trie my patience.

Fal. No, no, no: not so: I did not thinke, thou wast within hearing.

Prince. I shall driue you then to confesse the wilfull abuse, and then I know how to handle you.

Fal. No abuse (*Hall*) on mine Honor, no abuse.

Prince. Not to disprayse me? and call me Pantler, and Bread-chopper, and I know not what?

Fal. No abuse (*Hal.*)

Poin. No abuse?

Fal. No abuse (*Ned*) in the World: honest *Ned* none. I disprays'd him before the Wicked, that the Wicked might not fall in loue with him: In which doing, I haue done the part of a carefull Friend, and a true Subiect, and thy Father is to giue me thankes for it. No abuse (*Hal:*) none (*Ned*) none; no Boyes, none.

Prince. See now whether pure Feare, and entire Cowardise, doth not make thee wrong this vertuous Gentlewoman, to close with vs? Is shee of the Wicked? Is thine Hostesse heere, of the Wicked? Or is the Boy of the Wicked? Or honest *Bardolph* (whose Zeale burnes in his Nose) of the Wicked?

Poin. Answere thou dead Elme, answere.

Fal. The Fiend hath prickt downe *Bardolph* irrecouerable, and his Face is *Lucifers* Priuy-Kitchin, where hee doth nothing but rost Mault-Wormes: for the Boy, there is a good Angell about him, but the Deuill outbids him too.

Prince. For the Women?

Fal. For one of them, shee is in Hell alreadie, and burnes poore Soules: for the other, I owe her Money; and whether shee bee damn'd for that, I know not.

Host. No, I warrant you.

Fal. No,

Fal. No, I thinke thou art not: I thinke thou art quit for that. Marry, there is another Indictment vpon thee, for suffering flesh to bee eaten in thy house, contrary to the Law, for the which I thinke thou wilt howle.

Host. All Victuallers doe so: What is a Ioynt of Mutton, or two, in a whole Lent?

Prince. You, Gentlewoman.

Dol. What sayes your Grace?

Falst. His Grace sayes that, which his flesh rebells against.

Host. Who knocks so lowd at doore? Looke to the doore there, *Francis*?

Enter Peto.

Prince. Peto, how now? what newes?

Peto. The King, your Father, is at Westminster,
And there are twentie weake and wearied Postes,
Come from the North: and as I came along,
I met, and ouer-tooke a dozen Captaines,
Bare-headed, sweating, knocking at the Tauernes,
And asking euery one for Sir *Iohn Falstaffe.*

Prince. By Heauen (*Poines*) I feele me much to blame,
So idly to prophane the precious time,
When Tempest of Commotion, like the South,
Borne with black Vapour, doth begin to melt,
And drop vpon our bare vnarmed heads.
Giue me my Sword, and Cloake:
Falstaffe, good night. *Exit.*

Falst. Now comes in the sweetest Morsell of the night, and wee must hence, and leaue it vnpickt. More knocking at the doore? How now? what's the matter?

Bard. You must away to Court, Sir, presently,
A dozen Captaines stay at doore for you.

Falst. Pay the Musitians, Sirrha: farewell Hostesse, farewell *Dol.* You see (my good Wenches) how men of Merit are sought after: the vndeseruer may sleepe, when the man of Action is call'd on. Farewell good Wenches: if I be not sent away poste, I will see you againe, ere I goe.

Dol. I cannot speake: if my heart bee not readie to burst--- Well (sweete *Iacke*) haue a care of thy selfe.

Falst. Farewell, farewell. *Exit.*

Host. Well, fare thee well: I haue knowne thee these twentie nine yeeres, come Pescod-time: but an honester, and truer-hearted man---- Well, fare thee well.

Bard. Mistris *Teare-sheet.*

Host. What's the matter?

Bard. Bid Mistris *Teare-sheet* come to my Master.

Host. Oh runne *Dol*, runne: runne, good *Dol.*
Exeunt.

Actus Tertius. Scena Prima.

Enter the King, with a Page.

King. Goe, call the Earles of Surrey, and of Warwick:
But ere they come, bid them ore-reade these Letters,
And well consider of them: make good speed. *Exit.*
How many thousand of my poorest Subiects
Are at this howre asleepe? O Sleepe, O gentle Sleepe,
Natures soft Nurse, how haue I frighted thee,
That thou no more wilt weigh my eye-lids downe,
And steepe my Sences in Forgetfulnesse?
Why rather (Sleepe) lyest thou in smoakie Cribs,
Vpon vneasie Pallads stretching thee,
And huisht with bussing Night, flyes to thy slumber,
Then in the perfum'd Chambers of the Great?
Vnder the Canopies of costly State,
And lull'd with sounds of sweetest Melodie?
O thou dull God, why lyest thou with the vilde,
In loathsome Beds, and leau'st the Kingly Couch,
A Watch-case, or a common Larum-Bell?
Wilt thou, vpon the high and giddie Mast,
Seale vp the Ship-boyes Eyes, and rock his Braines,
In Cradle of the rude imperious Surge,
And in the visitation of the Windes,
Who take the Ruffian Billowes by the top,
Curling their monstrous heads, and hanging them
With deaff'ning Clamors in the slipp'ry Clouds,
That with the hurley, Death it selfe awakes?
Canst thou (O partiall Sleepe) giue thy Repose
To the wet Sea-Boy, in an houre so rude:
And in the calmest, and most stillest Night,
With all appliances, and meanes to boote,
Deny it to a King? Then happy Lowe, lye downe,
Vneasie lyes the Head that weares a Crowne.

Enter Warwicke and Surrey.

War. Many good-morrowes to your Maiestie.

King. Is it good-morrow, Lords?

War. 'Tis One a Clock, and past.

King. Why then good-morrow to you all (my Lords:)
Haue you read o're the Letters that I sent you?

War. We haue (my Liege.)

King. Then you perceiue the Body of our Kingdome,
How foule it is: what ranke Diseases grow,
And with what danger, neere the Heart of it?

War. It is but as a Body, yet distemper'd,
Which to his former strength may be restor'd,
With good aduice, and little Medicine:
My Lord *Northumberland* will soone be cool'd.

King. Oh Heauen, that one might read the Book of Fate,
And see the reuolution of the Times
Make Mountaines leuell, and the Continent
(Wearie of solide firmenesse) melt it selfe
Into the Sea: and other Times, to see
The beachie Girdle of the Ocean
Too wide for *Neptunes* hippes; how Chances mocks
And Changes fill the Cuppe of Alteration.
With diuers Liquors. 'Tis not tenne yeeres gone,
Since *Richard*, and *Northumberland*, great friends,
Did feast together; and in two yeeres after,
Were they at Warres. It is but eight yeeres since,
This *Percie* was the man, neerest my Soule,
Who, like a Brother, toyl'd in my Affaires,
And layd his Loue and Life vnder my foot:
Yea, for my sake, euen to the eyes of *Richard*
Gaue him defiance. But which of you was by
(You Cousin *Nevill*, as I may remember)
When *Richard*, with his Eye, brim-full of Teares,
(Then check'd, and rated by *Northumberland*)
Did speake these words (now prou'd a Prophecie:)
Northumberland, thou Ladder, by the which

My

My Cousin *Bullingbrooke* ascends my Throne:
(Though then, Heauen knowes, I had no such intent,
But that necessitie so bow'd the State,
That I and Greatnesse were compell'd to kisse:)
The Time shall come (thus did hee follow it)
The Time will come, that foule Sinne gathering head,
Shall breake into Corruption: so went on,
Fore-telling this same Times Condition,
And the diuision of our Amitie.

War. There is a Historie in all mens Liues,
Figuring the nature of the Times deceas'd:
The which obseru'd, a man may prophecie
With a neere ayme, of the maine chance of things,
As yet not come to Life, which in their Seedes
And weake beginnings lye entreasured:
Such things become the Hatch and Brood of Time;
And by the necessarie forme of this,
King *Richard* might create a perfect guesse,
That great *Northumberland*, then false to him,
Would of that Seed, grow to a greater falsenesse,
Which should not finde a ground to roote vpon,
Vnlesse on you.

King. Are these things then Necessities?
Then let vs meete them like Necessities;
And that same word, euen now cryes out on vs:
They say, the Bishop and *Northumberland*
Are fiftie thousand strong.

War. It cannot be (my Lord:)
Rumor doth double, like the Voice, and Eccho,
The numbers of the feared. Please it your Grace
To goe to bed, vpon my Life (my Lord)
The Pow'rs that you alreadie haue sent forth,
Shall bring this Prize in very easily.
To comfort you the more, I haue receiu'd
A certaine instance, that *Glendour* is dead.
Your Maiestie hath beene this fort-night ill,
And these vnseason'd howres perforce must adde
Vnto your Sicknesse.

King. I will take your counsaile:
And were these inward Warres once out of hand,
Wee would (deare Lords) vnto the Holy-Land.

Exeunt.

Scena Secunda.

Enter Shallow and Silence: with Mouldie, Shadow, Wart, Feeble, Bull-calfe.

Shal. Come-on, come-on, come-on: giue mee your Hand, Sir; giue mee your Hand, Sir: an early stirrer, by the Rood. And how doth my good Cousin *Silence*?

Sil. Good-morrow, good Cousin *Shallow*.

Shal. And how doth my Cousin, your Bed-fellow? and your fairest Daughter, and mine, my God-Daughter *Ellen*?

Sil. Alas, a blacke Ouzell (Cousin *Shallow*.)

Shal. By yea and nay, Sir, I dare say my Cousin *William* is become a good Scholler? hee is at Oxford still, is hee not?

Sil. Indeede Sir, to my cost.

Shal. Hee must then to the Innes of Court shortly: I was once of *Clements* Inne; where (I thinke) they will talke of mad *Shallow* yet.

Sil. You were call'd lustie *Shallow* then (Cousin.)

Shal. I was call'd any thing: and I would haue done any thing indeede too, and roundly too. There was I, and little *Iohn Doit* of Staffordshire, and blacke *George Bare*, and *Francis Pick-bone*, and *Will Squele* a Cot-sal-man, you had not foure such Swindge-bucklers in all the Innes of Court againe: And I may say to you, wee knew where the *Bona-Roba's* were, and had the best of them all at commandement. Then was *Iacke Falstaffe* (now Sir *Iohn*) a Boy, and Page to *Thomas Mowbray*, Duke of Norfolke.

Sil. This Sir *Iohn* (Cousin) that comes hither anon about Souldiers?

Shal. The same Sir *Iohn*, the very same: I saw him breake *Scoggan's* Head at the Court-Gate, when hee was a Crack, not thus high: and the very same day did I fight with one *Sampson Stock-fish*, a Fruiterer, behinde Greyes-Inne. Oh the mad dayes that I haue spent! and to see how many of mine olde Acquaintance are dead?

Sil. Wee shall all follow (Cousin.)

Shal. Certaine: 'tis certaine: very sure, very sure: Death is certaine to all, all shall dye. How a good Yoke of Bullocks at Stamford Fayre?

Sil. Truly Cousin, I was not there.

Shal. Death is certaine. Is old *Double* of your Towne liuing yet?

Sil. Dead, Sir.

Shal. Dead? See, see: hee drew a good Bow: and dead? hee shot a fine shoote. *Iohn* of Gaunt loued him well, and betted much Money on his head. Dead? hee would haue clapt in the Clowt at Twelue-score, and carryed you a fore-hand Shaft at foureteene, and foureteene and a halfe, that it would haue done a mans heart good to see. How a score of Ewes now?

Sil. Thereafter as they be: a score of good Ewes may be worth tenne pounds.

Shal. And is olde *Double* dead?

Enter Bardolph and his Boy.

Sil. Heere come two of Sir *Iohn Falstaffes* Men (as I thinke.)

Shal. Good-morrow, honest Gentlemen.

Bard. I beseech you, which is Iustice *Shallow*?

Shal. I am *Robert Shallow* (Sir) a poore Esquire of this Countie, and one of the Kings Iustices of the Peace: What is your good pleasure with me?

Bard. My Captaine (Sir) commends him to you: my Captaine, Sir *Iohn Falstaffe*: a tall Gentleman, and a most gallant Leader.

Shal. Hee greetes me well: (Sir) I knew him a good Back-Sword-man. How doth the good Knight? may I aske, how my Lady his Wife doth?

Bard. Sir, pardon: a Souldier is better accommodated, then with a Wife.

Shal. It is well said, Sir; and it is well said, indeede, too: Better accommodated? it is good, yea indeede is it: good phrases are surely, and euery where very commendable. Accommodated, it comes of *Accommodo*: very good, a good Phrase.

Bard. Pardon, Sir, I haue heard the word. Phrase call you it? by this Day, I know not the Phrase: but I will maintaine the Word with my Sword, to bee a Souldier-like Word, and a Word of exceeding good Command. Accommodated: that is, when a man is (as they say) accommodated: or, when a man is, being

whereby

whereby he thought to be accommodated, which is an excellent thing.

Enter Falstaffe.

Shal. It is very iust: Looke, heere comes good Sir *Iohn*. Giue me your hand, giue me your Worships good hand: Trust me, you looke well: and beare your yeares very well. Welcome, good Sir *Iohn*.

Fal. I am glad to see you well, good M. *Robert Shallow*: Master *Sure-card* as I thinke?

Shal. No sir *Iohn*, it is my Cosin *Silence*: in Commission with mee.

Fal. Good M. *Silence*, it well befits you should be of the peace.

Sil. Your good Worship is welcome.

Fal Fye, this is hot weather (Gentlemen) haue you prouided me heere halfe a dozen of sufficient men?

Shal. Marry haue we sir: Will you sit?

Fal. Let me see them, I beseech you.

Shal. Where's the Roll? Where's the Roll? Where's the Roll? Let me see, let me see, let me see: so, so, so, so: yea marry Sir. *Raphe Mouldie*: let them appeare as I call: let them do so, let them do so: Let mee see, Where is *Mouldie*?

Moul. Heere, if it please you.

Shal. What thinke you (Sir *Iohn*) a good limb'd fellow: yong, strong, and of good friends.

Fal. Is thy name *Mouldie*?

Moul. Yea, if it please you.

Fal. 'Tis the more time thou wert vs'd.

Shal. Ha, ha, ha, most excellent. Things that are mouldie, lacke vse: very singular good. Well saide Sir *Iohn*, very well said.

Fal. Pricke him.

Moul. I was prickt well enough before, if you could haue let me alone: my old Dame will be vndone now, for one to doe her Husbandry, and her Drudgery; you need not to haue prickt me, there are other men fitter to goe out, then I.

Fal. Go too: peace *Mouldie*, you shall goe. *Mouldie*, it is time you were spent.

Moul. Spent?

Shallow. Peace, fellow, peace; stand aside: Know you where you are? For the other sir *Iohn*: Let me see: *Simon Shadow*.

Fal. I marry, let me haue him to sit vnder: he's like to be a cold souldier.

Shal. Where's *Shadow*?

Shad. Heere sir.

Fal. *Shadow*, whose sonne art thou?

Shad. My Mothers sonne, Sir.

Falst. Thy Mothers sonne: like enough, and thy Fathers shadow: so the sonne of the Female, is the shadow of the Male: it is often so indeede, but not of the Fathers substance.

Shal. Do you like him, sir *Iohn*?

Falst. *Shadow* will serue for Summer: pricke him: For wee haue a number of shadowes to fill vppe the Muster-Booke.

Shal. *Thomas Wart*?

Falst. Where's he?

Wart. Heere sir.

Falst. Is thy name *Wart*?

Wart. Yea sir.

Fal. Thou art a very ragged Wart.

Shal. Shall I pricke him downe, Sir *Iohn*?

Falst. It were superfluous: for his apparrel is built vpon his backe, and the whole frame stands vpon pins: prick him no more.

Shal. Ha, ha, ha, you can do it sir: you can doe it: I commend you well.

Francis Feeble.

Feeble. Heere sir.

Shal. What Trade art thou *Feeble*?

Feeble. A Womans Taylor sir.

Shal. Shall I pricke him, sir?

Fal. You may:
But if he had beene a mans Taylor, he would haue prick'd you. Wilt thou make as many holes in an enemies Battaile, as thou hast done in a Womans petticote?

Feeble. I will doe my good will sir, you can haue no more.

Falst. Well said, good Womans Tailour: Well sayde Couragious *Feeble*: thou wilt bee as valiant as the wrathfull Doue, or most magnanimous Mouse. Pricke the womans Taylour well Master *Shallow*, deepe Maister *Shallow*.

Feeble. I would *Wart* might haue gone sir.

Fal. I would thou wert a mans Tailor, that ỳ might'st mend him, and make him fit to goe. I cannot put him to a priuate souldier, that is the Leader of so many thousands. Let that suffice, most Forcible *Feeble*.

Feeble. It shall suffice.

Falst. I am bound to thee, reuerend *Feeble*. Who is the next?

Shal. *Peter Bulcalfe* of the Greene.

Falst. Yea marry, let vs see *Bulcalfe*.

Bul. Heere sir.

Fal. Trust me, a likely Fellow. Come, pricke me *Bulcalfe* till he roare againe.

Bul. Oh, good my Lord Captaine.

Fal. What? do'st thou roare before th'art prickt.

Bul. Oh sir, I am a diseased man.

Fal. What disease hast thou?

Bul. A whorson cold sir, a cough sir, which I caught with Ringing in the Kings affayres, vpon his Coronation day, sir.

Fal. Come, thou shalt go to the Warres in a Gowne: we will haue away thy Cold, and I will take such order that thy friends shall ring for thee. Is heere all?

Shal. There is two more called then your number: you must haue but foure heere sir, and so I pray you go in with me to dinner.

Fal. Come, I will goe drinke with you, but I cannot tarry dinner. I am glad to see you in good troth, Master *Shallow*.

Shal. O sir *Iohn*, doe you remember since wee lay all night in the Winde-mill, in S Georges Field.

Falstaffe. No more of that good Master *Shallow*: No more of that.

Shal. Ha? it was a merry night. And is *Iane Nightworke* aliue?

Fal. She liues, M. *Shallow*.

Shal. She neuer could away with me.

Fal. Neuer, neuer: she would alwayes say shee could not abide M. *Shallow*.

Shal. I could anger her to the heart: shee was then a *Bona-Roba*. Doth she hold her owne well.

Fal. Old, old, M. *Shallow*.

Shal. Nay, she must be old, she cannot choose but be

old: certaine shee's old: and had *Robin Night-worke*, by old *Night-worke*, before I came to *Clements* Inne.

Sil. That's fiftie fiue yeeres agoe.

Shal. Hah, Cousin *Silence*, that thou hadst seene that, that this Knight and I haue seene: hah, Sir *Iohn*, said I well?

Falst. Wee haue heard the Chymes at mid-night, Master *Shallow*.

Shal. That wee haue, that wee haue; in faith, Sir *Iohn*, wee haue: our watch-word was, Hem-Boyes. Come, let's to Dinner; come, let's to Dinner: Oh the dayes that wee haue seene. Come, come.

Bul Good Master Corporate *Bardolph*, stand my friend, and heere is foure *Harry* tenne shillings in French Crownes for you: in very truth, sir, I had as lief be hang'd sir, as goe: and yet, for mine owne part, sir, I do not care; but rather, because I am vnwilling, and for mine owne part, haue a desire to stay with my friends: else, sir, I did not care, for mine owne part, so much.

Bard. Go-too: stand aside.

Mould. And good Master Corporall Captaine, for my old Dames sake, stand my friend: shee hath no body to doe any thing about her, when I am gone: and she is old, and cannot helpe her selfe: you shall haue fortie, sir.

Bard. Go-too: stand aside.

Feeble. I care not, a man can die but once: wee owe a death. I will neuer beare a base minde: if it be my destinie, so: if it be not, so: no man is too good to serue his Prince: and let it goe which way it will, he that dies this yeere, is quit for the next.

Bard. Well said, thou art a good fellow.

Feeble. Nay, I will beare no base minde.

Falst. Come sir, which men shall I haue?

Shal. Foure of which you please.

Bard. Sir, a word with you: I haue three pound, to free *Mouldie* and *Bull-calfe*.

Falst. Go-too: well.

Shal. Come, sir *Iohn*, which foure will you haue?

Falst. Doe you chuse for me.

Shal. Marry then, *Mouldie*, *Bull-calfe*, *Feeble*, and *Shadow*.

Falst. *Mouldie*, and *Bull-calfe*: for you *Mouldie*, stay at home, till you are past seruice: and for your part, *Bull-calfe*, grow till you come vnto it: I will none of you.

Shal. Sir *Iohn*, Sir *Iohn*, doe not your selfe wrong, they are your likelyest men, and I would haue you seru'd with the best.

Falst. Will you tell me (Master *Shallow*) how to chuse a man? Care I for the Limbe, the Thewes, the stature, bulke, and bigge assemblance of a man? giue mee the spirit (Master *Shallow*.) Where's *Wart*? you see what a ragged appearance it is: hee shall charge you, and discharge you, with the motion of a Pewterers Hammer: come off, and on, swifter then hee that gibbets on the Brewers Bucket. And this same halfe-fac'd fellow, *Shadow*, giue me this man: hee presents no marke to the Enemie, the foe-man may with as great ayme leuell at the edge of a Pen-knife: and for a Retrait, how swiftly will this *Feeble*, the Womans Taylor, runne off. O, giue me the spare men, and spare me the great ones. Put me a Calyuer into *Warts* hand, *Bardolph*.

Bard. Hold *Wart*, Trauerse: thus, thus, thus.

Falst. Come, manage me your Calyuer: so: very well, go-too, very good, exceeding good. O, giue me alwayes a little, leane, old, chopt, bald Shot. Well said *Wart*, thou art a good Scab: hold, there is a Tester for thee.

Shal. Hee is not his Crafts-master, hee doth not doe it right. I remember at Mile-end-Greene, when I lay at *Clements* Inne, I was then Sir *Dagonet* in *Arthurs* Show: there was a little quiuer fellow, and hee would manage you his Peece thus: and hee would about, and about, and come you in, and come you in: Rah, tah, tah, would hee say, Bownce would hee say, and away againe would hee goe, and againe would he come: I shall neuer see such a fellow.

Falst. These fellowes will doe well, Master *Shallow*. Farewell Master *Silence*, I will not vse many wordes with you: fare you well, Gentlemen both: I thanke you: I must a dozen mile to night. *Bardolph*, giue the Souldiers Coates.

Shal. Sir *Iohn*, Heauen blesse you, and prosper your Affaires, and send vs Peace. As you returne, visit my house. Let our old acquaintance be renewed: peraduenture I will with you to the Court.

Falst. I would you would, Master *Shallow*.

Shal. Go-too: I haue spoke at a word. Fare you well. *Exit.*

Falst. Fare you well, gentle Gentlemen. On *Bardolph*, leade the men away. As I returne, I will fetch off these Iustices: I doe see the bottome of Iustice *Shallow*. How subiect wee old men are to this vice of Lying? This same staru'd Iustice hath done nothing but prate to me of the wildenesse of his Youth, and the Feates hee hath done about Turnball-street, and euery third word a Lye, duer pay'd to the hearer, then the Turkes Tribute. I doe remember him at *Clements* Inne, like a man made after Supper, of a Cheese-paring. When hee was naked, hee was, for all the world, like a forked Radish, with a Head fantastically caru'd vpon it with a Knife. Hee was so forlorne, that his Dimensions (to any thicke sight) were inuincible. Hee was the very *Genius* of Famine: hee came euer in the rere-ward of the Fashion: And now is this Vices Dagger become a Squire, and talkes as familiarly of *Iohn* of Gaunt, as if hee had beene sworne Brother to him: and Ile be sworne hee neuer saw him but once in the Tilt-yard, and then he burst his Head, for crowding among the Marshals men. I saw it, and told *Iohn* of Gaunt, hee beat his owne Name, for you might haue truss'd him and all his Apparrell into an Eele-skinne: the Case of a Treble Hoeboy was a Mansion for him: a Court: and now hath hee Land, and Beeues. Well, I will be acquainted with him, if I returne: and it shall goe hard, but I will make him a Philosophers two Stones to me. If the young Dace be a Bayt for the old Pike, I see no reason, in the Law of Nature, but I may snap at him. Let time shape, and there an end. *Exeunt.*

Actus Quartus. Scena Prima.

Enter the Arch-bishop, Mowbray, Hastings, Westmerland, Coleuile.

Bish. What is this Forrest call'd?

Hast. 'Tis Gualtree Forrest, and't shall please your Grace.

Bish. Here stand (my Lords) and send discouerers forth, To know the numbers of our Enemies.

Hast. Wee

Hast. Wee haue sent forth alreadie.
Bish. 'Tis well done.
My Friends,and Brethren (in these great Affaires)
I must acquaint you,that I haue receiu'd
New-dated Letters from *Northumberland:*
Their cold intent,tenure,and substance thus.
Here doth hee wish his Person,with such Powers
As might hold sortance with his Qualitie,
The which hee could not leuie: whereupon
Hee is retyr'd,to ripe his growing Fortunes,
To Scotland; and concludes in heartie prayers,
That your Attempts may ouer-liue the hazard,
And fearefull meeting of their Opposite.
Mow. Thus do the hopes we haue in him,touch ground,
And dash themselues to pieces.

Enter a Messenger.

Hast. Now? what newes?
Mess. West of this Forrest,scarcely off a mile,
In goodly forme,comes on the Enemie:
And by the ground they hide, I iudge their number
Vpon,or neere,the rate of thirtie thousand.
Mow. The iust proportion that we gaue them out.
Let vs sway-on,and face them in the field.

Enter Westmerland.

Bish. What well-appointed Leader fronts vs here?
Mow. I thinke it is my Lord of Westmerland.
West. Health,and faire greeting from our Generall,
The Prince,Lord *Iohn*,and Duke of Lancaster.
Bish. Say on (my Lord of Westmerland) in peace:
What doth concerne your comming?
West. Then (my Lord)
Vnto your Grace doe I in chiefe addresse
The substance of my Speech. If that Rebellion
Came like it selfe,in base and abiect Routs,
Led on by bloodie Youth,guarded with Rage,
And countenanc'd by Boyes,and Beggerie:
I say,if damn'd Commotion so appeare,
In his true,natiue,and most proper shape,
You (Reuerend Father,and these Noble Lords)
Had not beene here,to dresse the ougly forme
Of base,and bloodie Insurrection,
With your faire Honors. You,Lord Arch-bishop,
Whose Sea is by a Ciuill Peace maintain'd,
Whose Beard,the Siluer Hand of Peace hath touch'd,
Whose Learning,and good Letters,Peace hath tutor'd,
Whose white Inuestments figure Innocence,
The Doue,and very blessed Spirit of Peace.
Wherefore doe you so ill translate your selfe,
Out of the Speech of Peace,that beares such grace,
Into the harsh and boystrous Tongue of Warre?
Turning your Bookes to Graues, your Inke to Blood,
Your Pennes to Launces,and your Tongue diuine
To a lowd Trumpet,and a Point of Warre.
Bish. Wherefore doe I this? so the Question stands.
Briefely to this end: Wee are all diseas'd,
And with our surfetting,and wanton howres,
Haue brought our selues into a burning Feuer,
And wee must bleede for it: of which Disease,
Our late King *Richard* (being infected) dy'd.
But (my most Noble Lord of Westmerland)
I take not on me here as a Physician,
Nor doe I,as an Enemie to Peace,
Troope in the Throngs of Militarie men:
But rather shew a while like fearefull Warre,
To dyet ranke Mindes,sicke of happinesse,
And purge th'obstructions, which begin to stop
Our very Veines of Life: heare me more plainely.
I haue in equall ballance iustly weigh'd,
What wrongs our Arms may do,what wrongs we suffer,
And finde our Griefes heauier then our Offences.
Wee see which way the streame of Time doth runne,
And are enforc'd from our most quiet there,
By the rough Torrent of Occasion,
And haue the summarie of all our Griefes
(When time shall serue) to shew in Articles;
Which long ere this,wee offer'd to the King,
And might,by no Suit,gayne our Audience:
When wee are wrong'd,and would vnfold our Griefes,
Wee are deny'd accesse vnto his Person,
Euen by those men,that most haue done vs wrong.
The dangers of the dayes but newly gone,
Whose memorie is written on the Earth
With yet appearing blood; and the examples
Of euery Minutes instance (present now)
Hath put vs in these ill-beseeming Armes:
Not to breake Peace,or any Branch of it,
But to establish here a Peace indeede,
Concurring both in Name and Qualitie.
West. When euer yet was your Appeale deny'd?
Wherein haue you beene galled by the King?
What Peere hath beene suborn'd,to grate on you,
That you should seale this lawlesse bloody Booke
Of forg'd Rebellion,with a Seale diuine?
Bish. My Brother generall,the Common-wealth,
I make my Quarrell,in particular.
West. There is no neede of any such redresse:
Or if there were,it not belongs to you.
Mow. Why not to him in part, and to vs all,
That feele the bruizes of the dayes before,
And suffer the Condition of these Times
To lay a heauie and vnequall Hand vpon our Honors?
West. O my good Lord *Mowbray*,
Construe the Times to their Necessities,
And you shall say (indeede) it is the Time,
And not the King,that doth you iniuries.
Yet for your part,it not appeares to me,
Either from the King,or in the present Time,
That you should haue an ynch of any ground
To build a Griefe on: were you not restor'd
To all the Duke of Norfolkes Seignories,
Your Noble,and right well-remembred Fathers?
Mow. What thing,in Honor,had my Father lost,
That need to be reuiu'd,and breath'd in me?
The King that lou'd him,as the State stood then,
Was forc'd,perforce compell'd to banish him:
And then,that *Henry Bullingbrooke* and hee
Being mounted,and both rowsed in their Seates,
Their neighing Coursers daring of the Spurre,
Their armed Staues in charge,their Beauers downe,
Their eyes of fire,sparkling through sights of Steele,
And the lowd Trumpet blowing them together:
Then,then,when there was nothing could haue stay'd
My Father from the Breast of *Bullingbrooke*;
O,when the King did throw his Warder downe,
(His owne Life hung vpon the Staffe hee threw)
Then threw hee downe himselfe,and all their Liues,
That by Indictment,and by dint of Sword,
Haue since mis-carryed vnder *Bullingbrooke*.

West. You speak (Lord *Mowbray*) now you know not what.
The Earle of Hereford was reputed then
In England the most valiant Gentleman.
Who knowes, on whom Fortune would then haue smil'd?
But if your Father had beene Victor there,
Hee ne're had borne it out of Couentry.
For all the Countrey, in a generall voyce,
Cry'd hate vpon him: and all their prayers, and loue,
Were set on *Herford*, whom they doted on,
And bless'd, and grac'd, and did more then the King.
But this is meere digression from my purpose.
Here come I from our Princely Generall,
To know your Griefes; to tell you, from his Grace,
That hee will giue you Audience: and wherein
It shall appeare, that your demands are iust,
You shall enioy them, euery thing set off,
That might so much as thinke you Enemies.

Mow. But hee hath forc'd vs to compell this Offer,
And it proceedes from Pollicy, not Loue.

West. *Mowbray*, you ouer-weene to take it so:
This Offer comes from Mercy, not from Feare.
For loe, within a Ken our Army lyes,
Vpon mine Honor, all too confident
To giue admittance to a thought of feare.
Our Battaile is more full of Names then yours,
Our Men more perfect in the vse of Armes,
Our Armor all as strong, our Cause the best;
Then Reason will, our hearts should be as good.
Say you not then, our Offer is compell'd.

Mow. Well, by my will, wee shall admit no Parley.

West. That argues but the shame of your offence:
A rotten Case abides no handling.

Hast. Hath the Prince *Iohn* a full Commission,
In very ample vertue of his Father,
To heare, and absolutely to determine
Of what Conditions wee shall stand vpon?

West. That is intended in the Generals Name:
I muse you make so slight a Question.

Bish. Then take (my Lord of Westmerland) this Schedule,
For this containes our generall Grieuances:
Each seuerall Article herein redress'd,
All members of our Cause, both here, and hence,
That are insinewed to this Action,
Acquitted by a true substantiall forme,
And present execution of our wills,
To vs, and to our purposes confin'd,
Wee come within our awfull Banks againe,
And knit our Powers to the Arme of Peace.

West. This will I shew the Generall. Please you Lords,
In sight of both our Battailes, wee may meete
At either end in peace: which Heauen so frame,
Or to the place of difference call the Swords,
Which must decide it.

Bish. My Lord, wee will doe so.

Mow. There is a thing within my Bosome tells me,
That no Conditions of our Peace can stand.

Hast. Feare you not, that if wee can make our Peace
Vpon such large termes, and so absolute,
As our Conditions shall consist vpon,
Our Peace shall stand as firme as Rockie Mountaines.

Mow. I, but our valuation shall be such,
That euery slight, and false-deriued Cause,
Yea, euery idle, nice, and wanton Reason,
Shall, to the King, taste of this Action:
That were our Royall faiths, Martyrs in Loue,
Wee shall be winnowed with so rough a winde,
That euen our Corne shall seeme as light as Chaffe,
And good from bad finde no partition.

Bish. No, no (my Lord) note this: the King is wearie
Of daintie, and such picking Grieuances:
For hee hath found, to end one doubt by Death,
Reuiues two greater in the Heires of Life.
And therefore will hee wipe his Tables cleane,
And keepe no Tell-tale to his Memorie,
That may repeat, and Historie his losse,
To new remembrance. For full well hee knowes,
Hee cannot so precisely weede this Land,
As his mis-doubts present occasion:
His foes are so en-rooted with his friends,
That plucking to vnfixe an Enemie,
Hee doth vnfasten so, and shake a friend.
So that this Land, like an offensiue wife,
That hath enrag'd him on, to offer strokes,
As he is striking, holds his Infant vp,
And hangs resolu'd Correction in the Arme,
That was vpreard to execution.

Hast. Besides, the King hath wasted all his Rods,
On late Offenders, that he now doth lacke
The very Instruments of Chasticement:
So that his power, like to a Fanglesse Lion
May offer, but not hold.

Bish. 'Tis very true:
And therefore be assur'd (my good Lord Marshal)
If we do now make our attonement well,
Our Peace, will (like a broken Limbe vnited)
Grow stronger, for the breaking.

Mow. Be it so:
Heere is return'd my Lord of Westmerland.

Enter Westmerland.

West. The Prince is here at hand: pleaseth your Lordship
To meet his Grace, iust distance 'tweene our Armies?

Mow. Your Grace of Yorke, in heauen's name then forward.

Bish. Before, and greet his Grace (my Lord) we come.

Enter Prince Iohn.

Iohn. You are wel encountred here (my cosin *Mowbray*)
Good day to you, gentle Lord Archbishop,
And so to you Lord *Hastings*, and to all.
My Lord of Yorke, it better shew'd with you,
When that your Flocke (assembled by the Bell)
Encircled you, to heare with reuerence
Your exposition on the holy Text,
Then now to see you heere an Iron man
Chearing a rowt of Rebels with your Drumme,
Turning the Word, to Sword; and Life to death:
That man that sits within a Monarches heart,
And ripens in the Sunne-shine of his fauor,
Would hee abuse the Countenance of the King,
Alack, what Mischiefes might hee set abroach,
In shadow of such Greatnesse? With you, Lord Bishop,
It is euen so. Who hath not heard it spoken,
How deepe you were within the Bookes of Heauen?
To vs, the Speaker in his Parliament;
To vs, th'imagine Voyce of Heauen it selfe:
The very Opener, and Intelligencer,
Betweene the Grace, the Sanctities of Heauen,
And our dull workings. O, who shall beleeue,
But you mis-vse the reuerence of your Place,
Employ the Countenance, and Grace of Heauen,
As a false Fauorite doth his Princes Name,
In deedes dis-honorable? You haue taken vp,

Vnder

Vnder the counterfeited Zeale of Heauen,
The Subiects of Heauens Substitute, my Father,
And both against the Peace of Heauen,and him,
Haue here vp-swarmed them.

Bish. Good my Lord of Lancaster,
I am not here against your Fathers Peace.
But (as I told my Lord of Westmerland)
The Time (mis-order'd) doth in common sence
Crowd vs,and crush vs,to this monstrous Forme,
To hold our safetie vp. I sent your Grace
The parcels, and particulars of our Griefe,
The which hath been with scorne shou'd from the Court:
Whereon this *Hydra*-Sonne of Warre is borne,
Whose dangerous eyes may well be charm'd asleepe,
With graunt of our most iust and right desires;
And true Obedience,of this Madnesse cur'd,
Stoope tamely to the foot of Maiestie.

Mow. If not,wee readie are to trye our fortunes,
To the last man.

Hast. And though wee here fall downe,
Wee haue Supplyes, to second our Attempt:
If they mis-carry,theirs shall second them.
And so,successe of Mischiefe shall be borne,
And Heire from Heire shall hold this Quarrell vp,
Whiles England shall haue generation.

Iohn. You are too shallow (*Hastings*)
Much too shallow,
To sound the bottome of the after-Times.

West. Pleaseth your Grace,to answere them directly,
How farre-forth you doe like their Articles.

Iohn. I like them all,and doe allow them well
And sweare here,by the honor of my blood,
My Fathers purposes haue beene mistooke,
And some,about him,haue too lauishly
Wrested his meaning,and Authoritie.
My Lord,these Griefes shall be with speed redrest:
Vpon my Life,they shall. If this may please you,
Discharge your Powers vnto their seuerall Counties,
As wee will ours: and here,betweene the Armies,
Let's drinke together friendly,and embrace,
That all their eyes may beare those Tokens home,
Of our restored Loue,and Amitie.

Bish. I take your Princely word,for these redresses,

Iohn. I giue it you,and will maintaine my word:
And thereupon I drinke vnto your Grace.

Hast. Goe Captaine,and deliuer to the Armie
This newes of Peace: let them haue pay,and part:
I know,it will well please them.
High thee Captaine. *Exit.*

Bish. To you,my Noble Lord of Westmerland,

West. I pledge your Grace:
And if you knew what paines I haue bestow'd,
To breede this present Peace,
You would drinke freely: but my loue to ye,
Shall shew it selfe more openly hereafter.

Bish. I doe not doubt you.

West. I am glad of it.
Health to my Lord,and gentle Cousin *Mowbray*.

Mow. You wish me health in very happy season,
For I am,on the sodaine,something ill.

Bish. Against ill Chances,men are euer merry,
But heauinesse fore-runnes the good euent.

West. Therefore be merry(Cooze)since sodaine sorrow
Serues to say thus: some good thing comes to morrow.

Bish. Beleeue me,I am passing light in spirit.

Mow. So much the worse,if your owne Rule be true.

Iohn. The word of Peace is render'd: hearke how they showt.

Mow. This had been chearefull,after Victorie.

Bish. A Peace is of the nature of a Conquest
For then both parties nobly are subdu'd,
And neither partie looser.

Iohn. Goe (my Lord)
And let our Army be discharged too:
And good my Lord(so please you)let our Traines
March by vs,that wee may peruse the men *Exit.*
Wee should haue coap'd withall.

Bish. Goe,good Lord *Hastings*:
And ere they be dismiss'd,let them march by. *Exit.*

Iohn. I trust(Lords)wee shall lye to night together.

Enter Westmerland.

Now Cousin,wherefore stands our Army still?

West. The Leaders hauing charge from you to stand,
Will not goe off,vntill they heare you speake.

Iohn. They know their duties. *Enter Hastings.*

Hast. Our Army is dispers'd:
Like youthfull Steeres,vnyoak'd, they tooke their course
East, West,North,South:or like a Schoole,broke vp,
Each hurryes towards his home,and sporting place.

West. Good tidings(my Lord *Hastings*)for the which,
I doe arrest thee(Traytor) of high Treason:
And you Lord Arch-bishop, and you Lord *Mowbray*,
Of Capitall Treason,I attach you both.

Mow. Is this proceeding iust,and honorable?

West. Is your Assembly so?

Bish. Will you thus breake your faith?

Iohn. I pawn'd thee none:
I promis'd you redresse of these same Grieuances
Whereof you did complaine; which,by mine Honor,
I will performe,with a most Christian care.
But for you(Rebels) looke to taste the due
Meet for Rebellion,and such Acts as yours.
Most shallowly did you these Armes commence,
Fondly brougnt here,and foolishly sent hence.
Strike vp our Drummes,pursue the scatter'd stray,
Heauen,and not wee,haue safely fought to day.
Some guard these Traitors to the Block of Death,
Treasons true Bed,and yeelder vp of breath. *Exeunt.*

Enter Falstaffe and Collevile.

Falst. What's your Name,Sir? of what Condition are you? and of what place,I pray?

Col. I am a Knight,Sir:
And my Name is *Collevile* of the Dale.

Falst. Well then, *Collevile* is your Name, a Knight is your Degree, and your Place,the Dale. *Collevile* shall still be your Name,a Traytor your Degree,and the Dungeon your Place,a place deepe enough: so shall you be still *Collevile* of the Dale.

Col. Are not you Sir *Iohn Falstaffe*?

Falst. As good a man as he sir, who ere I am: doe yee yeelde sir,or shall I sweate for you? if I doe sweate, they are the drops of thy Louers.and they weep for thy death, therefore rowze vp Feare and Trembling, and do obseruance to my mercy.

Col. I thinke you are Sir *Iohn Falstaffe*,& in that thought yeeld me.

Fal. I haue a whole Schoole of tongues in this belly of mine, and not a Tongue of them all, speakes anie other word but my name: and I had but a belly of any indifferencie, I were simply the most actiue fellow in Europe: my wombe, my wombe,my wombe vndoes mee. Heere comes our Generall.

Enter Prince Iohn, and Westmerland.

Iohn. The heat is past, follow no farther now:
Call in the Powers, good Cousin *Westmerland*.
Now *Falstaffe*, where haue you beene all this while?
When euery thing is ended, then you come.
These tardie Tricks of yours will (on my life)
One time, or other, breake some Gallowes back.

Falst. I would bee sorry (my Lord) but it should bee thus: I neuer knew yet, but rebuke and checke was the reward of Valour. Doe you thinke me a Swallow, an Arrow, or a Bullet? Haue I, in my poore and olde Motion, the expedition of Thought? I haue speeded hither with the very extremest ynch of possibilitie. I haue fowndred nine score and odde Postes: and heere (trauell-tainted as I am) haue, in my pure and immaculate Valour, taken Sir *Iohn Collevile* of the Dale, a most furious Knight, and valorous Enemie: But what of that? hee saw mee, and yeelded: that I may iustly say with the hooke-nos'd fellow of Rome, I came, saw, and ouer-came.

Iohn. It was more of his Courtesie, then your deseruing.

Falst. I know not: heere hee is, and heere I yeeld him: and I beseech your Grace, let it be book'd, with the rest of this dayes deedes; or I sweare, I will haue it in a particular Ballad, with mine owne Picture on the top of it (*Collevile* kissing my foot:) To the which course, if I be enforc'd, if you do not all shew like gilt two-pences to me; and I, in the cleare Skie of Fame, o're-shine you as much as the Full Moone doth the Cynders of the Element (which shew like Pinnes-heads to her) beleeue not the Word of the Noble: therefore let mee haue right, and let desert mount.

Iohn. Thine's too heauie to mount.

Falst. Let it shine then.

Iohn. Thine's too thick to shine.

Falst. Let it doe something (my good Lord) that may doe me good, and call it what you will.

Iohn. Is thy Name *Collevile*?

Col. It is (my Lord.)

Iohn. A famous Rebell art thou, *Collevile*.

Falst. And a famous true Subiect tooke him.

Col. I am (my Lord) but as my Betters are,
That led me hither: had they beene rul'd by me,
You should haue wonne them dearer then you haue.

Falst. I know not how they sold themselues, but thou like a kinde fellow, gau'st thy selfe away; and I thanke thee, for thee.

Enter Westmerland.

Iohn. Haue you left pursuit?

West. Retreat is made, and Execution stay'd.

Iohn. Send *Collevile*, with his Confederates,
To Yorke, to present Execution.
Blunt, leade him hence, and see you guard him sure.

Exit with Collevile.

And now dispatch we toward the Court (my Lords)
I heare the King, my Father, is sore sicke.
Our Newes shall goe before vs, to his Maiestie,
Which (Cousin) you shall beare, to comfort him:
And wee with sober speede will follow you.

Falst. My Lord, I beseech you, giue me leaue to goe through Gloucestershire: and when you come to Court, stand my good Lord, 'pray, in your good report.

Iohn. Fare you well, *Falstaffe*: I, in my condition,
Shall better speake of you, then you deserue. *Exit.*

Falst. I would you had but the wit: 'twere better then your Dukedome. Good faith, this same young sober-blooded Boy doth not loue me, nor a man cannot make him laugh: but that's no maruaile, hee drinkes no Wine. There's neuer any of these demure Boyes come to any proofe: for thinne Drinke doth so ouer-coole their blood, and making many Fish-Meales, that they fall into a kinde of Male Greene-sicknesse: and then, when they marry, they get Wenches. They are generally Fooles, and Cowards; which some of vs should be too, but for inflamation. A good Sherris-Sack hath a two-fold operation in it: it ascends me into the Braine, dryes me there all the foolish, and dull, and cruddie Vapours, which enuiron it: makes it apprehensiue, quicke, forgetiue, full of nimble, fierie, and delectable shapes; which deliuer'd o're to the Voyce, the Tongue, which is the Birth, becomes excellent Wit. The second propertie of your excellent Sherris, is, the warming of the Blood: which before (cold, and setled) left the Liuer white, and pale; which is the Badge of Pusillanimitie, and Cowardize: but the Sherris warmes it, and makes it course from the inwards, to the parts extremes: it illuminateth the Face, which (as a Beacon) giues warning to all the rest of this little Kingdome (Man) to Arme: and then the Vitall Commoners, and in-land pettie Spirits, muster me all to their Captaine, the Heart; who great, and puft vp with his Retinue, doth any Deed of Courage: and this Valour comes of Sherris. So, that skill in the Weapon is nothing, without Sack (for that sets it a-worke.) and Learning, a meere Hoord of Gold, kept by a Deuill, till Sack commences it, and sets it in act, and vse. Hereof comes it, that Prince *Harry* is valiant: for the cold blood hee did naturally inherite of his Father, hee hath, like leane, stirrill, and bare Land, manured, husbanded, and tyll'd, with excellent endeauour of drinking good, and good store of fertile Sherris, that hee is become very hot, and valiant. If I had a thousand Sonnes, the first Principle I would teach them, should be to forsweare thinne Potations, and to addict themselues to Sack. *Enter Bardolph.*
How now *Bardolph*?

Bard. The Armie is discharged all, and gone.

Falst. Let them goe: Ile through Gloucestershire, and there will I visit Master *Robert Shallow*, Esquire: I haue him alreadie tempering betweene my finger and my thombe, and shortly will I seale with him. Come away.

Exeunt.

Scena Secunda.

Enter King, Warwicke, Clarence, Gloucester.

King. Now Lords, if Heauen doth giue successefull end
To this Debate that bleedeth at our doores,
Wee will our Youth lead on to higher Fields,
And draw no Swords, but what are sanctify'd.
Our Nauie is addressed, our Power collected,
Our Substitutes, in absence, well inuested,
And euery thing lyes leuell to our wish;
Onely wee want a little personall Strength:
And pawse vs, till these Rebels, now a-foot,
Come vnderneath the yoake of Gouernment.

War. Both which we doubt not, but your Maiestie
Shall soone enioy.

King. Hum-

King. *Humphrey* (my Sonne of Gloucester) where is the Prince, your Brother?

Glo. I thinke hee's gone to hunt (my Lord) at Windsor.

King. And how accompanied?

Glo. I doe not know (my Lord.)

King. Is not his Brother, *Thomas* of Clarence, with him?

Glo. No (my good Lord) hee is in presence heere.

Clar. What would my Lord, and Father?

King. Nothing but well to thee, *Thomas* of Clarence.
How chance thou art not with the Prince, thy Brother?
Hee loues thee, and thou do'st neglect him (*Thomas.*)
Thou hast a better place in his Affection,
Then all thy Brothers: cherish it (my Boy)
And Noble Offices thou may'st effect
Of Mediation (after I am dead)
Betweene his Greatnesse, and thy other Brethren.
Therefore omit him not: blunt not his Loue,
Nor loose the good aduantage of his Grace,
By seeming cold, or carelesse of his will.
For hee is gracious, if hee be obseru'd:
Hee hath a Teare for Pitie, and a Hand
Open (as Day) for melting Charitie:
Yet notwithstanding, being incens'd, hee's Flint,
As humorous as Winter, and as sudden,
As Flawes congealed in the Spring of day.
His temper therefore must be well obseru'd:
Chide him for faults, and doe it reuerently,
When you perceiue his blood enclin'd to mirth:
But being moodie, giue him Line, and scope,
Till that his passions (like a Whale on ground)
Confound themselues with working. Learne this *Thomas*,
And thou shalt proue a shelter to thy friends,
A Hoope of Gold, to binde thy Brothers in:
That the vnited Vessell of their Blood
(Mingled with Venome of Suggestion,
As force, perforce, the Age will powre it in)
Shall neuer leake, though it doe worke as strong
As *Aconitum*, or rash Gun-powder.

Clar. I shall obserue him with all care, and loue.

King. Why art thou not at Windsor with him (*Thomas?*)

Clar. Hee is not there to day: hee dines in London.

King. And how accompanyed? Canst thou tell that?

Clar. With *Points*, and other his continuall followers.

King. Most subiect is the fattest Soyle to Weedes:
And hee (the Noble Image of my Youth)
Is ouer-spread with them: therefore my griefe
Stretches it selfe beyond the howre of death.
The blood weepes from my heart, when I doe shape
(In formes imaginarie) th'vnguided Dayes,
And rotten Times, that you shall looke vpon,
When I am sleeping with my Ancestors.
For when his head-strong Riot hath no Curbe,
When Rage and hot-Blood are his Counsailors,
When Meanes and lauish Manners meete together;
Oh, with what Wings shall his Affections flye
Towards fronting Perill, and oppos'd Decay?

War. My gracious Lord, you looke beyond him quite:
The Prince but studies his Companions,
Like a strange Tongue: wherein, to gaine the Language,
'Tis needfull, that the most immodest word
Be look'd vpon, and learn'd: which once attayn'd,
Your Highnesse knowes, comes to no farther vse,
But to be knowne, and hated. So, like grosse termes,
The Prince will, in the perfectnesse of time,
Cast off his followers: and their memorie
Shall as a Patterne, or a Measure, liue,
By which his Grace must mete the liues of others,
Turning past-euills to aduantages.

King. 'Tis seldome, when the Bee doth leaue her Combe
In the dead Carrion.

Enter Westmerland.

Who's heere? *Westmerland?*

West. Health to my Soueraigne, and new happinesse
Added to that, that I am to deliuer.
Prince *Iohn*, your Sonne, doth kisse your Graces Hand:
Mowbray, the Bishop, *Scroope*, *Hastings*, and all,
Are brought to the Correction of your Law.
There is not now a Rebels Sword vnsheath'd,
But Peace puts forth her Oliue euery where:
The manner how this Action hath beene borne,
Here (at more leysure) may your Highnesse reade,
With euery course, in his particular.

King. O *Westmerland*, thou art a Summer Bird,
Which euer in the haunch of Winter sings
The lifting vp of day.

Enter Harcourt.

Looke, heere's more newes.

Harc. From Enemies, Heauen keepe your Maiestie:
And when they stand against you, may they fall,
As those that I am come to tell you of.
The Earle *Northumberland*, and the Lord *Bardolfe*,
With a great Power of English, and of Scots,
Are by the Sherife of Yorkeshire ouerthrowne:
The manner, and true order of the fight,
This Packet (please it you) containes at large.

King. And wherefore should these good newes
Make me sicke?
Will Fortune neuer come with both hands full,
But write her faire words still in foulest Letters?
Shee eyther giues a Stomack, and no Foode,
(Such are the poore, in health) or else a Feast,
And takes away the Stomack (such are the Rich,
That haue aboundance, and enioy it not.)
I should reioyce now, at this happy newes,
And now my Sight fayles, and my Braine is giddie.
O me, come neere me, now I am much ill.

Glo. Comfort your Maiestie.

Cla. Oh, my Royall Father.

West. My Soueraigne Lord, cheare vp your selfe, looke vp.

War. Be patient (Princes) you doe know, these Fits
Are with his Highnesse very ordinarie.
Stand from him, giue him ayre:
Hee'le straight be well.

Clar. No, no, hee cannot long hold out: these pangs,
Th'incessant care, and labour of his Minde,
Hath wrought the Mure, that should confine it in,
So thinne, that Life lookes through, and will breake out.

Glo. The people feare me: for they doe obserue
Vnfather'd Heires, and loathly Births of Nature:
The Seasons change their manners, as the Yeere
Had found some Moneths asleepe, and leap'd them ouer.

Clar. The Riuer hath thrice flow'd, no ebbe betweene:
And the old folke (Times doting Chronicles)
Say it did so, a little time before
That our great Grand-sire *Edward* sick'd, and dy'de.

War. Speake lower (Princes) for the King recouers.
Glo. This Apoplexie will (certaine) be his end.
King. I pray you take me vp, and beare me hence
Into some other Chamber: softly 'pray.
Let there be no noyse made (my gentle friends)
Vnlesse some dull and fauourable hand
Will whisper Musicke to my wearie Spirit.
War. Call for the Musicke in the other Roome.
King. Set me the Crowne vpon my Pillow here.
Clar. His eye is hollow, and hee changes much.
War. Lesse noyse, lesse noyse.

Enter Prince Henry.

P.Hen. Who saw the Duke of Clarence?
Clar. I am here (Brother) full of heauinesse.
P.Hen. How now? Raine within doores, and none abroad? How doth the King?
Glo. Exceeding ill.
P.Hen. Heard hee the good newes yet?
Tell it him.
Glo. Hee alter'd much, vpon the hearing it.
P Hen. If hee be sicke with Ioy,
Hee'le recouer without Physicke.
War. Not so much noyse (my Lords)
Sweet Prince speake lowe.
The King, your Father, is dispos'd to sleepe.
Clar. Let vs with-draw into the other Roome.
War. Wil't please your Grace to goe along with vs?
P.Hen. No: I will sit, and watch here, by the King
Why doth the Crowne lye there, vpon his Pillow,
Being so troublesome a Bed fellow?
O pollish'd Perturbation! Golden Care!
That keep'st the Ports of Slumber open wide,
To many a watchfull Night: sleepe with it now,
Yet not so sound, and halfe so deepely sweete,
As hee whose Brow (with homely Biggen bound)
Snores out the Watch of Night. O Maiestie!
When thou do'st pinch thy Bearer, thou do'st sit
Like a rich Armor, worne in heat of day,
That scald'st with safetie: by his Gates of breath,
There lyes a dowlney feather, which stirres not:
Did hee suspire, that light and weightlesse dowlne
Perforce must moue. My gracious Lord, my Father,
This sleepe is sound indeede: this is a sleepe,
That from this Golden Rigoll hath diuorc'd
So many English Kings. Thy due, from me,
Is Teares, and heauie Sorrowes of the Blood,
Which Nature, Loue, and filiall tendernesse,
Shall (O deare Father) pay thee plenteously.
My due, from thee, is this Imperiall Crowne,
Which (as immediate from thy Place and Blood)
Deriues it selfe to me. Loe, heere it sits,
Which Heauen shall guard:
And put the worlds whole strength into one gyant Arme,
It shall not force this Lineall Honor from me.
This, from thee, will I to mine leaue,
As 'tis left to me. *Exit.*

Enter Warwicke, Gloucester, Clarence.

King. Warwicke, Gloucester, Clarence.
Clar. Doth the King call?
War. What would your Maiestie? how fares your Grace?
King. Why did you leaue me here alone (my Lords?)
Cla. We left the Prince (my Brother) here (my Liege)
Who vndertooke to sit and watch by you.
King. The Prince of Wales? where is hee? let mee see him.
War. This doore is open, hee is gone this way.
Glo. Hee came not through the Chamber where wee stayd.
King. Where is the Crowne? who tooke it from my Pillow?
War. When wee with-drew (my Liege) wee left it heere.
King. The Prince hath ta'ne it hence:
Goe seeke him out.
Is hee so hastie, that hee doth suppose
My sleepe, my death? Finde him (my Lord of Warwick)
Chide him hither: this part of his conioynes
With my disease, and helpes to end me.
See Sonnes, what things you are:
How quickly Nature falls into reuolt,
When Gold becomes her Obiect?
For this, the foolish ouer-carefull Fathers
Haue broke their sleepes with thoughts,
Their braines with care, their bones with industry.
For this, they haue ingrossed and pyl'd vp
The canker'd heapes of strange-atchieued Gold:
For this, they haue beene thoughtfull, to inuest
Their Sonnes with Arts, and Martiall Exercises:
When, like the Bee, culling from euery flower
The vertuous Sweetes, our Thighes packt with Wax,
Our Mouthes with Honey, wee bring it to the Hiue;
And like the Bees, are murthered for our paines.
This bitter taste yeelds his engrossements,
To the ending Father.

Enter Warwicke.

Now, where is hee, that will not stay so long,
Till his Friend Sicknesse hath determin'd me?
War. My Lord, I found the Prince in the next Roome,
Washing with kindly Teares his gentle Cheekes,
With such a deepe demeanure, in great sorrow,
That Tyranny, which neuer quafft but blood,
Would (by beholding him) haue wash'd his Knife
With gentle eye-drops. Hee is comming hither.
King. But wherefore did hee take away the Crowne?

Enter Prince Henry.

Loe, where hee comes. Come hither to me (*Harry.*)
Depart the Chamber, leaue vs heere alone. *Exit.*
P.Hen. I neuer thought to heare you speake againe.
King. Thy wish was Father (*Harry*) to that thought:
I stay too long by thee, I wearie thee.
Do'st thou so hunger for my emptie Chayre,
That thou wilt needes inuest thee with mine Honors,
Before thy howre be ripe? O foolish Youth!
Thou seek'st the Greatnesse, that will ouer-whelme thee.
Stay but a little: for my Cloud of Dignitie
Is held from falling, with so weake a winde,
That it will quickly drop: my Day is dimme.
Thou hast stolne that, which after some few howres
Were thine, without offence: and at my death
Thou hast seal'd vp my expectation.
Thy Life did manifest, thou lou'dst me not,
And thou wilt haue me dye assur'd of it.
Thou hid'st a thousand Daggers in thy thoughts,
Which thou hast whetted on thy stonie heart,
To stab at halfe an howre of my Life.
What? canst thou not forbeare me halfe an howre?

Then get thee gone, and digge my graue thy selfe,
And bid the merry Bels ring to thy eare
That thou art Crowned, not that I am dead.
Let all the Teares, that should bedew my Hearse
Be drops of Balme, to sanctifie thy head:
Onely compound me with forgotten dust.
Giue that, which gaue thee life, vnto the Wormes:
Plucke downe my Officers, breake my Decrees;
For now a time is come, to mocke at Forme.
Henry the fift is Crown'd: Vp Vanity,
Downe Royall State: All you sage Counsailors, hence:
And to the English Court, assemble now
From eu'ry Region, Apes of Idlenesse.
Now neignbor-Confines, purge you of your Scum:
Haue you a Ruffian that swill sweare? drinke? dance?
Reuell the night? Rob? Murder? and commit
The oldest sinnes, the newest kinde of wayes?
Be happy, he will trouble you no more:
England, shall double gill'd, his trebble guilt.
England, shall giue him Office, Honor, Might
For the Fift *Harry*, from curb'd License pluckes
The muzzle of Restraint; and the wilde Dogge
Shall flesh his tooth in euery Innocent.
O my poore Kingdome (sicke, with ciuill blowes)
When that my Care could not with-hold thy Ryots,
What wilt thou do, when Ryot is thy Care?
O, thou wilt be a Wildernesse againe,
Peopled with Wolues (thy old Inhabitants

Prince. O pardon me (my Liege)
But for my Teares,
The most Impediments vnto my Speech,
I had fore-stall'd this deere, and deepe Rebuke,
Ere you (with greefe) had spoke, and I had heard
The course of it so farre. There is your Crowne,
And he that weares the Crowne immortally,
Long guard it yours. If I affect it more,
Then as your Honour, and as your Renowne,
Let me no more from this Obedience rise,
Which my most true, and inward duteous Spirit
Teacheth this prostrate, and exteriour bending.
Heauen witnesse with me, when I heere came in,
And found no course of breath within your Maiestie,
How cold it strooke my heart. If I do faine,
O let me, in my present wildenesse, dye,
And neuer liue, to shew th'incredulous World,
The Noble change that I haue purposed.
Comming to looke on you, thinking you dead,
(And dead almost (my Liege) to thinke you were)
I spake vnto the Crowne (as hauing sense)
And thus vpbraided it. The Care on thee depending,
Hath fed vpon the body of my Father,
Therefore, thou best of Gold, art worst of Gold.
Other, lesse fine in Charract, is more precious,
Preseruing life, in Med'cine potable:
But thou, most Fine, most Honour'd, most Renown'd,
Hast eate the Bearer vp.
Thus (my Royall Liege)
Accusing it, I put it on my Head,
To try with it (as with an Enemie,
That had before my face murdred my Father)
The Quarrell of a true Inheritor.
But if it did infect my blood with Ioy,
Or swell my Thoughts, to any straine of Pride,
If any Rebell, or vaine spirit of mine,
Did, with the least Affection of a Welcome,
Giue entertainment to the might of it,
Let heauen, for euer, keepe it from my head,
And make me, as the poorest Vassaile is,
That doth with awe, and terror kneele to it.

King. O my Sonne!
Heauen put it in thy minde to take it hence,
That thou might'st ioyne the more, thy Fathers loue,
Pleading so wisely, in excuse of it.
Come hither *Harrie*, sit thou by my bedde,
And heare (I thinke, the very latest Counsell
That euer I shall breath: Heauen knowes, my Sonne)
By what by-pathes, and indirect crook'd-wayes
I met this Crowne: and I my selfe know well
How troublesome it sate vpon my head.
To thee, it shall descend with better Quiet,
Better Opinion, better Confirmation:
For all the soyle of the Atchieuement goes
With me, into the Earth. It seem'd in mee,
But as an Honour snatch'd with boyst'rous hand,
And I had many liuing, to vpbraide
My gaine of it, by their Assistances,
Which dayly grew to Quarrell, and to Blood-shed,
Wounding supposed Peace.
All these bold Feares,
Thou seest (with perill) I haue answered:
For all my Reigne, hath beene but as a Scene
Acting that argument. And now my death
Changes the Moode: For what in me, was purchas'd,
Falles vpon thee, in a more Fayrer sort.
So thou, the Garland wear'st successiu[illegible]
Yet, though thou stand'st more sure, the[illegible] could do,
Thou art not firme enough, since greefe[illegible]e greene:
And all thy Friends, which thou must ma[illegible]y Friends
Haue but their stings, and teeth, newly tak[illegible]t,
By whose fell working, I was first aduanc'[illegible]
And by whose power, I well might lodge a[illegible]
To be againe displac'd. Which to auoyd,
I cut them off: and had a purpose now
To leade out many to the Holy Land;
Least rest, and lying still, might make them looke
Too neere vnto my State.
Therefore (my *Harrie*)
Be it thy course to busie giddy Mindes
With Forraigne Quarrels: that Action hence borne out,
May waste the memory of the former dayes.
More would I, but my Lungs are wasted so,
That strength of Speech is vtterly deni'de mee.
How I came by the Crowne, O heauen forgiue:
And grant it may, with thee, in true peace liue.

Prince. My gracious Liege:
You wonne it, wore it: kept it, gaue it me,
Then plaine and right must my possession be;
Which I, with more, then with a Common paine,
'Gainst all the World, will rightfully maintaine.

Enter Lord Iohn of Lancaster, and Warwicke.

King. Looke, looke,
Heere comes my *Iohn* of Lancaster:

Iohn. Health, Peace, and Happinesse,
To my Royall Father.

King. Thou bring'st me happinesse and Peace (Sonne *Iohn*:
But health (alacke) with youthfull wings is flowne
From this bare, wither'd Trunke. Vpon thy sight
My worldly businesse makes a period.

Where

Where is my Lord of Warwicke?

Prin. My Lord of Warwicke.

King. Doth any name particular, belong
Vnto the Lodging, where I first did swoon'd?

War. 'Tis call'd *Ierusalem*, my Noble Lord.

King. Laud be to heauen:
Euen there my life must end.
It hath beene prophesi'de to me many yeares,
I should not dye, but in *Ierusalem*:
Which (vainly) I suppos'd the Holy-Land.
But beare me to that Chamber, there Ile lye:
In that *Ierusalem*, shall *Harry* dye. *Exeunt.*

Actus Quintus. Scœna Prima.

Enter Shallow, Silence, Falstaffe, Bardolfe, Page, and Dauie.

Shal. By Cocke and Pye, you shall not away to night. What *Dauy*, I say.

Fal. You must excuse me, M. *Robert Shallow.*

Shal. I will not excuse you: you shall not be excused. Excuses shall not be admitted: there is no excuse shall serue: you shall not be excus'd.
Why *Dauie.*

Dauie. Heere sir.

Shal. Dauy, Dauy, Dauy, let me see (*Dauy*) let me see: *William* Cooke, bid him come hither. Sir *Iohn*, you shal not be excus'd.

Dauy. Marry sir, thus: those Precepts cannot bee seru'd: and againe sir, shall we sowe the head-land with Wheate?

Shal. With red Wheate *Dauy*. But for *William* Cook: are there no yong Pigeons?

Dauy. Yes Sir.
Heere is now the Smithes note, for Shooing,
And Plough-Irons.

Shal. Let it be cast, and payde: Sir *Iohn*, you shall not be excus'd.

Dauy. Sir, a new linke to the Bucket must needes bee had: And Sir, doe you meane to stoppe any of *Williams* Wages, about the Sacke he lost the other day, at *Hinckley* Fayre?

Shal. He shall answer it:
Some Pigeons *Dauy*, a couple of short-legg'd Hennes: a Ioynt of Mutton, and any pretty little tine Kickshawes, tell *William* Cooke.

Dauy. Doth the man of Warre, stay all night sir?

Shal. Yes *Dauy*:
I will vse him well. A Friend i'th Court, is better then a penny in purse. Vse his men well *Dauy*, for they are arrant Knaues, and will backe-bite.

Dauy. No worse then they are bitten, sir: For they haue maruellous fowle linnen.

Shallow. Well conceited *Dauy*: about thy Businesse, *Dauy.*

Dauy. I beseech you sir,
To countenance *William Visor* of Woncot, against *Clement Perkes* of the hill.

Shal. There are many Complaints *Dauy*, against that *Visor*, that *Visor* is an arrant Knaue, on my knowledge.

Dauy. I graunt your Worship, that he is a knaue Sir:) But yet heauen forbid Sir, but a Knaue should haue some Countenance, at his Friends request. An honest man sir, is able to speake for himselfe, when a Knaue is not. I haue seru'd your Worshippe truely sir, these eight yeares: and if I cannot once or twice in a Quarter beare out a knaue, against an honest man, I haue but a very litle credite with your Worshippe. The Knaue is mine honest Friend Sir, therefore I beseech your Worship, let him bee Countenanc'd.

Shal. Go too,
I say he shall haue no wrong: Looke about *Dauy.*
Where are you Sir *Iohn*? Come, off with your Boots.
Giue me your hand M. *Bardolfe.*

Bard. I am glad to see your Worship.

Shal. I thanke thee, with all my heart, kinde Master *Bardolfe*: and welcome my tall Fellow:
Come Sir *Iohn.*

Falstaffe. Ile follow you, good Master *Robert Shallow*. *Bardolfe*, looke to our Horsses. If I were saw'de into Quantities, I should make foure dozen of such bearded Hermites staues, as Master *Shallow*. It is a wonderfull thing to see the semblable Coherence of his mens spirits, and his: They, by obseruing of him, do beare themselues like foolish Iustices: Hee, by conuersing with them, is turn'd into a Iustice-like Seruingman. Their spirits are so married in Coniunction, with the participation of Society, that they flocke together in consent, like so many Wilde-Geese. If I had a suite to Mayster *Shallow*, I would humour his men, with the imputation of beeing neere their Mayster. If to his Men, I would currie with Maister *Shallow*, that no man could better command his Seruants. It is certaine, that either wise bearing, or ignorant Carriage is caught, as men take diseases, one of another: therefore, let men take heede of their Companie. I will deuise matter enough out of this *Shallow*, to keepe Prince *Harry* in continuall Laughter, the wearing out of sixe Fashions (which is foure Tearmes) or two Actions, and he shall laugh with *Internallums*. O it is much that a Lye (with a slight Oath) and a iest (with a sadde brow) will doe, with a Fellow, that neuer had the Ache in his shoulders. O you shall see him laugh, till his Face be like a wet Cloake, ill laid vp.

Shal. Sir *Iohn.*

Falst. I come Master *Shallow*, I come Master *Shallow*.
Exeunt

Scena Secunda.

Enter the Earle of Warwicke, and the Lord Chiefe Iustice.

Warwicke. How now, my Lord Chiefe Iustice, whether away?

Ch.Iust. How doth the King?

Warw. Exceeding well: his Cares
Are now, all ended.

Ch.Iust. I hope, not dead.

Warw. Hee's walk'd the way of Nature,
And to our purposes, he liues no more.

Ch.Iust. I would his Maiesty had call'd me with him,
The seruice, that I truly did his life,
Hath left me open to all iniuries.

War.

War. Indeed I thinke the yong King loues you not.
Ch.Iust. I know he doth not, and do arme my selfe
To welcome the condition of the Time,
Which cannot looke more hideously vpon me,
Then I haue drawne it in my fantasie.

Enter Iohn of Lancaster, Glouceſter, and Clarence.

War. Heere come the heauy Issue of dead *Harrie:*
O, that the liuing *Harrie* had the temper
Of him, the worst of these three Gentlemen:
How many Nobles then, should hold their places,
That must strike saile, to Spirits of vilde sort?
Ch.Iust. Alas, I feare, all will be ouer-turn'd.
Iohn. Good morrow Cosin Warwick, good morrow.
Glou. Cla. Good morrow, Cosin.
Iohn. We meet, like men, that had forgot to speake.
War. We do remember: but our Argument
Is all too heauy, to admit much talke.
Ioh. Well: Peace be with him, that hath made vs heauy
Ch.Iust. Peace be with vs, least we be heauier.
Glou. O, good my Lord, you haue lost a friend indeed:
And I dare sweare, you borrow not that face
Of seeming sorrow, it is sure your owne.
Iohn. Though no man be assur'd what grace to finde,
You stand in coldest expectation.
I am the sorrier, would 'twere otherwise.
Cla. Wel, you must now speake Sir *Iohn Falstaffe* faire,
Which swimmes against your streame of Quality.
Ch.Iust. Sweet Princes: what I did, I did in Honor,
Led by th'Imperiall Conduct of my Soule,
And neuer shall you see, that I will begge
A ragged, and fore-stall'd Remission.
If Troth, and vpright Innocency fayle me,
Ile to the King (my Master) that is dead,
And tell him, who hath sent me after him.
War. Heere comes the Prince.

Enter Prince Henrie.

Ch.Iust. Good morrow: and heauen saue your Maiesty
Prince. This new, and gorgeous Garment, Maiesty,
Sits not so easie on me, as you thinke.
Brothers, you mixe your Sadnesse with some Feare:
This is the English, not the Turkish Court:
Not *Amurah,* an *Amurah* succeeds,
But *Harry, Harry*: Yet be sad (good Brothers)
For (to speake truth) it very well becomes you:
Sorrow, so Royally in you appeares,
That I will deeply put the Fashion on,
And weare it in my heart. Why then be sad,
But entertaine no more of it (good Brothers)
Then a ioynt burthen, laid vpon vs all.
For me, by Heauen (I bid you be assur'd)
Ile be your Father, and your Brother too:
Let me but beare your Loue, Ile beare your Cares;
But weepe that *Herrie's* dead, and so will I.
But *Harry* liues, that shall conuert those Teares
By number, into houres of Happinesse.
Iohn, &c. We hope no other from your Maiesty.
Prin. You all looke strangely on me: and you most,
You are (I thinke) assur'd, I loue you not.
Ch.Iust. I am assur'd (if I be measur'd rightly)
Your Maiesty hath no iust cause to hate mee.
Pr. No? How might a Prince of my great hopes forget
So great Indignities you laid vpon me?
What? Rate? Rebuke? and roughly send to Prison
Th'immediate Heire of England? Was this easie?
May this be wash'd in *Lethe,* and forgotten?
Ch.Iust. I then did vse the Person of your Father:
The Image of his power, lay then in me,
And in th'administration of his Law,
Whiles I was busie for the Commonwealth,
Your Highnesse pleased to forget my place,
The Maiesty, and power of Law, and Iustice,
The Image of the King, whom I presented,
And strooke me in my very Seate of Iudgement;
Whereon (as an Offender to your Father)
I gaue bold way to my Authority,
And did commit you. If the deed were ill,
Be you contented, wearing now the Garland,
To haue a Sonne, set your Decrees at naught?
To plucke downe Iustice from your awefull Bench?
To trip the course of Law, and blunt the Sword
That guards the peace, and safety of your Person?
Nay more, to spurne at your most Royall Image,
And mocke your workings, in a Second body?
Question your Royall Thoughts, make the case yours:
Be now the Father, and propose a Sonne:
Heare your owne dignity so much prophan'd,
See your most dreadfull Lawes, so loosely slighted;
Behold your selfe, so by a Sonne disdained:
And then imagine me, taking you part,
And in your power, soft silencing your Sonne:
After this cold considerance, sentence me;
And, as you are a King, speake in your State,
What I haue done, that misbecame my place,
My person, or my Lieges Soueraigntie.
Prin. You are right Iustice, and you weigh this well:
Therefore still beare the Ballance, and the Sword:
And I do wish your Honors may encrease,
Till you do liue, to see a Sonne of mine
Offend you, and obey you, as I did.
So shall I liue, to speake my Fathers words:
Happy am I, that haue a man so bold,
That dares do Iustice, on my proper Sonne;
And no lesse happy, hauing such a Sonne,
That would deliuer vp his Greatnesse so,
Into the hands of Iustice. You did commit me:
For which, I do commit into your hand,
Th'vnstained Sword that you haue vs'd to beare:
With this Remembrance; That you vse the same
With the like bold, iust, and impartiall Spirit
As you haue done 'gainst me. There is my hand,
You shall be as a Father, to my Youth:
My voice shall sound, as you do prompt mine eare,
And I will stoope, and humble my Intents,
To your well-practis'd, wise Directions.
And Princes all, beleeue me, I beseech you:
My Father is gone wilde into his Graue,
(For in his Tombe, lye my Affections)
And with his Spirits, sadly I suruiue,
To mocke the expectation of the World;
To frustrate Prophesies, and to race out
Rotten Opinion, who hath writ me downe
After my seeming. The Tide of Blood in me,
Hath prowdly flow'd in Vanity, till now.
Now doth it turne, and ebbe backe to the Sea,
Where it shall mingle with the state of Floods,
And flow henceforth in formall Maiesty.
Now call we our High Court of Parliament,
And let vs choose such Limbes of Noble Counsaile,
That

That the great Body of our State may go
In equall ranke, with the best gouern'd Nation,
That Warre, or Peace, or both at once may be
As things acquainted and familiar to vs,
In which you (Father) shall haue formost hand.
Our Coronation done, we will accite
(As I before remembred) all our State,
And heauen (consigning to my good intents)
No Prince nor Peere, shall haue iust cause to say,
Heauen shorten *Harries* happy life, one day. *Exeunt.*

Scena Tertia.

Enter Falstaffe, Shallow, Silence, Bardolfe, Page, and Pistoll.

Shal. Nay, you shall see mine Orchard: where, in an Arbor we will eate a last yeares Pippin of my owne graffing, with a dish of Carrawayes, and so forth (Come Cosin *Silence*, and then to bed.

Fal. You haue heere a goodly dwelling, and a rich.

Shal. Barren, barren, barren: Beggers all, beggers all Sir *Iohn*: Marry, good ayre. Spread *Dauy*, spread *Dauie*: Well said *Dauie*.

Falst. This *Dauie* serues you for good vses: he is your Seruingman, and your Husband.

Shal. A good Varlet, a good Varlet, a very good Varlet, Sir *Iohn*: I haue drunke too much Sacke at Supper. A good Varlet. Now sit downe, now sit downe: Come Cosin.

Sil. Ah sirra (quoth-a) we shall doe nothing but eate, and make good cheere, and praise heauen for the merrie yeere: when flesh is cheape, and Females deere, and lustie Lads rome heere, and there: so merrily, and euer among so merrily.

Fal. There's a merry heart, good M. *Silence*, Ile giue you a health for that anon.

Shal. Good M. *Bardolfe*: some wine, *Dauie*.

Da. Sweet sir, sit: Ile be with you anon: most sweete sir, sit. Master Page, good M Page, sit: Proface. What you want in meate, wee'l haue in drinke: but you beare, the heart's all.

Shal. Be merry M. *Bardolfe*, and my little Souldiour there, be merry.

Sil. Be merry, be merry, my wife ha's all.
For women are Shrewes, both short, and tall:
'Tis merry in Hall, when Beards wagge all;
And welcome merry Shrouetide. Be merry, be merry.

Fal. I did not thinke M. *Silence* had bin a man of this Mettle.

Sil. Who I? I haue beene merry twice and once, ere now.

Dauy. There is a dish of Lether-coats for you.

Shal. *Dauie.*

Dau. Your Worship: Ile be with you straight. A cup of Wine, sir?

Sil. A Cup of Wine, that's briske and fine, & drinke vnto the Leman mine: and a merry heart liues long-a.

Fal. Well said, M. *Silence*.

Sil. If we shall be merry, now comes in the sweete of the night.

Fal. Health, and long life to you, M. *Silence*.

Sil. Fill the Cuppe, and let it come. Ile pledge you a mile to the bottome.

Shal. Honest *Bardolfe*, welcome: If thou want'st any thing, and wilt not call, beshrew thy heart. Welcome my little tyne theefe, and welcome indeed too: Ile drinke to M. *Bardolfe*, and to all the Cauileroes about London.

Dau. I hope to see London, once ere I die.

Bar. If I might see you there, *Dauie*.

Shal. You'l cracke a quart together? Ha, will you not M. *Bardolfe*?

Bar. Yes Sir, in a pottle pot.

Shal. I thanke thee: the knaue will sticke by thee, I can assure thee that. He will not out, he is true bred.

Bar. And Ile sticke by him, sir.

Shal. Why there spoke a King: lack nothing, be merry. Looke, who's at doore there, ho: who knockes?

Fal Why now you haue done me right.

Sil. Do me right, and dub me Knight, *Samingo*. Is't not so?

Fal. 'Tis so.

Sil. Is't so? Why then say an old man can do somwhat.

Dav. If it please your Worshippe, there's one *Pistoll* come from the Court with newes.

Fal. From the Court? Let him come in.

Enter Pistoll.

How now Pistoll?

Pist. Sir *Iohn*, 'saue you sir.

Fal. What winde blew you hither, Pistoll?

Pist. Not the ill winde which blowes none to good, sweet Knight: Thou art now one of the greatest men in the Realme.

Sil. Indeed, I thinke he bee, but Goodman *Puffe* of Barson.

Pist. Puffe? puffe in thy teeth, most recreant Coward base. Sir *Iohn*, I am thy Pistoll, and thy Friend: helter skelter haue I rode to thee, and tydings do I bring, and luckie ioyes, and golden Times, and happie Newes of price.

Fal. I prethee now deliuer them, like a man of this World.

Pist. A footra for the World, and Worldlings base,
I speake of Affrica, and Golden ioyes.

Fal. O base Assyrian Knight, what is thy newes?
Let King *Couitha* know the truth thereof.

Sil. And Robin-hood, Scarlet, and Iohn.

Pist. Shall dunghill Curres confront the *Hellicons*?
And shall good newes be baffel'd?
Then Pistoll lay thy head in Furies lappe.

Shal. Honest Gentleman,
I know not your breeding.

Pist. Why then Lament therefore.

Shal. Giue me pardon, Sir.
If sir, you come with news from the Court, I take it, there is but two wayes, either to vtter them, or to conceale them. I am Sir, vnder the King, in some Authority.

Pist. Vnder which King?
Bezonian, speake, or dye.

Shal. Vnder King *Harry*.

Pist. *Harry* the Fourth? or Fift?

Shal *Harry* the Fourth.

Pist. A footra for thine Office.
Sir *Iohn*, thy tender Lamb-kinne, now is King,
Harry the Fift's the man, I speake the truth,
When Pistoll lyes, do this, and figge-me, like
The bragging Spaniard.

Fal.

Fal. What,is the old King dead?

Pist. As naile in doore.
The things I speake, are iust.

Fal. Away *Bardolfe*, Sadle my Horse,
Master *Robert Shallow*, choose what Office thou wilt
In the Land, 'tis thine. *Pistol*, I will double charge thee
With Dignities.

Bard. O ioyfull day:
I would not take a Knighthood for my Fortune.

Pist. What? I do bring good newes.

Fal. Carrie Master *Silence* to bed: Master *Shallow*, my Lord *Shallow*, be what thou wilt, I am Fortunes Steward. Get on thy Boots, wee'l ride all night. Oh sweet Pistoll: Away *Bardolfe*: Come Pistoll, vtter more to mee: and withall deuise something to do thy selfe good. Boote, boote Master *Shallow*, I know the young King is sick for mee. Let vs take any mans Horsses: The Lawes of England are at my command'ment. Happie are they, which haue beene my Friendes: and woe vnto my Lord Chiefe Iustice.

Pist. Let Vultures vil'de seize on his Lungs also:
Where is the life that late I led, say they?
Why heere it is, welcome those pleasant dayes. *Exeunt*

Scena Quarta.

Enter Hostesse Quickly, Dol Teare-sheete, and Beadles.

Hostesse. No, thou arrant knaue: I would I might dy, that I might haue thee hang'd: Thou hast drawne my shoulder out of ioynt.

Off. The Constables haue deliuer'd her ouer to mee: and shee shall haue Whipping cheere enough, I warrant her. There hath beene a man or two (lately) kill'd about her.

Dol. Nut-hooke, nut-hooke, you Lye: Come on, Ile tell thee what, thou damn'd Tripe-visag'd Rascall, if the Childe I now go with, do miscarrie, thou had'st better thou had'st strooke thy Mother, thou Paper-fac'd Villaine.

Host. O that Sir *Iohn* were come, hee would make this a bloody day to some body. But I would the Fruite of her Wombe might miscarry.

Officer. If it do, you shall haue a dozen of Cushions againe, you haue but eleuen now. Come, I charge you both go with me: for the man is dead, that you and Pistoll beate among you.

Dol. Ile tell thee what, thou thin man in a Censor; I will haue you as soundly swindg'd for this, you blew-Bottel'd Rogue: you filthy famish'd Correctioner, if you be not swing'd, Ile forsweare halfe Kirtles.

Off. Come, come, you shee-Knight-arrant, come.

Host. O, that right should thus o'recome might. Wel of sufferance, comes ease.

Dol. Come you Rogue, come:
Bring me to a Iustice.

Host. Yes, come you staru'd Blood-hound.

Dol. Goodman death, goodman Bones,

Host. Thou Anatomy, thou.

Dol. Come you thinne Thing:
Come you Rascall.

Off. Very well. *Exeunt.*

Scena Quinta.

Enter two Groomes.

1.*Groo.* More Rushes, more Rushes.

2.*Groo.* The Trumpets haue sounded twice.

1.*Groo.* It will be two of the Clocke, ere they come from the Coronation. *Exit Groo.*

Enter Falstaffe, Shallow, Pistoll, Bardolfe, and Page.

Falstaffe. Stand heere by me, M. *Robert Shallow*, I will make the King do you Grace. I will leere vpon him, as he comes by: and do but marke the countenance that hee will giue me.

Pistol. Blesse thy Lungs, good Knight.

Falst. Come heere *Pistol*, stand behind me. O if I had had time to haue made new Liueries, I would haue bestowed the thousand pound I borrowed of you. But it is no matter, this poore shew doth better: this doth inferre the zeale I had to see him.

Shal. It doth so.

Falst. It shewes my earnestnesse in affection.

Pist. It doth so.

Fal. My deuotion.

Pist. It doth, it doth, it doth.

Fal. As it were, to ride day and night,
And not to deliberate, not to remember,
Not to haue patience to shift me.

Shal. It is most certaine.

Fal. But to stand stained with Trauaile, and sweating with desire to see him, thinking of nothing else, putting all affayres in obliuion, as if there were nothing els to bee done, but to see him.

Pist. 'Tis *semper idem*: for *obsque hoc nihil est*. 'Tis all in euery part.

Shal. 'Tis so indeed.

Pist. My Knight, I will enflame thy Noble Liuer, and make thee rage. Thy *Dol*, and *Helen* of thy noble thoghts is in base Durance, and contagious prison: Hall'd thither by most Mechanicall and durty hand. Rowze vppe Reuenge from Ebon den, with fell Alecto's Snake, for *Dol* is in. Pistol, speakes nought but troth.

Fal. I will deliuer her.

Pistol. There roar'd the Sea: and Trumpet Clangour sounds.

The Trumpets sound. Enter King Henrie the Fift, Brothers, Lord Chiefe Iustice.

Falst. Saue thy Grace, King *Hall*, my Royall *Hall*.

Pist. The heauens thee guard, and keepe, most royall Impe of Fame.

Fal. 'Saue thee my sweet Boy.

King. My Lord Chiefe Iustice, speake to that vaine man.

Ch.Iust. Haue you your wits?
Know you what 'tis you speake?

Falst. My King, my Ioue; I speake to thee, my heart.

King. I know thee not, old man: Fall to thy Prayers:
How ill white haires become a Foole, and Iester?

I haue

I haue long dream'd of such a kinde of man,
So surfeit-swell'd, so old, and so prophane:
But being awake, I do despise my dreame.
Make lesse thy body (hence) and more thy Grace,
Leaue gourmandizing; Know the Graue doth gape
For thee, thrice wider then for other men.
Reply not to me, with a Foole-borne Iest,
Presume not, that I am the thing I was,
For heauen doth know (so shall the world perceiue)
That I haue turn'd away my former Selfe,
So will I those that kept me Companie.
When thou dost heare I am, as I haue bin,
Approach me, and thou shalt be as thou was't
The Tutor and the Feeder of my Riots:
Till then, I banish thee, on paine of death,
As I haue done the rest of my Misleaders,
Not to come neere our Person, by ten mile.
For competence of life, I will allow you,
That lacke of meanes enforce you not to euill:
And as we heare you do reforme your selues,
We will according to your strength, and qualities,
Giue you aduancement. Be it your charge (my Lord)
To see perform'd the tenure of our word. Set on.

Exit King.

Fal. Master *Shallow*, I owe you a thousand pound.

Shal. I marry Sir *Iohn*, which I beseech you to let me haue home with me.

Fal. That can hardly be, M. *Shallow*, do not you grieue at this: I shall be sent for in priuate to him: Looke you, he must seeme thus to the world: feare not your aduancement: I will be the man yet, that shall make you great.

Shal. I cannot well perceiue how, vnlesse you should giue me your Doublet, and stuffe me out with Straw. I beseech you, good Sir *Iohn*, let mee haue fiue hundred of my thousand.

Fal. Sir, I will be as good as my word. This that you heard, was but a colour.

Shall. A colour I feare, that you will dye, in Sir *Iohn*.

Fal. Feare no colours, go with me to dinner:
Come Lieutenant *Pistol*, come *Bardolfe*,
I shall be sent for soone at night.

Ch.Iust. Go carry Sir *Iohn Falstaffe* to the Fleete,
Take all his Company along with him.

Fal. My Lord, my Lord.

Ch.Iust. I cannot now speake, I will heare you soone:
Take them away.

Pist. *Si fortuna me tormento, spera me contento.*

Exit. Manet Lancaster and Chiefe Iustice.

Iohn. I like this faire proceeding of the Kings:
He hath intent his wonted Followers
Shall all be very well prouided for:
But all are banisht, till their conuersations
Appeare more wise, and modest to the world.

Ch.Iust. And so they are.

Iohn. The King hath call'd his Parliament,
My Lord.

Ch.Iust. He hath.

Iohn. I will lay oddes, that ere this yeere expire,
We beare our Ciuill Swords, and Natiue fire
As farre as France. I heare a Bird so sing,
Whose Musicke (to my thinking) pleas'd the King.
Come, will you hence?

Exeunt

FINIS.

EPILOGVE.

FIRST, my Feare: then, my Curtsie· last, my Speech. My Feare, is your Displeasure: My Curtsie, my Dutie: And my speech, to Begge your Pardons. If you looke for a good speech now, you vndoe me: For what I haue to say, is of mine owne making: and what (indeed) I should say, will (I doubt) prooue mine owne marring. But to the Purpose, and so to the Venture. Be it knowne to you (as it is very well) I was lately heere in the end of a displeasing Play, to pray your Patience for it, and to promise you a Better: I did meane (indeede) to pay you with this, which if (like an ill Venture) it come vnluckily home, I breake; and you, my gentle Creditors lose. Heere I promist you I would be, and heere I commit my Bodie to your Mercies: Bate me some, and I will pay you some, and (as most Debtors do) promise you infinitely.

If my Tongue cannot entreate you to acquit me: will you command me to vse my Legges? And yet that were but light payment, to Dance out of your debt: But a good Conscience, will make any possible satisfaction, and so will I. All the Gentlewomen heere, haue forgiuen me, if the Gentlemen will not, then the Gentlemen do not agree with the Gentlewowen, which was neuer seene before, in such an Assembly.

One word more, I beseech you: if you be not too much cloid with Fat Meate, our humble Author will continue the Story (with Sir Iohn in it) and make you merry, with faire Katherine of France: where (for any thing I know) Falstaffe shall dye of a sweat, vnlesse already he be kill'd with your hard Opinions: For Old-Castle dyed a Martyr, and this is not the man. My Tongue is wearie, when my Legs are too, I will bid you good night; and so kneele downe before you But (indeed) to pray for the Queene.

THE ACTORS NAMES.

RVMOVR the Presentor.
King *Henry* the Fourth.
Prince *Henry*, afterwards Crowned King *Henrie* the Fift.

Prince *Iohn* of Lancaster.
Humphrey of Gloucester.
Thomas of Clarence.
} Sonnes to *Henry* the Fourth, & brethren to *Henry* 5.

Northumberland.
The Arch Byshop of Yorke.
Mowbray.
Hastings.
Lord Bardolfe.
Trauers.
Morton.
Coleuile.
} Opposites against King *Henrie* the Fourth.

Warwicke.
Westmerland.
Surrey.
Gowre.
Harecourt.
Lord Chiefe Iustice.
} Of the Kings Partie.

Pointz.
Falstaffe.
Bardolphe.
Pistoll.
Peto.
Page.
} Irregular Humorists.

Shallow.
Silence.
} Both Country Iustices.

Dauie, Seruant to Shallow.
Phang, and Snare, 2. Serieants

Mouldie.
Shadow.
Wart.
Feeble.
Bullcalfe.
} Country Soldiers

Drawers
Beadles.
Groomes

Northumberlands Wife.
Percies Widdow.
Hostesse Quickly.
Doll Teare-sheete.
Epilogue.

The Life of Henry the Fift.

Enter Prologue.

O For a Muse of Fire, that would ascend
The brightest Heauen of Inuention:
A Kingdome for a Stage, Princes to Act,
And Monarchs to behold the swelling Scene.
Then should the Warlike Harry, *like himselfe,*
Assume the Port of Mars, *and at his heeles*
(Leasht in, like Hounds) should Famine, Sword, and Fire
Crouch for employment. But pardon, Gentles all:
The flat vnraysed Spirits, that hath dar'd,
On this vnworthy Scaffold, to bring forth
So great an Obiect. Can this Cock-Pit hold
The vastie fields of France? Or may we cramme
Within this Woodden O, the very Caskes
That did affright the Ayre at Agincourt?
O pardon: since a crooked Figure may
Attest in little place a Million,
And let vs, Cyphers to this great Accompt,
On your imaginarie Forces worke.
Suppose within the Girdle of these Walls
Are now confin'd two mightie Monarchies,
Whose high, vp-reared, and abutting Fronts,
The perillous narrow Ocean parts asunder.
Peece out our imperfections with your thoughts:
Into a thousand parts diuide one Man,
And make imaginarie Puissance.
Thinke when we talke of Horses, that you see them,
Printing their prowd Hoofes i'th' receiuing Earth:
For 'tis your thoughts that now must deck our Kings,
Carry them here and there: Iumping o're Times;
Turning th'accomplishment of many yeeres
Into an Howre-glasse: for the which supplie,
Admit me Chorus *to this Historie;*
Who Prologue-like, your humble patience pray,
Gently to heare, kindly to iudge our Play. *Exit.*

Actus Primus. Scœna Prima.

Enter the two Bishops of Canterbury and Ely.

Bish. Cant.

MY Lord, Ile tell you, that selfe Bill is vrg'd,
Which in th'eleueth yere of ye last Kings reign
Was like, and had indeed against vs past,
But that the scambling and vnquiet time
Did push it out of farther question.

Bish. Ely. But how my Lord shall we resist it now?

Bish. Cant. It must be thought on: if it passe against vs,
We loose the better halfe of our Possession:
For all the Temporall Lands, which men deuout
By Testament haue giuen to the Church,
Would they strip from vs; being valu'd thus,
As much as would maintaine, to the Kings honor,
Full fifteene Earles, and fifteene hundred Knights,
Six thousand and two hundred good Esquires:
And to reliefe of Lazars, and weake age
Of indigent faint Soules, past corporall toyle,
A hundred Almes-houses, right well supply'd:
And to the Coffers of the King beside,
A thousand pounds by th'yeere. Thus runs the Bill.

Bish. Ely. This would drinke deepe.

Bish. Cant. 'Twould drinke the Cup and all.

Bish. Ely. But what preuention?

Bish. Cant. The King is full of grace, and faire regard.

Bish. Ely. And a true louer of the holy Church.

Bish. Cant. The courses of his youth promis'd it not.
The breath no sooner left his Fathers body,
But that his wildnesse, mortify'd in him,
Seem'd to dye too: yea, at that very moment,
Consideration like an Angell came,
And whipt th'offending *Adam* out of him;
Leauing his body as a Paradise,
T'inuelop and containe Celestiall Spirits.
Neuer was such a sodaine Scholler made:
Neuer came Reformation in a Flood,
With such a heady currance scowring faults:
Nor neuer *Hidra*-headed Wilfulnesse
So soone did loose his Seat; and all at once;
As in this King.

Bish. Ely. We are blessed in the Change.

Bish. Cant. Heare him but reason in Diuinitie;
And all-admiring, with an inward wish
You would desire the King were made a Prelate:
Heare him debate of Common-wealth Affaires;
You would say, it hath been all in all his study:
List his discourse of Warre; and you shall heare
A fearefull Battaile rendred you in Musique.

Turne him to any Cause of Pollicy,
The Gordian Knot of it he will vnloose,
Familiar as his Garter: that when he speakes,
The Ayre, a Charter'd Libertine, is still,
And the mute Wonder lurketh in mens eares,
To steale his sweet and honyed Sentences:
So that the Art and Practique part of Life,
Must be the Mistresse to this Theorique.
Which is a wonder how his Grace should gleane it,
Since his addiction was to Courses vaine,
His Companies vnletter'd, rude, and shallow,
His Houres fill'd vp with Ryots, Banquets, Sports;
And neuer noted in him any studie,
Any retyrement, any sequestration,
From open Haunts and Popularitie.

B. Ely. The Strawberry growes vnderneath the Nettle,
And holesome Berryes thriue and ripen best,
Neighbour'd by Fruit of baser qualitie:
And so the Prince obscur'd his Contemplation
Vnder the Veyle of Wildnesse, which (no doubt)
Grew like the Summer Grasse, fastest by Night,
Vnseene, yet cressiue in his facultie.

B. Cant. It must be so; for Miracles are ceast:
And therefore we must needes admit the meanes,
How things are perfected.

B. Ely. But my good Lord:
How now for mittigation of this Bill,
Vrg'd by the Commons? doth his Maiestie
Incline to it, or no?

B. Cant. He seemes indifferent:
Or rather swaying more vpon our part,
Then cherishing th'exhibiters against vs;
For I haue made an offer to his Maiestie,
Vpon our Spirituall Conuocation,
And in regard of Causes now in hand,
Which I haue open'd to his Grace at large,
As touching France, to giue a greater Summe,
Then euer at one time the Clergie yet
Did to his Predecessors part withall.

B. Ely. How did this offer seeme receiu'd, my Lord?

B. Cant. With good acceptance of his Maiestie:
Saue that there was not time enough to heare,
As I perceiu'd his Grace would faine haue done,
The seueralls and vnhidden passages
Of his true Titles to some certaine Dukedomes,
And generally, to the Crowne and Seat of France,
Deriu'd from *Edward*, his great Grandfather.

B. Ely. What was th'impediment that broke this off?

B. Cant. The French Embassador vpon that instant
Crau'd audience; and the howre I thinke is come,
To giue him hearing: Is it foure a Clock?

B. Ely. It is.

B. Cant. Then goe we in, to know his Embassie:
Which I could with a ready guesse declare,
Before the Frenchman speake a word of it.

B. Ely. Ile wait vpon you, and I long to heare it.

Exeunt.

Enter the King, Humfrey, Bedford, Clarence, Warwick, Westmerland, and Exeter.

King. Where is my gracious Lord of Canterbury?

Exeter. Not here in presence.

King. Send for him, good Vnckle.

Westm. Shall we call in th'Ambassador, my Liege?

King. Not yet, my Cousin: we would be resolu'd,
Before we heare him, of some things of weight,
That taske our thoughts, concerning vs and France.

Enter two Bishops.

B. Cant. God and his Angels guard your sacred Throne,
And make you long become it.

King. Sure we thanke you.
My learned Lord, we pray you to proceed,
And iustly and religiously vnfold,
Why the Law *Salike*, that they haue in France,
Or should or should not barre vs in our Clayme:
And God forbid, my deare and faithfull Lord,
That you should fashion, wrest, or bow your reading,
Or nicely charge your vnderstanding Soule,
With opening Titles miscreate, whose right
Sutes not in natiue colours with the truth:
For God doth know, how many now in health,
Shall drop their blood, in approbation
Of what your reuerence shall incite vs to.
Therefore take heed how you impawne our Person,
How you awake our sleeping Sword of Warre;
We charge you in the Name of God take heed:
For neuer two such Kingdomes did contend,
Without much fall of blood, whose guiltlesse drops
Are euery one, a Woe, a sore Complaint,
'Gainst him, whose wrongs giues edge vnto the Swords,
That makes such waste in briefe mortalitie.
Vnder this Coniuration, speake my Lord:
For we will heare, note, and beleeue in heart,
That what you speake, is in your Conscience washt,
As pure as sinne with Baptisme.

B. Can. Then heare me gracious Soueraign, & you Peers,
That owe your selues, your liues, and seruices,
To this Imperiall Throne. There is no barre
To make against your Highnesse Clayme to France,
But this which they produce from *Pharamond*,
In terram Salicam Mulieres ne succedant,
No Woman shall succeed in *Salike* Land:
Which *Salike* Land, the French vniustly gloze
To be the Realme of France, and *Pharamond*
The founder of this Law, and Female Barre.
Yet their owne Authors faithfully affirme,
That the Land *Salike* is in Germanie,
Betweene the Floods of Sala and of Elue:
Where *Charles* the Great hauing subdu'd the Saxons,
There left behind and setled certaine French:
Who holding in disdaine the German Women,
For some dishonest manners of their life,
Establisht then this Law; to wit, No Female
Should be Inheritrix in *Salike* Land:
Which *Salike* (as I said) 'twixt Elue and Sala,
Is at this day in Germanie, call'd *Meisen*.
Then doth it well appeare, the *Salike* Law
Was not deuised for the Realme of France:
Nor did the French possesse the *Salike* Land,
Vntill foure hundred one and twentie yeeres
After defunction of King *Pharamond*,
Idly suppos'd the founder of this Law,
Who died within the yeere of our Redemption,
Foure hundred twentie six: and *Charles* the Great
Subdu'd the Saxons, and did seat the French
Beyond the Riuer Sala, in the yeere
Eight hundred fiue. Besides, their Writers say,
King *Pepin*, which deposed *Childerike*,
Did as Heire Generall, being descended
Of *Blithild*, which was Daughter to King *Clothair*,
Make Clayme and Title to the Crowne of France.
Hugh Capet also, who vsurpt the Crowne

Of

Of *Charles* the Duke of Loraine, sole Heire male
Of the true Line and Stock of *Charles* the Great:
To find his Title with some shewes of truth,
Though in pure truth it was corrupt and naught,
Conuey'd himselfe as th'Heire to th' Lady *Lingare*,
Daughter to *Charlemaine*, who was the Sonne
To *Lewes* the Emperour, and *Lewes* the Sonne
Of *Charles* the Great: also King *Lewes* the Tenth,
Who was sole Heire to the Vsurper *Capet*,
Could not keepe quiet in his conscience,
Wearing the Crowne of France, 'till satisfied,
That faire Queene *Isabel*, his Grandmother,
Was Lineall of the Lady *Ermengare*,
Daughter to *Charles* the foresaid Duke of Loraine:
By the which Marriage, the Lyne of *Charles* the Great
Was re-vnited to the Crowne of France.
So, that as cleare as is the Summers Sunne,
King *Pepins* Title, and *Hugh Capets* Clayme,
King *Lewes* his satisfaction, all appeare
To hold in Right and Title of the Female:
So doe the Kings of France vnto this day.
Howbeit, they would hold vp this Salique Law,
To barre your Highnesse clayming from the Female,
And rather chuse to hide them in a Net,
Then amply to imbarre their crooked Titles,
Vsurpt from you and your Progenitors.

King. May I with right and conscience make this claim?

Bish. Cant. The sinne vpon my head, dread Soueraigne:
For in the Booke of *Numbers* is it writ,
When the man dyes, let the Inheritance
Descend vnto the Daughter. Gracious Lord,
Stand for your owne, vnwind your bloody Flagge,
Looke back into your mightie Ancestors:
Goe my dread Lord, to your great Grandsires Tombe,
From whom you clayme; inuoke his Warlike Spirit,
And your Great Vnckles, *Edward* the Black Prince,
Who on the French ground play'd a Tragedie,
Making defeat on the full Power of France:
Whiles his most mightie Father on a Hill
Stood smiling, to behold his Lyons Whelpe
Forrage in blood of French Nobilitie.
O Noble English, that could entertaine
With halfe their Forces, the full pride of France,
And let another halfe stand laughing by,
All out of worke, and cold for action.

Bish. Awake remembrance of these valiant dead,
And with your puissant Arme renew their Feats;
You are their Heire, you sit vpon their Throne:
The Blood and Courage that renowned them,
Runs in your Veines: and my thrice-puissant Liege
Is in the very May-Morne of his Youth,
Ripe for Exploits and mightie Enterprises.

Exe. Your Brother Kings and Monarchs of the Earth
Doe all expect, that you should rowse your selfe,
As did the former Lyons of your Blood.

West. They know your Grace hath cause, and means, and (might;
So hath your Highnesse: neuer King of England
Had Nobles richer, and more loyall Subiects,
Whose hearts haue left their bodyes here in England,
And lye pauillion'd in the fields of France.

Bish. Can. O let their bodyes follow my deare Liege
With Bloods, and Sword and Fire, to win your Right:
In ayde whereof, we of the Spiritualtie
Will rayse your Highnesse such a mightie Summe,
As neuer did the Clergie at one time
Bring in to any of your Ancestors.

King. We must not onely arme t'inuade the French,
But lay downe our proportions, to defend
Against the Scot, who will make roade vpon vs,
With all aduantages.

Bish. Can. They of those Marches, gracious Soueraign,
Shall be a Wall sufficient to defend
Our in-land from the pilfering Borderers.

King. We do not meane the coursing snatchers onely,
But feare the maine intendment of the Scot,
Who hath been still a giddy neighbour to vs.
For you shall reade, that my great Grandfather
Neuer went with his forces into France,
But that the Scot, on his vnfurnisht Kingdome,
Came pouring like the Tyde into a breach,
With ample and brim fulnesse of his force,
Galling the gleaned Land with hot Assayes,
Girding with grieuous siege, Castles and Townes:
That England being emptie of defence,
Hath shooke and trembled at th'ill neighbourhood.

B. Can. She hath bin thē more fear'd thē harm'd, my Liege:
For heare her but exampl'd by her selfe,
When all her Cheualrie hath been in France,
And shee a mourning Widdow of her Nobles,
Shee hath her selfe not onely well defended,
But taken and impounded as a Stray,
The King of Scots: whom shee did send to France,
To fill King *Edwards* fame with prisoner Kings,
And make their Chronicle as rich with prayse,
As is the Owse and bottome of the Sea
With sunken Wrack, and sum-lesse Treasuries.

Bish. Ely. But there's a saying very old and true,
If that you will France win, then with Scotland first begin.
For once the Eagle (England) being in prey,
To her vnguarded Nest, the Weazell (Scot)
Comes sneaking, and so sucks her Princely Egges,
Playing the Mouse in absence of the Cat,
To tame and hauocke more then she can eate.

Exet. It followes then, the Cat must stay at home,
Yet that is but a crush'd necessity,
Since we haue lockes to safegard necessaries,
And pretty traps to catch the petty theeues.
While that the Armed hand doth fight abroad,
Th'aduised head defends it selfe at home:
For Gouernment, though high, and low, and lower,
Put into parts, doth keepe in one consent,
Congreeing in a full and natural close,
Like Musicke.

Cant. Therefore doth heauen diuide
The state of man in diuers functions,
Setting endeuour in continual motion:
To which is fixed as an ayme or butt,
Obedience: for so worke the Hony Bees,
Creatures that by a rule in Nature teach
The Act of Order to a peopled Kingdome.
They haue a King, and Officers of sorts,
Where some like Magistrates correct at home:
Others, like Merchants venter Trade abroad:
Others, like Souldiers armed in their stings,
Make boote vpon the Summers Veluet buddes:
Which pillage, they with merry march bring home
To the Tent-royal of their Emperor:
Who busied in his Maiesties surueyes
The singing Masons building roofes of Gold,
The ciuil Citizens kneading vp the hony;
The poore Mechanicke Porters, crowding in
Their heauy burthens at his narrow gate:

The sad-ey'd Iustice with his surly humme,
Deliuering ore to Executors pale
The lazie yawning Drone: I this inferre,
That many things hauing full reference
To one consent, may worke contrariously,
As many Arrowes loosed seuerall wayes
Come to one marke: as many wayes meet in one towne,
As many fresh streames meet in one salt sea;
As many Lynes close in the Dials center:
So may a thousand actions once a foote,
And in one purpose, and be all well borne
Without defeat. Therefore to France, my Liege,
Diuide your happy England into foure,
Whereof, take you one quarter into France,
And you withall shall make all Gallia shake.
If we with thrice such powers left at home,
Cannot defend our owne doores from the dogge,
Let vs be worried, and our Nation lose
The name of hardinesse and policie.

King. Call in the Messengers sent from the Dolphin.
Now are we well resolu'd, and by Gods helpe
And yours, the noble sinewes of our power,
France being ours, wee'l bend it to our Awe,
Or breake it all to peeces. Or there wee'l sit,
(Ruling in large and ample Emperie,
Ore France, and all her (almost) Kingly Dukedomes)
Or lay these bones in an vnworthy Vrne,
Tomblesse, with no remembrance ouer them:
Either our History shall with full mouth
Speake freely of our Acts, or else our graue
Like Turkish mute, shall haue a tonguelesse mouth,
Not worshipt with a waxen Epitaph.

Enter Ambassadors of France.

Now are we well prepar'd to know the pleasure
Of our faire Cosin Dolphin: for we heare,
Your greeting is from him, not from the King.

Amb. May't please your Maiestie to giue vs leaue
Freely to render what we haue in charge:
Or shall we sparingly shew you farre off
The Dolphins meaning, and our Embassie.

King. We are no Tyrant, but a Christian King,
Vnto whose grace our passion is as subiect
As is our wretches fettred in our prisons,
Therefore with franke and with vncurbed plainnesse,
Tell vs the *Dolphins* minde.

Amb. Thus than in few:
Your Highnesse lately sending into France,
Did claime some certaine Dukedomes, in the right
Of your great Predecessor, King *Edward* the third.
In answer of which claime, the Prince our Master
Sayes, that you sauour too much of your youth,
And bids you be aduis'd: There's nought in France,
That can be with a nimble Galliard wonne:
You cannot reuell into Dukedomes there.
He therefore sends you meeter for your spirit
This Tun of Treasure; and in lieu of this,
Desires you let the dukedomes that you claime
Heare no more of you. This the *Dolphin* speakes.

King. What Treasure Vncle?

Exe. Tennis balles, my Liege.

Kin, We are glad the *Dolphin* is so pleasant with vs,
His Present, and your paines we thanke you for:
When we haue matcht our Rackets to these Balles,
We will in France (by Gods grace) play a set,
Shall strike his fathers Crowne into the hazard.
Tell him, he hath made a match with such a Wrangler,
That all the Courts of France will be disturb'd
With Chaces. And we vnderstand him well,
How he comes o're vs with our wilder dayes,
Not measuring what vse we made of them.
We neuer valew'd this poore seate of England,
And therefore liuing hence, did giue our selfe
To barbarous license: As 'tis euer common,
That men are merriest, when they are from home.
But tell the *Dolphin*, I will keepe my State,
Be like a King, and shew my sayle of Greatnesse,
When I do rowse me in my Throne of France.
For that I haue layd by my Maiestie,
And plodded like a man for working dayes:
But I will rise there with so full a glorie,
That I will dazle all the eyes of France,
Yea strike the *Dolphin* blinde to looke on vs,
And tell the pleasant Prince, this Mocke of his
Hath turn'd his balles to Gun-stones, and his soule
Shall stand sore charged, for the wastefull vengeance
That shall flye with them: for many a thousand widows
Shall this his Mocke, mocke out of their deer husbands;
Mocke mothers from their sonnes, mock Castles downe:
And some are yet vngotten and vnborne,
That shal haue cause to curse the *Dolphins* scorne.
But this lyes all within the wil of God,
To whom I do appeale, and in whose name
Tel you the *Dolphin*, I am comming on,
To venge me as I may, and to put forth
My rightfull hand in a wel-hallow'd cause.
So get you hence in peace: And tell the *Dolphin*,
His Iest will sauour but of shallow wit,
When thousands weepe more then did laugh at it.
Conuey them with safe conduct. Fare you well.

Exeunt Ambassadors.

Exe. This was a merry Message.

King. We hope to make the Sender blush at it:
Therefore, my Lords, omit no happy howre,
That may giue furth'rance to our Expedition:
For we haue now no thought in vs but France,
Saue those to God, that runne before our businesse.
Therefore let our proportions for these Warres
Be soone collected, and all things thought vpon,
That may with reasonable swiftnesse adde
More Feathers to our Wings: for God before,
Wee'le chide this *Dolphin* at his fathers doore.
Therefore let euery man now taske his thought,
That this faire Action may on foot be brought. *Exeunt.*

Flourish. Enter Chorus.

Now all the Youth of England are on fire,
And silken Dalliance in the Wardrobe lyes:
Now thriue the Armorers, and Honors thought
Reignes solely in the breast of euery man.
They sell the Pasture now, to buy the Horse;
Following the Mirror of all Christian Kings,
With winged heeles, as English *Mercuries.*
For now sits Expectation in the Ayre,
And hides a Sword, from Hilts vnto the Point,
With Crownes Imperiall, Crownes and Coronets.
Promis'd to *Harry*, and his followers.
The French aduis'd by good intelligence
Of this most dreadfull preparation,
Shake in their feare, and with pale Pollicy
Seeke to diuert the English purposes.
O England: Modell to thy inward Greatnesse,
Like little Body with a mightie Heart:

What

What mightst thou do, that honour would thee do,
Were all thy children kinde and naturall:
But see, thy fault France hath in thee found out,
A nest of hollow bosomes, which he filles
With treacherous Crownes, and three corrupted men:
One, *Richard* Earle of Cambridge, and the second
Henry Lord *Scroope* of *Masham*, and the third
Sir *Thomas Grey* Knight of Northumberland,
Haue for the Gilt of France (O guilt indeed)
Confirm'd Conspiracy with fearefull France,
And by their hands, this grace of Kings must dye.
If Hell and Treason hold their promises,
Ere he take ship for France; and in Southampton.
Linger your patience on, and wee'l digest
Th'abuse of distance; force a play:
The summe is payde, the Traitors are agreed,
The King is set from London, and the Scene
Is now transported (Gentles) to Southampton,
There is the Play-house now, there must you sit,
And thence to France shall we conuey you safe,
And bring you backe: Charming the narrow seas
To giue you gentle Passe: for if we may,
Wee'l not offend one stomacke with our Play.
But till the King come forth, and not till then,
Vnto Southampton do we shift our Scene. *Exit*

Enter Corporall Nym, and Lieutenant Bardolfe.

Bar. Well met Corporall *Nym*.

Nym. Good morrow Lieutenant *Bardolfe*.

Bar. What, are Ancient *Pistoll* and you friends yet?

Nym. For my part, I care not: I say little: but when time shall serue there shall be smiles, but that shall be as it may. I dare not fight, but I will winke and holde out mine yron: it is a simple one, but what though? It will toste Cheese, and it will endure cold, as another mans sword will: and there's an end.

Bar. I will bestow a breakfast to make you friendes, and wee'l bee all three sworne brothers to France: Let't be so good Corporall *Nym*.

Nym. Faith, I will liue so long as I may, that's the certaine of it: and when I cannot liue any longer, I will doe as I may: That is my rest, that is the rendeuous of it.

Bar. It is certaine Corporall, that he is marryed to *Nell Quickly*, and certainly she did you wrong, for you were troth-plight to her.

Nym. I cannot tell, Things must be as they may: men may sleepe, and they may haue their throats about them at that time, and some say, kniues haue edges: It must be as it may, though patience be a tyred name, yet shee will plodde, there must be Conclusions, well, I cannot tell.

Enter Pistoll, & Quickly.

Bar. Heere comes Ancient *Pistoll* and his wife: good Corporall be patient heere. How now mine Hoaste *Pistoll*?

Pist. Base Tyke, cal'st thou mee Hoste, now by this hand I sweare I scorne the terme: nor shall my *Nel* keep Lodgers.

Host. No by my troth, not long: For we cannot lodge and board a dozen or fourteene Gentlewomen that liue honestly by the pricke of their Needles, but it will bee thought we keepe a Bawdy-house straight. O welliday Lady, if he be not hewne now, we shall see wilful adultery and murther committed.

Bar. Good Lieutenant, good Corporal offer nothing heere. *Nym.* Pish.

Pist. Pish for thee, Island dogge: thou prickeard cur of Island.

Host. Good Corporall *Nym* shew thy valor, and put vp your sword.

Nym. Will you shogge off? I would haue you solus.

Pist. Solus, egregious dog? O Viper vile; The solus in thy most meruailous face, the solus in thy teeth, and in thy throate, and in thy hatefull Lungs, yea in thy Maw perdy; and which is worse, within thy nastie mouth. I do retort the solus in thy bowels, for I can take, and *Pistols* cocke is vp, and flashing fire will follow.

Nym. I am not *Barbason*, you cannot coniure mee: I haue an humor to knocke you indifferently well: If you grow fowle with me Pistoll, I will scoure you with my Rapier, as I may, in fayre tearmes. If you would walke off, I would pricke your guts a little in good tearmes, as I may, and that's the humor of it.

Pist. O Braggard vile, and damned furious wight, The Graue doth gape, and doting death is neere, Therefore exhale.

Bar. Heare me, heare me what I say: Hee that strikes the first stroake, Ile run him vp to the hilts, as I am a soldier.

Pist. An oath of mickle might, and fury shall abate. Giue me thy fist, thy fore-foote to me giue: Thy spirites are most tall.

Nym. I will cut thy throate one time or other in faire termes, that is the humor of it.

Pistoll. *Couple a gorge*, that is the word. I defie thee againe. O hound of Creet, think'st thou my spouse to get? No, to the spittle goe, and from the Poudring tub of infamy, fetch forth the Lazar Kite of *Cressids* kinde, *Doll Teare-sheete*, she by name, and her espouse. I haue, and I will hold the *Quondam Quickely* for the onely shee: and *Pauca*, there's enough to go to.

Enter the Boy.

Boy. Mine Hoast *Pistoll*, you must come to my Mayster, and your Hostesse: He is very sicke, & would to bed. Good *Bardolfe*, put thy face betweene his sheets, and do the Office of a Warming-pan: Faith, he's very ill.

Bard. Away you Rogue.

Host. By my troth he'l yeeld the Crow a pudding one of these dayes: the King has kild his heart. Good Husband come home presently. *Exit*

Bar. Come, shall I make you two friends. Wee must to France together: why the diuel should we keep kniues to cut one anothers throats?

Pist. Let floods ore-swell, and fiends for food howle on.

Nym. You'l pay me the eight shillings I won of you at Betting?

Pist. Base is the Slaue that payes.

Nym. That now I wil haue: that's the humor of it.

Pist. As manhood shal compound: push home. *Draw*

Bard. By this sword, hee that makes the first thrust, Ile kill him: By this sword, I wil.

Pi. Sword is an Oath, & Oaths must haue their course

Bar. Coporall *Nym*, & thou wilt be friends be frends, and thou wilt not, why then be enemies with me to: prethee put vp.

Pist. A Noble shalt thou haue, and present pay, and Liquor likewise will I giue to thee, and friendshippe shall combyne, and brotherhood. Ile liue by *Nymme*, & *Nymme* shall liue by me, is not this iust? For I shal Sutler be vnto the Campe, and profits will accrue. Giue mee thy hand.

Nym. I shall haue my Noble?

Pist. In cash, most iustly payd.

Nym. Well, then that the humor of't.

Enter Hostesse.

Host. As euer you come of women, come in quickly to sir *Iohn*: A poore heart, hee is so shak'd of a burning quotidian Tertian, that it is most lamentable to behold. Sweet men, come to him.

Nym. The King hath run bad humors on the Knight, that's the euen of it.

Pist. Nym, thou hast spoke the right, his heart is fracted and corroborate.

Nym. The King is a good King, but it must bee as it may: he passes some humors, and carreeres.

Pist. Let vs condole the Knight, for (Lambekins) we will liue.

Enter Exeter, Bedford, & Westmerland.

Bed Fore God his Grace is bold to trust these traitors

Exe. They shall be apprehended by and by.

West. How smooth and euen they do bear themselues,
As if allegeance in their bosomes sate
Crowned with faith, and constant loyalty.

Bed. The King hath note of all that they intend,
By interception, which they dreame not of.

Exe. Nay, but the man that was his bedfellow,
Whom he hath dull'd and cloy'd with gracious fauours;
That he should for a forraigne purse, so sell
His Soueraignes life to death and treachery.

Sound Trumpets.

Enter the King, Scroope, Cambridge, and Gray.

King. Now sits the winde faire, and we will aboord.
My Lord of *Cambridge*, and my kinde Lord of *Masham*,
And you my gentle Knight, giue me your thoughts:
Thinke you not that the powres we beare with vs
Will cut their passage through the force of France?
Doing the execution, and the acte,
For which we haue in head assembled them.

Scro. No doubt my Liege, if each man do his best.

King. I doubt not that, since we are well perswaded
We carry not a heart with vs from hence,
That growes not in a faire consent with ours:
Nor leaue not one behinde, that doth not wish
Successe and Conquest to attend on vs.

Cam. Neuer was Monarch better fear'd and lou'd,
Then is your Maiesty; there's not I thinke a subiect
That sits in heart-greefe and vneasinesse
Vnder the sweet shade of your gouernment.

Kni. True: those that were your Fathers enemies,
Haue steep'd their gauls in hony, and do serue you
With hearts create of duty, and of zeale.

King. We therefore haue great cause of thankfulnes,
And shall forget the office of our hand
Sooner then quittance of desert and merit,
According to the weight and worthinesse.

Scro. So seruice shall with steeled sinewes toyle,
And labour shall refresh it selfe with hope
To do your Grace incessant seruices.

King. We Iudge no lesse. Vnkle of *Exeter*,
Inlarge the man committed yesterday,
That rayl'd against our person: We consider
It was excesse of Wine that set him on,
And on his more aduice, We pardon him.

Scro. That's mercy, but too much security:
Let him be punish'd Soueraigne, least example
Breed (by his sufferance) more of such a kind.

King. O let vs yet be mercifull.

Cam. So may your Highnesse, and yet punish too.

Grey. Sir, you shew great mercy if you giue him life,
After the taste of much correction.

King. Alas, your too much loue and care of me,
Are heauy Orisons 'gainst this poore wretch:
If little faults proceeding on distemper,
Shall not be wink'd at, how shall we stretch our eye
When capitall crimes, chew'd, swallow'd, and digested,
Appeare before vs? Wee'l yet inlarge that man,
Though *Cambridge, Scroope*, and *Gray*, in their deere care
And tender preseruation of our person
Wold haue him punish'd. And now to our French causes,
Who are the late Commissioners?

Cam. I one my Lord,
Your Highnesse bad me aske for it to day.

Scro. So did you me my Liege.

Gray. And I my Royall Soueraigne.

King. Then *Richard* Earle of *Cambridge*, there is yours:
There yours Lord *Scroope* of *Masham*, and Sir Knight:
Gray of *Northumberland*, this same is yours:
Reade them, and know I know your worthinesse.
My Lord of *Westmerland*, and Vnkle *Exeter*,
We will aboord to night. Why how now Gentlemen?
What see you in those papers, that you loose
So much complexion? Looke ye how they change:
Their cheekes are paper. Why, what reade you there,
That haue so cowarded and chac'd your blood
Out of apparance.

Cam. I do confesse my fault,
And do submit me to your Highnesse mercy.

Gray. Scro. To which we all appeale.

King. The mercy that was quicke in vs but late,
By your owne counsaile is supprest and kill'd:
You must not dare (for shame) to talke of mercy,
For your owne reasons turne into your bosomes,
As dogs vpon their maisters, worrying you:
See you my Princes, and my Noble Peeres,
These English monsters: My Lord of *Cambridge* heere,
You know how apt our loue was, to accord
To furnish with all appertinents
Belonging to his Honour; and this man,
Hath for a few light Crownes, lightly conspir'd
And sworne vnto the practises of France
To kill vs heere in Hampton. To the which,
This Knight no lesse for bounty bound to Vs
Then Cambridge is, hath likewise sworne. But O,
What shall I say to thee Lord *Scroope*, thou cruell,
Ingratefull, sauage, and inhumane Creature?
Thou that didst beare the key of all my counsailes,
That knew'st the very bottome of my soule,
That (almost) might'st haue coyn'd me into Golde,
Would'st thou haue practis'd on me, for thy vse?
May it be possible, that forraigne hyer
Could out of thee extract one sparke of euill
That might annoy my finger? 'Tis so strange,
That though the truth of it stands off as grosse
As blacke and white, my eye will scarsely see it.
Treason, and murther, euer kept together,
As two yoake diuels sworne to eythers purpose,
Working so grossely in an naturall cause,
That admiration did not hoope at them.
But thou (gainst all proportion) didst bring in
Wonder to waite on treason, and on murther:
And whatsoeuer cunning fiend it was
That wrought vpon thee so preposterously,
Hath got the voyce in hell for excellence:

And

And other diuels that suggest by treasons,
Do botch and bungle vp damnation,
With patches, colours, and with formes being fetcht
From glist'ring semblances of piety:
But he that temper'd thee, bad thee stand vp,
Gaue thee no instance why thou shouldst do treason,
Vnlesse to dub thee with the name of Traitor.
If that same Dæmon that hath gull'd thee thus,
Should with his Lyon-gate walke the whole world,
He might returne to vastie Tartar backe,
And tell the Legions, I can neuer win
A soule so easie as that Englishmans.
Oh, how hast thou with iealousie infected
The sweetnesse of affiance? Shew men dutifull,
Why so didst thou: seeme they graue and learned?
Why so didst thou. Come they of Noble Family?
Why so didst thou. Seeme they religious?
Why so didst thou. Or are they spare in diet,
Free from grosse passion, or of mirth, or anger,
Constant in spirit, not sweruing with the blood,
Garnish'd and deck'd in modest complement,
Not working with the eye, without the eare,
And but in purged iudgement trusting neither,
Such and so finely boulted didst thou seeme:
And thus thy fall hath left a kinde of blot,
To make thee full fraught man, and best indued
With some suspition, I will weepe for thee.
For this reuolt of thine, me thinkes is like
Another fall of Man. Their faults are open,
Arrest them to the answer of the Law,
And God acquit them of their practises.

Exe. I arrest thee of High Treason, by the name of *Richard* Earle of *Cambridge*.

I arrest thee of High Treason, by the name of *Thomas* Lord *Scroope* of *Marsham*.

I arrest thee of High Treason, by the name of *Thomas Grey*, Knight of *Northumberland*.

Scro. Our purposes, God iustly hath discouer'd,
And I repent my fault more then my death,
Which I beseech your Highnesse to forgiue,
Although my body pay the price of it.

Cam. For me, the Gold of France did not seduce,
Although I did admit it as a motiue,
The sooner to effect what I intended:
But God be thanked for preuention,
Which in sufferance heartily will reioyce,
Beseeching God, and you, to pardon mee.

Gray. Neuer did faithfull subiect more reioyce
At the discouery of most dangerous Treason,
Then I do at this houre ioy ore my selfe,
Preuented from a damned enterprize;
My fault, but not my body, pardon Soueraigne.

King. God quit you in his mercy: Hear your sentence
You haue conspir'd against Our Royall person,
Ioyn'd with an enemy proclaim'd, and from his Coffers,
Receyu'd the Golden Earnest of Our death:
Wherein you would haue sold your King to slaughter,
His Princes, and his Peeres to seruitude,
His Subiects to oppression, and contempt,
And his whole Kingdome into desolation:
Touching our person, seeke we no reuenge,
But we our Kingdomes safety must so tender,
Whose ruine you sought, that to her Lawes
We do deliuer you. Get you therefore hence,
(Poore miserable wretches) to your death:
The taste whereof, God of his mercy giue
You patience to indure, and true Repentance
Of all your deare offences. Beare them hence. *Exit.*
Now Lords for France: the enterprise whereof
Shall be to you as vs, like glorious.
We doubt not of a faire and luckie Warre,
Since God so graciously hath brought to light
This dangerous Treason, lurking in our way,
To hinder our beginnings. We doubt not now,
But euery Rubbe is smoothed on our way.
Then forth, deare Countreymen: Let vs deliuer
Our Puissance into the hand of God,
Putting it straight in expedition.
Chearely to Sea, the signes of Warre aduance,
No King of England, if not King of France. *Flourish.*

Enter Pistoll, Nim, Bardolph, Boy, and Hostesse.

Hostesse. 'Prythee honey sweet Husband, let me bring thee to Staines.

Pistoll. No: for my manly heart doth erne. *Bardolph*, be blythe: *Nim*, rowse thy vaunting Veines: Boy, bristle thy Courage vp: for *Falstaffe* hee is dead, and wee must erne therefore.

Bard. Would I were with him, wheresomere hee is, eyther in Heauen, or in Hell.

Hostesse. Nay sure, hee's not in Hell: hee's in *Arthurs* Bosome, if euer man went to *Arthurs* Bosome: a made a finer end, and went away and it had beene any Christome Child: a parted eu'n iust betweene Twelue and One, eu'n at the turning o'th' Tyde: for after I saw him fumble with the Sheets, and play with Flowers, and smile vpon his fingers end, I knew there was but one way: for his Nose was as sharpe as a Pen, and a Table of greene fields. How now Sir *Iohn* (quoth I?) what man? be a good cheare: so a cryed out, God, God, God, three or foure times: now I, to comfort him, bid him a should not thinke of God; I hop'd there was no neede to trouble himselfe with any such thoughts yet: so a bad me lay more Clothes on his feet: I put my hand into the Bed, and felt them, and they were as cold as any stone: then I felt to his knees, and so vp-peer'd, and vpward, and all was as cold as any stone.

Nim. They say he cryed out of Sack.

Hostesse. I, that a did.

Bard. And of Women.

Hostesse. Nay, that a did not.

Boy. Yes that a did, and said they were Deules incarnate.

Woman. A could neuer abide Carnation, 'twas a Colour he neuer lik'd.

Boy. A said once, the Deule would haue him about Women.

Hostesse. A did in some sort (indeed) handle Women: but then hee was rumatique, and talk'd of the Whore of Babylon.

Boy. Doe you not remember a saw a Flea sticke vpon *Bardolphs* Nose, and a said it was a blacke Soule burning in Hell.

Bard. Well, the fuell is gone that maintain'd that fire: that's all the Riches I got in his seruice.

Nim. Shall wee shogg? the King will be gone from Southampton.

Pist. Come, let's away. My Loue, giue me thy Lippes: Looke to my Chattels, and my Moueables: Let Sences rule: The world is, Pitch and pay: trust none: for Oathes are Strawes, mens Faiths are Wafer-Cakes, and hold-fast is the onely Dogge: My Ducke, therefore *Caueto* bee thy Counsailor. Goe, cleare thy Chrystalls. Yoke-fellowes in Armes, let vs to France, like Horse-leeches

leeches my Boyes, to sucke, to sucke, the very blood to sucke.

Boy. And that's but vnwholesome food, they say.

Pist. Touch her soft mouth, and march.

Bard. Farwell Hostesse.

Nim. I cannot kisse, that is the humor of it: but adieu.

Pist. Let Huswiferie appeare: keepe close, I thee command.

Hostesse. Farwell: adieu. *Exeunt*

Flourish.

Enter the French King, the Dolphin, the Dukes of Berry and Britaine.

King. Thus comes the English with full power vpon vs,
And more then carefully it vs concernes,
To answer Royally in our defences.
Therefore the Dukes of Berry and of Britaine,
Of Brabant and of Orleance, shall make forth,
And you Prince Dolphin, with all swift dispatch
To lyne and new repayre our Townes of Warre
With men of courage, and with meanes defendant:
For England his approaches makes as fierce,
As Waters to the sucking of a Gulfe.
It fits vs then to be as prouident,
As feare may teach vs, out of late examples
Left by the fatall and neglected English,
Vpon our fields.

Dolphin. My most redoubted Father,
It is most meet we arme vs 'gainst the Foe:
For Peace it selfe should not so dull a Kingdome,
(Though War nor no knowne Quarrel were in question)
But that Defences, Musters, Preparations,
Should be maintain'd, assembled, and collected,
As were a Warre in expectation.
Therefore I say, 'tis meet we all goe forth,
To view the sick and feeble parts of France:
And let vs doe it with no shew of feare,
No, with no more, then if we heard that England
Were busied with a Whitson Morris-dance:
For, my good Liege, shee is so idly King'd,
Her Scepter so phantastically borne,
By a vaine giddie shallow humorous Youth,
That feare attends her not.

Const. O peace, Prince Dolphin,
You are too much mistaken in this King:
Question your Grace the late Embassadors,
With what great State he heard their Embassie,
How well supply'd with Noble Councellors,
How modest in exception; and withall,
How terrible in constant resolution:
And you shall find, his Vanities fore-spent,
Were but the out-side of the Roman *Brutus*,
Couering Discretion with a Coat of Folly;
As Gardeners doe with Ordure hide those Roots
That shall first spring, and be most delicate.

Dolphin. Well, 'tis not so, my Lord High Constable.
But though we thinke it so, it is no matter:
In cases of defence, 'tis best to weigh
The Enemie more mightie then he seemes,
So the proportions of defence are fill'd:
Which of a weake and niggardly proiection,
Doth like a Miser spoyle his Coat, with scanting
A little Cloth.

King. Thinke we King *Harry* strong:
And Princes, looke you strongly arme to meet him.
The Kindred of him hath beene flesht vpon vs:
And he is bred out of that bloodie straine,
That haunted vs in our familiar Pathes:
Witnesse our too much memorable shame,
When Cressy Battell fatally was strucke,
And all our Princes captiu'd, by the hand
Of that black Name, *Edward*, black Prince of Wales:
Whiles that his Mountaine Sire, on Mountaine standing
Vp in the Ayre, crown'd with the Golden Sunne,
Saw his Heroicall Seed, and smil'd to see him
Mangle the Worke of Nature, and deface
The Patternes, that by God and by French Fathers
Had twentie yeeres been made. This is a Stem
Of that Victorious Stock: and let vs feare
The Natiue mightinesse and fate of him.

Enter a Messenger.

Mess. Embassadors from *Harry* King of England,
Doe craue admittance to your Maiestie.

King. Weele giue them present audience.
Goe, and bring them.
You see this Chase is hotly followed, friends.

Dolphin. Turne head, and stop pursuit: for coward Dogs
Most spend their mouths, whẽ what they seem to threaten
Runs farre before them. Good my Soueraigne
Take vp the English short, and let them know
Of what a Monarchie you are the Head:
Selfe-loue, my Liege, is not so vile a sinne,
As selfe-neglecting.

Enter Exeter.

King. From our Brother of England?

Exe. From him, and thus he greets your Maiestie:
He wills you in the Name of God Almightie,
That you deuest your selfe, and lay apart
The borrowed Glories, that by gift of Heauen,
By Law of Nature, and of Nations, longs
To him and to his Heires, namely, the Crowne,
And all wide-stretched Honors, that pertaine
By Custome, and the Ordinance of Times,
Vnto the Crowne of France: that you may know
'Tis no sinister, nor no awk-ward Clayme,
Pickt from the worme-holes of long-vanisht dayes,
Nor from the dust of old Obliuion rakt,
He sends you this most memorable Lyne,
In euery Branch truly demonstratiue;
Willing you ouer-looke this Pedigree:
And when you find him euenly deriu'd
From his most fam'd, of famous Ancestors,
Edward the third; he bids you then resigne
Your Crowne and Kingdome, indirectly held
From him the Natiue and true Challenger.

King. Or else what followes?

Exe. Bloody constraint: for if you hide the Crowne
Euen in your hearts, there will he rake for it.
Therefore in fierce Tempest is he comming,
In Thunder and in Earth-quake, like a *Ioue*:
That if requiring faile, he will compell.
And bids you, in the Bowels of the Lord,
Deliuer vp the Crowne, and to take mercie
On the poore Soules, for whom this hungry Warre
Opens his vastie Iawes: and on your head
Turning the Widdowes Teares, the Orphans Cryes,
The dead-mens Blood, the priuy Maidens Groanes,
For Husbands, Fathers, and betrothed Louers,
That shall be swallowed in this Controuersie.
This is his Clayme, his Threatning, and my Message:
Vnlesse the Dolphin be in presence here;
To whom expressely I bring greeting to.

King. For

King. For vs, we will consider of this further:
To morrow shall you beare our full intent
Back to our Brother of England.

Dolph. For the Dolphin,
I stand here for him: what to him from England?

Exe. Scorne and defiance, sleight regard, contempt,
And any thing that may not mis-become
The mightie Sender, doth he prize you at.
Thus sayes my King: and if your Fathers Highnesse
Doe not, in graunt of all demands at large,
Sweeten the bitter Mock you sent his Maiestie;
Hee'le call you to so hot an Answer of it,
That Caues and Wombie Vaultages of France
Shall chide your Trespas, and returne your Mock
In second Accent of his Ordinance.

Dolph. Say: if my Father render faire returne,
It is against my will: for I desire
Nothing but Oddes with England.
To that end, as matching to his Youth and Vanitie,
I did present him with the Paris-Balls.

Exe. Hee'le make your Paris Louer shake for it,
Were it the Mistresse Court of mightie Europe:
And be assur'd, you'le find a diff'rence,
As we his Subiects haue in wonder found,
Betweene the promise of his greener dayes,
And these he masters now: now he weighes Time
Euen to the vtmost Graine: that you shall reade
In your owne Losses, if he stay in France.

King. To morrow shall you know our mind at full.

Flourish.

Exe. Dispatch vs with all speed, least that our King
Come here himselfe to question our delay;
For he is footed in this Land already.

King. You shalbe soone dispatcht, with faire conditions.
A Night is but small breathe, and little pawse,
To answer matters of this consequence. *Exeunt.*

Actus Secundus.

Flourish. Enter Chorus.

Thus with imagin'd wing our swift Scene flyes,
In motion of no lesse celeritie then that of Thought.
Suppose, that you haue seene
The well-appointed King at Douer Peer,
Embarke his Royaltie: and his braue Fleet,
With silken Streamers, the young *Phebus* fayning;
Play with your Fancies: and in them behold,
Vpon the Hempen Tackle, Ship-boyes climbing;
Heare the shrill Whistle, which doth order giue
To sounds confus'd: behold the threaden Sayles,
Borne with th'inuisible and creeping Wind,
Draw the huge Bottomes through the furrowed Sea,
Bresting the loftie Surge. O, doe but thinke
You stand vpon the Riuage, and behold
A Citie on th'inconstant Billowes dauncing.
For so appeares this Fleet Maiesticall,
Holding due course to Harflew. Follow, follow:
Grapple your minds to sternage of this Nauie,
And leaue your England as dead Mid-night, still,
Guarded with Grandsires, Babyes, and old Women,
Eyther past, or not arriu'd to pyth and puissance:
For who is he, whose Chin is but enricht
With one appearing Hayre, that will not follow
These cull'd and choyse-drawne Caualiers to France?
Worke, worke your Thoughts, and therein see a Siege:
Behold the Ordenance on their Carriages,
With fatall mouthes gaping on girded Harflew.
Suppose th'Embassador from the French comes back:
Tells *Harry*, That the King doth offer him
Katherine his Daughter, and with her to Dowrie,
Some petty and vnprofitable Dukedomes.
The offer likes not: and the nimble Gunner
With Lynstock now the diuellish Cannon touches,

Alarum, and Chambers goe off.

And downe goes all before them. Still be kind,
And eech out our performance with your mind. *Exit.*

Enter the King, Exeter, Bedford, and Glocester.
Alarum: Scaling Ladders at Harflew.

King. Once more vnto the Breach,
Deare friends, once more;
Or close the Wall vp with our English dead:
In Peace, there's nothing so becomes a man,
As modest stillnesse, and humilitie:
But when the blast of Warre blowes in our eares,
Then imitate the action of the Tyger:
Stiffen the sinewes, commune vp the blood,
Disguise faire Nature with hard-fauour'd Rage:
Then lend the Eye a terrible aspect:
Let it pry through the portage of the Head,
Like the Brasse Cannon: let the Brow o'rewhelme it,
As fearefully, as doth a galled Rocke
O're-hang and iutty his confounded Base,
Swill'd with the wild and wastfull Ocean.
Now set the Teeth, and stretch the Nosthrill wide,
Hold hard the Breath, and bend vp euery Spirit
To his full height. On, on you Noblish English,
Whose blood is fet from Fathers of Warre-proofe:
Fathers, that like so many *Alexanders*,
Haue in these parts from Morne till Euen fought,
And sheath'd their Swords, for lack of argument.
Dishonour not your Mothers: now attest,
That those whom you call'd Fathers, did beget you.
Be Coppy now to me of grosser blood,
And teach them how to Warre. And you good Yeomen,
Whose Lyms were made in England; shew vs here
The mettell of your Pasture: let vs sweare,
That you are worth your breeding: which I doubt not:
For there is none of you so meane and base,
That hath not Noble luster in your eyes.
I see you stand like Grey-hounds in the slips,
Straying vpon the Start. The Game's afoot:
Follow your Spirit; and vpon this Charge,
Cry, God for *Harry*, England, and S. *George*.

Alarum, and Chambers goe off.

Enter Nim, Bardolph, Pistoll, and Boy.

Bard. On, on, on, on, on, to the breach, to the breach.

Nim. 'Pray thee Corporall stay, the Knocks are too hot: and for mine owne part, I haue not a Case of Liues: the humor of it is too hot, that is the very plaine-Song of it.

Pist. The plaine-Song is most iust: for humors doe abound: Knocks goe and come: Gods Vassals drop and dye: and Sword and Shield, in bloody Field, doth winne immortall fame.

Boy. Would I were in an Ale-house in London, I would giue all my fame for a Pot of Ale, and safetie.

Pist. And

Pist. And I: If wishes would preuayle with me, my purpose should not fayle with me; but thither would I high.

Boy. As duly, but not as truly, as Bird doth sing on bough.

Enter Fluellen.

Flu. Vp to the breach, you Dogges; auaunt you Cullions.

Pist. Be mercifull great Duke to men of Mould: abate thy Rage, abate thy manly Rage; abate thy Rage, great Duke. Good Bawcock bate thy Rage: vse lenitie sweet Chuck.

Nim. These be good humors: your Honor wins bad humors. *Exit.*

Boy. As young as I am, I haue obseru'd these three Swashers: I am Boy to them all three, but all they three, though they would serue me, could not be Man to me; for indeed three such Antiques doe not amount to a man: for *Bardolph*, hee is white-liuer'd, and red-fac'd; by the meanes whereof, a faces it out, but fights not: for *Pistoll*, hee hath a killing Tongue, and a quiet Sword; by the meanes whereof, a breakes Words, and keepes whole Weapons: for *Nim*, hee hath heard, that men of few Words are the best men, and therefore hee scornes to say his Prayers, lest a should be thought a Coward: but his few bad Words are matcht with as few good Deeds; for a neuer broke any mans Head but his owne, and that was against a Post, when he was drunke. They will steale any thing, and call it Purchase. *Bardolph* stole a Lute-case, bore it twelue Leagues, and sold it for three halfepence. *Nim* and *Bardolph* are sworne Brothers in filching: and in Callice they stole a fire-shouell. I knew by that peece of Seruice, the men would carry Coales. They would haue me as familiar with mens Pockets, as their Gloues or their Hand-kerchers: which makes much against my Manhood, if I should take from anothers Pocket, to put into mine; for it is plaine pocketting vp of Wrongs. I must leaue them, and seeke some better Seruice: their Villany goes against my weake stomacke, and therefore I must cast it vp. *Exit.*

Enter Gower.

Gower. Captaine *Fluellen*, you must come presently to the Mynes; the Duke of Gloucester would speake with you.

Flu. To the Mynes? Tell you the Duke, it is not so good to come to the Mynes: for looke you, the Mynes is not according to the disciplines of the Warre; the concauities of it is not sufficient: for looke you, th'athuersarie, you may discusse vnto the Duke, looke you, is digt himselfe foure yard vnder the Countermines: by *Cheshu*, I thinke a will plowe vp all, if there is not better directions.

Gower. The Duke of Gloucester, to whom the Order of the Siege is giuen, is altogether directed by an Irish man, a very valiant Gentleman yfaith.

Welch. It is Captaine *Makmorrice*, is it not?

Gower. I thinke it be.

Welch. By *Cheshu* he is an Asse, as in the World, I will verifie as much in his Beard: he ha's no more directions in the true disciplines of the Warres, looke you, of the Roman disciplines, then is a Puppy-dog.

Enter Makmorrice, and Captaine Iamy.

Gower. Here a comes, and the Scots Captaine, Captaine *Iamy*, with him.

Welch. Captaine *Iamy* is a maruellous falorous Gentleman, that is certain, and of great expedition and knowledge in th'aunchiant Warres, vpon my particular knowledge of his directions: by *Cheshu* he will maintaine his Argument as well as any Militarie man in the World, in the disciplines of the Pristine Warres of the Romans.

Scot. I say gudday, Captaine *Fluellen*.

Welch. Godden to your Worship, good Captaine *Iames*.

Gower. How now Captaine *Mackmorrice*, haue you quit the Mynes? haue the Pioners giuen o're?

Irish. By Chrish Law tish ill done: the Worke ish giue ouer, the Trompet sound the Retreat. By my Hand I sweare, and my fathers Soule, the Worke ish ill done: it ish giue ouer: I would haue blowed vp the Towne, so Chrish saue me law, in an houre. O tish ill done, tish ill done: by my Hand tish ill done.

Welch. Captaine *Mackmorrice*, I beseech you now, will you voutsafe me, looke you, a few disputations with you, as partly touching or concerning the disciplines of the Warre, the Roman Warres, in the way of Argument, looke you, and friendly communication: partly to satisfie my Opinion, and partly for the satisfaction, looke you, of my Mind: as touching the direction of the Militarie discipline, that is the Point.

Scot. It sall be vary gud, gud feith, gud Captens bath, and I sall quit you with gud leue, as I may pick occasion: that sall I mary.

Irish. It is no time to discourse, so Chrish saue me: the day is hot, and the Weather, and the Warres, and the King, and the Dukes: it is no time to discourse, the Town is beseech'd: and the Trumpet call vs to the breech, and we talke, and be Chrish do nothing, tis shame for vs all: so God sa'me tis shame to stand still, it is shame by my hand: and there is Throats to be cut, and Workes to be done, and there ish nothing done, so Christ sa'me law.

Scot. By the Mes, ere theise eyes of mine take themselues to slomber, ayle de gud seruice, or Ile ligge i'th' grund for it; ay, or goe to death: and Ile pay't as valorously as I may, that sal I suerly do, that is the breff and the long: mary, I wad full faine heard some question tween you tway.

Welch. Captaine *Mackmorrice*, I thinke, looke you, vnder your correction, there is not many of your Nation.

Irish. Of my Nation? What ish my Nation? Ish a Villaine, and a Basterd, and a Knaue, and a Rascall. What ish my Nation? Who talkes of my Nation?

Welch. Looke you, if you take the matter otherwise then is meant, Captaine *Mackmorrice*, peraduenture I shall thinke you doe not vse me with that affabilitie, as in discretion you ought to vse me, looke you, being as good a man as your selfe, both in the disciplines of Warre, and in the deriuation of my Birth, and in other particularities.

Irish. I doe not know you so good a man as my selfe: so Chrish saue me, I will cut off your Head.

Gower. Gentlemen both, you will mistake each other.

Scot. A, that's a foule fault. *A Parley.*

Gower. The Towne sounds a Parley.

Welch. Captaine *Mackmorrice*, when there is more better oportunitie to be required, looke you, I will be so bold as to tell you, I know the disciplines of Warre: and there is an end. *Exit.*

Enter the King and all his Traine before the Gates.

King. How yet resolues the Gouernour of the Towne? This is the latest Parle we will admit:

There-

Therefore to our beſt mercy giue your ſelues,
Or like to men prowd of deſtruction,
Defie vs to our worſt: for as I am a Souldier,
A Name that in my thoughts becomes me beſt;
If I begin the batt'rie once againe,
I will not leaue the halfe-atchieued Harflew,
Till in her aſhes ſhe lye buryed.
The Gates of Mercy ſhall be all ſhut vp,
And the fleſh'd Souldier, rough and hard of heart,
In libertie of bloody hand, ſhall raunge
With Conſcience wide as Hell, mowing like Graſſe
Your freſh faire Virgins, and your flowring Infants.
What is it then to me, if impious Warre,
Arrayed in flames like to the Prince of Fiends,
Doe with his ſmyrcht complexion all fell feats,
Enlynckt to waſt and deſolation?
What is't to me, when you your ſelues are cauſe,
If your pure Maydens fall into the hand
Of hot and forcing Violation?
What Reyne can hold licentious Wickedneſſe,
When downe the Hill he holds his fierce Carriere?
We may as bootleſſe ſpend our vaine Command
Vpon th'enraged Souldiers in their ſpoyle,
As ſend Precepts to the *Leuiathan*, to come aſhore.
Therefore, you men of Harflew,
Take pitty of your Towne and of your People,
Whiles yet my Souldiers are in my Command,
Whiles yet the coole and temperate Wind of Grace
O're-blowes the filthy and contagious Clouds
Of headly Murther, Spoyle, and Villany.
If not: why in a moment looke to ſee
The blind and bloody Souldier, with foule hand
Deſire the Locks of your ſhrill-ſhriking Daughters:
Your Fathers taken by the ſiluer Beards,
And their moſt reuerend Heads daſht to the Walls:
Your naked Infants ſpitted vpon Pykes,
Whiles the mad Mothers, with their howles confus'd,
Doe breake the Clouds; as did the Wiues of Iewry,
At *Herods* bloody-hunting ſlaughter-men.
What ſay you? Will you yeeld, and this auoyd?
Or guiltie in defence, be thus deſtroy'd.

Enter Gouernour.

Gouer. Our expectation hath this day an end:
The Dolphin, whom of Succours we entreated,
Returnes vs, that his Powers are yet not ready,
To rayſe ſo great a Siege: Therefore great King,
We yeeld our Towne and Liues to thy ſoft Mercy:
Enter our Gates, diſpoſe of vs and ours,
For we no longer are defenſible.

King. Open your Gates: Come Vnckle *Exeter*,
Goe you and enter Harflew; there remaine,
And fortifie it ſtrongly 'gainſt the French:
Vſe mercy to them all for vs, deare Vnckle.
The Winter comming on, and Sickneſſe growing
Vpon our Souldiers, we will retyre to Calis.
To night in Harflew will we be your Gueſt,
To morrow for the March are we addreſt.

Flouriſh, and enter the Towne.

Enter Katherine and an old Gentlewoman.

Kathe. *Alice, tu as eſte en Angleterre, & tu bien parlas le Language.*

Alice. *En peu Madame.*

Kath. *Ie te prie m'enſigniez, il faut que ie apprend a parlen: Comient appelle vous le main en Anglois?*

Alice. *Le main il & appelle de Hand.*

Kath. *De Hand.*

Alice. *E le doyts.*

Kat. *Le doyts, ma foy Ie oublie, e doyt mays, ie me ſouemeray le doyts ie penſe qu'ils ont appelle de fingres, ou de fingres.*

Alice. *Le main de Hand, le doyts le Fingres, ie penſe que ie ſuis le bon eſcholier.*

Kath. *L'ay gaynie diux mots d' Anglois viſtement, coment appelle vous le ongles?*

Alice. *Le ongles, les appellons de Nayles.*

Kath. *De Nayles eſcoute: dites moy, ſi ie parle bien: de Hand, de Fingres, e de Nayles.*

Alice. *C'eſt bien dict Madame, il & fort bon Anglois.*

Kath. *Dites moy l' Anglois pour le bras.*

Alice. *De Arme, Madame.*

Kath. *E de coudee.*

Alice. *D' Elbow.*

Kath. *D Elbow: Ie men fay le repiticio de touts les mots que vous maves, apprins des a preſent.*

Alice. *Il & trop difficile Madame, comme Ie penſe.*

Kath. *Excuſe moy Alice eſcoute, d'Hand, de Fingre, de Nayles, d' Arma, de Bilbow.*

Alice. *D'Elbow, Madame.*

Kath. *O Seigneur Dieu, ie men oublie d'Elbow, coment appelle vous le col.*

Alice. *De Nick, Madame.*

Kath. *De Nick, e le menton.*

Alice. *De Chin.*

Kath. *De Sin: le col de Nick, le menton de Sin.*

Alice. *Ouy. Sauf voſtre honneur en verite vous prononcies les mots auſi droict, que le Natifs d' Angleterre.*

Kath. *Ie ne doute point d apprendre par de grace de Dieu, & en peu de temps.*

Alice. *N'aue vos y deſia oublie ce que ie vous a enſignie.*

Kath. *Nome ie recitera a vous promptement, d' Hand, de Fingre, de Maylees.*

Alice. *De Nayles, Madame.*

Kath. *De Nayles, de Arme, de Ilbow.*

Alice. *Sans voſtre honeus d Elbow.*

Kath. *Ainſi de ie d Elbow, de Nick, & de Sin: coment appelle vous les pied & de roba.*

Alice. *Le Foot Madame, & le Count.*

Kath. *Le Foot, & le Count: O Seignieur Dieu, il ſont le mots de ſon mauvais corruptible groſſe & impudique, & non pour le Dames de Honeur d'vſer: Ie ne voudray prononcer ce mots deuant le Seigneurs de France, pour toute le monde, fo le Foot & le Count neant moys, Ie recitera vn autrefoys ma lecon enſembe, d' Hand, de Fingre, de Nayles, d' Arme, d' Elbow, de Nick, de Sin, de Foot, le Count.*

Alice. *Excellent, Madame.*

Kath. *C'eſt aſſes pour vne foyes, alons nous a diner.*

Exit.

Enter the King of France, the Dolphin, the Conſtable of France, and others.

King. Tis certaine he hath paſt the Riuer Some.

Conſt. And if he be not fought withall, my Lord,
Let vs not liue in France: let vs quit all,
And giue our Vineyards to a barbarous People.

Dolph. *O Dieu viuant:* Shall a few Sprayes of vs,
The emptying of our Fathers Luxurie,
Our Syens, put in wilde and ſauage Stock,
Spirt vp ſo ſuddenly into the Clouds,
And ouer-looke their Grafters?

Brit. Normans, but baſtard Normans, Norman baſtards:
Mort du ma vie, if they march along
Vnfought withall, but I will ſell my Dukedome,

To

To buy a slobbry and a durtie Farme
In that nooke-shotten Ile of Albion.

Const. *Dieu de Battailes*, where haue they this mettell?
Is not their Clymate foggy, raw, and dull?
On whom, as in despight, the Sunne lookes pale,
Killing their Fruit with frownes. Can sodden Water,
A Drench for sur-reyn'd Iades, their Barly broth,
Decoct their cold blood to such valiant heat?
And shall our quick blood, spirited with Wine,
Seeme frostie? O, for honor of our Land,
Let vs not hang like roping Isyckles
Vpon our Houses Thatch, whiles a more frostie People
Sweat drops of gallant Youth in our rich fields:
Poore we call them, in their Natiue Lords.

Dolphin. By Faith and Honor,
Our Madames mock at vs, and plainely say,
Our Mettell is bred out, and they will giue
Their bodyes to the Lust of English Youth,
To new-store France with Bastard Warriors.

Brit. They bid vs to the English Dancing-Schooles,
And teach *Lauolta's* high, and swift *Carranto's*,
Saying, our Grace is onely in our Heeles,
And that we are most loftie Run-awayes.

King. Where is *Montioy* the Herald? speed him hence,
Let him greet England with our sharpe defiance.
Vp Princes, and with spirit of Honor edged,
More sharper then your Swords, high to the field:
Charles Delabreth, High Constable of France,
You Dukes of *Orleance*, *Burbon*, and of *Berry*,
Alanson, *Brabant*, *Bar*, and *Burgonie*,
Iaques Chattillion, *Rambures*, *Vandemont*,
Beumont, *Grand Pree*, *Roussi*, and *Faulconbridge*,
Loys, *Lestrale*, *Bouciquall*, and *Charaloyes*,
High Dukes, great Princes, Barons, Lords, and Kings;
For your great Seats, now quit you of great shames:
Barre *Harry* England, that sweepes through our Land
With Penons painted in the blood of Harflew:
Rush on his Hoast, as doth the melted Snow
Vpon the Valleyes, whose low Vassall Seat,
The Alpes doth spit, and void his rhewme vpon.
Goe downe vpon him, you haue Power enough,
And in a Captiue Chariot, into Roan
Bring him our Prisoner.

Const. This becomes the Great.
Sorry am I his numbers are so few,
His Souldiers sick, and famisht in their March:
For I am sure, when he shall see our Army,
Hee'le drop his heart into the sinck of feare,
And for atchieuement, offer vs his Ransome.

King. Therefore Lord Constable, hast on *Montioy*,
And let him say to England, that we send,
To know what willing Ransome he will giue.
Prince *Dolphin*, you shall stay with vs in Roan.

Dolph. Not so, I doe beseech your Maiestie.

King. Be patient, for you shall remaine with vs.
Now forth Lord Constable, and Princes all,
And quickly bring vs word of Englands fall. *Exeunt.*

Enter Captaines, English and Welch, Gower and Fluellen.

Gower. How now Captaine *Fluellen*, come you from the Bridge?

Flu. I assure you, there is very excellent Seruices committed at the Bridge.

Gower. Is the Duke of Exeter safe?

Flu. The Duke of Exeter is as magnanimous as *Agamemnon*, and a man that I loue and honour with my soule, and my heart, and my dutie, and my liue, and my liuing, and my vttermost power. He is not, God be praysed and blessed, any hurt in the World, but keepes the Bridge most valiantly, with excellent discipline. There is an aunchient Lieutenant there at the Pridge, I thinke in my very conscience hee is as valiant a man as *Marke Anthony*, and hee is a man of no estimation in the World, but I did see him doe as gallant seruice.

Gower. What doe you call him?

Flu. Hee is call'd aunchient *Pistoll*.

Gower. I know him not.

Enter Pistoll.

Flu. Here is the man.

Pist. Captaine, I thee beseech to doe me fauours: the Duke of Exeter doth loue thee well.

Flu. I, I prayse God, and I haue merited some loue at his hands.

Pist. *Bardolph*, a Souldier firme and sound of heart, and of buxome valour, hath by cruell Fate, and giddie Fortunes furious fickle Wheele, that Goddesse blind, that stands vpon the rolling restlesse Stone.

Flu. By your patience, aunchient *Pistoll*: Fortune is painted blinde, with a Muffler afore his eyes, to signifie to you, that Fortune is blinde; and shee is painted also with a Wheele, to signifie to you, which is the Morall of it, that shee is turning and inconstant, and mutabilitie, and variation: and her foot, looke you, is fixed vpon a Sphericall Stone, which rowles, and rowles, and rowles: in good truth, the Poet makes a most excellent description of it: Fortune is an excellent Morall.

Pist. Fortune is *Bardolphs* foe, and frownes on him: for he hath stolne a Pax, and hanged must a be: a damned death: let Gallowes gape for Dogge, let Man goe free, and let not Hempe his Wind-pipe suffocate: but *Exeter* hath giuen the doome of death, for Pax of little price. Therefore goe speake, the Duke will heare thy voyce; and let not *Bardolphs* vitall thred bee cut with edge of Penny-Cord, and vile reproach. Speake Captaine for his Life, and I will thee requite.

Flu. Aunchient *Pistoll*, I doe partly vnderstand your meaning.

Pist. Why then reioyce therefore.

Flu. Certainly Aunchient, it is not a thing to reioyce at: for if, looke you, he were my Brother, I would desire the Duke to vse his good pleasure, and put him to execution; for discipline ought to be vsed.

Pist. Dye, and be dam'd, and *Figo* for thy friendship.

Flu. It is well.

Pist. The Figge of Spaine. *Exit.*

Flu. Very good.

Gower. Why, this is an arrant counterfeit Rascall, I remember him now: a Bawd, a Cut-purse.

Flu. Ile assure you, a vtt'red as praue words at the Pridge, as you shall see in a Summers day: but it is very well: what he ha's spoke to me, that is well I warrant you, when time is serue.

Gower. Why 'tis a Gull, a Foole, a Rogue, that now and then goes to the Warres, to grace himselfe at his returne into London, vnder the forme of a Souldier: and such fellowes are perfit in the Great Commanders Names, and they will learne you by rote where Seruices were done; at such and such a Sconce, at such a Breach, at such a Conuoy: who came off brauely, who was shot, who disgrac'd, what termes the Enemy stood on: and this they conne perfitly in the phrase of Warre; which they tricke vp with new-tuned Oathes: and what a Beard of the Generalls Cut, and a horride Sute of the Campe, will doe among foming Bottles, and Ale-washt Wits, is wonderfull to be thought on: but you must learne to know such slanders of the age, or else you may be maruellously mistooke.

Flu. I tell you what, Captaine *Gower*: I doe perceiue hee is not the man that hee would gladly make shew to the World hee is: if I finde a hole in his Coat, I will tell him my minde: hearke you, the King is comming, and I must speake with him from the Pridge.

Drum and Colours. Enter the King and his poore Souldiers.

Flu. God plesse your Maiestie.

King. How now *Fluellen*, cam'st thou from the Bridge?

Flu. I, so please your Maiestie: The Duke of Exeter ha's very gallantly maintain'd the Pridge; the French is gone off, looke you, and there is gallant and most praue passages: marry, th'athuersarie was haue possession of the Pridge, but he is enforced to retyre, and the Duke of Exeter is Master of the Pridge: I can tell your Maiestie, the Duke is a praue man.

King. What men haue you lost, *Fluellen*?

Flu. The perdition of th'athuersarie hath beene very great, reasonnable great: marry for my part, I thinke the Duke hath lost neuer a man, but one that is like to be executed for robbing a Church, one *Bardolph*, if your Maiestie know the man: his face is all bubukles and whelkes, and knobs, and flames a fire, and his lippes blowes at his nose, and it is like a coale of fire, sometimes plew, and sometimes red, but his nose is executed, and his fire's out.

King. Wee would haue all such offendors so cut off: and we giue expresse charge, that in our Marches through the Countrey, there be nothing compell'd from the Villages; nothing taken, but pay'd for: none of the French vpbrayded or abused in disdainefull Language; for when Leuitie and Crueltie play for a Kingdome, the gentler Gamester is the soonest winner.

Tucket. Enter Mountioy.

Mountioy. You know me by my habit.

King. Well then, I know thee: what shall I know of thee?

Mountioy. My Masters mind.

King. Vnfold it.

Mountioy. Thus sayes my King: Say thou to *Harry* of England, Though we seem'd dead, we did but sleepe: Aduantage is a better Souldier then rashnesse. Tell him, wee could haue rebuk'd him at Harflewe, but that wee thought not good to bruise an iniurie, till it were full ripe. Now wee speake vpon our Q. and our voyce is imperiall: England shall repent his folly, see his weakenesse, and admire our sufferance. Bid him therefore consider of his ransome, which must proportion the losses we haue borne, the subiects we haue lost, the disgrace we haue digested; which in weight to re-answer, his pettinesse would bow vnder. For our losses, his Exchequer is too poore; for th'effusion of our bloud, the Muster of his Kingdome too faint a number; and for our disgrace, his owne person kneeling at our feet, but a weake and worthlesse satisfaction. To this adde defiance: and tell him for conclusion, he hath betrayed his followers, whose condemnation is pronounc't: So farre my King and Master; so much my Office.

King. What is thy name? I know thy qualitie.

Mount. *Mountioy.*

King. Thou doo'st thy Office fairely. Turne thee back,
And tell thy King, I doe not seeke him now,
But could be willing to march on to Callice,
Without impeachment: for to say the sooth,
Though 'tis no wisdome to confesse so much
Vnto an enemie of Craft and Vantage,
My people are with sicknesse much enfeebled,
My numbers lessen'd: and those few I haue,
Almost no better then so many French;
Who when they were in health, I tell thee Herald,
I thought, vpon one payre of English Legges
Did march three Frenchmen. Yet forgiue me God,
That I doe bragge thus; this your ayre of France
Hath blowne that vice in me. I must repent:
Goe therefore tell thy Master, heere I am;
My Ransome, is this frayle and worthlesse Trunke;
My Army, but a weake and sickly Guard:
Yet God before, tell him we will come on,
Though France himselfe, and such another Neighbor
Stand in our way. There's for thy labour *Mountioy*.
Goe bid thy Master well aduise himselfe.
If we may passe, we will: if we be hindred,
We shall your tawnie ground with your red blood
Discolour: and so *Mountioy*, fare you well.
The summe of all our Answer is but this:
We would not seeke a Battaile as we are,
Nor as we are, we say we will not shun it:
So tell your Master.

Mount. I shall deliuer so: Thankes to your Highnesse.

Glouc. I hope they will not come vpon vs now.

King. We are in Gods hand, Brother, not in theirs:
March to the Bridge, it now drawes toward night,
Beyond the Riuer wee'le encampe our selues,
And on to morrow bid them march away. *Exeunt.*

Enter the Constable of France, the Lord Rambures, Orleance, Dolphin, with others.

Const. Tut, I haue the best Armour of the World: would it were day.

Orleance. You haue an excellent Armour: but let my Horse haue his due.

Const. It is the best Horse of Europe.

Orleance. Will it neuer be Morning?

Dolph. My Lord of Orleance, and my Lord High Constable, you talke of Horse and Armour?

Orleance. You are as well prouided of both, as any Prince in the World.

Dolph. What a long Night is this? I will not change my Horse with any that treades but on foure postures: ch' ha: he bounds from the Earth, as if his entrayles were hayres: *le Cheual volante*, the Pegasus, *ches les narines de feu*. When I bestryde him, I soare, I am a Hawke: he trots the ayre: the Earth sings, when he touches it: the basest horne of his hoofe, is more Musicall then the Pipe of *Hermes*.

Orleance. Hee's of the colour of the Nutmeg.

Dolph. And of the heat of the Ginger. It is a Beast for *Perseus*: hee is pure Ayre and Fire; and the dull Elements of Earth and Water neuer appeare in him, but only in patient stillnesse while his Rider mounts him: hee is indeede a Horse, and all other Iades you may call Beasts.

Const. Indeed my Lord, it is a most absolute and excellent Horse.

Dolph. It is the Prince of Palfrayes, his Neigh is like the bidding of a Monarch, and his countenance enforces Homage.

Orleance. No more Cousin.

Dolph. Nay, the man hath no wit, that cannot from the rising of the Larke to the lodging of the Lambe, varie deserued prayse on my Palfray: it is a Theame as fluent as the Sea: Turne the Sands into eloquent tongues, and my Horse is argument for them all: 'tis a subiect for a Soueraigne to reason on, and for a Soueraignes Soueraigne to ride on: And for the World, familiar to vs, and vnknowne, to lay apart their particular Functions, and wonder at him, I once writ a Sonnet in his prayse, and began thus, *Wonder of Nature*.

Orleance. I haue heard a Sonnet begin so to ones Mistresse.

Dolph. Then did they imitate that which I compos'd to my Courser, for my Horse is my Mistresse.

Orleance. Your Mistresse beares well.

Dolph. Me well, which is the prescript prayse and perfection of a good and particular Mistresse.

Const. Nay, for me thought yesterday your Mistresse shrewdly shooke your back.

Dolph. So perhaps did yours.

Const. Mine was not bridled.

Dolph. O then belike she was old and gentle, and you rode like a Kerne of Ireland, your French Hose off, and in your strait Strossers.

Const. You haue good iudgement in Horsemanship.

Dolph. Be warn'd by me then: they that ride so, and ride not warily, fall into foule Boggs: I had rather haue my Horse to my Mistresse.

Const. I had as liue haue my Mistresse a Iade.

Dolph. I tell thee Constable, my Mistresse weares his owne hayre.

Const. I could make as true a boast as that, if I had a Sow to my Mistresse.

Dolph. *Le chien est retourne a son propre vemissement est la leuye lauee au bourbier*: thou mak'st vse of any thing.

Const. Yet doe I not vse my Horse for my Mistresse, or any such Prouerbe, so little kin to the purpose.

Ramb. My Lord Constable, the Armour that I saw in your Tent to night, are those Starres or Sunnes vpon it?

Const. Starres my Lord.

Dolph. Some of them will fall to morrow, I hope.

Const. And yet my Sky shall not want.

Dolph. That may be, for you beare a many superfluously, and 'twere more honor some were away.

Const. Eu'n as your Horse beares your prayses, who would trot as well, were some of your bragges dismounted.

Dolph. Would I were able to loade him with his desert. Will it neuer be day? I will trot to morrow a mile, and my way shall be paued with English Faces.

Const. I will not say so, for feare I should be fac't out of my way: but I would it were morning, for I would faine be about the eares of the English.

Ramb. Who will goe to Hazard with me for twentie Prisoners?

Const. You must first goe your selfe to hazard, ere you haue them.

Dolph Tis Mid-night, Ile goe arme my selfe. *Exit*.

Orleance. The Dolphin longs for morning.

Ramb. He longs to eate the English.

Const. I thinke he will eate all he kills.

Orleance. By the white Hand of my Lady, hee's a gallant Prince.

Const. Sweare by her Foot, that she may tread out the Oath.

Orleance. He is simply the most actiue Gentleman of France.

Const. Doing is actiuitie, and he will still be doing.

Orleance. He neuer did harme, that I heard of.

Const. Nor will doe none to morrow: hee will keepe that good name still.

Orleance. I know him to be valiant.

Const. I was told that, by one that knowes him better then you.

Orleance. What's hee?

Const. Marry hee told me so himselfe, and hee sayd hee car'd not who knew it.

Orleance. Hee needes not, it is no hidden vertue in him.

Const. By my faith Sir, but it is: neuer any body saw it, but his Lacquey: 'tis a hooded valour, and when it appeares, it will bate.

Orleance. Ill will neuer sayd well.

Const. I will cap that Prouerbe with, There is flatterie in friendship.

Orleance. And I will take vp that with, Giue the Deuill his due.

Const. Well plac't: there stands your friend for the Deuill: haue at the very eye of that Prouerbe with, A Pox of the Deuill.

Orleance. You are the better at Prouerbs, by how much a Fooles Bolt is soone shot.

Const. You haue shot ouer.

Orleance. 'Tis not the first time you were ouer-shot.

Enter a Messenger.

Mess. My Lord high Constable, the English lye within fifteene hundred paces of your Tents.

Const. Who hath measur'd the ground?

Mess. The Lord *Grandpree*.

Const. A valiant and most expert Gentleman. Would it were day? Alas poore *Harry* of England: hee longs not for the Dawning, as wee doe.

Orleance. What a wretched and peeuish fellow is this King of England, to mope with his fat-brain'd followers so farre out of his knowledge.

Const. If the English had any apprehension, they would runne away.

Orleance. That they lack: for if their heads had any intellectuall Armour, they could neuer weare such heauie Head-pieces.

Ramb. That Iland of England breedes very valiant Creatures; their Mastiffes are of vnmatchable courage.

Orleance. Foolish Curres, that runne winking into the mouth of a Russian Beare, and haue their heads crusht like rotten Apples: you may as well say, that's a valiant Flea, that dare eate his breakefast on the Lippe of a Lyon.

Const. Iust, iust: and the men doe sympathize with the Mastiffes, in robustious and rough comming on, leauing their Wits with their Wiues: and then giue them great Meales of Beefe, and Iron and Steele; they will eate like Wolues, and fight like Deuils.

Orleance. I,

Orleance. I, but these English are shrowdly out of Beefe.

Const. Then shall we finde to morrow,they haue only stomackes to eate, and none to fight. Now is it time to arme: come,shall we about it?

Orleance. It is now two a Clock: but let me see,by ten Wee shall haue each a hundred English men. *Exeunt.*

Actus Tertius.

Chorus.

Now entertaine coniecture of a time,
When creeping Murmure and the poring Darke
Fills the wide Vessell of the Vniuerse.
From Camp to Camp,through the foule Womb of Night
The Humme of eyther Army stilly sounds;
That the fixt Centinels almost receiue
The secret Whispers of each others Watch.
Fire answers fire,and through their paly flames
Each Battaile sees the others vmber'd face.
Steed threatens Steed, in high and boastfull Neighs
Piercing the Nights dull Eare: and from the Tents,
The Armourers accomplishing the Knights,
With busie Hammers closing Riuets vp,
Giue dreadfull note of preparation.
The Countrey Cocks doe crow,the Clocks doe towle:
And the third howre of drowsie Morning nam'd,
Prowd of their Numbers,and secure in Soule,
The confident and ouer-lustie French,
Doe the low-rated English play at Dice;
And chide the creeple-tardy-gated Night,
Who like a foule and ougly Witch doth limpe
So tediously away. The poore condemned English,
Like Sacrifices,by their watchfull Fires
Sit patiently, and inly ruminate
The Mornings danger: and their gesture sad,
Inuesting lanke-leane Cheekes,and Warre-worne Coats,
Presented them vnto the gazing Moone
So many horride Ghosts. O now,who will behold
The Royall Captaine of this ruin'd Band
Walking from Watch to Watch,from Tent to Tent;
Let him cry,Prayse and Glory on his head:
For forth he goes,and visits all his Hoast,
Bids them good morrow with a modest Smyle,
And calls them Brothers,Friends,and Countreymen.
Vpon his Royall Face there is no note,
How dread an Army hath enrounded him;
Nor doth he dedicate one iot of Colour
Vnto the wearie and all-watched Night:
But freshly lookes,and ouer-beares Attaint,
With chearefull semblance,and sweet Maiestie:
That euery Wretch,pining and pale before,
Beholding him,plucks comfort from his Lookes.
A Largesse vniuersall,like the Sunne,
His liberall Eye doth giue to euery one,
Thawing cold feare,that meane and gentle all
Behold,as may vnworthinesse define.
A little touch of *Harry* in the Night,
And so our Scene must to the Battaile flye:
Where,O for pitty,we shall much disgrace,
With foure or fiue most vile and ragged foyles,
(Right ill dispos'd, in brawle ridiculous)
The Name of Agincourt: Yet sit and see,
Minding true things, by what their Mock'ries bee.
Exit.

Enter the King, Bedford, and Glocester.

King. *Gloster*,'tis true that we are in great danger,
The greater therefore should our Courage be.
God morrow Brother *Bedford*: God Almightie,
There is some soule of goodnesse in things euill,
Would men obseruingly distill it out.
For our bad Neighbour makes vs early stirrers,
Which is both healthfull, and good husbandry.
Besides,they are our outward Consciences,
And Preachers to vs all; admonishing,
That we should dresse vs fairely for our end.
Thus may we gather Honey from the Weed,
And make a Morall of the Diuell himselfe.

Enter Erpingham.

Good morrow old Sir *Thomas Erpingham*:
A good soft Pillow for that good white Head,
Were better then a churlish turfe of France.

Erping. Not so my Liege,this Lodging likes me better,
Since I may say, now lye I like a King.

King. 'Tis good for men to loue their present paines,
Vpon example,so the Spirit is eased:
And when the Mind is quickned,out of doubt
The Organs,though defunct and dead before,
Breake vp their drowsie Graue,and newly moue
With casted slough,and fresh legeritie.
Lend me thy Cloake Sir *Thomas*: Brothers both,
Commend me to the Princes in our Campe;
Doe my good morrow to them,and anon
Desire them all to my Pauillion.

Gloster. We shall,my Liege.

Erping. Shall I attend your Grace?

King. No,my good Knight:
Goe with my Brothers to my Lords of England:
I and my Bosome must debate a while,
And then I would no other company.

Erping. The Lord in Heauen blesse thee, Noble *Harry*. *Exeunt.*

King. God a mercy old Heart, thou speak'st cheare-fully. *Enter Pistoll.*

Pist. Che vous la?

King. A friend.

Pist. Discusse vnto me, art thou Officer, or art thou base,common,and popular?

King. I am a Gentleman of a Company.

Pist. Trayl'st thou the puissant Pyke?

King. Euen so: what are you?

Pist. As good a Gentleman as the Emperor.

King. Then you are a better then the King.

Pist. The King's a Bawcock, and a Heart of Gold, a Lad of Life, an Impe of Fame, of Parents good, of Fist most valiant: I kisse his durtie shooe, and from heart-string I loue the louely Bully. What is thy Name?

King. *Harry le Roy.*

Pist. *Le Roy?* a Cornish Name: art thou of Cornish Crew?

King. No, I am a Welchman.

Pist. Know'st thou *Fluellen*?

King. Yes.

Pist. Tell him Ile knock his Leeke about his Pate vpon S. *Dauies* day.

King. Doe not you weare your Dagger in your Cappe that day,least he knock that about yours.

Pist. Art thou his friend?

King. And his Kinsman too.

Pist. The *Figo* for thee then.

King. I thanke you: God be with you.

Pist. My name is *Pistol* call'd. *Exit.*

King. It sorts well with your fiercenesse.

Manet King.

Enter Fluellen and Gower.

Gower. Captaine *Fluellen.*

Flu. 'So, in the Name of Iesu Christ, speake fewer: it is the greatest admiration in the vniuersall World, when the true and aunchient Prerogatifes and Lawes of the Warres is not kept: if you would take the paines but to examine the Warres of *Pompey* the Great, you shall finde, I warrant you, that there is no tiddle tadle nor pibble babble in *Pompeyes* Campe: I warrant you, you shall finde the Ceremonies of the Warres, and the Cares of it, and the Formes of it, and the Sobrietie of it, and the Modestie of it, to be otherwise.

Gower. Why the Enemie is lowd, you heare him all Night.

Flu. If the Enemie is an Asse and a Foole, and a prating Coxcombe; is it meet, thinke you, that wee should also, looke you, be an Asse and a Foole, and a prating Coxcombe, in your owne conscience now?

Gow. I will speake lower.

Flu. I pray you, and beseech you, that you will. *Exit.*

King. Though it appeare a little out of fashion,
There is much care and valour in this Welchman.

Enter three Souldiers, Iohn Bates, Alexander Court, and Michael Williams.

Court. Brother *Iohn Bates*, is not that the Morning which breakes yonder?

Bates. I thinke it be: but wee haue no great cause to desire the approach of day.

Williams. Wee see yonder the beginning of the day, but I thinke wee shall neuer see the end of it. Who goes there?

King. A Friend.

Williams. Vnder what Captaine serue you?

King. Vnder Sir *Iohn Erpingham.*

Williams. A good old Commander, and a most kinde Gentleman: I pray you, what thinkes he of our estate?

King. Euen as men wrackt vpon a Sand, that looke to be washt off the next Tyde.

Bates. He hath not told his thought to the King?

King. No: nor it is not meet he should: for though I speake it to you, I thinke the King is but a man, as I am: the Violet smells to him, as it doth to me; the Element shewes to him, as it doth to me; all his Sences haue but humane Conditions: his Ceremonies layd by, in his Nakednesse he appeares but a man; and though his affections are higher mounted then ours, yet when they stoupe, they stoupe with the like wing: therefore, when he sees reason of feares, as we doe; his feares, out of doubt, be of the same rellish as ours are: yet in reason, no man should possesse him with any appearance of feare; least hee, by shewing it, should dis-hearten his Army.

Bates. He may shew what outward courage he will: but I beleeue, as cold a Night as 'tis, hee could wish himselfe in Thames vp to the Neck; and so I would he were, and I by him, at all aduentures, so we were quit here.

King. By my troth, I will speake my conscience of the King: I thinke hee would not wish himselfe any where, but where hee is.

Bates. Then I would he were here alone; so should he be sure to be ransomed, and a many poore mens liues saued.

King. I dare say, you loue him not so ill, to wish him here alone: howsoeuer you speake this to feele other mens minds, me thinks I could not dye any where so contented, as in the Kings company; his Cause being iust, and his Quarrell honorable.

Williams. That's more then we know.

Bates. I, or more then wee should seeke after; for wee know enough, if wee know wee are the Kings Subiects: if his Cause be wrong, our obedience to the King wipes the Cryme of it out of vs.

Williams. But if the Cause be not good, the King himselfe hath a heauie Reckoning to make, when all those Legges, and Armes and Heads, chopt off in a Battaile, shall ioyne together at the latter day, and cry all, Wee dyed at such a place, some swearing, some crying for a Surgean; some vpon their Wiues, left poore behind them; some vpon the Debts they owe, some vpon their Children rawly left: I am afear'd, there are few dye well, that dye in a Battaile: for how can they charitably dispose of any thing, when Blood is their argument? Now, if these men doe not dye well, it will be a black matter for the King, that led them to it; who to disobey, were against all proportion of subiection.

King. So, if a Sonne that is by his Father sent about Merchandize, doe sinfully miscarry vpon the Sea; the imputation of his wickednesse, by your rule, should be imposed vpon his Father that sent him: or if a Seruant, vnder his Masters command, transporting a summe of Money, be assayled by Robbers, and dye in many irreconcil'd Iniquities; you may call the businesse of the Master the author of the Seruants damnation: but this is not so: The King is not bound to answer the particular endings of his Souldiers, the Father of his Sonne, nor the Master of his Seruant; for they purpose not their death, when they purpose their seruices. Besides, there is no King, be his Cause neuer so spotlesse, if it come to the arbitrement of Swords, can trye it out with all vnspotted Souldiers: some (peraduenture) haue on them the guilt of premeditated and contriued Murther; some, of beguiling Virgins with the broken Seales of Periurie; some, making the Warres their Bulwarke, that haue before gored the gentle Bosome of Peace with Pillage and Robberie. Now, if these men haue defeated the Law, and outrunne Natiue punishment; though they can out-strip men, they haue no wings to flye from God. Warre is his Beadle, Warre is his Vengeance: so that here men are punisht, for before breach of the Kings Lawes, in now the Kings Quarrell: where they feared the death, they haue borne life away; and where they would bee safe, they perish. Then if they dye vnprouided, no more is the King guiltie of their damnation, then hee was before guiltie of those Impieties, for the which they are now visited. Euery Subiects Dutie is the Kings, but euery Subiects Soule is his owne. Therefore should euery Souldier in the Warres doe as euery sicke man in his Bed, wash euery Moth out of his Conscience: and dying so, Death is to him aduantage; or not dying, the time was blessedly lost, wherein such preparation was gayned: and in him that escapes, it were not sinne to thinke, that making God so free an offer, he let him outliue that day, to see his Greatnesse, and to teach others how they should prepare.

Will. 'Tis

Will. 'Tis certaine, euery man that dyes ill, the ill vpon his owne head, the King is not to answer it.

Bates. I doe not desire hee should answer for me, and yet I determine to fight lustily for him.

King. I my selfe heard the King say he would not be ransom'd.

Will. I, hee said so, to make vs fight chearefully: but when our throats are cut, hee may be ransom'd, and wee ne're the wiser.

King. If I liue to see it, I will neuer trust his word after.

Will. You pay him then: that's a perillous shot out of an Elder Gunne, that a poore and a priuate displeasure can doe against a Monarch: you may as well goe about to turne the Sunne to yce, with fanning in his face with a Peacocks feather: You'le neuer trust his word after; come, 'tis a foolish saying.

King. Your reproofe is something too round, I should be angry with you, if the time were conuenient.

Will. Let it bee a Quarrell betweene vs, if you liue.

King. I embrace it.

Will. How shall I know thee againe?

King. Giue me any Gage of thine, and I will weare it in my Bonnet: Then if euer thou dar'st acknowledge it, I will make it my Quarrell.

Will. Heere's my Gloue: Giue mee another of thine.

King. There.

Will. This will I also weare in my Cap: if euer thou come to me, and say, after to morrow, This is my Gloue, by this Hand I will take thee a box on the eare.

King. If euer I liue to see it, I will challenge it.

Will. Thou dar'st as well be hang'd.

King. Well, I will doe it, though I take thee in the Kings companie.

Will. Keepe thy word: fare thee well.

Bates. Be friends you English fooles, be friends, wee haue French Quarrels enow, if you could tell how to reckon. *Exit Souldiers.*

King. Indeede the French may lay twentie French Crownes to one, they will beat vs, for they beare them on their shoulders: but it is no English Treason to cut French Crownes, and to morrow the King himselfe will be a Clipper.

Vpon the King, let vs our Liues, our Soules,
Our Debts, our carefull Wiues,
Our Children, and our Sinnes, lay on the King:
We must beare all.
O hard Condition, Twin-borne with Greatnesse,
Subiect to the breath of euery foole, whose sence
No more can feele, but his owne wringing.
What infinite hearts-ease must Kings neglect,
That priuate men enioy?
And what haue Kings, that Priuates haue not too,
Saue Ceremonie, saue generall Ceremonie?
And what art thou, thou Idoll Ceremonie?
What kind of God art thou? that suffer'st more
Of mortall griefes, then doe thy worshippers.
What are thy Rents? what are thy Commings in?
O Ceremonie, shew me but thy worth.
What? is thy Soule of Odoration?
Art thou ought else but Place, Degree, and Forme,
Creating awe and feare in other men?
Wherein thou art lesse happy, being fear'd,
Then they in fearing.
What drink'st thou oft, in stead of Homage sweet,
But poyson'd flatterie? O, be sick, great Greatnesse,
And bid thy Ceremonie giue thee cure.
Thinks thou the fierie Feuer will goe out
With Titles blowne from Adulation?
Will it giue place to flexure and low bending?
Canst thou, when thou command'st the beggers knee,
Command the health of it? No, thou prowd Dreame,
That play'st so subtilly with a Kings Repose.
I am a King that find thee: and I know,
'Tis not the Balme, the Scepter, and the Ball,
The Sword, the Mase, the Crowne Imperiall,
The enter-tissued Robe of Gold and Pearle,
The farsed Title running 'fore the King,
The Throne he sits on: nor the Tyde of Pompe,
That beates vpon the high shore of this World:
No, not all these, thrice-gorgeous Ceremonie;
Not all these, lay'd in Bed Maiesticall,
Can sleepe so soundly, as the wretched Slaue:
Who with a body fill'd, and vacant mind,
Gets him to rest, cram'd with distressefull bread,
Neuer sees horride Night, the Child of Hell:
But like a Lacquey, from the Rise to Set,
Sweates in the eye of *Phebus*; and all Night
Sleepes in *Elizium*: next day after dawne,
Doth rise and helpe *Hiperio* to his Horse,
And followes so the euer-running yeere
With profitable labour to his Graue:
And but for Ceremonie, such a Wretch,
Winding vp Dayes with toyle, and Nights with sleepe
Had the fore-hand and vantage of a King.
The Slaue, a Member of the Countreyes peace,
Enioyes it; but in grosse braine little wots,
What watch the King keepes, to maintaine the peace;
Whose howres, the Pesant best aduantages.

Enter Erpingham.

Erp. My Lord, your Nobles iealous of your absence,
Seeke through your Campe to find you.

King. Good old Knight, collect them all together
At my Tent: Ile be before thee.

Erp. I shall doo't, my Lord. *Exit.*

King. O God of Battailes, steele my Souldiers hearts,
Possesse them not with feare: Take from them now
The sence of reckning of th'opposed numbers:
Pluck their hearts from them. Not to day, O Lord,
O not to day, thinke not vpon the fault
My Father made, in compassing the Crowne.
I *Richards* body haue interred new,
And on it haue bestowed more contrite teares,
Then from it issued forced drops of blood.
Fiue hundred poore I haue in yeerely pay,
Who twice a day their wither'd hands hold vp
Toward Heauen, to pardon blood:
And I haue built two Chauntries,
Where the sad and solemne Priests sing still
For *Richards* Soule. More will I doe:
Though all that I can doe, is nothing worth;
Since that my Penitence comes after all,
Imploring pardon.

Enter Gloucester.

Glouc. My Liege.

King. My Brother *Gloucesters* voyce? I:
I know thy errand, I will goe with thee:
The day, my friend, and all things stay for me.

Exeunt.

Enter the Dolphin, Orleance, Ramburs, and Beaumont.

Orleance. The Sunne doth gild our Armour vp, my Lords.

Dolph. Monte Cheual: My Horse, *Verlot Lacquay:* Ha.

Orleance. Oh braue Spirit.

Dolph. Via les ewes & terre.

Orleance. Rien puis le air & feu.

Dolph. Cein, Cousin Orleance. *Enter Constable.*
Now my Lord Constable?

Const. Hearke how our Steedes, for present Seruice neigh.

Dolph. Mount them, and make incision in their Hides,
That their hot blood may spin in English eyes,
And doubt them with superfluous courage: ha.

Ram. What, wil you haue them weep our Horses blood?
How shall we then behold their naturall teares?

Enter Messenger.

Messeng. The English are embattail'd, you French Peeres.

Const. To Horse you gallant Princes, straight to Horse.
Doe but behold yond poore and starued Band,
And your faire shew shall suck away their Soules,
Leauing them but the shales and huskes of men.
There is not worke enough for all our hands,
Scarce blood enough in all their sickly Veines,
To giue each naked Curtleax a stayne,
That our French Gallants shall to day draw out,
And sheath for lack of sport. Let vs but blow on them,
The vapour of our Valour will o're-turne them.
'Tis positiue against all exceptions, Lords,
That our superfluous Lacquies, and our Pesants,
Who in vnnecessarie action swarme
About our Squares of Battaile, were enow
To purge this field of such a hilding Foe;
Though we vpon this Mountaines Basis by,
Tooke stand for idle speculation:
But that our Honours must not. What's to say?
A very little little let vs doe,
And all is done: then let the Trumpets sound
The Tucket Sonuance, and the Note to mount:
For our approach shall so much dare the field,
That England shall couch downe in feare, and yeeld.

Enter Graundpree.

Grandpree. Why do you stay so long, my Lords of France?
Yond Iland Carrions, desperate of their bones,
Ill-fauoredly become the Morning field:
Their ragged Curtaines poorely are let loose,
And our Ayre shakes them passing scornefully.
Bigge *Mars* seemes banqu'rout in their begger'd Hoast,
And faintly through a rustie Beuer peepes.
The Horsemen sit like fixed Candlesticks,
With Torch-staues in their hand: and their poore Iades
Lob downe their heads, dropping the hides and hips:
The gumme downe roping from their pale-dead eyes,
And in their pale dull mouthes the Iymold Bitt
Lyes foule with chaw'd-grasse, still and motionlesse.
And their executors, the knauish Crowes,
Flye o're them all, impatient for their howre.
Description cannot sute it selfe in words,
To demonstrate the Life of such a Battaile,
In life so liuelesse, as it shewes it selfe.

Const. They haue said their prayers,
And they stay for death.

Dolph. Shall we goe send them Dinners, and fresh Sutes,
And giue their fasting Horses Prouender,
And after fight with them?

Const. I stay but for my Guard: on
To the field, I will the Banner from a Trumpet take,
And vse it for my haste. Come, come away,
The Sunne is high, and we out-weare the day. *Exeunt.*

Enter Gloucester, Bedford, Exeter, Erpingham with all his Hoast: Salisbury, and Westmerland.

Glouc. Where is the King?

Bedf. The King himselfe is rode to view their Battaile.

West. Of fighting men they haue full threescore thousand.

Exe. There's fiue to one, besides they all are fresh.

Salisb. Gods Arme strike with vs, 'tis a fearefull oddes.
God buy' you Princes all; Ile to my Charge:
If we no more meet, till we meet in Heauen;
Then ioyfully, my Noble Lord of Bedford,
My deare Lord Gloucester, and my good Lord Exeter,
And my kind Kinsman, Warriors all, adieu.

Bedf. Farwell good *Salisbury,* & good luck go with thee:
And yet I doe thee wrong, to mind thee of it,
For thou art fram'd of the firme truth of valour.

Exe. Farwell kind Lord: fight valiantly to day.

Bedf. He is as full of Valour as of Kindnesse,
Princely in both.

Enter the King.

West. O that we now had here
But one ten thousand of those men in England,
That doe no worke to day.

King. What's he that wishes so?
My Cousin *Westmerland.* No, my faire Cousin:
If we are markt to dye, we are enow
To doe our Countrey losse: and if to liue,
The fewer men, the greater share of honour.
Gods will, I pray thee wish not one man more.
By *Ioue,* I am not couetous for Gold,
Nor care I who doth feed vpon my cost:
It yernes me not, if men my Garments weare;
Such outward things dwell not in my desires.
But if it be a sinne to couet Honor,
I am the most offending Soule aliue.
No 'faith, my Couze, wish not a man from England:
Gods peace, I would not loose so great an Honor,
As one man more me thinkes would share from me,
For the best hope I haue. O, doe not wish one more:
Rather proclaime it (*Westmerland*) through my Hoast,
That he which hath no stomack to this fight,
Let him depart, his Pasport shall be made,
And Crownes for Conuoy put into his Purse:
We would not dye in that mans companie,
That feares his fellowship, to dye with vs.
This day is call'd the Feast of *Crispian:*
He that out-liues this day, and comes safe home,
Will stand a tip-toe when this day is named,
And rowse him at the Name of *Crispian.*
He that shall see this day, and liue old age,
Will yeerely on the Vigil feast his neighbours,
And say, to morrow is Saint *Crispian.*
Then will he strip his sleeue, and shew his skarres:
Old men forget; yet all shall be forgot:
But hee'le remember, with aduantages,
What feats he did that day. Then shall our Names,
Familiar in his mouth as houshold words,

Harry

Harry the King, *Bedford* and *Exeter*,
Warwick and *Talbot*, *Salisbury* and *Gloucester*,
Be in their flowing Cups freshly remembred.
This story shall the good man teach his sonne:
And *Crispine Crispian* shall ne're goe by,
From this day to the ending of the World,
But we in it shall be remembred;
We few, we happy few, we band of brothers:
For he to day that sheds his blood with me,
Shall be my brother: be he ne're so vile,
This day shall gentle his Condition.
And Gentlemen in England, now a bed,
Shall thinke themselues accurst they were not here;
And hold their Manhoods cheape, whiles any speakes,
That fought with vs vpon Saint *Crispines* day.

Enter Salisbury.

Sal. My Soueraign Lord, bestow your selfe with speed:
The French are brauely in their battailes set,
And will with all expedience charge on vs.

King. All things are ready, if our minds be so.

West. Perish the man, whose mind is backward now.

King. Thou do'st not wish more helpe from England, Couze?

West. Gods will, my Liege, would you and I alone,
Without more helpe, could fight this Royall battaile.

King. Why now thou hast vnwisht fiue thousand men:
Which likes me better, then to wish vs one.
You know your places: God be with you all.

Tucket. Enter Montioy.

Mont. Once more I come to know of thee King *Harry*,
If for thy Ransome thou wilt now compound,
Before thy most assured Ouerthrow:
For certainly, thou art so neere the Gulfe,
Thou needs must be englutted. Besides, in mercy
The Constable desires thee, thou wilt mind
Thy followers of Repentance; that their Soules
May make a peacefull and a sweet retyre
From off these fields: where (wretches) their poore bodies
Must lye and fester.

King. Who hath sent thee now?

Mont. The Constable of France.

King. I pray thee beare my former Answer back:
Bid them atchieue me, and then sell my bones.
Good God, why should they mock poore fellowes thus?
The man that once did sell the Lyons skin
While the beast liu'd, was kill'd with hunting him.
A many of our bodyes shall no doubt
Find Natiue Graues: vpon the which, I trust
Shall witnesse liue in Brasse of this dayes worke.
And those that leaue their valiant bones in France,
Dying like men, though buryed in your Dunghills,
They shall be fam'd: for there the Sun shall greet them,
And draw their honors reeking vp to Heauen,
Leauing their earthly parts to choake your Clyme,
The smell whereof shall breed a Plague in France.
Marke then abounding valour in our English:
That being dead, like to the bullets crasing,
Breake out into a second course of mischiefe,
Killing in relapse of Mortalitie.
Let me speake prowdly: Tell the Constable,
We are but Warriors for the working day:
Our Gaynesse and our Gilt are all besmyrcht
With raynie Marching in the painefull field.
There's not a piece of feather in our Hoast:
Good argument (I hope) we will not flye:
And time hath worne vs into slouenrie.
But by the Masse, our hearts are in the trim:
And my poore Souldiers tell me, yet ere Night,
They'le be in fresher Robes, or they will pluck
The gay new Coats o're the French Souldiers heads,
And turne them out of seruice. If they doe this,
As if God please, they shall; my Ransome then
Will soone be leuyed.
Herauld, saue thou thy labour:
Come thou no more for Ransome, gentle Herauld,
They shall haue none, I sweare, but these my ioynts:
Which if they haue, as I will leaue vm them,
Shall yeeld them little, tell the Constable.

Mont. I shall, King *Harry*. And so fare thee well:
Thou neuer shalt heare Herauld any more. *Exit.*

King. I feare thou wilt once more come againe for a Ransome.

Enter Yorke.

Yorke. My Lord, most humbly on my knee I begge
The leading of the Vaward.

King. Take it, braue *Yorke*.
Now Souldiers march away,
And how thou pleasest God, dispose the day. *Exeunt.*

Alarum. Excursions.
Enter Pistoll, French Souldier, Boy.

Pist. Yeeld Curre.

French. *Ie pense que vous estes le Gentilhome de bon qualitee.*

Pist. Qualtitie calmie custure me. Art thou a Gentleman? What is thy Name? discusse.

French. *O Seigneur Dieu.*

Pist. O Signieur Dewe should be a Gentleman: perpend my words O Signieur Dewe and marke: O Signieur Dewe, thou dyest on point of Fox, except O Signieur thou doe giue to me egregious Ransome.

French. *O prennes misericordie aye pitez de moy.*

Pist. Moy shall not serue, I will haue fortie Moyes: for I will fetch thy rymme out at thy Throat, in droppes of Crimson blood.

French. *Est il impossible d'eschapper le force de ton bras.*

Pist. Brasse, Curre? thou damned and luxurious Mountaine Goat, offer'st me Brasse?

French. *O perdonne moy.*

Pist. Say'st thou me so? is that a Tonne of Moyes? Come hither boy, aske me this slaue in French what is his Name.

Boy. *Escoute comment estes vous appelle?*

French. *Mounsieur le Fer.*

Boy. He sayes his Name is M. *Fer.*

Pist. M. *Fer:* Ile fer him, and firke him, and ferret him: discusse the same in French vnto him.

Boy. I doe not know the French for fer, and ferret, and firke.

Pist. Bid him prepare, for I will cut his throat.

French. *Que dit il Mounsieur?*

Boy. *Il me commande a vous dire que vous faite vous prest, car ce soldat icy est disposee tout asture de couppes vostre gorge.*

Pist. Owy, cuppele gorge permafoy pesant, vnlesse thou giue me Crownes, braue Crownes; or mangled shalt thou be by this my Sword.

French. *O Ie vous supplie pour l'amour de Dieu: ma pardonner, Ie suis le Gentilhome de bon maison, garde ma vie, & Ie vous donneray deux cent escus.*

Pist. What are his words

Boy. He

Boy. He prayes you to saue his life, he is a Gentleman of a good house, and for his ransom he will giue you two hundred Crownes.

Pist. Tell him my fury shall abate, and I the Crownes will take.

Fren. Petit Monsieur que dit il?

Boy. Encore qu'il et contra son Iurement, de pardonner aucune prisonner: neant-mons pour les escues que vous layt a promets, il est content a vous donnes le liberte le franchisement.

Fre. Sur mes genoux se vous donnes milles remercious, et Ie me estime heurex que Ie intombe, entre les main. d'vn Chevalier Ie pense le plus braue valiant et tres distinie signieur d'Angleterre.

Pist. Expound vnto me boy.

Boy. He giues you vpon his knees a thousand thanks, and he esteemes himselfe happy, that he hath falne into the hands of one (as he thinkes) the most braue, valorous and thrice-worthy signeur of England.

Pist. As I sucke blood, I will some mercy shew. Follow mee.

Boy. Saaue vous le grand Capitaine?
I did neuer know so full a voyce issue from so emptie a heart: but the saying is true, The empty vessel makes the greatest sound, *Bardolfe* and *Nym* had tenne times more valour, then this roaring diuell i'th olde play, that euerie one may payre his nayles with a woodden dagger, and they are both hang'd, and so would this be, if hee durst steale any thing aduenturously. I must stay with the Lackies with the luggage of our camp, the French might haue a good pray of vs, if he knew of it, for there is none to guard it but boyes. *Exit.*

Enter Constable, Orleance, Burbon, Dalphin, and Ramburs.

Con. O Diable.

Orl. O signeur le iour et perdia, toute et perdie.

Dol. Mor Dieu ma vie, all is confounded all,
Reproach, and euerlasting shame
Sits mocking in our Plumes. *A short Alarum.*
O meschante Fortune, do not runne away.

Con. Why all our rankes are broke.

Dol. O perdurable shame, let's stab our selues:
Be these the wretches that we plaid at dice for?

Orl. Is this the King we sent too, for his ransome?

Bur. Shame, and eternall shame, nothing but shame,
Let vs dye in once more backe againe,
And he that will not follow *Burbon* now,
Let him go hence, and with his cap in hand
Like a base Pander hold the Chamber doore,
Whilst a base slaue, no gentler then my dogge,
His fairest daughter is contaminated.

Con. Disorder that hath spoyl'd vs, friend vs now,
Let vs on heapes go offer vp our liues.

Orl. We are enow yet liuing in the Field,
To smother vp the English in our throngs,
If any order might be thought vpon.

Bur. The diuell take Order now, Ile to the throng;
Let life be short, else shame will be too long. *Exit.*

Alarum. Enter the King and his trayne, with Prisoners.

King. Well haue we done, thrice-valiant Countrimen,
But all's not done, yet keepe the French the field.

Exe The D. of York commends him to your Maiesty

King. Liues he good Vnckle: thrice within this houre
I saw him downe; thrice vp againe, and fighting,
From Helmet to the spurre, all blood he was.

Exe. In which array (braue Soldier) doth he lye,
Larding the plaine: and by his bloody side,
(Yoake-fellow to his honour-owing-wounds)
The Noble Earle of Suffolke also lyes.
Suffolke first dyed, and Yorke all hagled ouer
Comes to him, where in gore he lay insteeped,
And takes him by the Beard, kisses the gashes
That bloodily did yawne vpon his face.
He cryes aloud; Tarry my Cosin Suffolke,
My soule shall thine keepe company to heauen:
Tarry (sweet soule) for mine, then flye a-brest:
As in this glorious and well-foughten field
We kept together in our Chiualrie.
Vpon these words I came, and cheer'd him vp,
He smil'd me in the face, raught me his hand,
And with a feeble gripe, sayes: Deere my Lord,
Commend my seruice to my Soueraigne,
So did he turne, and ouer Suffolkes necke
He threw his wounded arme, and kist his lippes,
And so espous'd to death, with blood he seal'd
A Testament of Noble-ending-loue:
The prettie and sweet manner of it forc'd
Those waters from me, which I would haue stop'd,
But I had not so much of man in mee,
And all my mother came into mine eyes,
And gaue me vp to teares.

King. I blame you not,
For hearing this, I must perforce compound
With mixtfull eyes, or they will issue to. *Alarum*
But hearke, what new alarum is this same?
The French haue re-enforc'd their scatter'd men:
Then euery souldiour kill his Prisoners,
Giue the word through. *Exit*

Actus Quartus.

Enter Fluellen and Gower.

Flu. Kill the poyes and the luggage, 'Tis expressely against the Law of Armes, tis as arrant a peece of knauery marke you now, as can bee offert in your Conscience now, is it not?

Gow. Tis certaine, there's not a boy left aliue, and the Cowardly Rascalls that ranne from the battaile ha' done this slaughter: besides they haue burned and carried away all that was in the Kings Tent, wherefore the King most worthily hath caus'd euery soldiour to cut his prisoners throat. O 'tis a gallant King.

Flu. I, hee was porne at *Monmouth* Captaine *Gower*: What call you the Townes name where *Alexander* the pig was borne?

Gow. Alexander the Great.

Flu. Why I pray you, is not pig, great? The pig, or the great, or the mighty, or the huge, or the magnanimous, are all one reckonings, saue the phrase is a litle variations.

Gower. I thinke *Alexander* the Great was borne in *Macedon*, his Father was called *Phillip* of *Macedon*, as I take it.

Flu. I thinke it is in *Macedon* where *Alexander* is porne.

porne: I tell you Captaine, if you looke in the Maps of the Orld, I warrant you sall finde in the comparisons betweene *Macedon* & *Monmouth*, that the situations looke you, is both alike. There is a Riuer in *Macedon*, & there is also moreouer a Riuer at *Monmouth*, it is call'd Wye at *Monmouth*: but it is out of my praines, what is the name of the other Riuer: but 'tis all one, tis alike as my fingers is to my fingers, and there is Salmons in both. If you marke *Alexanders* life well, *Harry of Monmouthes* life is come after it indifferent well, for there is figures in all things. *Alexander* God knowes, and you know, in his rages, and his furies, and his wraths, and his chollers, and his moodes, and his displeasures, and his indignations, and also being a little intoxicates in his praines, did in his Ales and his angers (looke you) kill his best friend *Clytus*.

Gow. Our King is not like him in that, he neuer kill'd any of his friends.

Flu. It is not well done (marke you now) to take the tales out of my mouth, ere it is made and finished. I speak but in the figures, and comparisons of it: as *Alexander* kild his friend *Clytus*, being in his Ales and his Cuppes; so also *Harry Monmouth* being in his right wittes, and his good iudgements, turn'd away the fat Knight with the great belly doublet: he was full of iests, and gypes, and knaueries, and mockes, I haue forgot his name.

Gow. Sir *Iohn Falstaffe*.

Flu. That is he: Ile tell you, there is good men porne at *Monmouth*.

Gow. Heere comes his Maiesty.

Alarum. Enter King Harry and Burbon with prisoners. Flourish.

King. I was not angry since I came to France,
Vntill this instant. Take a Trumpet Herald,
Ride thou vnto the Horsemen on yond hill:
If they will fight with vs, bid them come downe,
Or voyde the field: they do offend our sight.
If they'l do neither, we will come to them,
And make them sker away, as swift as stones
Enforced from the old Assyrian slings:
Besides, wee'l cut the throats of those we haue,
And not a man of them that we shall take,
Shall taste our mercy. Go and tell them so.

Enter Montioy.

Exe. Here comes the Herald of the French, my Liege

Glou. His eyes are humbler then they vs'd to be.

King. How now, what meanes this Herald? Knowst thou not,
That I haue fin'd these bones of mine for ransome?
Com'st thou againe for ransome?

Her. No great King:
I come to thee for charitable License,
That we may wander ore this bloody field,
To booke our dead, and then to bury them,
To sort our Nobles from our common men.
For many of our Princes (woe the while)
Lye drown'd and soak'd in mercenary blood:
So do our vulgar drench their peasant limbes
In blood of Princes, and with wounded steeds
Fret fet-locke deepe in gore, and with wilde rage
Yerke out their armed heeles at their dead masters,
Killing them twice. O giue vs leaue great King,
To view the field in safety, and dispose
Of their dead bodies.

Kin. I tell thee truly Herald,
I know not if the day be ours or no,
For yet a many of your horsemen peere,
And gallop ore the field.

Her. The day is yours.

Kin. Praised be God, and not our strength for it:
What is this Castle call'd that stands hard by.

Her. They call it *Agincourt*.

King. Then call we this the field of *Agincourt*,
Fought on the day of *Crispin Crispianus*.

Flu. Your Grandfather of famous memory (an't please your Maiesty) and your great Vncle *Edward* the Placke Prince of Wales, as I haue read in the Chronicles, fought a most praue pattle here in France.

Kin. They did *Fluellen*.

Flu. Your Maiesty sayes very true: If your Maiesties is remembred of it, the Welchmen did good seruice in a Garden where Leekes did grow, wearing Leekes in their *Monmouth* caps, which your Maiesty know to this houre is an honourable badge of the seruice: And I do beleeue your Maiesty takes no scorne to weare the Leeke vppon S. Tauies day.

King. I weare it for a memorable honor:
For I am Welch you know good Countriman.

Flu. All the water in Wye, cannot wash your Maiesties Welsh plood out of your pody, I can tell you that: God plesse it, and preserue it, as long as it pleases his Grace, and his Maiesty too.

Kin. Thankes good my Countrymen.

Flu. By Ieshu, I am your Maiesties Countreyman, I care not who know it: I will confesse it to all the Orld, I need not to be ashamed of your Maiesty, praised be God so long as your Maiesty is an honest man.

King. Good keepe me so.

Enter Williams.

Our Heralds go with him,
Bring me iust notice of the numbers dead
On both our parts. Call yonder fellow hither.

Exe. Souldier, you must come to the King.

Kin Souldier, why wear'st thou that Gloue in thy Cappe?

Will. And't please your Maiesty, tis the gage of one that I should fight withall, if he be aliue.

Kin. An Englishman?

Wil. And't please your Maiesty, a Rascall that swagger'd with me last night: who if aliue, and euer dare to challenge this Gloue, I haue sworne to take him a boxe a'th ere: or if I can see my Gloue in his cappe, which he swore as he was a Souldier he would weare (if aliue) I wil strike it out soundly.

Kin. What thinke you Captaine *Fluellen*, is it fit this souldier keepe his oath.

Flu. Hee is a Crauen and a Villaine else, and't please your Maiesty in my conscience.

King. It may bee, his enemy is a Gentleman of great sort quite from the answer of his degree.

Flu. Though he be as good a Ientleman as the diuel is, as Lucifer and Belzebub himselfe, it is necessary (looke your Grace) that he keepe his vow and his oath: If hee bee periur'd (see you now) his reputation is as arrant a villaine and a Iacke sawce, as euer his blacke shoo trodd vpon Gods ground, and his earth, in my conscience law

King. Then keepe thy vow sirrah, when thou meet'st the fellow.

Wil. So, I wil my Liege, as I liue.

King. Who seru'st thou vnder?

Wil.

Will. Vnder Captaine *Gower*, my Liege.

Flu. *Gower* is a good Captaine, and is good knowledge and literatured in the Warres.

King. Call him hither to me, Souldier.

Will. I will my Liege. *Exit.*

King. Here *Fluellen*, weare thou this fauour for me, and sticke it in thy Cappe: when *Alanson* and my selfe were downe together, I pluckt this Gloue from his Helme: If any man challenge this, hee is a friend to *Alanson*, and an enemy to our Person; if thou encounter any such, apprehend him, and thou do'st me loue.

Flu. Your Grace doo's me as great Honors as can be desir'd in the hearts of his Subiects: I would faine see the man, that ha's but two legges, that shall find himselfe agreefd at this Gloue; that is all: but I would faine see it once, and please God of his grace that I might see.

King. Know'st thou *Gower*?

Flu. He is my deare friend, and please you.

King. Pray thee goe seeke him, and bring him to my Tent.

Flu. I will fetch him. *Exit.*

King. My Lord of *Warwick*, and my Brother *Gloster*,
Follow *Fluellen* closely at the heeles.
The Gloue which I haue giuen him for a fauour,
May haply purchase him a box a th'eare.
It is the Souldiers: I by bargaine should
Weare it my selfe. Follow good Cousin *Warwick*:
If that the Souldier strike him, as I iudge
By his blunt bearing, he will keepe his word;
Some sodaine mischiefe may arise of it:
For I doe know *Fluellen* valiant,
And toucht with Choler, hot as Gunpowder,
And quickly will returne an iniurie.
Follow, and see there be no harme betweene them.
Goe you with me, Vnckle of Exeter. *Exeunt.*

Enter Gower and Williams.

Will. I warrant it is to Knight you, Captaine.

Enter Fluellen.

Flu. Gods will, and his pleasure, Captaine, I beseech you now, come apace to the King: there is more good toward you peraduenture, then is in your knowledge to dreame of

Will. Sir, know you this Gloue?

Flu. Know the Gloue? I know the Gloue is a Gloue.

Will. I know this, and thus I challenge it.

Strikes him.

Flu. 'Sblud, an arrant Traytor as anyes in the Vniuersall World, or in France, or in England.

Gower. How now Sir? you Villaine.

Will. Doe you thinke Ile be forsworne?

Flu. Stand away Captaine *Gower*, I will giue Treason his payment into plowes, I warrant you.

Will. I am no Traytor.

Flu. That's a Lye in thy Throat. I charge you in his Maiesties Name apprehend him, he's a friend of the Duke *Alansons*.

Enter Warwick and Gloucester.

Warw. How now how now, what's the matter?

Flu. My Lord of Warwick, heere is, praysed be God for it, a most contagious Treason come to light, looke you, as you shall desire in a Summers day. Heere is his Maiestie. *Enter King and Exeter.*

King. How now, what's the matter?

Flu. My Liege, heere is a Villaine, and a Traytor, that looke your Grace, ha's strooke the Gloue which your Maiestie is take out of the Helmet of *Alanson*.

Will. My Liege, this was my Gloue, here is the fellow of it: and he that I gaue it to in change, promis'd to weare it in his Cappe: I promis'd to strike him, if he did: I met this man with my Gloue in his Cappe, and I haue been as good as my word.

Flu. Your Maiestie heare now, sauing your Maiesties Manhood, what an arrant rascally, beggerly, lowsie Knaue it is: I hope your Maiestie is peare me testimonie and witnesse, and will auouchment, that this is the Gloue of *Alanson*, that your Maiestie is giue me, in your Conscience now.

King. Giue me thy Gloue Souldier;
Looke, heere is the fellow of it:
'Twas I indeed thou promised'st to strike,
And thou hast giuen me most bitter termes.

Flu. And please your Maiestie, let his Neck answere for it, if there is any Marshall Law in the World.

King. How canst thou make me satisfaction?

Will. All offences, my Lord, come from the heart: neuer came any from mine, that might offend your Maiestie.

King. It was our selfe thou didst abuse.

Will. Your Maiestie came not like your selfe: you appear'd to me but as a common man; witnesse the Night, your Garments, your Lowlinesse: and what your Highnesse suffer'd vnder that shape, I beseech you take it for your owne fault, and not mine: for had you beene as I tooke you for, I made no offence; therefore I beseech your Highnesse pardon me.

King. Here Vnckle *Exeter*, fill this Gloue with Crownes,
And giue it to this fellow. Keepe it fellow,
And weare it for an Honor in thy Cappe,
Till I doe challenge it. Giue him the Crownes:
And Captaine, you must needs be friends with him.

Flu. By this Day and this Light, the fellow ha's mettell enough in his belly: Hold, there is twelue-pence for you, and I pray you to serue God, and keepe you out of prawles and prabbles, and quarrels and dissentions, and I warrant you it is the better for you.

Will. I will none of your Money.

Flu. It is with a good will: I can tell you it will serue you to mend your shooes: come, wherefore should you be so pashfull, your shooes is not so good: 'tis a good silling I warrant you, or I will change it.

Enter Herauld.

King. Now Herauld, are the dead numbred?

Herald. Heere is the number of the slaught'red French.

King. What Prisoners of good sort are taken Vnckle?

Exe. *Charles* Duke of Orleance, Nephew to the King,
John Duke of Burbon, and Lord *Bouchiquald*:
Of other Lords and Barons, Knights and Squires,
Full fifteene hundred, besides common men.

King. This Note doth tell me of ten thousand French
That in the field lye slaine: of Princes in this number,
And Nobles bearing Banners, there lye dead
One hundred twentie six: added to these,
Of Knights, Esquires, and gallant Gentlemen,
Eight thousand and foure hundred: of the which,
Fiue hundred were but yesterday dubb'd Knights.
So that in these ten thousand they haue lost,
There are but sixteene hundred Mercenaries:
The rest are Princes, Barons, Lords, Knights, Squires,

And

And Gentlemen of bloud and qualitie.
The Names of those their Nobles that lye dead:
Charles Delabreth, High Constable of France,
Iaques of Chatilion, Admirall of France,
The Master of the Crosse-bowes, Lord *Rambures*,
Great Master of France, the braue Sir *Guichard Dolphin*,
Iohn Duke of Alanson, *Anthonie* Duke of Brabant,
The Brother to the Duke of Burgundie,
And *Edward* Duke of Barr: of lustie Earles,
Grandpree and *Roussie*, *Fauconbridge* and *Foyes*,
Beaumont and *Marle*, *Vandemont* and *Lestrale*.
Here was a Royall fellowship of death.
Where is the number of our English dead?
Edward the Duke of Yorke, the Earle of Suffolke.
Sir *Richard Ketly*, *Dauy Gam* Esquire;
None else of name: and of all other men,
But fiue and twentie.
O God, thy Arme was heere:
And not to vs, but to thy Arme alone,
Ascribe we all: when, without stratagem,
But in plaine shock, and euen play of Battaile,
Was euer knowne so great and little losse?
On one part and on th'other, take it God,
For it is none but thine.

Exet. 'Tis wonderfull.

King. Come, goe me in procession to the Village:
And be it death proclaymed through our Hoast,
To boast of this, or take that prayse from God,
Which is his onely.

Flu. Is it not lawfull and please your Maiestie, to tell how many is kill'd?

King. Yes Captaine: but with this acknowledgement,
That God fought for vs.

Flu. Yes, my conscience, he did vs great good.

King. Doe we all holy Rights:
Let there be sung *Non nobis*, and *Te Deum*,
The dead with charitie enclos'd in Clay:
And then to Callice, and to England then,
Where ne're from France arriu'd more happy men.

Exeunt.

Actus Quintus.

Enter Chorus.

Vouchsafe to those that haue not read the Story,
That I may prompt them: and of such as haue,
I humbly pray them to admit th'excuse
Of time, of numbers, and due course of things,
Which cannot in their huge and proper life,
Be here presented. Now we beare the King
Toward Callice: Graunt him there; there seene,
Heaue him away vpon your winged thoughts,
Athwart the Sea: Behold the English beach
Pales in the flood; with Men, Wiues, and Boyes,
Whose shouts & claps out-voyce the deep-mouth'd Sea,
Which like a mightie Whiffler 'fore the King,
Seemes to prepare his way: So let him land,
And solemnly see him set on to London.
So swift a pace hath Thought, that euen now
You may imagine him vpon Black-Heath:
Where, that his Lords desire him, to haue borne
His bruised Helmet, and his bended Sword
Before him, through the Citie: he forbids it,
Being free from vain-nesse, and selfe-glorious pride;
Giuing full Trophee, Signall, and Ostent,
Quite from himselfe, to God. But now behold,
In the quick Forge and working-house of Thought,
How London doth powre out her Citizens,
The Maior and all his Brethren in best sort,
Like to the Senatours of th'antique Rome,
With the Plebeians swarming at their heeles,
Goe forth and fetch their Conqu'ring *Cæsar* in:
As by a lower, but by louing likelyhood,
Were now the Generall of our gracious Empresse,
As in good time he may, from Ireland comming,
Bringing Rebellion broached on his Sword;
How many would the peacefull Citie quit,
To welcome him? much more, and much more cause,
Did they this *Harry*. Now in London place him.
As yet the lamentation of the French
Inuites the King of Englands stay at home:
The Emperour's comming in behalfe of France,
To order peace betweene them: and omit
All the occurrences, what euer chanc't,
Till *Harryes* backe returne againe to France:
There must we bring him; and my selfe haue play'd
The *interim*, by remembring you 'tis past.
Then brooke abridgement, and your eyes aduance,
After your thoughts, straight backe againe to France.

Exit.

Enter Fluellen and Gower.

Gower. Nay, that's right: but why weare you your Leeke to day? S. *Dauies* day is past.

Flu. There is occasions and causes why and wherefore in all things: I will tell you asse my friend, Captaine *Gower*; the rascally, scauld, beggerly, lowsie, pragging Knaue *Pistoll*, which you and your selfe, and all the World, know to be no petter then a fellow, looke you now, of no merits: hee is come to me, and prings me pread and sault yesterday, looke you, and bid me eate my Leeke: it was in a place where I could not breed no contention with him; but I will be so bold as to weare it in my Cap till I see him once againe, and then I will tell him a little piece of my desires.

Enter Pistoll.

Gower. Why heere hee comes, swelling like a Turky-cock.

Flu. 'Tis no matter for his swellings, nor his Turky-cocks. God plesse you aunchient *Pistoll*: you scuruie lowsie Knaue, God plesse you.

Pist. Ha, art thou bedlam? doest thou thirst, base Troian, to haue me fold vp *Parcas* fatall Web? Hence; I am qualmish at the smell of Leeke.

Flu. I peseech you heartily, scuruie lowsie Knaue, at my desires, and my requests, and my petitions, to eate, looke you, this Leeke; because, looke you, you doe not loue it, nor your affections, and your appetites and your disgestions doo's not agree with it, I would desire you to eate it.

Pist. Not for *Cadwallader* and all his Goats.

Flu. There is one Goat for you. *Strikes him.*
Will you be so good, scauld Knaue, as eate it?

Pist. Base Troian, thou shalt dye.

Flu. You say very true, scauld Knaue, when Gods will is: I will desire you to liue in the meane time, and eate your Victuals: come, there is sawce for it. You call'd me yesterday Mountaine-Squier, but I will make you

you to day a squire of low degree. I pray you fall too, if you can mocke a Leeke, you can eate a Leeke.

Gour. Enough Captaine, you haue astonisht him.

Flu. I say, I will make him eate some part of my leeke, or I will peate his pate foure dayes: bite I pray you, it is good for your greene wound, and your ploodie Coxecombe.

Pist. Must I bite.

Flu. Yes certainly, and out of doubt and out of question too, and ambiguities.

Pist. By this Leeke, I will most horribly reuenge I eate and eate I sweare.

Flu. Eate I pray you, will you haue some more sauce to your Leeke: there is not enough Leeke to sweare by.

Pist. Quiet thy Cudgell, thou dost see I eate.

Flu. Much good do you scald knaue, heartily. Nay, pray you throw none away, the skinne is good for your broken Coxcombe; when you take occasions to see Leekes heereafter, I pray you mocke at 'em, that is all.

Pist. Good.

Flu. I, Leekes is good: hold you, there is a groat to heale your pate.

Pist. Me a groat?

Flu Yes verily, and in truth you shall take it, or I haue another Leeke in my pocket, which you shall eate,

Pist. I take thy groat in earnest of reuenge.

Flu. If I owe you any thing, I will pay you in Cudgels, you shall be a Woodmonger, and buy nothing of me but cudgels: God bu'y you, and keepe you, & heale your pate. *Exit*

Pist. All hell shall stirre for this.

Gow. Go, go, you are a counterfeit cowardly Knaue, will you mocke at an ancient Tradition began vppon an honourable respect, and worne as a memorable Trophee of predeceased valor, and dare not auouch in your deeds any of your words. I haue seene you gleeking & galling at this Gentleman twice or thrice. You thought, because he could not speake English in the natiue garb, he could not therefore handle an English Cudgell: you finde it otherwise, and henceforth let a Welsh correction, teach you a good English condition, fare ye well. *Exit*

Pist. Doeth fortune play the huswife with me now?
Newes haue I that my *Doll* is dead i'th Spittle of a malady of France, and there my rendeuous is quite cut off:
Old I do waxe, and from my wearie limbes honour is
Cudgeld. Well, Baud Ile turne, and something leane to
Cut-purse of quicke hand: To England will I steale, and
there Ile steale:
And patches will I get vnto these cudgeld scarres,
And swore I got them in the Gallia warres. *Exit.*

Enter at one doore, King Henry, Exeter, Bedford, Warwicke, and other Lords. At another, Queene Isabel, the King, the Duke of Bourgougne, and other French.

King. Peace to this meeting, wherefore we are met;
Vnto our brother France, and to our Sister
Health and faire time of day: Ioy and good wishes
To our most faire and Princely Cosine *Katherine*:
And as a branch and member of this Royalty,
By whom this great assembly is contriu'd,
We do salute you Duke of *Burgogne*,
And Princes French and Peeres health to you all.

Fra. Right ioyous are we to behold your face,
Most worthy brother England, fairely met,
So are you Princes (English) euery one.

Quee. So happy be the Issue brother Ireland
Of this good day, and of this gracious meeting,
As we are now glad to behold your eyes,
Your eyes which hitherto haue borne
In them against the French that met them in their bent,
The fatall Balls of murthering Basiliskes:
The venome of such Lookes we fairely hope
Haue lost their qualitie, and that this day
Shall change all griefes and quarrels into loue.

Eng. To cry Amen to that, thus we appeare.

Quee. You English Princes all, I doe salute you.

Burg. My dutie to you both, on equall loue.
Great Kings of France and England: that I haue labour'd
With all my wits, my paines, and strong endeuors,
To bring your most Imperiall Maiesties
Vnto this Barre, and Royall enterview;
Your Mightinesse on both parts best can witnesse.
Since then my Office hath so farre preuayl'd,
That Face to Face, and Royall Eye to Eye,
You haue congreeted: let it not disgrace me,
If I demand before this Royall view,
What Rub, or what Impediment there is,
Why that the naked, poore, and mangled Peace,
Deare Nourse of Arts, Plentyes, and ioyfull Births,
Should not in this best Garden of the World,
Our fertile France, put vp her louely Visage?
Alas, shee hath from France too long been chas'd,
And all her Husbandry doth lye on heapes,
Corrupting in it owne fertilitie.
Her Vine, the merry chearer of the heart,
Vnpruned, dyes: her Hedges euen pleach'd,
Like Prisoners wildly ouer-growne with hayre,
Put forth disorder'd Twigs: her fallow Leas,
The Darnell, Hemlock, and ranke Femetary,
Doth root vpon; while that the Culter rusts,
That should deracinate such Sauagery:
The euen Meade, that erst brought sweetly forth
The freckled Cowslip, Burnet, and greene Clouer,
Wanting the Sythe, withall vncorrected, ranke;
Conceiues by idlenesse, and nothing teemes,
But hatefull Docks, rough Thistles, Kecksyes, Burres,
Loosing both beautie and vtilitie;
And all our Vineyards, Fallowes, Meades, and Hedges,
Defectiue in their natures, grow to wildnesse.
Euen so our Houses, and our selues, and Children,
Haue lost, or doe not learne, for want of time,
The Sciences that should become our Countrey;
But grow like Sauages, as Souldiers will,
That nothing doe, but meditate on Blood,
To Swearing, and sterne Lookes, defus'd Attyre,
And euery thing that seemes vnnaturall.
Which to reduce into our former fauour,
You are assembled: and my speech entreats,
That I may know the Let, why gentle Peace
Should not expell these inconueniences,
And blesse vs with her former qualities.

Eng. If Duke of Burgonie, you would the Peace,
Whose want giues growth to th'imperfections
Which you haue cited; you must buy that Peace
With full accord to all our iust demands,
Whose Tenures and particular effects
You haue enschedul'd briefely in your hands.

Burg. The King hath heard them: to the which, as yet
There is no Answer made.

Eng. Well then: the Peace which you before so vrg'd,
Lyes in his Answer.

France. I haue but with a curselarie eye
O're-glanc't the Articles: Pleaseth your Grace
To appoint some of your Councell presently
To sit with vs once more, with better heed
To re-suruey them; we will suddenly
Passe our accept and peremptorie Answer.

England. Brother we shall. Goe Vnckle *Exeter*,
And Brother *Clarence*, and you Brother *Gloucester*,
Warwick, and *Huntington*, goe with the King,
And take with you free power, to ratifie,
Augment, or alter, as your Wisdomes best
Shall see aduantageable for our Dignitie,
Any thing in or out of our Demands,
And wee'le consigne thereto. Will you, faire Sister,
Goe with the Princes, or stay here with vs?

Quee. Our gracious Brother, I will goe with them:
Happily a Womans Voyce may doe some good,
When Articles too nicely vrg'd, be stood on.

England. Yet leaue our Cousin *Katherine* here with vs,
She is our capitall Demand, compris'd
Within the fore-ranke of our Articles.

Quee. She hath good leaue. *Exeunt omnes.*

Manet King and Katherine.

King. Faire *Katherine*, and most faire,
Will you vouchsafe to teach a Souldier tearmes,
Such as will enter at a Ladyes eare,
And pleade his Loue-suit to her gentle heart.

Kath. Your Maiestie shall mock at me, I cannot speake your England.

King. O faire *Katherine*. if you will loue me soundly with your French heart, I will be glad to heare you confesse it brokenly with your English Tongue. Doe you like me, *Kate*?

Kath. *Pardonne moy*, I cannot tell wat is like me.

King. An Angell is like you *Kate*, and you are like an Angell.

Kath. *Que dit il que Ie suis semblable a les Anges?*

Lady. *Ouy verayment (sauf vostre Grace) ainsi dit il.*

King. I said so, deare *Katherine*, and I must not blush to affirme it.

Kath. *O bon Dieu, les langues des hommes sont plein de tromperies.*

King. What sayes she, faire one? that the tongues of men are full of deceits?

Lady. *Ouy*, dat de tongeus of de mans is be full of deceits: dat is de Princesse.

King. The Princesse is the better English-woman: yfaith *Kate*, my wooing is fit for thy vnderstanding, I am glad thou canst speake no better English, for if thou could'st, thou would'st finde me such a plaine King, that thou wouldst thinke, I had sold my Farme to buy my Crowne. I know no wayes to mince it in loue, but directly to say, I loue you; then if you vrge me farther, then to say, Doe you in faith? I weare out my suite: Giue me your answer, yfaith doe, and so clap hands, and a bargaine: how say you, Lady?

Kath. *Sauf vostre honeur*, me vnderstand well.

King. Marry, if you would put me to Verses, or to Dance for your sake, *Kate*, why you vndid me: for the one I haue neither words nor measure; and for the other, I haue no strength in measure, yet a reasonable measure in strength. If I could winne a Lady at Leape-frogge, or by vawting into my Saddle, with my Armour on my backe; vnder the correction of bragging be it spoken, I should quickly leape into a Wife: Or if I might buffet for my Loue, or bound my Horse for her fauours, I could lay on like a Butcher, and sit like a Iack an Apes, neuer off. But before God *Kate*, I cannot looke greenely, nor gaspe out my eloquence, nor I haue no cunning in protestation; onely downe-right Oathes, which I neuer vse till vrg'd, nor neuer breake for vrging. If thou canst loue a fellow of this temper, *Kate*, whose face is not worth Sunne-burning? that neuer lookes in his Glasse, for loue of any thing he sees there? let thine Eye be thy Cooke. I speake to thee plaine Souldier: If thou canst loue me for this, take me? if not? to say to thee that I shall dye, is true; but for thy loue, by the L. No: yet I loue thee too. And while thou liu'st, deare *Kate*, take a fellow of plaine and vncoyned Constancie, for he perforce must do thee right, because he hath not the gift to wooe in other places: for these fellowes of infinit tongue, that can ryme themselues into Ladyes fauours, they doe alwayes reason themselues out againe. What? a speaker is but a prater, a Ryme is but a Ballad; a good Legge will fall, a strait Backe will stoope, a blacke Beard will turne white, a curl'd Pate will grow bald, a faire Face will wither, a full Eye will wax hollow: but a good Heart, *Kate*, is the Sunne and the Moone, or rather the Sunne, and not the Moone; for it shines bright, and neuer changes, but keepes his course truly. If thou would haue such a one, take me? and take me; take a Souldier: take a Souldier; take a King. And what say'st thou then to my Loue? speake my faire, and fairely, I pray thee.

Kath. Is it possible dat I sould loue de ennemie of Fraunce?

King. No, it is not possible you should loue the Enemie of France, *Kate*; but in louing me, you should loue the Friend of France: for I loue France so well, that I will not part with a Village of it; I will haue it all mine: and *Kate*, when France is mine, and I am yours; then yours is France, and you are mine.

Kath. I cannot tell wat is dat.

King. No, *Kate*? I will tell thee in French, which I am sure will hang vpon my tongue, like a new-married Wife about her Husbands Necke, hardly to be shooke off; *Ie quand sur le possession de Fraunce, & quand vous aues le possession de moy*, (Let mee see, what then? Saint *Dennis* bee my speede) *Donc vostre est Fraunce, & vous estes mienne.* It is as easie for me, *Kate*, to conquer the Kingdome, as to speake so much more French: I shall neuer moue thee in French, vnlesse it be to laugh at me.

Kath. *Sauf vostre honeur, le Francois ques vous parleis, il & melieus que l Anglois le quel Ie parle.*

King. No faith is't not, *Kate*: but thy speaking of my Tongue, and I thine, most truely falsely, must needes be graunted to be much at one. But *Kate*, doo'st thou vnderstand thus much English? Canst thou loue mee?

Kath. I cannot tell.

King. Can any of your Neighbours tell, *Kate*? Ile aske them. Come, I know thou louest me: and at night, when you come into your Closet, you'le question this Gentlewoman about me; and I know, *Kate*, you will to her disprayse those parts in me, that you loue with your heart: but good *Kate*, mocke me mercifully, the rather gentle Princesse, because I loue thee cruelly. If euer thou beest mine, *Kate*, as I haue a sauing Faith within me tells me thou shalt; I get thee with skambling, and thou must therefore needes proue a good Souldier-breeder: Shall not thou and I, betweene Saint *Dennis* and Saint *George*, compound a Boy, halfe French halfe English, that

that ſhall goe to Conſtantinople, and take the Turke by the Beard. Shall wee not? what ſay'ſt thou, my faire Flower-de-Luce.

Kate. I doe not know dat.

King. No:'tis hereafter to know, but now to promiſe: doe but now promiſe *Kate*, you will endeauour for your French part of ſuch a Boy; and for my Engliſh moytie, take the Word of a King, and a Batcheler. How anſwer you, *La plus belle Katherine du monde mon treſcher & deuin deeſſe.*

Kath. Your Maieſtee aue fauſe Frenche enough to deceiue de moſt ſage Damoiſeil dat is en Fraunce.

King. Now fye vpon my falſe French: by mine Honor in true Engliſh, I loue thee *Kate*; by which Honor, I dare not ſweare thou loueſt me, yet my blood begins to flatter me, that thou doo'ſt; notwithſtanding the poore and vntempering effect of my Viſage. Now beſhrew my Fathers Ambition, hee was thinking of Ciuill Warres when hee got me, therefore was I created with a ſtubborne out-ſide, with an aſpect of Iron, that when I come to wooe Ladyes, I fright them: but in faith *Kate*, the elder I wax, the better I ſhall appeare. My comfort is, that Old Age, that ill layer vp of Beautie, can doe no more ſpoyle vpon my Face. Thou haſt me, if thou haſt me, at the worſt; and thou ſhalt weare me, if thou weare me, better and better: and therefore tell me, moſt faire *Katherine*, will you haue me? Put off your Maiden Bluſhes, auouch the Thoughts of your Heart with the Lookes of an Empreſſe, take me by the Hand, and ſay, *Harry* of England, I am thine: which Word thou ſhalt no ſooner bleſſe mine Eare withall, but I will tell thee alowd, England is thine, Ireland is thine, France is thine, and *Henry Plantaginet* is thine; who, though I ſpeake it before his Face, if he be not Fellow with the beſt King, thou ſhalt finde the beſt King of Good-fellowes Come your Anſwer in broken Muſick; for thy Voyce is Muſick, and thy Engliſh broken: Therefore Queene of all, *Katherine*, breake thy minde to me in broken Engliſh; wilt thou haue me?

Kath. Dat is as it ſhall pleaſe *de Roy mon pere.*

King. Nay, it will pleaſe him well, *Kate*; it ſhall pleaſe him, *Kate.*

Kath. Den it ſall alſo content me.

King. Vpon that I kiſſe your Hand, and I call you my Queene.

Kath. Laiſſe mon Seigneur, laiſſe, laiſſe, may foy: Ie ne veus point que vous abbaiſſe voſtre grandeus, en baiſant le main d'une noſtre Seigneur indignie ſeruiteur excuſe moy. Ie vous ſupplie mon treſ-puiſſant Seigneur.

King. Then I will kiſſe your Lippes, *Kate.*

Kath. Les Dames & Damoiſels pour eſtre baiſee deuant leur nopceſe il net pas le coſtume de Fraunce.

King. Madame, my Interpreter, what ſayes ſhee?

Lady. Dat it is not be de faſhon pour le Ladies of Fraunce; I cannot tell wat is buiſſe en Angliſh.

King. To kiſſe.

Lady. Your Maieſtee *entendre bettre que moy.*

King. It is not a faſhion for the Maids in Fraunce to kiſſe before they are marryed, would ſhe ſay?

Lady. Ouy verayment.

King. O *Kate*, nice Cuſtomes curſie to great Kings. Deare *Kate*, you and I cannot bee confin'd within the weake Lyſt of a Countreyes faſhion: wee are the makers of Manners, *Kate*; and the libertie that followes our Places, ſtoppes the mouth of all finde-faults, as I will doe yours, for vpholding the nice faſhion of your Countrey, in denying me a Kiſſe: therefore patiently, and yeelding. You haue Witch-craft in your Lippes, *Kate*: there is more eloquence in a Sugar touch of them, then in the Tongues of the French Councell; and they ſhould ſooner perſwade *Harry* of England, then a generall Petition of Monarchs. Heere comes your Father.

Enter the French Power, and the Engliſh Lords.

Burg. God ſaue your Maieſtie, my Royall Couſin, teach you our Princeſſe Engliſh?

King. I would haue her learne, my faire Couſin, how perfectly I loue her, and that is good Engliſh.

Burg. Is ſhee not apt?

King. Our Tongue is rough, Coze, and my Condition is not ſmooth: ſo that hauing neyther the Voyce nor the Heart of Flatterie about me, I cannot ſo coniure vp the Spirit of Loue in her, that hee will appeare in his true likeneſſe.

Burg. Pardon the frankneſſe of my mirth, if I anſwer you for that. If you would coniure in her, you muſt make a Circle: if coniure vp Loue in her in his true likeneſſe, hee muſt appeare naked, and blinde. Can you blame her then, being a Maid, yet ros'd ouer with the Virgin Crimſon of Modeſtie, if ſhee deny the apparance of a naked blinde Boy in her naked ſeeing ſelfe? It were (my Lord) a hard Condition for a Maid to conſigne to.

King. Yet they doe winke and yeeld, as Loue is blind and enforces.

Burg. They are then excus'd, my Lord, when they ſee not what they doe.

King. Then good my Lord, teach your Couſin to conſent winking.

Burg. I will winke on her to conſent, my Lord, if you will teach her to know my meaning: for Maides well Summer'd, and warme kept, are like Flyes at Bartholomew-tyde, blinde, though they haue their eyes, and then they will endure handling, which before would not abide looking on.

King. This Morall tyes me ouer to Time, and a hot Summer; and ſo I ſhall catch the Flye, your Couſin, in the latter end, and ſhee muſt be blinde to.

Burg. As Loue is my Lord, before it loues.

King. It is ſo: and you may, ſome of you, thanke Loue for my blindneſſe, who cannot ſee many a faire French Citie for one faire French Maid that ſtands in my way.

French King. Yes my Lord, you ſee them perſpectiuely: the Cities turn'd into a Maid; for they are all gyrdled with Maiden Walls, that Warre hath entred.

England. Shall *Kate* be my Wife?

France. So pleaſe you.

England. I am content, ſo the Maiden Cities you talke of, may wait on her: ſo the Maid that ſtood in the way for my Wiſh, ſhall ſhew me the way to my Will.

France. Wee haue conſented to all tearmes of reaſon.

England. Is't ſo, my Lords of England?

Weſt. The King hath graunted euery Article:
His Daughter firſt; and in ſequele, all,
According to their firme propoſed natures.

Exet. Onely

Exet. Onely he hath not yet subscribed this:
Where your Maiestie demands, That the King of France hauing any occasion to write for matter of Graunt, shall name your Highnesse in this forme, and with this addition, in French: *Nostre trescher filz Henry Roy d'Angleterre Heretere de Fraunce:* and thus in Latine; *Praeclarissimus Filius noster Henricus Rex Angliae & Heres Franciae.*

France. Nor this I haue not Brother so deny'd,
But your request shall make me let it passe.

England. I pray you then, in loue and deare allyance,
Let that one Article ranke with the rest,
And thereupon giue me your Daughter.

France. Take her faire Sonne, and from her blood rayse vp
Issue to me, that the contending Kingdomes
Of France and England, whose very shoares looke pale,
With enuy of each others happinesse,
May cease their hatred; and this deare Coniunction
Plant Neighbour-hood and Christian-like accord
In their sweet Bosomes: that neuer Warre aduance
His bleeding Sword 'twixt England and faire France.

Lords. Amen.

King. Now welcome *Kate:* and beare me witnesse all,
That here I kisse her as my Soueraigne Queene.

Flourish.

Quee. God, the best maker of all Marriages,
Combine your hearts in one, your Realmes in one:
As Man and Wife being two, are one in loue,
So be there 'twixt your Kingdomes such a Spousall,
That neuer may ill Office, or fell Iealousie,
Which troubles oft the Bed of blessed Marriage,
Thrust in betweene the Pation of these Kingdomes,
To make diuorce of their incorporate League:
That English may as French, French Englishmen,
Receiue each other. God speake this Amen.

All. Amen.

King. Prepare we for our Marriage: on which day,
My Lord of Burgundy wee'le take your Oath
And all the Peeres, for suretie of our Leagues.
Then shall I sweare to *Kate*, and you to me,
And may our Oathes well kept and prosp'rous be.

Senet. Exeunt.

Enter Chorus.

Thus farre with rough, and all-vnable Pen,
Our bending Author hath pursu'd the Story,
In little roome confining mightie men,
Mangling by starts the full course of their glory.
Small time: but in that small, most greatly liued
This Starre of England. Fortune made his Sword;
By which, the Worlds best Garden he atchieued:
And of it left his Sonne Imperiall Lord.
Henry the Sixt, in Infant Bands crown'd King
Of France and England, did this King succeed:
Whose State so many had the managing,
That they lost France, and made his England bleed:
Which oft our Stage hath showne; and for their sake,
In your faire minds let this acceptance take.

FINIS.

The first Part of Henry the Sixt.

Actus Primus. Scœna Prima.

Dead March.

Enter the Funerall of King Henry the Fift, attended on by the Duke of Bedford, Regent of France; the Duke of Gloster, Protector; the Duke of Exeter Warwicke, the Bishop of Winchester, and the Duke of Somerset.

Bedford.

Hvng be ỹ heauens with black, yield day to night;
Comets importing change of Times and States,
Brandish your crystall Tresses in the Skie,
And with them scourge the bad reuolting Stars,
That haue consented vnto *Henries* death:
King *Henry* the Fift, too famous to liue long,
England ne're lost a King of so much worth.

Glost. England ne're had a King vntill his time:
Vertue he had, deseruing to command,
His brandisht Sword did blinde men with his beames,
His Armes spred wider then a Dragons Wings:
His sparkling Eyes, repleat with wrathfull fire,
More dazled and droue back his Enemies,
Then mid-day Sunne, fierce bent against their faces.
What should I say? his Deeds exceed all speech:
He ne're lift vp his Hand, but conquered.

Exe. We mourne in black, why mourn we not in blood?
Henry is dead, and neuer shall reuiue:
Vpon a Woodden Coffin we attend;
And Deaths dishonourable Victorie,
We with our stately presence glorifie,
Like Captiues bound to a Triumphant Carre.
What? shall we curse the Planets of Mishap,
That plotted thus our Glories ouerthrow?
Or shall we thinke the subtile-witted French,
Coniurers and Sorcerers, that afraid of him,
By Magick Verses haue contriu'd his end.

Winch. He was a King, blest of the King of Kings.
Vnto the French, the dreadfull Iudgement-Day
So dreadfull will not be, as was his sight.
The Battailes of the Lord of Hosts he fought:
The Churches Prayers made him so prosperous.

Glost. The Church? where is it?
Had not Church-men pray'd,
His thred of Life had not so soone decay'd.
None doe you like, but an effeminate Prince,
Whom like a Schoole-boy you may ouer-awe.

Winch. Gloster, what ere we like, thou art Protector,
And lookest to command the Prince and Realme.
Thy Wife is prowd, she holdeth thee in awe,
More then God or Religious Church-men may.

Glost. Name not Religion, for thou lou'st the Flesh,
And ne're throughout the yeere to Church thou go'st,
Except it be to pray against thy foes.

Bed. Cease, cease these Iarres, & rest your minds in peace:
Let's to the Altar: Heralds wayt on vs;
In stead of Gold, wee'le offer vp our Armes,
Since Armes auayle not, now that *Henry's* dead,
Posteritie await for wretched yeeres,
When at their Mothers moistned eyes, Babes shall suck,
Our Ile be made a Nourish of salt Teares,
And none but Women left to wayle the dead.
Henry the Fift, thy Ghost I inuocate:
Prosper this Realme, keepe it from Ciuill Broyles,
Combat with aduerse Planets in the Heauens;
A farre more glorious Starre thy Soule will make,
Then *Iulius Cæsar*, or bright----

Enter a Messenger.

Mess. My honourable Lords, health to you all:
Sad tidings bring I to you out of France,
Of losse of slaughter, and discomfiture:
Guyen, Champaigne, Rheimes, Orleance,
Paris, Guysors Poictiers, are all quite lost.

Bedf. What say'st thou man, before dead *Henry's* Coarse?
Speake softly, or the losse of those great Townes
Will make him burst his Lead, and rise from death.

Glost. Is Paris lost? is Roan yeelded vp?
If *Henry* were recall'd to life againe,
These news would cause him once more yeeld the Ghost.

Exe. How were they lost? what trecherie was vs'd?

Mess. No trecherie, but want of Men and Money.
Amongst the Souldiers this is muttered,
That here you maintaine seuerall Factions:
And whil'st a Field should be dispatcht and fought,
You are disputing of your Generals.
One would haue lingring Warres, with little cost;
Another would flye swift, but wanteth Wings:
A third thinkes, without expence at all,
By guilefull faire words, Peace may be obtayn'd.
Awake, awake, English Nobilitie,
Let not slouth dimme your Honors, new begot;
Cropt are the Flower-de-Luces in your Armes
Of Englands Coat, one halfe is cut away.

Exe. Were our Teares wanting to this Funerall,
These Tidings would call forth her flowing Tides.

Bedf. Me they concerne, Regent I am of France:
Giue me my steeled Coat, Ile fight for France.
Away with these disgracefull wayling Robes;
Wounds will I lend the French in stead of Eyes,
To weepe their intermissiue Miseries.

Enter

Enter to them another Messenger.

Mess. Lords view these Letters, full of bad mischance.
France is reuolted from the English quite,
Except some petty Townes, of no import.
The Dolphin *Charles* is crowned King in Rheimes:
The Bastard of Orleance with him is ioyn'd:
Reynold, Duke of Aniou, doth take his part,
The Duke of Alanson flyeth to his side. *Exit.*

Exe. The Dolphin crown'd King? all flye to him?
O whither shall we flye from this reproach?

Glost. We will not flye, but to our enemies throats.
Bedford, if thou be slacke, Ile fight it out.

Bed. *Gloster*, why doubtst thou of my forwardnesse?
An Army haue I muster'd in my thoughts,
Wherewith already France is ouer-run.

Enter another Messenger.

Mes. My gracious Lords, to adde to your laments,
Wherewith you now bedew King *Henries* hearse,
I must informe you of a dismall fight,
Betwixt the stout Lord *Talbot*, and the French.

Win. What? wherein *Talbot* ouercame, is't so?

3. *Mes.* O no: wherein Lord *Talbot* was o'rethrown:
The circumstance Ile tell you more at large.
The tenth of August last, this dreadfull Lord,
Retyring from the Siege of Orleance,
Hauing full scarce six thousand in his troupe,
By three and twentie thousand of the French
Was round incompassed, and set vpon:
No leysure had he to enranke his men.
He wanted Pikes to set before his Archers:
In stead whereof, sharpe Stakes pluckt out of Hedges
They pitched in the ground confusedly,
To keepe the Horsemen off, from breaking in.
More then three houres the fight continued:
Where valiant *Talbot*, aboue humane thought,
Enacted wonders with his Sword and Lance.
Hundreds he sent to Hell, and none durst stand him:
Here, there, and euery where enrag'd, he slew.
The French exclaym'd, the Deuill was in Armes,
All the whole Army stood agaz'd on him.
His Souldiers spying his vndaunted Spirit,
A *Talbot*, a *Talbot*, cry'd out amaine,
And rusht into the Bowels of the Battaile.
Here had the Conquest fully been seal'd vp,
If Sir *Iohn Falstaffe* had not play'd the Coward.
He being in the Vauward, plac't behinde,
With purpose to relieue and follow them,
Cowardly fled, not hauing struck one stroake.
Hence grew the generall wrack and massacre:
Enclosed were they with their Enemies.
A base Wallon, to win the Dolphins grace,
Thrust *Talbot* with a Speare into the Back,
Whom all France, with their chiefe assembled strength,
Durst not presume to looke once in the face.

Bedf. Is *Talbot* slaine then? I will slay my selfe,
For liuing idly here, in pompe and ease,
Whil'st such a worthy Leader, wanting ayd,
Vnto his dastard foe-men is betray'd.

3. *Mess.* O no, he liues, but is tooke Prisoner,
And Lord *Scales* with him, and Lord *Hungerford*:
Most of the rest slaughter'd, or tooke likewise.

Bedf. His Ransome there is none but I shall pay.
Ile hale the Dolphin headlong from his Throne,
His Crowne shall be the Ransome of my friend:
Foure of their Lords Ile change for one of ours.
Farwell my Masters, to my Taske will I,
Bonfires in France forthwith I am to make,
To keepe our great Saint *Georges* Feast withall.
Ten thousand Souldiers with me I will take,
Whose bloody deeds shall make all Europe quake.

3. *Mess.* So you had need, for Orleance is besieg'd,
The English Army is growne weake and faint:
The Earle of Salisbury craueth supply,
And hardly keepes his men from mutinie,
Since they so few, watch such a multitude.

Exe. Remember Lords your Oathes to *Henry* sworne:
Eyther to quell the Dolphin vtterly,
Or bring him in obedience to your yoake.

Bedf. I doe remember it, and here take my leaue,
To goe about my preparation. *Exit Bedford.*

Glost. Ile to the Tower with all the hast I can,
To view th'Artillerie and Munition,
And then I will proclayme young *Henry* King. *Exit Gloster.*

Exe. To Eltam will I, where the young King is,
Being ordayn'd his speciall Gouernor,
And for his safetie there Ile best deuise. *Exit.*

Winch. Each hath his Place and Function to attend:
I am left out; for me nothing remaines:
But long I will not be Iack out of Office.
The King from Eltam I intend to send,
And sit at chiefest Sterne of publique Weale. *Exit.*

Sound a Flourish.

Enter Charles, Alanson, and Reigneir, marching with Drum and Souldiers.

Charles. *Mars* his true mouing, euen as in the Heauens,
So in the Earth, to this day is not knowne.
Late did he shine vpon the English side:
Now we are Victors, vpon vs he smiles.
What Townes of any moment, but we haue?
At pleasure here we lye, neere Orleance:
Otherwhiles, the famisht English, like pale Ghosts,
Faintly besiege vs one houre in a moneth.

Alan. They want their Porredge, & their fat Bul Beeues:
Eyther they must be dyeted like Mules,
And haue their Prouender ty'd to their mouthes,
Or pitteous they will looke, like drowned Mice.

Reigneir. Let's rayse the Siege: why liue we idly here?
Talbot is taken, whom we wont to feare:
Remayneth none but mad-brayn'd *Salisbury*,
And he may well in fretting spend his gall,
Nor men nor Money hath he to make Warre.

Charles. Sound, sound Alarum, we will rush on them.
Now for the honour of the forlorne French:
Him I forgiue my death, that killeth me,
When he sees me goe back one foot, or flye. *Exeunt.*

Here Alarum, they are beaten back by the English, with great losse.

Enter Charles, Alanson, and Reigneir.

Charles. Who euer saw the like? what men haue I?
Dogges, Cowards, Dastards: I would ne're haue fled,
But that they left me 'midst my Enemies.

Reigneir. *Salisbury* is a desperate Homicide,
He fighteth as one weary of his life:
The other Lords, like Lyons wanting foode,
Doe rush vpon vs as their hungry prey.

Alanson. *Froysard*, a Countreyman of ours, records,
England all *Oliuers* and *Rowlands* breed,
During the time *Edward* the third did raigne:
More truly now may this be verified;
For none but *Samsons* and *Goliasses*
It sendeth forth to skirmish: one to tenne?
Leane raw-bon'd Rascals, who would e're suppose,
They had such courage and audacitie?

Charles. Let's leaue this Towne,
For they are hayre-brayn'd Slaues,
And hunger will enforce them to be more eager:
Of old I know them; rather with their Teeth
The Walls they'le teare downe, then forsake the Siege.

Reigneir. I thinke by some odde Gimmors or Deuice
Their Armes are set, like Clocks, still to strike on;
Else ne're could they hold out so as they doe:
By my consent, wee'le euen let them alone.

Alanson. Be it so.

Enter the Bastard of Orleance.

Bastard. Where's the Prince Dolphin? I haue newes for him.

Dolph. Bastard of Orleance, thrice welcome to vs.

Bast. Me thinks your looks are sad, your chear appal'd.
Hath the late ouerthrow wrought this offence?
Be not dismay'd, for succour is at hand:
A holy Maid hither with me I bring,
Which by a Vision sent to her from Heauen,
Ordayned is to rayse this tedious Siege,
And driue the English forth the bounds of France:
The spirit of deepe Prophecie she hath,
Exceeding the nine *Sibyls* of old Rome:
What's past, and what's to come, she can descry.
Speake, shall I call her in? beleeue my words,
For they are certaine, and vnfallible.

Dolph. Goe call her in: but first, to try her skill,
Reignier stand thou as Dolphin in my place;
Question her prowdly, let thy Lookes be sterne,
By this meanes shall we sound what skill she hath.

Enter Ioane Puzel.

Reigneir. Faire Maid, is't thou wilt doe these wondrous feats?

Puzel. *Reignier*, is't thou that thinkest to beguile me?
Where is the Dolphin? Come, come from behinde,
I know thee well, though neuer seene before.
Be not amaz'd, there's nothing hid from me;
In priuate will I talke with thee apart:
Stand back you Lords, and giue vs leaue a while.

Reigneir. She takes vpon her brauely at first dash.

Puzel. Dolphin, I am by birth a Shepheards Daughter,
My wit vntrayn'd in any kind of Art:
Heauen and our Lady gracious hath it pleas'd
To shine on my contemptible estate.
Loe, whilest I wayted on my tender Lambes,
And to Sunnes parching heat display'd my cheekes,
Gods Mother deigned to appeare to me,
And in a Vision full of Maiestie,
Will'd me to leaue my base Vocation,
And free my Countrey from Calamitie:
Her ayde she promis'd, and assur'd successe.
In compleat Glory shee reueal'd her selfe:
And whereas I was black and swart before,
With those cleare Rayes, which shee infus'd on me,
That beautie am I blest with, which you may see.
Aske me what question thou canst possible,
And I will answer vnpremeditated:
My Courage trie by Combat, if thou dar'st,
And thou shalt finde that I exceed my Sex.
Resolue on this, thou shalt be fortunate,
If thou receiue me for thy Warlike Mate.

Dolph. Thou hast astonisht me with thy high termes:
Onely this proofe Ile of thy Valour make,
In single Combat thou shalt buckle with me;
And if thou vanquishest, thy words are true,
Otherwise I renounce all confidence.

Puzel. I am prepar'd: here is my keene-edg'd Sword,
Deckt with fine Flower-de-Luces on each side,
The which at Touraine, in S. *Katherines* Church-yard,
Out of a great deale of old Iron, I chose forth.

Dolph. Then come a Gods name, I feare no woman.

Puzel. And while I liue, Ile ne're flye from a man.

Here they fight, and Ioane de Puzel overcomes.

Dolph. Stay, stay thy hands, thou art an Amazon,
And fightest with the Sword of *Debora*.

Puzel. Christs Mother helpes me, else I were too weake.

Dolph. Who e're helps thee, 'tis thou that must help me:
Impatiently I burne with thy desire,
My heart and hands thou hast at once subdu'd.
Excellent *Puzel*, if thy name be so,
Let me thy seruant, and not Soueraigne be,
'Tis the French Dolphin sueth to thee thus.

Puzel. I must not yeeld to any rights of Loue,
For my Profession's sacred from aboue:
When I haue chased all thy Foes from hence,
Then will I thinke vpon a recompence.

Dolph. Meane time looke gracious on thy prostrate Thrall.

Reigneir. My Lord me thinkes is very long in talke.

Alans. Doubtlesse he shriues this woman to her smock,
Else ne're could he so long protract his speech.

Reigneir. Shall wee disturbe him, since hee keepes no meane?

Alan. He may meane more then we poor men do know,
These women are shrewd tempters with their tongues.

Reigneir. My Lord, where are you? what deuise you on?
Shall we giue o're Orleance, or no?

Puzel. Why no, I say: distrustfull Recreants,
Fight till the last gaspe: Ile be your guard.

Dolph. What shee sayes, Ile confirme: wee'le fight it out.

Puzel. Assign'd am I to be the English Scourge.
This night the Siege assuredly Ile rayse:
Expect Saint *Martins* Summer, *Halcyons* dayes,
Since I haue entred into these Warres.
Glory is like a Circle in the Water,
Which neuer ceaseth to enlarge it selfe,
Till by broad spreading, it disperse to naught.
With *Henries* death, the English Circle ends,
Dispersed are the glories it included:
Now am I like that prowd insulting Ship,
Which *Cæsar* and his fortune bare at once.

Dolph. Was *Mahomet* inspired with a Doue?
Thou with an Eagle art inspired then.
Helen, the Mother of Great *Constantine*,
Nor yet S. *Philips* daughters were like thee.
Bright Starre of *Venus*, falne downe on the Earth,
How may I reuerently worship thee enough?

Alanson. Leaue off delayes, and let vs rayse the Siege.

Reigneir. Wo-

Reigneir. Woman, do what thou canst to saue our honors,
Driue them from Orleance, and be immortaliz'd.
Dolph. Presently wee'le try: come, let's away about it,
No Prophet will I trust, if shee proue false. *Exeunt.*

Enter Gloster, with his Seruing-men.

Glost. I am come to suruey the Tower this day;
Since *Henries* death, I feare there is Conueyance:
Where be these Warders, that they wait not here?
Open the Gates, 'tis *Gloster* that calls.
1. *Warder.* Who's there, that knocks so imperiously?
Glost. 1. *Man.* It is the Noble Duke of Gloster.
2. *Warder.* Who ere he be, you may not be let in.
1. *Man.* Villaines, answer you so the Lord Protector?
1. *Warder.* The Lord protect him, so we answer him,
We doe no otherwise then wee are will'd.
Glost. Who willed you? or whose will stands but mine?
There's none Protector of the Realme, but I:
Breake vp the Gates, Ile be your warrantize;
Shall I be flowted thus by dunghill Groomes?
Glosters men rush at the Tower Gates, and Wooduile the Lieutenant speakes within.
Wooduile. What noyse is this? what Traytors haue wee here?
Glost. Lieutenant, is it you whose voyce I heare?
Open the Gates, here's *Gloster* that would enter.
Wooduile. Haue patience Noble Duke, I may not open,
The Cardinall of Winchester forbids:
From him I haue expresse commandement,
That thou nor none of thine shall be let in.
Glost. Faint-hearted *Wooduile*, prizest him 'fore me?
Arrogant *Winchester* that haughtie Prelate,
Whom *Henry* our late Soueraigne ne're could brooke?
Thou art no friend to God, or to the King:
Open the Gates, or Ile shut thee out shortly.
Seruingmen. Open the Gates vnto the Lord Protector,
Or wee'le burst them open, if that you come not quickly.

Enter to the Protector at the Tower Gates Winchester and his men in Tawney Coates.

Winchest. How now ambitious *Vmpheir*, what meanes this?
Glost. Piel'd Priest, doo'st thou command me to be shut out?
Winch. I doe, thou most vsurping Proditor,
And not Protector of the King or Realme.
Glost. Stand back thou manifest Conspirator,
Thou that contriued'st to murther our dead Lord,
Thou that giu'st Whores Indulgences to sinne,
Ile canuas thee in thy broad Cardinalls Hat,
If thou proceed in this thy insolence.
Winch. Nay, stand thou back, I will not budge a foot:
This be Damascus, be thou cursed *Cain*,
To slay thy Brother *Abel*, if thou wilt.
Glost. I will not slay thee, but Ile driue thee back:
Thy Scarlet Robes, as a Childs bearing Cloth,
Ile vse, to carry thee out of this place.
Winch. Doe what thou dar'st, I beard thee to thy face.
Glost. What? am I dar'd, and bearded to my face?
Draw men, for all this priuiledged place,
Blew Coats to Tawny Coats. Priest, beware your Beard,
I meane to tugge it, and to cuffe you soundly.
Vnder my feet I stampe thy Cardinalls Hat:
In spight of Pope, or dignities of Church,
Here by the Cheekes Ile drag thee vp and downe.
Winch. *Gloster*, thou wilt answere this before the Pope.
Glost. Winchester Goose, I cry, a Rope, a Rope.
Now beat them hence, why doe you let them stay?
Thee Ile chase hence, thou Wolfe in Sheepes array.
Out Tawney-Coates, out Scarlet Hypocrite.

Here Glosters men beat out the Cardinalls men, and enter in the hurly-burly the Maior of London, and his Officers.

Maior. Fye Lords, that you being supreme Magistrates,
Thus contumeliously should breake the Peace.
Glost. Peace Maior, thou know'st little of my wrongs:
Here's *Beauford*, that regards nor God nor King,
Hath here distrayn'd the Tower to his vse.
Winch. Here's *Gloster*, a Foe to Citizens,
One that still motions Warre, and neuer Peace,
O're-charging your free Purses with large Fines;
That seekes to ouerthrow Religion,
Because he is Protector of the Realme;
And would haue Armour here out of the Tower,
To Crowne himselfe King, and suppresse the Prince.
Glost. I will not answer thee with words, but blowes.
Here they skirmish againe.
Maior. Naught rests for me, in this tumultuous strife,
But to make open Proclamation.
Come Officer, as lowd as e're thou canst, cry:
All manner of men, assembled here in Armes this day, against Gods Peace and the Kings, wee charge and command you, in his Highnesse Name, to repayre to your seuerall dwelling places, and not to weare, handle, or vse any Sword, Weapon, or Dagger hence-forward, vpon paine of death.
Glost. Cardinall, Ile be no breaker of the Law:
But we shall meet, and breake our minds at large.
Winch. *Gloster*, wee'le meet to thy cost, be sure:
Thy heart-blood I will haue for this dayes worke.
Maior. Ile call for Clubs, if you will not away:
This Cardinall's more haughtie then the Deuill.
Glost. Maior farewell: thou doo'st but what thou may'st.
Winch. Abhominable *Gloster*, guard thy Head,
For I intend to haue it ere long. *Exeunt.*
Maior. See the Coast clear'd, and then we will depart.
Good God, these Nobles should such stomacks beare,
I my selfe fight not once in fortie yeere. *Exeunt.*

Enter the Master Gunner of Orleance, and his Boy.

M.Gunner. Sirrha, thou know'st how Orleance is besieg'd,
And how the English haue the Suburbs wonne.
Boy. Father I know, and oft haue shot at them,
How e're vnfortunate, I miss'd my ayme.
M.Gunner. But now thou shalt not. Be thou rul'd by me:
Chiefe Master Gunner am I of this Towne,
Something I must doe to procure me grace:
The Princes espyals haue informed me,
How the English, in the Suburbs close entrencht,
Went through a secret Grate of Iron Barres,
In yonder Tower, to ouer-peere the Citie,
And thence discouer, how with most aduantage
They may vex vs with Shot or with Assault.
To intercept this inconuenience,
A Peece of Ordnance 'gainst it I haue plac'd,

And

And euen these three dayes haue I watcht,
If I could see them. Now doe thou watch,
For I can stay no longer.
If thou spy'st any, runne and bring me word,
And thou shalt finde me at the Gouernors. *Exit.*
Boy. Father, I warrant you, take you no care,
Ile neuer trouble you, if I may spye them. *Exit.*

Enter Salisbury and Talbot on the Turrets, with others.

Salisb. *Talbot*, my life, my ioy, againe return'd?
How wert thou handled, being Prisoner?
Or by what meanes got's thou to be releas'd?
Discourse I prethee on this Turrets top.
Talbot. The Earle of Bedford had a Prisoner,
Call'd the braue Lord *Ponton de Santrayle*,
For him was I exchang'd, and ransom'd.
But with a baser man of Armes by farre,
Once in contempt they would haue barter'd me:
Which I disdaining, scorn'd, and craued death,
Rather then I would be so pil'd esteem'd:
In fine, redeem'd I was as I desir'd.
But O, the trecherous *Falstaffe* wounds my heart,
Whom with my bare fists I would execute,
If I now had him brought into my power.
Salisb. Yet tell'st thou not, how thou wert entertain'd.
Tal. With scoffes and scornes, and contumelious taunts,
In open Market-place produc't they me,
To be a publique spectacle to all:
Here, sayd they, is the Terror of the French,
The Scar-Crow that affrights our Children so.
Then broke I from the Officers that led me,
And with my nayles digg'd stones out of the ground,
To hurle at the beholders of my shame.
My grisly countenance made others flye,
None durst come neere, for feare of suddaine death.
In Iron Walls they deem'd me not secure:
So great feare of my Name 'mongst them were spread,
That they suppos'd I could rend Barres of Steele,
And spurne in pieces Posts of Adamant.
Wherefore a guard of chosen Shot I had,
That walkt about me euery Minute while:
And if I did but stirre out of my Bed,
Ready they were to shoot me to the heart.

Enter the Boy with a Linstock.

Salisb. I grieue to heare what torments you endur'd,
But we will be reueng'd sufficiently.
Now it is Supper time in Orleance:
Here, through this Grate, I count each one,
And view the Frenchmen how they fortifie:
Let vs looke in, the sight will much delight thee:
Sir *Thomas Gargraue*, and Sir *William Glansdale*,
Let me haue your expresse opinions,
Where is best place to make our Batt'ry next?
Gargraue. I thinke at the North Gate, for there stands Lords.
Glansdale. And I heere, at the Bulwarke of the Bridge.
Talb. For ought I see, this Citie must be famisht,
Or with light Skirmishes enfeebled. *Here they shot, and Salisbury falls downe.*
Salisb. O Lord haue mercy on vs, wretched sinners.
Gargraue. O Lord haue mercy on me, wofull man.
Talb. What chance is this, that suddenly hath crost vs?
Speake *Salisbury*; at least, if thou canst, speake:
How far'st thou, Mirror of all Martiall men?
One of thy Eyes, and thy Cheekes side struck off?
Accursed Tower, accursed fatall Hand,
That hath contriu'd this wofull Tragedie.
In thirteene Battailes, *Salisbury* o'recame:
Henry the Fift he first trayn'd to the Warres.
Whil'st any Trumpe did sound, or Drum struck vp,
His Sword did ne're leaue striking in the field.
Yet liu'st thou *Salisbury*? though thy speech doth fayle,
One Eye thou hast to looke to Heauen for grace.
The Sunne with one Eye vieweth all the World.
Heauen be thou gracious to none aliue,
If *Salisbury* wants mercy at thy hands.
Beare hence his Body, I will helpe to bury it.
Sir *Thomas Gargraue*, hast thou any life?
Speake vnto *Talbot*, nay, looke vp to him.
Salisbury cheare thy Spirit with this comfort,
Thou shalt not dye whiles——
He beckens with his hand, and smiles on me:
As who should say, When I am dead and gone,
Remember to auenge me on the French.
Plantaginet I will, and like thee,
Play on the Lute, beholding the Townes burne:
Wretched shall France be onely in my Name.

Here an Alarum, and it Thunders and Lightens.

What stirre is this? what tumult's in the Heauens?
Whence commeth this Alarum, and the noyse?

Enter a Messenger.

Mess. My Lord, my Lord, the French haue gather'd head.
The Dolphin, with one *Ioane de Puzel* ioyn'd,
A holy Prophetesse, new risen vp,
Is come with a great Power, to rayse the Siege.

Here Salisbury lifteth himselfe vp, and groanes.

Talb. Heare, heare, how dying *Salisbury* doth groane,
It irkes his heart he cannot be reueng'd.
Frenchmen, Ile be a *Salisbury* to you.
Puzel or *Pussel*, Dolphin or Dog-fish,
Your hearts Ile stampe out with my Horses heeles,
And make a Quagmire of your mingled braines.
Conuey me *Salisbury* into his Tent,
And then wee'le try what these dastard Frenchmen dare.

Alarum. Exeunt.

Here an Alarum againe, and Talbot pursueth the Dolphin, and driueth him: Then enter Ioane de Puzel, driuing Englishmen before her. Then enter Talbot.

Talb. Where is my strength, my valour, and my force?
Our English Troupes retyre, I cannot stay them,
A Woman clad in Armour chaseth them.

Enter Puzel.

Here, here shee comes. Ile haue a bowt with thee:
Deuill, or Deuils Dam, Ile coniure thee:
Blood will I draw on thee, thou art a Witch,
And straightway giue thy Soule to him thou seru'st.
Puzel. Come, come, 'tis onely I that must disgrace thee. *Here they fight.*
Talb. Heauens, can you suffer Hell so to preuayle?
My brest Ile burst with straining of my courage,
And from my shoulders crack my Armes asunder,
But I will chastise this high-minded Strumpet.

They fight againe.

Puzel. *Talbot* farwell, thy houre is not yet come,
I must goe Victuall Orleance forthwith:

A short Alarum: then enter the Towne with Souldiers.

O're-

O're-take me if thou canst, I scorne thy strength.
Goe, goe, cheare vp thy hungry-starued men,
Helpe *Salisbury* to make his Testament,
This Day is ours, as many more shall be. *Exit.*

Talb. My thoughts are whirled like a Potters Wheele,
I know not where I am, nor what I doe:
A Witch by feare, not force, like *Hannibal*,
Driues back our troupes, and conquers as she lists:
So Bees with smoake, and Doues with noysome stench,
Are from their Hyues and Houses driuen away.
They call'd vs, for our fiercenesse, English Dogges,
Now like to Whelpes, we crying runne away.

A short Alarum.

Hearke Countreymen, eyther renew the fight,
Or teare the Lyons out of Englands Coat;
Renounce your Soyle, giue Sheepe in Lyons stead:
Sheepe run not halfe so trecherous from the Wolfe,
Or Horse or Oxen from the Leopard,
As you flye from your oft-subdued slaues.

Alarum. Here another Skirmish.

It will not be, retyre into your Trenches:
You all consented vnto *Salisburies* death,
For none would strike a stroake in his reuenge.
Puzel is entred into Orleance,
In spight of vs, or ought that we could doe.
O would I were to dye with *Salisbury*,
The shame hereof, will make me hide my head.

Exit Talbot.

Alarum, Retreat, Flourish.

Enter on the Walls, Puzel, Dolphin, Reigneir, Alanson, and Souldiers.

Puzel. Aduance our wauing Colours on the Walls,
Rescu'd is Orleance from the English.
Thus *Ioane de Puzel* hath perform'd her word.

Dolph. Diuinest Creature, *Astrea's* Daughter,
How shall I honour thee for this successe?
Thy promises are like *Adonis* Garden,
That one day bloom'd, and fruitfull were the next.
France, triumph in thy glorious Prophetesse,
Recouer'd is the Towne of Orleance,
More blessed hap did ne're befall our State.

Reigneir. Why ring not out the Bells alowd,
Throughout the Towne?
Dolphin command the Citizens make Bonfires,
And feast and banquet in the open streets,
To celebrate the ioy that God hath giuen vs.

Alans. All France will be repleat with mirth and ioy,
When they shall heare how we haue play'd the men.

Dolph. 'Tis *Ioane*, not we, by whom the day is wonne:
For which, I will diuide my Crowne with her,
And all the Priests and Fryers in my Realme,
Shall in procession sing her endlesse prayse.
A statelyer Pyramis to her Ile reare,
Then *Rhodophe's* or *Memphis* euer was.
In memorie of her, when she is dead,
Her Ashes, in an Vrne more precious
Then the rich-iewel'd Coffer of *Darius*,
Transported, shall be at high Festiuals
Before the Kings and Queenes of France.
No longer on Saint *Dennis* will we cry,
But *Ioane de Puzel* shall be France's Saint.
Come in, and let vs Banquet Royally,
After this Golden Day of Victorie.

Flourish. Exeunt.

Actus Secundus. Scena Prima.

Enter a Sergeant of a Band, with two Sentinels.

Ser. Sirs, take your places, and be vigilant:
If any noyse or Souldier you perceiue
Neere to the walles, by some apparant signe
Let vs haue knowledge at the Court of Guard.

Sent. Sergeant you shall. Thus are poore Seruitors
(When others sleepe vpon their quiet beds)
Constrain'd to watch in darknesse, raine, and cold.

Enter Talbot, Bedford, and Burgundy, with scaling Ladders: Their Drummes beating a Dead March.

Tal. Lord Regent, and redoubted *Burgundy*,
By whose approach, the Regions of *Artoys*,
Wallon, and *Picardy*, are friends to vs:
This happy night, the Frenchmen are secure,
Hauing all day carows'd and banquetted,
Embrace we then this opportunitie,
As fitting best to quittance their deceite,
Contriu'd by Art, and balefull Sorcerie.

Bed. Coward of France, how much he wrongs his fame,
Dispairing of his owne armes fortitude,
To ioyne with Witches, and the helpe of Hell.

Bur. Traitors haue neuer other company.
But what's that *Puzell* whom they tearme so pure?

Tal. A Maid, they say.

Bed. A Maid? And be so martiall?

Bur. Pray God she proue not masculine ere long:
If vnderneath the Standard of the French
She carry Armour, as she hath begun.

Tal. Well, let them practise and conuerse with spirits.
God is our Fortresse, in whose conquering name
Let vs resolue to scale their flinty bulwarkes.

Bed. Ascend braue *Talbot*, we will follow thee.

Tal. Not altogether: Better farre I guesse,
That we do make our entrance seuerall wayes:
That if it chance the one of vs do faile,
The other yet may rise against their force.

Bed. Agreed; Ile to yond corner.

Bur. And I to this.

Tal. And heere will *Talbot* mount, or make his graue.
Now *Salisbury*, for thee and for the right
Of English *Henry*, shall this night appeare
How much in duty, I am bound to both.

Sent. Arme, arme, the enemy doth make assault.

Cry, S. George, A Talbot.

The French leape ore the walles in their shirts. Enter seuerall wayes, Bastard, Alanson, Reignier, halfe ready, and halfe vnready.

Alan. How now my Lords? what all vnreadie so?

Bast. Vnready? I and glad we scap'd so well.

Reig. 'Twas time (I trow) to wake and leaue our beds,
Hearing Alarums at our Chamber doores.

Alan. Of all exploits since first I follow'd Armes,
Nere heard I of a warlike enterprize

More

More venturous, or desperate then this.
Bast. I thinke this *Talbot* be a Fiend of Hell.
Reig. If not of Hell, the Heauens sure fauour him.
Alans. Here commeth *Charles*, I maruell how he sped?

Enter Charles and Ioane.

Bast. Tut, holy *Ioane* was his defensiue Guard.
Charl. Is this thy cunning, thou deceitfull Dame?
Didst thou at first, to flatter vs withall,
Make vs partakers of a little gayne,
That now our losse might be ten times so much?
Ioane. Wherefore is *Charles* impatient with his friend?
At all times will you haue my Power alike?
Sleeping or waking, must I still preuayle,
Or will you blame and lay the fault on me?
Improuident Souldiors, had your Watch been good,
This sudden Mischiefe neuer could haue falne.
Charl. Duke of Alanson, this was your default,
That being Captaine of the Watch to Night,
Did looke no better to that weightie Charge.
Alans. Had all your Quarters been as safely kept,
As that whereof I had the gouernment,
We had not beene thus shamefully surpriz'd.
Bast. Mine was secure.
Reig. And so was mine, my Lord.
Charl. And for my selfe, most part of all this Night
Within her Quarter, and mine owne Precinct,
I was imploy'd in passing to and fro,
About relieuing of the Centinels.
Then how, or which way, should they first breake in?
Ioane. Question (my Lords) no further of the case,
How or which way; 'tis sure they found some place,
But weakely guarded, where the breach was made:
And now there rests no other shift but this,
To gather our Souldiors, scatter'd and disperc't,
And lay new Plat-formes to endammage them.
Exeunt.

Alarum. Enter a Souldier, crying, a Talbot, a Talbot: they flye, leauing their Clothes behind.

Sould. Ile be so bold to take what they haue left:
The Cry of *Talbot* serues me for a Sword,
For I haue loaden me with many Spoyles,
Vsing no other Weapon but his Name. *Exit.*

Enter Talbot, Bedford, Burgundie.

Bedf. The Day begins to breake, and Night is fled,
Whose pitchy Mantle ouer-vayl'd the Earth.
Here sound Retreat, and cease our hot pursuit. *Retreat.*
Talb. Bring forth the Body of old *Salisbury*,
And here aduance it in the Market-Place,
The middle Centure of this cursed Towne.
Now haue I pay'd my Vow vnto his Soule:
For euery drop of blood was drawne from him,
There hath at least fiue Frenchmen dyed to night.
And that hereafter Ages may behold
What ruine happened in reuenge of him,
Within their chiefest Temple Ile erect
A Tombe, wherein his Corps shall be interr'd:
Vpon the which, that euery one may reade,
Shall be engrau'd the sacke of Orleance,
The trecherous manner of his mournefull death,
And what a terror he had beene to France.
But Lords, in all our bloudy Massacre,
I muse we met not with the Dolphins Grace,
His new-come Champion, vertuous *Ioane* of Acre,
Nor any of his false Confederates.
Bedf. 'Tis thought Lord *Talbot*, when the fight began,
Rows'd on the sudden from their drowsie Beds,
They did amongst the troupes of armed men,
Leape o're the Walls for refuge in the field.
Burg. My selfe, as farre as I could well discerne,
For smoake, and duskie vapours of the night,
Am sure I scar'd the Dolphin and his Trull,
When Arme in Arme they both came swiftly running,
Like to a payre of louing Turtle-Doues,
That could not liue asunder day or night.
After that things are set in order here,
Wee'le follow them with all the power we haue.

Enter a Messenger.

Mess. All hayle, my Lords: which of this Princely trayne
Call ye the Warlike *Talbot*, for his Acts
So much applauded through the Realme of France?
Talb. Here is the *Talbot*, who would speak with him?
Mess. The vertuous Lady, Countesse of Ouergne,
With modestie admiring thy Renowne,
By me entreats (great Lord) thou would'st vouchsafe
To visit her poore Castle where she lyes,
That she may boast she hath beheld the man,
Whose glory fills the World with lowd report.
Burg. Is it euen so? Nay, then I see our Warres
Will turne vnto a peacefull Comick sport,
When Ladyes craue to be encountred with.
You may not (my Lord) despise her gentle suit.
Talb. Ne're trust me then: for when a World of men
Could not preuayle with all their Oratorie,
Yet hath a Womans kindnesse ouer-rul'd:
And therefore tell her, I returne great thankes,
And in submission will attend on her.
Will not your Honors beare me company?
Bedf. No, truly, 'tis more then manners will:
And I haue heard it sayd, Vnbidden Guests
Are often welcommest when they are gone.
Talb. Well then, alone (since there's no remedie)
I meane to proue this Ladyes courtesie.
Come hither Captaine, you perceiue my minde.
Whispers.
Capt. I doe my Lord, and meane accordingly.
Exeunt.

Enter Countesse.

Count. Porter, remember what I gaue in charge,
And when you haue done so, bring the Keyes to me.
Port. Madame, I will. *Exit.*
Count. The Plot is layd, if all things fall out right,
I shall as famous be by this exploit,
As Scythian *Tomyris* by *Cyrus* death.
Great is the rumour of this dreadfull Knight,
And his atchieuements of no lesse account:
Faine would mine eyes be witnesse with mine eares,
To giue their censure of these rare reports.

Enter Messenger and Talbot.

Mess. Madame, according as your Ladyship desir'd,
By Message crau'd, so is Lord *Talbot* come.
Count. And he is welcome: what? is this the man?
Mess. Madame, it is.
Count. Is this the Scourge of France?
Is this the *Talbot*, so much fear'd abroad?
That with his Name the Mothers still their Babes?
I see Report is fabulous and false.

I thought I should haue seene some *Hercules*,
A second *Hector*, for his grim aspect,
And large proportion of his strong knit Limbes.
Alas, this is a Child, a silly Dwarfe:
It cannot be, this weake and writhled shrimpe
Should strike such terror to his Enemies.

Talb. Madame, I haue beene bold to trouble you:
But since your Ladyship is not at leysure,
Ile sort some other time to visit you.

Count. What meanes he now?
Goe aske him, whither he goes?

Mess. Stay my Lord *Talbot*, for my Lady craues,
To know the cause of your abrupt departure?

Talb. Marry, for that shee's in a wrong beleefe,
I goe to certifie her *Talbot's* here.

Enter Porter with Keyes.

Count. If thou be he, then art thou Prisoner.

Talb. Prisoner? to whom?

Count. To me, blood-thirstie Lord:
And for that cause I trayn'd thee to my House.
Long time thy shadow hath been thrall to me,
For in my Gallery thy Picture hangs:
But now the substance shall endure the like,
And I will chayne these Legges and Armes of thine,
That hast by Tyrannie these many yeeres
Wasted our Countrey, slaine our Citizens,
And sent our Sonnes and Husbands captiuate.

Talb. Ha, ha, ha.

Count. Laughest thou Wretch?
Thy mirth shall turne to moane.

Talb. I laugh to see your Ladyship so fond,
To thinke, that you haue ought but *Talbots* shadow,
Whereon to practise your seueritie.

Count. Why? art not thou the man?

Talb. I am indeede.

Count. Then haue I substance too.

Talb. No, no, I am but shadow of my selfe:
You are deceiu'd, my substance is not here;
For what you see, is but the smallest part,
And least proportion of Humanitie:
I tell you Madame, were the whole Frame here,
It is of such a spacious loftie pitch,
Your Roofe were not sufficient to contayn't.

Count. This is a Riddling Merchant for the nonce,
He will be here, and yet he is not here:
How can these contrarieties agree?

Talb. That will I shew you presently.

Winds his Horne, Drummes strike vp, a Peale of Ordenance: Enter Souldiors.

How say you Madame? are you now perswaded,
That *Talbot* is but shadow of himselfe?
These are his substance, sinewes, armes, and strength,
With which he yoaketh your rebellious Neckes,
Razeth your Cities, and subuerts your Townes,
And in a moment makes them desolate.

Count. Victorious *Talbot*, pardon my abuse,
I finde thou art no lesse then Fame hath bruited,
And more then may be gathered by thy shape.
Let my presumption not prouoke thy wrath,
For I am sorry, that with reuerence
I did not entertaine thee as thou art.

Talb. Be not dismay'd, faire Lady, nor misconster
The minde of *Talbot*, as you did mistake
The outward composition of his body.
What you haue done, hath not offended me:
Nor other satisfaction doe I craue,
But onely with your patience, that we may
Taste of your Wine, and see what Cates you haue,
For Souldiers stomacks alwayes serue them well.

Count. With all my heart, and thinke me honored,
To feast so great a Warrior in my House. *Exeunt.*

Enter Richard Plantagenet, Warwick, Somerset, Poole, and others.

Yorke. Great Lords and Gentlemen,
What meanes this silence?
Dare no man answer in a Case of Truth?

Suff. Within the Temple Hall we were too lowd,
The Garden here is more conuenient.

York. Then say at once, if I maintain'd the Truth:
Or else was wrangling *Somerset* in th'error?

Suff. Faith I haue beene a Truant in the Law,
And neuer yet could frame my will to it,
And therefore frame the Law vnto my will.

Som. Iudge you, my Lord of Warwicke, then betweene vs.

War. Between two Hawks, which flyes the higher pitch,
Between two Dogs, which hath the deeper mouth,
Between two Blades, which beares the better temper,
Between two Horses, which doth beare him best,
Between two Girles, which hath the merryest eye,
I haue perhaps some shallow spirit of Iudgement:
But in these nice sharpe Quillets of the Law,
Good faith I am no wiser then a Daw.

York. Tut, tut, here is a mannerly forbearance:
The truth appeares so naked on my side,
That any purblind eye may find it out.

Som. And on my side it is so well apparrell'd,
So cleare, so shining, and so euident,
That it will glimmer through a blind-mans eye.

York. Since you are tongue-ty'd, and so loth to speake,
In dumbe significants proclayme your thoughts:
Let him that is a true-borne Gentleman,
And stands vpon the honor of his birth,
If he suppose that I haue pleaded truth,
From off this Bryer pluck a white Rose with me.

Som. Let him that is no Coward, nor no Flatterer,
But dare maintaine the partie of the truth,
Pluck a red Rose from off this Thorne with me.

War. I loue no Colours: and without all colour
Of base insinuating flatterie,
I pluck this white Rose with *Plantagenet*.

Suff. I pluck this red Rose, with young *Somerset*,
And say withall, I thinke he held the right.

Vernon. Stay Lords and Gentlemen, and pluck no more
Till you conclude, that he vpon whose side
The fewest Roses are cropt from the Tree,
Shall yeeld the other in the right opinion.

Som. Good Master *Vernon*, it is well obiected:
If I haue fewest, I subscribe in silence.

York. And I.

Vernon. Then for the truth, and plainnesse of the Case,
I pluck this pale and Maiden Blossome here,
Giuing my Verdict on the white Rose side.

Som. Prick not your finger as you pluck it off,
Least bleeding, you doe paint the white Rose red,
And fall on my side so against your will.

Vernon. If I, my Lord, for my opinion bleed,
Opinion shall be Surgeon to my hurt,
And keepe me on the side where still I am.

Som. Well, well, come on, who else?

Lawyer. Vn-

Lawyer. Vnlesse my Studie and my Bookes be false,
The argument you held, was wrong in you;
In signe whereof, I pluck a white Rose too.
Yorke. Now *Somerset*, where is your argument?
Som. Here in my Scabbard, meditating, that
Shall dye your white Rose in a bloody red.
York. Meane time your cheeks do counterfeit our Roses:
For pale they looke with feare, as witnessing
The truth on our side.
Som. No *Plantagenet*:
'Tis not for feare, but anger, that thy cheekes
Blush for pure shame, to counterfeit our Roses,
And yet thy tongue will not confesse thy error.
Yorke. Hath not thy Rose a Canker, *Somerset*?
Som. Hath not thy Rose a Thorne, *Plantagenet*?
Yorke. I, sharpe and piercing to maintaine his truth,
Whiles thy consuming Canker eates his falsehood.
Som. Well, Ile find friends to weare my bleeding Roses,
That shall maintaine what I haue said is true,
Where false *Plantagenet* dare not be seene.
Yorke. Now by this Maiden Blossome in my hand,
I scorne thee and thy fashion, peeuish Boy.
Suff. Turne not thy scornes this way, *Plantagenet*.
Yorke. Prowd *Poole*, I will, and scorne both him and thee.
Suff. Ile turne my part thereof into thy throat.
Som. Away, away, good *William de la Poole*,
We grace the Yeoman, by conuersing with him.
Warw. Now by Gods will thou wrong'st him, *Somerset*:
His Grandfather was *Lyonel* Duke of Clarence,
Third Sonne to the third *Edward* King of England:
Spring Crestlesse Yeomen from so deepe a Root?
Yorke. He beares him on the place's Priuiledge,
Or durst not for his crauen heart say thus.
Som. By him that made me, Ile maintaine my words
On any Plot of Ground in Christendome.
Was not thy Father, *Richard*, Earle of Cambridge,
For Treason executed in our late Kings dayes?
And by his Treason, stand'st not thou attainted,
Corrupted, and exempt from ancient Gentry?
His Trespas yet liues guiltie in thy blood,
And till thou be restor'd, thou art a Yeoman.
Yorke. My Father was attached, not attainted,
Condemn'd to dye for Treason, but no Traytor;
And that Ile proue on better men then *Somerset*,
Were growing time once ripened to my will.
For your partaker *Poole*, and you your selfe,
Ile note you in my Booke of Memorie,
To scourge you for this apprehension:
Looke to it well, and say you are well warn'd.
Som. Ah, thou shalt finde vs ready for thee still:
And know vs by these Colours for thy Foes,
For these, my friends in spight of thee shall weare.
Yorke. And by my Soule, this pale and angry Rose,
As Cognizance of my blood-drinking hate,
Will I for euer, and my Faction weare,
Vntill it wither with me to my Graue,
Or flourish to the height of my Degree.
Suff. Goe forward, and be choak'd with thy ambition:
And so farwell, vntill I meet thee next. *Exit.*
Som. Haue with thee *Poole*: Farwell ambitious *Richard*. *Exit.*
Yorke. How I am brau'd, and must perforce endure it?
Warw. This blot that they obiect against your House,
Shall be whipt out in the next Parliament,
Call'd for the Truce of *Winchester* and *Gloucester*:
And if thou be not then created *Yorke*
I will not liue to be accounted *Warwicke*.
Meane time, in signall of my loue to thee,
Against prowd *Somerset*, and *William Poole*,
Will I vpon thy partie weare this Rose.
And here I prophecie: this brawle to day,
Growne to this faction in the Temple Garden,
Shall send betweene the Red-Rose and the White,
A thousand Soules to Death and deadly Night.
Yorke. Good Master *Vernon*, I am bound to you,
That you on my behalfe would pluck a Flower.
Ver. In your behalfe still will I weare the same.
Lawyer. And so will I.
Yorke. Thankes gentle.
Come, let vs foure to Dinner: I dare say,
This Quarrell will drinke Blood another day.
Exeunt.

Enter Mortimer, brought in a Chayre, and Iaylors.

Mort. Kind Keepers of my weake decaying Age,
Let dying *Mortimer* here rest himselfe.
Euen like a man new haled from the Wrack,
So fare my Limbes with long Imprisonment:
And these gray Locks, the Pursuiuants of death,
Nestor-like aged, in an Age of Care,
Argue the end of *Edmund Mortimer*.
These Eyes, like Lampes, whose wasting Oyle is spent,
Waxe dimme, as drawing to their Exigent.
Weake Shoulders, ouer-borne with burthening Griefe,
And pyth-lesse Armes, like to a withered Vine,
That droupes his sappe-lesse Branches to the ground.
Yet are these Feet, whose strength-lesse stay is numme,
(Vnable to support this Lumpe of Clay)
Swift-winged with desire to get a Graue,
As witting I no other comfort haue.
But tell me, Keeper, will my Nephew come?
Keeper. *Richard Plantagenet*, my Lord, will come:
We sent vnto the Temple, vnto his Chamber,
And answer was return'd, that he will come.
Mort. Enough: my Soule shall then be satisfied.
Poore Gentleman, his wrong doth equall mine.
Since *Henry Monmouth* first began to reigne,
Before whose Glory I was great in Armes,
This loathsome sequestration haue I had;
And euen since then, hath *Richard* beene obscur'd,
Depriu'd of Honor and Inheritance.
But now, the Arbitrator of Despaires,
Iust Death, kinde Vmpire of mens miseries,
With sweet enlargement doth dismisse me hence:
I would his troubles likewise were expir'd,
That so he might recouer what was lost.

Enter Richard.

Keeper. My Lord, your louing Nephew now is come.
Mor. *Richard Plantagenet*, my friend, is he come?
Rich. I Noble Vnckle, thus ignobly vs'd,
Your Nephew, late despised *Richard*, comes.
Mort. Direct mine Armes, I may embrace his Neck,
And in his Bosome spend my latter gaspe.
Oh tell me when my Lippes doe touch his Cheekes,
That I may kindly giue one fainting Kisse.
And now declare sweet Stem from *Yorkes* great Stock,
Why didst thou say of late thou wert despis'd?

Rich. First

Rich. First, leane thine aged Back against mine Arme,
And in that ease, Ile tell thee my Disease.
This day in argument vpon a Case,
Some words there grew 'twixt *Somerset* and me:
Among which tearmes, he vs'd his lauish tongue,
And did vpbrayd me with my Fathers death;
Which obloquie set barres before my tongue,
Else with the like I had requited him.
Therefore good Vnckle, for my Fathers sake,
In honor of a true *Plantagenet*,
And for Alliance sake, declare the cause
My Father, Earle of Cambridge, lost his Head.

Mort. That cause (faire Nephew) that imprison'd me,
And hath detayn'd me all my flowring Youth,
Within a loathsome Dungeon, there to pyne,
Was cursed Instrument of his decease.

Rich. Discouer more at large what cause that was,
For I am ignorant, and cannot guesse.

Mort. I will, if that my fading breath permit,
And Death approach not, ere my Tale be done.
Henry the Fourth, Grandfather to this King,
Depos'd his Nephew *Richard*, *Edwards* Sonne,
The first begotten, and the lawfull Heire
Of *Edward* King, the Third of that Descent.
During whose Reigne, the *Percies* of the North,
Finding his Vsurpation most vniust,
Endeuour'd my aduancement to the Throne.
The reason mou'd these Warlike Lords to this,
Was, for that (young *Richard* thus remou'd,
Leauing no Heire begotten of his Body)
I was the next by Birth and Parentage:
For by my Mother, I deriued am
From *Lionel* Duke of Clarence, third Sonne
To King *Edward* the Third; whereas hee,
From *Iohn* of Gaunt doth bring his Pedigree,
Being but fourth of that Heroick Lyne.
But marke: as in this haughtie great attempt,
They laboured, to plant the rightfull Heire,
I lost my Libertie, and they their Liues.
Long after this, when *Henry* the Fift
(Succeeding his Father *Bullingbrooke*) did reigne;
Thy Father, Earle of Cambridge, then deriu'd
From famous *Edmund Langley*, Duke of Yorke,
Marrying my Sister, that thy Mother was;
Againe, in pitty of my hard distresse,
Leuied an Army, weening to redeeme,
And haue install'd me in the Diademe:
But as the rest, so fell that Noble Earle,
And was beheaded. Thus the *Mortimers*,
In whom the Title rested, were supprest.

Rich. Of which, my Lord, your Honor is the last.

Mort. True; and thou seest, that I no Issue haue,
And that my fainting words doe warrant death:
Thou art my Heire; the rest, I wish thee gather:
But yet be wary in thy studious care.

Rich. Thy graue admonishments preuayle with me:
But yet me thinkes, my Fathers execution
Was nothing lesse then bloody Tyranny.

Mort. With silence, Nephew, be thou pollitick.
Strong fixed is the House of *Lancaster*,
And like a Mountaine, not to be remou'd.
But now thy Vnckle is remouing hence,
As Princes doe their Courts, when they are cloy'd
With long continuance in a setled place.

Rich. O Vnckle, would some part of my young yeeres
Might but redeeme the passage of your Age.

Mort. Thou do'st then wrong me, as ÿ slaughterer doth,
Which giueth many Wounds, when one will kill.
Mourne not, except thou sorrow for my good,
Onely giue order for my Funerall.
And so farewell, and faire be all thy hopes,
And prosperous be thy Life in Peace and Warre. *Dyes.*

Rich. And Peace, no Warre, befall thy parting Soule.
In Prison hast thou spent a Pilgrimage,
And like a Hermite ouer-past thy dayes.
Well, I will locke his Councell in my Brest,
And what I doe imagine, let that rest.
Keepers conuey him hence, and I my selfe
Will see his Buryall better then his Life. *Exit.*
Here dyes the duskie Torch of *Mortimer*,
Choakt with Ambition of the meaner sort.
And for those Wrongs, those bitter Iniuries,
Which *Somerset* hath offer'd to my House,
I doubt not, but with Honor to redresse.
And therefore haste I to the Parliament,
Eyther to be restored to my Blood,
Or make my will th'aduantage of my good. *Exit.*

Actus Tertius. Scena Prima.

Flourish. Enter King, Exeter, Gloster, Winchester, Warwick, Somerset, Suffolk, Richard Plantagenet. Gloster offers to put vp a Bill: Winchester snatches it, teares it.

Winch. Com'st thou with deepe premeditated Lines?
With written Pamphlets, studiously deuis'd?
Humfrey of Gloster, if thou canst accuse,
Or ought intend'st to lay vnto my charge,
Doe it without inuention, suddenly,
As I with sudden, and extemporall speech,
Purpose to answer what thou canst obiect.

Glo. Presumptuous Priest, this place comands my patiēce,
Or thou should'st finde thou hast dis-honor'd me.
Thinke not, although in Writing I preferr'd
The manner of thy vile outragious Crymes,
That therefore I haue forg'd, or am not able
Verbatim to rehearse the Methode of my Penne.
No Prelate, such is thy audacious wickednesse,
Thy lewd, pestiferous, and dissentious prancks,
As very Infants prattle of thy pride.
Thou art a most pernitious Vsurer,
Froward by nature, Enemie to Peace,
Lasciuious, wanton, more then well beseemes
A man of thy Profession, and Degree.
And for thy Trecherie, what's more manifest?
In that thou layd'st a Trap to take my Life,
As well at London Bridge, as at the Tower.
Beside, I feare me, if thy thoughts were sifted,
The King, thy Soueraigne, is not quite exempt
From enuious mallice of thy swelling heart.

Winch. *Gloster*, I doe defie thee. Lords vouchsafe
To giue me hearing what I shall reply.
If I were couetous, ambitious, or peruerse,
As he will haue me: how am I so poore?
Or how haps it, I seeke not to aduance
Or rayse my selfe? but keepe my wonted Calling.
And for Dissention, who preferreth Peace
More then I doe? except I be prouok'd.
No, my good Lords, it is not that offends,
It is not that, that hath incens'd the Duke:
It is because no one should sway but hee,
No one, but hee, should be about the King;
And that engenders Thunder in his breast,

And makes him rore these Accusations forth.
But he shall know I am as good.
Glost. As good?
Thou Bastard of my Grandfather.
Winch. I, Lordly Sir: for what are you, I pray,
But one imperious in anothers Throne?
Glost. Am I not Protector, sawcie Priest?
Winch. And am not I a Prelate of the Church?
Glost. Yes, as an Out-law in a Castle keepes,
And vseth it, to patronage his Theft.
Winch. Vnreuerent *Glocester*.
Glost. Thou art reuerent,
Touching thy Spirituall Function, not thy Life.
Winch. Rome shall remedie this.
Warw. Roame thither then.
My Lord, it were your dutie to forbeare.
Som. I, see the Bishop be not ouer-borne:
Me thinkes my Lord should be Religious,
And know the Office that belongs to such.
Warw. Me thinkes his Lordship should be humbler,
It fitteth not a Prelate so to plead.
Som. Yes, when his holy State is toucht so neere.
Warw. State holy, or vnhallow'd, what of that?
Is not his Grace Protector to the King?
Rich. *Plantagenet* I see must hold his tongue,
Least it be said, Speake Sirrha when you should:
Must your bold Verdict entertalke with Lords?
Else would I haue a fling at *Winchester*.
King. Vnckles of *Gloster*, and of *Winchester*,
The speciall Watch-men of our English Weale,
I would preuayle, if Prayers might preuayle,
To ioyne your hearts in loue and amitie.
Oh, what a Scandall is it to our Crowne,
That two such Noble Peeres as ye should iarre?
Beleeue me, Lords, my tender yeeres can tell,
Ciuill dissention is a viperous Worme,
That gnawes the Bowels of the Common-wealth.

A noyse within, Downe with the Tawny-Coats.

King. What tumult's this?
Warw. An Vprore, I dare warrant,
Begun through malice of the Bishops men.

A noyse againe, Stones, Stones.

Enter Maior.

Maior. Oh my good Lords, and vertuous *Henry*,
Pitty the Citie of London, pitty vs:
The Bishop, and the Duke of Glosters men,
Forbidden late to carry any Weapon,
Haue fill'd their Pockets full of peeble stones;
And banding themselues in contrary parts,
Doe pelt so fast at one anothers Pate,
That many haue their giddy braynes knockt out:
Our Windowes are broke downe in euery Street,
And we, for feare, compell'd to shut our Shops.

Enter in skirmish with bloody Pates.

King. We charge you, on allegeance to our selfe,
To hold your slaughtring hands, and keepe the Peace:
Pray' Vnckle *Gloster* mittigate this strife.
1. Seruing. Nay, if we be forbidden Stones, wee'le fall to it with our Teeth.
2. Seruing. Doe what ye dare, we are as resolute.

Skirmish againe.

Glost. You of my houshold, leaue this peeuish broyle,
And set this vnaccustom'd fight aside.
3. Seru. My Lord, we know your Grace to be a man
Iust, and vpright; and for your Royall Birth,
Inferior to none, but to his Maiestie:
And ere that we will suffer such a Prince,
So kinde a Father of the Common-weale,
To be disgraced by an Inke-horne Mate,
Wee and our Wiues and Children all will fight,
And haue our bodyes slaughtred by thy foes.
1. Seru. I, and the very parings of our Nayles
Shall pitch a Field when we are dead.

Begin againe.

Glost. Stay, stay, I say:
And if you loue me, as you say you doe,
Let me perswade you to forbeare a while.
King. Oh, how this discord doth afflict my Soule.
Can you, my Lord of Winchester, behold
My sighes and teares, and will not once relent?
Who should be pittifull, if you be not?
Or who should study to preferre a Peace,
If holy Church-men take delight in broyles?
Warw. Yeeld my Lord Protector, yeeld *Winchester*,
Except you meane with obstinate repulse
To slay your Soueraigne, and destroy the Realme.
You see what Mischiefe, and what Murther too,
Hath beene enacted through your enmitie:
Then be at peace, except ye thirst for blood.
Winch. He shall submit, or I will neuer yeeld.
Glost. Compassion on the King commands me stoupe,
Or I would see his heart out, ere the Priest
Should euer get that priuiledge of me.
Warw. Behold my Lord of Winchester, the Duke
Hath banisht moodie discontented fury,
As by his smoothed Browes it doth appeare:
Why looke you still so sterne, and tragicall?
Glost. Here *Winchester*, I offer thee my Hand.
King. Fie Vnckle *Beauford*, I haue heard you preach,
That Mallice was a great and grieuous sinne:
And will not you maintaine the thing you teach?
But proue a chiefe offendor in the same.
Warw. Sweet King: the Bishop hath a kindly gyrd:
For shame my Lord of Winchester relent;
What, shall a Child instruct you what to doe?
Winch. Well, Duke of Gloster, I will yeeld to thee
Loue for thy Loue, and Hand for Hand I giue.
Glost. I, but I feare me with a hollow Heart.
See here my Friends and louing Countreymen,
This token serueth for a Flagge of Truce,
Betwixt our selues, and all our followers:
So helpe me God, as I dissemble not.
Winch. So helpe me God, as I intend it not.
King. Oh louing Vnckle, kinde Duke of Gloster,
How ioyfull am I made by this Contract.
Away my Masters, trouble vs no more,
But ioyne in friendship, as your Lords haue done.
1. Seru. Content, Ile to the Surgeons.
2. Seru. And so will I.
3. Seru. And I will see what Physick the Tauerne affords. *Exeunt.*
Warw. Accept this Scrowle, most gracious Soueraigne,
Which in the Right of *Richard Plantagenet*,
We doe exhibite to your Maiestie.
Glo. Well vrg'd, my Lord of Warwick: for sweet Prince,
And if your Grace marke euery circumstance,
You haue great reason to doe *Richard* right,
Especially for those occasions
At Eltam Place I told your Maiestie.

King. And those occasions, Vnckle, were of force:
Therefore my louing Lords, our pleasure is,
That *Richard* be restored to his Blood.

Warw. Let *Richard* be restored to his Blood,
So shall his Fathers wrongs be recompenc't.

Winch. As will the rest, so willeth *Winchester*.

King. If *Richard* will be true, not that all alone.
But all the whole Inheritance I giue,
That doth belong vnto the House of *Yorke*,
From whence you spring, by Lineall Descent.

Rich. Thy humble seruant vowes obedience,
And humble seruice, till the point of death.

King. Stoope then, and set your Knee against my Foot,
And in reguerdon of that dutie done,
I gyrt thee with the valiant Sword of *Yorke*:
Rise *Richard*, like a true *Plantagenet*,
And rise created Princely Duke of *Yorke*.

Rich. And so thriue *Richard*, as thy foes may fall,
And as my dutie springs, so perish they,
That grudge one thought against your Maiesty.

All. Welcome high Prince, the mighty Duke of *Yorke*.

Som. Perish base Prince, ignoble Duke of *Yorke*.

Glost. Now will it best auaile your Maiestie,
To crosse the Seas, and to be Crown'd in France:
The presence of a King engenders loue
Amongst his Subiects, and his loyall Friends,
As it dis-animates his Enemies.

King. When *Gloster* sayes the word, King *Henry* goes,
For friendly counsaile cuts off many Foes.

Glost. Your Ships alreadie are in readinesse.

Senet. Flourish. Exeunt.

Manet Exeter.

Exet. I, we may march in England, or in France,
Not seeing what is likely to ensue:
This late dissention growne betwixt the Peeres,
Burnes vnder fained ashes of forg'd loue,
And will at last breake out into a flame,
As festred members rot but by degree,
Till bones and flesh and sinewes fall away,
So will this base and enuious discord breed.
And now I feare that fatall Prophecie,
Which in the time of *Henry*, nam'd the Fift,
Was in the mouth of euery sucking Babe,
That *Henry* borne at Monmouth should winne all,
And *Henry* borne at Windsor, loose all:
Which is so plaine, that *Exeter* doth wish,
His dayes may finish, ere that haplesse time. *Exit.*

Scœna Secunda.

Enter Pucell disguis'd, with foure Souldiors with Sacks vpon their backs.

Pucell. These are the Citie Gates, the Gates of Roan,
Through which our Pollicy must make a breach.
Take heed, be wary how you place your words,
Talke like the vulgar sort of Market men,
That come to gather Money for their Corne.
If we haue entrance, as I hope we shall,
And that we finde the slouthfull Watch but weake,
Ile by a signe giue notice to our friends,
That *Charles* the Dolphin may encounter them.

Souldier. Our Sacks shall be a meane to sack the City,
And we be Lords and Rulers ouer Roan,
Therefore wee'le knock. *Knock.*

Watch. *Che la.*

Pucell. *Peasauns la pouure gens de Fraunce*,
Poore Market folkes that come to sell their Corne.

Watch. Enter, goe in, the Market Bell is rung.

Pucell. Now Roan, Ile shake thy Bulwarkes to the ground. *Exeunt.*

Enter Charles, Bastard, Alanson.

Charles. Saint *Dennis* blesse this happy Stratageme,
And once againe wee'le sleepe secure in Roan.

Bastard. Here entred *Pucell*, and her Practisants:
Now she is there, how will she specifie?
Here is the best and safest passage in.

Reig. By thrusting out a Torch from yonder Tower,
Which once discern'd, shewes that her meaning is,
No way to that (for weaknesse) which she entred.

Enter Pucell on the top, thrusting out a Torch burning.

Pucell. Behold, this is the happy Wedding Torch,
That ioyneth Roan vnto her Countreymen,
But burning fatall to the *Talbonites*.

Bastard. See Noble *Charles* the Beacon of our friend,
The burning Torch in yonder Turret stands.

Charles. Now shine it like a Commet of Reuenge,
A Prophet to the fall of all our Foes.

Reig. Deferre no time, delayes haue dangerous ends,
Enter and cry, the Dolphin, presently,
And then doe execution on the Watch. *Alarum.*

An Alarum. Talbot in an Excursion.

Talb. France, thou shalt rue this Treason with thy teares,
If *Talbot* but suruiue thy Trecherie.
Pucell that Witch, that damned Sorceresse,
Hath wrought this Hellish Mischiefe vnawares,
That hardly we escap't the Pride of France. *Exit.*

An Alarum: Excursions. Bedford brought in sicke in a Chayre.

Enter Talbot and Burgonie without: within, Pucell, Charles, Bastard, and Reigneir on the Walls.

Pucell. God morrow Gallants, want ye Corn for Bread?
I thinke the Duke of Burgonie will fast,
Before hee'le buy againe at such a rate.
'Twas full of Darnell: doe you like the taste?

Burg. Scoffe on vile Fiend, and shamelesse Curtizan,
I trust ere long to choake thee with thine owne,
And make thee curse the Haruest of that Corne.

Charles. Your Grace may starue (perhaps) before that time.

Bedf. Oh let no words, but deedes, reuenge this Treason.

Pucell. What will you doe, good gray-beard?
Breake a Launce, and runne a-Tilt at Death,
Within a Chayre.

Talb. Foule Fiend of France, and Hag of all despight,
Incompass'd with thy lustfull Paramours,
Becomes it thee to taunt his valiant Age,
And twit with Cowardise a man halfe dead?
Damsell, Ile haue a bowt with you againe,
Or else let *Talbot* perish with this shame.

Pucell Are ye so hot, Sir: yet *Pucell* hold thy peace,
If *Talbot* doe but Thunder, Raine will follow.

They whisper together in counsell.

God speed the Parliament: who shall be the Speaker?

Talb. Dare yee come forth,and meet vs in the field?
Pucell. Belike your Lordship takes vs then for fooles,
To try if that our owne be ours,or no.
Talb. I speake not to that rayling *Hecate*,
But vnto thee *Alanson*, and the rest.
Will ye,like Souldiors,come and fight it out?
Alans. Seignior no.
Talb. Seignior hang: base Muleters of France,
Like Pesant foot-Boyes doe they keepe the Walls,
And dare not take vp Armes,like Gentlemen.
Pucell. Away Captaines,let's get vs from the Walls,
For *Talbot* meanes no goodnesse by his Lookes.
God b'uy my Lord, we came but to tell you
That wee are here. *Exeunt from the Walls.*
Talb. And there will we be too,ere it be long,
Or else reproach be *Talbots* greatest fame.
Vow *Burgonie*, by honor of thy House,
Prickt on by publike Wrongs sustain'd in France,
Either to get the Towne againe,or dye.
And I,as sure as English *Henry* liues,
And as his Father here was Conqueror;
As sure as in this late betrayed Towne,
Great *Cordelions* Heart was buryed;
So sure I sweare,to get the Towne,or dye.
Burg. My Vowes are equall partners with thy Vowes.
Talb. But ere we goe,regard this dying Prince,
The valiant Duke of Bedford: Come my Lord,
We will bestow you in some better place,
Fitter for sicknesse,and for crasie age.
Bedf. Lord *Talbot*,doe not so dishonour me:
Here will I sit,before the Walls of Roan,
And will be partner of your weale or woe.
Burg. Couragious *Bedford*, let vs now perswade you.
Bedf. Not to be gone from hence: for once I read,
That stout *Pendragon*,in his Litter sick,
Came to the field,and vanquished his foes.
Me thinkes I should reuiue the Souldiors hearts,
Because I euer found them as my selfe.
Talb Vndaunted spirit in a dying breast,
Then be it so: Heauens keepe old *Bedford* safe
And now no more adoe, braue *Burgonie*,
But gather we our Forces out of hand,
And set vpon our boasting Enemie. *Exit.*

An Alarum: Excursions. Enter Sir Iohn Falstaffe, and a Captaine.

Capt. Whither away Sir *Iohn Falstaffe*,in such haste?
Falst. Whither away? to saue my selfe by flight,
We are like to haue the ouerthrow againe.
Capt. What? will you flye,and leaue Lord *Talbot*?
Falst. I,all the *Talbots* in the World,to saue my life. *Exit.*
Capt. Cowardly Knight,ill fortune follow thee. *Exit.*

Retreat. Excursions. Pucell, Alanson, and Charles flye.

Bedf. Now quiet Soule,depart when Heauen please,
For I haue seene our Enemies ouerthrow.
What is the trust or strength of foolish man?
They that of late were daring with their scoffes,
Are glad and faine by flight to saue themselues.
Bedford dyes,and is carryed in by two in his Chaire.

An Alarum. Enter Talbot, Burgonie, and the rest.

Talb. Lost,and recouered in a day againe,
This is a double Honor, *Burgonie*:
Yet Heauens haue glory for this Victorie.
Burg. Warlike and Martiall *Talbot*, *Burgonie*
Inshrines thee in his heart,and there erects
Thy noble Deeds,as Valors Monuments.
Talb. Thanks gentle Duke: but where is *Pucel* now?
I thinke her old Familiar is asleepe.
Now where's the Bastards braues,and *Charles* his glikes?
What all amort? Roan hangs her head for griefe,
That such a valiant Company are fled.
Now will we take some order in the Towne,
Placing therein some expert Officers,
And then depart to Paris, to the King,
For there young *Henry* with his Nobles lye.
Burg. What wills Lord *Talbot*,pleaseth *Burgonie*.
Talb. But yet before we goe,let's not forget
The Noble Duke of Bedford,late deceas'd,
But see his Exequies fulfill'd in Roan.
A brauer Souldier neuer couched Launce,
A gentler Heart did neuer sway in Court.
But Kings and mightiest Potentates must die,
For that's the end of humane miserie. *Exeunt.*

Scæna Tertia.

Enter Charles, Bastard, Alanson, Pucell.

Pucell. Dismay not (Princes) at this accident,
Nor grieue that Roan is so recouered:
Care is no cure,but rather corrosiue,
For things that are not to be remedy'd.
Let frantike *Talbot* triumph for a while,
And like a Peacock sweepe along his tayle,
Wee'le pull his Plumes,and take away his Trayne,
If Dolphin and the rest will be but rul'd.
Charles. We haue been guided by thee hitherto,
And of thy Cunning had no diffidence,
One sudden Foyle shall neuer breed distrust.
Bastard. Search out thy wit for secret pollicies,
And we will make thee famous through the World.
Alans. Wee'le set thy Statue in some holy place,
And haue thee reuerenc't like a blessed Saint.
Employ thee then,sweet Virgin, for our good.
Pucell. Then thus it must be, this doth *Ioane* deuise:
By faire perswasions, mixt with sugred words,
We will entice the Duke of Burgonie
To leaue the *Talbot*,and to follow vs.
Charles. I marry Sweeting, if we could doe that,
France were no place for *Henryes* Warriors,
Nor should that Nation boast it so with vs,
But be extirped from our Prouinces.
Alans. For euer should they be expuls'd from France,
And not haue Title of an Earledome here.
Pucell. Your Honors shall perceiue how I will worke,
To bring this matter to the wished end.
Drumme sounds a farre off.
Hearke,by the sound of Drumme you may perceiue
Their Powers are marching vnto Paris-ward.
Here sound an English March.
There goes the *Talbot*, with his Colours spred,
And all the Troupes of English after him.

French March.

Now in the Rereward comes the Duke and his:
Fortune in fauor makes him lagge behinde.
Summon a Parley, we will talke with him.

Trumpets sound a Parley.

Charles. A Parley with the Duke of Burgonie.

Burg. Who craues a Parley with the Burgonie?

Pucell. The Princely *Charles* of France, thy Countrey-man.

Burg. What say'st thou *Charles*? for I am marching hence.

Charles. Speake *Pucell*, and enchaunt him with thy words.

Pucell. Braue *Burgonie*, vndoubted hope of France,
Stay, let thy humble Hand-maid speake to thee.

Burg. Speake on, but be not ouer-tedious.

Pucell. Looke on thy Country, look on fertile France,
And see the Cities and the Townes defac't,
By wasting Ruine of the cruell Foe,
As lookes the Mother on her lowly Babe,
When Death doth close his tender-dying Eyes.
See, see the pining Maladie of France:
Behold the Wounds, the most vnnaturall Wounds,
Which thou thy selfe hast giuen her wofull Brest.
Oh turne thy edged Sword another way,
Strike those that hurt, and hurt not those that helpe:
One drop of Blood drawne from thy Countries Bosome,
Should grieue thee more then streames of forraine gore.
Returne thee therefore with a floud of Teares,
And wash away thy Countries stayned Spots.

Burg. Either she hath bewitcht me with her words,
Or Nature makes me suddenly relent.

Pucell. Besides, all French and France exclaimes on thee,
Doubting thy Birth and lawfull Progenie.
Who ioyn'st thou with, but with a Lordly Nation,
That will not trust thee, but for profits sake?
When *Talbot* hath set footing once in France,
And fashion'd thee that Instrument of Ill,
Who then, but English *Henry*, will be Lord,
And thou be thrust out, like a Fugitiue?
Call we to minde, and marke but this for proofe:
Was not the Duke of Orleance thy Foe?
And was he not in England Prisoner?
But when they heard he was thine Enemie,
They set him free, without his Ransome pay'd,
In spight of *Burgonie* and all his friends.
See then, thou fight'st against thy Countreymen,
And ioyn'st with them will be thy slaughter-men.
Come, come, returne; returne thou wandering Lord,
Charles and the rest will take thee in their armes.

Burg. I am vanquished:
These haughtie wordes of hers
Haue batt'red me like roaring Cannon-shot,
And made me almost yeeld vpon my knees.
Forgiue me Countrey, and sweet Countreymen:
And Lords accept this heartie kind embrace.
My Forces and my Power of Men are yours.
So farwell *Talbot*, Ile no longer trust thee.

Pucell. Done like a Frenchman: turne and turne againe.

Charles. Welcome braue Duke, thy friendship makes vs fresh.

Bastard. And doth beget new Courage in our Breasts.

Alans. *Pucell* hath brauely play'd her part in this,
And doth deserue a Coronet of Gold.

Charles. Now let vs on, my Lords,
And ioyne our Powers,
And seeke how we may preiudice the Foe. *Exeunt.*

Scœna Quarta.

Enter the King, Gloucester, Winchester, Yorke, Suffolke, Somerset, Warwicke, Exeter: To them, with his Souldiors, Talbot.

Talb. My gracious Prince, and honorable Peeres,
Hearing of your arriuall in this Realme,
I haue a while giuen Truce vnto my Warres,
To doe my dutie to my Soueraigne.
In signe whereof, this Arme, that hath reclaym'd
To your obedience, fiftie Fortresses,
Twelue Cities, and seuen walled Townes of strength,
Beside fiue hundred Prisoners of esteeme;
Lets fall his Sword before your Highnesse feet:
And with submissiue loyaltie of heart
Ascribes the Glory of his Conquest got,
First to my God, and next vnto your Grace.

King. Is this the Lord *Talbot* Vnckle *Gloucester*,
That hath so long beene resident in France?

Glost. Yes, if it please your Maiestie, my Liege.

King. Welcome braue Captaine, and victorious Lord.
When I was young (as yet I am not old)
I doe remember how my Father said,
A stouter Champion neuer handled Sword.
Long since we were resolued of your truth,
Your faithfull seruice, and your toyle in Warre:
Yet neuer haue you tasted our Reward,
Or beene reguerdon'd with so much as Thanks,
Because till now, we neuer saw your face.
Therefore stand vp, and for these good deserts,
We here create you Earle of Shrewsbury,
And in our Coronation take your place.

Senet. Flourish. Exeunt.

Manet Vernon and Basset.

Vern. Now Sir, to you that were so hot at Sea,
Disgracing of these Colours that I weare,
In honor of my Noble Lord of Yorke|
Dar'st thou maintaine the former words thou spak'st?

Bass. Yes Sir, as well as you dare patronage
The enuious barking of your sawcie Tongue,
Against my Lord the Duke of Somerset.

Vern. Sirrha, thy Lord I honour as he is.

Bass. Why, what is he? as good a man as *Yorke*.

Vern. Hearke ye: not so: in witnesse take ye that.

Strikes him.

Bass. Villaine, thou knowest
The Law of Armes is such,
That who so drawes a Sword, 'tis present death,
Or else this Blow should broach thy dearest Bloud.
But Ile vnto his Maiestie, and craue,
I may haue libertie to venge this Wrong,
When thou shalt see, Ile meet thee to thy cost.

Vern. Well miscreant, Ile be there as soone as you,
And after meete you, sooner then you would.

Exeunt.

Actus Quartus. Scena Prima.

Enter King, Glocester, Winchester, Yorke, Suffolke, Somerset, Warwicke, Talbot, and Gouernor Exeter.

Glo. Lord Bishop set the Crowne vpon his head.
Win. God saue King *Henry* of that name the sixt.
Glo. Now Gouernour of Paris take your oath,
That you elect no other King but him;
Esteeme none Friends, but such as are his Friends,
And none your Foes, but such as shall pretend
Malicious practises against his State:
This shall ye do, so helpe you righteous God.

Enter Falstaffe.

Fal. My gracious Soueraigne, as I rode from Calice,
To haste vnto your Coronation:
A Letter was deliuer'd to my hands,
Writ to your Grace, from th'Duke of Burgundy.
Tal. Shame to the Duke of Burgundy, and thee:
I vow'd (base Knight) when I did meete the next,
To teare the Garter from thy Crauens legge,
Which I haue done, because (vnworthily)
Thou was't installed in that High Degree.
Pardon me Princely *Henry*, and the rest:
This Dastard, at the battell of *Poictiers*,
When (but in all) I was sixe thousand strong,
And that the French were almost ten to one,
Before we met, or that a stroke was giuen,
Like to a trustie Squire, did run away.
In which assault, we lost twelue hundred men.
My selfe, and diuers Gentlemen beside,
Were there surpriz'd, and taken prisoners.
Then iudge (great Lords) if I haue done amisse:
Or whether that such Cowards ought to weare
This Ornament of Knighthood, yea or no?
Glo. To say the truth, this fact was infamous,
And ill beseeming any common man;
Much more a Knight, a Captaine, and a Leader.
Tal. When first this Order was ordain'd my Lords,
Knights of the Garter were of Noble birth;
Valiant, and Vertuous, full of haughtie Courage,
Such as were growne to credit by the warres:
Not fearing Death, nor shrinking for Distresse,
But alwayes resolute, in most extreames.
He then, that is not furnish'd in this sort,
Doth but vsurpe the Sacred name of Knight,
Prophaning this most Honourable Order,
And should (if I were worthy to be Iudge)
Be quite degraded, like a Hedge-borne Swaine,
That doth presume to boast of Gentle blood.
K. Staine to thy Countrymen, thou hear'st thy doom:
Be packing therefore, thou that was't a knight:
Henceforth we banish thee on paine of death.
And now Lord Protector, view the Letter
Sent from our Vnckle Duke of Burgundy.
Glo. What meanes his Grace, that he hath chaung'd his Stile?
No more but plaine and bluntly? (*To the King.*)
Hath he forgot he is his Soueraigne?
Or doth this churlish Superscription
Pretend some alteration in good will?
What's heere? *I haue vpon especiall cause,*
Mou'd with compassion of my Countries wracke,
Together with the pittifull complaints
Of such as your oppression feedes vpon,
Forsaken your pernitious Faction,
And ioyn'd with Charles, the rightfull king of France.
O monstrous Treachery: Can this be so?
That in alliance, amity, and oathes,
There should be found such false dissembling guile?
King. What? doth my Vnckle Burgundy reuolt?
Glo. He doth my Lord, and is become your foe.
King. Is that the worst this Letter doth containe?
Glo. It is the worst, and all (my Lord) he writes.
King. Why then Lord *Talbot* there shal talk with him,
And giue him chasticement for this abuse.
How say you (my Lord) are you not content?
Tal. Content, my Liege? Yes: But ẏ I am preuented,
I should haue begg'd I might haue bene employd.
King. Then gather strength, and march vnto him straight:
Let him perceiue how ill we brooke his Treason,
And what offence it is to flout his Friends.
Tal. I go my Lord, in heart desiring still
You may behold confusion of your foes.

Enter Vernon and Bassit.

Ver. Grant me the Combate, gracious Soueraigne.
Bas. And me (my Lord) grant me the Combate too
Yorke. This is my Seruant, heare him Noble Prince.
Som. And this is mine (sweet *Henry*) fauour him.
King. Be patient Lords, and giue them leaue to speak.
Say Gentlemen, what makes you thus exclaime,
And wherefore craue you Combate? Or with whom?
Ver. With him (my Lord) for he hath done me wrong.
Bas. And I with him, for he hath done me wrong.
King. What is that wrong, wherof you both complain
First let me know, and then Ile answer you.
Bas. Crossing the Sea, from England into France,
This Fellow heere with enuious carping tongue,
Vpbraided me about the Rose I weare,
Saying, the sanguine colour of the Leaues
Did represent my Masters blushing cheekes:
When stubbornly he did repugne the truth,
About a certaine question in the Law,
Argu'd betwixt the Duke of Yorke, and him:
With other vile and ignominious tearmes.
In confutation of which rude reproach,
And in defence of my Lords worthinesse,
I craue the benefit of Law of Armes.
Ver. And that is my petition (Noble Lord:)
For though he seeme with forged queint conceite
To set a glosse vpon his bold intent,
Yet know (my Lord) I was prouok'd by him,
And he first tooke exceptions at this badge,
Pronouncing that the palenesse of this Flower,
Bewray'd the faintnesse of my Masters heart.
Yorke. Will not this malice Somerset be left?
Som. Your priuate grudge my Lord of York, wil out,
Though ne're so cunningly you smother it.
King. Good Lord, what madnesse rules in braine-sicke men,
When for so slighr and friuolous a cause,
Such factious æmulations shall arise?
Good Cosins both of Yorke and Somerset,
Quiet your selues (I pray) and be at peace.
Yorke. Let this dissention first be tried by fight,
And then your Highnesse shall command a Peace.
Som. The quarrell toucheth none but vs alone,
Betwixt our selues let vs decide it then.
Yorke. There is my pledge, accept it Somerset.
Ver. Nay, let it rest where it began at first.

Bass. Confirme it so, mine honourable Lord.
Glo. Confirme it so? Confounded be your strife,
And perish ye with your audacious prate,
Presumptuous vassals, are you not asham'd
With this immodest clamorous outrage,
To trouble and disturbe the King, and Vs?
And you my Lords, me thinkes you do not well
To beare with their peruerse Obiections:
Much lesse to take occasion from their mouthes,
To raise a mutiny betwixt your selues.
Let me perswade you take a better course.
Exet. It greeues his Highnesse,
Good my Lords, be Friends.
King. Come hither you that would be Combatants:
Henceforth I charge you, as you loue our fauour,
Quite to forget this Quarrell, and the cause.
And you my Lords: Remember where we are,
In France, amongst a fickle wauering Nation:
If they perceyue dissention in our lookes,
And that within our selues we disagree;
How will their grudging stomackes be prouok'd
To wilfull Disobedience, and Rebell?
Beside, What infamy will there arise,
When Forraigne Princes shall be certified,
That for a toy, a thing of no regard,
King *Henries* Peeres, and cheefe Nobility,
Destroy'd themselues, and lost the Realme of France?
Oh thinke vpon the Conquest of my Father,
My tender yeares, and let vs not forgoe
That for a trifle, that was bought with blood.
Let me be Vmper in this doubtfull strife:
I see no reason if I weare this Rose,
That any one should therefore be suspitious
I more incline to Somerset, than Yorke:
Both are my kinsmen, and I loue them both.
As well they may vpbray'd me with my Crowne,
Because (forsooth) the King of Scots is Crown'd.
But your discretions better can perswade,
Then I am able to instruct or teach:
And therefore, as we hither came in peace,
So let vs still continue peace, and loue.
Cosin of Yorke, we institute your Grace
To be our Regent in these parts of France:
And good my Lord of Somerset, vnite
Your Troopes of horsemen, with his Bands of foote,
And like true Subiects, sonnes of your Progenitors,
Go cheerefully together, and digest
Your angry Choller on your Enemies.
Our Selfe, my Lord Protector, and the rest,
After some respit, will returne to Calice;
From thence to England, where I hope ere long
To be presented by your Victories,
With *Charles*, *Alanson*, and that Traiterous rout.
Exeunt. Manet, Yorke, Warwick, Exeter, Vernon.
War. My Lord of Yorke, I promise you the King
Prettily (me thought) did play the Orator.)
Yorke. And so he did, but yet I like it not,
In that he weares the badge of Somerset.
War. Tush, that was but his fancie, blame him not,
I dare presume (sweet Prince) he thought no harme.
York. And if I wish he did. But let it rest,
Other affayres must now be managed. *Exeunt.*
Flourish. Manet Exeter.
Exet. Well didst thou *Richard* to suppresse thy voice:
For had the passions of thy heart burst out,
I feare we should haue seene decipher'd there
More rancorous spight, more furious raging broyles,
Then yet can be imagin'd or suppos'd:
But howsoere, no simple man that sees
This iarring discord of Nobilitie,
This shouldering of each other in the Court,
This factious bandying of their Fauourites,
But that it doth presage some ill euent.
'Tis much, when Scepters are in Childrens hands:
But more, when Enuy breeds vnkinde deuision,
There comes the ruine, there begins confusion. *Exit.*

Enter Talbot with Trumpe and Drumme, before Burdeaux.

Talb. Go to the Gates of Burdeaux Trumpeter,
Summon their Generall vnto the Wall. *Sounds.*
Enter Generall aloft.
English *John Talbot* (Captaines) call you forth,
Seruant in Armes to *Harry* King of England,
And thus he would. Open your Citie Gates,
Be humble to vs, call my Soueraigne yours,
And do him homage as obedient Subiects,
And Ile withdraw me, and my bloody power.
But if you frowne vpon this proffer'd Peace,
You tempt the fury of my three attendants,
Leane Famine, quartering Steele, and climbing Fire,
Who in a moment, eeuen with the earth,
Shall lay your stately, and ayre-brauing Towers,
If you forsake the offer of their loue.
Cap. Thou ominous and fearefull Owle of death,
Our Nations terror, and their bloody scourge,
The period of thy Tyranny approacheth,
On vs thou canst not enter but by death:
For I protest we are well fortified,
And strong enough to issue out and fight.
If thou retire, the Dolphin well appointed,
Stands with the snares of Warre to tangle thee.
On either hand thee, there are squadrons pitcht,
To wall thee from the liberty of Flight;
And no way canst thou turne thee for redresse,
But death doth front thee with apparant spoyle,
And pale destruction meets thee in the face:
Ten thousand French haue tane the Sacrament,
To ryue their dangerous Artillerie
Vpon no Christian soule but English *Talbot*:
Loe, there thou standst a breathing valiant man
Of an inuincible vnconquer'd spirit:
This is the latest Glorie of thy praise,
That I thy enemy dew thee withall:
For ere the Glasse that now begins to runne,
Finish the processe of his sandy houre,
These eyes that see thee now well coloured,
Shall see thee withered, bloody, pale, and dead.
Drum a farre off.
Harke, harke, the Dolphins drumme, a warning bell,
Sings heauy Musicke to thy timorous soule,
And mine shall ring thy dire departure out. *Exit*
Tal. He Fables not, I heare the enemie:
Out some light Horsemen, and peruse their Wings.
O negligent and heedlesse Discipline,
How are we park'd and bounded in a pale?
A little Heard of Englands timorous Deere,
Maz'd with a yelping kennell of French Curres.
If we be English Deere, be then in blood,
Not Rascall-like to fall downe with a pinch,
But rather moodie mad: And desperate Stagges,

Turne

Turne on the bloody Hounds with heads of Steele,
And make the Cowards stand aloofe at bay:
Sell euery man his life as deere as mine,
And they shall finde deere Deere of vs my Friends.
God, and S. *George*, *Talbot* and Englands right,
Prosper our Colours in this dangerous fight.

Enter a Messenger that meets Yorke. Enter Yorke with Trumpet, and many Soldiers.

Yorke. Are not the speedy scouts return'd againe,
That dog'd the mighty Army of the Dolphin?

Mess. They are return'd my Lord, and giue it out,
That he is march'd to Burdeaux with his power
To fight with *Talbot* as he march'd along.
By your espyals were discouered
Two mightier Troopes then that the Dolphin led,
Which ioyn'd with him, and made their march for (Burdeaux

Yorke. A plague vpon that Villaine Somerset,
That thus delayes my promised supply
Of horsemen, that were leuied for this siege.
Renowned *Talbot* doth expect my ayde,
And I am lowted by a Traitor Villaine,
And cannot helpe the noble Cheualier:
God comfort him in this necessity:
If he miscarry, farewell Warres in France.

Enter another Messenger.

2.Mes. Thou Princely Leader of our English strength,
Neuer so needfull on the earth of France,
Spurre to the rescue of the Noble *Talbot*,
Who now is girdled with a waste of Iron,
And hem'd about with grim destruction:
To Burdeaux warlike Duke, to Burdeaux Yorke,
Else farwell *Talbot*, France, and Englands honor.

Yorke. O God, that Somerset who in proud heart
Doth stop my Cornets, were in *Talbots* place,
So should wee saue a valiant Gentleman,
By forfeyting a Traitor, and a Coward:
Mad ire, and wrathfull fury makes me weepe,
That thus we dye, while remisse Traitors sleepe.

Mes. O send some succour to the distrest Lord.

Yorke. He dies, we loose: I breake my warlike word:
We mourne, France smiles: We loose, they dayly get,
All long of this vile Traitor Somerset.

Mes. Then God take mercy on braue *Talbots* soule,
And on his Sonne yong *Iohn*, who two houres since,
I met in trauaile toward his warlike Father;
This seuen yeeres did not *Talbot* see his sonne,
And now they meete where both their liues are done.

Yorke. Alas, what ioy shall noble *Talbot* haue,
To bid his yong sonne welcome to his Graue:
Away, vexation almost stoppes my breath,
That sundred friends greete in the houre of death.
Lucie farewell, no more my fortune can,
But curse the cause I cannot ayde the man.
Maine, *Bloys*, *Poytiers*, and *Toures*, are wonne away,
Long all of Somerset, and his delay. *Exit*

Mes. Thus while the Vulture of sedition,
Feedes in the bosome of such great Commanders,
Sleeping neglection doth betray to losse:
The Conquest of our scarse-cold Conqueror,
That euer-liuing man of Memorie,
Henrie the fift: Whiles they each other crosse,
Liues, Honours, Lands, and all, hurrie to losse.

Enter Somerset with his Armie.

Som. It is too late, I cannot send them now:
This expedition was by *Yorke* and *Talbot*,
Too rashly plotted. All our generall force,
Might with a sally of the very Towne
Be buckled with: the ouer-daring *Talbot*
Hath sullied all his glosse of former Honor
By this vnheedfull, desperate, wilde aduenture:
Yorke set him on to fight, and dye in shame,
That *Talbot* dead, great *Yorke* might beare the name.

Cap. Heere is Sir *William Lucie*, who with me
Set from our ore-matcht forces forth for ayde.

Som. How now Sir *William*, whether were you sent?

Lu. Whether my Lord, from bought & sold L. *Talbot*,
Who ring'd about with bold aduersitie,
Cries out for noble Yorke and Somerset,
To beate assayling death from his weake Regions,
And whiles the honourable Captaine there
Drops bloody swet from his warre-wearied limbes,
And in aduantage lingring lookes for rescue,
You his false hopes, the trust of Englands honor,
Keepe off aloofe with worthlesse emulation:
Let not your priuate discord keepe away
The leuied succours that should lend him ayde,
While he renowned Noble Gentleman
Yeeld vp his life vnto a world of oddes.
Orleance the Bastard, *Charles*, *Burgundie*,
Alanson, *Reignard*, compasse him about,
And *Talbot* perisheth by your default.

Som. Yorke set him on, Yorke should haue sent him ayde.

Luc. And Yorke as fast vpon your Grace exclaimes,
Swearing that you with-hold his leuied hoast,
Collected for this expidition.

Som. York lyes: He might haue sent, & had the Horse:
I owe him little Dutie, and lesse Loue,
And take foule scorne to fawne on him by sending.

Lu. The fraud of England, not the force of France,
Hath now intrapt the Noble-minded *Talbot*:
Neuer to England shall he beare his life,
But dies betraid to fortune by your strife.

Som. Come go, I will dispatch the Horsemen strait:
Within sixe houres, they will be at his ayde.

Lu. Too late comes rescue, he is tane or slaine.
For flye he could not, if he would haue fled:
And flye would *Talbot* neuer though he might.

Som. If he be dead, braue *Talbot* then adieu.

Lu. His Fame liues in the world. His Shame in you. *Exeunt.*

Enter Talbot and his Sonne.

Tal. O yong *Iohn Talbot*, I did send for thee
To tutor thee in stratagems of Warre,
That *Talbots* name might be in thee reuiu'd,
When saplesse Age, and weake vnable limbes
Should bring thy Father to his drooping Chaire.
But O malignant and ill-boading Starres,
Now thou art come vnto a Feast of death,
A terrible and vnauoyded danger:
Therefore deere Boy, mount on my swiftest horse,
And Ile direct thee how thou shalt escape
By sodaine flight. Come, dally not, be gone.

Iohn. Is my name *Talbot*? and am I your Sonne?

Shall

And shall I flye? O, if you loue my Mother,
Dishonor not her Honorable Name,
To make a Bastard, and a Slaue of me:
The World will say, he is not *Talbots* blood,
That basely fled, when Noble *Talbot* stood.

Talb. Flye, to reuenge my death, if I be slaine.

Iohn. He that flyes so, will ne're returne againe.

Talb. If we both stay, we both are sure to dye.

Iohn. Then let me stay, and Father doe you flye:
Your losse is great, so your regard should be;
My worth vnknowne, no losse is knowne in me.
Vpon my death, the French can little boast;
In yours they will, in you all hopes are lost.
Flight cannot stayne the Honor you haue wonne,
But mine it will, that no Exploit haue done.
You fled for Vantage, euery one will sweare:
But if I bow, they'le say it was for feare.
There is no hope that euer I will stay,
If the first howre I shrinke and run away:
Here on my knee I begge Mortalitie,
Rather then Life, preseru'd with Infamie.

Talb. Shall all thy Mothers hopes lye in one Tombe?

Iohn. I rather then Ile shame my Mothers Wombe.

Talb. Vpon my Blessing I command thee goe.

Iohn. To fight I will, but not to flye the Foe.

Talb. Part of thy Father may be sau'd in thee.

Iohn. No part of him, but will be shame in mee.

Talb. Thou neuer hadst Renowne, nor canst not lose it.

Iohn. Yes, your renowned Name: shall flight abuse it?

Talb. Thy Fathers charge shal cleare thee from ẏ staine.

Iohn. You cannot witnesse for me, being slaine.
If Death be so apparant, then both flye.

Talb. And leaue my followers here to fight and dye?
My Age was neuer tainted with such shame.

Iohn. And shall my Youth be guiltie of such blame?
No more can I be seuered from your side,
Then can your selfe, your selfe in twaine diuide:
Stay, goe, doe what you will, the like doe I;
For liue I will not, if my Father dye.

Talb. Then here I take my leaue of thee, faire Sonne,
Borne to eclipse thy Life this afternoone:
Come, side by side, together liue and dye,
And Soule with Soule from France to Heauen flye. *Exit.*

Alarum: Excursions, wherein Talbots Sonne is hemm'd about, and Talbot rescues him.

Talb. Saint *George*, and Victory; fight Souldiers, fight:
The Regent hath with *Talbot* broke his word,
And left vs to the rage of France his Sword.
Where is *Iohn Talbot*? pawse, and take thy breath,
I gaue thee Life, and rescu'd thee from Death.

Iohn. O twice my Father, twice am I thy Sonne:
The Life thou gau'st me first, was lost and done,
Till with thy Warlike Sword, despight of Fate,
To my determin'd time thou gau'st new date.

Talb. When frõ the *Dolphins* Crest thy Sword struck fire,
It warm'd thy Fathers heart with prowd desire
Of bold-fac't Victorie. Then Leaden Age,
Quicken'd with Youthfull Spleene, and Warlike Rage,
Beat downe *Alanson, Orleance, Burgundie*,
And from the Pride of Gallia rescued thee.
The irefull Bastard *Orleance*, that drew blood
From thee my Boy, and had the Maidenhood
Of thy first fight, I soone encountred,
And interchanging blowes, I quickly shed
Some of his Bastard blood, and in disgrace
Bespoke him thus: Contaminated, base,
And mis-begotten blood, I spill of thine,
Meane and right poore, for that pure blood of mine,
Which thou didst force from *Talbot*, my braue Boy.
Here purposing the Bastard to destroy,
Came in strong rescue. Speake thy Fathers care:
Art thou not wearie, *Iohn*? How do'st thou fare?
Wilt thou yet leaue the Battaile, Boy, and flie,
Now thou art seal'd the Sonne of Chiualrie?
Flye, to reuenge my death when I am dead,
The helpe of one stands me in little stead.
Oh, too much folly is it, well I wot,
To hazard all our liues in one small Boat.
If I to day dye not with Frenchmens Rage,
To morrow I shall dye with mickle Age.
By me they nothing gaine, and if I stay,
'Tis but the shortning of my Life one day.
In thee thy Mother dyes, our Housholds Name,
My Deaths Reuenge, thy Youth, and Englands Fame:
All these, and more, we hazard by thy stay;
All these are sau'd, if thou wilt flye away.

Iohn. The Sword of *Orleance* hath not made me smart,
These words of yours draw Life-blood from my Heart.
On that aduantage, bought with such a shame,
To saue a paltry Life, and slay bright Fame,
Before young *Talbot* from old *Talbot* flye,
The Coward Horse that beares me, fall and dye:
And like me to the pesant Boyes of France,
To be Shames scorne, and subiect of Mischance.
Surely, by all the Glorie you haue wonne,
And if I flye, I am not *Talbots* Sonne.
Then talke no more of flight, it is no boot,
If Sonne to *Talbot*, dye at *Talbots* foot.

Talb. Then follow thou thy desp'rate Syre of Creet,
Thou *Icarus*, thy Life to me is sweet:
If thou wilt fight, fight by thy Fathers side,
And commendable prou'd, let's dye in pride. *Exit.*

Alarum. Excursions. Enter old Talbot led.

Talb. Where is my other Life? mine owne is gone.
O, where's young *Talbot*? where is valiant *Iohn*?
Triumphant Death, smear'd with Captiuitie,
Young *Talbots* Valour makes me smile at thee.
When he perceiu'd me shrinke, and on my Knee,
His bloodie Sword he brandisht ouer mee,
And like a hungry Lyon did commence
Rough deeds of Rage, and sterne Impatience:
But when my angry Guardant stood alone,
Tendring my ruine, and assayl'd of none,
Dizzie-ey'd Furie, and great rage of Heart,
Suddenly made him from my side to start
Into the clustring Battaile of the French:
And in that Sea of Blood, my Boy did drench
His ouer-mounting Spirit; and there di'de
My *Icarus*, my Blossome, in his pride.

Enter with Iohn Talbot, borne.

Seru. O my deare Lord, loe where your Sonne is borne.

Tal. Thou antique Death, which laugh'st vs here to scorn,
Anon from thy insulting Tyrannie,
Coupled in bonds of perpetuitie,
Two *Talbots* winged through the lither Skie,
In thy despight shall scape Mortalitie.

O thou whose wounds become hard fauoured death,
Speake to thy father, ere thou yeeld thy breath,
Braue death by speaking, whither he will or no:
Imagine him a Frenchman, and thy Foe.
Poore Boy, he smiles, me thinkes, as who should say,
Had Death bene French, then Death had dyed to day.
Come, come, and lay him in his Fathers armes,
My spirit can no longer beare these harmes.
Souldiers adieu: I haue what I would haue,
Now my old armes are yong *Iohn Talbots* graue. *Dyes*

Enter Charles, Alanson, Burgundie, Bastard, and Pucell.

Char. Had Yorke and Somerset brought rescue in,
We should haue found a bloody day of this.
Bast. How the yong whelpe of *Talbots* raging wood,
Did flesh his punie-sword in Frenchmens blood.
Puc. Once I encountred him, and thus I said:
Thou Maiden youth, be vanquisht by a Maide.
But with a proud Maiesticall high scorne
He answer'd thus: Yong *Talbot* was not borne
To be the pillage of a Giglot Wench:
So rushing in the bowels of the French,
He left me proudly, as vnworthy fight.
Bur. Doubtlesse he would haue made a noble Knight:
See where he lyes inherced in the armes
Of the most bloody Nursser of his harmes.
Bast. Hew them to peeces, hack their bones assunder,
Whose life was Englands glory, Gallia's wonder.
Char. Oh no forbeare: For that which we haue fled
During the life, let vs not wrong it dead.

Enter Lucie.

Lu. Herald, conduct me to the Dolphins Tent,
To know who hath obtain'd the glory of the day.
Char. On what submissiue message art thou sent?
Lucy. Submission Dolphin? Tis a meere French word:
We English Warriours wot not what it meanes.
I come to know what Prisoners thou hast tane,
And to suruey the bodies of the dead.
Char. For prisoners askst thou? Hell our prison is.
But tell me whom thou seek'st?
Luc. But where's the great Alcides of the field,
Valiant Lord *Talbot* Earle of Shrewsbury?
Created for his rare successe in Armes,
Great Earle of *Washford, Waterford*, and *Valence*,
Lord *Talbot* of *Goodrig* and *Vrchinfield*,
Lord *Strange* of *Blackmere*, Lord *Verdon* of *Alton*,
Lord *Cromwell* of *Wingefield*, Lord *Furniuall* of *Sheffeild*,
The thrice victorious Lord of *Falconbridge*,
Knight of the Noble Order of *S. George*,
Worthy S. *Michael*, and the *Golden Fleece*,
Great Marshall to *Henry* the sixt,
Of all his Warres within the Realme of France.
Puc. Heere's a silly stately stile indeede:
The Turke that two and fiftie Kingdomes hath,
Writes not so tedious a Stile as this.
Him that thou magnifi'st with all these Titles,
Stinking and fly-blowne lyes heere at our feete.
Lucy. Is *Talbot* slaine, the Frenchmens only Scourge,
Your Kingdomes terror, and blacke *Nemesis*?
Oh were mine eye-balles into Bullets turn'd,
That I in rage might shoot them at your faces.
Oh, that I could but call these dead to life,
It were enough to fright the Realme of France.
Were but his Picture left amongst you here,
It would amaze the prowdest of you all.
Giue me their Bodyes, that I may beare them hence,
And giue them Buriall, as beseemes their worth.
Pucel. I thinke this vpstart is old *Talbots* Ghost,
He speakes with such a proud commanding spirit:
For Gods sake let him haue him, to keepe them here,
They would but stinke, and putrifie the ayre.
Char. Go take their bodies hence.
Lucy. Ile beare them hence: but from their ashes shal be reard
A Phœnix that shall make all France affear'd.
Char. So we be rid of them, do with him what ye wilt.
And now to Paris in this conquering vaine,
All will be ours, now bloody *Talbots* slaine. *Exit.*

Scena secunda.

SENNET.

Enter King, Glocester, and Exeter.

King. Haue you perus'd the Letters from the Pope,
The Emperor, and the Earle of Arminack?
Glo. I haue my Lord, and their intent is this,
They humbly sue vnto your Excellence,
To haue a godly peace concluded of,
Betweene the Realmes of England, and of France.
King. How doth your Grace affect their motion?
Glo. Well (my good Lord) and as the only meanes
To stop effusion of our Christian blood,
And stablish quietnesse on euery side.
King. I marry Vnckle, for I alwayes thought
It was both impious and vnnaturall,
That such immanity and bloody strife
Should reigne among Professors of one Faith.
Glo. Beside my Lord, the sooner to effect,
And surer binde this knot of amitie,
The Earle of Arminacke neere knit to *Charles*,
A man of great Authoritie in France,
Proffers his onely daughter to your Grace,
In marriage, with a large and sumptuous Dowrie.
King. Marriage Vnckle? Alas my yeares are yong:
And fitter is my studie, and my Bookes,
Than wanton dalliance with a Paramour.
Yet call th'Embassadors, and as you please,
So let them haue their answeres euery one:
I shall be well content with any choyce
Tends to Gods glory, and my Countries weale.

Enter Winchester, and three Ambassadors.

Exet. What, is my Lord of *Winchester* install'd,
And call'd vnto a Cardinalls degree?
Then I perceiue, that will be verified
Henry the Fift did sometime prophesie.
If once he come to be a Cardinall,
Hee'l make his cap coequall with the Crowne.
King. My Lords Ambassadors, your seuerall suites
Haue bin consider'd and debated on,
Your purpose is both good and reasonable:
And therefore are we certainly resolu'd,
To draw conditions of a friendly peace,

Which

Which by my Lord of Winchester we meane
Shall be transported presently to France.

Glo. And for the proffer of my Lord your Master,
I haue inform'd his Highnesse so at large,
As liking of the Ladies vertuous gifts,
Her Beauty, and the valew of her Dower,
He doth intend she shall be Englands Queene.

King. In argument and proofe of which contract,
Beare her this Iewell, pledge of my affection.
And so my Lord Protector see them guarded,
And safely brought to *Douer*, wherein ship'd
Commit them to the fortune of the sea. *Exeunt.*

Win. Stay my Lord Legate, you shall first receiue
The summe of money which I promised
Should be deliuered to his Holinesse,
For cloathing me in these graue Ornaments.

Legat. I will attend vpon your Lordships leysure.

Win. Now Winchester will not submit, I trow,
Or be inferiour to the proudest Peere;
Humfrey of Gloster, thou shalt well perceiue,
That neither in birth, or for authoritie,
The Bishop will be ouer-borne by thee:
Ile either make thee stoope, and bend thy knee,
Or sacke this Country with a mutiny. *Exeunt*

Scœna Tertia.

Enter Charles, Burgundy, Alanson, Bastard, Reignier, and Ione.

Char. These newes (my Lords) may cheere our drooping spirits:
'Tis said, the stout Parisians do reuolt,
And turne againe vnto the warlike French.

Alan. Then march to Paris Royall *Charles* of France,
And keepe not backe your powers in dalliance.

Pucel. Peace be amongst them if they turne to vs,
Else ruine combate with their Pallaces.

Enter Scout.

Scout. Successe vnto our valiant Generall,
And happinesse to his accomplices.

Char. What tidings send our Scouts? I prethee speak.

Scout. The English Army that diuided was
Into two parties, is now conioyn'd in one,
And meanes to giue you battell presently.

Char. Somewhat too sodaine Sirs, the warning is,
But we will presently prouide for them.

Bur. I trust the Ghost of *Talbot* is not there:
Now he is gone my Lord, you neede not feare.

Pucel. Of all base passions, Feare is most accurst.
Command the Conquest *Charles*, it shall be thine:
Let *Henry* fret, and all the world repine.

Char. Then on my Lords, and France be fortunate.
Exeunt. Alarum. Excursions.

Enter Ione de Pucell.

Puc. The Regent conquers, and the Frenchmen flye.
Now helpe ye charming Spelles and Periapts,
And ye choise spirits that admonish me,
And giue me signes of future accidents. *Thunder.*
You speedy helpers, that are substitutes
Vnder the Lordly Monarch of the North,
Appeare, and ayde me in this enterprize.

Enter Fiends.

This speedy and quicke appearance argues proofe
Of your accustom'd diligence to me.
Now ye Familiar Spirits, that are cull'd
Out of the powerfull Regions vnder earth,
Helpe me this once, that France may get the field.

They walke, and speake not.

Oh hold me not with silence ouer-long:
Where I was wont to feed you with my blood,
Ile lop a member off, and giue it you,
In earnest of a further benefit:
So you do condiscend to helpe me now.

They hang their heads.

No hope to haue redresse? My body shall
Pay recompence, if you will graunt my suite.

They shake their heads.

Cannot my body, nor blood-sacrifice,
Intreate you to your wonted furtherance?
Then take my soule; my body, soule, and all,
Before that England giue the French the foyle.

They depart.

See, they forsake me. Now the time is come,
That France must vale her lofty plumed Crest,
And let her head fall into Englands lappe.
My ancient Incantations are too weake,
And hell too strong for me to buckle with:
Now France, thy glory droopeth to the dust. *Exit.*

Excursions. Burgundie and Yorke fight hand to hand. French flye.

Yorke. Damsell of France, I thinke I haue you fast,
Vnchaine your spirits now with spelling Charmes,
And try if they can gaine your liberty.
A goodly prize, fit for the diuels grace.
See how the vgly Witch doth bend her browes,
As if with *Circe*, she would change my shape.

Puc. Chang'd to a worser shape thou canst not be:

Yor. Oh, *Charles* the Dolphin is a proper man,
No shape but his can please your dainty eye.

Puc. A plaguing mischeefe light on *Charles*, and thee,
And may ye both be sodainly surpriz'd
By bloudy hands, in sleeping on your beds.

Yorke. Fell banning Hagge, Inchantresse hold thy tongue.

Puc. I prethee giue me leaue to curse awhile.

Yorke. Curse Miscreant, when thou comst to the stake
Exeunt.

Alarum. Enter Suffolke with Margaret in his hand.

Suff. Be what thou wilt, thou art my prisoner.

Gazes on her.

Oh Fairest Beautie, do not feare, nor flye:
For I will touch thee but with reuerend hands,
I kisse these fingers for eternall peace,
And lay them gently on thy tender side.
Who art thou, say? that I may honor thee.

Mar. Margaret my name, and daughter to a King,
The King of Naples, who so ere thou art.

Suff. An Earle I am, and Suffolke am I call'd.
Be not offended Natures myracle,
Thou art alotted to be tane by me:
So doth the Swan her downie Signets saue,

Oh stay:

Keeping them prisoner vnderneath his wings:
Yet if this seruile vsage once offend,
Go, and be free againe, as Suffolkes friend. *She is going*
Oh stay: I haue no power to let her passe,
My hand would free her, but my heart sayes no.
As playes the Sunne vpon the glassie streames,
Twinkling another counterfetted beame,
So seemes this gorgeous beauty to mine eyes.
Faine would I woe her, yet I dare not speake:
Ile call for Pen and Inke, and write my minde:
Fye *De la Pole*, disable not thy selfe:
Hast not a Tongue? Is she not heere?
Wilt thou be daunted at a Womans sight?
I: Beauties Princely Maiesty is such,
'Confounds the tongue, and makes the senses rough.

Mar. Say Earle of Suffolke, if thy name be so,
What ransome must I pay before I passe?
For I perceiue I am thy prisoner.

Suf. How canst thou tell she will deny thy suite,
Before thou make a triall of her loue?

M. Why speak'st thou not? What ransom must I pay?

Suf. She's beautifull; and therefore to be Wooed:
She is a Woman; therefore to be Wonne.

Mar. Wilt thou accept of ransome, yea or no?

Suf. Fond man, remember that thou hast a wife,
Then how can *Margaret* be thy Paramour?

Mar. I were best to leaue him, for he will not heare.

Suf. There all is marr'd: there lies a cooling card.

Mar. He talkes at randon: sure the man is mad.

Suf. And yet a dispensation may bee had.

Mar. And yet I would that you would answer me:

Suf. Ile win this Lady *Margaret*. For whom?
Why for my King: Tush, that's a woodden thing.

Mar. He talkes of wood: It is some Carpenter.

Suf. Yet so my fancy may be satisfied,
And peace established betweene these Realmes.
But there remaines a scruple in that too:
For though her Father be the King of *Naples*,
Duke of *Anion* and *Mayne*, yet is he poore,
And our Nobility will scorne the match.

Mar. Heare ye Captaine? Are you not at leysure?

Suf. It shall be so, disdaine they ne're so much:
Henry is youthfull, and will quickly yeeld.
Madam, I haue a secret to reueale.

Mar. What though I be inthral'd, he seems a knight
And will not any way dishonor me.

Suf. Lady, vouchsafe to listen what I say.

Mar. Perhaps I shall be rescu'd by the French,
And then I need not craue his curtesie.

Suf. Sweet Madam, giue me hearing in a cause.

Mar. Tush, women haue bene captiuate ere now.

Suf. Lady, wherefore talke you so?

Mar. I cry you mercy, 'tis but *Quid* for *Quo*.

Suf. Say gentle Princesse, would you not suppose
Your bondage happy, to be made a Queene?

Mar. To be a Queene in bondage, is more vile,
Than is a slaue, in base seruility:
For Princes should be free.

Suf. And so shall you,
If happy Englands Royall King be free.

Mar. Why what concernes his freedome vnto mee?

Suf. Ile vndertake to make thee *Henries* Queene,
To put a Golden Scepter in thy hand,
And set a precious Crowne vpon thy head,
If thou wilt condiscend to be my———

Mar. What?

Suf. His loue.

Mar. I am vnworthy to be *Henries* wife.

Suf. No gentle Madam, I vnworthy am
To woe so faire a Dame to be his wife,
And haue no portion in the choice my selfe.
How say you Madam, are ye so content?

Mar. And if my Father please, I am content.

Suf. Then call our Captaines and our Colours forth,
And Madam, at your Fathers Castle walles,
Wee'l craue a parley, to conferre with him.

Sound. Enter Reignier on the Walles.

See *Reignier* see, thy daughter prisoner.

Reig. To whom?

Suf. To me.

Reig. Suffolke, what remedy?
I am a Souldier, and vnapt to weepe,
Or to exclaime on Fortunes ficklenesse.

Suf. Yes, there is remedy enough my Lord,
Consent, and for thy Honor giue consent,
Thy daughter shall be wedded to my King,
Whom I with paine haue wooed and wonne thereto:
And this her easie held imprisonment,
Hath gain'd thy daughter Princely libertie.

Reig. Speakes Suffolke as he thinkes?

Suf. Faire *Margaret* knowes,
That Suffolke doth not flatter, face, or faine.

Reig. Vpon thy Princely warrant, I descend,
To giue thee answer of thy iust demand.

Suf. And heere I will expect thy comming.

Trumpets sound. Enter Reignier.

Reig. Welcome braue Earle into our Territories,
Command in *Anion* what your Honor pleases.

Suf. Thankes *Reignier*, happy for so sweet a Childe,
Fit to be made companion with a King:
What answer makes your Grace vnto my suite?

Reig. Since thou dost daigne to woe her little worth,
To be the Princely Bride of such a Lord:
Vpon condition I may quietly
Enioy mine owne, the Country *Maine* and *Anion*,
Free from oppression, or the stroke of Warre,
My daughter shall be *Henries*, if he please.

Suf. That is her ransome, I deliuer her,
And those two Counties I will vndertake
Your Grace shall well and quietly enioy.

Reig. And I againe in *Henries* Royall name,
As Deputy vnto that gracious King,
Giue thee her hand for signe of plighted faith.

Suf. *Reignier* of France, I giue thee Kingly thankes,
Because this is in Trafficke of a King.
And yet me thinkes I could be well content
To be mine owne Atturney in this case.
Ile ouer then to England with this newes.
And make this marriage to be solemniz'd:
So farewell *Reignier*, set this Diamond safe
In Golden Pallaces as it becomes.

Reig. I do embrace thee, as I would embrace
The Christian Prince King *Henrie* were he heere.

Mar. Farewell my Lord good wishes, praise, & praiers,
Shall Suffolke euer haue of *Margaret*. *Shee is going.*

Suf. Farwell sweet Madam: but hearke you *Margaret*,
No Princely commendations to my King?

Mar. Such commendations as becomes a Maide,
A Virgin, and his Seruant, say to him.

Suf. Words sweetly plac'd, and modestie directed,
But

But Madame, I must trouble you againe,
No louing Token to his Maiestie?

Mar. Yes, my good Lord, a pure vnspotted heart,
Neuer yet taint with loue, I send the King.

Suf. And this withall. *Kisse her.*

Mar. That for thy selfe, I will not so presume,
To send such peeuish tokens to a King.

Suf. Oh wert thou for my selfe: but *Suffolke* stay,
Thou mayest not wander in that Labyrinth,
There Minotaurs and vgly Treasons lurke,
Solicite *Henry* with her wonderous praise.
Bethinke thee on her Vertues that surmount,
Mad naturall Graces that extinguish Art,
Repeate their semblance often on the Seas,
That when thou com'st to kneele at *Henries* feete,
Thou mayest bereaue him of his wits with wonder. *Exit*

Enter Yorke, Warwicke, Shepheard, Pucell.

Yor. Bring forth that Sorceresse condemn'd to burne.

Shep. Ah *Ione*, this kils thy Fathers heart out-right,
Haue I sought euery Country farre and neere,
And now it is my chance to finde thee out,
Must I behold thy timelesse cruell death:
Ah *Ione*, sweet daughter *Ione*, Ile die with thee.

Pucel. Decrepit Miser, base ignoble Wretch,
I am descended of a gentler blood.
Thou art no Father, nor no Friend of mine.

Shep. Out, out: My Lords, and please you, 'tis not so
I did beget her, all the Parish knowes:
Her Mother liueth yet, can testifie
She was the first fruite of my Bach'ler-ship.

War. Gracelesse, wilt thou deny thy Parentage?

Yorke. This argues what her kinde of life hath beene,
Wicked and vile, and so her death concludes.

Shep. Fye *Ione*, that thou wilt be so obstacle:
God knowes, thou art a collop of my flesh,
And for thy sake haue I shed many a teare:
Deny me not, I prythee, gentle *Ione*.

Pucell. Pezant auant. You haue suborn'd this man
Of purpose, to obscure my Noble birth.

Shep. 'Tis true, I gaue a Noble to the Priest,
The morne that I was wedded to her mother.
Kneele downe and take my blessing, good my Gyrle.
Wilt thou not stoope? Now cursed be the time
Of thy natiuitie: I would the Milke
Thy mother gaue thee when thou suck'st her brest,
Had bin a little Rats-bane for thy sake.
Or else, when thou didst keepe my Lambes a-field,
I wish some rauenous Wolfe had eaten thee.
Doest thou deny thy Father, cursed Drab?
O burne her, burne her, hanging is too good. *Exit.*

Yorke. Take her away, for she hath liu'd too long,
To fill the world with vicious qualities.

Puc. First let me tell you whom you haue condemn'd;
Not me, begotten of a Shepheard Swaine,
But issued from the Progeny of Kings.
Vertuous and Holy, chosen from aboue,
By inspiration of Celestiall Grace,
To worke exceeding myracles on earth.
I neuer had to do with wicked Spirits.
But you that are polluted with your lustes,
Stain'd with the guiltlesse blood of Innocents,
Corrupt and tainted with a thousand Vices:
Because you want the grace that others haue,
You iudge it straight a thing impossible
To compasse Wonders, but by helpe of diuels.
No misconceyued, *Ione* of *Aire* hath beene
A Virgin from her tender infancie,
Chaste, and immaculate in very thought,
Whose Maiden-blood thus rigorously effus'd,
Will cry for Vengeance, at the Gates of Heauen.

Yorke. I, I: away with her to execution.

War. And hearke ye sirs: because she is a Maide,
Spare for no Faggots, let there be enow:
Place barrelles of pitch vpon the fatall stake,
That so her torture may be shortned.

Puc. Will nothing turne your vnrelenting hearts?
Then *Ione* discouer thine infirmity,
That warranteth by Law, to be thy priuiledge.
I am with childe ye bloody Homicides:
Murther not then the Fruite within my Wombe,
Although ye hale me to a violent death.

Yor. Now heauen forfend, the holy Maid with child?

War. The greatest miracle that ere ye wrought.
Is all your strict precisenesse come to this?

Yorke. She and the Dolphin haue bin iugling,
I did imagine what would be her refuge.

War. Well go too, we'll haue no Bastards liue,
Especially since *Charles* must Father it.

Puc. You are deceyu'd, my childe is none of his,
It was *Alanson* that inioy'd my loue.

Yorke. *Alanson* that notorious Macheuile?
It dyes, and if it had a thousand liues.

Puc. Oh giue me leaue, I haue deluded you,
'Twas neyther *Charles*, nor yet the Duke I nam'd,
But *Reignier* King of *Naples* that preuayl'd.

War. A married man, that's most intollerable.

Yor. Why here's a Gyrle: I think she knowes not wel
(There were so many) whom she may accuse.

War. It's signe she hath beene liberall and free.

Yor. And yet forsooth she is a Virgin pure.
Strumpet, thy words condemne thy Brat, and thee.
Vse no intreaty, for it is in vaine.

Pu. Then lead me hence: with whom I leaue my curse.
May neuer glorious Sunne reflex his beames
Vpon the Countrey where you make abode:
But darknesse, and the gloomy shade of death
Inuiron you, till Mischeefe and Dispaire,
Driue you to break your necks, or hang your selues. *Exit*

Enter Cardinall.

Yorke. Breake thou in peeces, and consume to ashes,
Thou fowle accursed minister of Hell.

Car. Lord Regent, I do greete your Excellence
With Letters of Commission from the King.
For know my Lords, the States of Christendome,
Mou'd with remorse of these out-ragious broyles,
Haue earnestly implor'd a generall peace,
Betwixt our Nation, and the aspyring French;
And heere at hand, the Dolphin and his Traine
Approacheth, to conferre about some matter.

Yorke. Is all our trauell turn'd to this effect,
After the slaughter of so many Peeres,
So many Captaines, Gentlemen, and Soldiers,
That in this quarrell haue beene ouerthrowne,
And sold their bodyes for their Countryes benefit,
Shall we at last conclude effeminate peace?
Haue we not lost most part of all the Townes,
By Treason, Falshood, and by Treacherie,
Our great Progenitors had conquered:
Oh Warwicke, Warwicke, I foresee with greefe
The vtter losse of all the Realme of France.

War. Be patient Yorke, if we conclude a Peace

It shall be with such strict and seuere Couenants,
As little shall the Frenchmen gaine thereby.

Enter Charles, Alanson, Bastard, Reignier.

Char. Since Lords of England, it is thus agreed,
That peacefull truce shall be proclaim'd in France,
We come to be informed by your selues,
What the conditions of that league must be.
Yorke. Speake Winchester, for boyling choller chokes
The hollow passage of my poyson'd voyce,
By sight of these our balefull enemies.
Win. *Charles*, and the rest, it is enacted thus:
That in regard King *Henry* giues consent,
Of meere compassion, and of lenity,
To ease your Countrie of distressefull Warre,
And suffer you to breath in fruitfull peace,
You shall become true Liegemen to his Crowne.
And *Charles*, vpon condition thou wilt sweare
To pay him tribute, and submit thy selfe,
Thou shalt be plac'd as Viceroy vnder him,
And still enioy thy Regall dignity.
Alan. Must he be then as shadow of himselfe?
Adorne his Temples with a Coronet,
And yet in substance and authority,
Retaine but priuiledge of a priuate man?
This proffer is absurd, and reasonlesse.
Char. 'Tis knowne already that I am possest
With more then halfe the Gallian Territories,
And therein reuerenc'd for their lawfull King.
Shall I for lucre of the rest vn-vanquisht,
Detract so much from that prerogatiue,
As to be call'd but Viceroy of the whole?
No Lord Ambassador, Ile rather keepe
That which I haue, than coueting for more
Be cast from possibility of all.
Yorke. Insulting *Charles*, hast thou by secret meanes
Vs'd intercession to obtaine a league,
And now the matter growes to compremize,
Stand'st thou aloofe vpon Comparison.
Either accept the Title thou vsurp'st,
Of benefit proceeding from our King,
And not of any challenge of Desert,
Or we will plague thee with incessant Warres.
Reig. My Lord, you do not well in obstinacy,
To cauill in the course of this Contract:
If once it be neglected, ten to one
We shall not finde like opportunity.
Alan. To say the truth, it is your policie,
To saue your Subiects from such massacre
And ruthlesse slaughters as are dayly seene
By our proceeding in Hostility,
And therefore take this compact of a Truce,
Although you breake it, when your pleasure serues.
War. How sayst thou *Charles*?
Shall our Condition stand?
Char. It Shall:
Onely reseru'd, you claime no interest
In any of our Townes of Garrison.
Yor. Then sweare Allegeance to his Maiesty,
As thou art Knight, neuer to disobey,
Nor be Rebellious to the Crowne of England,
Thou nor thy Nobles, to the Crowne of England.
So, now dismisse your Army when ye please:
Hang vp your Ensignes, let your Drummes be still,
For heere we entertaine a solemne peace. *Exeunt*

Actus Quintus.

Enter Suffolke in conference with the King, Glocester, and Exeter.

King. Your wondrous rare description (noble Earle)
Of beauteous *Margaret* hath astonish'd me:
Her vertues graced with externall gifts,
Do breed Loues setled passions in my heart,
And like as rigour of tempestuous gustes
Prouokes the mightiest Hulke against the tide,
So am I driuen by breath of her Renowne,
Either to suffer Shipwracke, or arriue
Where I may haue fruition of her Loue.
Suf. Tush my good Lord, this superficiall tale,
Is but a preface of her worthy praise:
The cheefe perfections of that louely Dame,
(Had I sufficient skill to vtter them)
Would make a volume of inticing lines,
Able to rauish any dull conceit.
And which is more, she is not so Diuine,
So full repleate with choice of all delights,
But with as humble lowlinesse of minde,
She is content to be at your command:
Command I meane, of Vertuous chaste intents,
To Loue, and Honor *Henry* as her Lord.
King. And otherwise, will *Henry* ne're presume:
Therefore my Lord Protector, giue consent,
That *Marg'ret* may be Englands Royall Queene.
Glo. So should I giue consent to flatter sinne,
You know (my Lord) your Highnesse is betroath'd
Vnto another Lady of esteeme,
How shall we then dispense with that contract,
And not deface your Honor with reproach?
Suf As doth a Ruler with vnlawfull Oathes,
Or one that at a Triumph, hauing vow'd
To try his strength, forsaketh yet the Listes
By reason of his Aduersaries oddes.
A poore Earles daughter is vnequall oddes,
And therefore may be broke without offence.
Gloucester. Why what (I pray) is *Margaret* more then that?
Her Father is no better than an Earle,
Although in glorious Titles he excell.
Suf. Yes my Lord, her Father is a King,
The King of Naples, and Ierusalem,
And of such great Authoritie in France,
As his alliance will confirme our peace,
And keepe the Frenchmen in Allegeance.
Glo. And so the Earle of Arminacke may doe,
Because he is neere Kinsman vnto *Charles*.
Exet. Beside, his wealth doth warrant a liberal dower,
Where *Reignier* sooner will receyue, than giue.
Suf. A Dowre my Lords? Disgrace not so your King,
That he should be so abiect, base, and poore,
To choose for wealth, and not for perfect Loue.
Henry is able to enrich his Queene,
And not to seeke a Queene to make him rich,
So worthlesse Pezants bargaine for their Wiues,
As Market men for Oxen, Sheepe, or Horse.
Marriage is a matter of more worth,
Then to be dealt in by Attturney-ship:
Not whom we will, but whom his Grace affects,

Must

Must be companion of his Nuptiall bed.
And therefore Lords, since he affects her most,
Most of all these reasons bindeth vs,
In our opinions she should be preferr'd.
For what is wedlocke forced? but a Hell,
An Age of discord and continuall strife,
Whereas the contrarie bringeth blisse,
And is a patterne of Celestiall peace.
Whom should we match with *Henry* being a King,
But *Margaret*, that is daughter to a King:
Her peerelesse feature, ioyned with her birth,
Approues her fit for none, but for a King.
Her valiant courage, and vndaunted spirit,
(More then in women commonly is seene)
Will answer our hope in issue of a King.
For *Henry*, sonne vnto a Conqueror,
Is likely to beget more Conquerors,
If with a Lady of so high resolue,
(As is faire *Margaret*) he be link'd in loue.
Then yeeld my Lords, and heere conclude with mee,
That *Margaret* shall be Queene, and none but shee.

King. Whether it be through force of your report,
My Noble Lord of Suffolke: Or for that
My tender youth was neuer yet attaint
With any passion of inflaming loue,
I cannot tell: but this I am assur'd,
I feele such sharpe dissention in my breast,
Such fierce alarums both of Hope and Feare,
As I am sicke with working of my thoughts.
Take therefore shipping, poste my Lord to France,
Agree to any couenants, and procure
That Lady *Margaret* do vouchsafe to come
To crosse the Seas to England, and be crown'd
King *Henries* faithfull and annointed Queene.
For your expences and sufficient charge,
Among the people gather vp a tenth.
Be gone I say, for till you do returne,
I rest perplexed with a thousand Cares.
And you (good Vnckle) banish all offence:
If you do censure me, by what you were,
Not what you are, I know it will excuse
This sodaine execution of my will.
And so conduct me, where from company,
I may reuolue and ruminate my greefe. *Exit.*

Glo. I greefe I feare me, both at first and last.

Exit Glocester.

Suf. Thus Suffolke hath preuail'd, and thus he goes
As did the youthfull *Paris* once to Greece,
With hope to finde the like euent in loue,
But prosper better than the Troian did:
Margaret shall now be Queene, and rule the King:
But I will rule both her, the King, and Realme. *Exit*

FINIS.

The second Part of Henry the Sixt, with the death of the Good Duke HVMFREY.

Actus Primus. Scœna Prima.

Flourish of Trumpets: Then Hoboyes.

Enter King, Duke Humfrey, Salisbury, Warwicke, and Beauford on the one side.
The Queene, Suffolke, Yorke, Somerset, and Buckingham, on the other.

Suffolke.

AS by your high Imperiall Maiesty,
I had in charge at my depart for France,
As Procurator to your Excellence,
To marry Princes *Margaret* for your Grace;
So in the Famous Ancient City, *Toures*,
In presence of the Kings of *France*, and *Sicill*,
The Dukes of *Orleance*, *Calaber*, *Britaigne*, and *Alanson*,
Seuen Earles, twelue Barons, & twenty reuerend Bishops
I haue perform'd my Taske, and was espous'd,
And humbly now vpon my bended knee,
In sight of England, and her Lordly Peeres,
Deliuer vp my Title in the Queene
To your most gracious hands, that are the Substance
Of that great Shadow I did represent:
The happiest Gift, that euer Marquesse gaue,
The Fairest Queene, that euer King receiu'd.

King. Suffolke arise. Welcome Queene *Margaret*,
I can expresse no kinder signe of Loue
Then this kinde kisse: O Lord, that lends me life,
Lend me a heart repleate with thankfulnesse:
For thou hast giuen me in this beauteous Face
A world of earthly blessings to my soule,
If Simpathy of Loue vnite our thoughts.

Queen. Great King of England, & my gracious Lord,
The mutuall conference that my minde hath had,
By day, by night; waking, and in my dreames,
In Courtly company, or at my Beades,
With you mine *Alder liefest* Soueraigne,
Makes me the bolder to salute my King,
With ruder termes, such as my wit affoords,
And ouer ioy of heart doth minister.

King. Her sight did rauish, but her grace in Speech,
Her words yclad with wisedomes Maiesty,
Makes me from Wondring, fall to Weeping ioyes,
Such is the Fulnesse of my hearts content.
Lords, with one cheerefull voice, Welcome my Loue.

All kneel. Long liue Qu. *Margaret*, Englands happines.

Queene. We thanke you all. *Florish*

Suf. My Lord Protector, so it please your Grace,
Heere are the Articles of contracted peace,
Betweene our Soueraigne, and the French King *Charles*,
For eighteene moneths concluded by consent.

Glo. Reads. Inprimis, *It is agreed betweene the French K. Charles, and William de la Pole Marquesse of Suffolke, Ambassador for Henry King of England, That the said Henry shal espouse the Lady Margaret, daughter vnto Reignier King of Naples, Sicillia, and Ierusalem, and Crowne her Queene of England, ere the thirtieth of May next ensuing.*

Item, *That the Dutchy of Anion, and the County of Main, shall be released and deliuered to the King her father.*

King. Vnkle, how now?

Glo. Pardon me gracious Lord,
Some sodaine qualme hath strucke me at the heart,
And dim'd mine eyes, that I can reade no further.

King. Vnckle of Winchester, I pray read on.

Win. Item, *It is further agreed betweene them, That the Dutchesse of Aniou and Maine, shall be released and deliuered ouer to the King her Father, and shee sent ouer of the King of Englands owne proper Cost and Charges, without hauing any Dowry.*

King. They please vs well. Lord Marques kneel down,
We heere create thee the first Duke of Suffolke,
And girt thee with the Sword. Cosin of Yorke,
We heere discharge your Grace from being Regent
I'th parts of France, till terme of eighteene Moneths
Be full expyr'd. Thankes Vncle Winchester,
Gloster, Yorke, Buckingham, Somerset,
Salisburie, and Warwicke.
We thanke you all for this great fauour done,
In entertainment to my Princely Queene.
Come, let vs in, and with all speede prouide
To see her Coronation be perform'd.

Exit King, Queene, and Suffolke.

Manet the rest.

Glo. Braue Peeres of England, Pillars of the State,
To you Duke *Humfrey* must vnload his greefe:
Your greefe, the common greefe of all the Land.
What? did my brother *Henry* spend his youth,
His valour, coine, and people in the warres?
Did he so often lodge in open field:
In Winters cold, and Summers parching heate,
To conquer France, his true inheritance?
And did my brother *Bedford* toyle his wits,

To

To keepe by policy what *Henrie* got:
Haue you your selues, *Somerset*, *Buckingham*,
Braue *Yorke*, *Salisbury*, and victorious *Warwicke*,
Receiud deepe scarres in France and Normandie:
Or hath mine Vnckle *Beauford*, and my selfe,
With all the Learned Counsell of the Realme,
Studied so long, sat in the Councell house,
Early and late, debating too and fro
How France and Frenchmen might be kept in awe,
And hath his Highnesse in his infancie,
Crowned in Paris in despight of foes,
And shall these Labours, and these Honours dye?
Shall *Henries* Conquest, *Bedfords* vigilance,
Your Deeds of Warre, and all our Counsell dye?
O Peeres of England, shamefull is this League,
Fatall this Marriage, cancelling your Fame,
Blotting your names from Bookes of memory,
Racing the Charracters of your Renowne,
Defacing Monuments of Conquer'd France,
Vndoing all as all had neuer bin.

Car. Nephew, what meanes this passionate discourse?
This preroration with such circumstance:
For France, 'tis ours; and we will keepe it still.

Glo. I Vnckle, we will keepe it, if we can:
But now it is impossible we should.
Suffolke, the new made Duke that rules the rost,
Hath giuen the Dutchy of *Aniou* and *Mayne*,
Vnto the poore King *Reignier*, whose large style
Agrees not with the leannesse of his purse.

Sal. Now by the death of him that dyed for all,
These Counties were the Keyes of *Normandie*:
But wherefore weepes *Warwicke*, my valiant sonne?

War. For greefe that they are past recouerie.
For were there hope to conquer them againe,
My sword should shed hot blood, mine eyes no teares.
Anion and *Maine*? My selfe did win them both:
Those Prouinces, these Armes of mine did conquer,
And are the Citties that I got with wounds,
Deliuer'd vp againe with peacefull words?
Mort Dieu.

Yorke. For Suffolkes Duke, may he be suffocate,
That dims the Honor of this Warlike Isle:
France should haue torne and rent my very hart,
Before I would haue yeelded to this League.
I neuer read but Englands Kings haue had
Large summes of Gold, and Dowries with their wiues,
And our King *Henry* giues away his owne,
To match with her that brings no vantages.

Hum. A proper iest, and neuer heard before,
That Suffolke should demand a whole Fifteenth,
For Costs and Charges in transporting her:
She should haue staid in France, and steru'd in France
Before———

Car. My Lord of Gloster, now ye grow too hot,
It was the pleasure of my Lord the King.

Hum. My Lord of Winchester I know your minde.
'Tis not my speeches that you do mislike:
But 'tis my presence that doth trouble ye,
Rancour will out, proud Prelate, in thy face
I see thy furie: If I longer stay,
We shall begin our ancient bickerings:
Lordings farewell, and say when I am gone,
I prophesied, France will be lost ere long. *Exit Humfrey.*

Car. So, there goes our Protector in a rage:
'Tis knowne to you he is mine enemy:
Nay more, an enemy vnto you all,
And no great friend, I feare me to the King;
Consider Lords, he is the next of blood,
And heyre apparant to the English Crowne:
Had *Henrie* got an Empire by his marriage,
And all the wealthy Kingdomes of the West,
There's reason he should be displeas'd at it:
Looke to it Lords, let not his smoothing words
Bewitch your hearts, be wise and circumspect.
What though the common people fauour him,
Calling him, *Humfrey the good Duke of Gloster*,
Clapping their hands, and crying with loud voyce,
Iesu maintaine your Royall Excellence,
With God preserue the good Duke *Humfrey*:
I feare me Lords, for all this flattering glosse,
He will be found a dangerous Protector.

Buc. Why should he then protect our Soueraigne?
He being of age to gouerne of himselfe.
Cosin of Somerset, ioyne you with me,
And altogether with the Duke of Suffolke,
Wee'l quickly hoyse Duke *Humfrey* from his seat.

Car. This weighty businesse will not brooke delay,
Ile to the Duke of Suffolke presently. *Exit Cardinall.*

Som. Cosin of Buckingham, though *Humfries* pride
And greatnesse of his place be greefe to vs,
Yet let vs watch the haughtie Cardinall,
His insolence is more intollerable
Then all the Princes in the Land beside,
If Gloster be displac'd, hee'l be Protector.

Buc. Or thou, or I Somerset will be Protectors,
Despite Duke *Humfrey*, or the Cardinall.

Exit Buckingham, and Somerset.

Sal. Pride went before, Ambition followes him.
While these do labour for their owne preferment,
Behooues it vs to labor for the Realme.
I neuer saw but Humfrey Duke of Gloster,
Did beare him like a Noble Gentleman:
Oft haue I seene the haughty Cardinall,
More like a Souldier then a man o'th'Church,
As stout and proud as he were Lord of all,
Sweare like a Ruffian, and demeane himselfe
Vnlike the Ruler of a Common-weale.
Warwicke my sonne, the comfort of my age,
Thy deeds, thy plainnesse, and thy house-keeping,
Hath wonne the greatest fauour of the Commons,
Excepting none but good Duke Humfrey.
And Brother Yorke, thy Acts in Ireland,
In bringing them to ciuill Discipline:
Thy late exploits done in the heart of France,
When thou wert Regent for our Soueraigne,
Haue made thee fear'd and honor'd of the people,
Ioyne we together for the publike good,
In what we can, to bridle and suppresse
The pride of Suffolke, and the Cardinall,
With Somersets and Buckinghams Ambition,
And as we may, cherish Duke Humfries deeds,
While they do tend the profit of the Land.

War. So God helpe Warwicke, as he loues the Land,
And common profit of his Countrey

Yor. And so sayes Yorke,
For he hath greatest cause.

Salisbury. Then lets make hast away,
And looke vnto the maine.

Warwicke. Vnto the maine?
Oh Father, *Maine* is lost,
That *Maine*, which by maine force Warwicke did winne,
And would haue kept, so long as breath did last:

Main-chance father you meant, but I meant *Maine*,
Which I will win from France, or else be slaine.

Exit Warwicke, and Salisbury. Manet Yorke.

Yorke. *Anion* and *Maine* are giuen to the French,
Paris is lost, the state of *Normandie*
Stands on a tickle point, now they are gone:
Suffolke concluded on the Articles,
The Peeres agreed, and *Henry* was well pleas'd,
To change two Dukedomes for a Dukes faire daughter.
I cannot blame them all, what is't to them?
'Tis thine they giue away, and not their owne.
Pirates may make cheape penyworths of their pillage,
And purchase Friends, and giue to Curtezans,
Still reuelling like Lords till all be gone,
While as the silly Owner of the goods
Weepes ouer them, and wrings his haplesse hands,
And shakes his head, and trembling stands aloofe,
While all is shar'd, and all is borne away,
Ready to sterue, and dare not touch his owne.
So Yorke must sit, and fret, and bite his tongue,
While his owne Lands are bargain'd for, and sold:
Me thinkes the Realmes of England, France, & Ireland,
Beare that proportion to my flesh and blood,
As did the fatall brand *Althaea* burnt,
Vnto the Princes heart of *Calidon*:
Anion and *Maine* both giuen vnto the French?
Cold newes for me: for I had hope of France,
Euen as I haue of fertile Englands soile.
A day will come, when Yorke shall claime his owne,
And therefore I will take the *Neuils* parts,
And make a shew of loue to proud Duke *Humfrey*,
And when I spy aduantage, claime the Crowne,
For that's the Golden marke I seeke to hit:
Nor shall proud Lancaster vsurpe my right,
Nor hold the Scepter in his childish Fist,
Nor weare the Diadem vpon his head,
Whose Church-like humors fits not for a Crowne.
Then Yorke be still a-while, till time do serue:
Watch thou, and wake when others be asleepe,
To prie into the secrets of the State,
Till *Henrie* surfetting in ioyes of loue,
With his new Bride, & Englands deere bought Queen,
And *Humfrey* with the Peeres be falne at iarres:
Then will I raise aloft the Milke-white-Rose,
With whose sweet smell the Ayre shall be perfum'd,
And in my Standard beare the Armes of Yorke,
To grapple with the house of Lancaster,
And force perforce Ile make him yeeld the Crowne,
Whose bookish Rule, hath pull'd faire England downe.

Exit Yorke.

Enter Duke Humfrey and his wife Elianor.

Elia. Why droopes my Lord like ouer-ripen'd Corn,
Hanging the head at Ceres plenteous load?
Why doth the Great Duke *Humfrey* knit his browes,
As frowning at the Fauours of the world?
Why are thine eyes fixt to the sullen earth,
Gazing on that which seemes to dimme thy sight?
What seest thou there? King *Henries* Diadem,
Inchac'd with all the Honors of the world?
If so, Gaze on, and grouell on thy face,
Vntill thy head be circled with the same.
Put forth thy hand, reach at the glorious Gold.
What, is't too short? Ile lengthen it with mine,
And hauing both together heau'd it vp,
Wee'l both together lift our heads to heauen,
And neuer more abase our sight so low,
As to vouchsafe one glance vnto the ground.

Hum. O *Nell*, sweet *Nell*, if thou dost loue thy Lord,
Banish the Canker of ambitious thoughts:
And may that thought, when I imagine ill
Against my King and Nephew, vertuous *Henry*,
Be my last breathing in this mortall world.
My troublous dreames this night, doth make me sad.

Eli. What dream'd my Lord, tell me, and Ile requite it
With sweet rehearsall of my mornings dreame?

Hum. Me thought this staffe mine Office-badge in Court
Was broke in twaine: by whom, I haue forgot,
But as I thinke, it was by'th Cardinall,
And on the peeces of the broken Wand
Were plac'd the heads of *Edmond* Duke of Somerset,
And *William de la Pole* first Duke of Suffolke.
This was my dreame, what it doth bode God knowes.

Eli. Tut, this was nothing but an argument,
That he that breakes a sticke of Glosters groue,
Shall loose his head for his presumption.
But list to me my *Humfrey*, my sweete Duke:
Me thought I sate in Seate of Maiesty,
In the Cathedrall Church of Westminster,
And in that Chaire where Kings & Queens wer crownd,
Where *Henrie* and Dame *Margaret* kneel'd to me,
And on my head did set the Diadem.

Hum. Nay *Elinor*, then must I chide outright:
Presumptuous Dame, ill-nurter'd *Elianor*,
Art thou not second Woman in the Realme?
And the Protectors wife belou'd of him?
Hast thou not worldly pleasure at command,
Aboue the reach or compasse of thy thought?
And wilt thou still be hammering Treachery,
To tumble downe thy husband, and thy selfe,
From top of Honor, to Disgraces feete?
Away from me, and let me heare no more.

Elia. What, what, my Lord? Are you so chollericke
With *Elianor*, for telling but her dreame?
Next time Ile keepe my dreames vnto my selfe,
And not be check'd.

Hum. Nay be not angry, I am pleas'd againe.

Enter Messenger.

Mess. My Lord Protector, 'tis his Highnes pleasure,
You do prepare to ride vnto S. *Albons*,
Where as the King and Queene do meane to Hawke.

Hu. I go. Come *Nel* thou wilt ride with vs? *Ex. Hum*

Eli. Yes my good Lord, Ile follow presently.
Follow I must, I cannot go before,
While Gloster beares this base and humble minde.
Were I a Man, a Duke, and next of blood,
I would remoue these tedious stumbling blockes,
And smooth my way vpon their headlesse neckes.
And being a woman, I will not be slacke
To play my part in Fortunes Pageant.
Where are you there? Sir *Iohn*; nay feare not man,
We are alone, here's none but thee, & I. *Enter Hume.*

Hume. Iesus preserue your Royall Maiesty.

Elia. What saist thou? Maiesty: I am but Grace.

Hume. But by the grace of God, and *Humes* aduice,
Your Graces Title shall be multiplied.

Elia. What saist thou man? Hast thou as yet confer'd
With *Margerie Iordane* the cunning Witch,
With *Roger Bollingbrooke* the Coniurer?
And will they vndertake to do me good?

Hume. This they haue promised to shew your Highnes
A Spirit rais'd from depth of vnder ground,

That

That shall make answere to such Questions,
As by your Grace shall be propounded him.

Elianor. It is enough, Ile thinke vpon the Questions:
When from Saint *Albones* wee doe make returne,
Wee'le see these things effected to the full.
Here *Hume*, take this reward, make merry man
With thy Confederates in this weightie cause.

Exit Elianor.

Hume. *Hume* must make merry with the Duchesse Gold:
Marry and shall: but how now, Sir *Iohn Hume*?
Seale vp your Lips, and giue no words but Mum,
The businesse asketh silent secrecie.
Dame *Elianor* giues Gold, to bring the Witch:
Gold cannot come amisse, were she a Deuill.
Yet haue I Gold flyes from another Coast:
I dare not say, from the rich Cardinall,
And from the great and new-made Duke of Suffolke;
Yet I doe finde it so: for to be plaine,
They (knowing Dame *Elianors* aspiring humor)
Haue hyred me to vnder-mine the Duchesse,
And buzze these Coniurations in her brayne.
They say, A craftie Knaue do's need no Broker,
Yet am I *Suffolke* and the Cardinalls Broker.
Hume, if you take not heed, you shall goe neere
To call them both a payre of craftie Knaues.
Well, so it stands: and thus I feare at last,
Humes Knauerie will be the Duchesse Wracke,
And her Attainture, will be *Humphreyes* fall:
Sort how it will, I shall haue Gold for all. *Exit*

Enter three or foure Petitioners, the Armorers Man being one.

1. Pet. My Masters, let's stand close, my Lord Protector will come this way by and by, and then wee may deliuer our Supplications in the Quill.

2. Pet. Marry the Lord protect him, for hee's a good man, Iesu blesse him.

Enter Suffolke, and Queene.

Peter. Here a comes me thinkes, and the Queene with him: Ile be the first sure.

2. Pet. Come backe foole, this is the Duke of Suffolk, and not my Lord Protector.

Suff. How now fellow: would'st any thing with me?

1. Pet. I pray my Lord pardon me, I tooke ye for my Lord Protector.

Queene. To my Lord Protector? Are your Supplications to his Lordship? Let me see them: what is thine?

1. Pet. Mine is, and't please your Grace, against *Iohn Goodman*, my Lord Cardinals Man, for keeping my House, and Lands, and Wife and all, from me.

Suff. Thy Wife too? that's some Wrong indeede. What's yours? What's heere? Against the Duke of Suffolke, for enclosing the Commons of Melforde. How now, Sir Knaue?

2. Pet. Alas Sir, I am but a poore Petitioner of our whole Towneship.

Peter. Against my Master *Thomas Horner*, for saying, That the Duke of Yorke was rightfull Heire to the Crowne.

Queene. What say'st thou? Did the Duke of Yorke say, hee was rightfull Heire to the Crowne?

Peter. That my Mistresse was? No forsooth: my Master said, That he was, and that the King was an Vsurper.

Suff. Who is there?

Enter Seruant.

Take this fellow in, and send for his Master with a Purseuant presently: wee'le heare more of your matter before the King. *Exit.*

Queene. And as for you that loue to be protected
Vnder the Wings of our Protectors Grace,
Begin your Suites anew, and sue to him.

Teare the Supplication.

Away, base Cullions: *Suffolke* let them goe.

All. Come, let's be gone. *Exit.*

Queene. My Lord of Suffolke, say, is this the guise?
Is this the Fashions in the Court of England?
Is this the Gouernment of Britaines Ile?
And this the Royaltie of *Albions* King?
What, shall King *Henry* be a Pupill still,
Vnder the surly *Glosters* Gouernance?
Am I a Queene in Title and in Stile,
And must be made a Subiect to a Duke?
I tell thee *Poole*, when in the Citie *Tours*
Thou ran'st a-tilt in honor of my Loue,
And stol'st away the Ladies hearts of France;
I thought King *Henry* had resembled thee,
In Courage, Courtship, and Proportion:
But all his minde is bent to Holinesse,
To number *Aue-Maries* on his Beades:
His Champions, are the Prophets and Apostles,
His Weapons, holy Sawes of sacred Writ,
His Studie is his Tilt-yard, and his Loues
Are brazen Images of Canonized Saints.
I would the Colledge of the Cardinalls
Would chuse him Pope, and carry him to Rome,
And set the Triple Crowne vpon his Head;
That were a State fit for his Holinesse.

Suff. Madame be patient: as I was cause
Your Highnesse came to England, so will I
In England worke your Graces full content.

Queene. Beside the haughtie Protector, haue we *Beauford*
The imperious Churchman; *Somerset*, *Buckingham*,
And grumbling *Yorke*: and not the least of these,
But can doe more in England then the King.

Suff. And he of these, that can doe most of all,
Cannot doe more in England then the *Neuils*:
Salisbury and *Warwick* are no simple Peeres.

Queene. Not all these Lords do vex me halfe so much,
As that prowd Dame, the Lord Protectors Wife:
She sweepes it through the Court with troups of Ladies,
More like an Empresse, then Duke *Humphreyes* Wife:
Strangers in Court, doe take her for the Queene:
She beares a Dukes Reuenewes on her backe,
And in her heart she scornes our Pouertie:
Shall I not liue to be aueng'd on her?
Contemptuous base-borne Callot as she is,
She vaunted 'mongst her Minions t'other day,
The very trayne of her worst wearing Gowne,
Was better worth then all my Fathers Lands,
Till *Suffolke* gaue two Dukedomes for his Daughter.

Suff. Madame, my selfe haue lym'd a Bush for her,
And plac't a Quier of such enticing Birds,
That she will light to listen to the Layes,
And neuer mount to trouble you againe.
So let her rest: and Madame list to me,
For I am bold to counsaile you in this;
Although we fancie not the Cardinall,
Yet must we ioyne with him and with the Lords,
Till we haue brought Duke *Humphrey* in disgrace.

As

As for the Duke of Yorke, this late Complaint
Will make but little for his benefit:
So one by one wee'le weed them all at last,
And you your selfe shall steere the happy Helme. *Exit.*

Sound a Sennet.

Enter the King, Duke Humfrey, Cardinall, Buckingham, Yorke, Salisbury, Warwicke, and the Duchesse.

King. For my part, Noble Lords, I care not which,
Or *Somerset*, or *Yorke*, all's one to me.
Yorke. If *Yorke* haue ill demean'd himselfe in France,
Then let him be denay'd the Regent-ship.
Som. If *Somerset* be vnworthy of the Place,
Let *Yorke* be Regent, I will yeeld to him.
Warw. Whether your Grace be worthy, yea or no,
Dispute not that, *Yorke* is the worthyer.
Card. Ambitious *Warwicke*, let thy betters speake.
Warw. The Cardinall's not my better in the field.
Buck. All in this presence are thy betters, *Warwicke*.
Warw. *Warwicke* may liue to be the best of all.
Salisb. Peace Sonne, and shew some reason *Buckingham*
Why *Somerset* should be preferr'd in this?
Queene. Because the King forsooth will haue it so.
Humf. Madame, the King is old enough himselfe
To giue his Censure: These are no Womens matters.
Queene. If he be old enough, what needs your Grace
To be Protector of his Excellence?
Humf. Madame, I am Protector of the Realme,
And at his pleasure will resigne my Place.
Suff. Resigne it then, and leaue thine insolence.
Since thou wert King; as who is King, but thou?
The Common-wealth hath dayly run to wrack,
The Dolphin hath preuayl'd beyond the Seas,
And all the Peeres and Nobles of the Realme
Haue beene as Bond-men to thy Soueraigntie.
Card. The Commons hast thou rackt, the Clergies Bags
Are lanke and leane with thy Extortions.
Som. Thy sumptuous Buildings, and thy Wiues Attyre
Haue cost a masse of publique Treasurie.
Buck. Thy Crueltie in execution
Vpon Offendors, hath exceeded Law,
And left thee to the mercy of the Law.
Queene. Thy sale of Offices and Townes in France,
If they were knowne, as the suspect is great,
Would make thee quickly hop without thy Head.
Exit Humfrey.
Giue me my Fanne: what, Mynion, can ye not?
She giues the Duchesse a box on the eare.
I cry you mercy, Madame: was it you?
Duch. Was't I? yea, I it was, prowd French-woman:
Could I come neere your Beautie with my Nayles,
I could set my ten Commandements in your face.
King. Sweet Aunt be quiet, 'twas against her will.
Duch. Against her will, good King? looke to't in time,
Shee'le hamper thee, and dandle thee like a Baby:
Though in this place most Master weare no Breeches,
She shall not strike Dame *Elianor* vnreueng'd.
Exit Elianor.
Buck. Lord Cardinall, I will follow *Elianor*,
And listen after *Humfrey*, how he proceedes:
Shee's tickled now, her Fume needs no spurres,
Shee'le gallop farre enough to her destruction.
Exit Buckingham.

Enter Humfrey.

Humf. Now Lords, my Choller being ouer-blowne,
With walking once about the Quadrangle,
I come to talke of Common-wealth Affayres.
As for your spightfull false Obiections,
Proue them, and I lye open to the Law:
But God in mercie so deale with my Soule,
As I in dutie loue my King and Countrey.
But to the matter that we haue in hand:
I say, my Soueraigne, *Yorke* is meetest man
To be your Regent in the Realme of France.
Suff. Before we make election, giue me leaue
To shew some reason, of no little force,
That *Yorke* is most vnmeet of any man.
Yorke. Ile tell thee, *Suffolke*, why I am vnmeet.
First, for I cannot flatter thee in Pride:
Next, if I be appointed for the Place,
My Lord of Somerset will keepe me here,
Without Discharge, Money, or Furniture,
Till France be wonne into the Dolphins hands:
Last time I danc't attendance on his will,
Till Paris was besieg'd, famisht, and lost.
Warw. That can I witnesse, and a fouler fact
Did neuer Traytor in the Land commit.
Suff. Peace head-strong *Warwicke*.
Warw. Image of Pride, why should I hold my peace?

Enter Armorer and his Man.

Suff. Because here is a man accused of Treason,
Pray God the Duke of Yorke excuse himselfe.
Yorke. Doth any one accuse *Yorke* for a Traytor?
King. What mean'st thou, *Suffolke*? tell me, what are these?
Suff. Please it your Maiestie, this is the man
That doth accuse his Master of High Treason;
His words were these: That *Richard*, Duke of Yorke,
Was rightfull Heire vnto the English Crowne,
And that your Maiestie was an Vsurper.
King. Say man, were these thy words?
Armorer. And't shall please your Maiestie, I neuer sayd nor thought any such matter: God is my witnesse, I am falsely accus'd by the Villaine.
Peter. By these tenne bones, my Lords, hee did speake them to me in the Garret one Night, as wee were scowring my Lord of Yorkes Armor.
Yorke. Base Dunghill Villaine, and Mechanicall,
Ile haue thy Head for this thy Traytors speech:
I doe beseech your Royall Maiestie,
Let him haue all the rigor of the Law.
Armorer. Alas, my Lord, hang me if euer I spake the words: my accuser is my Prentice, and when I did correct him for his fault the other day, he did vow vpon his knees he would be euen with me: I haue good witnesse of this; therefore I beseech your Maiestie, doe not cast away an honest man for a Villaines accusation.
King. Vnckle, what shall we say to this in law?
Humf. This doome, my Lord, if I may iudge:
Let *Somerset* be Regent o're the French,
Because in *Yorke* this breedes suspition;
And let these haue a day appointed them
For single Combat, in conuenient place,
For he hath witnesse of his seruants malice:
This is the Law, and this Duke *Humfreyes* doome.

Som. I humbly thanke your Royall Maiestie.

Armorer. And I accept the Combat willingly.

Peter. Alas, my Lord, I cannot fight; for Gods sake pitty my case: the spight of man preuayleth against me. O Lord haue mercy vpon me, I shall neuer be able to fight a blow: O Lord my heart.

Humf. Sirrha, or you must fight, or else be hang'd.

King. Away with them to Prison: and the day of Combat, shall be the last of the next moneth. Come *Somerset*, wee'le see thee sent away.

Flourish. Exeunt.

Enter the Witch, the two Priests, and Bullingbrooke.

Hume. Come my Masters, the Duchesse I tell you expects performance of your promises.

Bulling. Master *Hume*, we are therefore prouided: will her Ladyship behold and heare our Exorcismes?

Hume. I, what else? feare you not her courage.

Bulling. I haue heard her reported to be a Woman of an inuincible spirit: but it shall be conuenient, Master *Hume*, that you be by her aloft, while wee be busie below; and so I pray you goe in Gods Name, and leaue vs.

Exit Hume.

Mother *Iordan*, be you prostrate, and grouell on the Earth; *Iohn Southwell* reade you, and let vs to our worke.

Enter Elianor aloft.

Elianor. Well said my Masters, and welcome all: To this geere, the sooner the better.

Bullin. Patience, good Lady, Wizards know their times:
Deepe Night, darke Night, the silent of the Night,
The time of Night when Troy was set on fire,
The time when Screech-owles cry, and Bandogs howle,
And Spirits walke, and Ghosts breake vp their Graues;
That time best fits the worke we haue in hand.
Madame, sit you, and feare not: whom wee rayse,
Wee will make fast within a hallow'd Verge.

Here doe the Ceremonies belonging, and make the Circle, Bullingbrooke or Southwell reades, Coniuro te, &c. *It Thunders and Lightens terribly: then the Spirit riseth.*

Spirit. *Ad sum.*

Witch. *Asmath*, by the eternall God,
Whose name and power thou tremblest at,
Answere that I shall aske: for till thou speake,
Thou shalt not passe from hence.

Spirit. Aske what thou wilt; that I had sayd, and done.

Bulling. First of the King: What shall of him become?

Spirit. The Duke yet liues, that *Henry* shall depose:
But him out-liue, and dye a violent death.

Bulling. What fates await the Duke of Suffolke?

Spirit. By Water shall he dye, and take his end.

Bulling. What shall befall the Duke of Somerset?

Spirit. Let him shun Castles,
Safer shall he be vpon the sandie Plaines,
Then where Castles mounted stand.
Haue done, for more I hardly can endure.

Bulling. Discend to Darknesse, and the burning Lake:
False Fiend auoide.

Thunder and Lightning. Exit Spirit.

Enter the Duke of Yorke and the Duke of Buckingham with their Guard, and breake in.

Yorke. Lay hands vpon these Traytors, and their trash:
Beldam I thinke we watcht you at an ynch.
What Madame, are you there? the King & Commonweale
Are deepely indebted for this peece of paines;
My Lord Protector will, I doubt it not,
See you well guerdon'd for these good deserts.

Elianor. Not halfe so bad as thine to Englands King,
Iniurious Duke, that threatest where's no cause.

Buck. True Madame, none at all: what call you this?
Away with them, let them be clapt vp close,
And kept asunder: you Madame shall with vs.
Stafford take her to thee.
Wee'le see your Trinkets here all forth-comming.
All away. *Exit.*

Yorke. Lord *Buckingham*, me thinks you watcht her well:
A pretty Plot, well chosen to build vpon.
Now pray my Lord, let's see the Deuils Writ.
What haue we here? *Reades.*
The Duke yet liues, that Henry *shall depose:*
But him out-liue, and dye a violent death.
Why this is iust *Aio Æacida Romanos vincere posso.*
Well, to the rest:
Tell me what fate awaits the Duke of Suffolke?
By Water shall he dye, and take his end.
What shall betide the Duke of Somerset?
Let him shunne Castles,
Safer shall he be vpon the sandie Plaines,
Then where Castles mounted stand.
Come, come, my Lords,
These Oracles are hardly attain'd,
And hardly vnderstood.
The King is now in progresse towards Saint *Albones*,
With him, the Husband of this louely Lady:
Thither goes these Newes,
As fast as Horse can carry them:
A sorry Breakfast for my Lord Protector.

Buck. Your Grace shal giue me leaue, my Lord of York,
To be the Poste, in hope of his reward.

Yorke. At your pleasure, my good Lord.
Who's within there, hoe?

Enter a Seruingman.

Inuite my Lords of Salisbury and Warwick
To suppe with me to morrow Night. Away.

Exeunt.

Enter the King, Queene, Protector, Cardinall, and Suffolke, with Faulkners hallowing.

Queene. Beleeue me Lords, for flying at the Brooke,
I saw not better sport these seuen yeeres day:
Yet by your leaue, the Winde was very high,
And ten to one, old *Ioane* had not gone out.

King. But what a point, my Lord, your Faulcon made,
And what a pytch she flew aboue the rest:
To see how God in all his Creatures workes,
Yea Man and Birds are fayne of climbing high.

Suff. No maruell, and it like your Maiestie,
My Lord Protectors Hawkes doe towre so well,
They know their Master loues to be aloft,
And beares his thoughts aboue his Faulcons Pitch.

Glost. My Lord, 'tis but a base ignoble minde,
That mounts no higher then a Bird can sore:

Card. I thought as much, hee would be aboue the Clouds.

Glost. I my Lord Cardinall, how thinke you by that?
Were it not good your Grace could flye to Heauen?

King. The Treasurie of euerlasting Ioy.

Card. Thy Heauen is on Earth, thine Eyes & Thoughts
Beat on a Crowne, the Treasure of thy Heart,
Pernitious Protector, dangerous Peere,
That smooth'st it so with King and Common-weale.

Glost. What, Cardinall?
Is your Priest-hood growne peremptorie?
Tantane animis Cœlestibus iræ, Church-men so hot?
Good Vnckle hide such mallice:
With such Holynesse can you doe it?

Suff. No mallice Sir, no more then well becomes
So good a Quarrell, and so bad a Peere.

Glost. As who, my Lord?

Suff. Why, as you, my Lord,
An't like your Lordly Lords Protectorship.

Glost. Why *Suffolke*, England knowes thine insolence.

Queene. And thy Ambition, *Gloster*.

King. I prythee peace, good Queene,
And whet not on these furious Peeres,
For blessed are the Peace-makers on Earth.

Card. Let me be blessed for the Peace I make
Against this prowd Protector with my Sword.

Glost. Faith holy Vnckle, would't were come to that.

Card. Marry, when thou dar'st.

Glost. Make vp no factious numbers for the matter,
In thine owne person answere thy abuse.

Card. I, where thou dar'st not peepe:
And if thou dar'st, this Euening,
On the East side of the Groue.

King. How now, my Lords?

Card. Beleeue me, Cousin *Gloster*,
Had not your man put vp the Fowle so suddenly,
We had had more sport.
Come with thy two hand Sword.

Glost. True Vnckle, are ye aduis'd?
The East side of the Groue:
Cardinall, I am with you.

King. Why how now, Vnckle *Gloster*?

Glost. Talking of Hawking; nothing else, my Lord
Now by Gods Mother, Priest,
Ile shaue your Crowne for this,
Or all my Fence shall fayle.

Card. *Medice teipsum*, Protector see to't well, protect your selfe.

King. The Windes grow high,
So doe your Stomacks, Lords:
How irkesome is this Musick to my heart?
When such Strings iarre, what hope of Harmony?
I pray my Lords let me compound this strife.

Enter one crying a Miracle.

Glost. What meanes this noyse?
Fellow, what Miracle do'st thou proclayme?

One. A Miracle, a Miracle.

Suffolke. Come to the King, and tell him what Miracle.

One. Forsooth, a blinde man at Saint *Albones* Shrine,
Within this halfe houre hath receiu'd his sight,
A man that ne're saw in his life before.

King. Now God be prays'd, that to beleeuing Soules
Giues Light in Darknesse, Comfort in Despaire.

Enter the Maior of Saint Albones, and his Brethren, bearing the man betweene two in a Chayre.

Card. Here comes the Townes-men, on Procession,
To present your Highnesse with the man.

King. Great is his comfort in this Earthly Vale,
Although by his sight his sinne be multiplyed.

Glost. Stand by, my Masters, bring him neere the King,
His Highnesse pleasure is to talke with him.

King Good-fellow, tell vs here the circumstance,
That we for thee may glorifie the Lord.
What, hast thou beene long blinde, and now restor'd?

Simpc. Borne blinde, and't please your Grace.

Wife. I indeede was he.

Suff. What Woman is this?

Wife. His Wife, and't like your Worship.

Glost. Hadst thou been his Mother, thou could'st haue better told.

King. Where wert thou borne?

Simpc. At Barwick in the North, and't like your Grace.

King. Poore Soule,
Gods goodnesse hath beene great to thee:
Let neuer Day nor Night vnhallowed passe,
But still remember what the Lord hath done.

Queene. Tell me, good-fellow,
Cam'st thou here by Chance, or of Deuotion,
To this holy Shrine?

Simpc. God knowes of pure Deuotion,
Being call'd a hundred times, and oftner,
In my sleepe, by good Saint *Albon*:
Who said; *Symon*, come; come offer at my Shrine,
And I will helpe thee.

Wife. Most true, forsooth:
And many time and oft my selfe haue heard a Voyce,
To call him so.

Card. What, art thou lame?

Simpc. I, God Almightie helpe me.

Suff. How cam'st thou so?

Simpc. A fall off of a Tree.

Wife. A Plum-tree, Master.

Glost. How long hast thou beene blinde?

Simpc. O borne so, Master.

Glost. What, and would'st climbe a Tree?

Simpc. But that in all my life, when I was a youth.

Wife. Too true, and bought his climbing very deare.

Glost. 'Masse, thou lou'dst Plummes well, that would'st venture so.

Simpc. Alas, good Master, my Wife desired some Damsons, and made me climbe, with danger of my Life.

Glost. A subtill Knaue, but yet it shall not serue:
Let me see thine Eyes; winck now, now open them,
In my opinion, yet thou seest not well.

Simpc. Yes Master, cleare as day, I thanke God and Saint *Albones*.

Glost. Say'st thou me so: what Colour is this Cloake of?

Simpc. Red Master, Red as Blood.

Glost. Why that's well said: What Colour is my Gowne of?

Simpc. Black forsooth, Coale-Black, as Iet.

King. Why then, thou know'st what Colour Iet is of?

Suff. And yet I thinke, Iet did he neuer see.

Glost. But

Glost. But Cloakes and Gownes, before this day, a many.
Wife. Neuer before this day, in all his life.
Glost. Tell me Sirrha, what's my Name?
Simpc. Alas Master, I know not.
Glost. What's his Name?
Simpc. I know not.
Glost. Nor his?
Simpc. No indeede, Master.
Glost. What's thine owne Name?
Simpc. *Saunder Simpcoxe*, and if it please you, Master.
Glost. Then *Saunder*, sit there,
The lying'st Knaue in Christendome.
If thou hadst beene borne blinde,
Thou might'st as well haue knowne all our Names,
As thus to name the seuerall Colours we doe weare.
Sight may distinguish of Colours:
But suddenly to nominate them all,
It is impossible.
My Lords, Saint *Albone* here hath done a Miracle:
And would ye not thinke it, Cunning to be great,
That could restore this Cripple to his Legges againe.
Simpc. O Master, that you could?
Glost. My Masters of Saint *Albones*,
Haue you not Beadles in your Towne,
And Things call'd Whippes?
Maior. Yes, my Lord, if it please your Grace.
Glost. Then send for one presently.
Maior. Sirrha, goe fetch the Beadle hither straight.
Exit.
Glost. Now fetch me a Stoole hither by and by.
Now Sirrha, if you meane to saue your selfe from Whipping, leape me ouer this Stoole, and runne away.
Simpc. Alas Master, I am not able to stand alone:
You goe about to torture me in vaine.

Enter a Beadle with Whippes.

Glost. Well Sir, we must haue you finde your Legges.
Sirrha Beadle, whippe him till he leape ouer that same Stoole.
Beadle. I will, my Lord.
Come on Sirrha, off with your Doublet, quickly.
Simpc. Alas Master, what shall I doe? I am not able to stand.

After the Beadle hath hit him once, he leapes ouer the Stoole, and runnes away: and they follow, and cry, A Miracle.

King. O God, seest thou this, and bearest so long?
Queene. It made me laugh, to see the Villaine runne.
Glost. Follow the Knaue, and take this Drab away.
Wife. Alas Sir, we did it for pure need.
Glost. Let thẽ be whipt through euery Market Towne,
Till they come to Barwick, from whence they came.
Exit.
Card. Duke *Humfrey* ha's done a Miracle to day.
Suff. True: made the Lame to leape and flye away.
Glost. But you haue done more Miracles then I:
You made in a day, my Lord, whole Townes to flye.

Enter Buckingham.

King. What Tidings with our Cousin *Buckingham*?
Buck. Such as my heart doth tremble to vnfold:
A sort of naughtie persons, lewdly bent,
Vnder the Countenance and Confederacie
Of Lady *Elianor*, the Protectors Wife,
The Ring-leader and Head of all this Rout,
Haue practis'd dangerously against your State,
Dealing with Witches and with Coniurers,
Whom we haue apprehended in the Fact,
Raysing vp wicked Spirits from vnder ground,
Demanding of King *Henries* Life and Death,
And other of your Highnesse Priuie Councell,
As more at large your Grace shall vnderstand.
Card. And so my Lord Protector, by this meanes
Your Lady is forth-comming, yet at London.
This Newes I thinke hath turn'd your Weapons edge;
'Tis like, my Lord, you will not keepe your houre.
Glost. Ambitious Church-man, leaue to afflict my heart:
Sorrow and griefe haue vanquisht all my powers;
And vanquisht as I am, I yeeld to thee,
Or to the meanest Groome.
King. O God, what mischiefes work the wicked ones?
Heaping confusion on their owne heads thereby.
Queene. *Gloster*, see here the Tainture of thy Nest,
And looke thy selfe be faultlesse, thou wert best.
Glost. Madame, for my selfe, to Heauen I doe appeale,
How I haue lou'd my King, and Common-weale:
And for my Wife, I know not how it stands,
Sorry I am to heare what I haue heard.
Noble shee is: but if shee haue forgot
Honor and Vertue, and conuers't with such,
As like to Pytch, defile Nobilitie;
I banish her my Bed, and Companie,
And giue her as a Prey to Law and Shame,
That hath dis-honored *Glosters* honest Name.
King. Well, for this Night we will repose vs here:
To morrow toward London, back againe,
To looke into this Businesse thorowly,
And call these foule Offendors to their Answeres;
And poyse the Cause in Iustice equall Scales,
Whose Beame stands sure, whose rightful cause preuailes.
Flourish. Exeunt.

Enter Yorke, Salisbury, and Warwick.

Yorke. Now my good Lords of Salisbury & Warwick,
Our simple Supper ended, giue me leaue,
In this close Walke, to satisfie my selfe,
In crauing your opinion of my Title,
Which is infallible, to Englands Crowne.
Salisb. My Lord, I long to heare it at full.
Warw. Sweet *Yorke* begin: and if thy clayme be good,
The *Neuills* are thy Subiects to command.
Yorke. Then thus:
Edward the third, my Lords, had seuen Sonnes:
The first, *Edward* the Black-Prince, Prince of Wales;
The second, *William* of Hatfield; and the third,
Lionel, Duke of Clarence; next to whom,
Was *Iohn* of Gaunt, the Duke of Lancaster;
The fift, was *Edmond Langley*, Duke of Yorke;
The sixt, was *Thomas* of Woodstock, Duke of Gloster;
William of Windsor was the seuenth, and last.
Edward the Black-Prince dyed before his Father,
And left behinde him *Richard*, his onely Sonne,
Who after *Edward* the third's death, raign'd as King,
Till *Henry Bullingbrooke*, Duke of Lancaster,
The eldest Sonne and Heire of *Iohn* of Gaunt,
Crown'd by the Name of *Henry* the fourth,
Seiz'd on the Realme, depos'd the rightfull King,
Sent his poore Queene to France, from whence she came,

And him to Pumfret; where, as all you know,
Harmelesse *Richard* was murthered traiterously.

Warw. Father, the Duke hath told the truth;
Thus got the House of *Lancaster* the Crowne.

Yorke. Which now they hold by force, and not by right:
For *Richard*, the first Sonnes Heire, being dead,
The Issue of the next Sonne should haue reign'd.

Salisb. But *William* of Hatfield dyed without an Heire.

Yorke. The third Sonne, Duke of Clarence,
From whose Line I clayme the Crowne,
Had Issue *Phillip*, a Daughter,
Who marryed *Edmond Mortimer*, Earle of March:
Edmond had Issue, *Roger*, Earle of March;
Roger had Issue, *Edmond, Anne*, and *Elianor*.

Salisb. This *Edmond*, in the Reigne of *Bullingbrooke*,
As I haue read, layd clayme vnto the Crowne,
And but for *Owen Glendour*, had beene King;
Who kept him in Captiuitie, till he dyed.
But, to the rest.

Yorke. His eldest Sister, *Anne*,
My Mother, being Heire vnto the Crowne,
Marryed *Richard*, Earle of Cambridge,
Who was to *Edmond Langley*,
Edward the thirds fift Sonnes Sonne;
By her I clayme the Kingdome:
She was Heire to *Roger*, Earle of March,
Who was the Sonne of *Edmond Mortimer*,
Who marryed *Phillip*, sole Daughter
Vnto *Lionel*, Duke of Clarence.
So, if the Issue of the elder Sonne
Succeed before the younger, I am King.

Warw. What plaine proceedings is more plain then this?
Henry doth clayme the Crowne from *Iohn* of Gaunt,
The fourth Sonne, *Yorke* claymes it from the third.
Till *Lionels* Issue fayles, his should not reigne.
It fayles not yet, but flourishes in thee,
And in thy Sonnes, faire slippes of such a Stock.
Then Father *Salisbury*, kneele we together,
And in this priuate Plot be we the first,
That shall salute our rightfull Soueraigne
With honor of his Birth-right to the Crowne.

Both. Long liue our Soueraigne *Richard*, Englands King.

Yorke. We thanke you Lords:
But I am not your King, till I be Crown'd,
And that my Sword be stayn'd
With heart-blood of the House of *Lancaster*:
And that's not suddenly to be perform'd,
But with aduice and silent secrecie.
Doe you as I doe in these dangerous dayes,
Winke at the Duke of Suffolkes insolence,
At *Beaufords* Pride, at *Somersets* Ambition,
At *Buckingham*, and all the Crew of them,
Till they haue snar'd the Shepheard of the Flock,
That vertuous Prince, the good Duke *Humfrey*:
'Tis that they seeke; and they, in seeking that,
Shall finde their deaths, if *Yorke* can prophecie.

Salisb. My Lord, breake we off; we know your minde at full.

Warw. My heart assures me, that the Earle of Warwick
Shall one day make the Duke of Yorke a King.

Yorke. And *Neuill*, this I doe assure my selfe,
Richard shall liue to make the Earle of Warwick
The greatest man in England, but the King.

Exeunt.

Sound Trumpets. Enter the King and State,
with Guard, to banish the Duchesse.

King. Stand forth Dame *Elianor Cobham*,
Glosters Wife:
In sight of God, and vs, your guilt is great,
Receiue the Sentence of the Law for sinne,
Such as by Gods Booke are adiudg'd to death.
You foure from hence to Prison, back againe;
From thence, vnto the place of Execution:
The Witch in Smithfield shall be burnt to ashes,
And you three shall be strangled on the Gallowes.
You Madame, for you are more Nobly borne,
Despoyled of your Honor in your Life,
Shall, after three dayes open Penance done,
Liue in your Countrey here, in Banishment,
With Sir *Iohn Stanly*, in the Ile of Man.

Elianor. Welcome is Banishment, welcome were my Death.

Glost. *Elianor*, the Law thou seest hath iudged thee,
I cannot iustifie whom the Law condemnes:
Mine eyes are full of teares, my heart of griefe.
Ah *Humfrey*, this dishonor in thine age,
Will bring thy head with sorrow to the ground.
I beseech your Maiestie giue me leaue to goe;
Sorrow would sollace, and mine Age would ease.

King. Stay *Humfrey*, Duke of Gloster,
Ere thou goe, giue vp thy Staffe,
Henry will to himselfe Protector be,
And God shall be my hope, my stay, my guide,
And Lanthorne to my feete:
And goe in peace, *Humfrey*, no lesse belou'd,
Then when thou wert Protector to thy King.

Queene. I see no reason, why a King of yeeres
Should be to be protected like a Child,
God and King *Henry* gouerne Englands Realme:
Giue vp your Staffe, Sir, and the King his Realme.

Glost. My Staffe? Here, Noble *Henry*, is my Staffe:
As willingly doe I the same resigne,
As ere thy Father *Henry* made it mine;
And euen as willingly at thy feete I leaue it,
As others would ambitiously receiue it.
Farewell good King: when I am dead, and gone,
May honorable Peace attend thy Throne.

Exit Gloster.

Queene. Why now is *Henry* King, and *Margaret* Queen,
And *Humfrey*, Duke of Gloster, scarce himselfe,
That beares so shrewd a mayme: two Pulls at once;
His Lady banisht, and a Limbe lopt off.
This Staffe of Honor raught, there let it stand,
Where it best fits to be, in *Henries* hand.

Suff. Thus droupes this loftie Pyne, & hangs his sprayes,
Thus *Elianors* Pride dyes in her youngest dayes.

Yorke. Lords, let him goe. Please it your Maiestie,
This is the day appointed for the Combat,
And ready are the Appellant and Defendant,
The Armorer and his Man, to enter the Lists,
So please your Highnesse to behold the fight.

Queene. I, good my Lord: for purposely therefore
Left I the Court, to see this Quarrell try'de.

King. A Gods Name see the Lysts and all things fit,
Here let them end it, and God defend the right.

Yorke. I neuer saw a fellow worse bestead,
Or more afraid to fight, then is the Appellant,
The seruant of this Armorer, my Lords.

Enter at one Doore the Armorer and his Neighbors, drinking to him so much, that hee is drunke; and he enters with a Drumme before him, and his Staffe, with a Sand-bagge fastened to it: and at the other Doore his Man, with a Drumme and Sand-bagge, and Prentices drinking to him.

1. *Neighbor.* Here Neighbour *Horner*, I drinke to you in a Cup of Sack; and feare not Neighbor, you shall doe well enough.

2. *Neighbor.* And here Neighbour, here's a Cuppe of Charneco.

3. *Neighbor.* And here's a Pot of good Double-Beere Neighbor: drinke, and feare not your Man.

Armorer. Let it come yfaith, and Ile pledge you all, and a figge for *Peter.*

1. *Prent.* Here *Peter*, I drinke to thee, and be not afraid.

2. *Prent.* Be merry *Peter*, and feare not thy Master, Fight for credit of the Prentices.

Peter. I thanke you all: drinke, and pray for me, I pray you, for I thinke I haue taken my last Draught in this World. Here *Robin*, and if I dye, I giue thee my Aporne; and *Will*, thou shalt haue my Hammer: and here *Tom*, take all the Money that I haue. O Lord blesse me, I pray God, for I am neuer able to deale with my Master, hee hath learnt so much fence already.

Salub. Come, leaue your drinking, and fall to blowes. Sirrha, what's thy Name?

Peter. *Peter* forsooth.

Salub. *Peter*? what more?

Peter. *Thumpe.*

Salisb. *Thumpe*? Then see thou thumpe thy Master well.

Armorer. Masters, I am come hither as it were vpon my Mans instigation, to proue him a Knaue, and my selfe an honest man: and touching the Duke of Yorke, I will take my death, I neuer meant him any ill, nor the King, nor the Queene: and therefore *Peter* haue at thee with a downe-right blow.

Yorke. Dispatch, this Knaues tongue begins to double. Sound Trumpets, Alarum to the Combattants.

They fight, and Peter strikes him downe.

Armorer. Hold *Peter*, hold, I confesse, I confesse Treason.

Yorke. Take away his Weapon: Fellow thanke God, and the good Wine in thy Masters way.

Peter. O God, haue I ouercome mine Enemies in this presence? O *Peter*, thou hast preuayl'd in right.

King. Goe, take hence that Traytor from our sight,
For by his death we doe perceiue his guilt,
And God in Iustice hath reueal'd to vs
The truth and innocence of this poore fellow,
Which he had thought to haue murther'd wrongfully.
Come fellow, follow vs for thy Reward.

Sound a flourish. *Exeunt.*

Enter Duke Humfrey and his Men in Mourning Cloakes.

Glost. Thus sometimes hath the brightest day a Cloud:
And after Summer, euermore succeedes
Barren Winter, with his wrathfull nipping Cold;
So Cares and Ioyes abound, as Seasons fleet.
Sirs, what's a Clock?

Seru. Tenne, my Lord.

Glost. Tenne is the houre that was appointed me,
To watch the comming of my punisht Duchesse:
Vneath may shee endure the Flintie Streets,
To treade them with her tender-feeling feet.
Sweet *Nell*, ill can thy Noble Minde abrooke
The abiect People, gazing on thy face,
With enuious Lookes laughing at thy shame,
That erst did follow thy prowd Chariot-Wheeles,
When thou didst ride in triumph through the streets.
But soft, I thinke she comes, and Ile prepare
My teare-stayn'd eyes, to see her Miseries.

Enter the Duchesse in a white Sheet, and a Taper burning in her hand, with the Sherife and Officers.

Seru. So please your Grace, wee'le take her from the Sherife.

Gloster. No, stirre not for your liues, let her passe by.

Elianor. Come you, my Lord, to see my open shame?
Now thou do'st Penance too. Looke how they gaze,
See how the giddy multitude doe point,
And nodde their heads, and throw their eyes on thee.
Ah *Gloster*, hide thee from their hatefull lookes,
And in thy Closet pent vp, rue my shame,
And banne thine Enemies, both mine and thine.

Glost. Be patient, gentle *Nell*, forget this griefe.

Elianor. Ah *Gloster*, teach me to forget my selfe:
For whilest I thinke I am thy married Wife,
And thou a Prince, Protector of this Land;
Me thinkes I should not thus be led along,
Mayl'd vp in shame, with Papers on my back,
And follow'd with a Rabble, that reioyce
To see my teares, and heare my deepe-fet groanes.
The ruthlesse Flint doth cut my tender feet,
And when I start, the enuious people laugh,
And bid me be aduised how I treade.
Ah *Humfrey*, can I beare this shamefull yoake?
Trowest thou, that ere Ile looke vpon the World,
Or count them happy, that enioyes the Sunne?
No: Darke shall be my Light, and Night my Day.
To thinke vpon my Pompe, shall be my Hell.
Sometime Ile say, I am Duke *Humfreyes* Wife,
And he a Prince, and Ruler of the Land:
Yet so he rul'd, and such a Prince he was,
As he stood by, whilest I, his forlorne Duchesse,
Was made a wonder, and a pointing stock
To euery idle Rascall follower.
But be thou milde, and blush not at my shame,
Nor stirre at nothing, till the Axe of Death
Hang ouer thee, as sure it shortly will.
For *Suffolke*, he that can doe all in all
With her, that hateth thee and hates vs all,
And *Yorke*, and impious *Beauford*, that false Priest,
Haue all lym'd Bushes to betray thy Wings,
And flye thou how thou canst, they'le tangle thee.
But feare not thou, vntill thy foot be snar'd,
Nor neuer seeke preuention of thy foes.

Glost. Ah *Nell*, forbeare: thou aymest all awry.
I must offend, before I be attainted:
And had I twentie times so many foes,
And each of them had twentie times their power,
All these could not procure me any scathe,
So long as I am loyall, true, and crimelesse.
Would'st haue me rescue thee from this reproach?

Why yet thy scandall were not wipt away,
But I in danger for the breach of Law.
Thy greatest helpe is quiet, gentle *Nell*:
I pray thee sort thy heart to patience,
These few dayes wonder will be quickly worne.

Enter a Herald.

Her. I summon your Grace to his Maiesties Parliament,
Holden at Bury, the first of this next Moneth.

Glost. And my consent ne're ask'd herein before?
This is close dealing. Well, I will be there.
My *Nell*, I take my leaue: and Master Sherife,
Let not her Penance exceede the Kings Commission.

Sh. And't please your Grace, here my Commission stayes:
And Sir *Iohn Stanly* is appointed now,
To take her with him to the Ile of Man.

Glost. Must you, Sir *Iohn*, protect my Lady here?

Stanly. So am I giuen in charge, may't please your Grace.

Glost. Entreat her not the worse, in that I pray
You vse her well: the World may laugh againe,
And I may liue to doe you kindnesse, if you doe it her.
And so Sir *Iohn*, farewell.

Elianor. What, gone my Lord, and bid me not farewell?

Glost. Witnesse my teares, I cannot stay to speake.

Exit Gloster.

Elianor. Art thou gone to? all comfort goe with thee,
For none abides with me: my Ioy, is Death;
Death, at whose Name I oft haue beene afear'd,
Because I wish'd this Worlds eternitie.
Stanley, I prethee goe, and take me hence,
I care not whither, for I begge no fauor;
Onely conuey me where thou art commanded.

Stanley. Why, Madame, that is to the Ile of Man,
There to be vs'd according to your State.

Elianor. That's bad enough, for I am but reproach:
And shall I then be vs'd reproachfully?

Stanley. Like to a Duchesse, and Duke *Humfreyes* Lady,
According to that State you shall be vs'd.

Elianor. Sherife farewell, and better then I fare,
Although thou hast beene Conduct of my shame.

Sherife. It is my Office, and Madame pardon me.

Elianor. I, I, farewell, thy Office is discharg'd:
Come *Stanley*, shall we goe?

Stanley. Madame, your Penance done,
Throw off this Sheet,
And goe we to attyre you for our Iourney.

Elianor. My shame will not be shifted with my Sheet:
No, it will hang vpon my richest Robes,
And shew it selfe, attyre me how I can.
Goe, leade the way, I long to see my Prison. *Exeunt*

Sound a Senet. Enter King, Queene, Cardinall, Suffolke, Yorke, Buckingham, Salisbury, and Warwicke, to the Parliament.

King. I muse my Lord of Gloster is not come:
'Tis not his wont to be the hindmost man,
What e're occasion keepes him from vs now.

Queene. Can you not see? or will ye not obserue
The strangenesse of his alter'd Countenance?
With what a Maiestie he beares himselfe,
How insolent of late he is become,
How prowd, how peremptorie, and vnlike himselfe.
We know the time since he was milde and affable,
And if we did but glance a farre-off Looke,
Immediately he was vpon his Knee,
That all the Court admir'd him for submission.
But meet him now, and be it in the Morne,
When euery one will giue the time of day,
He knits his Brow, and shewes an angry Eye,
And passeth by with stiffe vnbowed Knee,
Disdaining dutie that to vs belongs.
Small Curres are not regarded when they grynne,
But great men tremble when the Lyon rores,
And *Humfrey* is no little Man in England.
First note, that he is neere you in discent,
And should you fall, he is the next will mount.
Me seemeth then, it is no Pollicie,
Respecting what a rancorous minde he beares,
And his aduantage following your decease,
That he should come about your Royall Person,
Or be admitted to your Highnesse Councell.
By flatterie hath he wonne the Commons hearts:
And when he please to make Commotion,
'Tis to be fear'd they all will follow him.
Now 'tis the Spring, and Weeds are shallow-rooted,
Suffer them now, and they'le o're-grow the Garden,
And choake the Herbes for want of Husbandry.
The reuerent care I beare vnto my Lord,
Made me collect these dangers in the Duke.
If it be fond, call it a Womans feare:
Which feare, if better Reasons can supplant,
I will subscribe, and say I wrong'd the Duke.
My Lord of Suffolke, Buckingham, and Yorke,
Reproue my allegation, if you can,
Or else conclude my words effectuall.

Suff. Well hath your Highnesse seene into this Duke:
And had I first beene put to speake my minde,
I thinke I should haue told your Graces Tale.
The Duchesse, by his subornation,
Vpon my Life began her diuellish practises:
Or if he were not priuie to those Faults,
Yet by reputing of his high discent,
As next the King, he was successiue Heire,
And such high vaunts of his Nobilitie,
Did instigate the Bedlam braine-sick Duchesse,
By wicked meanes to frame our Soueraignes fall.
Smooth runnes the Water, where the Brooke is deepe,
And in his simple shew he harbours Treason.
The Fox barkes not, when he would steale the Lambe.
No, no, my Soueraigne, *Glouster* is a man
Vnsounded yet, and full of deepe deceit.

Card. Did he not, contrary to forme of Law,
Deuise strange deaths, for small offences done?

Yorke. And did he not, in his Protectorship,
Leuie great summes of Money through the Realme,
For Souldiers pay in France, and neuer sent it?
By meanes whereof, the Townes each day reuolted.

Buck. Tut, these are petty faults to faults vnknowne,
Which time will bring to light in smooth Duke *Humfrey*.

King. My Lords at once: the care you haue of vs,
To mowe downe Thornes that would annoy our Foot,
Is worthy prayse: but shall I speake my conscience,
Our Kinsman *Gloster* is as innocent,
From meaning Treason to our Royall Person,
As is the sucking Lambe, or harmelesse Doue:
The Duke is vertuous, milde, and too well giuen,
To dreame on euill, or to worke my downefall.

Qu. Ah what's more dangerous, then this fond affiance?
Seemes he a Doue? his feathers are but borrow'd,
For hee's disposed as the hatefull Rauen.
Is he a Lambe? his Skinne is surely lent him,

For

For hee's enclin'd as is the rauenous Wolues.
Who cannot steale a shape, that meanes deceit?
Take heed, my Lord, the welfare of vs all,
Hangs on the cutting short that fraudfull man.

Enter Somerset.

Som. All health vnto my gracious Soueraigne.
King. Welcome Lord *Somerset*: What Newes from France?
Som. That all your Interest in those Territories,
Is vtterly bereft you: all is lost.
King. Cold Newes, Lord *Somerset*: but Gods will be done.
Yorke. Cold Newes for me: for I had hope of France,
As firmely as I hope for fertile England.
Thus are my Blossomes blasted in the Bud,
And Caterpillers eate my Leaues away:
But I will remedie this geare ere long,
Or sell my Title for a glorious Graue.

Enter Gloucester

Glost. All happinesse vnto my Lord the King:
Pardon, my Liege, that I haue stay'd so long.
Suff. Nay *Gloster*, know that thou art come too soone,
Vnlesse thou wert more loyall then thou art:
I doe arrest thee of High Treason here.
Glost. Well *Suffolke*, thou shalt not see me blush,
Nor change my Countenance for this Arrest:
A Heart vnspotted, is not easily daunted.
The purest Spring is not so free from mudde,
As I am cleare from Treason to my Soueraigne.
Who can accuse me? wherein am I guiltie?
Yorke. 'Tis thought, my Lord,
That you tooke Bribes of France,
And being Protector, stay'd the Souldiers pay,
By meanes whereof, his Highnesse hath lost France.
Glost. Is it but thought so?
What are they that thinke it?
I neuer rob'd the Souldiers of their pay,
Nor euer had one penny Bribe from France.
So helpe me God, as I haue watcht the Night,
I, Night by Night, in studying good for England.
That Doyt that ere I wrested from the King,
Or any Groat I hoorded to my vse,
Be brought against me at my Tryall day.
No: many a Pound of mine owne proper store,
Because I would not taxe the needie Commons,
Haue I dis-pursed to the Garrisons,
And neuer ask'd for restitution.
Card. It serues you well, my Lord, to say so much.
Glost. I say no more then truth, so helpe me God.
Yorke. In your Protectorship, you did deuise
Strange Tortures for Offendors, neuer heard of,
That England was defam'd by Tyrannie.
Glost. Why 'tis well known, that whiles I was Protector,
Pittie was all the fault that was in me:
For I should melt at an Offendors teares,
And lowly words were Ransome for their fault:
Vnlesse it were a bloody Murtherer,
Or foule felonious Theefe, that fleec'd poore passengers,
I neuer gaue them condigne punishment.
Murther indeede, that bloodie sinne, I tortur'd
Aboue the Felon, or what Trespas else.
Suff. My Lord, these faults are easie, quickly answer'd:
But mightier Crimes are lay'd vnto your charge,
Whereof you cannot easily purge your selfe.
I doe arrest you in his Highnesse Name,
And here commit you to my Lord Cardinall
To keepe, vntill your further time of Tryall.
King. My Lord of Gloster, 'tis my speciall hope,
That you will cleare your selfe from all suspence,
My Conscience tells me you are innocent.
Glost. Ah gracious Lord, these dayes are dangerous:
Vertue is choakt with foule Ambition,
And Charitie chas'd hence by Rancours hand;
Foule Subornation is predominant,
And Equitie exil'd your Highnesse Land.
I know, their Complot is to haue my Life:
And if my death might make this Iland happy,
And proue the Period of their Tyrannie,
I would expend it with all willingnesse.
But mine is made the Prologue to their Play
For thousands more, that yet suspect no perill,
Will not conclude their plotted Tragedie.
Beaufords red sparkling eyes blab his hearts mallice,
And *Suffolks* cloudie Brow his stormie hate;
Sharpe *Buckingham* vnburthens with his tongue,
The enuious Load that lyes vpon his heart:
And dogged *Yorke*, that reaches at the Moone,
Whose ouer-weening Arme I haue pluckt back,
By false accuse doth leuell at my Life.
And you, my Soueraigne Lady, with the rest,
Causelesse haue lay'd disgraces on my head,
And with your best endeuour haue stirr'd vp
My liefest Liege to be mine Enemie:
I, all of you haue lay'd your heads together,
My selfe had notice of your Conuenticles,
And all to make away my guiltlesse Life.
I shall not want false Witnesse, to condemne me,
Nor store of Treasons, to augment my guilt:
The ancient Prouerbe will be well effected,
A Staffe is quickly found to beat a Dogge.
Card. My Liege, his rayling is intollerable.
If those that care to keepe your Royall Person
From Treasons secret Knife, and Traytors Rage,
Be thus vpbrayded, chid, and rated at,
And the Offendor graunted scope of speech,
'Twill make them coole in zeale vnto your Grace.
Suff. Hath he not twit our Soueraigne Lady here
With ignominious words, though Clarkely coucht?
As if she had suborned some to sweare
False allegations, to o'rethrow his state.
Qu. But I can giue the loser leaue to chide.
Glost. Farre truer spoke then meant: I lose indeede,
Beshrew the winners, for they play'd me false,
And well such losers may haue leaue to speake.
Buck. Hee'le wrest the sence, and hold vs here all day.
Lord Cardinall, he is your Prisoner.
Card. Sirs, take away the Duke, and guard him sure.
Glost. Ah, thus King *Henry* throwes away his Crutch,
Before his Legges be firme to beare his Body.
Thus is the Shepheard beaten from thy side,
And Wolues are gnarling, who shall gnaw thee first.
Ah that my feare were false, ah that it were;
For good King *Henry*, thy decay I feare. *Exit Gloster.*
King. My Lords, what to your wisdomes seemeth best,
Doe, or vndoe, as if our selfe were here.
Queene. What, will your Highnesse leaue the Parliament?
King. I *Margaret*: my heart is drown'd with griefe,
Whose floud begins to flowe within mine eyes;
My Body round engyrt with miserie:

For what's more miserable then Discontent?
Ah Vnckle *Humfrey*, in thy face I see
The Map of Honor, Truth, and Loyaltie:
And yet, good *Humfrey*, is the houre to come,
That ere I prou'd thee false, or fear'd thy faith.
What lowring Starre now enuies thy estate?
That these great Lords, and *Margaret* our Queene,
Doe seeke subuersion of thy harmelesse Life.
Thou neuer didst them wrong, nor no man wrong:
And as the Butcher takes away the Calfe,
And binds the Wretch, and beats it when it strayes,
Bearing it to the bloody Slaughter-house;
Euen so remorselesse haue they borne him hence:
And as the Damme runnes lowing vp and downe,
Looking the way her harmelesse young one went,
And can doe naught but wayle her Darlings losse;
Euen so my selfe bewayles good *Glosters* case
With sad vnhelpefull teares, and with dimn'd eyes:
Looke after him, and cannot doe him good:
So mightie are his vowed Enemies.
His fortunes I will weepe, and 'twixt each groane,
Say, who's a Traytor? *Gloster* he is none. *Exit.*

Queene. Free Lords:
Cold Snow melts with the Sunnes hot Beames:
Henry, my Lord, is cold in great Affaires,
Too full of foolish pittie: and *Glosters* shew
Beguiles him, as the mournefull Crocodile
With sorrow snares relenting passengers;
Or as the Snake, roll'd in a flowring Banke,
With shining checker'd slough doth sting a Child,
That for the beautie thinkes it excellent.
Beleeue me Lords, were none more wise then I,
And yet herein I iudge mine owne Wit good;
This *Gloster* should be quickly rid the World,
To rid vs from the feare we haue of him.

Card. That he should dye, is worthie pollicie,
But yet we want a Colour for his death:
'Tis meet he be condemn'd by course of Law.

Suff. But in my minde, that were no pollicie:
The King will labour still to saue his Life,
The Commons haply rise, to saue his Life;
And yet we haue but triuiall argument,
More then mistrust, that shewes him worthy death.

Yorke. So that by this, you would not haue him dye.

Suff. Ah *Yorke*, no man aliue, so faine as I.

Yorke. 'Tis *Yorke* that hath more reason for his death.
But my Lord Cardinall, and you my Lord of Suffolke,
Say as you thinke, and speake it from your Soules:
Wer't not all one, an emptie Eagle were set,
To guard the Chicken from a hungry Kyte,
As place Duke *Humfrey* for the Kings Protector?

Queene. So the poore Chicken should be sure of death.

Suff. Madame 'tis true: and wer't not madnesse then,
To make the Fox surueyor of the Fold?
Who being accus'd a craftie Murtherer,
His guilt should be but idly posted ouer,
Because his purpose is not executed.
No: let him dye, in that he is a Fox,
By nature prou'd an Enemie to the Flock,
Before his Chaps be stayn'd with Crimson blood,
As *Humfrey* prou'd by Reasons to my Liege.
And doe not stand on Quillets how to slay him:
Be it by Gynnes, by Snares, by Subtletie,
Sleeping, or Waking 'tis no matter how,
So he be dead; for that is good deceit,
Which mates him first, that first intends deceit.

Queene. Thrice Noble *Suffolke*, 'tis resolutely spoke.

Suff. Not resolute, except so much were done,
For things are often spoke, and seldome meant,
But that my heart accordeth with my tongue,
Seeing the deed is meritorious,
And to preserue my Soueraigne from his Foe,
Say but the word, and I will be his Priest.

Card. But I would haue him dead, my Lord of Suffolke,
Ere you can take due Orders for a Priest:
Say you consent, and censure well the deed,
And Ile prouide his Executioner,
I tender so the safetie of my Liege.

Suff. Here is my Hand, the deed is worthy doing.

Queene. And so say I.

Yorke. And I: and now we three haue spoke it,
It skills not greatly who impugnes our doome.

Enter a Poste.

Post. Great Lords, from Ireland am I come amaine,
To signifie, that Rebels there are vp,
And put the Englishmen vnto the Sword.
Send Succours (Lords) and stop the Rage betime,
Before the Wound doe grow vncurable;
For being greene, there is great hope of helpe.

Card. A Breach that craues a quick expedient stoppe,
What counsaile giue you in this weightie cause?

Yorke. That *Somerset* be sent as Regent thither:
'Tis meet that luckie Ruler be imploy'd,
Witnesse the fortune he hath had in France.

Som. If *Yorke*, with all his farre-fet pollicie,
Had beene the Regent there, in stead of me,
He neuer would haue stay'd in France so long.

Yorke. No, not to lose it all, as thou hast done.
I rather would haue lost my Life betimes,
Then bring a burthen of dis-honour home,
By staying there so long, till all were lost.
Shew me one skarre, character'd on thy Skinne,
Mens flesh preseru'd so whole, doe seldome winne.

Qu. Nay then, this sparke will proue a raging fire,
If Wind and Fuell be brought, to feed it with:
No more, good *Yorke*; sweet *Somerset* be still.
Thy fortune, *Yorke*, hadst thou beene Regent there,
Might happily haue prou'd farre worse then his.

Yorke. What, worse then naught? nay, then a shame take all.

Somerset. And in the number, thee, that wishest shame.

Card. My Lord of Yorke, trie what your fortune is:
Th'vnciuill Kernes of Ireland are in Armes,
And temper Clay with blood of Englishmen.
To Ireland will you leade a Band of men,
Collected choycely, from each Countie some,
And trie your hap against the Irishmen?

Yorke. I will, my Lord, so please his Maiestie.

Suff. Why, our Authoritie is his consent,
And what we doe establish, he confirmes:
Then, Noble *Yorke*, take thou this Taske in hand.

Yorke. I am content: Prouide me Souldiers, Lords,
Whiles I take order for mine owne affaires.

Suff. A charge, Lord *Yorke*, that I will see perform'd.
But now returne we to the false Duke *Humfrey*.

Card. No more of him: for I will deale with him,
That henceforth he shall trouble vs no more:
And so breake off, the day is almost spent,
Lord *Suffolke*, you and I must talke of that euent.

Yorke. My

Yorke. My Lord of Suffolke, within foureteene dayes
At Bristow I expect my Souldiers,
For there Ile shippe them all for Ireland.

Suff. Ile see it truly done, my Lord of Yorke. *Exeunt.*

Manet Yorke.

Yorke. Now *Yorke*, or neuer, steele thy fearfull thoughts,
And change misdoubt to resolution;
Be that thou hop'st to be, or what thou art;
Resigne to death, it is not worth th'enioying:
Let pale-fac't feare keepe with the meane-borne man,
And finde no harbor in a Royall heart.
Faster the Spring-time showres, comes thoght on thoght,
And not a thought, but thinkes on Dignitie.
My Brayne, more busie then the laboring Spider,
Weaues tedious Snares to trap mine Enemies.
Well Nobles, well: 'tis politikely done,
To send me packing with an Hoast of men:
I feare me, you but warme the starued Snake,
Who cherisht in your breasts, will sting your hearts.
'Twas men I lackt, and you will giue them me;
I take it kindly: yet be well assur'd,
You put sharpe Weapons in a mad-mans hands.
Whiles I in Ireland nourish a mightie Band,
I will stirre vp in England some black Storme,
Shall blowe ten thousand Soules to Heauen, or Hell;
And this fell Tempest shall not cease to rage,
Vntill the Golden Circuit on my Head,
Like to the glorious Sunnes transparant Beames,
Doe calme the furie of this mad-bred Flawe.
And for a minister of my intent,
I haue seduc'd a head-strong Kentishman,
Iohn Cade of Ashford,
To make Commotion, as full well he can,
Vnder the Title of *Iohn Mortimer*.
In Ireland haue I seene this stubborne *Cade*
Oppose himselfe against a Troupe of Kernes,
And fought so long, till that his thighes with Darts
Were almost like a sharpe-quill'd Porpentine:
And in the end being rescued, I haue seene
Him capre vpright, like a wilde Morisco,
Shaking the bloody Darts, as he his Bells.
Full often, like a shag-hayr'd craftie Kerne,
Hath he conuersed with the Enemie,
And vndiscouer'd, come to me againe,
And giuen me notice of their Villanies.
This Deuill here shall be my substitute;
For that *Iohn Mortimer*, which now is dead,
In face, in gate, in speech he doth resemble.
By this, I shall perceiue the Commons minde,
How they affect the House and Clayme of *Yorke*.
Say he be taken, rackt, and tortured;
I know, no paine they can inflict vpon him,
Will make him say, I mou'd him to those Armes.
Say that he thriue, as 'tis great like he will,
Why then from Ireland come I with my strength,
And reape the Haruest which that Rascall sow'd.
For *Humfrey*; being dead, as he shall be,
And *Henry* put apart: the next for me. *Exit.*

Enter two or three running ouer the Stage, from the Murther of Duke Humfrey

1. Runne to my Lord of Suffolke: let him know
We haue dispatcht the Duke, as he commanded.

2. Oh, that it were to doe: what haue we done?
Didst euer heare a man so penitent? *Enter Suffolke.*

1. Here comes my Lord.

Suff. Now Sirs, haue you dispatcht this thing?

1. I, my good Lord, hee's dead.

Suff. Why that's well said. Goe, get you to my House,
I will reward you for this venturous deed:
The King and all the Peeres are here at hand.
Haue you layd faire the Bed? Is all things well,
According as I gaue directions?

1. 'Tis, my good Lord.

Suff. Away, be gone. *Exeunt.*

Sound Trumpets. Enter the King, the Queene, Cardinall, Suffolke, Somerset, with Attendants.

King. Goe call our Vnckle to our presence straight:
Say, we intend to try his Grace to day,
If he be guiltie, as 'tis published.

Suff. Ile call him presently, my Noble Lord. *Exit.*

King. Lords take your places: and I pray you all
Proceed no straiter 'gainst our Vnckle *Gloster*,
Then from true euidence, of good esteeme,
He be approu'd in practise culpable.

Queene. God forbid any Malice should preuayle,
That faultlesse may condemne a Noble man:
Pray God he may acquit him of suspition.

King. I thanke thee *Nell*, these wordes content mee much.

Enter Suffolke.

How now? why look'st thou pale? why tremblest thou?
Where is our Vnckle? what's the matter, *Suffolke*?

Suff. Dead in his Bed, my Lord: *Gloster* is dead.

Queene. Marry God forfend.

Card. Gods secret Iudgement: I did dreame to Night,
The Duke was dumbe, and could not speake a word.

King sounds.

Qu. How fares my Lord? Helpe Lords, the King is dead.

Som. Rere vp his Body, wring him by the Nose.

Qu. Runne, goe, helpe, helpe: Oh *Henry* ope thine eyes.

Suff. He doth reuiue againe, Madame be patient.

King. Oh Heauenly God.

Qu. How fares my gracious Lord?

Suff. Comfort my Soueraigne, gracious *Henry* comfort.

King. What, doth my Lord of Suffolke comfort me?
Came he right now to sing a Rauens Note,
Whose dismall tune bereft my Vitall powres:
And thinkes he, that the chirping of a Wren,
By crying comfort from a hollow breast,
Can chase away the first-conceiued sound?
Hide not thy poyson with such sugred words,
Lay not thy hands on me: forbeare I say,
Their touch affrights me as a Serpents sting.
Thou balefull Messenger, out of my sight:
Vpon thy eye-balls, murderous Tyrannie
Sits in grim Maiestie, to fright the World.
Looke not vpon me, for thine eyes are wounding;
Yet doe not goe away: come Basiliske,
And kill the innocent gazer with thy sight:
For in the shade of death, I shall finde ioy;
In life, but double death, now *Gloster's* dead.

Queene. Why do you rate my Lord of Suffolke thus?
Although the Duke was enemie to him,
Yet he most Christian-like laments his death:
And for my selfe, Foe as he was to me,
Might liquid teares, or heart-offending groanes,
Or blood-consuming sighes recall his Life;

I would be blinde with weeping, sicke with grones,
Looke pale as Prim-rose with blood-drinking sighes,
And all to haue the Noble Duke aliue.
What know I how the world may deeme of me?
For it is knowne we were but hollow Friends:
It may be iudg'd I made the Duke away,
So shall my name with Slanders tongue be wounded,
And Princes Courts be fill'd with my reproach:
This get I by his death: Aye me vnhappie,
To be a Queene, and Crown'd with infamie.

King. Ah woe is me for Gloster, wretched man.

Queen. Be woe for me, more wretched then he is.
What, Dost thou turne away, and hide thy face?
I am no loathsome Leaper, looke on me.
What? Art thou like the Adder waxen deafe?
Be poysonous too, and kill thy forlorne Queene.
Is all thy comfort shut in Glosters Tombe?
Why then Dame *Elianor* was neere thy ioy.
Erect his Statue, and worship it,
And make my Image but an Ale-house signe.
Was I for this nye wrack'd vpon the Sea,
And twice by aukward winde from Englands banke
Droue backe againe vnto my Natiue Clime.
What boaded this? but well fore-warning winde
Did seeme to say, seeke not a Scorpions Nest,
Nor set no footing on this vnkinde Shore.
What did I then? But curst the gentle gusts,
And he that loos'd them forth their Brazen Caues,
And bid them blow towards Englands blessed shore,
Or turne our Sterne vpon a dreadfull Rocke:
Yet Æolus would not be a murtherer,
But left that hatefull office vnto thee.
The pretty vaulting Sea refus'd to drowne me,
Knowing that thou wouldst haue me drown'd on shore
With teares as salt as Sea, through thy vnkindnesse.
The splitting Rockes cowr'd in the sinking sands,
And would not dash me with their ragged sides,
Because thy flinty heart more hard then they,
Might in thy Pallace, perish *Elianor*.
As farre as I could ken thy Chalky Cliffes,
When from thy Shore, the Tempest beate vs backe,
I stood vpon the Hatches in the storme:
And when the duskie sky, began to rob
My earnest-gaping-sight of thy Lands view,
I tooke a costly Iewell from my necke,
A Hart it was bound in with Diamonds,
And threw it towards thy Land: The Sea receiu'd it,
And so I wish'd thy body might my Heart:
And euen with this, I lost faire Englands view,
And bid mine eyes be packing with my Heart,
And call'd them blinde and duskie Spectacles,
For loosing ken of *Albions* wished Coast.
How often haue I tempted Suffolkes tongue
(The agent of thy foule inconstancie)
To sit and watch me as *Ascanius* did,
When he to madding *Dido* would vnfold
His Fathers Acts, commenc'd in burning Troy.
Am I not witcht like her? Or thou not false like him?
Aye me, I can no more: Dye *Elinor*,
For *Henry* weepes, that thou dost liue so long.

Noyse within. Enter Warwicke, and many Commons.

War. It is reported, mighty Soueraigne,
That good Duke *Humfrey* Traiterously is murdred
By Suffolke, and the Cardinall *Beaufords* meanes:
The Commons like an angry Hiue of Bees
That want their Leader, scatter vp and downe,
And care not who they sting in his reuenge.
My selfe haue calm'd their spleenfull mutinie,
Vntill they heare the order of his death.

King. That he is dead good Warwick, 'tis too true,
But how he dyed, God knowes, not *Henry*:
Enter his Chamber, view his breathlesse Corpes,
And comment then vpon his sodaine death.

War. That shall I do my Liege; Stay Salsburie
With the rude multitude, till I returne.

King. O thou that iudgest all things, stay my thoghts:
My thoughts, that labour to perswade my soule,
Some violent hands were laid on *Humfries* life:
If my suspect be false, forgiue me God,
For iudgement onely doth belong to thee:
Faine would I go to chafe his palie lips,
With twenty thousand kisses, and to draine
Vpon his face an Ocean of salt teares,
To tell my loue vnto his dumbe deafe trunke,
And with my fingers feele his hand, vnfeeling:
But all in vaine are these meane Obsequies,

Bed put forth.

And to suruey his dead and earthy Image:
What were it but to make my sorrow greater?

Warw. Come hither gracious Soueraigne, view this body.

King. That is to see how deepe my graue is made,
For with his soule fled all my worldly solace:
For seeing him, I see my life in death.

War. As surely as my soule intends to liue
With that dread King that tooke our state vpon him,
To free vs from his Fathers wrathfull curse,
I do beleeue that violent hands were laid
Vpon the life of this thrice-famed Duke.

Suf. A dreadfull Oath, sworne with a solemn tongue:
What instance giues Lord Warwicke for his vow.

War. See how the blood is setled in his face.
Oft haue I seene a timely-parted Ghost,
Of ashy semblance, meager, pale, and bloodlesse,
Being all descended to the labouring heart,
Who in the Conflict that it holds with death,
Attracts the same for aydance 'gainst the enemy,
Which with the heart there cooles, and ne're returneth,
To blush and beautifie the Cheeke againe.
But see, his face is blacke, and full of blood:
His eye-balles further out, than when he liued,
Staring full gastly, like a strangled man:
His hayre vp rear'd, his nostrils stretcht with strugling:
His hands abroad display'd, as one that graspt
And tugg'd for Life, and was by strength subdude.
Looke on the sheets his haire (you see) is sticking,
His well proportion'd Beard, made ruffe and rugged,
Like to the Summers Corne by Tempest lodged:
It cannot be but he was murdred heere,
The least of all these signes were probable.

Suf. Why Warwicke, who should do the D. to death?
My selfe and *Beauford* had him in protection,
And we I hope sir, are no murtherers.

War. But both of you were vowed D. Humfries foes,
And you (forsooth) had the good Duke to keepe:
Tis like you would not feast him like a friend,
And 'tis well seene, he found an enemy.

Queen. Than you belike suspect these Noblemen,
As guilty of Duke *Humfries* timelesse death.

War.

Warw. Who finds the Heyfer dead, and bleeding fresh,
And sees fast-by, a Butcher with an Axe,
But will suspect, 'twas he that made the slaughter?
Who finds the Partridge in the Puttocks Nest,
But may imagine how the Bird was dead,
Although the Kyte soare with vnbloudied Beake?
Euen so suspitious is this Tragedie.

Qu. Are you the Butcher, *Suffolk?* where's your Knife?
Is *Beauford* tearm'd a Kyte? where are his Tallons?

Suff. I weare no Knife, to slaughter sleeping men,
But here's a vengefull Sword, rusted with ease,
That shall be scowred in his rancorous heart,
That slanders me with Murthers Crimson Badge.
Say, if thou dar'st, prowd Lord of Warwickshire,
That I am faultie in Duke *Humfreyes* death.

Warw. What dares not *Warwick*, if false *Suffolke* dare him?

Qu. He dares not calme his contumelious Spirit,
Nor cease to be an arrogant Controller,
Though *Suffolke* dare him twentie thousand times.

Warw. Madame be still: with reuerence may I say,
For euery word you speake in his behalfe,
Is slander to your Royall Dignitie.

Suff. Blunt-witted Lord, ignoble in demeanor,
If euer Lady wrong'd her Lord so much,
Thy Mother tooke into her blamefull Bed
Some sterne vntutur'd Churle; and Noble Stock
Was graft with Crab-tree slippe, whose Fruit thou art,
And neuer of the *Neuils* Noble Race.

Warw. But that the guilt of Murther bucklers thee,
And I should rob the Deaths-man of his Fee,
Quitting thee thereby of ten thousand shames,
And that my Soueraignes presence makes me milde,
I would, false murd'rous Coward, on thy Knee
Make thee begge pardon for thy passed speech,
And say, it was thy Mother that thou meant'st,
That thou thy selfe wast borne in Bastardie;
And after all this fearefull Homage done,
Giue thee thy hyre, and send thy Soule to Hell,
Pernicious blood-sucker of sleeping men.

Suff. Thou shalt be waking, while I shed thy blood,
If from this presence thou dar'st goe with me.

Warw. Away euen now, or I will drag thee hence:
Vnworthy though thou art, Ile cope with thee,
And doe some seruice to Duke *Humfreyes* Ghost.

Exeunt.

King. What stronger Brest-plate then a heart vntainted?
Thrice is he arm'd, that hath his Quarrell iust;
And he but naked, though lockt vp in Steele,
Whose Conscience with Iniustice is corrupted.

A noyse within.

Queene. What noyse is this?

Enter Suffolke and Warwicke, with their Weapons drawne.

King. Why how now Lords?
Your wrathfull Weapons drawne,
Here in our presence? Dare you be so bold?
Why what tumultuous clamor haue we here?

Suff. The trayt'rous *Warwick*, with the men of Bury,
Set all vpon me, mightie Soueraigne.

Enter Salisbury.

Salisb. Sirs stand apart, the King shall know your minde.
Dread Lord, the Commons send you word by me,
Vnlesse Lord *Suffolke* straight be done to death,
Or banished faire Englands Territories,
They will by violence teare him from your Pallace,
And torture him with grieuous lingring death.
They say, by him the good Duke *Humfrey* dy'de:
They say, in him they feare your Highnesse death;
And meere instinct of Loue and Loyaltie,
Free from a stubborne opposite intent,
As being thought to contradict your liking,
Makes them thus forward in his Banishment.
They say, in care of your most Royall Person,
That if your Highnesse should intend to sleepe,
And charge, that no man should disturbe your rest,
In paine of your dislike, or paine of death;
Yet notwithstanding such a strait Edict,
Were there a Serpent seene, with forked Tongue,
That slyly glyded towards your Maiestie,
It were but necessarie you were wak't:
Least being suffer'd in that harmefull slumber,
The mortall Worme might make the sleepe eternall.
And therefore doe they cry, though you forbid,
That they will guard you, where you will, or no,
From such fell Serpents as false *Suffolke* is;
With whose inuenomed and fatall sting,
Your louing Vnckle, twentie times his worth,
They say is shamefully bereft of life.

Commons within. An answer from the King, my Lord of Salisbury.

Suff. 'Tis like the Commons, rude vnpolisht Hindes,
Could send such Message to their Soueraigne:
But you, my Lord, were glad to be imploy'd,
To shew how queint an Orator you are.
But all the Honor *Salisbury* hath wonne,
Is, that he was the Lord Embassador,
Sent from a sort of Tinkers to the King.

Within. An answer from the King, or wee will all breake in.

King. Goe *Salisbury*, and tell them all from me,
I thanke them for their tender louing care;
And had I not beene cited so by them,
Yet did I purpose as they doe entreat:
For sure, my thoughts doe hourely prophecie,
Mischance vnto my State by *Suffolkes* meanes.
And therefore by his Maiestie I sweare,
Whose farre-vnworthie Deputie I am,
He shall not breathe infection in this ayre,
But three dayes longer, on the paine of death.

Qu. Oh *Henry*, let me pleade for gentle *Suffolke*.

King. Vngentle Queene, to call him gentle *Suffolke*.
No more I say: if thou do'st pleade for him,
Thou wilt but adde encrease vnto my Wrath.
Had I but sayd, I would haue kept my Word;
But when I sweare, it is irreuocable:
If after three dayes space thou here bee'st found,
On any ground that I am Ruler of,
The World shall not be Ransome for thy Life.
Come *Warwicke*, come good *Warwicke*, goe with mee,
I haue great matters to impart to thee. *Exit.*

Qu. Mischance and Sorrow goe along with you,
Hearts Discontent, and sowre Affliction,
Be play-fellowes to keepe you companie:
There's two of you, the Deuill make a third,
And three-fold Vengeance tend vpon your steps.

Suff. Cease, gentle Queene, these Execrations,
And let thy *Suffolke* take his heauie leaue.

Queene. Fye

Queen. Fye Coward woman, and soft harted wretch,
Hast thou not spirit to curse thine enemy.
Suf. A plague vpon them: wherefore should I cursse them?
Would curses kill, as doth the Mandrakes grone,
I would inuent as bitter searching termes,
As curst, as harsh, and horrible to heare,
Deliuer'd strongly through my fixed teeth,
With full as many signes of deadly hate,
As leane-fac'd enuy in her loathsome caue.
My tongue should stumble in mine earnest words,
Mine eyes should sparkle like the beaten Flint,
Mine haire be fixt an end as one distract:
I, euery ioynt should seeme to curse and ban,
And euen now my burthen'd heart would breake
Should I not curse them. Poyson be their drinke.
Gall, worse then Gall, the daintiest that they taste:
Their sweetest shade, a groue of Cypresse Trees:
Their cheefest Prospect, murd'ring Basiliskes:
Their softest Touch, as smart as Lyzards stings:
Their Musicke, frightfull as the Serpents hisse,
And boading Screech-Owles, make the Consort full.
All the foule terrors in darke seated hell———
Q. Enough sweet Suffolke, thou torment'st thy selfe,
And these dread curses like the Sunne 'gainst glasse,
Or like an ouer-charged Gun, recoile,
And turnes the force of them vpon thy selfe.
Suf. You bad me ban, and will you bid me leaue?
Now by the ground that I am banish'd from,
Well could I curse away a Winters night,
Though standing naked on a Mountaine top,
Where byting cold would neuer let grasse grow,
And thinke it but a minute spent in sport.
Qu. Oh, let me intreat thee cease, giue me thy hand,
That I may dew it with my mournfull teares:
Nor let the raine of heauen wet this place,
To wash away my wofull Monuments.
Oh, could this kisse be printed in thy hand,
That thou might'st thinke vpon these by the Seale,
Through whom a thousand sighes are breath'd for thee.
So get thee gone, that I may know my greefe,
'Tis but surmiz'd, whiles thou art standing by,
As one that surfets, thinking on a want:
I will repeale thee, or be well assur'd,
Aduenture to be banished my selfe:
And banished I am, if but from thee.
Go, speake not to me; euen now be gone.
Oh go not yet. Euen thus, two Friends condemn'd,
Embrace, and kisse, and take ten thousand leaues,
Loather a hundred times to part then dye;
Yet now farewell, and farewell Life with thee.
Suf. Thus is poore Suffolke ten times banished,
Once by the King, and three times thrice by thee.
'Tis not the Land I care for, wer't thou thence,
A Wildernesse is populous enough,
So Suffolke had thy heauenly company:
For where thou art, there is the World it selfe,
With euery seuerall pleasure in the World:
And where thou art not, Desolation.
I can no more: Liue thou to ioy thy life;
My selfe no ioy in nought, but that thou liu'st.

Enter Vaux.

Queene. Whether goes *Vaux* so fast? What newes I prethee?
Vaux. To signifie vnto his Maiesty,
That Cardinall *Beauford* is at point of death:
For sodainly a greeuous sicknesse tooke him,
That makes him gaspe, and stare, and catch the aire,
Blaspheming God, and cursing men on earth.
Sometime he talkes, as if Duke *Humfries* Ghost
Were by his side: Sometime, he calles the King,
And whispers to his pillow, as to him,
The secrets of his ouer-charged soule,
And I am sent to tell his Maiestie,
That euen now he cries alowd for him.
Qu. Go tell this heauy Message to the King. *Exit*
Aye me! What is this World? What newes are these?
But wherefore greeue I at an houres poore losse,
Omitting Suffolkes exile, my soules Treasure?
Why onely Suffolke mourne I not for thee?
And with the Southerne clouds, contend in teares?
Theirs for the earths encrease, mine for my sorrowes.
Now get thee hence, the King thou know'st is comming,
If thou be found by me, thou art but dead.
Suf. If I depart from thee, I cannot liue,
And in thy sight to dye, what were it else,
But like a pleasant slumber in thy lap?
Heere could I breath my soule into the ayre,
As milde and gentle as the Cradle-babe,
Dying with mothers dugge betweene it's lips.
Where from thy sight, I should be raging mad,
And cry out for thee to close vp mine eyes:
To haue thee with thy lippes to stop my mouth:
So should'st thou eyther turne my flying soule,
Or I should breathe it so into thy body,
And then it liu'd in sweete Elizium.
To dye by thee, were but to dye in iest,
From thee to dye, were torture more then death:
Oh let me stay, befall what may befall.
Queen. Away: Though parting be a fretfull corosiue,
It is applyed to a deathfull wound.
To France sweet Suffolke: Let me heare from thee:
For wheresoere thou art in this worlds Globe,
Ile haue an *Iris* that shall finde thee out.
Suf. I go.
Qu. And take my heart with thee.
Suf. A Iewell lockt into the wofulst Caske,
That euer did containe a thing of worth,
Euen as a splitted Barke, so sunder we:
This way fall I to death.
Qu. This way for me. *Exeunt*

Enter the King, Salisbury, and Warwicke, to the Cardinal in bed.

King. How fare's my Lord? Speake *Beauford* to thy Soueraigne.
Ca. If thou beest death, Ile giue thee Englands Treasure,
Enough to purchase such another Island,
So thou wilt let me liue, and feele no paine.
King. Ah, what a signe it is of euill life,
Where death's approach is seene so terrible.
War. *Beauford*, it is thy Soueraigne speakes to thee.
Beau. Bring me vnto my Triall when you will.
Dy'de he not in his bed? Where should he dye?
Can I make men liue where they will or no?
Oh torture me no more, I will confesse.
Aliue againe? Then shew me where he is,
Ile giue a thousand pound to looke vpon him.
He hath no eyes, the dust hath blinded them.

Combe downe his haire; looke,looke, it ftands vpright,
Like Lime-twigs fet to catch my winged foule:
Giue me fome drinke, and bid the Apothecarie
Bring the ftrong poyfon that I bought of him.

King. Oh thou eternall mouer of the heauens,
Looke with a gentle eye vpon this Wretch,
Oh beate away the bufie medling Fiend,
That layes ftrong fiege vnto this wretches foule,
And from his bofome purge this blacke difpaire.

War. See how the pangs of death do make him grin.

Sal. Difturbe him not, let him paffe peaceably.

King. Peace to his foule, if Gods good pleafure be.
Lord Card'nall, if thou think'ft on heauens bliffe,
Hold vp thy hand, make fignall of thy hope.
He dies and makes no figne: Oh God forgiue him.

War. So bad a death, argues a monftrous life.

King. Forbeare to iudge, for we are finners all.
Clofe vp his eyes, and draw the Curtaine clofe,
And let vs all to Meditation. *Exeunt.*

Alarum Fight at Sea. Ordnance goes off.

Enter Lieutenant, Suffolke, and others.

Lieu. The gaudy blabbing and remorfefull day,
Is crept into the bofome of the Sea:
And now loud houling Wolues arroufe the Iades
That dragge the Tragicke melancholy night:
Who with their drowfie, flow,and flagging wings
Cleape dead-mens graues, and from their mifty Iawes,
Breath foule contagious darkneffe in the ayre:
Therefore bring forth the Souldiers of our prize,
For whilft our Pinnace Anchors in the Downes,
Heere fhall they make their ranfome on the fand,
Or with their blood ftaine this difcoloured fhore.
Maifter, this Prifoner freely giue I thee,
And thou that art his Mate, make boote of this:
The other *Walter Whitmore* is thy fhare.

1.Gent. What is my ranfome Mafter,let me know.

Ma. A thoufand Crownes, or elfe lay down your head

Mate. And fo much fhall you giue,or off goes yours.

Lieu. What thinke you much to pay 2000.Crownes,
And beare the name and port of Gentlemen?
Cut both the Villaines throats, for dy you fhall:
The liues of thofe which we haue loft in fight,
Be counter-poys'd with fuch a pettie fumme.

1.Gent. Ile giue it fir, and therefore fpare my life.

2.Gent. And fo will I,and write home for it ftraight.

Whitm. I loft mine eye in laying the prize aboord,
And therefore to reuenge it, fhalt thou dye,
And fo fhould thefe, if I might haue my will.

Lieu. Be not fo rafh, take ranfome, let him liue.

Suf. Looke on my George, I am a Gentleman,
Rate me at what thou wilt, thou fhalt be payed

Whit. And fo am I: my name is *Walter Whitmore*.
How now? why ftarts thou? What doth death affright?

Suf. Thy name affrights me, in whofe found is death:
A cunning man did calculate my birth,
And told me that by Water I fhould dye:
Yet let not this make thee be bloody-minded,
Thy name is *Gualtier*, being rightly founded.

Whit. *Gualtier* or *Walter*, which it is I care not,
Neuer yet did bafe difhonour blurre our name,
But with our fword we wip'd away the blot.
Therefore, when Merchant-like I fell reuenge,
Broke be my fword, my Armes torne and defac'd,
And I proclaim'd a Coward through the world.

Suf. Stay *Whitmore*, for thy Prifoner is a Prince,
The Duke of Suffolke, *William de la Pole*.

Whit. The Duke of Suffolke, muffled vp in ragges?

Suf. I, but thefe ragges are no part of the Duke.

Lieu. But Ioue was neuer flaine as thou fhalt be,
Obfcure and lowfie Swaine, King *Henries* blood.

Suf. The honourable blood of Lancafter
Muft not be fhed by fuch a iaded Groome:
Haft thou not kift thy hand, and held my ftirrop?
Bare-headed plodded by my foot-cloth Mule,
And thought thee happy when I fhooke my head.
How often haft thou waited at my cup,
Fed from my Trencher, kneel'd downe at the boord,
When I haue feafted with Queene *Margaret*?
Remember it, and let it make thee Creft-falne,
I, and alay this thy abortiue Pride:
How in our voyding Lobby haft thou ftood,
And duly wayted for my comming forth?
This hand of mine hath writ in thy behalfe,
And therefore fhall it charme thy riotous tongue.

Whit. Speak Captaine, fhall I ftab the forlorn Swain.

Lieu. Firft let my words ftab him,as he hath me.

Suf. Bafe flaue, thy words are blunt,and fo art thou.

Lieu. Conuey him hence,and on our long boats fide,
Strike off his head. *Suf*. Thou dar'ft not for thy owne.

Lieu. *Poole*, Sir *Poole*? Lord,
I kennell, puddle, finke, whofe filth and dirt
Troubles the filuer Spring, where England drinkes:
Now will I dam vp this thy yawning mouth,
For fwallowing the Treafure of the Realme.
Thy lips that kift the Queene, fhall fweepe the ground:
And thou that fmil'dft at good Duke *Humfries* death,
Againft the fenfeleffe windes fhall grin in vaine,
Who in contempt fhall hiffe at thee againe.
And wedded be thou to the Hagges of hell,
For daring to affye a mighty Lord
Vnto the daughter of a worthleffe King,
Hauing neyther Subiect, Wealth, nor Diadem:
By diuellifh policy art thou growne great,
And like ambitious Sylla ouer-gorg'd,
With gobbets of thy Mother-bleeding heart.
By thee *Anion* and *Maine* were fold to France.
The falfe reuolting Normans thorough thee,
Difdaine to call vs Lord, and *Piccardie*
Hath flaine their Gouernors, furpriz'd our Forts,
And fent the ragged Souldiers wounded home.
The Princely Warwicke, and the *Neuils* all,
Whofe dreadfull fwords were neuer drawne in vaine,
As hating thee, and rifing vp in armes.
And now the Houfe of Yorke thruft from the Crowne,
By fhamefull murther of a guiltleffe King,
And lofty proud incroaching tyranny,
Burnes with reuenging fire, whofe hopefull colours
Aduance our halfe-fac'd Sunne, ftriuing to fhine;
Vnder the which is writ, *Inuitis nubibus*.
The Commons heere in Kent are vp in armes,
And to conclude, Reproach and Beggerie,
Is crept into the Pallace of our King,
And all by thee: away, conuey him hence.

Suf. O that I were a God, to fhoot forth Thunder
Vpon thefe paltry, feruile, abiect Drudges:
Small things make bafe men proud. This Villaine heere,
Being Captaine of a Pinnace, threatens more
Then *Bargulus* the ftrong Illyrian Pyrate.
Drones fucke not Eagles blood, but rob Bee-hiues:
It is impoffible that I fhould dye

By

By such a lowly Vassall as thy selfe.
Thy words moue Rage, and not remorse in me:
I go of Message from the Queene to France:
I charge thee waft me safely crosse the Channell.

Lieu. Water: W. Come Suffolke, I must waft thee to thy death.

Suf. *Pine gelidus timor occupat artus*, it is thee I feare.

Wal. Thou shalt haue cause to feare before I leaue thee. What, are ye danted now? Now will ye stoope.

1.Gent. My gracious Lord intreat him, speak him fair.

Suf. Suffolkes Imperiall tongue is sterne and rough:
Vs'd to command, vntaught to pleade for fauour.
Farre be it, we should honor such as these
With humble suite: no, rather let my head
Stoope to the blocke, then these knees bow to any,
Saue to the God of heauen, and to my King:
And sooner dance vpon a bloody pole,
Then stand vncouer'd to the Vulgar Groome.
True Nobility, is exempt from feare:
More can I beare, then you dare execute.

Lieu. Hale him away, and let him talke no more:
Come Souldiers, shew what cruelty ye can.

Suf. That this my death may neuer be forgot,
Great men oft dye by vilde Bezonions.
A Romane Sworder, and Bandetto slaue
Murder'd sweet *Tully*. *Brutus* Bastard hand
Stab'd *Iulius Cæsar*. Sauage Islanders
Pompey the Great, and *Suffolke* dyes by Pyrats.

Exit Water with Suffolke.

Lieu. And as for these whose ransome we haue set,
It is our pleasure one of them depart:
Therefore come you with vs, and let him go.

Exit Lieutenant, and the rest.

Manet the first Gent. *Enter Walter with the body.*

Wal. There let his head, and liuelesse bodie lye,
Vntill the Queene his Mistris bury it. *Exit Walter.*

1.Gent. O barbarous and bloudy spectacle,
His body will I beare vnto the King:
If he reuenge it not, yet will his Friends,
So will the Queene, that liuing, held him deere.

Enter Beuis, and Iohn Holland.

Beuis. Come and get thee a sword, though made of a Lath, they haue bene vp these two dayes.

Hol. They haue the more neede to sleepe now then.

Beuis. I tell thee, *Iacke Cade* the Cloathier, meanes to dresse the Common-wealth and turne it, and set a new nap vpon it.

Hol. So he had need, for 'tis thred-bare. Well, I say, it was neuer merrie world in England, since Gentlemen came vp.

Beuis. O miserable Age: Vertue is not regarded in Handy-crafts men.

Hol. The Nobilitie thinke scorne to goe in Leather Aprons.

Beuis. Nay more, the Kings Councell are no good Workemen.

Hol. True: and yet it is said, Labour in thy Vocation: which is as much to say, as let the Magistrates be labouring men, and therefore should we be Magistrates.

Beuis. Thou hast hit it: for there's no better signe of a braue minde, then a hard hand.

Hol. I see them, I see them: There's *Bests* Sonne, the Tanner of Wingham.

Beuis. Hee shall haue the skinnes of our enemies, to make Dogges Leather of.

Hol. And Dicke the Butcher.

Beuis. Then is sin strucke downe like an Oxe, and iniquities throate cut like a Calfe.

Hol. And Smith the Weauer.

Beu. Argo, their thred of life is spun.

Hol. Come, come, let's fall in with them.

Drumme. Enter Cade, Dicke Butcher, Smith the Weauer, and a Sawyer, with infinite numbers.

Cade. Wee *Iohn Cade*, so tearm'd of our supposed Father.

But. Or rather of stealing a Cade of Herrings.

Cade. For our enemies shall faile before vs, inspired with the spirit of putting down Kings and Princes. Command silence.

But. Silence.

Cade. My Father was a *Mortimer*.

But. He was an honest man, and a good Bricklayer.

Cade. My mother a *Plantagenet*.

Butch. I knew her well, she was a Midwife.

Cade. My wife descended of the *Lacies*.

But. She was indeed a Pedlers daughter, & sold many Laces.

Weauer. But now of late, not able to trauell with her furr'd Packe, she washes buckes here at home.

Cade. Therefore am I of an honorable house.

But. I by my faith, the field is honourable, and there was he borne, vnder a hedge: for his Father had neuer a house but the Cage.

Cade. Valiant I am.

Weauer. A must needs, for beggery is valiant.

Cade. I am able to endure much.

But. No question of that: for I haue seene him whipt three Market dayes together.

Cade. I feare neither sword, nor fire.

Wea. He neede not feare the sword, for his Coate is of proofe.

But. But me thinks he should stand in feare of fire, being burnt i'th hand for stealing of Sheepe.

Cade. Be braue then, for your Captaine is Braue, and Vowes Reformation. There shall be in England, seuen halfe peny Loaues sold for a peny: the three hoop'd pot, shall haue ten hoopes, and I wil make it Fellony to drink small Beere. All the Realme shall be in Common, and in Cheapside shall my Palfrey go to grasse: and when I am King, as King I will be.

All. God saue your Maiesty.

Cade. I thanke you good people. There shall bee no mony, all shall eate and drinke on my score, and I will apparrell them all in one Liuery, that they may agree like Brothers, and worship me their Lord.

But. The first thing we do, let's kill all the Lawyers.

Cade. Nay, that I meane to do. Is not this a lamentable thing, that of the skin of an innocent Lambe should be made Parchment; that Parchment being scribeld ore, should vndoe a man. Some say the Bee stings, but I say, 'tis the Bees waxe: for I did but seale once to a thing, and I was neuer mine owne man since. How now? Who's there?

Enter a Clearke.

Weauer. The Clearke of Chartam: hee can write and reade, and cast accompt.

Cade. O monstrous.

Wea. We tooke him setting of boyes Copies.

Cade.

Cade. Here's a Villaine.

Wea. Ha's a Booke in his pocket with red Letters in't

Cade. Nay then he is a Coniurer.

But. Nay, he can make Obligations, and write Court hand.

Cade. I am sorry for't: The man is a proper man of mine Honour: vnlesse I finde him guilty, he shall not die. Come hither sirrah, I must examine thee: What is thy name?

Clearke. *Emanuell.*

But. They vse to writ it on the top of Letters: 'Twill go hard with you.

Cade. Let me alone: Dost thou vse to write thy name? Or hast thou a marke to thy selfe, like a honest plain dealing man?

Clearke. Sir I thanke God, I haue bin so well brought vp, that I can write my name.

All. He hath confest: away with him: he's a Villaine and a Traitor.

Cade. Away with him I say: Hang him with his Pen and Inke-horne about his necke.

Exit one with the Clearke

Enter Michael.

Mich. Where's our Generall?

Cade. Heere I am thou particular fellow.

Mich. Fly, fly, fly, Sir *Humfrey Stafford* and his brother are hard by, with the Kings Forces.

Cade. Stand villaine, stand, or Ile fell thee downe: he shall be encountred with a man as good as himselfe. He is but a Knight, is a?

Mich. No.

Cade. To equall him I will make my selfe a knight, presently; Rise vp Sir *Iohn Mortimer.* Now haue at him.

Enter Sir Humfrey Stafford, and his Brother, with Drum and Soldiers.

Staf. Rebellious Hinds, the filth and scum of Kent,
Mark'd for the Gallowes: Lay your Weapons downe,
Home to your Cottages: forsake this Groome.
The King is mercifull, if you reuolt,

Bro. But angry, wrathfull, and inclin'd to blood,
If you go forward: therefore yeeld, or dye.

Cade. As for these silken-coated slaues I passe not,
It is to you good people, that I speake,
Ouer whom (in time to come) I hope to raigne:
For I am rightfull heyre vnto the Crowne.

Staff. Villaine, thy Father was a Playsterer,
And thou thy selfe a Sheareman, art thou not?

Cade. And *Adam* was a Gardiner.

Bro. And what of that?

Cade. Marry, this *Edmund Mortimer* Earle of March, married the Duke of *Clarence* daughter, did he not?

Staf. I sir.

Cade. By her he had two children at one birth.

Bro. That's false.

Cade. I, there's the question; But I say, 'tis true:
The elder of them being put to nurse,
Was by a begger-woman stolne away,
And ignorant of his birth and parentage,
Became a Bricklayer, when he came to age.
His sonne am I, deny it if you can.

But. Nay, 'tis too true, therefore he shall be King.

Wea. Sir, he made a Chimney in my Fathers house, & the brickes are aliue at this day to testifie it: therefore deny it not.

Staf. And will you credit this base Drudges Wordes, that speakes he knowes not what.

All. I marry will we: therefore get ye gone.

Bro. *Iacke Cade,* the D. of York hath taught you this.

Cade. He lyes, for I inuented it my selfe. Go too Sirrah, tell the King from me, that for his Fathers sake *Henry* the fift, (in whose time, boyes went to Span-counter for French Crownes) I am content he shall raigne, but Ile be Protector ouer him.

Butcher. And furthermore, wee'l haue the Lord *Sayes* head, for selling the Dukedome of *Maine.*

Cade And good reason: for thereby is England main'd
And faine to go with a staffe, but that my puissance holds it vp. Fellow-Kings, I tell you, that that Lord *Say* hath gelded the Commonwealth, and made it an Eunuch: & more then that, he can speake French, and therefore hee is a Traitor.

Staf. O grosse and miserable ignorance.

Cade. Nay answer if you can: The Frenchmen are our enemies: go too then, I ask but this: Can he that speaks with the tongue of an enemy, be a good Councellour, or no?

All. No, no, and therefore wee'l haue his head.

Bro. Well, seeing gentle words will not preuayle,
Assaile them with the Army of the King.

Staf. Herald away, and throughout euery Towne,
Proclaime them Traitors that are vp with *Cade,*
That those which flye before the battell ends,
May euen in their Wiues and Childrens sight,
Be hang'd vp for example at their doores:
And you that be the Kings Friends follow me. *Exit.*

Cade. And you that loue the Commons, follow me:
Now shew your selues men, 'tis for Liberty.
We will not leaue one Lord, one Gentleman:
Spare none, but such as go in clouted shooen,
For they are thrifty honest men, and such
As would (but that they dare not) take our parts.

But. They are all in order, and march toward vs.

Cade. But then are we in order, when we are most out of order. Come, march forward.

Alarums to the fight, wherein both the Staffords are slaine. Enter Cade and the rest.

Cade. Where's Dicke, the Butcher of Ashford?

But. Heere sir.

Cade. They fell before thee like Sheepe and Oxen, & thou behaued'st thy selfe, as if thou hadst beene in thine owne Slaughter-house: Therfore thus will I reward thee, the Lent shall bee as long againe as it is, and thou shalt haue a License to kill for a hundred lacking one.

But. I desire no more.

Cade. And to speake truth, thou deseru'st no lesse.
This Monument of the victory will I beare, and the bodies shall be dragg'd at my horse heeles, till I do come to London, where we will haue the Maiors sword born before vs.

But. If we meane to thriue, and do good, breake open the Gaoles, and let out the Prisoners.

Cade. Feare not that I warrant thee. Come, let's march towards London. *Exeunt.*

Enter the King with a Supplication, and the Queene with Suffolkes head, the Duke of Buckingham, and the Lord Say.

Queene. Oft haue I heard that greefe softens the mind,

And makes it fearefull and degenerate,
Thinke therefore on reuenge, and cease to weepe.
But who can cease to weepe, and looke on this.
Heere may his head lye on my throbbing brest:
But where's the body that I should imbrace?

Buc. What answer makes your Grace to the Rebells Supplication?

King. Ile send some holy Bishop to intreat:
For God forbid, so many simple soules
Should perish by the Sword. And I my selfe,
Rather then bloody Warre shall cut them short,
Will parley with *Iacke Cade* their Generall.
But stay, Ile read it ouer once againe.

Qu. Ah barbarous villaines: Hath this louely face,
Rul'd like a wandering Plannet ouer me,
And could it not inforce them to relent,
That were vnworthy to behold the same.

King. Lord *Say*, *Iacke Cade* hath sworne to huae thy head.

Say. I, but I hope your Highnesse shall haue his.

King. How now Madam?
Still lamenting and mourning for Suffolkes death?
I feare me (Loue) if that I had beene dead,
Thou would'st not haue mourn'd so much for me.

Qu. No my Loue, I should not mourne, but dye for thee.

Enter a Messenger.

King. How now? What newes? Why com'st thou in such haste?

Mes. The Rebels are in Southwarke: Fly my Lord:
Iacke Cade proclaimes himselfe Lord *Mortimer*,
Descended from the Duke of *Clarence* house,
And calles your Grace Vsurper, openly,
And vowes to Crowne himselfe in Westminster.
His Army is a ragged multitude
Of Hindes and Pezants, rude and mercilesse:
Sir *Humfrey Stafford*, and his Brothers death,
Hath giuen them heart and courage to proceede:
All Schollers, Lawyers, Courtiers, Gentlemen,
They call false Catterpillers, and intend their death.

Kin. Oh gracelesse men: they know not what they do.

Buck. My gracious Lord, retire to Killingworth,
Vntill a power be rais'd to put them downe.

Qu. Ah were the Duke of Suffolke now aliue,
These Kentish Rebels would be soone appeas'd.

King. Lord *Say*, the Traitors hateth thee,
Therefore away with vs to Killingworth.

Say. So might your Graces person be in danger;
The sight of me is odious in their eyes:
And therefore in this Citty will I stay,
And liue alone as secret as I may.

Enter another Messenger.

Mess. *Iacke Cade* hath gotten London-bridge.
The Citizens flye and forsake their houses:
The Rascall people, thirsting after prey,
Ioyne with the Traitor, and they ioyntly sweare
To spoyle the City, and your Royall Court.

Buc. Then linger not my Lord, away, take horse.

King. Come *Margaret*, God our hope will succor vs.

Qu. My hope is gone, now Suffolke is deceast.

King. Farewell my Lord, trust not the Kentish Rebels

Buc. Trust no body for feare you betraid.

Say. The trust I haue, is in mine innocence,
And therefore am I bold and resolute. *Exeunt.*

Enter Lord Scales vpon the Tower walking. Then enters two or three Citizens below.

Scales. How now? Is *Iacke Cade* slaine?

1.Cit. No my Lord, nor likely to be slaine:
For they haue wonne the Bridge,
Killing all those that withstand them:
The L. Maior craues ayd of your Honor from the Tower
To defend the City from the Rebels.

Scales. Such ayd as I can spare you shall command,
But I am troubled heere with them my selfe,
The Rebels haue assay'd to win the Tower.
But get you to Smithfield, and gather head,
And thither I will send you *Mathew Goffe*.
Fight for your King, your Countrey, and your Liues,
And so farwell, for I must hence againe. *Exeunt*

Enter Iacke Cade and the rest, and strikes his staffe on London stone.

Cade. Now is *Mortimer* Lord of this City,
And heere sitting vpon London Stone,
I charge and command, that of the Cities cost
The pissing Conduit run nothing but Clarret Wine
This first yeare of our raigne.
And now henceforward it shall be Treason for any,
That calles me other then Lord *Mortimer*.

Enter a Soldier running.

Soul. *Iacke Cade, Iacke Cade.*

Cade. Knocke him downe there. *They kill him.*

But. If this Fellow be wise, hee'l neuer call yee *Iacke Cade* more, I thinke he hath a very faire warning.

Dicke. My Lord, there's an Army gathered together in Smithfield.

Cade. Come, then let's go fight with them:
But first, go and set London Bridge on fire,
And if you can, burne downe the Tower too.
Come, let's away, *Exeunt omnes.*

Alarums. Mathew Goffe is slain, and all the rest. Then enter Iacke Cade, with his Company.

Cade. So sirs: now go some and pull down the Sauoy:
Others to'th Innes of Court, downe with them all.

But. I haue a suite vnto your Lordship.

Cade. Bee it a Lordshippe, thou shalt haue it for that word.

But. Onely that the Lawes of England may come out of your mouth.

Iohn. Masse 'twill be sore Law then, for he was thrust in the mouth with a Speare, and 'tis not whole yet.

Smith. Nay *Iohn*, it wil be stinking Law, for his breath stinkes with eating toasted cheese.

Cade. I haue thought vpon it, it shall bee so. Away, burne all the Records of the Realme, my mouth shall be the Parliament of England.

Iohn. Then we are like to haue biting Statutes
Vnlesse his teeth be pull'd out.

Cade. And hence-forward all things shall be in Common. *Enter a Messenger.*

Mes. My Lord, a prize, a prize, heeres the Lord *Say*, which sold the Townes in France. He that made vs pay one and twenty Fifteenes, and one shilling to the pound, the last Subsidie.

Enter

Enter George, with the Lord Say.

Cade. Well, hee shall be beheaded for it ten times: Ah thou Say, thou Surge, nay thou Buckram Lord, now art thou within point-blanke of our Iurisdiction Regall. What canst thou answer to my Maiesty, for giuing vp of Normandie vnto Mounsieur *Basimecu*, the Dolphine of France? Be it knowne vnto thee by these presence, euen the presence of Lord *Mortimer*, that I am the Beesome that must sweepe the Court cleane of such filth as thou art: Thou hast most traiterously corrupted the youth of the Realme, in erecting a Grammar Schoole: and whereas before, our Fore-fathers had no other Bookes but the Score and the Tally, thou hast caused printing to be vs'd, and contrary to the King, his Crowne, and Dignity, thou hast built a Paper-Mill. It will be prooued to thy Face, that thou hast men about thee, that vsually talke of a Nowne and a Verbe, and such abhominable wordes, as no Christian eare can endure to heare. Thou hast appointed Iustices of Peace, to call poore men before them, about matters they were not able to answer. Moreouer, thou hast put them in prison, and because they could not reade, thou hast hang'd them, when (indeede) onely for that cause they haue beene most worthy to liue. Thou dost ride in a foot-cloth, dost thou not?

Say. What of that?

Cade. Marry thou ought'st not to let thy horse weare a Cloake, when honester men then thou go in their Hose and Doublets.

Dicke. And worke in their shirt to, as my selfe for example, that am a butcher.

Say. You men of Kent.

Dic. What say you of Kent.

Say. Nothing but this: 'Tis *bona terra, mala gens*.

Cade. Away with him, away with him, he speaks Latine.

Say. Heare me but speake, and beare mee wher'e you will:
Kent, in the Commentaries *Cæsar* writ,
Is term'd the ciuel'st place of all this Isle:
Sweet is the Covntry, because full of Riches,
The People Liberall, Valiant, Actiue, Wealthy,
Which makes me hope you are not void of pitty.
I sold not *Maine*, I lost not *Normandie*,
Yet to recouer them would loose my life:
Iustice with fauour haue I alwayes done,
Prayres and Teares haue mou'd me, Gifts could neuer.
When haue I ought exacted at your hands?
Kent to maintaine, the King, the Realme and you,
Large gifts haue I bestow'd on learned Clearkes,
Because my Booke preferr'd me to the King.
And seeing Ignorance is the curse of God,
Knowledge the Wing wherewith we flye to heauen.
Vnlesse you be possest with diuellish spirits,
You cannot but forbeare to murther me:
This Tongue hath parlied vnto Forraigne Kings
For your behoofe.

Cade. Tut, when struck'st thou one blow in the field?

Say. Great men haue reaching hands: oft haue I struck
Those that I neuer saw, and strucke them dead.

Geo. O monstrous Coward! What, to come behinde Folkes?

Say. These cheekes are pale for watching for your good

Cade. Giue him a box o'th'eare, and that wil make 'em red againe.

Say. Long sitting to determine poore mens causes,
Hath made me full of sicknesse and diseases.

Cade. Ye shall haue a hempen Candle then, & the help of hatchet.

Dicke. Why dost thou quiuer man?

Say. The Palsie, and not feare prouokes me.

Cade. Nay, he noddes at vs, as who should say, Ile be euen with you. Ile see if his head will stand steddier on a pole, or no: Take him away, and behead him.

Say. Tell me: wherein haue I offended most?
Haue I affected wealth, or honor? Speake.
Are my Chests fill'd vp with extorted Gold?
Is my Apparrell sumptuous to behold?
Whom haue I iniur'd, that ye seeke my death?
These hands are free from guiltlesse bloodshedding,
This breast from harbouring foule deceitfull thoughts.
O let me liue.

Cade. I feele remorse in my selfe with his words: but Ile bridle it: he shall dye, and it bee but for pleading so well for his life. Away with him, he ha's a Familiar vnder his Tongue, he speakes not a Gods name. Goe, take him away I say, and strike off his head presently, and then breake into his Sonne in Lawes house, Sir *Iames Cromer*, and strike off his head, and bring them both vppon two poles hither.

All. It shall be done.

Say. Ah Countrimen: If when you make your prair's,
God should be so obdurate as your selues:
How would it fare with your departed soules,
And therefore yet relent, and saue my life.

Cade. Away with him, and do as I command ye: the proudest Peere in the Realme, shall not weare a head on his shoulders, vnlesse he pay me tribute: there shall not a maid be married, but she shall pay to me her Maydenhead ere they haue it: Men shall hold of mee in Capite. And we charge and command, that their wiues be as free as heart can wish, or tongue can tell.

Dicke. My Lord,
When shall we go to Cheapside, and take vp commodities vpon our billes?

Cade. Marry presently.

All. O braue.

Enter one with the heads.

Cade. But is not this brauer:
Let them kisse one another: For they lou'd well
When they were aliue. Now part them againe,
Least they consult about the giuing vp
Of some more Townes in France. Soldiers,
Deferre the spoile of the Citie vntill night:
For with these borne before vs, in steed of Maces,
Will we ride through the streets, & at euery Corner
Haue them kisse. Away. *Exit*

Alarum, and Retreat. Enter againe Cade, and all his rabblement.

Cade. Vp Fish-streete, downe Saint Magnes corner, kill and knocke downe, throw them into Thames:

Sound a parley.

What noise is this I heare?
Dare any be so bold to sound Retreat or Parley
When I command them kill?

Enter Buckingham, and old Clifford.

Buc. I heere they be, that dare and will disturb thee:
Know *Cade*, we come Ambassadors from the King
Vnto the Commons, whom thou hast misled,
And heere pronounce free pardon to them all,
That will forsake thee, and go home in peace.

Clif. What say ye Countrimen, will ye relent
And yeeld to mercy, whil'st 'tis offered you,
Or let a rabble leade you to your deaths.
Who loues the King, and will imbrace his pardon,
Fling vp his cap. and say, God saue his Maiesty.
Who hateth him, and honors not his Father,
Henry the fift, that made all France to quake,
Shake he his weapon at vs, and passe by.

All. God saue the King, God saue the King.

Cade. What Buckingham and Clifford are ye so braue? And you base Pezants, do ye beleeue him, will you needs be hang'd with your Pardons about your neckes? Hath my sword therefore broke through London gates, that you should leaue me at the White-heart in Southwarke. I thought ye would neuer haue giuen out these Armes til you had recouered your ancient Freedome. But you are all Recreants and Dastards, and delight to liue in slauerie to the Nobility. Let them breake your backes with burthens, take your houses ouer your heads, rauish your Wiues and Daughters before your faces. For me, I will make shift for one, and so Gods Cursse light vppon you all.

All Wee'l follow *Cade*,
Wee'l follow *Cade*.

Clif. Is *Cade* the sonne of *Henry* the fift,
That thus you do exclaime you'l go with him.
Will he conduct you through the heart of France,
And make the meanest of you Earles and Dukes?
Alas, he hath no home, no place to flye too:
Nor knowes he how to liue, but by the spoile,
Vnlesse by robbing of your Friends, and vs.
Wer't not a shame, that whilst you liue at iarre,
The fearfull French, whom you late vanquished
Should make a start ore-seas, and vanquish you?
Me thinkes alreadie in this ciuill broyle,
I see them Lording it in London streets,
Crying *Villiago* vnto all they meete.
Better ten thousand base-borne *Cades* miscarry,
Then you should stoope vnto a Frenchmans mercy.
To France, to France, and get what you haue lost:
Spare England, for it is your Natiue Coast:
Henry hath mony, you are strong and manly:
God on our side, doubt not of Victorie.

All. A Clifford, a Clifford,
Wee'l follow the King, and Clifford.

Cade. Was euer Feather so lightly blowne too & fro, as this multitude? The name of Henry the fift, hales them to an hundred mischiefes, and makes them leaue mee desolate. I see them lay their heades together to surprize me. My sword make way for me, for heere is no staying: in despight of the diuels and hell, haue through the verie middest of you, and heauens and honor be witnesse, that no want of resolution in mee, but onely my Followers base and ignominious treasons, makes me betake mee to my heeles. *Exit*

Buck. What, is he fled? Go some and follow him,
And he that brings his head vnto the King,
Shall haue a thousand Crownes for his reward.

Exeunt some of them.

Follow me souldiers, wee'l deuise a meane,
To reconcile you all vnto the King. *Exeunt omnes.*

Sound Trumpets. Enter King, Queene, and Somerset on the Tarras.

King. Was euer King that ioy'd an earthly Throne,
And could command no more content then I?
No sooner was I crept out of my Cradle,
But I was made a King, at nine months olde.
Was neuer Subiect long'd to be a King,
As I do long and wish to be a Subiect.

Enter Buckingham and Clifford.

Buc. Health and glad tydings to your Maiesty.

Kin. Why Buckingham, is the Traitor *Cade* surpris'd?
Or is he but retir'd to make him strong?

Enter Multitudes with Halters about their Neckes.

Clif. He is fled my Lord, and all his powers do yeeld,
And humbly thus with halters on their neckes,
Expect your Highnesse doome of life, or death.

King. Then heauen set ope thy euerlasting gates,
To entertaine my vowes of thankes and praise.
Souldiers, this day haue you redeem'd your liues,
And shew'd how well you loue your Prince & Countrey:
Continue still in this so good a minde,
And *Henry* though he be infortunate,
Assure your selues will neuer be vnkinde:
And so with thankes, and pardon to you all,
I do dismisse you to your seuerall Countries.

All. God saue the King, God saue the King.

Enter a Messenger.

Mes. Please it your Grace to be aduertised,
The Duke of Yorke is newly come from Ireland,
And with a puissant and a mighty power
Of Gallow-glasses and stout Kernes,
Is marching hitherward in proud array,
And still proclaimeth as he comes along,
His Armes are onely to remoue from thee
The Duke of Somerset, whom he tearmes a Traitor.

King. Thus stands my state, 'twixt Cade and Yorke distrest,
Like to a Ship, that hauing scap'd a Tempest,
Is straight way calme, and boorded with a Pyrate.
But now is Cade driuen backe, his men dispierc'd,
And now is Yorke in Armes, to second him.
I pray thee Buckingham go and meete him,
And aske him what's the reason of these Armes:
Tell him, Ile send Duke *Edmund* to the Tower,
And *Somerset* we will commit thee thither,
Vntill his Army be dismist from him.

Somerset. My Lord
Ile yeelde my selfe to prison willingly,
Or vnto death, to do my Countrey good.

King. In any case, be not to rough in termes,
For he is fierce, and cannot brooke hard Language.

Buc. I will my Lord, and doubt not so to deale,
As all things shall redound vnto your good.

King. Come wife, let's in, and learne to gouern better,
For yet may England curse my wretched raigne.

Flourish. Exeunt.

Enter

Enter Cade.

Cade. Fye on Ambitions: fie on my selfe, that haue a sword, and yet am ready to famish. These fiue daies haue I hid me in these Woods, and durst not peepe out, for all the Country is laid for me: but now am I so hungry, that if I might haue a Lease of my life for a thousand yeares, I could stay no longer. Wherefore on a Bricke wall haue I climb'd into this Garden, to see if I can eate Grasse, or picke a Sallet another while, which is not amisse to coole a mans stomacke this hot weather: and I think this word Sallet was borne to do me good. for many a time but for a Sallet, my braine-pan had bene cleft with a brown Bill; and many a time when I haue beene dry, & brauely marching, it hath seru'd me insteede of a quart pot to drinke in: and now the word Sallet must serue me to feed on.

Enter Iden.

Iden. Lord, who would liue turmoyled in the Court,
And may enioy such quiet walkes as these?
This small inheritance my Father left me,
Contenteth me, and worth a Monarchy.
I seeke not to waxe great by others warning,
Or gather wealth I care not with what enuy:
Sufficeth, that I haue maintaines my state,
And sends the poore well pleased from my gate.

Cade. Heere's the Lord of the soile come to seize me for a stray, for entering his Fee-simple without leaue. A Villaine, thou wilt betray me, and get a 1000. Crownes of the King by carrying my head to him, but Ile make thee eate Iron like an Ostridge, and swallow my Sword like a great pin ere thou and I part.

Iden. Why rude Companion, whatsoere thou be,
I know thee not, why then should I betray thee?
Is't not enough to breake into my Garden,
And like a Theefe to come to rob my grounds:
Climbing my walles inspight of me the Owner,
But thou wilt braue me with these sawcie termes?

Cade. Braue thee? I by the best blood that euer was broach'd, and beard thee to. Looke on mee well, I haue eate no meate these fiue dayes, yet come thou and thy fiue men, and if I doe not leaue you all as dead as a doore naile, I pray God I may neuer eate grasse more.

Iden. Nay, it shall nere be said, while England stands,
That *Alexander Iden* an Esquire of Kent,
Tooke oddes to combate a poore famisht man.
Oppose thy stedfast gazing eyes to mine,
See if thou canst out-face me with thy lookes:
Set limbe to limbe, and thou art farre the lesser:
Thy hand is but a finger to my fist,
Thy legge a sticke compared with this Truncheon,
My foote shall fight with all the strength thou hast,
And if mine arme be heaued in the Ayre,
Thy graue is digg'd already in the earth:
As for words, whose greatnesse answer's words,
Let this my sword report what speech forbeares.

Cade. By my Valour: the most compleate Champion that euer I heard. Steele, if thou turne the edge, or cut not out the burly bon'd Clowne in chines of Beefe, ere thou sleepe in thy Sheath, I beseech Ioue on my knees thou mayst be turn'd to Hobnailes.

Heere they Fight.

O I am slaine, Famine and no other hath slaine me, let ten thousand diuelles come against me, and giue me but the ten meales I haue lost, and I'de defie them all. Wither Garden, and be henceforth a burying place to all that do dwell in this house, because the vnconquered soule of *Cade* is fled.

Iden. Is't *Cade* that I haue slain, that monstrous traitor?
Sword, I will hallow thee for this thy deede,
And hang thee o're my Tombe, when I am dead.
Ne're shall this blood be wiped from thy point,
But thou shalt weare it as a Heralds coate,
To emblaze the Honor that thy Master got.

Cade. *Iden* farewell, and be proud of thy victory: Tell Kent from me, she hath lost her best man, and exhort all the World to be Cowards: For I that neuer feared any, am vanquished by Famine, not by Valour. *Dyes.*

Id. How much thou wrong'st me, heauen be my iudge;
Die damned Wretch, the curse of her that bare thee:
And as I thrust thy body in with my sword,
So wish I, I might thrust thy soule to hell.
Hence will I dragge thee headlong by the heeles
Vnto a dunghill, which shall be thy graue,
And there cut off thy most vngracious head,
Which I will beare in triumph to the King,
Leauing thy trunke for Crowes to feed vpon. *Exit.*

Enter Yorke, and his Army of Irish, with Drum and Colours.

Yor. From Ireland thus comes York to claim his right,
And plucke the Crowne from feeble *Henries* head.
Ring Belles alowd, burne Bonfires cleare and bright
To entertaine great Englands lawfull King.
Ah *Sancta Maiestas*! who would not buy thee deere?
Let them obey, that knowes not how to Rule.
This hand was made to handle nought but Gold.
I cannot giue due action to my words,
Except a Sword or Scepter ballance it.
A Scepter shall it haue, haue I a soule,
On which Ile tosse the Fleure-de-Luce of France.

Enter Buckingham.

Whom haue we heere? Buckingham to disturbe me?
The king hath sent him sure: I must dissemble.

Buc. Yorke, if thou meanest wel, I greet thee well.

Yor. *Humfrey* of Buckingham, I accept thy greeting.
Art thou a Messenger, or come of pleasure.

Buc. A Messenger from *Henry*, our dread Liege,
To know the reason of these Armes in peace.
Or why, thou being a Subiect, as I am,
Against thy Oath, and true Allegeance sworne,
Should raise so great a power without his leaue?
Or dare to bring thy Force so neere the Court?

Yor. Scarse can I speake, my Choller is so great.
Oh I could hew vp Rockes, and fight with Flint,
I am so angry at these abiect tearmes.
And now like *Aiax Telamonius*,
On Sheepe or Oxen could I spend my furie.
I am farre better borne then is the king:
More like a King, more Kingly in my thoughts.
But I must make faire weather yet a while,
Till *Henry* be more weake, and I more strong.
Buckingham, I prethee pardon me,
That I haue giuen no answer all this while:
My minde was troubled with deepe Melancholly.
The cause why I haue brought this Armie hither,

Is to remoue proud Somerset from the King,
Seditious to his Grace, and to the State.

Buc. That is too much presumption on thy part:
But if thy Armes be to no other end,
The King hath yeelded vnto thy demand:
The Duke of Somerset is in the Tower.

Yorke. Vpon thine Honor is he Prisoner?

Buck. Vpon mine Honor he is Prisoner.

Yorke. Then Buckingham I do dismisse my Powres.
Souldiers, I thanke you all: disperse your selues:
Meet me to morrow in S. Georges Field,
You shall haue pay, and euery thing you wish.
And let my Soueraigne, vertuous *Henry*,
Command my eldest sonne, nay all my sonnes,
As pledges of my Fealtie and Loue,
Ile send them all as willing as I liue:
Lands, Goods, Horse, Armor, any thing I haue
Is his to vse, so Somerset may die.

Buc. Yorke, I commend this kinde submission,
We twaine will go into his Highnesse Tent.

Enter King and Attendants.

King. Buckingham, doth Yorke intend no harme to vs
That thus he marcheth with thee arme in arme?

Yorke. In all submission and humility,
Yorke doth present himselfe vnto your Highnesse.

K. Then what intends these Forces thou dost bring?

Yor. To heaue the Traitor Somerset from hence,
And fight against that monstrous Rebell *Cade*,
Who since I heard to be discomfited.

Enter Iden with Cades head.

Iden If one so rude, and of so meane condition
May passe into the presence of a King:
Loe, I present your Grace a Traitors head,
The head of *Cade*, whom I in combat slew.

King. The head of *Cade*? Great God, how iust art thou?
Oh let me view his Visage being dead,
That liuing wrought me such exceeding trouble.
Tell me my Friend, art thou the man that slew him?

Iden. I was, an't like your Maiesty.

King. How art thou call'd? And what is thy degree?

Iden. *Alexander Iden*, that's my name,
A poore Esquire of Kent, that loues his King.

Buc. So please it you my Lord, 'twere not amisse
He were created Knight for his good seruice.

King. *Iden*, kneele downe, rise vp a Knight:
We giue thee for reward a thousand Markes,
And will, that thou henceforth attend on vs.

Iden. May *Iden* liue to merit such a bountie,
And neuer liue but true vnto his Liege.

Enter Queene and Somerset.

K. See Buckingham, Somerset comes with th'Queene,
Go bid her hide him quickly from the Duke.

Qu. For thousand Yorkes he shall not hide his head,
But boldly stand, and front him to his face.

Yor. How now? is Somerset at libertie?
Then Yorke vnloose thy long imprisoned thoughts,
And let thy tongue be equall with thy heart.
Shall I endure the sight of Somerset?
False King, why hast thou broken faith with me,
Knowing how hardly I can brooke abuse?
King did I call thee? No: thou art not King:
Not fit to gouerne and rule multitudes,
Which dar'st not, no nor canst not rule a Traitor.
That Head of thine doth not become a Crowne:
Thy Hand is made to graspe a Palmers staffe,
And not to grace an awefull Princely Scepter.
That Gold, must round engirt these browes of mine,
Whose Smile and Frowne, like to *Achilles* Speare
Is able with the change, to kill and cure.
Heere is a hand to hold a Scepter vp,
And with the same to acte controlling Lawes:
Giue place: by heauen thou shalt rule no more
O're him, whom heauen created for thy Ruler.

Som. O monstrous Traitor! I arrest thee Yorke
Of Capitall Treason 'gainst the King and Crowne:
Obey audacious Traitor, kneele for Grace.

York. Wold'st haue me kneele? First let me ask of thee,
If they can brooke I bow a knee to man:
Sirrah, call in my sonne to be my bale:
I know ere they will haue me go to Ward,
They'l pawne their swords of my infranchisement.

Qu. Call hither *Clifford*, bid him come amaine,
To say, if that the Bastard boyes of Yorke
Shall be the Surety for their Traitor Father.

Yorke. O blood-bespotted Neopolitan,
Out-cast of *Naples*, Englands bloody Scourge,
The sonnes of Yorke, thy betters in their birth,
Shall be their Fathers baile, and bane to those
That for my Surety will refuse the Boyes.

Enter Edward and Richard.

See where they come, Ile warrant they'l make it good.

Enter Clifford.

Qu. And here comes *Clifford* to deny their baile.

Clif. Health, and all happinesse to my Lord the King.

Yor. I thanke thee *Clifford*: Say, what newes with thee?
Nay, do not fright vs with an angry looke:
We are thy Soueraigne *Clifford*, kneele againe;
For thy mistaking so, We pardon thee.

Clif. This is my King Yorke, I do not mistake,
But thou mistakes me much to thinke I do,
To Bedlem with him, is the man growne mad.

King. I Clifford, a Bedlem and ambitious humor
Makes him oppose himselfe against his King.

Clif. He is a Traitor, let him to the Tower,
And chop away that factious pate of his.

Qu. He is arrested, but will not obey:
His sonnes (he sayes) shall giue their words for him.

Yor. Will you not Sonnes?

Edw. I Noble Father, if our words will serue.

Rich. And if words will not, then our Weapons shal.

Clif. Why what a brood of Traitors haue we heere?

Yorke. Looke in a Glasse, and call thy Image so.
I am thy King, and thou a false-heart Traitor:
Call hither to the stake my two braue Beares,
That with the very shaking of their Chaines,
They may astonish these fell-lurking Curres,
Bid Salsbury and Warwicke come to me.

Enter the Earles of Warwicke, and Salisbury.

Clif. Are these thy Beares? Wee'l bate thy Bears to death,
And manacle the Berard in their Chaines,
If thou dar'st bring them to the bayting place.

Rich. Oft haue I seene a hot ore-weening Curre,
Run backe and bite, because he was with-held,
Who being suffer'd with the Beares fell paw,
Hath clapt his taile, betweene his legges and cride,
And such a peece of seruice will you do,

If

If you oppoſe your ſelues to match Lord Warwicke.
Clif. Hence heape of wrath, foule indigeſted lumpe,
As crooked in thy manners, as thy ſhape.
Yor. Nay we ſhall heate you thorowly anon.
Clif. Take heede leaſt by your heate you burne your ſelues:
King. Why Warwicke, hath thy knee forgot to bow?
Old Salsbury, ſhame to thy ſiluer haire,
Thou mad miſleader of thy brain-ſicke ſonne,
What wilt thou on thy death-bed play the Ruffian?
And ſeeke for ſorrow with thy Spectacles?
Oh where is Faith? Oh, where is Loyalty?
If it be baniſht from the froſtie head,
Where ſhall it finde a harbour in the earth?
Wilt thou go digge a graue to finde out Warre,
And ſhame thine honourable Age with blood?
Why art thou old, and want'ſt experience?
Or wherefore doeſt abuſe it, if thou haſt it?
For ſhame in dutie bend thy knee to me,
That bowes vnto the graue with mickle age.
Sal. My Lord, I haue conſidered with my ſelfe
The Title of this moſt renowned Duke,
And in my conſcience, do repute his grace
The rightfull heyre to Englands Royall ſeate.
King. Haſt thou not ſworne Allegeance vnto me?
Sal. I haue.
Ki. Canſt thou diſpenſe with heauen for ſuch an oath?
Sal. It is great ſinne, to ſweare vnto a ſinne:
But greater ſinne to keepe a ſinfull oath:
Who can be bound by any ſolemne Vow
To do a murd'rous deede, to rob a man,
To force a ſpotleſſe Virgins Chaſtitie,
To reaue the Orphan of his Patrimonie,
To wring the Widdow from her cuſtom'd right,
And haue no other reaſon for this wrong,
But that he was bound by a ſolemne Oath?
Qu. A ſubtle Traitor needs no Sophiſter.
King. Call Buckingham, and bid him arme himſelfe.
Yorke. Call Buckingham, and all the friends thou haſt,
I am reſolu'd for death and dignitie.
Old Clif. The firſt I warrant thee, if dreames proue true
War. You were beſt to go to bed, and dreame againe,
To keepe thee from the Tempeſt of the field.
Old Clif. I am reſolu'd to beare a greater ſtorme,
Then any thou canſt coniure vp to day:
And that Ile write vpon thy Burgonet,
Might I but know thee by thy houſed Badge.
War. Now by my Fathers badge, old *Neuils* Creſt,
The rampant Beare chain'd to the ragged ſtaffe,
This day Ile weare aloft my Burgonet,
As on a Mountaine top, the Cedar ſhewes,
That keepes his leaues inſpight of any ſtorme,
Euen to affright thee with the view thereof.
Old Clif. And from thy Burgonet Ile rend thy Beare,
And tread it vnder foot with all contempt,
Deſpight the Bearard, that protects the Beare.
Yo. Clif. And ſo to Armes victorious Father,
To quell the Rebels, and their Complices.
Rich. Fie, Charitie for ſhame, ſpeake not in ſpight,
For you ſhall ſup with Ieſu Chriſt to night.
Yo Clif. Foule ſtygmaticke that's more then thou canſt tell.
Ric. If not in heauen, you'l ſurely ſup in hell. *Exeunt*

Enter Warwicke.

War. Clifford of Cumberland, 'tis Warwicke calles:
And if thou doſt not hide thee from the Beare,
Now when the angrie Trumpet ſounds alarum,
And dead mens cries do fill the emptie ayre,
Clifford I ſay, come forth and fight with me,
Proud Northerne Lord, Clifford of Cumberland,
Warwicke is hoarſe with calling thee to armes.

Enter Yorke.

War. How now my Noble Lord? What all a-foot.
Yor. The deadly handed Clifford ſlew my Steed:
But match to match I haue encountred him,
And made a prey for Carrion Kytes and Crowes
Euen of the bonnie beaſt he loued ſo well.

Enter Clifford.

War. Of one or both of vs the time is come.
Yor. Hold Warwick: ſeek thee out ſome other chace
For I my ſelfe muſt hunt this Deere to death.
War. Then nobly Yorke, 'tis for a Crown thou fighſt:
As I intend Clifford to thriue to day,
It greeues my ſoule to leaue theee vnaſſail'd. *Exit War.*
Clif. What ſeeſt thou in me Yorke?
Why doſt thou pauſe?
Yorke. With thy braue bearing ſhould I be in loue,
But that thou art ſo faſt mine enemie.
Clif. Nor ſhould thy proweſſe want praiſe & eſteeme,
But that 'tis ſhewne ignobly, and in Treaſon.
Yorke. So let it helpe me now againſt thy ſword,
As I in iuſtice, and true right expreſſe it.
Clif. My ſoule and bodie on the action both.
Yor. A dreadfull lay, addreſſe thee inſtantly.
Clif. *La fin Corrone les eumenes.*
Yor. Thus Warre hath giuen thee peace, for ŷ art ſtill,
Peace with his ſoule, heauen if it be thy will.

Enter yong Clifford.

Clif. Shame and Confuſion all is on the rout,
Feare frames diſorder, and diſorder wounds
Where it ſhould guard. O Warre, thou ſonne of hell,
Whom angry heauens do make their miniſter,
Throw in the frozen boſomes of our part,
Hot Coales of Vengeance. Let no Souldier flye.
He that is truly dedicate to Warre,
Hath no ſelfe loue: nor he that loues himſelfe,
Hath not eſſentially, but by circumſtance
The name of Valour. O let the vile world end,
And the premiſed Flames of the Laſt day,
Knit earth and heauen together.
Now let the generall Trumpet blow his blaſt,
Particularities, and pettie ſounds
To ceaſe. Was't thou ordain'd (deere Father)
To looſe thy youth in peace, and to atcheeue
The Siluer Liuery of aduiſed Age,
And in thy Reuerence, and thy Chaire-dayes, thus
To die in Ruffian battell? Euen at this ſight,
My heart is turn'd to ſtone: and while 'tis mine,
It ſhall be ſtony. Yorke, not our old men ſpares:
No more will I their Babes, Teares Virginall,
Shall be to me, euen as the Dew to Fire,
And Beautie, that the Tyrant oft reclaimes,
Shall to my flaming wrath, be Oyle and Flax:
Henceforth, I will not haue to do with pitty.
Meet I an infant of the houſe of Yorke,
Into as many gobbits will I cut it
As wilde *Medea* yong *Abſirtis* did.
In cruelty, will I ſeeke out my Fame.
Come thou new ruine of olde Cliffords houſe:
As did *Æneas* old *Anchyſes* beare,
So beare I thee vpon my manly ſhoulders:
But then, *Æneas* bare a liuing loade;

Nothing so heauy as these woes of mine.

Enter Richard, and Somerset to fight.

Rich. So lye thou there:
For vnderneath an Ale-house paltry signe,
The Castle in S. *Albons*, Somerset
Hath made the Wizard famous in his death:
Sword, hold thy temper; Heart, be wrathfull still:
Priests pray for enemies, but Princes kill.

Fight. Excursions.

Enter King, Queene, and others.

Qu. Away my Lord, you are slow, for shame away.

King. Can we outrun the Heauens? Good *Margaret* stay.

Qu. What are you made of? You'l nor fight nor fly:
Now is it manhood, wisedome, and defence,
To giue the enemy way, and to secure vs
By what we can, which can no more but flye.

Alarum a farre off.

If you be tane, we then should see the bottome
Of all our Fortunes: but if we haply scape,
(As well we may, if not through your neglect)
We shall to London get, where you are lou'd,
And where this breach now in our Fortunes made
May readily be stopt.

Enter Clifford.

Clif. But that my hearts on future mischeefe set,
I would speake blasphemy ere bid you flye:
But flye you must: Vncureable discomfite
Reignes in the hearts of all our present parts.
Away for your releefe, and we will liue
To see their day, and them our Fortune giue.
Away my Lord, away. *Exeunt*

Alarum. Retreat. Enter Yorke, Richard, Warwicke, and Soldiers, with Drum & Colours.

Yorke. Of Salsbury, who can report of him,
That Winter Lyon, who in rage forgets
Aged contusions, and all brush of Time:
And like a Gallant, in the brow of youth,
Repaires him with Occasion. This happy day
Is not it selfe, nor haue we wonne one foot,
If Salsbury be lost.

Rich. My Noble Father:
Three times to day I holpe him to his horse,
Three times bestrid him: Thrice I led him off,
Perswaded him from any further act:
But still where danger was, still there I met him,
And like rich hangings in a homely house,
So was his Will, in his old feeble body,
But Noble as he is, looke where he comes.

Enter Salisbury.

Sal. Now by my Sword, well hast thou fought to day:
By'th'Masse so did we all. I thanke you *Richard*.
God knowes how long it is I haue to liue:
And it hath pleas'd him that three times to day
You haue defended me from imminent death.
Well Lords, we haue not got that which we haue,
'Tis not enough our foes are this time fled,
Being opposites of such repayring Nature.

Yorke. I know our safety is to follow them,
For (as I heare) the King is fled to London,
To call a present Court of Parliament:
Let vs pursue him ere the Writs go forth.
What sayes Lord Warwicke, shall we after them?

War. After them: nay before them if we can:
Now by my hand (Lords) 'twas a glorious day.
Saint Albons battell wonne by famous Yorke,
Shall be eterniz'd in all Age to come.
Sound Drumme and Trumpets, and to London all,
And more such dayes as these, to vs befall. *Exeunt.*

FINIS.

The third Part of Henry the Sixt, with the death of the Duke of YORKE.

Actus Primus. Scœna Prima.

Alarum.

Enter Plantagenet, Edward, Richard, Norfolke, Mountague, Warwicke, and Souldiers.

Warwicke.

I Wonder how the King escap'd our hands?

Pl. While we pursu'd the Horsmen of y North,
He slyly stole away, and left his men:
Whereat the great Lord of Northumberland,
Whose Warlike eares could neuer brooke retreat,
Chear'd vp the drouping Army, and himselfe,
Lord *Clifford* and Lord *Stafford* all a-brest
Charg'd our maine Battailes Front: and breaking in,
Were by the Swords of common Souldiers slaine.

Edw. Lord *Staffords* Father, Duke of *Buckingham*,
Is either slaine or wounded dangerous.
I cleft his Beauer with a down-right blow:
That this is true (Father) behold his blood.

Mount. And Brother, here's the Earle of Wilshires
Whom I encountred as the Battels ioyn'd. (blood,

Rich. Speake thou for me, and tell them what I did.

Plan. *Richard* hath best deseru'd of all my sonnes:
But is your Grace dead, my Lord of Somerset?

Nor. Such hope haue all the line of *Iohn of Gaunt*.

Rich. Thus do I hope to shake King *Henries* head.

Warw. And so doe I, victorious Prince of *Yorke*.
Before I see thee seated in that Throne,
Which now the House of *Lancaster* vsurpes,
I vow by Heauen, these eyes shall neuer close.
This is the Pallace of the fearefull King,
And this the Regall Seat: possesse it *Yorke*,
For this is thine, and not King *Henries* Heires.

Plant. Assist me then, sweet *Warwick*, and I will,
For hither we haue broken in by force.

Norf. Wee'le all assist you: he that flyes, shall dye.

Plant. Thankes gentle *Norfolke*, stay by me my Lords,
And Souldiers stay and lodge by me this Night.

They goe vp.

Warw. And when the King comes, offer him no violence,
Vnlesse he seeke to thrust you out perforce.

Plant. The Queene this day here holds her Parliament,
But little thinkes we shall be of her counsaile,
By words or blowes here let vs winne our right.

Rich. Arm'd as we are, let's stay within this House.

Warw. The bloody Parliament shall this be call'd,
Vnlesse *Plantagenet*, Duke of Yorke, be King,
And bashfull *Henry* depos'd, whose Cowardize
Hath made vs by-words to our enemies.

Plant. Then leaue me not, my Lords be resolute,
I meane to take possession of my Right.

Warw. Neither the King, nor he that loues him best,
The prowdest hee that holds vp *Lancaster*,
Dares stirre a Wing, if *Warwick* shake his Bells.
Ile plant *Plantagenet*, root him vp who dares:
Resolue thee *Richard*, clayme the English Crowne.

Flourish. Enter King Henry, Clifford, Northumberland, Westmerland, Exeter, and the rest.

Henry. My Lords, looke where the sturdie Rebell sits,
Euen in the Chayre of State: belike he meanes,
Backt by the power of *Warwicke*, that false Peere,
To aspire vnto the Crowne, and reigne as King.
Earle of Northumberland, he slew thy Father,
And thine, Lord *Clifford*, & you both haue vow'd reuenge
On him, his sonnes, his fauorites, and his friends.

Northumb. If I be not, Heauens be reueng'd on me.

Clifford. The hope thereof, makes *Clifford* mourne in Steele.

Westm. What, shall we suffer this? lets pluck him down,
My heart for anger burnes, I cannot brooke it.

Henry. Be patient, gentle Earle of Westmerland.

Clifford. Patience is for Poultroones, such as he:
He durst not sit there, had your Father liu'd.
My gracious Lord, here in the Parliament
Let vs assayle the Family of *Yorke*.

North Well hast thou spoken, Cousin be it so.

Henry. Ah, know you not the Citie fauours them,
And they haue troupes of Souldiers at their beck?

Westm. But when the Duke is slaine, they'le quickly flye.

Henry. Farre be the thought of this from *Henries* heart,
To make a Shambles of the Parliament House.
Cousin of Exeter, frownes, words, and threats,
Shall be the Warre that *Henry* meanes to vse.
Thou factious Duke of Yorke descend my Throne,
And kneele for grace and mercie at my feet,
I am thy Soueraigne.

Yorke. I am thine.

Exet. For shame come downe, he made thee Duke of Yorke.

Yorke. It was my Inheritance, as the Earledome was.

Exet. Thy

Exet. Thy Father was a Traytor to the Crowne.

Warw. *Exeter* thou art a Traytor to the Crowne, In following this vsurping *Henry*.

Clifford. Whom should hee follow, but his naturall King?

Warw. True *Clifford*, that's *Richard* Duke of Yorke.

Henry. And shall I stand, and thou sit in my Throne?

Yorke. It must and shall be so, content thy selfe.

Warw. Be Duke of Lancaster, let him be King.

Westm. He is both King, and Duke of Lancaster, And that the Lord of Westmerland shall maintaine.

Warw. And *Warwick* shall disproue it. You forget, That we are those which chas'd you from the field, And slew your Fathers, and with Colours spread Marcht through the Citie to the Pallace Gates.

Northumb. Yes *Warwicke*, I remember it to my griefe, And by his Soule, thou and thy House shall rue it.

Westm. *Plantagenet*, of thee and these thy Sonnes, Thy Kinsmen, and thy Friends, Ile haue more liues Then drops of bloud were in my Fathers Veines.

Cliff. Vrge it no more, lest that in stead of words, I send thee, *Warwicke*, such a Messenger, As shall reuenge his death, before I stirre.

Warw. Poore *Clifford*, how I scorne his worthlesse Threats.

Plant. Will you we shew our Title to the Crowne? If not, our Swords shall pleade it in the field.

Henry. What Title hast thou Traytor to the Crowne? My Father was as thou art, Duke of Yorke, Thy Grandfather *Roger Mortimer*, Earle of March. I am the Sonne of *Henry* the Fift, Who made the Dolphin and the French to stoupe, And seiz'd vpon their Townes and Prouinces.

Warw. Talke not of France, sith thou hast lost it all.

Henry. The Lord Protector lost it, and not I: When I was crown'd, I was but nine moneths old.

Rich. You are old enough now, And yet me thinkes you loose: Father teare the Crowne from the Vsurpers Head.

Edward. Sweet Father doe so, set it on your Head.

Mount. Good Brother, As thou lou'st and honorest Armes, Let's fight it out, and not stand cauilling thus.

Richard. Sound Drummes and Trumpets, and the King will flye.

Plant. Sonnes peace.

Henry. Peace thou, and giue King *Henry* leaue to speake.

Warw. *Plantagenet* shal speake first: Heare him Lords, And be you silent and attentiue too, For he that interrupts him, shall not liue.

Hen. Think'st thou, that I will leaue my Kingly Throne, Wherein my Grandsire and my Father sat? No: first shall Warre vnpeople this my Realme; I, and their Colours often borne in France, And now in England, to our hearts great sorrow, Shall be my Winding-sheet. Why faint you Lords? My Title's good, and better farre then his.

Warw. Proue it *Henry*, and thou shalt be King.

Hen. *Henry* the Fourth by Conquest got the Crowne.

Plant. 'Twas by Rebellion against his King.

Henry. I know not what to say, my Titles weake: Tell me, may not a King adopt an Heire?

Plant. What then?

Henry. And if he may, then am I lawfull King: For *Richard*, in the view of many Lords, Resign'd the Crowne to *Henry* the Fourth, Whose Heire my Father was, and I am his.

Plant. He rose against him, being his Soueraigne, And made him to resigne his Crowne perforce.

Warw. Suppose, my Lords, he did it vnconstrayn'd, Thinke you 'twere preiudiciall to his Crowne?

Exet. No: for he could not so resigne his Crowne, But that the next Heire should succeed and reigne.

Henry. Art thou against vs, Duke of Exeter?

Exet. His is the right, and therefore pardon me.

Plant. Why whisper you, my Lords, and answer not?

Exet. My Conscience tells me he is lawfull King.

Henry. All will reuolt from me, and turne to him.

Northumb. *Plantagenet*, for all the Clayme thou lay'st, Thinke not, that *Henry* shall be so depos'd.

Warw. Depos'd he shall be, in despight of all.

Northumb. Thou art deceiu'd: 'Tis not thy Southerne power Of Essex, Norfolke, Suffolke, nor of Kent, Which makes thee thus presumptuous and prowd, Can set the Duke vp in despight of me.

Clifford. King *Henry*, be thy Title right or wrong, Lord *Clifford* vowes to fight in thy defence: May that ground gape, and swallow me aliue, Where I shall kneele to him that slew my Father.

Henry. Oh *Clifford*, how thy words reuiue my heart.

Plant. *Henry* of Lancaster, resigne thy Crowne: What mutter you, or what conspire you Lords?

Warw. Doe right vnto this Princely Duke of Yorke, Or I will fill the House with armed men, And ouer the Chayre of State, where now he sits, Write vp his Title with vsurping blood.

He stampes with his foot, and the Souldiers shew themselues.

Henry. My Lord of Warwick, heare but one word, Let me for this my life time reigne as King.

Plant. Confirme the Crowne to me and to mine Heires, And thou shalt reigne in quiet while thou liu'st.

Henry. I am content: *Richard Plantagenet* Enioy the Kingdome after my decease.

Clifford What wrong is this vnto the Prince, your Sonne?

Warw. What good is this to England, and himselfe?

Westm. Base, fearefull, and despayring *Henry*.

Clifford. How hast thou iniur'd both thy selfe and vs?

Westm. I cannot stay to heare these Articles.

Northumb. Nor I.

Clifford. Come Cousin, let vs tell the Queene these Newes.

Westm. Farwell faint-hearted and degenerate King, In whose cold blood no sparke of Honor bides.

Northumb. Be thou a prey vnto the House of *Yorke*, And dye in Bands, for this vnmanly deed.

Cliff. In dreadfull Warre may'st thou be ouercome, Or liue in peace abandon'd and despis'd.

Warw. Turne this way *Henry*, and regard them not.

Exeter. They seeke reuenge, and therefore will not yeeld.

Henry. Ah *Exeter*.

Warw. Why should you sigh, my Lord?

Henry. Not for my selfe Lord *Warwick*, but my Sonne, Whom I vnnaturally shall dis-inherite. But be it as it may: I here entayle The Crowne to thee and to thine Heires for euer, Conditionally, that heere thou take an Oath, To cease this Ciuill Warre: and whil'st I liue,

To honor me as thy King, and Soueraigne:
And neyther by Treason nor Hostilitie,
To seeke to put me downe, and reigne thy selfe.

Plant. This Oath I willingly take, and will performe.

Warw. Long liue King *Henry*: *Plantagenet* embrace him.

Henry. And long liue thou, and these thy forward Sonnes.

Plant. Now *Yorke* and *Lancaster* are reconcil'd.

Exet. Accurst be he that seekes to make them foes.

Senet. Here they come downe.

Plant. Farewell my gracious Lord, Ile to my Castle.

Warw. And Ile keepe London with my Souldiers.

Norf. And I to Norfolke with my followers.

Mount. And I vnto the Sea, from whence I came.

Henry. And I with griefe and sorrow to the Court.

Enter the Queene.

Exeter. Heere comes the Queene,
Whose Lookes bewray her anger:
Ile steale away.

Henry. *Exeter* so will I.

Queene. Nay, goe not from me, I will follow thee.

Henry. Be patient gentle Queene, and I will stay.

Queene. Who can be patient in such extreames?
Ah wretched man, would I had dy'de a Maid?
And neuer seene thee, neuer borne thee Sonne,
Seeing thou hast prou'd so vnnaturall a Father.
Hath he deseru'd to loose his Birth-right thus?
Hadst thou but lou'd him halfe so well as I,
Or felt that paine which I did for him once,
Or nourisht him, as I did with my blood;
Thou would'st haue left thy dearest heart-blood there,
Rather then haue made that sauage Duke thine Heire,
And dis-inherited thine onely Sonne.

Prince. Father, you cannot dis-inherite me:
If you be King, why should not I succeede?

Henry. Pardon me *Margaret*, pardon me sweet Sonne,
The Earle of Warwick and the Duke enforc't me.

Quee. Enforc't thee? Art thou King, and wilt be forc't?
I shame to heare thee speake: ah timorous Wretch,
Thou hast vndone thy selfe, thy Sonne, and me,
And giu'n vnto the House of *Yorke* such head,
As thou shalt reigne but by their sufferance.
To entayle him and his Heires vnto the Crowne,
What is it, but to make thy Sepulcher,
And creepe into it farre before thy time?
Warwick is Chancelor, and the Lord of Callice,
Sterne *Falconbridge* commands the Narrow Seas,
The Duke is made Protector of the Realme,
And yet shalt thou be safe? Such safetie findes
The trembling Lambe, inuironned with Wolues.
Had I beene there, which am a silly Woman,
The Souldiers should haue toss'd me on their Pikes,
Before I would haue granted to that Act.
But thou preferr'st thy Life, before thine Honor.
And seeing thou do'st, I here diuorce my selfe,
Both from thy Table *Henry*, and thy Bed,
Vntill that Act of Parliament be repeal'd,
Whereby my Sonne is dis-inherited.
The Northerne Lords, that haue forsworne thy Colours,
Will follow mine, if once they see them spread:
And spread they shall be, to thy foule disgrace,
And vtter ruine of the House of *Yorke*:
Thus doe I leaue thee: Come Sonne, let's away,
Our Army is ready; come, wee'le after them.

Henry. Stay gentle *Margaret*, and heare me speake.

Queene. Thou hast spoke too much already: get thee gone.

Henry. Gentle Sonne *Edward*, thou wilt stay me?

Queene. I, to be murther'd by his Enemies.

Prince. When I returne with victorie to the field,
Ile see your Grace: till then, Ile follow her.

Queene. Come Sonne away, we may not linger thus.

Henry. Poore Queene,
How loue to me, and to her Sonne,
Hath made her breake out into termes of Rage.
Reueng'd may she be on that hatefull Duke,
Whose haughtie spirit, winged with desire,
Will cost my Crowne, and like an emptie Eagle,
Tyre on the flesh of me, and of my Sonne.
The losse of those three Lords torments my heart:
Ile write vnto them, and entreat them faire;
Come Cousin, you shall be the Messenger.

Exet. And I, I hope, shall reconcile them all. *Exit.*

Flourish. Enter Richard, Edward, and Mountague.

Richard. Brother, though I bee youngest, giue mee leaue.

Edward. No, I can better play the Orator.

Mount. But I haue reasons strong and forceable.

Enter the Duke of Yorke.

Yorke. Why how now Sonnes, and Brother, at a strife?
What is your Quarrell? how began it first?

Edward. No Quarrell, but a slight Contention.

Yorke. About what?

Rich. About that which concernes your Grace and vs,
The Crowne of England, Father, which is yours.

Yorke. Mine Boy? not till King *Henry* be dead.

Richard. Your Right depends not on his life, or death.

Edward. Now you are Heire, therefore enioy it now:
By giuing the House of *Lancaster* leaue to breathe,
It will out-runne you, Father, in the end.

Yorke. I tooke an Oath, that hee should quietly reigne.

Edward. But for a Kingdome any Oath may be broken:
I would breake a thousand Oathes, to reigne one yeere.

Richard. No: God forbid your Grace should be forsworne.

Yorke. I shall be, if I clayme by open Warre.

Richard. Ile proue the contrary, if you'le heare mee speake.

Yorke. Thou canst not, Sonne: it is impossible.

Richard. An Oath is of no moment, being not tooke
Before a true and lawfull Magistrate,
That hath authoritie ouer him that sweares.
Henry had none, but did vsurpe the place.
Then seeing 'twas he that made you to depose,
Your Oath, my Lord, is vaine and friuolous.
Therefore to Armes: and Father doe but thinke,
How sweet a thing it is to weare a Crowne,
Within whose Circuit is *Elizium*,
And all that Poets faine of Blisse and Ioy.
Why doe we linger thus? I cannot rest,
Vntill the White Rose that I weare, be dy'de
Euen in the luke-warme blood of *Henries* heart.

Yorke. *Richard* ynough: I will be King, or dye.
Brother, thou shalt to London presently,
And whet on *Warwick* to this Enterprise.

Thou

Thou *Richard* shalt to the Duke of Norfolke,
And tell him priuily of our intent.
You *Edward* shall vnto my Lord *Cobham*,
With whom the Kentishmen will willingly rise.
In them I trust: for they are Souldiors,
Wittie, courteous, liberall, full of spirit.
While you are thus imploy'd, what resteth more?
But that I seeke occasion how to rise,
And yet the King not priuie to my Drift,
Nor any of the House of *Lancaster*.

Enter Gabriel.

But stay, what Newes? Why comm'st thou in such poste?

Gabriel. The Queene,
With all the Northerne Earles and Lords,
Intend here to besiege you in your Castle.
She is hard by, with twentie thousand men:
And therefore fortifie your Hold, my Lord.

Yorke. I, with my Sword.
What? think'st thou, that we feare them?
Edward and *Richard*, you shall stay with me,
My Brother *Mountague* shall poste to London.
Let Noble *Warwicke*, *Cobham*, and the rest,
Whom we haue left Protectors of the King,
With powrefull Pollicie strengthen themselues,
And trust not simple *Henry*, nor his Oathes.

Mount. Brother, I goe: Ile winne them, feare it not.
And thus most humbly I doe take my leaue.

Exit Mountague.

Enter Mortimer, and his Brother.

York. Sir *Iohn*, and Sir *Hugh Mortimer*, mine Vnckles,
You are come to Sandall in a happie houre.
The Armie of the Queene meane to besiege vs.

Iohn. Shee shall not neede, wee'le meete her in the field.

Yorke. What, with fiue thousand men?

Richard. I, with fiue hundred, Father, for a neede.
A Womans generall: what should we feare?

A March afarre off.

Edward. I heare their Drummes:
Let's set our men in order,
And issue forth, and bid them Battaile straight.

Yorke. Fiue men to twentie: though the oddes be great,
I doubt not, Vnckle, of our Victorie.
Many a Battaile haue I wonne in France,
When as the Enemie hath beene tenne to one:
Why should I not now haue the like successe?

Alarum. Exit.

Enter Rutland, and his Tutor.

Rutland. Ah, whither shall I flye, to scape their hands?
Ah Tutor, looke where bloody *Clifford* comes.

Enter Clifford.

Clifford Chaplaine away, thy Priesthood saues thy life.
As for the Brat of this accursed Duke,
Whose Father slew my Father, he shall dye.

Tutor. And I, my Lord, will beare him company.

Clifford. Souldiers, away with him.

Tutor. Ah *Clifford*, murther not this innocent Child,
Least thou be hated both of God and Man. *Exit.*

Clifford. How now? is he dead alreadie?
Or is it feare, that makes him close his eyes?
Ile open them.

Rutland. So looks the pent-vp Lyon o're the Wretch,
That trembles vnder his deuouring Pawes:
And so he walkes, insulting o're his Prey,
And so he comes, to rend his Limbes asunder.
Ah gentle *Clifford*, kill me with thy Sword,
And not with such a cruell threatning Looke.
Sweet *Clifford* heare me speake, before I dye:
I am too meane a subiect for thy Wrath,
Be thou reueng'd on men, and let me liue.

Clifford. In vaine thou speak'st, poore Boy:
My Fathers blood hath stopt the passage
Where thy words should enter.

Rutland. Then let my Fathers blood open it againe,
He is a man, and *Clifford* cope with him.

Clifford. Had I thy Brethren here, their liues and thine
Were not reuenge sufficient for me:
No, if I digg'd vp thy fore-fathers Graues,
And hung their rotten Coffins vp in Chaynes,
It could not slake mine ire, nor ease my heart.
The sight of any of the House of *Yorke*,
Is as a furie to torment my Soule:
And till I root out their accursed Line,
And leaue not one aliue, I liue in Hell.
Therefore---

Rutland. Oh let me pray, before I take my death:
To thee I pray; sweet *Clifford* pitty me.

Clifford. Such pitty as my Rapiers point affords.

Rutland. I neuer did thee harme: why wilt thou slay me?

Clifford. Thy Father hath.

Rutland. But 'twas ere I was borne.
Thou hast one Sonne, for his sake pitty me,
Least in reuenge thereof, sith God is iust,
He be as miserably slaine as I.
Ah, let me liue in Prison all my dayes,
And when I giue occasion of offence,
Then let me dye, for now thou hast no cause.

Clifford. No cause? thy Father slew my Father: therefore dye.

Rutland. Dij faciant laudis summa sit ista tua.

Clifford. *Plantagenet*, I come *Plantagenet*:
And this thy Sonnes blood cleauing to my Blade,
Shall rust vpon my Weapon, till thy blood
Congeal'd with this, doe make me wipe off both. *Exit.*

Alarum. Enter Richard, Duke of Yorke.

Yorke. The Army of the Queene hath got the field:
My Vnckles both are slaine, in rescuing me;
And all my followers, to the eager foe
Turne back, and flye, like Ships before the Winde,
Or Lambes pursu'd by hunger-starued Wolues.
My Sonnes, God knowes what hath bechanced them:
But this I know, they haue demean'd themselues
Like men borne to Renowne, by Life or Death.
Three times did *Richard* make a Lane to me,
And thrice cry'de, Courage Father, fight it out:
And full as oft came *Edward* to my side,
With Purple Faulchion, painted to the Hilt,
In blood of those that had encountred him:
And when the hardyest Warriors did retyre,
Richard cry'de, Charge, and giue no foot of ground,
And cry'de, A Crowne, or else a glorious Tombe,

A

A Scepter, or an Earthly Sepulchre.
With this we charg'd againe: but out alas,
We bodg'd againe, as I haue seene a Swan
With bootlesse labour swimme against the Tyde,
And spend her strength with ouer-matching Waues.
A short Alarum within.
Ah hearke, the fatall followers doe pursue,
And I am faint, and cannot flye their furie:
And were I strong, I would not shunne their furie.
The Sands are numbred, that makes vp my Life,
Here must I stay, and here my Life must end.

Enter the Queene, Clifford, Northumberland, the young Prince, and Souldiers.

Come bloody *Clifford*, rough *Northumberland*,
I dare your quenchlesse furie to more rage.
I am your Butt, and I abide your Shot.

Northumb. Yeeld to our mercy, proud *Plantagenet*.

Clifford. I, to such mercy, as his ruthlesse Arme
With downe-right payment, shew'd vnto my Father.
Now *Phaeton* hath tumbled from his Carre,
And made an Euening at the Noone-tide Prick.

Yorke. My ashes, as the Phoenix, may bring forth
A Bird, that will reuenge vpon you all:
And in that hope, I throw mine eyes to Heauen,
Scorning what ere you can afflict me with.
Why come you not? what, multitudes, and feare?

Cliff. So Cowards fight, when they can flye no further,
So Doues doe peck the Faulcons piercing Tallons,
So desperate Theeues, all hopelesse of their Liues,
Breathe out Inuectiues 'gainst the Officers.

Yorke. Oh *Clifford*, but bethinke thee once againe,
And in thy thought ore-run my former time:
And if thou canst, for blushing, view this face,
And bite thy tongue, that slanders him with Cowardice,
Whose frowne hath made thee faint and flye ere this.

Clifford. I will not bandie with thee word for word,
But buckler with thee blowes twice two for one.

Queene. Hold valiant *Clifford*, for a thousand causes
I would prolong a while the Traytors Life:
Wrath makes him deafe; speake thou *Northumberland*.

Northumb. Hold *Clifford*, doe not honor him so much,
To prick thy finger, though to wound his heart.
What valour were it, when a Curre doth grinne,
For one to thrust his Hand betweene his Teeth,
When he might spurne him with his Foot away?
It is Warres prize, to take all Vantages,
And tenne to one, is no impeach of Valour.

Clifford. I, I, so striues the Woodcocke with the Gynne.

Northumb. So doth the Connie struggle in the Net.

York. So triumph Theeues vpon their conquer'd Booty,
So True men yeeld with Robbers, so o're-matcht.

Northumb. What would your Grace haue done vnto him now?

Queene. Braue Warriors, *Clifford* and *Northumberland*,
Come make him stand vpon this Mole-hill here,
That raught at Mountaines with out-stretched Armes,
Yet parted but the shadow with his Hand.
What, was it you that would be Englands King?
Was't you that reuell'd in our Parliament,
And made a Preachment of your high Descent?
Where are your Messe of Sonnes, to back you now,
The wanton *Edward*, and the lustie *George*?
And where's that valiant Crook-back Prodigie,
Dickie, your Boy, that with his grumbling voyce
Was wont to cheare his Dad in Mutinies?
Or with the rest, where is your Darling, *Rutland*?
Looke *Yorke*, I stayn'd this Napkin with the blood
That valiant *Clifford*, with his Rapiers point,
Made issue from the Bosome of the Boy:
And if thine eyes can water for his death,
I giue thee this to drie thy Cheekes withall.
Alas poore *Yorke*, but that I hate thee deadly,
I should lament thy miserable state.
I prythee grieue, to make me merry, *Yorke*.
What, hath thy fierie heart so parcht thine entrayles,
That not a Teare can fall, for *Rutlands* death?
Why art thou patient, man? thou should'st be mad:
And I, to make thee mad, doe mock thee thus.
Stampe, raue, and fret, that I may sing and dance.
Thou would'st be fee'd, I see, to make me sport:
Yorke cannot speake, vnlesse he weare a Crowne.
A Crowne for *Yorke*; and Lords, bow lowe to him:
Hold you his hands, whilest I doe set it on.
I marry Sir, now lookes he like a King:
I, this is he that tooke King *Henries* Chaire,
And this is he was his adopted Heire.
But how is it, that great *Plantagenet*
Is crown'd so soone, and broke his solemne Oath?
As I bethinke me, you should not be King,
Till our King *Henry* had shooke hands with Death.
And will you pale your head in *Henries* Glory,
And rob his Temples of the Diademe,
Now in his Life, against your holy Oath?
Oh 'tis a fault too too vnpardonable.
Off with the Crowne; and with the Crowne, his Head,
And whilest we breathe, take time to doe him dead.

Clifford. That is my Office, for my Fathers sake.

Queene. Nay stay, let's heare the Orizons hee makes.

Yorke. Shee-Wolfe of France,
But worse then Wolues of France,
Whose Tongue more poysons then the Adders Tooth:
How ill-beseeming is it in thy Sex,
To triumph like an Amazonian Trull,
Vpon their Woes, whom Fortune captiuates?
But that thy Face is Vizard-like, vnchanging,
Made impudent with vse of euill deedes,
I would assay, prowd Queene, to make thee blush.
To tell thee whence thou cam'st, of whom deriu'd,
Were shame enough, to shame thee,
Wert thou not shamelesse.
Thy Father beares the type of King of Naples,
Of both the Sicils, and Ierusalem,
Yet not so wealthie as an English Yeoman.
Hath that poore Monarch taught thee to insult?
It needes not, nor it bootes thee not, prowd Queene,
Vnlesse the Adage must be verify'd,
That Beggers mounted, runne their Horse to death.
'Tis Beautie that doth oft make Women prowd,
But God he knowes, thy share thereof is small.
'Tis Vertue, that doth make them most admir'd,
The contrary, doth make thee wondred at.
'Tis Gouernment that makes them seeme Diuine,
The want thereof, makes thee abhominable.
Thou art as opposite to euery good,
As the *Antipodes* are vnto vs,
Or as the South to the *Septentrion*.
Oh Tygres Heart, wrapt in a Womans Hide,

How

How could'st thou drayne the Life-blood of the Child,
To bid the Father wipe his eyes withall,
And yet be seene to beare a Womans face?
Women are soft, milde, pittifull, and flexible;
Thou, sterne, obdurate, flintie, rough, remorselesse.
Bidst thou me rage? why now thou hast thy wish.
Would'st haue me weepe? why now thou hast thy will.
For raging Wind blowes vp incessant showers,
And when the Rage allayes, the Raine begins.
These Teares are my sweet *Rutlands* Obsequies,
And euery drop cryes vengeance for his death,
'Gainst thee fell *Clifford*, and thee false French-woman.

Northumb. Beshrew me, but his passions moues me so,
That hardly can I check my eyes from Teares.

Yorke. That Face of his,
The hungry Caniballs would not haue toucht,
Would not haue stayn'd with blood:
But you are more inhumane, more inexorable,
Oh, tenne times more then Tygers of Hyrcania.
See, ruthlesse Queene, a haplesse Fathers Teares:
This Cloth thou dipd'st in blood of my sweet Boy,
And I with Teares doe wash the blood away.
Keepe thou the Napkin, and goe boast of this,
And if thou tell'st the heauie storie right,
Vpon my Soule, the hearers will shed Teares:
Yea, euen my Foes will shed fast-falling Teares,
And say, Alas, it was a pittious deed.
There, take the Crowne, and with the Crowne, my Curse,
And in thy need, such comfort come to thee,
As now I reape at thy too cruell hand.
Hard-hearted *Clifford*, take me from the World,
My Soule to Heauen, my Blood vpon your Heads.

Northumb. Had he been slaughter-man to all my Kinne,
I should not for my Life but weepe with him,
To see how inly Sorrow gripes his Soule.

Queen. What, weeping ripe, my Lord *Northumberland*?
Thinke but vpon the wrong he did vs all,
And that will quickly drie thy melting Teares.

Clifford. Heere's for my Oath, heere's for my Fathers Death.

Queene. And heere's to right our gentle-hearted King.

Yorke. Open thy Gate of Mercy, gracious God,
My Soule flyes through these wounds, to seeke out thee.

Queene. Off with his Head, and set it on Yorke Gates,
So *Yorke* may ouer-looke the Towne of Yorke.

Flourish. Exit.

A March. Enter Edward, Richard, and their power.

Edward. I wonder how our Princely Father scap't:
Or whether he be scap't away, or no,
From *Cliffords* and *Northumberlands* pursuit?
Had he been ta'ne, we should haue heard the newes;
Had he beene slaine, we should haue heard the newes:
Or had he scap't, me thinkes we should haue heard
The happy tidings of his good escape.
How fares my Brother? why is he so sad?

Richard. I cannot ioy, vntill I be resolu'd
Where our right valiant Father is become.
I saw him in the Battaile range about,
And watcht him how he singled *Clifford* forth.
Me thought he bore him in the thickest troupe,
As doth a Lyon in a Heard of Neat,
Or as a Beare encompass'd round with Dogges:
Who hauing pincht a few, and made them cry,
The rest stand all aloofe, and barke at him.
So far'd our Father with his Enemies,
So fled his Enemies my Warlike Father:
Me thinkes 'tis prize enough to be his Sonne.
See how the Morning opes her golden Gates,
And takes her farwell of the glorious Sunne.
How well resembles it the prime of Youth,
Trimm'd like a Yonker, prauncing to his Loue?

Ed. Dazle mine eyes, or doe I see three Sunnes?

Rich. Three glorious Sunnes, each one a perfect Sunne,
Not seperated with the racking Clouds,
But seuer'd in a pale cleare-shining Skye.
See, see, they ioyne, embrace, and seeme to kisse,
As if they vow'd some League inuiolable.
Now are they but one Lampe, one Light, one Sunne:
In this, the Heauen figures some euent.

Edward. 'Tis wondrous strange,
The like yet neuer heard of.
I thinke it cites vs (Brother) to the field,
That wee, the Sonnes of braue *Plantagenet*,
Each one alreadie blazing by our meedes,
Should notwithstanding ioyne our Lights together,
And ouer-shine the Earth, as this the World.
What ere it bodes, hence-forward will I beare
Vpon my Targuet three faire shining Sunnes.

Richard. Nay, beare three Daughters:
By your leaue, I speake it,
You loue the Breeder better then the Male.

Enter one blowing.

But what art thou, whose heauie Lookes fore-tell
Some dreadfull story hanging on thy Tongue?

Mess. Ah, one that was a wofull looker on,
When as the Noble Duke of Yorke was slaine,
Your Princely Father, and my louing Lord.

Edward. Oh speake no more, for I haue heard too much.

Richard. Say how he dy'de, for I will heare it all.

Mess. Enuironed he was with many foes,
And stood against them, as the hope of Troy
Against the Greekes, that would haue entred Troy.
But *Hercules* himselfe must yeeld to oddes:
And many stroakes, though with a little Axe,
Hewes downe and fells the hardest-tymber'd Oake.
By many hands your Father was subdu'd,
But onely slaught'red by the irefull Arme
Of vn-relenting *Clifford*, and the Queene:
Who crown'd the gracious Duke in high despight,
Laugh'd in his face: and when with griefe he wept,
The ruthlesse Queene gaue him, to dry his Cheekes,
A Napkin, steeped in the harmelesse blood
Of sweet young *Rutland*, by rough *Clifford* slaine:
And after many scornes, many foule taunts,
They tooke his Head, and on the Gates of Yorke
They set the same, and there it doth remaine,
The saddest spectacle that ere I view'd.

Edward. Sweet Duke of Yorke, our Prop to leane vpon,
Now thou art gone, wee haue no Staffe, no Stay.
Oh *Clifford*, boyst'rous *Clifford* thou hast slaine
The flowre of Europe, for his Cheualrie,
And trecherously hast thou vanquisht him,
For hand to hand he would haue vanquisht thee.
Now my Soules Pallace is become a Prison:
Ah, would she breake from hence, that this my body

Might

Might in the ground be closed vp in rest:
For neuer henceforth shall I ioy againe:
Neuer, oh neuer shall I see more ioy.

Rich. I cannot weepe: for all my bodies moysture
Scarse serues to quench my Furnace-burning hart:
Nor can my tongue vnloade my hearts great burthen,
For selfe-same winde that I should speake withall,
Is kindling coales that fires all my brest,
And burnes me vp with flames, that tears would quench.
To weepe, is to make lesse the depth of greefe:
Teares then for Babes; Blowes,and Reuenge for mee.
Richard, I beare thy name, Ile venge thy death,
Or dye renowned by attempting it.

Ed. His name that valiant Duke hath left with thee:
His Dukedome, and his Chaire with me is left.

Rich. Nay,if thou be that Princely Eagles Bird,
Shew thy descent by gazing 'gainst the Sunne:
For Chaire and Dukedome, Throne and Kingdome say,
Either that is thine, or else thou wer't not his.

March. Enter Warwicke,Marquesse Mountacute, and their Army.

Warwick. How now faire Lords? What faire? What newes abroad?

Rich. Great Lord of Warwicke,if we should recompt
Our balefull newes, and at each words deliuerance
Stab Poniards in our flesh, till all were told,
The words would adde more anguish then the wounds.
O valiant Lord,the Duke of Yorke is slaine.

Edw. O Warwicke, Warwicke, that *Plantagenet*
Which held thee deerely, as his Soules Redemption,
Is by the sterne Lord *Clifford* done to death.

War. Ten dayes ago, I drown'd these newes in teares,
And now to adde more measure to your woes,
I come to tell you things sith then befalne.
After the bloody Fray at Wakefield fought,
Where your braue Father breath'd his latest gaspe,
Tydings, as swiftly as the Postes could runne,
Were brought me of your Losse, and his Depart.
I then in London, keeper of the King,
Muster'd my Soldiers, gathered flockes of Friends,
Marcht toward S. Albons,to intercept the Queene
Bearing the King in my behalfe along:
For by my Scouts, I was aduertised
That she was comming with a full intent
To dash our late Decree in Parliament,
Touching King *Henries* Oath,and your Succesion:
Short Tale to make, we at S. Albons met,
Our Battailes ioyn'd, and both sides fiercely fought:
But whether 'twas the coldnesse of the King,
Who look'd full gently on his warlike Queene,
That robb'd my Soldiers of their heated Spleene.
Or whether 'twas report of her successe,
Or more then common feare of *Cliffords* Rigour,
Who thunders to his Captiues,Blood and Death,
I cannot iudge: but to conclude with truth,
Their Weapons like to Lightning, came and went:
Our Souldiers like the Night-Owles lazie flight,
Or like a lazie Thresher with a Flaile,
Fell gently downe,as if they strucke their Friends.
I cheer'd them vp with iustice of our Cause,
With promise of high pay,and great Rewards:
But all in vaine, they had no heart to fight,
And we (in them) no hope to win the day,
So that we fled: the King vnto the Queene,
Lord *George*, your Brother, Norfolke, and my Selfe,
In haste, post haste, are come to ioyne with you:
For in the Marches heere we heard you were,
Making another Head, to fight againe.

Ed. Where is the Duke of Norfolke, gentle Warwick?
And when came *George* from Burgundy to England?

War. Some six miles off the Duke is with the Soldiers,
And for your Brother he was lately sent
From your kinde Aunt Dutchesse of Burgundie,
With ayde of Souldiers to this needfull Warre.

Rich. 'Twas oddes belike, when valiant Warwick fled;
Oft haue I heard his praises in Pursuite,
But ne're till now, his Scandall of Retire.

War. Nor now my Scandall *Richard*, dost thou heare:
For thou shalt know this strong right hand of mine,
Can plucke the Diadem from faint *Henries* head,
And wring the awefull Scepter from his Fist,
Were he as famous, and as bold in Warre,
As he is fam d for Mildnesse, Peace,and Prayer.

Rich. I know it well Lord Warwick,blame me not,
'Tis loue I beare thy glories make me speake:
But in this troublous time, what's to be done?
Shall we go throw away our Coates of Steele,
And wrap our bodies in blacke mourning Gownes,
Numb'ring our Aue-Maries with our Beads?
Or shall we on the Helmets of our Foes
Tell our Deuotion with reuengefull Armes?
If for the last, say I, and to it Lords.

War. Why therefore Warwick came to seek you out,
And therefore comes my Brother *Mountague*:
Attend me Lords, the proud insulting Queene,
With *Clifford*, and the haught Northumberland,
And of their Feather, many moe proud Birds,
Haue wrought the easie-melting King, like Wax.
He swore consent to your Succession,
His Oath enrolled in the Parliament.
And now to London all the crew are gone,
To frustrate both his Oath,and what beside
May make against the house of Lancaster.
Their power (I thinke)is thirty thousand strong:
Now, if the helpe of Norfolke,and my selfe,
With all the Friends that thou braue Earle of March,
Among'st the louing Welshmen can'st procure,
Will but amount to fiue and twenty thousand,
Why Via, to London will we march,
And once againe, bestride our foaming Steeds,
And once againe cry Charge vpon our Foes,
But neuer once againe turne backe and flye.

Rich. I, now me thinks I heare great Warwick speak;
Ne're may he liue to see a Sun-shine day,
That cries Retire, if Warwicke bid him stay.

Ed. Lord Warwicke, on thy shoulder will I leane,
And when thou failst (as God forbid the houre)
Must *Edward* fall, which perill heauen forefend.

War. No longer Earle of March,but Duke of Yorke:
The next degree,is Englands Royall Throne:
For King of England shalt thou be proclaim'd
In euery Burrough as we passe along,
And he that throwes not vp his cap for ioy,
Shall for the Fault make forfeit of his head,
King *Edward*, valiant *Richard Mountague*:
Stay we no longer, dreaming of Renowne,
But sound the Trumpets,and about our Taske.

Rich. Then *Clifford*, were thy heart as hard as Steele,
As thou hast shewne it flintie by thy deeds,
I come to pierce it, or to giue thee mine.

Ed. Then strike vp Drums,God and S.George for vs.

Enter a Messenger.

War. How now? what newes?

Mes. The Duke of Norfolke sends you word by me,
The Queene is comming with a puissant Hoast,
And craues your company, for speedy counsell.

War. Why then it sorts, braue Warriors, let's away.

Exeunt Omnes.

Flourish. Enter the King, the Queene, Clifford, Northum- and Yong Prince, with Drumme and Trumpettes.

Qu. Welcome my Lord, to this braue town of Yorke,
Yonders the head of that Arch-enemy,
That sought to be incompast with your Crowne.
Doth not the obiect cheere your heart, my Lord.

K. I, as the rockes cheare them that feare their wrack,
To see this sight, it irkes my very soule:
With-hold reuenge (deere God) 'tis not my fault,
Nor wittingly haue I infring'd my Vow.

Clif. My gracious Liege, this too much lenity
And harmfull pitty must be layd aside:
To whom do Lyons cast their gentle Lookes?
Not to the Beast, that would vsurpe their Den.
Whose hand is that the Forrest Beare doth licke?
Not his that spoyles her yong before her face.
Who scapes the lurking Serpents mortall sting?
Not he that sets his foot vpon her backe.
The smallest Worme will turne, being troden on,
And Doues will pecke in safegard of their Brood.
Ambitious Yorke, did leuell at thy Crowne,
Thou smiling, while he knit his angry browes.
He but a Duke, would haue his Sonne a King,
And raise his issue like a louing Sire.
Thou being a King, blest with a goodly sonne,
Did'st yeeld consent to disinherit him:
Which argued thee a most vnlouing Father.
Vnreasonable Creatures feed their young,
And though mans face be fearefull to their eyes,
Yet in protection of their tender ones,
Who hath not seene them euen with those wings,
Which sometime they haue vs'd with fearfull flight,
Make warre with him that climb'd vnto their nest,
Offering their owne liues in their yongs defence?
For shame, my Liege, make them your President:
Were it not pitty that this goodly Boy
Should loose his Birth-right by his Fathers fault,
And long heereafter say vnto his childe,
What my great Grandfather, and Grandsire got,
My carelesse Father fondly gaue away.
Ah, what a shame were this? Looke on the Boy,
And let his manly face, which promiseth
Successefull Fortune steele thy melting heart,
To hold thine owne, and leaue thine owne with him.

King. Full well hath *Clifford* plaid the Orator,
Inferring arguments of mighty force:
But *Clifford* tell me, did'st thou neuer heare,
That things ill got, had euer bad successe.
And happy alwayes was it for that Sonne,
Whose Father for his hoording went to hell:
Ile leaue my Sonne my Vertuous deeds behinde,
And would my Father had left me no more:
For all the rest is held at such a Rate,
As brings a thousand fold more care to keepe,
Then in possession any iot of pleasure.
Ah Cosin Yorke, would thy best Friends did know,
How it doth greeue me that thy head is heere.

Qu. My Lord cheere vp your spirits, our foes are nye,
And this soft courage makes your Followers faint:
You promist Knighthood to our forward sonne,
Vnsheath your sword, and dub him presently.
Edward, kneele downe.

King. *Edward Plantagenet*, arise a Knight,
And learne this Lesson; Draw thy Sword in right.

Prin. My gracious Father, by your Kingly leaue,
Ile draw it as Apparant to the Crowne,
And in that quarrell, vse it to the death.

Clif. Why that is spoken like a toward Prince.

Enter a Messenger.

Mess. Royall Commanders, be in readinesse,
For with a Band of thirty thousand men,
Comes Warwicke backing of the Duke of Yorke,
And in the Townes as they do march along,
Proclaimes him King, and many flye to him,
Darraigne your battell, for they are at hand.

Clif. I would your Highnesse would depart the field,
The Queene hath best successe when you are absent.

Qu. I good my Lord, and leaue vs to our Fortune.

King. Why, that's my fortune too, therefore Ile stay.

North. Be it with resolution then to fight.

Prin. My Royall Father, cheere these Noble Lords,
And hearten those that fight in your defence:
Vnsheath your Sword, good Father: Cry S. George.

March. Enter Edward, Warwicke, Richard, Clarence, Norfolke, Mountague, and Soldiers.

Edw. Now periur'd *Henry*, wilt thou kneel for grace?
And set thy Diadem vpon my head?
Or bide the mortall Fortune of the field.

Qu. Go rate thy Minions, proud insulting Boy,
Becomes it thee to be thus bold in termes,
Before thy Soueraigne, and thy lawfull King?

Ed. I am his King, and he should bow his knee:
I was adopted Heire by his consent.

Cla. Since when, his Oath is broke: for as I heare,
You that are King, though he do weare the Crowne,
Haue caus'd him by new Act of Parliament,
To blot out me, and put his owne Sonne in.

Clif. And reason too,
Who should succeede the Father, but the Sonne.

Rich. Are you there Butcher? O, I cannot speake.

Clif. I Crooke-back, here I stand to answer thee,
Or any he, the proudest of thy sort.

Rich. 'Twas you that kill'd yong Rutland, was it not?

Clif. I, and old Yorke, and yet not satisfied.

Rich. For Gods sake Lords giue signall to the fight.

War. What say'st thou *Henry*,
Wilt thou yeeld the Crowne?

Qu. Why how now long-tongu'd Warwicke, dare you speak?
When you and I, met at S. *Albons* last,
Your legges did better seruice then your hands.

War. Then 'twas my turne to fly, and now 'tis thine:

Clif. You said so much before, and yet you fled.

War. 'Twas not your valor *Clifford* droue me thence.

Nor. No, nor your manhood that durst make you stay.

Rich. Northumberland, I hold thee reuerently,
Breake off the parley, for scarse I can refraine
The execution of my big-swolne heart
Vpon that *Clifford*, that cruell Child-killer.

Clif. I slew thy Father, cal'st thou him a Child?

Rich.

Rich. I like a Dastard, and a treacherous Coward,
As thou didd'st kill our tender Brother Rutland,
But ere Sunset, Ile make thee curse the deed.

King. Haue done with words (my Lords) and heare me speake.

Qu. Defie them then, or els hold close thy lips.

King. I prythee giue no limits to my Tongue,
I am a King, and priuiledg'd to speake.

Clif. My Liege, the wound that bred this meeting here,
Cannot be cur'd by Words, therefore be still.

Rich. Then Executioner vnsheath thy sword:
By him that made vs all, I am resolu'd,
That *Cliffords* Manhood, lyes vpon his tongue.

Ed. Say *Henry*, shall I haue my right, or no:
A thousand men haue broke their Fasts to day,
That ne're shall dine, vnlesse thou yeeld the Crowne.

War. If thou deny, their Blood vpon thy head,
For Yorke in iustice put's his Armour on.

Pr.Ed. If that be right, which Warwick saies is right,
There is no vvrong, but euery thing is right.

War. Who euer got thee, there thy Mother stands,
For well I vvot, thou hast thy Mothers tongue.

Qu. But thou art neyther like thy Sire nor Damme,
But like a foule mishapen Stygmaticke,
Mark'd by the Destinies to be auoided,
As venome Toades, or Lizards dreadfull stings.

Rich. Iron of Naples, hid with English gilt,
Whose Father beares the Title of a King,
(As if a Channell should be call'd the Sea)
Sham'st thou not, knowing whence thou art extraught,
To let thy tongue detect thy base-borne heart.

Ed. A wispe of straw were worth a thousand Crowns,
To make this shamelesse Callet know her selfe:
Helen of Greece was fayrer farre then thou,
Although thy Husband may be *Menelaus*;
And ne're was *Agamemnons* Brother wrong'd
By that false Woman, as this King by thee.
His Father reuel'd in the heart of France,
And tam'd the King, and made the Dolphin stoope:
And had he match'd according to his State,
He might haue kept that glory to this day.
But when he tooke a begger to his bed,
And grac'd thy poore Sire with his Bridall day,
Euen then that Sun-shine brew'd a showre for him,
That washt his Fathers fortunes forth of France,
And heap'd sedition on his Crowne at home:
For what hath broach'd this tumult but thy Pride?
Had'st thou bene meeke, our Title still had slept,
And we in pitty of the Gentle King,
Had slipt our Claime, vntill another Age.

Cla. But when we saw, our Sunshine made thy Spring,
And that thy Summer bred vs no increase,
We set the Axe to thy vsurping Roote:
And though the edge hath something hit our selues,
Yet know thou, since we haue begun to strike,
Wee'l neuer leaue, till we haue hewne thee downe,
Or bath'd thy growing, with our heated bloods.

Edw. And in this resolution, I defie thee,
Not willing any longer Conference,
Since thou denied'st the gentle King to speake.
Sound Trumpets, let our bloody Colours waue,
And either Victorie, or else a Graue.

Qu. Stay *Edward*.

Ed. No wrangling Woman, wee'l no longer stay,
These words will cost ten thousand liues this day.

Exeunt omnes.

Alarum. Excursions. Enter Warwicke.

War. Fore-spent with Toile, as Runners with a Race,
I lay me downe a little while to breath:
For strokes receiu'd, and many blowes repaid,
Haue robb'd my strong knit sinewes of their strength,
And spight of spight, needs must I rest a-while.

Enter Edward running.

Ed. Smile gentle heauen, or strike vngentle death,
For this world frownes, and *Edwards* Sunne is clowded.

War. How now my Lord, what happe? what hope of good?

Enter Clarence.

Cla. Our hap is losse, our hope but sad dispaire,
Our rankes are broke, and ruine followes vs.
What counsaile giue you? whether shall we flye?

Ed. Bootlesse is flight, they follow vs with Wings,
And weake we are, and cannot shun pursuite.

Enter Richard.

Rich. Ah Warwicke, why hast ÿ withdrawn thy selfe?
Thy Brothers blood the thirsty earth hath drunk,
Broach'd with the Steely point of *Cliffords* Launce:
And in the very pangs of death, he cryde,
Like to a dismall Clangor heard from farre,
Warwicke, reuenge; Brother, reuenge my death.
So vnderneath the belly of their Steeds,
That stain'd their Fetlockes in his smoaking blood,
The Noble Gentleman gaue vp the ghost.

War. Then let the earth be drunken with our blood:
Ile kill my Horse, because I will not flye:
Why stand we like soft-hearted women heere,
Wayling our losses, whiles the Foe doth Rage,
And looke vpon, as if the Tragedie
Were plaid in iest, by counterfetting Actors.
Heere on my knee, I vow to God aboue,
Ile neuer pawse againe, neuer stand still,
Till either death hath clos'd these eyes of mine,
Or Fortune giuen me measure of Reuenge.

Ed. Oh Warwicke, I do bend my knee with thine,
And in this vow do chaine my soule to thine:
And ere my knee rise from the Earths cold face,
I throw my hands, mine eyes, my heart to thee,
Thou setter vp, and plucker downe of Kings:
Beseeching thee (if with thy will it stands)
That to my Foes this body must be prey,
Yet that thy brazen gates of heauen may ope,
And giue sweet passage to my sinfull soule.
Now Lords, take leaue vntill we meete againe,
Where ere it be, in heauen, or in earth.

Rich. Brother,
Giue me thy hand, and gentle Warwicke,
Let me imbrace thee in my weary armes:
I that did neuer weepe, now melt with wo,
That Winter should cut off our Spring-time so.

War. Away, away:
Once more sweet Lords farwell.

Cla. Yet let vs altogether to our Troopes,
And giue them leaue to flye, that will not stay:
And call them Pillars that will stand to vs:
And if we thriue, promise them such rewards
As Victors weare at the Olympian Games.
This may plant courage in their quailing breasts,
For yet is hope of Life and Victory:

Foreslow no longer, make we hence amaine. *Exeunt*

Excursions. Enter Richard and Clifford.

Rich. Now *Clifford*, I haue singled thee alone,
Suppose this arme is for the Duke of Yorke,
And this for Rutland, both bound to reuenge,
Wer't thou inuiron'd with a Brazen wall.

Clif. Now *Richard*, I am with thee heere alone,
This is the hand that stabb'd thy Father Yorke,
And this the hand, that slew thy Brother Rutland,
And here's the heart, that triumphs in their death,
And cheeres these hands, that slew thy Sire and Brother,
To execute the like vpon thy selfe,
And so haue at thee.

They Fight, Warwicke comes, Clifford flies.

Rich. Nay Warwicke, single out some other Chace,
For I my selfe will hunt this Wolfe to death. *Exeunt.*

Alarum. Enter King Henry alone.

Hen. This battell fares like to the mornings Warre,
When dying clouds contend, with growing light,
What time the Shepheard blowing of his nailes,
Can neither call it perfect day, nor night.
Now swayes it this way, like a Mighty Sea,
Forc'd by the Tide, to combat with the Winde:
Now swayes it that way, like the selfe-same Sea,
Forc'd to retyre by furie of the Winde.
Sometime, the Flood preuailes; and than the Winde:
Now, one the better: then, another best;
Both tugging to be Victors, brest to brest:
Yet neither Conqueror, nor Conquered.
So is the equall poise of this fell Warre.
Heere on this Mole-hill will I sit me downe,
To whom God will, there be the Victorie:
For *Margaret* my Queene, and *Clifford* too
Haue chid me from the Battell: Swearing both,
They prosper best of all when I am thence.
Would I were dead, if Gods good will were so;
For what is in this world, but Greefe and Woe.
Oh God! me thinkes it were a happy life,
To be no better then a homely Swaine,
To sit vpon a hill, as I do now,
To carue out Dialls queintly, point by point,
Thereby to see the Minutes how they runne:
How many makes the Houre full compleate,
How many Houres brings about the Day,
How many Dayes will finish vp the Yeare,
How many Yeares, a Mortall man may liue.
When this is knowne, then to diuide the Times:
So many Houres, must I tend my Flocke;
So many Houres, must I take my Rest:
So many Houres, must I Contemplate:
So many Houres, must I Sport my selfe:
So many Dayes, my Ewes haue bene with yong:
So many weekes, ere the poore Fooles will Eane:
So many yeares, ere I shall sheere the Fleece:
So Minutes, Houres, Dayes, Monthes, and Yeares,
Past ouer to the end they were created,
Would bring white haires, vnto a Quiet graue.
Ah! what a life were this? How sweet? how louely?
Giues not the Hawthorne bush a sweeter shade
To Shepheards, looking on their silly Sheepe,
Then doth a rich Imbroider'd Canopie
To Kings, that feare their Subiects treacherie?
Oh yes, it doth; a thousand fold it doth.
And to conclude, the Shepherds homely Curds,
His cold thinne drinke out of his Leather Bottle,
His wonted sleepe, vnder a fresh trees shade,
All which secure, and sweetly he enioyes,
Is farre beyond a Princes Delicates:
His Viands sparkling in a Golden Cup,
His bodie couched in a curious bed,
When Care, Mistrust, and Treason waits on him.

Alarum. Enter a Sonne that hath kill'd his Father, at one doore: and a Father that hath kill'd his Sonne at another doore.

Son. Ill blowes the winde that profits no body,
This man whom hand to hand I slew in fight,
May be possessed with some store of Crownes,
And I that (haply) take them from him now,
May yet (ere night) yeeld both my Life and them
To some man else, as this dead man doth me.
Who's this? Oh God! It is my Fathers face,
Whom in this Conflict, I (vnwares) haue kill'd:
Oh heauy times! begetting such Euents.
From London, by the King was I prest forth,
My Father being the Earle of Warwickes man,
Came on the part of Yorke, prest by his Master:
And I, who at his hands receiu'd my life,
Haue by my hands, of Life bereaued him.
Pardon me God, I knew not what I did:
And pardon Father, for I knew not thee.
My Teares shall wipe away these bloody markes:
And no more words, till they haue flow'd their fill.

King. O pitteous spectacle! O bloody Times!
Whiles Lyons Warre, and battaile for their Dennes,
Poore harmlesse Lambes abide their enmity.
Weepe wretched man: Ile ayde thee Teare for Teare,
And let our hearts and eyes, like Ciuill Warre,
Be blinde with teares, and break ore-charg'd with griefe

Enter Father, bearing of his Sonne.

Fa. Thou that so stoutly hath resisted me,
Giue me thy Gold, if thou hast any Gold:
For I haue bought it with an hundred blowes.
But let me see: Is this our Foe-mans face?
Ah, no, no, no, it is mine onely Sonne.
Ah Boy, if any life be left in thee,
Throw vp thine eye: see, see, what showres arise,
Blowne with the windie Tempest of my heart,
Vpon thy wounds, that killes mine Eye, and Heart.
O pitty God, this miserable Age!
What Stragems? how fell? how Butcherly?
Erreoneous, mutinous, and vnnaturall,
This deadly quarrell daily doth beget?
O Boy! thy Father gaue thee life too soone,
And hath bereft thee of thy life too late.

King. Wo aboue wo: greefe, more thẽ common greefe
O that my death would stay these ruthfull deeds:
O pitty, pitty, gentle heauen pitty:
The Red Rose and the White are on his face,
The fatall Colours of our striuing Houses:
The one, his purple Blood right well resembles,
The other his pale Cheekes (me thinkes) presenteth:
Wither one Rose, and let the other flourish:
If you contend, a thousand liues must wither.

Son. How will my Mother, for a Fathers death
Take on with me, and ne're be satisfi'd?

Fa. How will my Wife, for slaughter of my Sonne,
Shed seas of Teares, and ne're be satisfi'd?

King. How will the Country, for these woful chances,

Mis-thinke

Mis-thinke the King, and not be satisfied?
Son. Was euer sonne, so rew'd a Fathers death?
Fath. Was euer Father so bemoan'd his Sonne?
Hen. Was euer King so greeu'd for Subiects woe?
Much is your sorrow; Mine, ten times so much.
Son. Ile beare thee hence, where I may weepe my fill.
Fath. These armes of mine shall be thy winding sheet:
My heart (sweet Boy) shall be thy Sepulcher,
For from my heart, thine Image ne're shall go.
My sighing brest, shall be thy Funerall bell;
And so obsequious will thy Father be,
Men for the losse of thee, hauing no more,
As *Priam* was for all his Valiant Sonnes,
Ile beare thee hence, and let them fight that will,
For I haue murthered where I should not kill. *Exit*
Hen. Sad-hearted-men, much ouergone with Care;
Heere sits a King, more wofull then you are.

Alarums. Excursions. Enter the Queen, the Prince, and Exeter.

Prin. Fly Father, flye: for all your Friends are fled.
And Warwicke rages like a chafed Bull:
Away, for death doth hold vs in pursuite.
Qu. Mount you my Lord, towards Barwicke post amaine:
Edward and *Richard* like a brace of Grey-hounds,
Hauing the fearfull flying Hare in sight,
With fiery eyes, sparkling for very wrath,
And bloody steele graspt in their yrefull hands
Are at our backes, and therefore hence amaine.
Exet. Away: for vengeance comes along with them.
Nay, stay not to expostulate, make speed,
Or else come after, Ile away before.
Hen. Nay take me with thee, good sweet Exeter:
Not that I feare to stay, but loue to go
Whether the Queene intends. Forward, away. *Exeunt*

A lowd alarum. Enter Clifford Wounded.

Clif. Heere burnes my Candle out; I, heere it dies,
Which whiles it lasted, gaue King *Henry* light.
O Lancaster! I feare thy ouerthrow,
More then my Bodies parting with my Soule:
My Loue and Feare, glew'd many Friends to thee,
And now I fall. Thy tough Commixtures melts,
Impairing *Henry*, strength'ning misproud Yorke;
And whether flye the Gnats, but to the Sunne?
And who shines now, but *Henries* Enemies?
O Phoebus! had'st thou neuer giuen consent,
That *Phaeton* should checke thy fiery Steeds,
Thy burning Carre neuer had scorch'd the earth.
And *Henry*, had'st thou sway'd as Kings should do,
Or as thy Father, and his Father did,
Giuing no ground vnto the house of Yorke,
They neuer then had sprung like Sommer Flyes:
I, and ten thousand in this lucklesse Realme,
Hed left no mourning Widdowes for our death,
And thou this day, had'st kept thy Chaire in peace.
For what doth cherrish Weeds, but gentle ayre?
And what makes Robbers bold, but too much lenity?
Bootlesse are Plaints, and Curelesse are my Wounds:
No way to flye, nor strength to hold out flight:
The Foe is mercilesse, and will not pitty:
For at their hands I haue deseru'd no pitty.
The ayre hath got into my deadly Wounds,
And much effuse of blood, doth make me faint:
Come *Yorke*, and *Richard*, *Warwicke* and the rest,
I stab'd your Fathers bosomes; Split my brest.

Alarum & Retreat. Enter Edward, Warwicke, Richard, and Soldiers, Montague, & Clarence.

Ed. Now breath we Lords, good fortune bids vs pause,
And smooth the frownes of War, with peacefull lookes:
Some Troopes pursue the bloody-minded Queene,
That led calme *Henry*, though he were a King,
As doth a Saile, fill'd with a fretting Gust
Command an Argosie to stemme the Waues.
But thinke you (Lords) that Clifford fled with them?
War. No, 'tis impossible he should escape:
(For though before his face I speake the words)
Your Brother *Richard* markt him for the Graue.
And wheresoere he is, hee's surely dead. *Clifford grones*
Rich. Whose soule is that which takes hir heauy leaue?
A deadly grone, like life and deaths departing.
See who it is.
Ed. And now the Battailes ended,
If Friend or Foe, let him be gently vsed.
Rich. Reuoke that doome of mercy, for 'tis *Clifford*,
Who not contented that he lopp'd the Branch
In hewing Rutland, when his leaues put forth,
But set his murth'ring knife vnto the Roote,
From whence that tender spray did sweetly spring,
I meane our Princely Father, Duke of Yorke.
War. From off the gates of Yorke, fetch down ẏ head,
Your Fathers head, which *Clifford* placed there:
In stead whereof, let this supply the roome,
Measure for measure, must be answered.
Ed. Bring forth that fatall Schreechowle to our house,
That nothing sung but death, to vs and ours:
Now death shall stop his dismall threatning sound,
And his ill-boading tongue, no more shall speake.
War. I thinke is vnderstanding is bereft:
Speake *Clifford*, dost thou know who speakes to thee?
Darke cloudy death ore-shades his beames of life,
And he nor sees, nor heares vs, what we say.
Rich. O would he did, and so (perhaps) he doth,
'Tis but his policy to counterfet,
Because he would auoid such bitter taunts
Which in the time of death he gaue our Father.
Cla If so thou think'st,
Vex him with eager Words.
Rich. *Clifford*, aske mercy, and obtaine no grace.
Ed. *Clifford*, repent in bootlesse penitence.
War. *Clifford*, deuise excuses for thy faults.
Cla. While we deuise fell Tortures for thy faults.
Rich. Thou didd'st loue Yorke, and I am son to Yorke.
Edw. Thou pittied'st Rutland, I will pitty thee.
Cla. Where's Captaine *Margaret*, to fence you now?
War. They mocke thee *Clifford*,
Sweare as thou was't wont.
Ric. What, not an Oath? Nay then the world go's hard
When *Clifford* cannot spare his Friends an oath:
I know by that he's dead, and by my Soule,
If this right hand would buy two houres life,
That I (in all despight) might rayle at him,
This hand should chop it off: & with the issuing Blood
Stifle the Villaine, whose vnstanched thirst
Yorke, and yong Rutland could not satisfie
War. I, but he's dead. Of with the Traitors head,
And reare it in the place your Fathers stands.
And now to London with Triumphant march,

There to be crowned Englands Royall King:
From whence, shall Warwicke cut the Sea to France,
And aske the Ladie *Bona* for thy Queene:
So shalt thou sinow both these Lands together,
And hauing France thy Friend, thou shalt not dread
The scattred Foe, that hopes to rise againe:
For though they cannot greatly sting to hurt,
Yet looke to haue them buz to offend thine eares:
First, will I see the Coronation,
And then to Britanny Ile crosse the Sea,
To effect this marriage, so it please my Lord.

Ed. Euen as thou wilt sweet Warwicke, let it bee:
For in thy shoulder do I builde my Seate;
And neuer will I vndertake the thing
Wherein thy counsaile and consent is wanting:
Richard I will create thee Duke of Gloucester,
And *George* of Clarence; *Warwicke* as our Selfe,
Shall do, and vndo as him pleaseth best.

Rich. Let me be Duke of Clarence, *George* of Gloster,
For Glosters Dukedome is too ominous.

War. Tut, that's a foolish obseruation:
Richard, be Duke of Gloster: Now to London,
To see these Honors in possession. *Exeunt*

Enter Sinklo, and Humfrey, with Crosse-bowes in their hands.

Sink. Vnder this thicke growne brake, wee'l shrowd (our selues:
For through this Laund anon the Deere will come,
And in this couert will we make our Stand,
Culling the principall of all the Deere.

Hum. Ile stay aboue the hill, so both may shoot.

Sink. That cannot be, the noise of thy Crosse-bow
Will scarre the Heard, and so my shoot is lost:
Heere stand we both, and ayme we at the best:
And for the time shall not seeme tedious,
Ile tell thee what befell me on a day,
In this selfe-place, where now we meane to stand.

Sink. Heere comes a man, let's stay till he be past:

Enter the King with a Prayer booke.

Hen. From Scotland am I stolne euen of pure loue,
To greet mine owne Land with my wishfull sight:
No *Harry, Harry*, 'tis no Land of thine,
Thy place is fill'd, thy Scepter wrung from thee,
Thy Balme washt off, wherewith thou was Annointed:
No bending knee will call thee *Cæsar* now,
No humble suters prease to speake for right:
No, not a man comes for redresse of thee:
For how can I helpe them, and not my selfe?

Sink. I, heere's a Deere, whose skin's a Keepers Fee:
This is the quondam King; Let's seize vpon him.

Hen. Let me embrace the sower Aduersaries,
For Wise men say, it is the wisest course.

Hum. Why linger we? Let vs lay hands vpon him.

Sink. Forbeare a-while, wee'l heare a little more.

Hen. My Queene and Son are gone to France for aid:
And (as I heare) the great Commanding Warwicke
I: thither gone, to craue the French Kings Sister
To wife for *Edward*. If this newes be true,
Poore Queene, and Sonne, your labour is but lost:
For Warwicke is a subtle Orator:
And *Lewis* a Prince soone wonne with mouing words:
By this account then, *Margaret* may winne him,
For she's a woman to be pittied much:
Her sighes will make a batt'ry in his brest,
Her teares will pierce into a Marble heart:
The Tyger will be milde, whiles she doth mourne;
And *Nero* will be tainted with remorse,
To heare and see her plaints, her Brinish Teares.
I, but shee's come to begge, Warwicke to giue
Shee on his left side, crauing ayde for *Henrie*;
He on his right, asking a wife for *Edward*.
Shee Weepes, and sayes, her *Henry* is depos'd:
He Smiles, and sayes, his *Edward* is instaul'd;
That she (poore Wretch) for greefe can speake no more.
Whiles Warwicke tels his Title, smooths the Wrong,
Inferreth arguments of mighty strength,
And in conclusion winnes the King from her,
With promise of his Sister, and what else,
To strengthen and support King *Edwards* place.
O *Margaret*, thus 'twill be, and thou (poore soule)
Art then forsaken, as thou went'st forlorne.

Hum. Say, what art thou talk'st of Kings & Queens?

King. More then I seeme, and lesse then I was born to:
A man at least, for lesse I should not be;
And men may talke of Kings, and why not I?

Hum. I, but thou talk'st, as if thou wer't a King.

King. Why so I am (in Minde) and that's enough.

Hum. But if thou be a King, where is thy Crowne?

King. My Crowne is in my heart, not on my head:
Not deck'd with Diamonds, and Indian stones:
Nor to be seene: my Crowne, is call'd Content,
A Crowne it is, that sildome Kings enioy.

Hum. Well, if you be a King crown'd with Content,
Your Crowne Content, and you, must be contented
To go along with vs. For (as we thinke)
You are the king King *Edward* hath depos'd:
And we his subiects, sworne in all Allegeance,
Will apprehend you, as his Enemie.

King. But did you neuer sweare, and breake an Oath.

Hum. No, neuer such an Oath, nor will not now.

King. Where did you dwell when I was K. of England?

Hum. Heere in this Country, where we now remaine.

King. I was annointed King at nine monthes old,
My Father, and my Grandfather were Kings:
And you were sworne true Subiects vnto me:
And tell me then, haue you not broke your Oathes?

Sin. No, for we were Subiects, but while you wer king

King. Why? Am I dead? Do I not breath a Man?
Ah simple men, you know not what you sweare:
Looke, as I blow this Feather from my Face,
And as the Ayre blowes it to me againe,
Obeying with my winde when I do blow,
And yeelding to another, when it blowes,
Commanded alwayes by the greater gust:
Such is the lightnesse of you, common men.
But do not breake your Oathes, for of that sinne,
My milde intreatie shall not make you guiltie.
Go where you will, the king shall be commanded,
And be you kings, command, and Ile obey.

Sinklo. We are true Subiects to the king,
King *Edward*.

King. So would you be againe to *Henrie*,
If he were seated as king *Edward* is.

Sinklo. We charge you in Gods name & the Kings,
To go with vs vnto the Officers.

King. In Gods name lead, your Kings name be obeyd,
And what God will, that let your King performe,
And what he will, I humbly yeeld vnto. *Exeunt*

Enter K. Edward, Gloster, Clarence, Lady Gray.

King. Brother of Gloster, at S. Albons field

This

This Ladyes Husband, Sir *Richard Grey*, was slaine,
His Land then seiz'd on by the Conqueror,
Her suit is now, to repossesse those Lands,
Which wee in Iustice cannot well deny,
Because in Quarrell of the House of *Yorke*,
The worthy Gentleman did lose his Life.

Rich. Your Highnesse shall doe well to graunt her suit:
It were dishonor to deny it her.

King. It were no lesse, but yet Ile make a pawse.

Rich. Yea, is it so:
I see the Lady hath a thing to graunt,
Before the King will graunt her humble suit.

Clarence. Hee knowes the Game, how true hee keepes the winde?

Rich. Silence.

King. Widow, we will consider of your suit,
And come some other time to know our minde.

Wid. Right gracious Lord, I cannot brooke delay:
May it please your Highnesse to resolue me now,
And what your pleasure is, shall satisfie me.

Rich. I Widow? then Ile warrant you all your Lands,
And if what pleases him, shall pleasure you:
Fight closer, or good faith you'le catch a Blow.

Clarence. I feare her not, vnlesse she chance to fall.

Rich. God forbid that, for hee'le take vantages.

King. How many Children hast thou, Widow? tell me.

Clarence. I thinke he meanes to begge a Child of her.

Rich. Nay then whip me: hee'le rather giue her two.

Wid. Three, my most gracious Lord.

Rich. You shall haue foure, if you'le be rul'd by him.

King. 'Twere pittie they should lose their Fathers Lands.

Wid. Be pittifull, dread Lord, and graunt it then.

King. Lords giue vs leaue, Ile trye this Widowes wit.

Rich. I, good leaue haue you, for you will haue leaue,
Till Youth take leaue, and leaue you to the Crutch.

King. Now tell me, Madame, doe you loue your Children?

Wid. I, full as dearely as I loue my selfe.

King. And would you not doe much to doe them good?

Wid. To doe them good, I would sustayne some harme.

King. Then get your Husbands Lands, to doe them good.

Wid. Therefore I came vnto your Maiestie.

King. Ile tell you how these Lands are to be got.

Wid. So shall you bind me to your Highnesse seruice.

King. What seruice wilt thou doe me, if I giue them?

Wid. What you command, that rests in me to doe.

King. But you will take exceptions to my Boone.

Wid. No, gracious Lord, except I cannot doe it.

King. I, but thou canst doe what I meane to aske.

Wid. Why then I will doe what your Grace commands.

Rich. Hee plyes her hard, and much Raine weares the Marble.

Clar. As red as fire? nay then, her Wax must melt.

Wid. Why stoppes my Lord? shall I not heare my Taske?

King. An easie Taske, 'tis but to loue a King.

Wid. That's soone perform'd, because I am a Subiect.

King. Why then, thy Husbands Lands I freely giue thee.

Wid. I take my leaue with many thousand thankes.

Rich. The Match is made, shee seales it with a Cursie.

King. But stay thee, 'tis the fruits of loue I meane.

Wid. The fruits of Loue, I meane, my louing Liege.

King. I, but I feare me in another sence.
What Loue, think'st thou, I sue so much to get?

Wid. My loue till death, my humble thanks, my prayers,
That loue which Vertue begges, and Vertue graunts.

King. No, by my troth, I did not meane such loue.

Wid. Why then you meane not, as I thought you did.

King. But now you partly may perceiue my minde.

Wid. My minde will neuer graunt what I perceiue
Your Highnesse aymes at, if I ayme aright.

King. To tell thee plaine, I ayme to lye with thee.

Wid. To tell you plaine, I had rather lye in Prison.

King. Why then thou shalt not haue thy Husbands Lands.

Wid. Why then mine Honestie shall be my Dower,
For by that losse, I will not purchase them.

King. Therein thou wrong'st thy Children mightily.

Wid. Herein your Highnesse wrongs both them & me:
But mightie Lord, this merry inclination
Accords not with the sadnesse of my suit:
Please you dismisse me, eyther with I, or no.

King. I, if thou wilt say I to my request:
No, if thou do'st say No to my demand.

Wid. Then No, my Lord: my suit is at an end.

Rich. The Widow likes him not, shee knits her Browes.

Clarence. Hee is the bluntest Wooer in Christendome.

King. Her Looks doth argue her replete with Modesty,
Her Words doth shew her Wit incomparable,
All her perfections challenge Soueraigntie,
One way, or other, shee is for a King,
And shee shall be my Loue, or else my Queene.
Say, that King *Edward* take thee for his Queene?

Wid. 'Tis better said then done, my gracious Lord:
I am a subiect fit to ieast withall,
But farre vnfit to be a Soueraigne.

King. Sweet Widow, by my State I sweare to thee,
I speake no more then what my Soule intends,
And that is, to enioy thee for my Loue.

Wid. And that is more then I will yeeld vnto:
I know, I am too meane to be your Queene,
And yet too good to be your Concubine.

King. You cauill, Widow, I did meane my Queene.

Wid. 'Twill grieue your Grace, my Sonnes should call you Father.

King. No more, then when my Daughters
Call thee Mother.
Thou art a Widow, and thou hast some Children,
And by Gods Mother, I being but a Batchelor,
Haue other-some. Why, 'tis a happy thing,
To be the Father vnto many Sonnes:
Answer no more, for thou shalt be my Queene.

Rich. The Ghostly Father now hath done his Shrift.

Clarence. When hee was made a Shriuer, 'twas for shift.

King. Brothers, you muse what Chat wee two haue had.

Rich. The Widow likes it not, for shee lookes very sad.

King. You'ld thinke it strange, if I should marrie her.

Clarence. To who, my Lord?

King. Why *Clarence*, to my selfe.

Rich. That

Rich. That would be tenne dayes wonder at the least.
Clarence. That's a day longer then a Wonder lasts.
Rich By so much is the Wonder in extremes.
King. Well, ieast on Brothers: I can tell you both,
Her suit is graunted for her Husbands Lands.

Enter a Noble man.

Nob. My gracious Lord, *Henry* your Foe is taken,
And brought your Prisoner to your Pallace Gate.
King. See that he be conuey'd vnto the Tower:
And goe wee Brothers to the man that tooke him,
To question of his apprehension.
Widow goe you along: Lords vse her honourable.

Exeunt.

Manet Richard.

Rich. I, *Edward* will vse Women honourably:
Would he were wasted, Marrow, Bones, and all,
That from his Loynes no hopefull Branch may spring,
To crosse me from the Golden time I looke for:
And yet, betweene my Soules desire, and me,
The lustfull *Edwards* Title buryed,
Is *Clarence*, *Henry*, and his Sonne young *Edward*,
And all the vnlook'd-for Issue of their Bodies,
To take their Roomes, ere I can place my selfe:
A cold premeditation for my purpose.
Why then I doe but dreame on Soueraigntie,
Like one that stands vpon a Promontorie,
And spyes a farre-off shore, where hee would tread,
Wishing his foot were equall with his eye,
And chides the Sea, that sunders him from thence,
Saying hee'le lade it dry, to haue his way:
So doe I wish the Crowne, being so farre off,
And so I chide the meanes that keepes me from it,
And so (I say) Ile cut the Causes off,
Flattering me with impossibilities:
My Eyes too quicke, my Heart o're-weenes too much,
Vnlesse my Hand and Strength could equall them.
Well, say there is no Kingdome then for *Richard:*
What other Pleasure can the World affoord?
Ile make my Heauen in a Ladies Lappe,
And decke my Body in gay Ornaments,
And 'witch sweet Ladies with my Words and Lookes.
Oh miserable Thought! and more vnlikely,
Then to accomplish twentie Golden Crownes.
Why Loue forswore me in my Mothers Wombe:
And for I should not deale in her soft Lawes,
Shee did corrupt frayle Nature with some Bribe,
To shrinke mine Arme vp like a wither'd Shrub,
To make an enuious Mountaine on my Back,
Where sits Deformitie to mocke my Body;
To shape my Legges of an vnequall size,
To dis-proportion me in euery part:
Like to a Chaos, or an vn-lick'd Beare-whelpe,
That carryes no impression like the Damme.
And am I then a man to be belou'd?
Oh monstrous fault, to harbour such a thought.
Then since this Earth affoords no Ioy to me,
But to command, to check, to o're-beare such,
As are of better Person then my selfe:
Ile make my Heauen, to dreame vpon the Crowne,
And whiles I liue, t'account this World but Hell,
Vntill my mis-shap'd Trunke, that beares this Head,
Be round impaled with a glorious Crowne.
And yet I know not how to get the Crowne,
For many Liues stand betweene me and home:
And I, like one lost in a Thornie Wood,
That rents the Thornes, and is rent with the Thornes,
Seeking a way, and straying from the way,
Not knowing how to finde the open Ayre,
But toyling desperately to finde it out,
Torment my selfe, to catch the English Crowne:
And from that torment I will free my selfe,
Or hew my way out with a bloody Axe.
Why I can smile, and murther whiles I smile,
And cry, Content, to that which grieues my Heart,
And wet my Cheekes with artificiall Teares,
And frame my Face to all occasions.
Ile drowne more Saylers then the Mermaid shall,
Ile slay more gazers then the Basiliske,
Ile play the Orator as well as *Nestor*,
Deceiue more slyly then *Vlisses* could,
And like a *Synon*, take another Troy.
I can adde Colours to the Camelion,
Change shapes with *Proteus*, for aduantages,
And set the murtherous *Macheuill* to Schoole.
Can I doe this, and cannot get a Crowne?
Tut, were it farther off, Ile plucke it downe. *Exit.*

Flourish.

Enter Lewis the French King, his Sister Bona, his Admirall, call'd Bourbon: Prince Edward, Queene Margaret, and the Earle of Oxford. Lewis sits, and riseth vp againe.

Lewis. Faire Queene of England, worthy *Margaret*,
Sit downe with vs: it ill befits thy State,
And Birth, that thou should'st stand, while *Lewis* doth sit.
Marg. No, mightie King of France: now *Margaret*
Must strike her sayle, and learne a while to serue,
Where Kings command. I was (I must confesse)
Great Albions Queene, in former Golden dayes:
But now mischance hath trod my Title downe,
And with dis-honor layd me on the ground,
Where I must take like Seat vnto my fortune,
And to my humble Seat conforme my selfe.
Lewis. Why say, faire Queene, whence springs this deepe despaire?
Marg. From such a cause, as fills mine eyes with teares,
And stops my tongue, while heart is drown'd in cares.
Lewis. What ere it be, be thou still like thy selfe,
And sit thee by our side. *Seats her by him.*
Yeeld not thy necke to Fortunes yoake,
But let thy dauntlesse minde still ride in triumph,
Ouer all mischance.
Be plaine, Queene *Margaret*, and tell thy griefe,
It shall be eas'd, if France can yeeld reliefe.
Marg. Those gracious words
Reuiue my drooping thoughts,
And giue my tongue-ty'd sorrowes leaue to speake.
Now therefore be it knowne to Noble *Lewis*,
That *Henry*, sole possessor of my Loue,
Is, of a King, become a banisht man,
And forc'd to liue in Scotland a Forlorne;
While prowd ambitious *Edward*, Duke of Yorke,
Vsurpes the Regall Title, and the Seat
Of Englands true anoynted lawfull King.
This is the cause that I, poore *Margaret*,
With this my Sonne, Prince *Edward*, *Henries* Heire,
Am come to craue thy iust and lawfull ayde:
And if thou faile vs, all our hope is done.
Scotland hath will to helpe, but cannot helpe:

Our People, and our Peeres, are both mis-led,
Our Treasure seiz'd, our Souldiors put to flight,
And (as thou seest) our selues in heauie plight.

Lewis. Renowned Queene,
With patience calme the Storme,
While we bethinke a meanes to breake it off.

Marg. The more wee stay, the stronger growes our Foe.

Lewis. The more I stay, the more Ile succour thee.

Marg. O, but impatience waiteth on true sorrow.
And see where comes the breeder of my sorrow.

Enter Warwicke.

Lewis. What's hee approacheth boldly to our presence?

Marg. Our Earle of Warwicke, *Edwards* greatest Friend.

Lewis. Welcome braue *Warwicke*, what brings thee to France? *Hee descends. Shee ariseth.*

Marg. I now begins a second Storme to rise,
For this is hee that moues both Winde and Tyde.

Warw. From worthy *Edward*, King of Albion,
My Lord and Soueraigne, and thy vowed Friend,
I come (in Kindnesse, and vnfayned Loue)
First, to doe greetings to thy Royall Person,
And then to craue a League of Amitie:
And lastly, to confirme that Amitie
With Nuptiall Knot, if thou vouchsafe to graunt
That vertuous Lady *Bona*, thy faire Sister,
To Englands King, in lawfull Marriage.

Marg. If that goe forward, *Henries* hope is done.

Warw. And gracious Madame, *Speaking to Bona.*
In our Kings behalfe,
I am commanded, with your leaue and fauor,
Humbly to kisse your Hand, and with my Tongue
To tell the passion of my Soueraignes Heart;
Where Fame, late entring at his heedfull Eares,
Hath plac'd thy Beauties Image, and thy Vertue.

Marg. King *Lewis*, and Lady *Bona*, heare me speake,
Before you answer *Warwicke*. His demand
Springs not from *Edwards* well-meant honest Loue,
But from Deceit, bred by Necessitie:
For how can Tyrants safely gouerne home,
Vnlesse abroad they purchase great allyance?
To proue him Tyrant, this reason may suffice,
That *Henry* liueth still: but were hee dead,
Yet here Prince *Edward* stands, King *Henries* Sonne.
Looke therefore *Lewis*, that by this League and Mariage
Thou draw not on thy Danger, and Dis-honor:
For though Vsurpers sway the rule a while,
Yet Heau'ns are iust, and Time suppresseth Wrongs.

Warw. Iniurious *Margaret.*

Edw. And why not Queene?

Warw. Because thy Father *Henry* did vsurpe,
And thou no more art Prince, then shee is Queene.

Oxf. Then *Warwicke* disanulls great *Iohn* of Gaunt,
Which did subdue the greatest part of Spaine;
And after *Iohn* of Gaunt, *Henry* the Fourth,
Whose Wisdome was a Mirror to the wisest:
And after that wise Prince, *Henry* the Fift,
Who by his Prowesse conquered all France:
From these, our *Henry* lineally descends.

Warw. *Oxford*, how haps it in this smooth discourse,
You told not, how *Henry* the Sixt hath lost
All that, which *Henry* the Fift had gotten:
Me thinkes these Peeres of France should smile at that.
But for the rest: you tell a Pedigree
Of threescore and two yeeres, a silly time
To make prescription for a Kingdomes worth.

Oxf. Why *Warwicke*, canst thou speak against thy Liege,
Whom thou obeyd'st thirtie and six yeeres,
And not bewray thy Treason with a Blush?

Warw. Can *Oxford*, that did euer fence the right,
Now buckler Falsehood with a Pedigree?
For shame leaue *Henry*, and call *Edward* King.

Oxf. Call him my King, by whose iniurious doome
My elder Brother, the Lord *Aubrey Vere*
Was done to death? and more then so, my Father,
Euen in the downe-fall of his mellow'd yeeres,
When Nature brought him to the doore of Death?
No *Warwicke*, no: while Life vpholds this Arme,
This Arme vpholds the House of *Lancaster.*

Warw. And I the House of *Yorke.*

Lewis. Queene *Margaret*, Prince *Edward*, and *Oxford*,
Vouchsafe at our request, to stand aside,
While I vse further conference with *Warwicke.*

They stand aloofe.

Marg. Heauens graunt, that *Warwickes* wordes bewitch him not.

Lew. Now *Warwicke*, tell me euen vpon thy conscience
Is *Edward* your true King? for I were loth
To linke with him, that were not lawfull chosen.

Warw. Thereon I pawne my Credit, and mine Honor.

Lewis. But is hee gracious in the Peoples eye?

Warw. The more, that *Henry* was vnfortunate.

Lewis. Then further: all dissembling set aside,
Tell me for truth, the measure of his Loue
Vnto our Sister *Bona.*

War. Such it seemes,
As may beseeme a Monarch like himselfe.
My selfe haue often heard him say, and sweare,
That this his Loue was an externall Plant,
Whereof the Root was fixt in Vertues ground,
The Leaues and Fruit maintain'd with Beauties Sunne,
Exempt from Enuy, but not from Disdaine,
Vnlesse the Lady *Bona* quit his paine.

Lewis. Now Sister, let vs heare your firme resolue.

Bona. Your graunt, or your denyall, shall be mine.
Yet I confesse, that often ere this day, *Speaks to War.*
When I haue heard your Kings desert recounted,
Mine eare hath tempted iudgement to desire.

Lewis. Then *Warwicke*, thus:
Our Sister shall be *Edwards.*
And now forthwith shall Articles be drawne,
Touching the Ioynture that your King must make,
Which with her Dowrie shall be counter-poys'd:
Draw neere, Queene *Margaret*, and be a witnesse,
That *Bona* shall be Wife to the English King.

Pr. Edw. To *Edward*, but not to the English King.

Marg. Deceitfull *Warwicke*, it was thy deuice,
By this alliance to make void my suit:
Before thy comming, *Lewis* was *Henries* friend.

Lewis. And still is friend to him, and *Margaret.*
But if your Title to the Crowne be weake,
As may appeare by *Edwards* good successe:
Then 'tis but reason, that I be releas'd
From giuing ayde, which late I promised.
Yet shall you haue all kindnesse at my hand,
That your Estate requires, and mine can yeeld.

Warw. *Henry* now liues in Scotland, at his ease;

Where

Where hauing nothing, nothing can he lose.
And as for you your selfe (our quondam Queene)
You haue a Father able to maintaine you,
And better 'twere, you troubled him, then France.

Mar. Peace impudent, and shamelesse Warwicke,
Proud setter vp, and puller downe of Kings,
I will not hence, till with my Talke and Teares
(Both full of Truth) I make King *Lewis* behold
Thy slye conueyance, and thy Lords false loue,

Post blowing a horne Within.

For both of you are Birds of selfe-same Feather.

Lewes. Warwicke, this is some poste to vs, or thee.

Enter the Poste.

Post. My Lord Ambassador,
These Letters are for you. *Speakes to Warwick,*
Sent from your Brother Marquesse *Montague.*
These from our King, vnto your Maiesty. *To Lewis.*
And Madam, these for you: *To Margaret*
From whom, I know not.

They all reade their Letters.

Oxf. I like it well, that our faire Queene and Mistris
Smiles at her newes, while *Warwicke* frownes at his.

Prince Ed. Nay marke how *Lewis* stampes as he were netled. I hope, all's for the best.

Lew. Warwicke, what are thy Newes?
And yours, faire Queene.

Mar. Mine such, as fill my heart with vnhop'd ioyes.

War. Mine full of sorrow, and hearts discontent.

Lew. What? has your King married the Lady *Grey*?
And now to sooth your Forgery, and his,
Sends me a Paper to perswade me Patience?
Is this th'Alliance that he seekes with France?
Dare he presume to scorne vs in this manner?

Mar. I told your Maiesty as much before:
This proueth *Edwards* Loue, and Warwickes honesty.

War. King *Lewis*, I heere protest in sight of heauen,
And by the hope I haue of heauenly blisse,
That I am cleere from this misdeed of *Edwards*;
No more my King, for he dishonors me,
But most himselfe, if he could see his shame.
Did I forget, that by the House of Yorke
My Father came vntimely to his death?
Did I let passe th'abuse done to my Neece?
Did I impale him with the Regall Crowne?
Did I put *Henry* from his Natiue Right?
And am I guerdon'd at the last, with Shame?
Shame on himselfe, for my Desert is Honor.
And to repaire my Honor lost for him,
I heere renounce him, and returne to *Henry.*
My Noble Queene, let former grudges passe,
And henceforth, I am thy true Seruitour:
I will reuenge his wrong to Lady *Bona,*
And replant *Henry* in his former state.

Mar. Warwicke,
These words haue turn'd my Hate, to Loue,
And I forgiue, and quite forget old faults,
And ioy that thou becom'st King *Henries* Friend.

War. So much his Friend, I, his vnfained Friend,
That if King *Lewis* vouchsafe to furnish vs
With some few Bands of chosen Soldiours,
Ile vndertake to Land them on our Coast,
And force the Tyrant from his seat by Warre.
'Tis not his new-made Bride shall succour him,
And as for *Clarence*, as my Letters tell me,
Hee's very likely now to fall from him,
For matching more for wanton Lust, then Honor,
Or then for strength and safety of our Country.

Bona. Deere Brother, how shall *Bona* be reueng'd,
But by thy helpe to this distressed Queene?

Mar. Renowned Prince, how shall Poore *Henry* liue,
Vnlesse thou rescue him from foule dispaire?

Bona. My quarrel, and this English Queens, are one.

War. And mine faire Lady *Bona*, ioynes with yours.

Lew. And mine, with hers, and thine, and *Margarets.*
Therefore, at last, I firmely am resolu'd
You shall haue ayde.

Mar. Let me giue humble thankes for all, at once.

Lew. Then Englands Messenger, returne in Poste,
And tell false *Edward*, thy supposed King,
That *Lewis* of France, is sending ouer Maskers
To reuell it with him, and his new Bride.
Thou seest what's past, go feare thy King withall.

Bona. Tell him, in hope hee'l proue a widower shortly,
I weare the Willow Garland for his sake.

Mar. Tell him, my mourning weeds are layde aside,
And I am ready to put Armor on.

War. Tell him from me, that he hath done me wrong,
And therefore Ile vn-Crowne him, er't be long.
There's thy reward, be gone. *Exit Post.*

Lew. But Warwicke,
Thou and Oxford, with fiue thousand men
Shall crosse the Seas, and bid false *Edward* battaile:
And as occasion serues, this Noble Queen
And Prince, shall follow with a fresh Supply.
Yet ere thou go, but answer me one doubt:
What Pledge haue we of thy firme Loyalty?

War. This shall assure my constant Loyalty,
That if our Queene, and this young Prince agree,
Ile ioyne mine eldest daughter, and my Ioy,
To him forthwith, in holy Wedlocke bands.

Mar. Yes, I agree, and thanke you for your Motion.
Sonne *Edward*, she is Faire and Vertuous,
Therefore delay not, giue thy hand to Warwicke,
And with thy hand, thy faith irreuocable,
That onely Warwickes daughter shall be thine.

Prin. Ed. Yes, I accept her, for she well deserues it,
And heere to pledge my Vow, I giue my hand.

He giues his hand to Warw.

Lew. Why stay we now? These soldiers shalbe leuied,
And thou Lord Bourbon, our High Admirall
Shall waft them ouer with our Royall Fleete.
I long till *Edward* fall by Warres mischance,
For mocking Marriage with a Dame of France.

Exeunt. Manet Warwicke.

War. I came from *Edward* as Ambassador,
But I returne his sworne and mortall Foe:
Matter of Marriage was the charge he gaue me,
But dreadfull Warre shall answer his demand.
Had he none else to make a stale but me?
Then none but I, shall turne his Iest to Sorrow.
I was the Cheefe that rais'd him to the Crowne,
And Ile be Cheefe to bring him downe againe:
Not that I pitty *Henries* misery,
But seeke Reuenge on *Edwards* mockery. *Exit.*

Enter Richard, Clarence, Somerset, and Mountague.

Rich. Now tell me Brother *Clarence*, what thinke you
Of this new Marriage with the Lady *Gray*?
Hath not our Brother made a worthy choice?

Cla. Alas, you know, tis farre from hence to France,

How could he stay till *Warwicke* made returne?

Som. My Lords, forbeare this talke: heere comes the King.

Flourish.

Enter King Edward, Lady Grey, Penbrooke, Stafford, Hastings: foure stand on one side, and foure on the other.

Rich. And his well-chosen Bride.

Clarence. I minde to tell him plainly what I thinke.

King. Now Brother of Clarence,
How like you our Choyce,
That you stand pensiue, as halfe malecontent?

Clarence. As well as *Lewis* of France,
Or the Earle of Warwicke,
Which are so weake of courage, and in iudgement,
That they'le take no offence at our abuse.

King. Suppose they take offence without a cause:
They are but *Lewis* and *Warwicke*, I am *Edward*,
Your King and *Warwickes*, and must haue my will.

Rich. And shall haue your will, because our King:
Yet hastie Marriage seldome prooueth well.

King. Yea, Brother *Richard*, are you offended too?

Rich. Not I: no:
God forbid, that I should wish them seuer'd,
Whom God hath ioyn'd together:
I, and 'twere pittie, to sunder them,
That yoake so well together.

King. Setting your skornes, and your mislike aside,
Tell me some reason, why the Lady *Grey*
Should not become my Wife, and Englands Queene?
And you too, *Somerset*, and *Mountague*,
Speake freely what you thinke.

Clarence. Then this is mine opinion:
That King *Lewis* becomes your Enemie,
For mocking him about the Marriage
Of the Lady *Bona*.

Rich. And *Warwicke*, doing what you gaue in charge,
Is now dis-honored by this new Marriage.

King. What, if both *Lewis* and *Warwick* be appeas'd,
By such inuention as I can deuise?

Mount. Yet, to haue ioyn'd with France in such alliance,
Would more haue strength'ned this our Commonwealth
'Gainst forraine stormes, then any home-bred Marriage.

Hast. Why, knowes not *Mountague*, that of it selfe,
England is safe, if true within it selfe?

Mount. But the safer, when 'tis back'd with France.

Hast. 'Tis better vsing France, then trusting France:
Let vs be back'd with God, and with the Seas,
Which he hath giu'n for fence impregnable,
And with their helpes, onely defend our selues:
In them, and in our selues, our safetie lyes.

Clar. For this one speech, Lord *Hastings* well deserues
To haue the Heire of the Lord *Hungerford*.

King. I, what of that? it was my will, and graunt,
And for this once, my Will shall stand for Law.

Rich. And yet me thinks, your Grace hath not done well,
To giue the Heire and Daughter of Lord *Scales*
Vnto the Brother of your louing Bride;
Shee better would haue fitted me, or *Clarence*:
But in your Bride you burie Brotherhood.

Clar. Or else you would not haue bestow'd the Heire
Of the Lord *Bonuill* on your new Wiues Sonne,
And leaue your Brothers to goe speede elsewhere.

King. Alas, poore *Clarence*: is it for a Wife
That thou art malecontent? I will prouide thee.

Clarence. In chusing for your selfe,
You shew'd your iudgement:
Which being shallow, you shall giue me leaue
To play the Broker in mine owne behalfe;
And to that end, I shortly minde to leaue you.

King. Leaue me, or tarry, *Edward* will be King,
And not be ty'd vnto his Brothers will.

Lady Grey. My Lords, before it pleas'd his Maiestie
To rayse my State to Title of a Queene,
Doe me but right, and you must all confesse,
That I was not ignoble of Descent,
And meaner then my selfe haue had like fortune.
But as this Title honors me and mine,
So your dislikes, to whom I would be pleasing,
Doth cloud my ioyes with danger, and with sorrow.

King. My Loue, forbeare to fawne vpon their frownes:
What danger, or what sorrow can befall thee,
So long as *Edward* is thy constant friend,
And their true Soueraigne, whom they must obey?
Nay, whom they shall obey, and loue thee too,
Vnlesse they seeke for hatred at my hands:
Which if they doe, yet will I keepe thee safe,
And they shall feele the vengeance of my wrath.

Rich. I heare, yet say not much, but thinke the more.

Enter a Poste.

King. Now Messenger, what Letters, or what Newes from France?

Post. My Soueraigne Liege, no Letters, & few words,
But such, as I (without your speciall pardon)
Dare not relate.

King. Goe too, wee pardon thee:
Therefore, in briefe, tell me their words,
As neere as thou canst guesse them.
What answer makes King *Lewis* vnto our Letters?

Post. At my depart, these were his very words:
Goe tell false *Edward*, the supposed King,
That *Lewis* of France is sending ouer Maskers,
To reuell it with him, and his new Bride.

King. Is *Lewis* so braue? belike he thinkes me *Henry*.
But what said Lady *Bona* to my Marriage?

Post. These were her words, vtt'red with mild disdaine:
Tell him, in hope hee'le proue a Widower shortly,
Ile weare the Willow Garland for his sake.

King. I blame not her; she could say little lesse:
She had the wrong. But what said *Henries* Queene?
For I haue heard, that she was there in place.

Post. Tell him (quoth she)
My mourning Weedes are done,
And I am readie to put Armour on.

King. Belike she minds to play the Amazon.
But what said *Warwicke* to these iniuries?

Post. He, more incens'd against your Maiestie,
Then all the rest, discharg'd me with these words:
Tell him from me, that he hath done me wrong,
And therefore Ile vncrowne him, er't be long.

King. Ha? durst the Traytor breath out so prowd words?
Well, I will arme me, being thus fore-warn'd:
They shall haue Warres, and pay for their presumption.
But say, is *Warwicke* friends with *Margaret*?

Post. I, gracious Soueraigne,
They are so link'd in friendship,
That yong Prince *Edward* marryes *Warwicks* Daughter.

Clarence. Belike, the elder;
Clarence will haue the younger.

Now Brother King farewell, and sit you fast,
For I will hence to *Warwickes* other Daughter,
That though I want a Kingdome, yet in Marriage
I may not proue inferior to your selfe.
You that loue me, and *Warwicke*, follow me.
Exit Clarence, and Somerset followes.
Rich. Not I:
My thoughts ayme at a further matter:
I stay not for the loue of *Edward*, but the Crowne.
King. *Clarence* and *Somerset* both gone to *Warwicke*?
Yet am I arm'd against the worst can happen:
And haste is needfull in this desp'rate case.
Pembrooke and *Stafford*, you in our behalfe
Goe leuie men, and make prepare for Warre;
They are alreadie, or quickly will be landed:
My selfe in person will straight follow you.
Exeunt Pembrooke and Stafford.
But ere I goe, *Hastings* and *Mountague*
Resolue my doubt: you twaine, of all the rest,
Are neere to *Warwicke*, by bloud, and by allyance:
Tell me, if you loue *Warwicke* more then me;
If it be so, then both depart to him:
I rather wish you foes, then hollow friends.
But if you minde to hold your true obedience,
Giue me assurance with some friendly Vow,
That I may neuer haue you in suspect.
Mount. So God helpe *Mountague*, as hee proues true.
Hast. And *Hastings*, as hee fauours *Edwards* cause.
King. Now, Brother *Richard*, will you stand by vs?
Rich. I, in despight of all that shall withstand you.
King. Why so: then am I sure of Victorie.
Now therefore let vs hence, and lose no howre,
Till wee meet *Warwicke*, with his forreine powre.
Exeunt.

Enter Warwicke and Oxford in England, with French Souldiors.

Warw. Trust me, my Lord, all hitherto goes well,
The common people by numbers swarme to vs.
Enter Clarence and Somerset.
But see where *Somerset* and *Clarence* comes:
Speake suddenly, my Lords, are wee all friends?
Clar. Feare not that, my Lord.
Warw. Then gentle *Clarence*, welcome vnto *Warwicke*,
And welcome *Somerset*: I hold it cowardize,
To rest mistrustfull, where a Noble Heart
Hath pawn'd an open Hand, in signe of Loue;
Else might I thinke, that *Clarence*, *Edwards* Brother,
Were but a fained friend to our proceedings:
But welcome sweet *Clarence*, my Daughter shall be thine.
And now, what rests? but in Nights Couerture,
Thy Brother being carelessely encamp'd,
His Souldiors lurking in the Towne about,
And but attended by a simple Guard,
Wee may surprize and take him at our pleasure,
Our Scouts haue found the aduenture very easie:
That as *Vlysses*, and stout *Diomede*,
With sleight and manhood stole to *Rhesus* Tents,
And brought from thence the Thracian fatall Steeds;
So wee, well couer'd with the Nights black Mantle,
At vnawares may beat downe *Edwards* Guard,
And seize himselfe: I say not, slaughter him,
For I intend but onely to surprize him.
You that will follow me to this attempt,
Applaud the Name of *Henry*, with your Leader.
They all cry, Henry.
Why then, let's on our way in silent sort,
For *Warwicke* and his friends, God and Saint *George*.
Exeunt.

Enter three Watchmen to guard the Kings Tent.

1. *Watch.* Come on my Masters, each man take his stand,
The King by this, is set him downe to sleepe.
2. *Watch.* What, will he not to Bed?
1. *Watch.* Why, no: for he hath made a solemne Vow,
Neuer to lye and take his naturall Rest,
Till *Warwicke*, or himselfe, be quite supprest.
2. *Watch.* To morrow then belike shall be the day,
If *Warwicke* be so neere as men report.
3. *Watch.* But say, I pray, what Noble man is that,
That with the King here resteth in his Tent?
1. *Watch.* 'Tis the Lord *Hastings*, the Kings chiefest friend.
3. *Watch.* O, is it so? but why commands the King,
That his chiefe followers lodge in Townes about him,
While he himselfe keepes in the cold field?
2. *Watch.* 'Tis the more honour, because more dangerous.
3. *Watch.* I, but giue me worship, and quietnesse,
I like it better then a dangerous honor.
If *Warwicke* knew in what estate he stands,
'Tis to be doubted he would waken him.
1. *Watch.* Vnlesse our Halberds did shut vp his passage.
2. *Watch.* I: wherefore else guard we his Royall Tent,
But to defend his Person from Night-foes?

Enter Warwicke, Clarence, Oxford, Somerset, and French Souldiors, silent all.

Warw. This is his Tent, and see where stand his Guard:
Courage my Masters: Honor now, or neuer:
But follow me, and *Edward* shall be ours.
1. *Watch.* Who goes there?
2. *Watch.* Stay, or thou dyest.
Warwicke and the rest cry all, Warwicke, Warwicke, and set vpon the Guard, who flye, crying, Arme, Arme, Warwicke and the rest following them.

The Drumme playing, and Trumpet sounding.
Enter Warwicke, Somerset, and the rest, bringing the King out in his Gowne, sitting in a Chaire: Richard and Hastings flyes ouer the Stage.
Som. What are they that flye there?
Warw. *Richard* and *Hastings*: let them goe, heere is the Duke.
K. Edw. The Duke?
Why *Warwicke*, when wee parted,
Thou call'dst me King.
Warw. I, but the case is alter'd.
When you disgrac'd me in my Embassade,
Then I degraded you from being King,
And come now to create you Duke of Yorke.
Alas, how should you gouerne any Kingdome,
That know not how to vse Embassadors,
Nor how to be contented with one Wife,
Nor how to vse your Brothers Brotherly,
Nor how to studie for the Peoples Welfare,
Nor how to shrowd your selfe from Enemies?

K. Edw. Yea, Brother of Clarence,
Art thou here too?
Nay then I see, that *Edward* needs must downe.
Yet *Warwicke*, in despight of all mischance,
Of thee thy selfe, and all thy Complices,
Edward will alwayes beare himselfe as King:
Though Fortunes mallice ouerthrow my State,
My minde exceedes the compasse of her Wheele.
Warw. Then for his minde, be *Edward* Englands King,

Takes off his Crowne.

But *Henry* now shall weare the English Crowne,
And be true King indeede: thou but the shadow.
My Lord of Somerset, at my request,
See that forthwith Duke *Edward* be conuey'd
Vnto my Brother Arch-Bishop of Yorke:
When I haue fought with *Pembrooke*, and his fellowes,
Ile follow you, and tell what answer
Lewis and the Lady *Bona* send to him.
Now for a-while farewell good Duke of Yorke.
They leade him out forcibly.
K.Ed. What Fates impose, that men must needs abide;
It boots not to resist both winde and tide. *Exeunt.*
Oxf. What now remaines my Lords for vs to do,
But march to London with our Soldiers?
War. I, that's the first thing that we haue to do,
To free King *Henry* from imprisonment,
And see him seated in the Regall Throne. *exit.*

Enter Riuers, and Lady Gray.

Riu. Madam, what makes you in this sodain change?
Gray. Why Brother *Riuers*, are you yet to learne
What late misfortune is befalne King *Edward*?
Riu. What losse of some pitcht battell
Against *Warwicke*?
Gray. No, but the losse of his owne Royall person.
Riu. Then is my Soueraigne slaine?
Gray. I almost slaine, for he is taken prisoner.
Either betrayd by falshood of his Guard,
Or by his Foe surpriz'd at vnawares:
And as I further haue to vnderstand,
Is new committed to the Bishop of Yorke,
Fell Warwickes Brother, and by that our Foe.
Riu. These Newes I must confesse are full of greefe,
Yet gracious Madam, beare it as you may,
Warwicke may loose, that now hath wonne the day.
Gray. Till then, faire hope must hinder liues decay:
And I the rather waine me from dispaire
For loue of *Edwards* Off-spring in my wombe:
This is it that makes me bridle passion,
And beare with Mildnesse my misfortunes crosse:
I, I, for this I draw in many a teare,
And stop the rising of blood-sucking sighes,
Least with my sighes or teares, I blast or drowne
King *Edwards* Fruite, true heyre to th'English Crowne.
Riu. But Madam,
Where is Warwicke then become?
Gray. I am inform'd that he comes towards London,
To set the Crowne once more on *Henries* head,
Guesse thou the rest, King *Edwards* Friends must downe.
But to preuent the Tyrants violence,
(For trust not him that hath once broken Faith)
Ile hence forthwith vnto the Sanctuary,
To saue (at least) the heire of *Edwards* right:
There shall I rest secure from force and fraud:
Come therefore let vs flye, while we may flye,
If Warwicke take vs, we are sure to dye. *exeunt.*

Enter Richard, Lord Hastings, and Sir William Stanley.

Rich. Now my Lord *Hastings*, and Sir *William Stanley*
Leaue off to wonder why I drew you hither,
Into this cheefest Thicket of the Parke.
Thus stand the case: you know our King, my Brother,
Is prisoner to the Bishop here, at whose hands
He hath good vsage, and great liberty,
And often but attended with weake guard,
Come hunting this way to disport himselfe.
I haue aduertis'd him by secret meanes,
That if about this houre he make this way,
Vnder the colour of his vsuall game,
He shall heere finde his Friends with Horse and Men,
To set him free from his Captiuitie.

Enter King Edward, and a Huntsman with him.

Huntsman. This way my Lord,
For this way lies the Game.
King Edw. Nay this way man,
See where the Huntsmen stand.
Now Brother of Gloster, Lord Hastings, and the rest,
Stand you thus close to steale the Bishops Deere?
Rich. Brother, the time and case, requireth hast,
Your horse stands ready at the Parke-corner.
King Ed. But whether shall we then?
Hast. To Lyn my Lord,
And shipt from thence to Flanders.
Rich. Wel guest beleeue me, for that was my meaning
K.Ed. *Stanley*, I will requite thy forwardnesse.
Rich. But wherefore stay we? 'tis no time to talke.
K.Ed. Huntsman, what say'st thou?
Wilt thou go along?
Hunts. Better do so, then tarry and be hang'd.
Rich. Come then away, lets ha no more adoo.
K.Ed. Bishop farwell,
Sheeld thee from *Warwickes* frowne,
And pray that I may re-possesse the Crowne. *exeunt*

Flourish. Enter King Henry the sixt, Clarence, Warwicke, Somerset, young Henry, Oxford, Mountague, and Lieutenant.

K.Hen. M. Lieutenant, now that God and Friends
Haue shaken *Edward* from the Regall seate,
And turn'd my captiue state to libertie,
My feare to hope, my sorrowes vnto ioyes,
At our enlargement what are thy due Fees?
Lieu. Subiects may challenge nothing of their Sou'rains
But, if an humble prayer may preuaile,
I then craue pardon of your Maiestie.
K.Hen. For what, Lieutenant? For well vsing me?
Nay, be thou sure, Ile well requite thy kindnesse.
For that it made my imprisonment, a pleasure:
I, such a pleasure, as incaged Birds
Conceiue; when after many moody Thoughts,
At last, by Notes of Houshold harmonie,
They quite forget their losse of Libertie.

But *Warwicke*, after God, thou set'st me free,
And chiefely therefore, I thanke God, and thee,
He was the Author, thou the Instrument.
Therefore that I may conquer Fortunes spight,
By liuing low, where Fortune cannot hurt me,
And that the people of this blessed Land
May not be punisht with my thwarting starres,
Warwicke, although my Head still weare the Crowne,
I here resigne my Gouernment to thee,
For thou art fortunate in all thy deeds.

Warw. Your Grace hath still beene fam'd for vertuous,
And now may seeme as wise as vertuous,
By spying and auoiding Fortunes malice,
For few men rightly temper with the Starres:
Yet in this one thing let me blame your Grace,
For chusing me, when *Clarence* is in place.

Clar. No *Warwicke*, thou art worthy of the sway,
To whom the Heau'ns in thy Natiuitie,
Adiudg'd an Oliue Branch, and Lawrell Crowne,
As likely to be blest in Peace and Warre:
And therefore I yeeld thee my free consent.

Warw. And I chuse *Clarence* onely for Protector.

King. *Warwick* and *Clarence*, giue me both your Hands:
Now ioyne your Hands, & with your Hands your Hearts,
That no dissention hinder Gouernment:
I make you both Protectors of this Land,
While I my selfe will lead a priuate Life,
And in deuotion spend my latter dayes,
To sinnes rebuke, and my Creators prayse.

Warw. What answeres *Clarence* to his Soueraignes will?

Clar. That he consents, if *Warwicke* yeeld consent,
For on thy fortune I repose my selfe.

Warw. Why then, though loth, yet must I be content:
Wee'le yoake together, like a double shadow
To *Henries* Body, and supply his place;
I meane, in bearing weight of Gouernment,
While he enioyes the Honor, and his ease.
And *Clarence*, now then it is more then needfull,
Forthwith that *Edward* be pronounc'd a Traytor,
And all his Lands and Goods confiscate.

Clar. What else? and that Succession be determined.

Warw. I, therein *Clarence* shall not want his part.

King. But with the first, of all your chiefe affaires,
Let me entreat (for I command no more)
That *Margaret* your Queene, and my Sonne *Edward*,
Be sent for, to returne from France with speed:
For till I see them here, by doubtfull feare,
My ioy of libertie is halfe eclips'd.

Clar. It shall bee done, my Soueraigne, with all speede.

King. My Lord of Somerset, what Youth is that,
Of whom you seeme to haue so tender care?

Somers. My Liege, it is young *Henry*, Earle of Richmond.

King. Come hither, Englands Hope:

Layes his Hand on his Head.

If secret Powers suggest but truth
To my diuining thoughts,
This prettie Lad will proue our Countries blisse.
His Lookes are full of peacefull Maiestie,
His Head by nature fram'd to weare a Crowne,
His Hand to wield a Scepter, and himselfe
Likely in time to blesse a Regall Throne:
Make much of him, my Lords; for this is hee
Must helpe you more, then you are hurt by mee.

Enter a Poste.

Warw. What newes, my friend?

Poste. That *Edward* is escaped from your Brother,
And fled (as hee heares since) to Burgundie.

Warw. Vnsauorie newes: but how made he escape?

Poste. He was conuey'd by *Richard*, Duke of Gloster,
And the Lord *Hastings*, who attended him
In secret ambush, on the Forrest side,
And from the Bishops Huntsmen rescu'd him:
For Hunting was his dayly Exercise.

Warw. My Brother was too carelesse of his charge.
But let vs hence, my Soueraigne, to prouide
A salue for any sore, that may betide. *Exeunt.*

Manet Somerset, Richmond, and Oxford.

Som. My Lord, I like not of this flight of *Edwards*:
For doubtlesse, *Burgundie* will yeeld him helpe,
And we shall haue more Warres befor't be long.
As *Henries* late presaging Prophecie
Did glad my heart, with hope of this young *Richmond*:
So doth my heart mis-giue me, in these Conflicts,
What may befall him, to his harme and ours.
Therefore, Lord *Oxford*, to preuent the worst,
Forthwith wee'le send him hence to Brittanie,
Till stormes be past of Ciuill Enmitie.

Oxf. I: for if *Edward* re-possesse the Crowne,
'Tis like that *Richmond*, with the rest, shall downe.

Som. It shall be so: he shall to Brittanie.
Come therefore, let's about it speedily. *Exeunt.*

Flourish. Enter Edward, Richard, Hastings, and Souldiers.

Edw. Now Brother *Richard*, Lord *Hastings*, and the rest,
Yet thus farre Fortune maketh vs amends,
And sayes, that once more I shall enterchange
My wained state, for *Henries* Regall Crowne.
Well haue we pass'd, and now re-pass'd the Seas,
And brought desired helpe from Burgundie.
What then remaines, we being thus arriu'd
From Rauenspurre Hauen, before the Gates of Yorke,
But that we enter, as into our Dukedome?

Rich. The Gates made fast?
Brother, I like not this.
For many men that stumble at the Threshold,
Are well fore-told, that danger lurkes within.

Edw. Tush man, aboadments must not now affright vs:
By faire or foule meanes we must enter in,
For hither will our friends repaire to vs.

Hast. My Liege, Ile knocke once more, to summon them.

Enter on the Walls, the Maior of Yorke, and his Brethren.

Maior. My Lords,
We were fore-warned of your comming,
And shut the Gates, for safetie of our selues;
For now we owe allegeance vnto *Henry*.

Edw. But, Master Maior, if *Henry* be your King,
Yet *Edward*, at the least, is Duke of Yorke.

Maior. True, my good Lord, I know you for no lesse.

Edw. Why, and I challenge nothing but my Dukedome,
As being well content with that alone.

Rich. But when the Fox hath once got in his Nose,
Hee'le soone finde meanes to make the Body follow.
Hast. Why, Master Maior, why stand you in a doubt?
Open the Gates, we are King *Henries* friends.
Maior. I, say you so? the Gates shall then be opened.
He descends.
Rich. A wise stout Captaine, and soone perswaded.
Hast. The good old man would faine that all were wel,
So 'twere not long of him: but being entred,
I doubt not I, but we'shall soone perswade
Both him, and all his Brothers, vnto reason.

Enter the Maior, and two Aldermen.

Edw. So, Master Maior: these Gates must not be shut,
But in the Night, or in the time of Warre.
What, feare not man, but yeeld me vp the Keyes,
Takes his Keyes.
For *Edward* will defend the Towne, and thee,
And all those friends, that deine to follow mee.

March. Enter Mountgomerie, with Drumme and Souldiers.

Rich. Brother, this is Sir *Iohn Mountgomerie*,
Our trustie friend, vnlesse I be deceiu'd.
Edw. Welcome Sir *Iohn*: but why come you in Armes?
Mount. To helpe King *Edward* in his time of storme,
As euery loyall Subiect ought to doe.
Edw. Thankes good *Mountgomerie*:
But we now forget our Title to the Crowne,
And onely clayme our Dukedome,
Till God please to send the rest.
Mount. Then fare you well, for I will hence againe,
I came to serue a King, and not a Duke:
Drummer strike vp, and let vs march away.
The Drumme begins to march.
Edw. Nay stay, Sir *Iohn*, a while, and wee'le debate
By what safe meanes the Crowne may be recouer'd.
Mount. What talke you of debating? in few words,
If you'le not here proclaime your selfe our King,
Ile leaue you to your fortune, and be gone,
To keepe them back, that come to succour you.
Why shall we fight, if you pretend no Title?
Rich. Why Brother, wherefore stand you on nice points?
Edw. When wee grow stronger,
Then wee'le make our Clayme:
Till then, 'tis wisdome to conceale our meaning.
Hast. Away with scrupulous Wit, now Armes must rule.
Rich. And fearelesse minds clyme soonest vnto Crowns.
Brother, we will proclaime you out of hand,
The bruit thereof will bring you many friends.
Edw. Then be it as you will: for 'tis my right,
And *Henry* but vsurpes the Diademe.
Mount. I, now my Soueraigne speaketh like himselfe,
And now will I be *Edwards* Champion.
Hast. Sound Trumpet, *Edward* shal be here proclaim'd:
Come, fellow Souldior, make thou proclamation.
Flourish. Sound.
Soul. Edward *the Fourth, by the Grace of God, King of England and France, and Lord of Ireland, &c.*
Mount. And whosoe're gainsayes King *Edwards* right,
By this I challenge him to single fight.
Throwes downe his Gauntlet.
All. Long liue *Edward* the Fourth.
Edw. Thankes braue *Mountgomery*,
And thankes vnto you all:
If fortune serue me, Ile requite this kindnesse.
Now for this Night, let's harbor here in Yorke:
And when the Morning Sunne shall rayse his Carre
Aboue the Border of this Horizon,
Wee'le forward towards *Warwicke*, and his Mates;
For well I wot, that *Henry* is no Souldier.
Ah froward *Clarence*, how euill it beseemes thee,
To flatter *Henry*, and forsake thy Brother?
Yet as wee may, wee'le meet both thee and *Warwicke*.
Come on braue Souldiors: doubt not of the Day,
And that once gotten, doubt not of large Pay. *Exeunt.*

Flourish. Enter the King, Warwicke, Mountague, Clarence, Oxford, and Somerset.

War. What counsaile, Lords? *Edward* from Belgia,
With hastie Germanes, and blunt Hollanders,
Hath pass'd in safetie through the Narrow Seas,
And with his troupes doth march amaine to London,
And many giddie people flock to him.
King. Let's leuie men, and beat him backe againe,
Clar. A little fire is quickly trodden out,
Which being suffer'd, Riuers cannot quench.
War. In Warwickshire I haue true-hearted friends,
Not mutinous in peace, yet bold in Warre,
Those will I muster vp: and thou Sonne *Clarence*
Shalt stirre vp in Suffolke, Norfolke, and in Kent,
The Knights and Gentlemen, to come with thee.
Thou Brother *Mountague*, in Buckingham,
Northampton, and in Leicestershire, shalt find
Men well enclin'd to heare what thou command'st.
And thou, braue *Oxford*, wondrous well belou'd,
In Oxfordshire shalt muster vp thy friends.
My Soueraigne, with the louing Citizens,
Like to his Iland, gyrt in with the Ocean,
Or modest *Dyan*, circled with her Nymphs,
Shall rest in London, till we come to him:
Faire Lords take leaue, and stand not to reply.
Farewell my Soueraigne.
King. Farewell my *Hector*, and my Troyes true hope.
Clar. In signe of truth, I kisse your Highnesse Hand.
King. Well-minded *Clarence*, be thou fortunate.
Mount. Comfort, my Lord, and so I take my leaue.
Oxf. And thus I seale my truth, and bid adieu.
King. Sweet *Oxford*, and my louing *Mountague*,
And all at once, once more a happy farewell.
War. Farewell, sweet Lords, let's meet at Couentry.
Exeunt.
King. Here at the Pallace will I rest a while.
Cousin of *Exeter*, what thinkes your Lordship?
Me thinkes, the Power that *Edward* hath in field,
Should not be able to encounter mine.
Exet. The doubt is, that he will seduce the rest.
King. That's not my feare, my meed hath got me fame:
I haue not stopt mine eares to their demands,
Nor posted off their suites with slow delayes,
My pittie hath beene balme to heale their wounds,
My mildnesse hath allay'd their swelling griefes,
My mercie dry'd their water-flowing teares.
I haue not been desirous of their wealth,
Nor much opprest them with great Subsidies,
Nor forward of reuenge, though they much err'd.
Then why should they loue *Edward* more then me?
No *Exeter*, these Graces challenge Grace:

And when the Lyon fawnes vpon the Lambe,
The Lambe will neuer ceaſe to follow him.

Shout within, A Lancaſter, A Lancaſter.

Exet. Hearke, hearke, my Lord, what Shouts are theſe?

Enter Edward and his Souldiers.

Edw. Seize on the ſhamefac'd *Henry*, beare him hence,
And once againe proclaime vs King of England.
You are the Fount, that makes ſmall Brookes to flow,
Now ſtops thy Spring, my Sea ſhall ſuck them dry,
And ſwell ſo much the higher, by their ebbe.
Hence with him to the Tower, let him not ſpeake.

Exit with King Henry.

And Lords, towards Couentry bend we our courſe,
Where peremptorie *Warwicke* now remaines:
The Sunne ſhines hot, and if we vſe delay,
Cold biting Winter marres our hop'd-for Hay.

Rich. Away betimes, before his forces ioyne,
And take the great-growne Traytor vnawares:
Braue Warriors, march amaine towards Couentry.

Exeunt.

Enter Warwicke, the Maior of Couentry, two Meſſengers, and others vpon the Walls.

War. Where is the Poſt that came from valiant *Oxford*?
How farre hence is thy Lord, mine honeſt fellow?

Meſſ. 1. By this at Dunſmore, marching hitherward.

War. How farre off is our Brother *Mountague*?
Where is the Poſt that came from *Mountague*?

Meſſ. 2. By this at Daintry, with a puiſſant troope.

Enter Someruile.

War. Say *Someruile*, what ſayes my louing Sonne?
And by thy gueſſe, how nigh is *Clarence* now?

Somerv. At Southam I did leaue him with his forces,
And doe expect him here ſome two howres hence.

War. Then *Clarence* is at hand, I heare his Drumme.

Somerv. It is not his, my Lord, here Southam lyes:
The Drum your Honor heares, marcheth from *Warwicke*.

War. Who ſhould that be? belike vnlook'd for friends.

Somerv. They are at hand, and you ſhall quickly know.

March. Flouriſh. Enter Edward, Richard, and Souldiers.

Edw. Goe, Trumpet, to the Walls, and ſound a Parle.

Rich. See how the ſurly *Warwicke* mans the Wall.

War. Oh vnbid ſpight, is ſportfull *Edward* come?
Where ſlept our Scouts, or how are they ſeduc'd,
That we could heare no newes of his repayre.

Edw. Now *Warwicke*, wilt thou ope the Citie Gates,
Speake gentle words, and humbly bend thy Knee,
Call *Edward* King, and at his hands begge Mercy,
And he ſhall pardon thee theſe Outrages?

War. Nay rather, wilt thou draw thy forces hence,
Confeſſe who ſet thee vp, and pluckt thee downe,
Call *Warwicke* Patron, and be penitent,
And thou ſhalt ſtill remaine the Duke of Yorke.

Rich. I thought at leaſt he would haue ſaid the King,
Or did he make the Ieaſt againſt his will?

War. Is not a Dukedome, Sir, a goodly gift?

Rich. I, by my faith, for a poore Earle to giue,
Ile doe thee ſeruice for ſo good a gift.

War. 'Twas I that gaue the Kingdome to thy Brother.

Edw. Why then 'tis mine, if but by *Warwickes* gift.

War. Thou art no *Atlas* for ſo great a weight:
And Weakeling, *Warwicke* takes his gift againe,
And *Henry* is my King, *Warwicke* his Subiect.

Edw. But *Warwickes* King is *Edwards* Priſoner:
And gallant *Warwicke*, doe but anſwer this,
What is the Body, when the Head is off?

Rich. Alas, that *Warwicke* had no more fore-caſt,
But whiles he thought to ſteale the ſingle Ten,
The King was ſlyly finger'd from the Deck:
You left poore *Henry* at the Biſhops Pallace,
And tenne to one you'le meet him in the Tower.

Edw. 'Tis euen ſo, yet you are *Warwicke* ſtill.

Rich. Come *Warwicke*,
Take the time, kneele downe, kneele downe:
Nay when? ſtrike now, or elſe the Iron cooles.

War. I had rather chop this Hand off at a blow
And with the other, fling it at thy face,
Then beare ſo low a ſayle, to ſtrike to thee.

Edw. Sayle how thou canſt,
Haue Winde and Tyde thy friend,
This Hand, faſt wound about thy coale-black hayre,
Shall, whiles thy Head is warme, and new cut off,
Write in the duſt this Sentence with thy blood,
Wind-changing *Warwicke* now can change no more.

Enter Oxford, with Drumme and Colours.

War. Oh chearefull Colours, ſee where *Oxford* comes.

Oxf. *Oxford, Oxford*, for *Lancaſter*.

Rich. The Gates are open, let vs enter too.

Edw. So other foes may ſet vpon our backs.
Stand we in good array: for they no doubt
Will iſſue out againe, and bid vs battaile;
If not, the Citie being but of ſmall defence,
Wee'le quickly rowze the Traitors in the ſame.

War. Oh welcome *Oxford*, for we want thy helpe.

Enter Mountague, with Drumme and Colours.

Mount. *Mountague, Mountague*, for *Lancaſter*.

Rich. Thou and thy Brother both ſhall buy this Treaſon
Euen with the deareſt blood your bodies beare.

Edw. The harder matcht, the greater Victorie,
My minde preſageth happy gaine, and Conqueſt.

Enter Somerſet, with Drumme and Colours.

Som. *Somerſet, Somerſet*, for *Lancaſter*.

Rich. Two of thy Name, both Dukes of Somerſet,
Haue ſold their Liues vnto the Houſe of *Yorke*,
And thou ſhalt be the third, if this Sword hold.

Enter Clarence, with Drumme and Colours.

War. And loe, where *George* of Clarence ſweepes along,
Of force enough to bid his Brother Battaile:
With whom, in vpright zeale to right, preuailes
More then the nature of a Brothers Loue.
Come *Clarence*, come: thou wilt, if *Warwicke* call.

Clar. Father of Warwick, know you what this meanes?
Looke here, I throw my infamie at thee:
I will not ruinate my Fathers Houſe,
Who gaue his blood to lyme the ſtones together,
And ſet vp *Lancaſter*. Why, troweſt thou, *Warwicke*,
That *Clarence* is ſo harſh, ſo blunt, vnnaturall,
To bend the fatall Inſtruments of Warre

Against his Brother, and his lawfull King.
Perhaps thou wilt obiect my holy Oath:
To keepe that Oath, were more impietie,
Then *Iephah*, when he sacrific'd his Daughter.
I am so sorry for my Trespas made,
That to deserue well at my Brothers hands,
I here proclayme my selfe thy mortall foe:
With resolution, wheresoe're I meet thee,
(As I will meet thee, if thou stirre abroad)
To plague thee, for thy foule mis-leading me.
And so, prowd-hearted *Warwicke*, I defie thee,
And to my Brother turne my blushing Cheekes.
Pardon me *Edward*, I will make amends:
And *Richard*, doe not frowne vpon my faults,
For I will henceforth be no more vnconstant.

Edw. Now welcome more, and ten times more belou'd,
Then if thou neuer hadst deseru'd our hate.

Rich. Welcome good *Clarence*, this is Brother-like.

Warw. Oh passing Traytor, periur'd and vniust.

Edw. What *Warwicke*,
Wilt thou leaue the Towne, and fight?
Or shall we beat the Stones about thine Eares?

Warw. Alas, I am not coop'd here for defence:
I will away towards Barnet presently,
And bid thee Battaile, *Edward*, if thou dar'st.

Edw. Yes *Warwicke*, *Edward* dares, and leads the way:
Lords to the field: Saint *George*, and Victorie. *Exeunt.*

March. Warwicke and his companie followes.

Alarum, and Excursions. Enter Edward bringing forth Warwicke wounded.

Edw. So, lye thou there: dye thou, and dye our feare,
For *Warwicke* was a Bugge that fear'd vs all.
Now *Mountague* sit fast, I seeke for thee,
That *Warwickes* Bones may keepe thine companie. *Exit.*

Warw. Ah, who is nigh? come to me, friend, or foe,
And tell me who is Victor, *Yorke*, or *Warwicke*?
Why aske I that? my mangled body shewes,
My blood, my want of strength, my sicke heart shewes,
That I must yeeld my body to the Earth,
And by my fall, the conquest to my foe.
Thus yeelds the Cedar to the Axes edge,
Whose Armes gaue shelter to the Princely Eagle,
Vnder whose shade the ramping Lyon slept,
Whose top-branch ouer-peer'd *Ioues* spreading Tree,
And kept low Shrubs from Winters pow'rfull Winde.
These Eyes, that now are dim'd with Deaths black Veyle,
Haue beene as piercing as the Mid-day Sunne,
To search the secret Treasons of the World:
The Wrinckles in my Browes, now fill'd with blood,
Were lik'ned oft to Kingly Sepulchers:
For who liu'd King, but I could digge his Graue?
And who durst smile, when *Warwicke* bent his Brow?
Loe, now my Glory smear'd in dust and blood.
My Parkes, my Walkes, my Mannors that I had,
Euen now forsake me; and of all my Lands,
Is nothing left me, but my bodies length.
Why, what is Pompe, Rule, Reigne, but Earth and Dust?
And liue we how we can, yet dye we must.

Enter Oxford and Somerset.

Som. Ah *Warwicke*, *Warwicke*, wert thou as we are,
We might recouer all our Losse againe:
The Queene from France hath brought a puissant power.
Euen now we heard the newes: ah, could'st thou flye.

Warw. Why then I would not flye. Ah *Mountague*,
If thou be there, sweet Brother, take my Hand,
And with thy Lippes keepe in my Soule a while.
Thou lou'st me not: for, Brother, if thou didst,
Thy teares would wash this cold congealed blood,
That glewes my Lippes, and will not let me speake.
Come quickly *Mountague*, or I am dead.

Som. Ah *Warwicke*, *Mountague* hath breath'd his last,
And to the latest gaspe, cry'd out for *Warwicke*:
And said, Commend me to my valiant Brother.
And more he would haue said, and more he spoke,
Which sounded like a Cannon in a Vault,
That mought not be distinguisht: but at last,
I well might heare, deliuered with a groane,
Oh farewell *Warwicke*.

Warw. Sweet rest his Soule:
Flye Lords, and saue your selues,
For *Warwicke* bids you all farewell, to meet in Heauen.

Oxf. Away, away, to meet the Queenes great power.

Here they beare away his Body. Exeunt.

Flourish. Enter King Edward in triumph, with Richard, Clarence, and the rest.

King. Thus farre our fortune keepes an vpward course,
And we are grac'd with wreaths of Victorie:
But in the midst of this bright-shining Day,
I spy a black suspicious threatning Cloud,
That will encounter with our glorious Sunne,
Ere he attaine his easefull Westerne Bed:
I meane, my Lords, those powers that the Queene
Hath rays'd in Gallia, haue arriued our Coast,
And, as we heare, march on to fight with vs.

Clar. A little gale will soone disperse that Cloud,
And blow it to the Source from whence it came,
Thy very Beames will dry those Vapours vp,
For euery Cloud engenders not a Storme.

Rich. The Queene is valued thirtie thousand strong,
And *Somerset*, with *Oxford*, fled to her:
If she haue time to breathe, be well assur'd
Her faction will be full as strong as ours.

King. We are aduertis'd by our louing friends,
That they doe hold their course toward Tewksbury.
We hauing now the best at Barnet field,
Will thither straight, for willingnesse rids way,
And as we march, our strength will be augmented:
In euery Countie as we goe along,
Strike vp the Drumme, cry courage, and away. *Exeunt.*

Flourish. March. Enter the Queene, young Edward, Somerset, Oxford, and Souldiers.

Qu. Great Lords, wise men ne'r sit and waile their losse,
But chearely seeke how to redresse their harmes.
What though the Mast be now blowne ouer-boord,
The Cable broke, the holding-Anchor lost,
And halfe our Saylors swallow'd in the flood?
Yet liues our Pilot still. Is't meet, that hee
Should leaue the Helme, and like a fearefull Lad,
With tearefull Eyes adde Water to the Sea,
And giue more strength to that which hath too much,
Whiles in his moane, the Ship splits on the Rock,
Which Industrie and Courage might haue sau'd?
Ah what a shame, ah what a fault were this.
Say *Warwicke* was our Anchor: what of that?

And *Mountague* our Top-Mast: what of him?
Our slaught'red friends, the Tackles: what of these?
Why is not *Oxford* here, another Anchor?
And *Somerset*, another goodly Mast?
The friends of France our Shrowds and Tacklings?
And though vnskilfull, why not *Ned* and I,
For once allow'd the skilfull Pilots Charge?
We will not from the Helme, to sit and weepe,
But keepe our Course (though the rough Winde say no)
From Shelues and Rocks, that threaten vs with Wrack.
As good to chide the Waues, as speake them faire.
And what is *Edward*, but a ruthlesse Sea?
What *Clarence*, but a Quick-sand of Deceit?
And *Richard*, but a raged fatall Rocke?
All these, the Enemies to our poore Barke.
Say you can swim, alas 'tis but a while:
Tread on the Sand, why there you quickly sinke,
Bestride the Rock, the Tyde will wash you off,
Or else you famish, that's a three-fold Death.
This speake I (Lords) to let you vnderstand,
If case some one of you would flye from vs,
That there's no hop'd-for Mercy with the Brothers,
More then with ruthlesse Waues, with Sands and Rocks.
Why courage then, what cannot be auoided,
'Twere childish weakenesse to lament, or feare.

Prince. Me thinkes a Woman of this valiant Spirit,
Should, if a Coward heard her speake these words,
Infuse his Breast with Magnanimitie,
And make him, naked, foyle a man at Armes.
I speake not this, as doubting any here:
For did I but suspect a fearefull man,
He should haue leaue to goe away betimes,
Least in our need he might infect another,
And make him of like spirit to himselfe.
If any such be here, as God forbid,
Let him depart, before we neede his helpe.

Oxf. Women and Children of so high a courage,
And Warriors faint, why 'twere perpetuall shame.
Oh braue young Prince: thy famous Grandfather
Doth liue againe in thee; long may'st thou liue,
To beare his Image, and renew his Glories.

Som. And he that will not fight for such a hope,
Goe home to Bed, and like the Owle by day,
If he arise, be mock'd and wondred at.

Qu. Thankes gentle *Somerset*, sweet *Oxford* thankes.

Prince. And take his thankes, that yet hath nothing else.

Enter a Messenger.

Mess. Prepare you Lords, for *Edward* is at hand,
Readie to fight: therefore be resolute.

Oxf. I thought no lesse: it is his Policie,
To haste thus fast, to finde vs vnprouided.

Som. But hee's deceiu'd, we are in readinesse.

Qu. This cheares my heart, to see your forwardnesse.

Oxf. Here pitch our Battaile, hence we will not budge.

Flourish, and march. Enter Edward, Richard, Clarence, and Souldiers.

Edw. Braue followers, yonder stands the thornie Wood,
Which by the Heauens assistance, and your strength,
Must by the Roots be hew'ne vp yet ere Night.
I need not adde more fuell to your fire,
For well I wot, ye blaze, to burne them out:
Giue signall to the fight, and to it Lords.

Qu. Lords, Knights, and Gentlemen, what I should say,
My teares gaine-say: for euery word I speake,
Ye see I drinke the water of my eye.
Therefore no more but this: *Henry* your Soueraigne
Is Prisoner to the Foe, his State vsurp'd,
His Realme a slaughter-house, his Subiects slaine,
His Statutes cancell'd, and his Treasure spent:
And yonder is the Wolfe, that makes this spoyle.
You fight in Iustice: then in Gods Name, Lords,
Be valiant, and giue signall to the fight.

Alarum, Retreat, Excursions. Exeunt.

Flourish. Enter Edward, Richard, Queene, Clarence, Oxford, Somerset.

Edw. Now here a period of tumultuous Broyles.
Away with *Oxford* to Hames Castle straight:
For *Somerset*, off with his guiltie Head.
Goe beare them hence, I will not heare them speake.

Oxf. For my part, Ile not trouble thee with words.

Som. Nor I, but stoupe with patience to my fortune.

Exeunt.

Qu. So part we sadly in this troublous World,
To meet with Ioy in sweet Ierusalem.

Edw. Is Proclamation made, That who finds *Edward*,
Shall haue a high Reward, and he his Life?

Rich. It is, and loe where youthfull *Edward* comes.

Enter the Prince.

Edw. Bring forth the Gallant, let vs heare him speake.
What? can so young a Thorne begin to prick?
Edward, what satisfaction canst thou make,
For bearing Armes, for stirring vp my Subiects,
And all the trouble thou hast turn'd me to?

Prince. Speake like a Subiect, prowd ambitious *Yorke*.
Suppose that I am now my Fathers Mouth,
Resigne thy Chayre, and where I stand, kneele thou,
Whil'st I propose the selfe-same words to thee,
Which (Traytor) thou would'st haue me answer to.

Qu. Ah, that thy Father had beene so resolu'd.

Rich. That you might still haue worne the Petticoat,
And ne're haue stolne the Breech from *Lancaster*.

Prince. Let *Æsop* fable in a Winters Night,
His Currish Riddles sorts not with this place.

Rich. By Heauen, Brat, Ile plague ye for that word.

Qu. I, thou wast borne to be a plague to men.

Rich. For Gods sake, take away this Captiue Scold.

Prince. Nay, take away this scolding Crooke-backe, rather.

Edw. Peace wilfull Boy, or I will charme your tongue.

Clar. Vntutor'd Lad, thou art too malapert.

Prince. I know my dutie, you are all vndutifull:
Lasciuious *Edward*, and thou periur'd *George*,
And thou mis-shapen *Dicke*, I tell ye all,
I am your better, Traytors as ye are,
And thou vsurp'st my Fathers right and mine.

Edw. Take that, the likenesse of this Rayler here.

Stabs him.

Rich. Sprawl'st thou? take that, to end thy agonie.

Rich. stabs him.

Clar. And ther's for twitting me with periurie.

Clar. stabs him.

Qu. Oh, kill me too.

Rich. Marry, and shall. *Offers to kill her.*

Edw. Hold, *Richard*, hold, for we haue done too much.

Rich. Why should shee liue, to fill the World with words.

Edw. What? doth shee swowne? vse meanes for her recouerie.

Rich. *Clarence* excuse me to the King my Brother:
Ile hence to London on a serious matter,
Ere ye come there, be sure to heare some newes.

Cla. What? what?

Rich Tower, the Tower. *Exit.*

Qu. Oh *Ned*, sweet *Ned*, speake to thy Mother Boy.
Can'st thou not speake? O Traitors, Murtherers!
They that stabb'd *Cæsar*, shed no blood at all:
Did not offend, nor were not worthy Blame,
If this foule deed were by, to equall it.
He was a Man; this (in respect) a Childe,
And Men, ne're spend their fury on a Childe.
What's worse then Murtherer, that I may name it?
No, no, my heart will burst, and if I speake,
And I will speake, that so my heart may burst.
Butchers and Villaines, bloudy Caniballes,
How sweet a Plant haue you vntimely cropt:
You haue no children (Butchers) if you had,
The thought of them would haue stirr'd vp remorse,
But if you euer chance to haue a Childe,
Looke in his youth to haue him so cut off.
As deathsmen you haue rid this sweet yong Prince.

King. Away with her, go beare her hence perforce.

Qu. Nay, neuer beare me hence, dispatch me heere:
Here sheath thy Sword, Ile pardon thee my death:
What? wilt thou not? Then *Clarence* do it thou.

Cla. By heauen, I will not do thee so much ease.

Qu. Good *Clarence* do: sweet *Clarence* do thou do it.

Cla. Did'st thou not heare me sweare I would not do it?

Qu. I, but thou vsest to forsweare thy selfe.
'Twas Sin before, but now 'tis Charity.
What wilt ŷ not? Where is that diuels butcher *Richard*?
Hard fauor'd *Richard*? *Richard*, where art thou?
Thou art not heere; Murther is thy Almes-deed:
Petitioners for Blood, thou ne're put'st backe.

Ed. Away I say, I charge ye beare her hence,

Qu. So come to you, and yours, as to this Prince.

Exit Queene.

Ed. Where's *Richard* gone.

Cla. To London all in post, and as I guesse,
To make a bloody Supper in the Tower.

Ed. He's sodaine if a thing comes in his head.
Now march we hence, discharge the common sort
With Pay and Thankes, and let's away to London,
And see our gentle Queene how well she fares,
By this (I hope) she hath a Sonne for me. *Exit.*

Enter Henry the sixt, and Richard, with the Lieutenant on the Walles.

Rich. Good day, my Lord, what at your Booke so hard?

Hen. I my good Lord: my Lord I should say rather,
Tis sinne to flatter, Good was little better:
Good Gloster, and good Deuill, were alike,
And both preposterous: therefore, not Good Lord.

Rich. Sirra, leaue vs to our selues, we must conferre.

Hen. So flies the wreaklesse shepherd from ŷ Wolfe
So first the harmlesse Sheepe doth yeeld his Fleece,
And next his Throate, vnto the Butchers Knife.
What Scene of death hath *Rostius* now to Acte?

Rich. Suspition alwayes haunts the guilty minde,
The Theefe doth feare each bush an Officer,

Hen. The Bird that hath bin limed in a bush,
With trembling wings misdoubteth euery bush:
And I the haplesse Male to one sweet Bird,
Haue now the fatall Obiect in my eye,
Where my poore yong was lim'd, was caught, and kill'd.

Rich. Why what a peeuish Foole was that of Creet,
That taught his Sonne the office of a Fowle,
And yet for all his wings, the Foole was drown'd.

Hen. I *Dedalus*, my poore Boy *Icarus*,
Thy Father *Minos*, that deni'de our course,
The Sunne that sear'd the wings of my sweet Boy.
Thy Brother *Edward*, and thy Selfe, the Sea
Whose enuious Gulfe did swallow vp his life:
Ah, kill me with thy Weapon, not with words,
My brest can better brooke thy Daggers point,
Then can my eares that Tragicke History.
But wherefore dost thou come? Is't for my Life?

Rich. Think'st thou I am an Executioner?

Hen. A Persecutor I am sure thou art,
If murthering Innocents be Executing,
Why then thou art an Executioner.

Rich. Thy Son I kill'd for his presumption.

Hen. Hadst thou bin kill'd, when first ŷ didst presume,
Thou had'st not liu'd to kill a Sonne of mine:
And thus I prophesie, that many a thousand,
Which now mistrust no parcell of my feare,
And many an old mans sighe, and many a Widdowes,
And many an Orphans water-standing-eye,
Men for their Sonnes, Wiues for their Husbands,
Orphans, for their Parents timeles death,
Shall rue the houre that euer thou was't borne.
The Owle shriek'd at thy birth, an euill signe,
The Night-Crow cry'de, aboding luckelesse time,
Dogs howl'd, and hiddeous Tempest shook down Trees:
The Rauen rook'd her on the Chimnies top,
And chatt'ring Pies in dismall Discords sung:
Thy Mother felt more then a Mothers paine,
And yet brought forth lesse then a Mothers hope,
To wit, an indigested and deformed lumpe,
Not like the fruit of such a goodly Tree.
Teeth had'st thou in thy head, when thou was't borne,
To signifie, thou cam'st to bite the world:
And if the rest be true, which I haue heard,
Thou cam'st——

Rich. Ile heare no more:
Dye Prophet in thy speech, *Stabbes him.*
For this (among'st the rest) was I ordain'd.

Hen. I, and for much more slaughter after this,
O God forgiue my sinnes, and pardon thee. *Dyes.*

Rich. What? will the aspiring blood of Lancaster
Sinke in the ground? I thought it would haue mounted.
See how my sword weepes for the poore Kings death.
O may such purple teares be alway shed
From those that wish the downfall of our house.
If any sparke of Life be yet remaining,
Downe, downe to hell, and say I sent thee thither.

Stabs him againe.

I that haue neyther pitty, loue, nor feare,
Indeed 'tis true that *Henrie* told me of:
For I haue often heard my Mother say,
I came into the world with my Legges forward.
Had I not reason (thinke ye) to make hast,
And seeke their Ruine, that vsurp'd our Right?
The Midwife wonder'd, and the Women cri'de
O Iesus blesse vs, he is borne with teeth,

And

And so I was, which plainly signified,
That I should snarle, and bite, and play the dogge:
Then since the Heauens haue shap'd my Body so,
Let Hell make crook'd my Minde to answer it.
I haue no Brother, I am like no Brother:
And this word [Loue] which Gray-beards call Diuine,
Be resident in men like one another,
And not in me: I am my selfe alone.
Clarence beware, thou keept'st me from the Light,
But I will sort a pitchy day for thee:
For I will buzze abroad such Prophesies,
That *Edward* shall be fearefull of his life,
And then to purge his feare, Ile be thy death.
King *Henry*, and the Prince his Son are gone,
Clarence thy turne is next, and then the rest,
Counting my selfe but bad, till I be best.
Ile throw thy body in another roome,
And Triumph *Henry*, in thy day of Doome. *Exit.*

Flourish. Enter King, Queene, Clarence, Richard, Hastings, Nurse, and Attendants.

King. Once more we sit in Englands Royall Throne,
Re-purchac'd with the Blood of Enemies:
What valiant Foe-men, like to Autumnes Corne,
Haue we mow'd downe in tops of all their pride?
Three Dukes of Somerset, threefold Renowne,
For hardy and vndoubted Champions:
Two *Cliffords*, as the Father and the Sonne,
And two Northumberlands: two brauer men,
Ne're spurr'd their Coursers at the Trumpets sound.
With them, the two braue Beares, *Warwick* & *Montague*,
That in their Chaines fetter'd the Kingly Lyon,
And made the Forrest tremble when they roar'd.
Thus haue we swept Suspition from our Seate,
And made our Footstoole of Security.
Come hither *Besse*, and let me kisse my Boy:
Yong *Ned*, for thee, thine Vnckles, and my selfe,
Haue in our Armors watcht the Winters night,
Went all afoote in Summers scalding heate,
That thou might'st repossesse the Crowne in peace,
And of our Labours thou shalt reape the gaine.

Rich. Ile blast his Haruest, if your head were laid,
For yet I am not look'd on in the world.
This shoulder was ordain'd so thicke, to heaue,
And heaue it shall some waight, or breake my backe,
Worke thou the way, and that shalt execute.

King. *Clarence* and *Gloster*, loue my louely Queene,
And kis your Princely Nephew Brothers both.

Cla. The duty that I owe vnto your Maiesty,
I Seale vpon the lips of this sweet Babe.

Cla. Thanke Noble *Clarence*, worthy brother thanks.

Rich. And that I loue the tree frõ whence ÿ sprang'st:
Witnesse the louing kisse I giue the Fruite,
To say the truth, so *Iudas* kist his master,
And cried all haile, when as he meant all harme.

King. Now am I seated as my soule delights,
Hauing my Countries peace, and Brothers loues.

Cla. What will your Grace haue done with *Margaret*,
Reynard her Father, to the King of France
Hath pawn'd the Sicils and Ierusalem,
And hither haue they sent it for her ransome.

King. Away with her, and waft her hence to France:
And now what rests, but that we spend the time
With stately Triumphes, mirthfull Comicke shewes,
Such as befits the pleasure of the Court.
Sound Drums and Trumpets, farwell sowre annoy,
For heere I hope begins our lasting ioy. *Exeunt omnes*

FINIS.

The Tragedy of Richard the Third: with the Landing of Earle Richmond, and the Battell at Bosworth Field.

Actus Primus. Scœna Prima.

Enter Richard Duke of Gloster, solus.

NOw is the Winter of our Discontent,
Made glorious Summer by this Son of Yorke:
And all the clouds that lowr'd vpon our house
In the deepe bosome of the Ocean buried.
Now are our browes bound with Victorious Wreathes,
Our bruised armes hung vp for Monuments;
Our sterne Alarums chang'd to merry Meetings;
Our dreadfull Marches, to delightfull Measures.
Grim-visag'd Warre, hath smooth'd his wrinkled Front:
And now, in stead of mounting Barbed Steeds,
To fright the Soules of fearfull Aduersaries,
He capers nimbly in a Ladies Chamber,
To the lasciuious pleasing of a Lute.
But I, that am not shap'd for sportiue trickes,
Nor made to court an amorous Looking-glasse:
I, that am Rudely stampt, and want loues Maiesty,
To strut before a wonton ambling Nymph:
I, that am curtail'd of this faire Proportion,
Cheated of Feature by dissembling Nature,
Deform'd, vn-finish'd, sent before my time
Into this breathing World, scarse halfe made vp,
And that so lamely and vnfashionable,
That dogges barke at me, as I halt by them.
Why I (in this weake piping time of Peace)
Haue no delight to passe away the time,
Vnlesse to see my Shadow in the Sunne,
And descant on mine owne Deformity.
And therefore, since I cannot proue a Louer,
To entertaine these faire well spoken dayes,
I am determined to proue a Villaine,
And hate the idle pleasures of these dayes.
Plots haue I laide, Inductions dangerous,
By drunken Prophesies, Libels, and Dreames,
To set my Brother *Clarence* and the King
In deadly hate, the one against the other:
And if King *Edward* be as true and iust,
As I am Subtle, False, and Treacherous,
This day should *Clarence* closely be mew'd vp:
About a Prophesie, which sayes that G,
Of *Edwards* heyres the murtherer shall be.
Diue thoughts downe to my soule, here *Clarence* comes.

Enter Clarence, and Brakenbury, guarded.

Brother, good day: What meanes this armed guard
That waites vpon your Grace?
Cla. His Maiesty tendring my persons safety,
Hath appointed this Conduct, to conuey me to th'Tower
Rich. Vpon what cause?
Cla. Because my name is *George*.
Rich. Alacke my Lord, that fault is none of yours:
He should for that commit your Godfathers.
O belike, his Maiesty hath some intent,
That you should be new Christned in the Tower.
But what's the matter *Clarence*, may I know?
Cla. Yea *Richard*, when I know: but I protest
As yet I do not: But as I can learne,
He hearkens after Prophesies and Dreames,
And from the Crosse-row pluckes the letter G:
And sayes, a Wizard told him, that by G,
His issue disinherited should be.
And for my name of *George* begins with G,
It followes in his thought, that I am he.
These (as I learne) and such like toyes as these,
Hath moou'd his H ghnesse to commit me now.
Rich. Why this it is, when men are rul'd by Women:
'Tis not the King that sends you to the Tower,
My Lady *Grey* his Wife, *Clarence* 'tis shee.
That tempts him to this harsh Extremity.
Was it not shee, and that good man of Worship,
Anthony Woodeuile her Brother there,
That made him send Lord *Hastings* to the Tower?
From whence this present day he is deliuered?
We are not safe *Clarence*, we are not safe.
Cla. By heauen, I thinke there is no man secure
But the Queenes Kindred, and night-walking Heralds,
That trudge betwixt the King, and Mistris *Shore*.
Heard you not what an humble Suppliant
Lord *Hastings* was, for her deliuery?
Rich. Humbly complaining to her Deitie,
Got my Lord Chamberlaine his libertie.
Ile tell you what, I thinke it is our way,
If we will keepe in fauour with the King,
To be her men, and weare her Liuery.
The iealous ore-worne Widdow, and her selfe,
Since that our Brother dub'd them Gentlewomen,
Are mighty Gossips in our Monarchy.
Bra. I beseech your Graces both to pardon me,
His Maiesty hath straightly giuen in charge,
That no man shall haue priuate Conference
(Of what degree soeuer) with your Brother.

Rich. Euen so, and please your Worship *Brakenbury*,
You may partake of any thing we say:
We speake no Treason man; We say the King
Is wise and vertuous, and his Noble Queene
Well strooke in yeares, faire, and not iealious.
We say, that *Shores* Wife hath a pretty Foot,
A cherry Lip, a bonny Eye, a passing pleasing tongue:
And that the Queenes Kindred are made gentle Folkes.
How say you sir? can you deny all this?

Bra. With this (my Lord) my selfe haue nought to doo.

Rich. Naught to do with Mistris *Shore*?
I tell thee Fellow, he that doth naught with her
(Excepting one) were best to do it secretly alone.

Bra. What one, my Lord?

Rich. Her Husband Knaue, would'st thou betray me?

Bra. I do beseech your Grace
To pardon me, and withall forbeare
Your Conference with the Noble Duke.

Cla. We know thy charge *Brakenbury*, and wil obey.

Rich. We are the Queenes abiects, and must obey.
Brother farewell, I will vnto the King,
And whatsoe're you will imploy me in,
Were it to call King *Edwards* Widdow, Sister,
I will performe it to infranchise you.
Meane time, this deepe disgrace in Brotherhood,
Touches me deeper then you can imagine.

Cla. I know it pleaseth neither of vs well.

Rich. Well, your imprisonment shall not be long,
I will deliuer you, or else lye for you:
Meane time, haue patience.

Cla. I must perforce: Farewell. *Exit Clar.*

Rich Go treade the path that thou shalt ne're return:
Simple plaine *Clarence*, I do loue thee so,
That I will shortly send thy Soule to Heauen,
If Heauen will take the present at our hands.
But who comes heere? the new deliuered *Hastings*?

Enter Lord Hastings.

Hast. Good time of day vnto my gracious Lord.

Rich. As much vnto my good Lord Chamberlaine:
Well are you welcome to this open Ayre,
How hath your Lordship brook'd imprisonment?

Hast. With patience (Noble Lord) as prisoners must:
But I shall liue (my Lord) to giue them thankes
That were the cause of my imprisonment.

Rich. No doubt, no doubt, and so shall *Clarence* too,
For they that were your Enemies, are his,
And haue preuail'd as much on him, as you,

Hast. More pitty, that the Eagles should be mew'd,
Whiles Kites and Buzards play at liberty.

Rich. What newes abroad?

Hast. No newes so bad abroad, as this at home:
The King is sickly, weake, and melancholly,
And his Physitians feare him mightily.

Rich. Now by S. Iohn, that Newes is bad indeed.
O he hath kept an euill Diet long,
And ouer-much consum'd his Royall Person:
'Tis very greeuous to be thought vpon.
Where is he, in his bed?

Hast. He is.

Rich. Go you before, and I will follow you.

Exit Hastings.

He cannot liue I hope, and must not dye,
Till *George* be pack'd with post-horse vp to Heauen.
Ile in to vrge his hatred more to *Clarence*,
With Lyes well steel'd with weighty Arguments,
And if I faile not in my deepe intent,
Clarence hath not another day to liue:
Which done, God take King *Edward* to his mercy,
And leaue the world for me to bussle in.
For then, Ile marry Warwickes yongest daughter.
What though I kill'd her Husband, and her Father,
The readiest way to make the Wench amends,
Is to become her Husband, and her Father:
The which will I, not all so much for loue,
As for another secret close intent,
By marrying her, which I must reach vnto.
But yet I run before my horse to Market:
Clarence still breathes, *Edward* still liues and raignes,
When they are gone, then must I count my gaines. *Exit*

Scena Secunda.

Enter the Coarse of Henrie the sixt with Halberds to guard it, Lady Anne being the Mourner.

Anne. Set downe, set downe your honourable load,
If Honor may be shrowded in a Herse;
Whil'st I a-while obsequiously lament
Th'vntimely fall of Vertuous Lancaster.
Poore key-cold Figure of a holy King,
Pale Ashes of the House of Lancaster;
Thou bloodlesse Remnant of that Royall Blood,
Be it lawfull that I inuocate thy Ghost,
To heare the Lamentations of poore *Anne*,
Wife to thy *Edward*, to thy slaughtred Sonne,
Stab'd by the selfesame hand that made these wounds.
Loe, in these windowes that let forth thy life,
I powre the helplesse Balme of my poore eyes.
O cursed be the hand that made these holes:
Cursed the Heart, that had the heart to do it:
Cursed the Blood, that let this blood from hence:
More direfull hap betide that hated Wretch
That makes vs wretched by the death of thee,
Then I can wish to Wolues, to Spiders, Toades,
Or any creeping venom'd thing that liues.
If euer he haue Childe, Abortiue be it,
Prodigeous, and vntimely brought to light,
Whose vgly and vnnaturall Aspect
May fright the hopefull Mother at the view,
And that be Heyre to his vnhappinesse.
If euer he haue Wife, let her be made
More miserable by the death of him,
Then I am made by my young Lord, and thee.
Come now towards Chertsey with your holy Lode,
Taken from Paules, to be interred there.
And still as you are weary of this waight,
Rest you, whiles I lament King *Henries* Coarse.

Enter Richard Duke of Gloster.

Rich. Stay you that beare the Coarse, & set it down.

An. What blacke Magitian coniures vp this Fiend,
To stop deuoted charitable deeds?

Rich. Villaines set downe the Coarse, or by S. Paul.
Ile make a Coarse of him that disobeyes.

Gen. My Lord stand backe, and let the Coffin passe.
Rich. Vnmanner'd Dogge,
Stand'st thou when I commaund:
Aduance thy Halbert higher then my brest,
Or by S. Paul Ile strike thee to my Foote,
And spurne vpon thee Begger for thy boldnesse.
Anne. What do you tremble? are you all affraid?
Alas, I blame you not, for you are Mortall,
And Mortall eyes cannot endure the Diuell.
Auant thou dreadfull minister of Hell;
Thou had'st but power ouer his Mortall body,
His Soule thou canst not haue: Therefore be gone.
Rich. Sweet Saint, for Charity, be not so curst.
An. Foule Diuell,
For Gods sake hence, and trouble vs not,
For thou hast made the happy earth thy Hell:
Fill'd it with cursing cries, and deepe exclaimes:
If thou delight to view thy heynous deeds,
Behold this patterne of thy Butcheries.
Oh Gentlemen, see, see dead *Henries* wounds,
Open their congeal'd mouthes, and bleed afresh.
Blush, blush, thou lumpe of fowle Deformitie:
For 'tis thy presence that exhales this blood
From cold and empty Veines where no blood dwels.
Thy Deeds inhumane and vnnaturall,
Prouokes this Deluge most vnnaturall.
O God! which this Blood mad'st, reuenge his death:
O Earth! which this Blood drink'st, reuenge his death.
Either Heau'n with Lightning strike the murth'rer dead:
Or Earth gape open wide, and eate him quicke,
As thou dost swallow vp this good Kings blood,
Which his Hell-gouern'd arme hath butchered.
Rich. Lady, you know no Rules of Charity,
Which renders good for bad, Blessings for Curses.
An. Villaine, thou know'st nor law of God nor Man,
No Beast so fierce, but knowes some touch of pitty.
Rich. But I know none, and therefore am no Beast.
An. O wonderfull, when diuels tell the truth!
Rich. More wonderfull, when Angels are so angry:
Vouchsafe (diuine perfection of a Woman)
Of these supposed Crimes, to giue me leaue
By circumstance, but to acquit my selfe.
An. Vouchsafe (defus'd infection of man)
Of these knowne euils, but to giue me leaue
By circumstance, to curse thy cursed Selfe.
Rich. Fairer then tongue can name thee, let me haue
Some patient leysure to excuse my selfe.
An. Fouler then heart can thinke thee,
Thou can'st make no excuse currant,
But to hang thy selfe.
Rich. By such dispaire, I should accuse my selfe.
An. And by dispairing shalt thou stand excused,
For doing worthy Vengeance on thy selfe,
That did'st vnworthy slaughter vpon others.
Rich. Say that I slew them not.
An. Then say they were not slaine:
But dead they are, and diuellish slaue by thee.
Rich. I did not kill your Husband.
An. Why then he is aliue.
Rich. Nay, he is dead, and slaine by Edwards hands.
An. In thy foule throat thou Ly'st,
Queene *Margaret* saw
Thy murd'rous Faulchion smoaking in his blood:
The which, thou once didd'st bend against her brest,
But that thy Brothers beate aside the point.
Rich. I was prouoked by her sland'rous tongue,
That laid their guilt, vpon my guiltlesse Shoulders.
An. Thou was't prouoked by thy bloody minde,
That neuer dream'st on ought but Butcheries:
Did'st thou not kill this King?
Rich. I graunt ye.
An. Do'st grant me Hedge-hogge,
Then God graunt me too
Thou may'st be damned for that wicked deede,
O he was gentle, milde, and vertuous.
Rich. The better for the King of heauen that hath him.
An. He is in heauen, where thou shalt neuer come.
Rich. Let him thanke me, that holpe to send him thither:
For he was fitter for that place then earth.
An. And thou vnfit for any place, but hell.
Rich. Yes one place else, if you will heare me name it.
An. Some dungeon.
Rich. Your Bed-chamber.
An. Ill rest betide the chamber where thou lyest.
Rich. So will it Madam, till I lye with you.
An. I hope so.
Rich. I know so. But gentle Lady *Anne*,
To leaue this keene encounter of our wittes,
And fall something into a slower method.
Is not the causer of the timelesse deaths
Of these *Plantagenets*, *Henrie* and *Edward*,
As blamefull as the Executioner.
An. Thou was't the cause, and most accurst effect.
Rich. Your beauty was the cause of that effect:
Your beauty, that did haunt me in my sleepe,
To vndertake the death of all the world,
So I might liue one houre in your sweet bosome.
An. If I thought that, I tell thee Homicide,
These Nailes should rent that beauty from my Cheekes.
Rich. These eyes could not endure ẏ beauties wrack,
You should not blemish it, if I stood by;
As all the world is cheared by the Sunne,
So I by that: It is my day, my life.
An. Blacke night ore-shade thy day, & death thy life.
Rich. Curse not thy selfe faire Creature,
Thou art both.
An. I would I were, to be reueng'd on thee.
Rich. It is a quarrell most vnnaturall,
To be reueng'd on him that loueth thee.
An. It is a quarrell iust and reasonable,
To be reueng'd on him that kill'd my Husband.
Rich. He that bereft the Lady of thy Husband,
Did it to helpe thee to a better Husband.
An. His better doth not breath vpon the earth.
Rich. He liues, that loues thee better then he could.
An. Name him.
Rich. *Plantagenet.*
An. Why that was he.
Rich. The selfesame name, but one of better Nature.
An. Where is he?
Rich. Heere: *Spits at him.*
Why dost thou spit at me.
An. Would it were mortall poyson, for thy sake.
Rich. Neuer came poyson from so sweet a place.
An. Neuer hung poyson on a fowler Toade.
Out of my sight, thou dost infect mine eyes.
Rich. Thine eyes (sweet Lady) haue infected mine.
An. Would they were Basiliskes, to strike thee dead.
Rich. I would they were, that I might dye at once:
For now they kill me with a liuing death.
Those eyes of thine, from mine haue drawne salt Teares;

Sham'd their Aspects with store of childish drops:
These eyes, which neuer shed remorsefull teare,
No, when my Father Yorke, and *Edward* wept,
To heare the pittious moane that Rutland made
When black-fac'd *Clifford* shooke his sword at him.
Nor when thy warlike Father like a Childe,
Told the sad storie of my Fathers death,
And twenty times, made pause to sob and weepe:
That all the standers by had wet their cheekes
Like Trees bedash'd with raine. In that sad time,
My manly eyes did scorne an humble teare:
And what these sorrowes could not thence exhale,
Thy Beauty hath, and made them blinde with weeping.
I neuer sued to Friend, nor Enemy:
My Tongue could neuer learne sweet smoothing word.
But now thy Beauty is propos'd my Fee,
My proud heart sues, and prompts my tongue to speake.
She lookes scornfully at him.
Teach not thy lip such Scorne; for it was made
For kissing Lady, not for such contempt.
If thy reuengefull heart cannot forgiue,
Loe heere I lend thee this sharpe-pointed Sword,
Which if thou please to hide in this true brest,
And let the Soule forth that adoreth thee,
I lay it naked to the deadly stroke,
And humbly begge the death vpon my knee,
He layes his brest open, she offers at with his sword.
Nay do not pause: For I did kill King *Henrie*,
But 'twas thy Beauty that prouoked me.
Nay now dispatch: 'Twas I that stabb'd yong *Edward*,
But 'twas thy Heauenly face that set me on.
She fals the Sword.
Take vp the Sword againe, or take vp me.
An. Arise Dissembler, though I wish thy death,
I will not be thy Executioner.
Rich. Then bid me kill my selfe, and I will do it.
An. I haue already.
Rich. That was in thy rage:
Speake it againe, and euen with the word,
This hand, which for thy loue, did kill thy Loue,
Shall for thy loue, kill a farre truer Loue,
To both their deaths shalt thou be accessary.
An. I would I knew thy heart.
Rich. 'Tis figur'd in my tongue.
An. I feare me, both are false.
Rich. Then neuer Man was true.
An. Well, well, put vp your Sword.
Rich. Say then my Peace is made.
An. That shalt thou know heereafter.
Rich. But shall I liue in hope.
An. All men I hope liue so.
Vouchsafe to weare this Ring.
Rich. Looke how my Ring incompasseth thy Finger,
Euen so thy Brest incloseth my poore heart:
Weare both of them, for both of them are thine.
And if thy poore deuoted Seruant may
But beg one fauour at thy gracious hand,
Thou dost confirme his happinesse for euer.
An. What is it?
Rich. That it may please you leaue these sad designes,
To him that hath most cause to be a Mourner,
And presently repayre to Crosbie House:
Where (after I haue solemnly interr'd
At Chertsey Monast'ry this Noble King,
And wet his Graue with my Repentant Teares)
I will with all expedient duty see you,
For diuers vnknowne Reasons, I beseech you,
Grant me this Boon.
An. With all my heart, and much it ioyes me too,
To see you are become so penitent.
Tressel and *Barkley*, go along with me.
Rich. Bid me farwell.
An. 'Tis more then you deserue:
But since you teach me how to flatter you,
Imagine I haue saide farewell already.
Exit two with Anne.
Gent. Towards Chertsey, Noble Lord?
Rich. No: to White Friars, there attend my comming
Exit Coarse
Was euer woman in this humour woo'd?
Was euer woman in this humour wonne?
Ile haue her, but I will not keepe her long.
What? I that kill'd her Husband, and his Father,
To take her in her hearts extreamest hate,
With curses in her mouth, Teares in her eyes,
The bleeding witnesse of my hatred by,
Hauing God, her Conscience, and these bars against me,
And I, no Friends to backe my suite withall,
But the plaine Diuell, and dissembling lookes?
And yet to winne her? All the world to nothing.
Hah!
Hath she forgot alreadie that braue Prince,
Edward, her Lord, whom I (some three monthes since)
Stab'd in my angry mood, at Tewkesbury?
A sweeter, and a louelier Gentleman,
Fram'd in the prodigallity of Nature:
Yong, Valiant, Wise, and (no doubt) right Royal,
The spacious World cannot againe affoord:
And will she yet abase her eyes on me,
That cropt the Golden prime of this sweet Prince,
And made her Widdow to a wofull Bed?
On me, whose All not equals *Edwards* Moytie?
On me, that halts, and am mishapen thus?
My Dukedome, to a Beggerly denier!
I do mistake my person all this while:
Vpon my life she findes (although I cannot)
My selfe to be a maru'llous proper man.
Ile be at Charges for a Looking-glasse,
And entertaine a score or two of Taylors,
To study fashions to adorne my body:
Since I am crept in fauour with my selfe,
I will maintaine it with some little cost.
But first Ile turne yon Fellow in his Graue,
And then returne lamenting to my Loue.
Shine out faire Sunne, till I haue bought a glasse,
That I may see my Shadow as I passe. *exit.*

Scena Tertia.

Enter the Queene Mother, Lord Riuers, and Lord Gray.

Riu. Haue patience Madam, ther's no doubt his Maiesty
Will soone recouer his accustom'd health.
Gray. In that you brooke it ill, it makes him worse,
Therefore for Gods sake entertaine good comfort,
And cheere his Grace with quicke and merry eyes
Qu. If he were dead, what would betide on me?

Gray.

If he were dead, what would betide on me?
Gray. No other harme, but losse of such a Lord.
Qu. The losse of such a Lord, includes all harmes.
Gray. The Heauens haue blest you with a goodly Son,
To be your Comforter, when he is gone.
Qu. Ah! he is yong; and his minority
Is put vnto the trust of *Richard Glouster*,
A man that loues not me, nor none of you.
Riu. Is it concluded he shall be Protector?
Qu. It is determin'd, not concluded yet:
But so it must be, if the King miscarry.

Enter Buckingham and Derby.

Gray. Here comes the Lord of Buckingham & Derby.
Buc. Good time of day vnto your Royall Grace.
Der. God make your Maiesty ioyful, as you haue bin
Qu. The Countesse *Richmond*, good my L. of *Derby*.
To your good prayer, will scarsely say, Amen.
Yet *Derby*, notwithstanding shee's your wife,
And loues not me, be you good Lord assur'd,
I hate not you for her proud arrogance.
Der. I do beseech you, either not beleeue
The enuious slanders of her false Accusers:
Or if she be accus'd on true report,
Beare with her weaknesse, which I thinke proceeds
From wayward sicknesse, and no grounded malice.
Qu. Saw you the King to day my Lord of *Derby*.
Der. But now the Duke of Buckingham and I,
Are come from visiting his Maiesty.
Que. What likelyhood of his amendment Lords.
Buc. Madam good hope, his Grace speaks chearfully.
Qu. God grant him health, did you confer with him?
Buc. I Madam, he desires to make attonement
Betweene the Duke of Glouster, and your Brothers,
And betweene them, and my Lord Chamberlaine,
And sent to warne them to his Royall presence.
Qu. Would all were well, but that will neuer be,
I feare our happinesse is at the height.

Enter Richard.

Rich. They do me wrong, and I will not indure it,
Who is it that complaines vnto the King,
That I (forsooth) am sterne, and loue them not?
By holy *Paul*, they loue his Grace but lightly,
That fill his eares with such dissentious Rumors.
Because I cannot flatter, and looke faire,
Smile in mens faces, smooth, deceiue, and cogge,
Ducke with French nods, and Apish curtesie,
I must be held a rancorous Enemy.
Cannot a plaine man liue, and thinke no harme,
But thus his simple truth must be abus'd,
With silken, slye, insinuating Iackes?
Grey. To who in all this presence speaks your Grace?
Rich. To thee, that hast not Honesty, nor Grace:
When haue I iniur'd thee? When done thee wrong?
Or thee? or thee? or any of your Faction?
A plague vpon you all. His Royall Grace
(Whom God preserue better then you would wish)
Cannot be quiet scarse a breathing while,
But you must trouble him with lewd complaints.
Qu. Brother of Glouster, you mistake the matter:
The King on his owne Royall disposition,
(And not prouok'd by any Sutor else)
Ayming (belike) at your interiour hatred,
That in your outward action shewes it selfe
Against my Children, Brothers, and my Selfe,
Makes him to send, that he may learne the ground.
Rich. I cannot tell, the world is growne so bad,
That Wrens make prey, where Eagles dare not pearch.
Since euerie Iacke became a Gentleman,
There's many a gentle person made a Iacke.
Qu. Come, come, we know your meaning Brother (Glotter
You enuy my aduancement, and my friends:
God grant we neuer may haue neede of you.
Rich. Meane time, God grants that I haue need of you.
Our Brother is imprison'd by your meanes,
My selfe disgrac'd, and the Nobilitie
Held in contempt, while great Promotions
Are daily giuen to ennoble those
That scarse some two dayes since were worth a Noble.
Qu. By him that rais'd me to this carefull height,
From that contented hap which I inioy'd,
I neuer did incense his Maiestie
Against the Duke of *Clarence*, but haue bin
An earnest aduocate to plead for him.
My Lord you do me shamefull iniurie,
Falsely to draw me in these vile suspects.
Rich. You may deny that you were not the meane
Of my Lord *Hastings* late imprisonment.
Riu. She may my Lord, for——
Rich. She may Lord *Riuers*, why who knowes not so?
She may do more sir then denying that:
She may helpe you to many faire preferments,
And then deny her ayding hand therein,
And lay those Honors on your high desert.
What may she not, she may, I marry may she.
Riu. What marry may she?
Ric. What marrie may she? Marrie with a King,
A Batcheller, and a handsome stripling too,
I wis your Grandam had a worser match.
Qu. My Lord of Glouster, I haue too long borne
Your blunt vpbraidings, and your bitter scoffes:
By heauen, I will acquaint his Maiestie
Of those grosse taunts that oft I haue endur'd.
I had rather be a Countrie seruant maide
Then a great Queene, with this condition,
To be so baited, scorn'd, and stormed at,
Small ioy haue I in being Englands Queene.

Enter old Queene Margaret.

Mar. And lesned be that small, God I beseech him,
Thy honor, state, and seate, is due to me.
Rich. What? threat you me with telling of the King?
I will auouch't in presence of the King:
I dare aduenture to be sent to th'Towre.
'Tis time to speake,
My paines are quite forgot.
Margaret. Out Diuell,
I do remember them too well:
Thou kill'dst my Husband *Henrie* in the Tower,
And *Edward* my poore Son, at Tewkesburie.
Rich. Ere you were Queene,
I, or your Husband King:
I was a packe-horse in his great affaires:
A weeder out of his proud Aduersaries,
A liberall rewarder of his Friends,
To royalize his blood, I spent mine owne.
Margaret. I and much better blood
Then his, or thine.

Rich.

Rich. In all which time, you and your Husband *Grey*
Were factious, for the House of *Lancaster*;
And *Riuers*, so were you: Was not your Husband,
In *Margarets* Battaile, at Saint *Albons*, slaine?
Let me put in your mindes, if you forget
What you haue beene ere this, and what you are:
Withall, what I haue beene, and what I am.

Q.M. A murth'rous Villaine, and so still thou art.

Rich. Poore *Clarence* did forsake his Father *Warwicke*,
I, and forswore himselfe (which Iesu pardon.)

Q.M. Which God reuenge.

Rich. To fight on *Edwards* partie, for the Crowne,
And for his meede, poore Lord, he is mewed vp:
I would to God my heart were Flint, like *Edwards*,
Or *Edwards* soft and pittifull, like mine;
I am too childish foolish for this World.

Q.M. High thee to Hell for shame, & leaue this World
Thou Cacodemon, there thy Kingdome is.

Riu. My Lord of Gloster: in those busie dayes,
Which here you vrge, to proue vs Enemies,
We follow'd then our Lord, our Soueraigne King,
So should we you, if you should be our King.

Rich. If I should be? I had rather be a Pedler:
Farre be it from my heart, the thought thereof.

Qu. As little ioy (my Lord) as you suppose
You should enioy, were you this Countries King,
As little ioy you may suppose in me,
That I enioy, being the Queene thereof.

Q.M. A little ioy enioyes the Queene thereof,
For I am shee, and altogether ioylesse:
I can no longer hold me patient.
Heare me, you wrangling Pyrates, that fall out,
In sharing that which you haue pill'd from me:
Which off you trembles not, that lookes on me?
If not, that I am Queene, you bow like Subiects;
Yet that by you depos'd, you quake like Rebells.
Ah gentle Villaine, doe not turne away.

Rich. Foule wrinckled Witch, what mak'st thou in my (sight?

Q.M. But repetition of what thou hast marr'd,
That will I make, before I let thee goe.

Rich. Wert thou not banished, on paine of death?

Q.M. I was: but I doe find more paine in banishment,
Then death can yeeld me here, by my abode.
A Husband and a Sonne thou ow'st to me,
And thou a Kingdome; all of you, allegeance:
This Sorrow that I haue, by right is yours,
And all the Pleasures you vsurpe, are mine.

Rich. The Curse my Noble Father layd on thee,
When thou didst Crown his Warlike Brows with Paper,
And with thy scornes drew'st Riuers from his eyes,
And then to dry them, gau'st the Duke a Clowt,
Steep'd in the faultlesse blood of prettie *Rutland*:
His Curses then, from bitternesse of Soule,
Denounc'd against thee, are all falne vpon thee:
And God, not we, hath plagu'd thy bloody deed.

Qu. So iust is God, to right the innocent.

Hast. O, 'twas the foulest deed to slay that Babe,
And the most mercilesse, that ere was heard of.

Riu. Tyrants themselues wept when it was reported.

Dors. No man but prophecied reuenge for it.

Buck. *Northumberland*, then present, wept to see it.

Q.M. What? were you snarling all before I came,
Ready to catch each other by the throat,
And turne you all your hatred now on me?
Did *Yorkes* dread Curse preuaile so much with Heauen,
That *Henries* death, my louely *Edwards* death,
Their Kingdomes losse, my wofull Banishment,
Should all but answer for that peeuish Brat?
Can Curses pierce the Clouds, and enter Heauen?
Why then giue way dull Clouds to my quick Curses.
Though not by Warre, by Surfet dye your King,
As ours by Murther, to make him a King.
Edward thy Sonne, that now is Prince of Wales,
For *Edward* our Sonne, that was Prince of Wales,
Dye in his youth, by like vntimely violence.
Thy selfe a Queene, for me that was a Queene,
Out-liue thy glory, like my wretched selfe:
Long may'st thou liue, to wayle thy Childrens death,
And see another, as I see thee now,
Deck'd in thy Rights, as thou art stall'd in mine.
Long dye thy happie dayes, before thy death,
And after many length'ned howres of griefe,
Dye neyther Mother, Wife, nor Englands Queene.
Riuers and *Dorset*, you were standers by,
And so wast thou, Lord *Hastings*, when my Sonne
Was stab'd with bloody Daggers: God, I pray him,
That none of you may liue his naturall age,
But by some vnlook'd accident cut off.

Rich. Haue done thy Charme, ỳ hateful wither'd Hagge.

Q.M. And leaue out thee? stay Dog, for ỳ shalt heare me.
If Heauen haue any grieuous plague in store,
Exceeding those that I can wish vpon thee,
O let them keepe it, till thy sinnes be ripe,
And then hurle downe their indignation
On thee, the troubler of the poore Worlds peace.
The Worme of Conscience still begnaw thy Soule,
Thy Friends suspect for Traytors while thou liu'st,
And take deepe Traytors for thy dearest Friends:
No sleepe close vp that deadly Eye of thine,
Vnlesse it be while some tormenting Dreame
Affrights thee with a Hell of ougly Deuills.
Thou eluish mark'd, abortiue rooting Hogge,
Thou that wast seal'd in thy Natiuitie
The slaue of Nature, and the Sonne of Hell:
Thou slander of thy heauie Mothers Wombe,
Thou loathed Issue of thy Fathers Loynes,
Thou Ragge of Honor, thou detested--

Rich. *Margaret.*

Q.M. *Richard.* *Rich.* Ha.

Q.M. I call thee not.

Rich. I cry thee mercie then: for I did thinke,
That thou hadst call'd me all these bitter names.

Q.M. Why so I did, but look'd for no reply.
Oh let me make the Period to my Curse.

Rich. 'Tis done by me, and ends in *Margaret*.

Qu. Thus haue you breath'd your Curse against your self.

Q.M. Poore painted Queen, vain flourish of my fortune,
Why strew'st thou Sugar on that Bottel'd Spider,
Whose deadly Web ensnareth thee about?
Foole, foole, thou whet'st a Knife to kill thy selfe:
The day will come, that thou shalt wish for me,
To helpe thee curse this poysonous Bunch-backt Toade.

Hast. False boding Woman, end thy frantick Curse,
Least to thy harme, thou moue our patience.

Q.M. Foule shame vpon you, you haue all mou'd mine.

Ri. Were you wel seru'd, you would be taught your duty.

Q.M To serue me well, you all should do me duty,
Teach me to be your Queene, and you my Subiects:
O serue me well, and teach your selues that duty.

Dors. Dispute not with her, shee is lunaticke.

Q.M. Peace Master Marquesse, you are malapert,
Your fire-new stampe of Honor is scarce currant.

O that your yong Nobility could iudge
What 'twere to lose it, and be miserable.
They that stand high, haue many blasts to shake them,
And if they fall, they dash themselues to peeces.

Rich. Good counsaile marry, learne it, learne it Marquesse.

Dor. It touches you my Lord, as much as me.

Rich. I, and much more: but I was borne so high:
Our ayerie buildeth in the Cedars top,
And dallies with the winde, and scornes the Sunne.

Mar. And turnes the Sun to shade: alas, alas,
Witnesse my Sonne, now in the shade of death,
Whose bright out-shining beames, thy cloudy wrath
Hath in eternall darknesse folded vp.
Your ayery buildeth in our ayeries Nest:
O God that seest it, do not suffer it,
As it is wonne with blood, lost be it so.

Buc. Peace, peace for shame: If not, for Charity.

Mar. Vrge neither charity, nor shame to me:
Vncharitably with me haue you dealt,
And shamefully my hopes (by you) are butcher'd.
My Charity is outrage, Life my shame,
And in that shame, still liue my sorrowes rage.

Buc. Haue done, haue done.

Mar. O Princely Buckingham, Ile kisse thy hand,
In signe of League and amity with thee:
Now faire befall thee, and thy Noble house:
Thy Garments are not spotted with our blood:
Nor thou within the compasse of my curse.

Buc. Nor no one heere: for Curses neuer passe
The lips of those that breath them in the ayre.

Mar. I will not thinke but they ascend the sky,
And there awake Gods gentle sleeping peace.
O Buckingham, take heede of yonder dogge:
Looke when he fawnes, he bites; and when he bites,
His venom tooth will rankle to the death.
Haue not to do with him, beware of him,
Sinne, death, and hell haue set their markes on him,
And all their Ministers attend on him.

Rich. What doth she say, my Lord of Buckingham.

Buc. Nothing that I respect my gracious Lord.

Mar. What dost thou scorne me
For my gentle counsell?
And sooth the diuell that I warne thee from.
O but remember this another day:
When he shall split thy very heart with sorrow:
And say (poore *Margaret*) was a Prophetesse:
Liue each of you the subiects to his hate,
And he to yours, and all of you to Gods. *Exit.*

Buc. My haire doth stand an end to heare her curses.

Riu. And so doth mine, I muse why she's at libertie.

Rich. I cannot blame her, by Gods holy mother,
She hath had too much wrong, and I repent
My part thereof, that I haue done to her.

Mar I neuer did her any to my knowledge.

Rich. Yet you haue all the vantage of her wrong:
I was too hot, to do somebody good,
That is too cold in thinking of it now:
Marry as for *Clarence*, he is well repayed:
He is frank'd vp to fatting for his paines,
God pardon them, that are the cause thereof.

Riu. A vertuous, and a Christian-like conclusion
To pray for them that haue done scath to vs.

Rich. So do I euer, being well aduis'd.

Speakes to himselfe.

For had I curst now, I had curst my selfe.

Enter Catesby.

Cates. Madam, his Maiesty doth call for you,
And for your Grace, and yours my gracious Lord.

Qu. *Catesby* I come, Lords will you go with mee.

Riu. We wait vpon your Grace.

Exeunt all but Gloster.

Rich. I do the wrong, and first begin to brawle.
The secret Mischeefes that I set abroach,
I lay vnto the greeuous charge of others.
Clarence, who I indeede haue cast in darknesse,
I do beweepe to many simple Gulles,
Namely to *Derby*, *Hastings*, *Buckingham*,
And tell them 'tis the Queene, and her Allies,
That stirre the King against the Duke my Brother.
Now they beleeue it, and withall whet me
To be reueng'd on *Riuers*, *Dorset*, *Grey*.
But then I sigh, and with a peece of Scripture,
Tell them that God bids vs do good for euill:
And thus I cloath my naked Villanie
With odde old ends, stolne forth of holy Writ,
And seeme a Saint, when most I play the deuill.

Enter two murtherers.

But soft, heere come my Executioners,
How now my hardy stout resolued Mates,
Are you now going to dispatch this thing?

Vil. We are my Lord, and come to haue the Warrant,
That we may be admitted where he is.

Ric. Well thought vpon, I haue it heare about me:
When you haue done, repayre to *Crosby* place;
But sirs be sodaine in the execution,
Withall obdurate, do not heare him pleade;
For *Clarence* is well spoken, and perhappes
May moue your hearts to pitty, if you marke him.

Vil. Tut, tut, my Lord, we will not stand to prate,
Talkers are no good dooers, be assur'd:
We go to vse our hands, and not our tongues.

Rich. Your eyes drop Mill-stones, when Fooles eyes fall Teares:
I like you Lads, about your businesse straight.
Go, go, dispatch.

Vil. We will my Noble Lord.

Scena Quarta.

Enter Clarence and Keeper.

Keep. Why lookes your Grace so heauily to day.

Cla. O, I haue past a miserable night,
So full of fearefull Dreames, of vgly sights,
That as I am a Christian faithfull man,
I would not spend another such a night
Though 'twere to buy a world of happy daies:
So full of dismall terror was the time.

Keep. What was your dream my Lord, I pray you tel me

Cla. Me thoughts that I had broken from the Tower,
And was embark'd to crosse to Burgundy,
And in my company my Brother Glouster,
Who from my Cabin tempted me to walke,
Vpon the Hatches: There we look'd toward England,
And cited vp a thousand heauy times,

During the warres of Yorke and Lancaster
That had befalne vs. As we pac'd along
Vpon the giddy footing of the Hatches,
Me thought that Glouster stumbled, and in falling
Strooke me (that thought to stay him) ouer-boord,
Into the tumbling billowes of the maine.
O Lord, me thought what paine it was to drowne,
What dreadfull noise of water in mine eares,
What sights of vgly death within mine eyes.
Me thoughts, I saw a thousand fearfull wrackes:
A thousand men that Fishes gnaw'd vpon:
Wedges of Gold, great Anchors, heapes of Pearle,
Inestimable Stones, vnvalewed Iewels,
All scattred in the bottome of the Sea,
Some lay in dead-mens Sculles, and in the holes
Where eyes did once inhabit, there were crept
(As 'twere in scorne of eyes) reflecting Gemmes,
That woo'd the slimy bottome of the deepe,
And mock'd the dead bones that lay scattred by.

Keep. Had you such leysure in the time of death
To gaze vpon these secrets of the deepe?

Cla. Me thought I had, and often did I striue
To yeeld the Ghost: but still the enuious Flood
Stop'd in my soule, and would not let it forth
To find the empty, vast, and wand'ring ayre:
But smother'd it within my panting bulke,
Who almost burst, to belch it in the Sea.

Keep. Awak'd you not in this sore Agony?

Clar. No, no, my Dreame was lengthen'd after life.
O then, began the Tempest to my Soule.
I past (me thought) the Melancholly Flood,
With that sowre Ferry-man which Poets write of,
Vnto the Kingdome of perpetuall Night.
The first that there did greet my Stranger-soule,
Was my great Father-in-Law, renowned Warwicke,
Who spake alowd: What scourge for Periurie,
Can this darke Monarchy affoord false *Clarence*?
And so he vanish'd. Then came wand'ring by,
A Shadow like an Angell, with bright hayre
Dabbel'd in blood, and he shriek'd out alowd
Clarence is come, false, fleeting, periur'd *Clarence*,
That stabb'd me in the field by Tewkesbury:
Seize on him Furies, take him vnto Torment.
With that (me thought) a Legion of foule Fiends
Inuiron'd me, and howled in mine eares
Such hiddeous cries, that with the very Noise,
I (trembling) wak'd, and for a season after,
Could not beleeue, but that I was in Hell,
Such terrible Impression made my Dreame.

Keep. No maruell Lord, though it affrighted you,
I am affraid (me thinkes) to heare you tell it.

Cla. Ah Keeper, Keeper, I haue done these things
(That now giue euidence against my Soule)
For *Edwards* sake, and see how he requits mee.
O God! if my deepe prayres cannot appease thee,
But thou wilt be aueng'd on my misdeeds,
Yet execute thy wrath in me alone:
O spare my guiltlesse Wife, and my poore children.
Keeper, I prythee sit by me a-while,
My Soule is heauy, and I faine would sleepe.

Keep. I will my Lord, God giue your Grace good rest.

Enter Brakenbury the Lieutenant.

Bra. Sorrow breakes Seasons, and reposing houres,
Makes the Night Morning, and the Noon-tide night:
Princes haue but their Titles for their Glories,
An outward Honor, for an inward Toyle,
And for vnfelt Imaginations
They often feele a world of restlesse Cares:
So that betweene their Titles, and low Name,
There's nothing differs, but the outward fame.

Enter two Murtherers.

1. *Mur.* Ho, who's heere?

Bra. What would'st thou Fellow? And how camm'st thou hither.

2. *Mur.* I would speak with *Clarence*, and I came hither on my Legges.

Bra. What so breefe?

1. 'Tis better (Sir) then to be tedious:
Let him see our Commission, and talke no more. *Reads*

Bra. I am in this, commanded to deliuer
The Noble Duke of *Clarence* to your hands.
I will not reason what is meant heereby,
Because I will be guiltlesse from the meaning.
There lies the Duke asleepe, and there the Keyes.
Ile to the King, and signifie to him,
That thus I haue resign'd to you my charge. *Exit.*

1 You may sir, 'tis a point of wisedome:
Far you well.

2 What, shall we stab him as he sleepes.

1 No: hee'l say 'twas done cowardly, when he wakes

2 Why he shall neuer wake, vntill the great Iudgement day.

1 Why then hee'l say, we stab'd him sleeping.

2 The vrging of that word Iudgement, hath bred a kinde of remorse in me.

1 What? art thou affraid?

2 Not to kill him, hauing a Warrant,
But to be damn'd for killing him, from the which
No Warrant can defend me.

1 I thought thou had'st bin resolute.

2 So I am, to let him liue.

1 Ile backe to the Duke of Glouster, and tell him so.

2 Nay, I prythee stay a little:
I hope this passionate humor of mine, will change,
It was wont to hold me but while one tels twenty.

1 How do'st thou feele thy selfe now?

2 Some certaine dregges of conscience are yet within mee.

1 Remember our Reward, when the deed's done.

2 Come, he dies: I had forgot the Reward.

1 Where's thy conscience now.

2 O, in the Duke of Glousters purse.

1 When hee opens his purse to giue vs our Reward, thy Conscience flyes out.

2 'Tis no matter, let it goe: There's few or none will entertaine it.

1 What if it come to thee againe?

2 Ile not meddle with it, it makes a man a Coward: A man cannot steale, but it accuseth him: A man cannot Sweare, but it Checkes him: A man cannot lye with his Neighbours Wife, but it detects him. 'Tis a blushing shamefac'd spirit, that mutinies in a mans bosome: It filles a man full of Obstacles. It made me once restore a Pursse of Gold that (by chance) I found: It beggars any man that keepes it: It is turn'd out of Townes and Citties for a dangerous thing, and euery man that means to liue well, endeuours to trust to himselfe, and liue vvithout it.

1 'Tis euen now at my elbow, perswading me not to kill the Dkue.

2 Take the diuell in thy minde,and beleeue him not: He would insinuate with thee but to make thee sigh.

1 I am strong fram'd,he cannot preuaile with me.

2 Spoke like a tall man,that respects thy reputation. Come,shall we fall to worke?

1 Take him on the Costard, with the hiltes of thy Sword,and then throw him into the Malmesey-Butte in the next roome.

2 O excellent deuice; and make a sop of him.

1 Soft,he wakes.

2 Strike.

1 No,wee'l reason with him.

Cla. Where art thou Keeper? Giue me a cup of wine.

2 You shall haue Wine enough my Lord anon.

Cla. In Gods name,what art thou?

1 A man,as you are.

Cla. But not as I am Royall.

1 Nor you as we are, Loyall.

Cla. Thy voice is Thunder,but thy looks are humble.

1 My voice is now the Kings,my lookes mine owne.

Cla. How darkly,and how deadly dost thou speake?
Your eyes do menace me: why looke you pale?
Who sent you hither? Wherefore do you come?

2 To,to,to——

Cla. To murther me?

Both. I,I.

Cla. You scarsely haue the hearts to tell me so,
And therefore cannot haue the hearts to do it.
Wherein my Friends haue I offended you?

1 Offended vs you haue not,but the King.

Cla. I shall be reconcil'd to him againe.

2 Neuer my Lord, therefore prepare to dye.

Cla. Are you drawne forth among a world of men
To slay the innocent? What is my offence?
Where is the Euidence that doth accuse me?
What lawfull Quest haue giuen their Verdict vp
Vnto the frowning Iudge? Or who pronounc'd
The bitter sentence of poore *Clarence* death,
Before I be conuict by course of Law?
To threaten me with death, is most vnlawfull.
I charge you, as you hope for any goodnesse,
That you depart,and lay no hands on me:
The deed you vndertake is damnable.

1 What we will do,we do vpon command.

2 And he that hath commanded,is our King.

Cla. Erroneous Vassals,the great King of Kings
Hath in the Table of his Law commanded
That thou shalt do no murther. Will you then
Spurne at his Edict,and fulfill a Mans?
Take heed: for he holds Vengeance in his hand,
To hurle vpon their heads that breake his Law.

2 And that same Vengeance doth he hurle on thee,
For false Forswearing,and for murther too:
Thou did'st receiue the Sacrament, to fight
In quarrell of the House of Lancaster.

1 And like a Traitor to the name of God,
Did'st breake that Vow,and with thy treacherous blade,
Vnrip'st the Bowels of thy Sou'raignes Sonne.

2 Whom thou was't sworne to cherish and defend.

1 How canst thou vrge Gods dreadfull Law to vs,
When thou hast broke it in such deere degree?

Cla. Alas! for whose sake did I that ill deede?
For *Edward*, for my Brother, for his sake.
He sends you not to murther me for this:
For in that sinne, he is as deepe as I.
If God will be auenged for the deed,
O know you yet,he doth it publiquely,
Take not the quarrell from his powrefull arme:
He needs no indirect,or lawlesse course,
To cut off those that haue offended him.

1 Who made thee then a bloudy minister,
When gallant springing braue *Plantagenet*,
That Princely Nouice was strucke dead by thee?

Cla. My Brothers loue,the Diuell,and my Rage.

1 Thy Brothers Loue,our Duty, and thy Faults,
Prouoke vs hither now,to slaughter thee.

Cla. If you do loue my Brother,hate not me:
I am his Brother, and I loue him well.
If you are hyr'd for meed, go backe againe,
And I will send you to my Brother Glouster:
Who shall reward you better for my life,
Then *Edward* will for tydings of my death.

2 You are deceiu'd,
Your Brother Glouster hates you.

Cla. Oh no,he loues me, and he holds me deere:
Go you to him from me.

1 I so we will.

Cla. Tell him,when that our Princely Father Yorke,
Blest his three Sonnes with his victorious Arme,
He little thought of this diuided Friendship:
Bid Glouster thinke on this, and he will weepe.

1 I Milstones,as he lessoned vs to weepe.

Cla. O do not slander him,for he is kinde.

1 Right,as Snow in Haruest:
Come, you deceiue your selfe,
'Tis he that sends vs to destroy you heere.

Cla. It cannot be, for he bewept my Fortune,
And hugg'd me in his armes,and swore with sobs,
That he would labour my deliuery.

1 Why so he doth, when he deliuers you
From this earths thraldome, to the ioyes of heauen.

2 Make peace with God,for you must die my Lord.

Cla. Haue you that holy feeling in your soules,
To counsaile me to make my peace with God,
And are you yet to your owne soules so blinde,
That you will warre with God,by murd'ring me.
O sirs consider, they that set you on
To do this deede, will hate you for the deede.

2 What shall we do?

Clar. Relent,and saue your soules:
Which of you, if you were a Princes Sonne,
Being pent from Liberty,as I am now,
If two such murtherers as your selues came to you,
Would not intreat for life, as you would begge
Were you in my distresse.

1 Relent? no: 'Tis cowardly and womanish.

Cla. Not to relent, is beastly,sauage,diuellish
My Friend, I spy some pitty in thy lookes:
O, if thine eye be not a Flatterer,
Come thou on my side, and intreate for mee,
A begging Prince,what begger pitties not.

2 Looke behinde you,my Lord.

1 Take that,and that,if all this will not do, *Stabs him.*
Ile drowne you in the Malmesey-But within. *Exit.*

2 A bloody deed,and desperately dispatcht:
How faine (like *Pilate*) would I wash my hands
Of this most greeuous murther. *Enter 1.Murtherer*

1 How now? what mean'st thou that thou help'st me not? By Heauen the Duke shall know how slacke you haue beene.

2.Mur. I would he knew that I had sau'd his brother,
Take thou the Fee, and tell him what I say,
For I repent me that the Duke is slaine. *Exit.*

1.Mur. So do not I: go Coward as thou art.
Well, Ile go hide the body in some hole,
Till that the Duke giue order for his buriall:
And when I haue my meede, I will away,
For this will out, and then I must not stay. *Exit*

Actus Secundus. Scœna Prima.

Flourish.
Enter the King sicke, the Queene, Lord Marquesse Dorset, Riuers, Hastings, Catesby, Buckingham, Wooduill.

King. Why so: now haue I done a good daies work.
You Peeres, continue this vnited League:
I, euery day expect an Embassage
From my Redeemer, to redeeme me hence.
And more to peace my soule shall part to heauen,
Since I haue made my Friends at peace on earth.
Dorset and *Riuers*, take each others hand,
Dissemble not your hatred, Sweare your loue.

Riu. By heauen, my soule is purg'd from grudging hate
And with my hand I seale my true hearts Loue.

Hast. So thriue I, as I truly sweare the like.

King. Take heed you dally not before your King,
Lest he that is the supreme King of Kings
Confound your hidden falshood, and award
Either of you to be the others end.

Hast. So prosper I, as I sweare perfect loue.

Ri. And I, as I loue *Hastings* with my heart,

King. Madam, your selfe is not exempt from this:
Nor you Sonne *Dorset*, *Buckingham* nor you;
You haue bene factious one against the other.
Wife, loue Lord *Hastings*, let him kisse your hand,
And what you do, do it vnfeignedly.

Qu. There *Hastings*, I will neuer more remember
Our former hatred, so thriue I, and mine.

King. *Dorset*, imbrace him:
Hastings, loue Lord Marquesse.

Dor. This interchange of loue, I heere protest
Vpon my part, shall be inuiolable.

Hast. And so sweare I.

King. Now Princely *Buckingham*, seale ỹ this league
With thy embracements to my wiues Allies,
And make me happy in your vnity.

Buc. When euer *Buckingham* doth turne his hate
Vpon your Grace, but with all dutious loue,
Doth cherish you, and yours, God punish me
With hate in those where I expect most loue,
When I haue most need to imploy a Friend,
And most assured that he is a Friend,
Deepe, hollow, treacherous, and full of guile,
Be he vnto me: This do I begge of heauen,
When I am cold in loue, to you, or yours. *Embrace*

King. A pleasing Cordiall, Princely *Buckingham*
Is this thy Vow, vnto my sickely heart:
There wanteth now our Brother Gloster heere,
To make the blessed period of this peace.

Buc. And in good time,
Heere comes Sir *Richard Ratcliffe*, and the Duke.

Enter Ratcliffe, and Gloster.

Rich. Good morrow to my Soueraigne King & Queen
And Princely Peeres, a happy time of day.

King. Happy indeed, as we haue spent the day:
Gloster, we haue done deeds of Charity,
Made peace of enmity, faire loue of hate,
Betweene these swelling wrong incensed Peeres.

Rich. A blessed labour my most Soueraigne Lord:
Among this Princely heape, if any heere
By false intelligence, or wrong surmize
Hold me a Foe: If I vnwillingly, or in my rage,
Haue ought committed that is hardly borne,
To any in this presence, I desire
To reconcile me to his Friendly peace:
'Tis death to me to be at enmitie:
I hate it, and desire all good mens loue,
First Madam, I intreate true peace of you,
Which I will purchase with my dutious seruice.
Of you my Noble Cosin Buckingham,
If euer any grudge were lodg'd betweene vs.
Of you and you, Lord *Riuers* and of *Dorset*,
That all without desert haue frown'd on me:
Of you Lord *Wooduill*, and Lord *Scales* of you,
Dukes, Earles, Lords, Gentlemen, indeed of all.
I do not know that Englishman aliue,
With whom my soule is any iot at oddes,
More then the Infant that is borne to night:
I thanke my God for my Humility.

Qu. A holy day shall this be kept heereafter:
I would to God all strifes were well compounded.
My Soueraigne Lord, I do beseech your Highnesse
To take our Brother *Clarence* to your Grace.

Rich Why Madam, haue I offred loue for this,
To be so flowted in this Royall presence?
Who knowes not that the gentle Duke is dead? *They*
You do him iniurie to scorne his Coarse. *all start.*

King. Who knowes not he is dead?
Who knowes he is?

Qu. All-seeing heauen, what a world is this?

Buc. Looke I so pale Lord *Dorset*, as the rest?

Dor. I my good Lord, and no man in the presence,
But his red colour hath forsooke his cheekes.

King. Is *Clarence* dead? The Order was reuerst.

Rich. But he (poore man) by your first order dyed,
And that a winged Mercurie did beare:
Some tardie Cripple bare the Countermand,
That came too lagge to see him buried.
God grant, that some lesse Noble, and lesse Loyall,
Neerer in bloody thoughts, and not in blood,
Deserue not worse then wretched *Clarence* did,
And yet go currant from Suspition.

Enter Earle of Derby.

Der. A boone my Soueraigne for my seruice done.

King. I prethee peace, my soule is full of sorrow.

Der. I will not rise, vnlesse your Highnes heare me.

King. Then say at once, what is it thou requests.

Der. The forfeit (Soueraigne) of my seruants life,
Who slew to day a Riotous Gentleman,
Lately attendant on the Duke of Norfolke.

King. Haue I a tongue to doome my Brothers death?
And shall that tongue giue pardon to a slaue?
My Brother kill'd no man, his fault was Thought,
And yet his punishment was bitter death.

Who

Who sued to me for him? Who (in my wrath)
Kneel'd and my feet, and bid me be aduis'd?
Who spoke ot Brother-hood? who spoke of loue?
Who told me how the poore soule did forsake
The mighty Warwicke, and did fight for me?
Who told me in the field at Tewkesbury,
When Oxford had me downe, he rescued me:
And said deare Brother liue, and be a King?
Who told me, when we both lay in the Field,
Frozen (almost) to death, how he did lap me
Euen in his Garments, and did giue himselfe
(All thin and naked) to the numbe cold night?
All this from my Remembrance, brutish wrath
Sinfully pluckt, and not a man of you
Had so much grace to put it in my minde.
But when your Carters, or your wayting Vassalls
Haue done a drunken Slaughter, and defac'd
The precious Image of our deere Redeemer,
You straight are on your knees for Pardon, pardon,
And I (vniustly too) must grant it you.
But for my Brother, not a man would speake,
Nor I (vngracious) speake vnto my selfe
For him poore Soule. The proudest of you all,
Haue bin beholding to him in his life:
Yet none of you, would once begge for his life.
O God! I feare thy iustice will take hold
On me, and you; and mine, and yours for this.
Come *Hastings* helpe me to my Closset.
Ah poore *Clarence*. *Exeunt some with K. & Queen.*

Rich. This is the fruits of rashnes: Markt you not,
How that the guilty Kindred of the Queene
Look'd pale, when they did heare of *Clarence* death.
O! they did vrge it still vnto the King,
God will reuenge it. Come Lords will you go,
To comfort *Edward* with our company.

Buc. We wait vpon your Grace. *exeunt.*

Scena Secunda.

Enter the old Dutchesse of Yorke, with the two children of Clarence.

Edw. Good Grandam tell vs, is our Father dead?

Dutch. No Boy.

Daugh. Why do weepe so oft? And beate your Brest?
And cry, O *Clarence*, my vnhappy Sonne.

Boy. Why do you looke on vs, and shake your head,
And call vs Orphans, Wretches, Castawayes,
If that our Noble Father were aliue?

Dut. My pretty Cosins, you mistake me both,
I do lament the sicknesse of the King,
As loath to lose him, not your Fathers death:
It were lost sorrow to waile one that's lost.

Boy. Then you conclude, (my Grandam) he is dead:
The King mine Vnckle is too blame for it.
God will reuenge it, whom I will importune
With earnest prayers, all to that effect.

Daugh. And so will I.

Dut. Peace children peace, the King doth loue you wel.
Incapeable, and shallow Innocents,
You cannot guesse who caus'd your Fathers death.

Boy. Grandam we can: for my good Vnkle Gloster
Told me, the King prouok'd to it by the Queene,
Deuis'd impeachments to imprison him;
And when my Vnckle told me so, he wept,
And pittied me, and kindly kist my cheeke:
Bad me rely on him, as on my Father,
And he would loue me deerely as a childe.

Dut. Ah! that Deceit should steale such gentle shape,
And with a vertuous Vizor hide deepe vice.
He is my sonne, I, and therein my shame,
Yet from my dugges, he drew not this deceit.

Boy. Thinke you my Vnkle did dissemble Grandam?

Dut. I Boy.

Boy. I cannot thinke it. Hearke, what noise is this?

Enter the Queene with her haire about her ears, Riuers & Dorset after her.

Qu. Ah! who shall hinder me to waile and weepe?
To chide my Fortune, and torment my Selfe.
Ile ioyne with blacke dispaire against my Soule,
And to my selfe, become an enemie.

Dut. What meanes this Scene of rude impatience?

Qu. To make an act of Tragicke violence.
Edward my Lord, thy Sonne, our King is dead.
Why grow the Branches, when the Roote is gone?
Why wither not the leaues that want their sap?
If you will liue, Lament: if dye, be breefe,
That our swift-winged Soules may catch the Kings,
Or like obedient Subiects follow him,
To his new Kingdome of nere-changing night.

Dut. Ah so much interest haue in thy sorrow,
As I had Title in thy Noble Husband:
I haue bewept a worthy Husbands death,
And liu'd with looking on his Images:
But now two Mirrors of his Princely semblance,
Are crack'd in pieces, by malignant death,
And I for comfort, haue but one false Glasse,
That greeues me, when I see my shame in him.
Thou art a Widdow: yet thou art a Mother,
And hast the comfort of thy Children left,
But death hath snatch'd my Husband from mine Armes,
And pluckt two Crutches from my feeble hands,
Clarence, and *Edward*. O, what cause haue I,
(Thine being but a moity of my moane)
To ouer-go thy woes, and drowne thy cries.

Boy. Ah Aunt! you wept not for our Fathers death:
How can we ayde you with our Kindred teares?

Daugh. Our fatherlesse distresse was left vnmoan'd,
Your widdow-dolour, likewise be vnwept.

Qu. Giue me no helpe in Lamentation,
I am not barren to bring forth complaints:
All Springs reduce their currents to mine eyes,
That I being gouern'd by the waterie Moone,
May send forth plenteous teares to drowne the World.
Ah, for my Husband, for my deere Lord *Edward*.

Chil. Ah for our Father, for our deere Lord *Clarence*.

Dut. Alas for both, both mine *Edward* and *Clarence*.

Qu. What stay had I but *Edward*, and hee's gone?

Chil. What stay had we but *Clarence*? and he's gone

Dut. What stayes had I, but they? and they are gone.

Qu. Was neuer widdow had so deere a losse.

Chil. Were neuer Orphans had so deere a losse.

Dut. Was neuer Mother had so deere a losse.
Alas! I am the Mother of these Greefes,
Their woes are parcell'd, mine is generall.
She for an *Edward* weepes, and so do I:

I for a *Clarence* weepes, so doth not shee:
These Babes for *Clarence* weepe, so do not they.
Alas! you three, on me threefold distrest:
Power all your teares, I am your sorrowes Nurse,
And I will pamper it with Lamentation.

Dor. Comfort deere Mother, God is much displeas'd,
That you take with vnthankfulnesse his doing.
In common worldly things, 'tis call'd vngratefull,
With dull vnwillingnesse to repay a debt,
Which with a bounteous hand was kindly lent:
Much more to be thus opposite with heauen,
For it requires the Royall debt it lent you.

Riuers. Madam, bethinke you like a carefull Mother
Of the young Prince your sonne: send straight for him,
Let him be Crown'd, in him your comfort liues.
Drowne desperate sorrow in dead *Edwards* graue,
And plant your ioyes in liuing *Edwards* Throne.

Enter Richard, Buckingham, Derbie, Hastings, and Ratcliffe.

Rich. Sister haue comfort, all of vs haue cause
To waile the dimming of our shining Starre:
But none can helpe our harmes by wayling them.
Madam, my Mother, I do cry you mercie,
I did not see your Grace. Humbly on my knee,
I craue your Blessing.

Dut. God blesse thee, and put meeknes in thy breast,
Loue Charity, Obedience, and true Dutie.

Rich. Amen, and make me die a good old man,
That is the butt-end of a Mothers blessing;
I maruell that her Grace did leaue it out.

Buc. You clowdy-Princes, & hart-sorowing-Peeres,
That beare this heauie mutuall loade of Moane,
Now cheere each other, in each others Loue:
Though we haue spent our Haruest of this King,
We are to reape the Haruest of his Sonne.
The broken rancour of your high-swolne hates,
But lately splinter'd, knit, and ioyn'd together,
Must gently be preseru'd, cherisht and kept:
Me seemeth good, that with some little Traine,
Forthwith from Ludlow, the young Prince be fet
Hither to London, to be crown'd our King.

Riuers. Why with some little Traine,
My Lord of Buckingham?

Buc. Marrie my Lord, least by a multitude,
The new-heal'd wound of Malice should breake out,
Which would be so much the more dangerous,
By how much the estate is greene, and yet vngouern'd.
Where euery Horse beares his commanding Reine,
And may direct his course as please himselfe,
As well the feare of harme, as harme apparant,
In my opinion, ought to be preuented.

Rich. I hope the King made peace with all of vs,
And the compact is firme, and true in me.

Riu. And so in me, and so (I thinke) in all.
Yet since it is but greene, it should be put
To no apparant likely-hood of breach,
Which haply by much company might be vrg'd:
Therefore I say with Noble Buckingham,
That it is meete so few should fetch the Prince.

Hast. And so say I.

Rich. Then be it so, and go we to determine
Who they shall be that strait shall poste to London.
Madam, and you my Sister, will you go
To giue your censures in this businesse. *Exeunt.*

Manet Buckingham, and Richard.

Buc. My Lord, who euer iournies to the Prince,
For God sake let not vs two stay at home:
For by the way, Ile sort occasion,
As Index to the story we late talk'd of,
To part the Queenes proud Kindred from the Prince.

Rich. My other selfe, my Counsailes Consistory,
My Oracle, My Prophet, my deere Cosin,
I, as a childe, will go by thy direction,
Toward London then, for wee'l not stay behinde. *Exeunt*

Scena Tertia.

Enter one Citizen at one doore, and another at the other.

1.*Cit.* Good morrow Neighbour, whether away so fast?

2.*Cit.* I promise you, I scarsely know my selfe:
Heare you the newes abroad?

1. Yes, that the King is dead.

2. Ill newes byrlady, seldome comes the better:
I feare, I feare, 'twill proue a giddy world.

Enter another Citizen.

3. Neighbours, God speed.

1. Giue you good morrow sir.

3. Doth the newes hold of good king *Edwards* death?

2. I sir, it is too true, God helpe the while.

3. Then Masters looke to see a troublous world.

1. No, no, by Gods good grace, his Son shall reigne.

3. Woe to that Land that's gouern'd by a Childe.

2. In him there is a hope of Gouernment,
Which in his nonage, counsell vnder him,
And in his full and ripened yeares, himselfe
No doubt shall then, and till then gouerne well.

1. So stood the State, when *Henry* the sixt
Was crown'd in Paris, but at nine months old.

3. Stood the State so? No, no, good friends, God wot
For then this Land was famously enrich'd
With politike graue Counsell; then the King
Had vertuous Vnkles to protect his Grace.

1. Why so hath this, both by his Father and Mother.

3. Better it were they all came by his Father:
Or by his Father there were none at all:
For emulation, who shall now be neerest,
Will touch vs all too neere, if God preuent not.
O full of danger is the Duke of Glouster,
And the Queenes Sons, and Brothers, haught and proud:
And were they to be rul'd, and not to rule,
This sickly Land, might solace as before.

1. Come, come, we feare the worst: all will be well.

3. When Clouds are seen, wisemen put on their clokes;
When great leaues fall, then Winter is at hand;
When the Sun sets, who doth not looke for night?
Vntimely stormes, makes men expect a Dearth:
All may be well; but if God sort it so,
'Tis more then we deserue, or I expect.

2. Truly, the hearts of men are full of feare:
You cannot reason (almost) with a man,
That lookes not heauily, and full of dread.

3. Before the dayes of Change, still is it so,
By a diuine instinct, mens mindes mistrust

Ensuing

Purſuing danger: as by proofe we ſee
The Water ſwell before a boyſt'rous ſtorme:
But leaue it all to God. Whither away?
2 Marry we were ſent for to the Iuſtices.
3 And ſo was I: Ile beare you company. *Exeunt.*

Scena Quarta.

Enter Arch-biſhop, yong Yorke, the Queene, and the Dutcheſſe

Arch. Laſt night I heard they lay at Stony Stratford,
And at Northampton they do reſt to night:
To morrow, or next day, they will be heere.
Dut. I long with all my heart to ſee the Prince:
I hope he is much growne ſince laſt I ſaw him.
Qu. But I heare no, they ſay my ſonne of Yorke
Ha's almoſt ouertane him in his growth.
Yorke. I Mother, but I would not haue it ſo.
Dut. Why my good Coſin, it is good to grow.
Yor. Grandam, one night as we did ſit at Supper,
My Vnkle *Riuers* talk'd how I did grow
More then my Brother. I, quoth my Vnkle Glouſter,
Small Herbes haue grace, great Weeds do grow apace.
And ſince, me thinkes I would not grow ſo faſt,
Becauſe ſweet Flowres are ſlow, and Weeds make haſt.
Dut. Good faith, good faith, the ſaying did not hold
In him that did obiect the ſame to thee.
He was the wretched'ſt thing when he was yong,
So long a growing, and ſo leyſurely,
That if his rule were true, he ſhould be gracious.
Yor. And ſo no doubt he is, my gracious Madam.
Dut. I hope he is, but yet let Mothers doubt.
Yor. Now by my troth, if I had beene remembred,
I could haue giuen my Vnkles Grace, a flout,
To touch his growth, neerer then he toucht mine.
Dut. How my yong Yorke,
I prythee let me heare it.
Yor. Marry (they ſay) my Vnkle grew ſo faſt,
That he could gnaw a cruſt at two houres old,
'Twas full two yeares ere I could get a tooth.
Grandam, this would haue beene a byting Ieſt.
Dut. I prythee pretty Yorke, who told thee this?
Yor. Grandam, his Nurſſe.
Dut. His Nurſe? why ſhe was dead, ere ẏ waſt borne.
Yor. If 'twere not ſhe, I cannot tell who told me.
Qu. A parlous Boy: go too, you are too ſhrew'd.
Dut. Good Madam, be not angry with the Childe.
Qu. Pitchers haue eares.

Enter a Meſſenger.

Arch. Heere comes a Meſſenger: What Newes?
Meſ. Such newes my Lord, as greeues me to report.
Qu. How doth the Prince?
Meſ. Well Madam, and in health.
Dut. What is thy Newes?
Meſ. Lord *Riuers*, and Lord *Grey*,
Are ſent to Pomfret, and with them,
Sir *Thomas Vaughan*, Priſoners.
Dut. Who hath committed them?
Meſ. The mighty Dukes, *Glouſter* and *Buckingham*.
Arch. For what offence?
Meſ. The ſumme of all I can, I haue diſclos'd:
Why, or for what, the Nobles were committed,
Is all vnknowne to me, my gracious Lord.
Qu. Aye me! I ſee the ruine of my Houſe:
The Tyger now hath ſeiz'd the gentle Hinde,
Inſulting Tiranny beginnes to Iutt
Vpon the innocent and aweleſſe Throne:
Welcome Deſtruction, Blood, and Maſſacre,
I ſee (as in a Map) the end of all.
Dut. Accurſed, and vnquiet wrangling dayes,
How many of you haue mine eyes beheld?
My Husband loſt his life, to get the Crowne,
And often vp and downe my ſonnes were toſt
For me to ioy, and weepe, their gaine and loſſe.
And being ſeated, and Domeſticke broyles
Cleane ouer-blowne, themſelues the Conquerors,
Make warre vpon themſelues, Brother to Brother;
Blood to blood, ſelfe againſt ſelfe: O prepoſterous
And franticke outrage, end thy damned ſpleene,
Or let me dye, to looke on earth no more.
Qu. Come, come my Boy, we will to Sanctuary.
Madam, farwell.
Dut. Stay, I will go with you.
Qu. You haue no cauſe.
Arch. My gracious Lady go,
And thether beare your Treaſure and your Goodes,
For my part, Ile reſigne vnto your Grace
The Seale I keepe, and ſo betide to me,
As well I tender you, and all of yours.
Go, Ile conduct you to the Sanctuary. *Exeunt*

Actus Tertius. Scœna Prima.

The Trumpets ſound.
Enter yong Prince, the Dukes of Glouceſter, and Buckingham, Lord Cardinall, with others.

Buc. Welcome ſweete Prince to London,
To your Chamber.
Rich. Welcome deere Coſin, my thoughts Soueraign
The wearie way hath made you Melancholly.
Prin. No Vnkle, but our croſſes on the way,
Haue made it tedious, wearíſome, and heauie.
I want more Vnkles heere to welcome me.
Rich. Sweet Prince, the vntainted vertue of your yeers
Hath not yet diu'd into the Worlds deceit:
No more can you diſtinguiſh of a man,
Then of his outward ſhew, which God he knowes,
Seldome or neuer iumpeth with the heart.
Thoſe Vnkles which you want, were dangerous:
Your Grace attended to their Sugred words,
But look'd not on the poyſon of their hearts:
God keepe you from them, and from ſuch falſe Friends.
Prin. God keepe me from falſe Friends,
But they were none.
Rich. My Lord, the Maior of London comes to greet you.

Enter Lord Maior.

Lo. Maior. God bleſſe your Grace, with health and happie dayes.
Prin. I thanke you, good my Lord, and thank you all:

I thought my Mother, and my Brother *Yorke*,
Would long, ere this, haue met vs on the way.
Fie, what a Slug is *Hastings*, that he comes not
To tell vs, whether they will come, or no.

Enter Lord Hastings.

Buck. And in good time, heere comes the sweating Lord.

Prince. Welcome, my Lord: what, will our Mother come?

Hast. On what occasion God he knowes, not I;
The Queene your Mother, and your Brother *Yorke*,
Haue taken Sanctuarie: The tender Prince
Would faine haue come with me, to meet your Grace,
But by his Mother was perforce with-held.

Buck. Fie, what an indirect and peeuish course
Is this of hers? Lord Cardinall, will your Grace
Perswade the Queene, to send the Duke of Yorke
Vnto his Princely Brother presently?
If she denie, Lord *Hastings* goe with him,
And from her iealous Armes pluck him perforce.

Card. My Lord of Buckingham, if my weake Oratorie
Can from his Mother winne the Duke of Yorke,
Anon expect him here: but if she be obdurate
To milde entreaties, God forbid
We should infringe the holy Priuiledge
Of blessed Sanctuarie: not for all this Land,
Would I be guiltie of so great a sinne.

Buck. You are too senceless obstinate, my Lord,
Too ceremonious, and traditionall.
Weigh it but with the grossenesse of this Age,
You breake not Sanctuarie, in seizing him:
The benefit thereof is alwayes granted
To those, whose dealings haue deseru'd the place,
And those who haue the wit to clayme the place:
This Prince hath neyther claym'd it, nor deseru'd it,
And therefore, in mine opinion, cannot haue it.
Then taking him from thence, that is not there,
You breake no Priuiledge, nor Charter there:
Oft haue I heard of Sanctuarie men,
But Sanctuarie children, ne're till now.

Card. My Lord, you shall o're-rule my mind for once.
Come on, Lord *Hastings*, will you goe with me?

Hast. I goe, my Lord. *Exit Cardinall and Hastings.*

Prince. Good Lords, make all the speedie hast you may.
Say, Vnckle *Glocester*, if our Brother come,
Where shall we soiourne, till our Coronation?

Glo. Where it think'st best vnto your Royall selfe.
If I may counsaile you, some day or two
Your Highnesse shall repose you at the Tower:
Then where you please, and shall be thought most fit
For your best health, and recreation.

Prince. I doe not like the Tower, of any place:
Did *Iulius Cæsar* build that place, my Lord?

Buck. He did, my gracious Lord, begin that place,
Which since, succeeding Ages haue re-edify'd.

Prince. Is it vpon record? or else reported
Successiuely from age to age, he built it?

Buck. Vpon record, my gracious Lord.

Prince. But say, my Lord, it were not registred,
Me thinkes the truth should liue from age to age,
As 'twere retayl'd to all posteritie,
Euen to the generall ending day.

Glo. So wise, so young, they say doe neuer liue long.

Prince. What say you, Vnckle?

Glo. I say, without Characters, Fame liues long.
Thus, like the formall Vice, Iniquitie,
I morallize two meanings in one word.

Prince. That *Iulius Cæsar* was a famous man,
With what his Valour did enrich his Wit,
His Wit set downe, to make his Valour liue:
Death makes no Conquest of his Conqueror,
For now he liues in Fame, though not in Life.
Ile tell you what, my Cousin *Buckingham*.

Buck. What, my gracious Lord?

Prince. And if I liue vntill I be a man,
Ile win our ancient Right in France againe,
Or dye a Souldier, as I liu'd a King.

Glo. Short Summers lightly haue a forward Spring.

Enter young Yorke, Hastings, and Cardinall.

Buck. Now in good time, heere comes the Duke of Yorke.

Prince. *Richard* of Yorke, how fares our Noble Brother?

Yorke. Well, my deare Lord, so must I call you now.

Prince. I, Brother, to our griefe, as it is yours:
Too late he dy'd, that might haue kept that Title,
Which by his death hath lost much Maiestie.

Glo. How fares our Cousin, Noble Lord of Yorke?

Yorke. I thanke you, gentle Vnckle. O my Lord,
You said, that idle Weeds are fast in growth:
The Prince, my Brother, hath out-growne me farre.

Glo. He hath, my Lord.

Yorke. And therefore is he idle?

Glo. Oh my faire Cousin, I must not say so.

Yorke. Then he is more beholding to you, then I.

Glo. He may command me as my Soueraigne,
But you haue power in me, as in a Kinsman.

Yorke. I pray you, Vnckle, giue me this Dagger.

Glo. My Dagger, little Cousin? with all my heart.

Prince. A Begger, Brother?

Yorke. Of my kind Vnckle, that I know will giue,
And being but a Toy, which is no griefe to giue.

Glo. A greater gift then that, Ile giue my Cousin.

Yorke. A greater gift? O, that's the Sword to it.

Glo. I, gentle Cousin, were it light enough.

Yorke. O then I see, you will part but with light gifts,
In weightier things you'le say a Begger nay.

Glo. It is too weightie for your Grace to weare.

Yorke. I weigh it lightly, were it heauier.

Glo. What, would you haue my Weapon, little Lord?

Yorke. I would that I might thanke you, as, as, you call me.

Glo. How?

Yorke. Little.

Prince. My Lord of Yorke will still be crosse in talke:
Vnckle, your Grace knowes how to beare with him.

Yorke. You meane to beare me, not to beare with me:
Vnckle, my Brother mockes both you and me,
Because that I am little, like an Ape,
He thinkes that you should beare me on your shoulders.

Buck. With what a sharpe prouided wit he reasons:
To mittigate the scorne he giues his Vnckle,
He prettily and aptly taunts himselfe:
So cunning, and so young, is wonderfull.

Glo. My Lord, wilt please you passe along?
My selfe, and my good Cousin *Buckingham*,
Will to your Mother, to entreat of her
To meet you at the Tower, and welcome you.

Yorke. What,

Yorke. What, will you goe vnto the Tower, my Lord?
Prince. My Lord Protector will haue it so.
Yorke. I shall not sleepe in quiet at the Tower.
Glo. Why, what should you feare?
Yorke. Marry, my Vnckle *Clarence* angry Ghost:
My Grandam told me he was murther'd there.
Prince. I feare no Vnckles dead.
Glo. Nor none that liue, I hope.
Prince. And if they liue, I hope I need not feare.
But come my Lord: and with a heauie heart,
Thinking on them, goe I vnto the Tower.
A Senet. Exeunt Prince, Yorke, Hastings, and Dorset.

Manet Richard, Buckingham, and Catesby.

Buck. Thinke you, my Lord, this little prating *Yorke*
Was not incensed by his subtile Mother,
To taunt and scorne you thus opprobriously?
Glo. No doubt, no doubt: Oh 'tis a perillous Boy,
Bold, quicke, ingenious, forward, capable:
Hee is all the Mothers, from the top to toe.
Buck. Well, let them rest: Come hither *Catesby*,
Thou art sworne as deepely to effect what we intend,
As closely to conceale what we impart:
Thou know'st our reasons vrg'd vpon the way.
What think'st thou? is it not an easie matter,
To make *William* Lord *Hastings* of our minde,
For the installment of this Noble Duke
In the Seat Royall of this famous Ile?
Cates. He for his fathers sake so loues the Prince,
That he will not be wonne to ought against him.
Buck. What think'st thou then of *Stanley*? Will not hee?
Cates. Hee will doe all in all as *Hastings* doth.
Buck. Well then, no more but this:
Goe gentle *Catesby*, and as it were farre off,
Sound thou Lord *Hastings*,
How he doth stand affected to our purpose,
And summon him to morrow to the Tower,
To sit about the Coronation.
If thou do'st finde him tractable to vs,
Encourage him, and tell him all our reasons:
If he be leaden, ycie, cold, vnwilling,
Be thou so too, and so breake off the talke,
And giue vs notice of his inclination:
For we to morrow hold diuided Councels,
Wherein thy selfe shalt highly be employ'd.
Rich. Commend me to Lord *William*: tell him *Catesby*,
His ancient Knot of dangerous Aduersaries
To morrow are let blood at Pomfret Castle,
And bid my Lord, for ioy of this good newes,
Giue Mistresse *Shore* one gentle Kisse the more.
Buck. Good *Catesby*, goe effect this businesse soundly.
Cates. My good Lords both, with all the heed I can.
Rich. Shall we heare from you, *Catesby*, ere we sleepe?
Cates. You shall, my Lord.
Rich. At *Crosby* House, there shall you find vs both.
Exit Catesby.
Buck. Now, my Lord,
What shall wee doe, if wee perceiue
Lord *Hastings* will not yeeld to our Complots?
Rich Chop off his Head:
Something wee will determine:
And looke when I am King, clayme thou of me
The Earledome of Hereford, and all the moueables
Whereof the King, my Brother, was possest.
Buck. Ile clayme that promise at your Graces hand.
Rich. And looke to haue it yeelded with all kindnesse.
Come, let vs suppe betimes, that afterwards
Wee may digest our complots in some forme.
Exeunt.

Scena Secunda.

Enter a Messenger to the Doore of Hastings.

Mess. My Lord, my Lord.
Hast. Who knockes:
Mess. One from the Lord *Stanley*.
Hast. What is't a Clocke?
Mess. Vpon the stroke of foure.

Enter Lord Hastings.

Hast. Cannot my Lord *Stanley* sleepe these tedious Nights?
Mess. So it appeares, by that I haue to say:
First, he commends him to your Noble selfe.
Hast. What then?
Mess. Then certifies your Lordship, that this Night
He dreamt, the Bore had rased off his Helme:
Besides, he sayes there are two Councels kept;
And that may be determin'd at the one,
Which may make you and him to rue at th'other.
Therefore he sends to know your Lordships pleasure,
If you will presently take Horse with him,
And with all speed post with him toward the North,
To shun the danger that his Soule diuines.
Hast. Goe fellow, goe, returne vnto thy Lord,
Bid him not feare the seperated Councell:
His Honor and my selfe are at the one,
And at the other, is my good friend *Catesby*;
Where nothing can proceede, that toucheth vs,
Whereof I shall not haue intelligence:
Tell him his Feares are shallow, without instance.
And for his Dreames, I wonder hee's so simple,
To trust the mock'ry of vnquiet slumbers.
To flye the Bore, before the Bore pursues,
Were to incense the Bore to follow vs,
And make pursuit, where he did meane no chase.
Goe, bid thy Master rise, and come to me,
And we will both together to the Tower,
Where he shall see the Bore will vse vs kindly.
Mess. Ile goe, my Lord, and tell him what you say.
Exit.

Enter Catesby.

Cates. Many good morrowes to my Noble Lord.
Hast. Good morrow *Catesby*, you are early stirring:
What newes, what newes, in this our tott'ring State?
Cates. It is a reeling World indeed, my Lord:
And I beleeue will neuer stand vpright,
Till *Richard* weare the Garland of the Realme.
Hast. How weare the Garland?
Doest thou meane the Crowne?
Cates. I, my good Lord,
Hast. Ile haue this Crown of mine cut frō my shoulders,
Before Ile see the Crowne so foule mis-plac'd:
But canst thou guesse, that he doth ayme at it?
Cates. I,

Cates. I,on my life, and hopes to find you forward,
Vpon his partie,for the gaine thereof:
And thereupon he sends you this good newes,
That this same very day your enemies,
The Kindred of the Queene,must dye at Pomfret.

Hast. Indeed I am no mourner for that newes,
Because they haue beene still my aduersaries:
But,that Ile giue my voice on *Richards* side,
To barre my Masters Heires in true Descent,
God knowes I will not doe it,to the death.

Cates. God keepe your Lordship in that gracious minde.

Hast. But I shall laugh at this a twelue-month hence,
That they which brought me in my Masters hate,
I liue to looke vpon their Tragedie.
Well *Catesby*,ere a fort-night make me older,
Ile send some packing,that yet thinke not on't.

Cates. 'Tis a vile thing to dye,my gracious Lord,
When men are vnprepar'd,and looke not for it.

Hast. O monstrous,monstrous! and so falls it out
With *Riuers,Vaughan,Grey*: and so 'twill doe
With some men else,that thinke themselues as safe
As thou and I,who(as thou know'st) are deare
To Princely *Richard*,and to *Buckingham*.

Cates. The Princes both make high account of you,
For they account his Head vpon the Bridge.

Hast. I know they doe,and I haue well deseru'd it.

Enter Lord Stanley.

Come on,come on,where is your Bore-speare man?
Feare you the Bore,and goe so vnprouided?

Stan. My Lord good morrow,good morrow *Catesby*:
You may ieast on, but by the holy Rood,
I doe not like these seuerall Councels,I.

Hast. My Lord,I hold my Life as deare as yours,
And neuer in my dayes,I doe protest,
Was it so precious to me,as 'tis now:
Thinke you,but that I know our state secure,
I would be so triumphant as I am?

*Sta.*The Lords at Pomfret,whē they rode from London,
Were iocund,and suppos'd their states were sure,
And they indeed had no cause to mistrust:
But yet you see,how soone the Day o're-cast.
This sudden stab of Rancour I misdoubt:
Pray God (I say) I proue a needlesse Coward.
What,shall we toward the Tower? the day is spent.

Hast. Come,come,haue with you:
Wot you what,my Lord,
To day the Lords you talke of,are beheaded.

*Sta.*They,for their truth,might better wear their Heads,
Then some that haue accus'd them,weare their Hats.
But come,my Lord,let's away.

Enter a Pursuiuant.

Hast. Goe on before,Ile talke with this good fellow.
Exit Lord Stanley,and Catesby.
How now,Sirrha? how goes the World with thee?

*Purs.*The better,that your Lordship please to aske.

Hast. I tell thee man,'tis better with me now,
Then when thou met'st me last,where now we meet:
Then was I going Prisoner to the Tower,
By the suggestion of the Queenes Allyes.
But now I tell thee (keepe it to thy selfe)
This day those Enemies are put to death,
And I in better state then ere I was.

Purs. God hold it, to your Honors good content.

Hast. Gramercie fellow: there,drinke that for me.
Throwes him his Purse.

Purs. I thanke your Honor. *Exit Pursuiuant.*

Enter a Priest.

Priest. Well met,my Lord,I am glad to see your Honor.

Hast. I thanke thee,good Sir *Iohn*,with all my heart.
I am in your debt,for your last Exercise:
Come the next Sabboth,and I will content you.

Priest. Ile wait vpon your Lordship.

Enter Buckingham.

Buc. What,talking with a Priest,Lord Chamberlaine?
Your friends at Pomfret,they doe need the Priest,
Your Honor hath no shriuing worke in hand.

Hast. Good faith,and when I met this holy man,
The men you talke of,came into my minde.
What,goe you toward the Tower?

Buc. I doe,my Lord,but long I cannot stay there:
I shall returne before your Lordship,thence.

Hast. Nay like enough,for I stay Dinner there.

Buc. And Supper too,although thou know'st it not.
Come,will you goe?

Hast. Ile wait vpon your Lordship. *Exeunt.*

Scena Tertia.

Enter Sir Richard Ratcliffe,with Halberds,carrying the Nobles to death at Pomfret.

Riuers. Sir *Richard Ratcliffe*,let me tell thee this,
To day shalt thou behold a Subiect die,
For Truth,for Dutie,and for Loyaltie.

Grey. God blesse the Prince from all the Pack of you,
A Knot you are,of damned Blood-suckers.

Vaugh. You liue,that shall cry woe for this heere-after.

Rat. Dispatch,the limit of your Liues is out.

Riuers. O Pomfret,Pomfret! O thou bloody Prison!
Fatall and ominous to Noble Peeres:
Within the guiltie Closure of thy Walls,
Richard the Second here was hackt to death:
And for more slander to thy dismall Seat,
Wee giue to thee our guiltlesse blood to drinke.

Grey. Now *Margarets* Curse is falne vpon our Heads,
When shee exclaim'd on *Hastings*,you,and I,
For standing by,when *Richard* stab'd her Sonne.

Riuers. Then curs'd shee *Richard*,
Then curs'd shee *Buckingham*,
Then curs'd shee *Hastings*. Oh remember God,
To heare her prayer for them,as now for vs:
And for my Sister,and her Princely Sonnes,
Be satisfy'd,deare God,with our true blood,
Which,as thou know'st,vniustly must be spilt.

Rat. Make haste,the houre of death is expiate.

Riuers. Come *Grey*,come *Vaughan*,let vs here embrace,
Farewell,vntill we meet againe in Heauen.

Exeunt.

Scæna Quarta.

Enter Buckingham, Darby, Hastings, Bishop of Ely, Norfolke, Ratcliffe, Louell, with others, at a Table.

Hast. Now Noble Peeres, the cause why we are met,
Is to determine of the Coronation:
In Gods Name speake, when is the Royall day?
Buck. Is all things ready for the Royall time?
Darb. It is, and wants but nomination.
Ely. To morrow then I iudge a happie day.
Buck. Who knowes the Lord Protectors mind herein?
Who is most inward with the Noble Duke?
Ely. Your Grace, we thinke, should soonest know his minde.
Buck. We know each others Faces: for our Hearts,
He knowes no more of mine, then I of yours,
Or I of his, my Lord, then you of mine:
Lord *Hastings*, you and he are neere in loue.
Hast. I thanke his Grace, I know he loues me well:
But for his purpose in the Coronation,
I haue not sounded him, nor he deliuer'd
His gracious pleasure any way therein:
But you, my Honorable Lords, may name the time,
And in the Dukes behalfe Ile giue my Voice,
Which I presume hee'le take in gentle part.

Enter Gloucester.

Ely. In happie time, here comes the Duke himselfe.
Rich. My Noble Lords, and Cousins all, good morrow:
I haue beene long a sleeper: but I trust,
My absence doth neglect no great designe,
Which by my presence might haue beene concluded.
Buck. Had you not come vpon your Q my Lord,
William, Lord *Hastings*, had pronounc'd your part;
I meane your Voice, for Crowning of the King.
Rich. Then my Lord *Hastings*, no man might be bolder,
His Lordship knowes me well, and loues me well.
My Lord of Ely, when I was last in Holborne,
I saw good Strawberries in your Garden there,
I doe beseech you, send for some of them.
Ely. Mary and will, my Lord, with all my heart.
Exit Bishop.
Rich. Cousin of Buckingham, a word with you.
Catesby hath sounded *Hastings* in our businesse,
And findes the testie Gentleman so hot,
That he will lose his Head, ere giue consent
His Masters Child, as worshipfully he tearmes it,
Shall lose the Royaltie of Englands Throne.
Buck. Withdraw your selfe a while, Ile goe with you.
Exeunt.
Darb. We haue not yet set downe this day of Triumph:
To morrow, in my iudgement, is too sudden,
For I my selfe am not so well prouided,
As else I would be, were the day prolong'd.

Enter the Bishop of Ely.

Ely. Where is my Lord, the Duke of Gloster?
I haue sent for these Strawberries.
Ha. His Grace looks chearfully & smooth this morning,
There's some conceit or other likes him well,
When that he bids good morrow with such spirit.
I thinke there's neuer a man in Christendome
Can lesser hide his loue, or hate, then hee,
For by his Face straight shall you know his Heart.
Darb. What of his Heart perceiue you in his Face,
By any liuelyhood he shew'd to day?
Hast. Mary, that with no man here he is offended:
For were he, he had shewne it in his Lookes.

Enter Richard, and Buckingham.

Rich. I pray you all, tell me what they deserue,
That doe conspire my death with diuellish Plots
Of damned Witchcraft, and that haue preuail'd
Vpon my Body with their Hellish Charmes.
Hast. The tender loue I beare your Grace, my Lord,
Makes me most forward, in this Princely presence,
To doome th'Offendors, whosoe're they be:
I say, my Lord, they haue deserued death.
Rich. Then be your eyes the witnesse of their euill.
Looke how I am bewitch'd: behold, mine Arme
Is like a blasted Sapling, wither'd vp:
And this is *Edwards* Wife, that monstrous Witch,
Consorted with that Harlot, Strumpet *Shore*,
That by their Witchcraft thus haue marked me.
Hast. If they haue done this deed, my Noble Lord.
Rich If? thou Protector of this damned Strumpet,
Talk'st thou to me of Ifs: thou art a Traytor
Off with his Head; now by Saint *Paul* I sweare,
I will not dine, vntill I see the same.
Louell and *Ratcliffe*, looke that it be done: *Exeunt.*
The rest that loue me, rise, and follow me.

Manet Louell and Ratcliffe, with the Lord Hastings.

Hast. Woe, woe for England, not a whit for me,
For I, too fond, might haue preuented this:
Stanley did dreame, the Bore did rowse our Helmes,
And I did scorne it, and disdaine to flye:
Three times to day my Foot-Cloth-Horse did stumble,
And started, when he look'd vpon the Tower,
As loth to beare me to the slaughter-house.
O now I need the Priest, that spake to me
I now repent I told the Pursuiuant,
As too triumphing, how mine Enemies
To day at Pomfret bloodily were butcher'd,
And I my selfe secure, in grace and fauour.
Oh *Margaret*, *Margaret*, now thy heauie Curse
Is lighted on poore *Hastings* wretched Head.
Ra. Come, come, dispatch, the Duke would be at dinner:
Make a short Shrift, he longs to see your Head.
Hast. O momentarie grace of mortall men,
Which we more hunt for, then the grace of God!
Who builds his hope in ayre of your good Lookes,
Liues like a drunken Sayler on a Mast,
Readie with euery Nod to tumble downe,
Into the fatall Bowels of the Deepe.
Lou. Come, come, dispatch, 'tis bootlesse to exclaime.
Hast. O bloody *Richard:* miserable England,
I prophecie the fearefull'st time to thee,
That euer wretched Age hath look'd vpon.
Come, lead me to the Block, beare him my Head,
They smile at me, who shortly shall be dead.
Exeunt.

Enter Richard, and Buckingham, in rotten Armour, maruellous ill-fauoured.

Richard. Come Cousin,
Canst thou quake, and change thy colour,
Murther thy breath in middle of a word,
And then againe begin, and stop againe,
As if thou were distraught, and mad with terror?

Buck. Tut, I can counterfeit the deepe Tragedian,
Speake, and looke backe, and prie on euery side,
Tremble and start at wagging of a Straw:
Intending deepe suspition, gastly Lookes
Are at my seruice, like enforced Smiles;
And both are readie in their Offices,
At any time to grace my Stratagemes.
But what, is *Catesby* gone?

Rich. He is, and see he brings the Maior along.

Enter the Maior, and Catesby.

Buck. Lord Maior.

Rich. Looke to the Draw-Bridge there.

Buck. Hearke, a Drumme.

Rich. *Catesby*, o're-looke the Walls.

Buck. Lord Maior, the reason we haue sent.

Rich. Looke back, defend thee, here are Enemies.

Buck. God and our Innocencie defend, and guard vs.

Enter Louell and Ratcliffe, with Hastings Head.

Rich. Be patient, they are friends: *Ratcliffe*, and *Louell.*

Louell. Here is the Head of that ignoble Traytor,
The dangerous and vnsuspected *Hastings.*

Rich. So deare I lou'd the man, that I must weepe:
I tooke him for the plainest harmelesse Creature,
That breath'd vpon the Earth, a Christian.
Made him my Booke, wherein my Soule recorded
The Historie of all her secret thoughts.
So smooth he dawb'd his Vice with shew of Vertue,
That his apparant open Guilt omitted,
I meane, his Conuersation with *Shores* Wife,
He liu'd from all attainder of suspects.

Buck. Well, well, he was the couertst sheltred Traytor
That euer liu'd.
Would you imagine, or almost beleeue,
Wert not, that by great preseruation
We liue to tell it, that the subtill Traytor
This day had plotted, in the Councell-House,
To murther me, and my good Lord of Gloster.

Maior. Had he done so?

Rich. What? thinke you we are Turkes, or Infidels?
Or that we would, against the forme of Law,
Proceed thus rashly in the Villaines death,
But that the extreme perill of the case,
The Peace of England, and our Persons safetie,
Enforc'd vs to this Execution.

Maior. Now faire befall you, he deseru'd his death,
And your good Graces both haue well proceeded,
To warne false Traytors from the like Attempts.

Buck. I neuer look'd for better at his hands,
After he once fell in with Mistresse *Shore:*
Yet had we not determin'd he should dye,
Vntill your Lordship came to see his end,
Which now the louing haste of these our friends,
Something against our meanings, haue preuented;
Because, my Lord, I would haue had you heard
The Traytor speake, and timorously confesse
The manner and the purpose of his Treasons:
That you might well haue signify'd the same
Vnto the Citizens, who haply may
Misconster vs in him, and wayle his death.

Ma. But, my good Lord, your Graces words shal serue,
As well as I had seene, and heard him speake:
And doe not doubt, right Noble Princes both,
But Ile acquaint our dutious Citizens
With all your iust proceedings in this case.

Rich. And to that end we wish'd your Lordship here,
T'auoid the Censures of the carping World.

Buck. Which since you come too late of our intent,
Yet witnesse what you heare we did intend:
And so, my good Lord Maior, we bid farwell.

Exit Maior.

Rich. Goe after, after, Cousin *Buckingham.*
The Maior towards Guild-Hall hyes him in all poste:
There, at your meetest vantage of the time,
Inferre the Bastardie of *Edwards* Children:
Tell them, how *Edward* put to death a Citizen,
Onely for saying, he would make his Sonne
Heire to the Crowne, meaning indeed his House,
Which, by the Signe thereof, was tearmed so.
Moreouer, vrge his hatefull Luxurie,
And beastiall appetite in change of Lust,
Which stretcht vnto their Seruants, Daughters, Wiues,
Euen where his raging eye, or sauage heart,
Without controll, lusted to make a prey.
Nay, for a need, thus farre come neere my Person:
Tell them, when that my Mother went with Child
Of that insatiate *Edward*; Noble *Yorke*,
My Princely Father, then had Warres in France,
And by true computation of the time,
Found, that the Issue was not his begot:
Which well appeared in his Lineaments,
Being nothing like the Noble Duke, my Father:
Yet touch this sparingly, as 'twere farre off,
Because, my Lord, you know my Mother liues.

Buck. Doubt not, my Lord, Ile play the Orator,
As if the Golden Fee, for which I plead,
Were for my selfe: and so, my Lord, adue.

Rich. If you thriue wel, bring them to Baynards Castle,
Where you shall finde me well accompanied
With reuerend Fathers, and well-learned Bishops.

Buck. I goe, and towards three or foure a Clocke
Looke for the Newes that the Guild-Hall affoords.

Exit Buckingham.

Rich. Goe *Louell* with all speed to Doctor *Shaw*,
Goe thou to Fryer *Peuker*, bid them both
Meet me within this houre at Baynards Castle. *Exit.*
Now will I goe to take some priuie order,
To draw the Brats of *Clarence* out of sight,
And to giue order, that no manner person
Haue any time recourse vnto the Princes. *Exeunt.*

Enter a Scriuener.

Scr. Here is the Indictment of the good Lord *Hastings*,
Which in a set Hand fairely is engross'd,
That it may be to day read o're in *Paules.*
And marke how well the sequell hangs together:
Eleuen houres I haue spent to write it ouer,
For yester-night by *Catesby* was it sent me,
The Precedent was full as long a doing,
And yet within these fiue houres *Hastings* liu'd,
Vntainted, vnexamin'd, free, at libertie.
Here's a good World the while.
Who is so grosse, that cannot see this palpable deuice?

Yet who so bold, but sayes he sees it not?
Bad is the World, and all will come to nought,
When such ill dealing must be seene in thought. *Exit.*

Enter Richard and Buckingham at seuerall Doores.

Rich. How now, how now, what say the Citizens?
Buck. Now by the holy Mother of our Lord,
The Citizens are mum, say not a word.
Rich. Toucht you the Bastardie of *Edwards* Children?
Buck. I did, with his Contract with Lady *Lucy*,
And his Contract by Deputie in France,
Th'vnsatiate greedinesse of his desire,
And his enforcement of the Citie Wiues,
His Tyrannie for Trifles, his owne Bastardie,
As being got, your Father then in France,
And his resemblance, being not like the Duke.
Withall, I did inferre your Lineaments,
Being the right *Idea* of your Father,
Both in your forme, and Noblenesse of Minde:
Layd open all your Victories in Scotland,
Your Discipline in Warre, Wisdome in Peace,
Your Bountie, Vertue, faire Humilitie:
Indeed, left nothing fitting for your purpose,
Vntoucht, or sleightly handled in discourse.
And when my Oratorie drew toward end,
I bid them that did loue their Countries good,
Cry, God saue *Richard*, Englands Royall King.
Rich. And did they so?
Buck. No, so God helpe me, they spake not a word,
But like dumbe Statues, or breathing Stones,
Star'd each on other, and look'd deadly pale:
Which when I saw, I reprehended them,
And ask'd the Maior, what meant this wilfull silence?
His answer was, the people were not vsed
To be spoke to, but by the Recorder.
Then he was vrg'd to tell my Tale againe:
Thus sayth the Duke, thus hath the Duke inferr'd,
But nothing spoke, in warrant from himselfe.
When he had done, some followers of mine owne,
At lower end of the Hall, hurld vp their Caps,
And some tenne voyces cry'd, God saue King *Richard*:
And thus I tooke the vantage of those few.
Thankes gentle Citizens, and friends, quoth I,
This generall applause, and chearefull showt,
Argues your wisdome, and your loue to *Richard*:
And euen here brake off, and came away.
Rich. What tongue-lesse Blockes were they,
Would they not speake?
Will not the Maior then, and his Brethren, come?
Buck. The Maior is here at hand: intend some feare,
Be not you spoke with, but by mightie suit:
And looke you get a Prayer-Booke in your hand,
And stand betweene two Church-men, good my Lord,
For on that ground Ile make a holy Descant:
And be not easily wonne to our requests,
Play the Maids part, still answer nay, and take it.
Rich. I goe: and if you plead as well for them,
As I can say nay to thee for my selfe,
No doubt we bring it to a happie issue.
Buck. Go, go vp to the Leads, the Lord Maior knocks.

Enter the Maior, and Citizens.

Welcome, my Lord, I dance attendance here,
I thinke the Duke will not be spoke withall.

Enter Catesby.

Buck. Now *Catesby*, what sayes your Lord to my request?
Catesby. He doth entreat your Grace, my Noble Lord,
To visit him to morrow, or next day:
He is within, with two right reuerend Fathers,
Diuinely bent to Meditation,
And in no Worldly suites would he be mou'd,
To draw him from his holy Exercise.
Buck. Returne, good *Catesby*, to the gracious Duke,
Tell him, my selfe, the Maior and Aldermen,
In deepe designes, in matter of great moment,
No lesse importing then our generall good,
Are come to haue some conference with his Grace.
Catesby. Ile signifie so much vnto him straight. *Exit.*
Buck. Ah ha, my Lord, this Prince is not an *Edward*,
He is not lulling on a lewd Loue-Bed,
But on his Knees, at Meditation:
Not dallying with a Brace of Curtizans,
But meditating with two deepe Diuines
Not sleeping, to engrosse his idle Body,
But praying, to enrich his watchfull Soule.
Happie were England, would this vertuous Prince
Take on his Grace the Soueraigntie thereof.
But sure I feare we shall not winne him to it.
Maior. Marry God defend his Grace should say vs nay.
Buck. I feare he will: here *Catesby* comes againe.

Enter Catesby.

Now *Catesby*, what sayes his Grace?
Catesby. He wonders to what end you haue assembled
Such troopes of Citizens, to come to him,
His Grace not being warn'd thereof before:
He feares, my Lord, you meane no good to him.
Buck. Sorry I am, my Noble Cousin should
Suspect me, that I meane no good to him:
By Heauen, we come to him in perfit loue,
And so once more returne, and tell his Grace. *Exit.*
When holy and deuout Religious men
Are at their Beades, 'tis much to draw them thence,
So sweet is zealous Contemplation.

Enter Richard aloft, betweene two Bishops.

Maior. See where his Grace stands, tweene two Clergie men.
Buck. Two Props of Vertue, for a Christian Prince,
To stay him from the fall of Vanitie:
And see a Booke of Prayer in his hand,
True Ornaments to know a holy man.
Famous *Plantagenet*, most gracious Prince,
Lend fauourable eare to our requests,
And pardon vs the interruption
Of thy Deuotion, and right Christian Zeale.
Rich. My Lord, there needes no such Apologie:
I doe beseech your Grace to pardon me,
Who earnest in the seruice of my God,
Deferr'd the visitation of my friends.
But leauing this, what is your Graces pleasure?
Buck. Euen that (I hope) which pleaseth God aboue,
And all good men, of this vngouern'd Ile.
Rich. I doe suspect I haue done some offence,
That seemes disgracious in the Cities eye,
And that you come to reprehend my ignorance.

Buck. You haue, my Lord:
Would it might please your Grace,
On our entreaties, to amend your fault.

Rich. Else wherefore breathe I in a Christian Land.

Buck. Know then, it is your fault, that you resigne
The Supreme Seat, the Throne Maiesticall,
The Sceptred Office of your Ancestors,
Your State of Fortune, and your Deaw of Birth,
The Lineall Glory of your Royall House,
To the corruption of a blemisht Stock;
Whiles in the mildnesse of your sleepie thoughts,
Which here we waken to our Countries good,
The Noble Ile doth want his proper Limmes:
His Face defac'd with skarres of Infamie,
His Royall Stock graft with ignoble Plants,
And almost shouldred in the swallowing Gulfe
Of darke Forgetfulnesse, and deepe Obliuion.
Which to recure, we heartily solicite
Your gracious selfe to take on you the charge
And Kingly Gouernment of this your Land:
Not as Protector, Steward, Substitute,
Or lowly Factor, for anothers gaine;
But as successiuely, from Blood to Blood,
Your Right of Birth, your Empyrie, your owne.
For this, consorted with the Citizens,
Your very Worshipfull and louing friends,
And by their vehement instigation,
In this iust Cause come I to moue your Grace.

Rich. I cannot tell, if to depart in silence,
Or bitterly to speake in your reproofe,
Best fitteth my Degree, or your Condition.
If not to answer, you might haply thinke,
Tongue-ty'd Ambition, not replying, yeelded
To beare the Golden Yoake of Soueraigntie,
Which fondly you would here impose on me.
If to reproue you for this suit of yours,
So season'd with your faithfull loue to me,
Then on the other side I check'd my friends.
Therefore to speake, and to auoid the first,
And then in speaking, not to incurre the last,
Definitiuely thus I answer you.
Your loue deserues my thankes, but my desert
Vnmeritable, shunnes your high request.
First, if all Obstacles were cut away,
And that my Path were euen to the Crowne,
As the ripe Reuenue, and due of Birth:
Yet so much is my pouertie of spirit,
So mightie, and so manie my defects,
That I would rather hide me from my Greatnesse,
Being a Barke to brooke no mightie Sea;
Then in my Greatnesse couet to be hid,
And in the vapour of my Glory smother'd.
But God be thank'd, there is no need of me,
And much I need to helpe you, were there need:
The Royall Tree hath left vs Royall Fruit,
Which mellow'd by the stealing howres of time,
Will well become the Seat of Maiestie,
And make (no doubt) vs happy by his Reigne.
On him I lay that, you would lay on me,
The Right and Fortune of his happie Starres,
Which God defend that I should wring from him.

Buck. My Lord, this argues Conscience in your Grace,
But the respects thereof are nice, and triuiall,
All circumstances well considered.
You say, that *Edward* is your Brothers Sonne,
So say we too, but not by *Edwards* Wife:
For first was he contract to Lady *Lucie*,
Your Mother liues a Witnesse to his Vow;
And afterward by substitute betroth'd
To *Bona*, Sister to the King of France.
These both put off, a poore Petitioner,
A Care-cras'd Mother to a many Sonnes,
A Beautie-waining, and distressed Widow,
Euen in the after-noone of her best dayes,
Made prize and purchase of his wanton Eye,
Seduc'd the pitch, and height of his degree,
To base declension, and loath'd Bigamie.
By her, in his vnlawfull Bed, he got
This *Edward*, whom our Manners call the Prince.
More bitterly could I expostulate,
Saue that for reuerence to some aliue,
I giue a sparing limit to my Tongue.
Then good, my Lord, take to your Royall selfe
This proffer'd benefit of Dignitie:
If not to blesse vs and the Land withall,
Yet to draw forth your Noble Ancestrie
From the corruption of abusing times,
Vnto a Lineall true deriued course.

Maior. Do good my Lord, your Citizens entreat you.

Buck. Refuse not, mightie Lord, this proffer'd loue.

Catesb. O make them ioyfull, grant their lawfull suit.

Rich. Alas, why would you heape this Care on me?
I am vnfit for State, and Maiestie:
I doe beseech you take it not amisse,
I cannot, nor I will not yeeld to you.

Buck. If you refuse it, as in loue and zeale,
Loth to depose the Child, your Brothers Sonne,
As well we know your tendernesse of heart,
And gentle, kinde, effeminate remorse,
Which we haue noted in you to your Kindred,
And egally indeede to all Estates:
Yet know, where you accept our suit, or no,
Your Brothers Sonne shall neuer reigne our King,
But we will plant some other in the Throne,
To the disgrace and downe-fall of your House:
And in this resolution here we leaue you.
Come Citizens, we will entreat no more. *Exeunt.*

Catesb. Call him againe, sweet Prince, accept their suit:
If you denie them, all the Land will rue it.

Rich. Will you enforce me to a world of Cares.
Call them againe, I am not made of Stones,
But penetrable to your kinde entreaties,
Albeit against my Conscience and my Soule.

Enter Buckingham, and the rest.

Cousin of Buckingham, and sage graue men,
Since you will buckle fortune on my back,
To beare her burthen, where I will or no.
I must haue patience to endure the Load:
But if black Scandall, or foule-fac'd Reproach,
Attend the sequell of your Imposition,
Your meere enforcement shall acquittance me
From all the impure blots and staynes thereof;
For God doth know, and you may partly see,
How farre I am from the desire of this.

Maior. God blesse your Grace, wee see it, and will say it.

Rich. In saying so, you shall but say the truth.

Buck. Then I salute you with this Royall Title,
Long liue King *Richard*, Englands worthie King.

All. Amen.

Buck. To morrow may it please you to be Crown'd.

Rich. Euen when you please, for you will haue it so.

Buck. To

Buck. To morrow then we will attend your Grace,
And so most ioyfully we take our leaue.

Rich. Come, let vs to our holy Worke againe.
Farewell my Cousins, farewell gentle friends. *Exeunt.*

Actus Quartus. Scena Prima.

Enter the Queene, Anne Duchesse of Gloucester, the Duchesse of Yorke, and Marquesse Dorset.

Duch.Yorke. Who meetes vs heere?
My Neece *Plantagenet,*
Led in the hand of her kind Aunt of Gloster?
Now, for my Life, shee's wandring to the Tower,
On pure hearts loue, to greet the tender Prince.
Daughter, well met.

Anne. God giue your Graces both, a happie
And a ioyfull time of day.

Qu. As much to you, good Sister: whither away?

Anne. No farther then the Tower, and as I guesse,
Vpon the like deuotion as your selues,
To gratulate the gentle Princes there.

Qu. Kind Sister thankes, wee'le enter all together:

Enter the Lieutenant.

And in good time, here the Lieutenant comes.
Master Lieutenant, pray you, by your leaue,
How doth the Prince, and my young Sonne of *Yorke*?

Lieu. Right well, deare Madame: by your patience,
I may not suffer you to visit them,
The King hath strictly charg'd the contrary.

Qu. The King? who's that?

Lieu. I meane, the Lord Protector.

Qu. The Lord protect him from that Kingly Title.
Hath he set bounds betweene their loue, and me?
I am their Mother, who shall barre me from them?

Duch.Yorke. I am their Fathers Mother, I will see them.

Anne. Their Aunt I am in law, in loue their Mother:
Then bring me to their sights, Ile beare thy blame,
And take thy Office from thee, on my perill.

Lieu. No, Madame, no; I may not leaue it so:
I am bound by Oath, and therefore pardon me.
Exit Lieutenant.

Enter Stanley.

Stanley. Let me but meet you Ladies one howre hence,
And Ile salute your Grace of Yorke as Mother,
And reuerend looker on of two faire Queenes.
Come Madame, you must straight to Westminster,
There to be crowned *Richards* Royall Queene.

Qu. Ah, cut my Lace asunder,
That my pent heart may haue some scope to beat,
Or else I swoone with this dead-killing newes.

Anne. Despightfull tidings, O vnpleasing newes.

Dors. Be of good cheare: Mother, how fares your Grace?

Qu. O *Dorset*, speake not to me, get thee gone,
Death and Destruction dogges thee at thy heeles,
Thy Mothers Name is ominous to Children.
If thou wilt out-strip Death, goe crosse the Seas,
And liue with *Richmond*, from the reach of Hell.
Goe hye thee, hye thee from this slaughter-house,
Lest thou encreasse the number of the dead,
And make me dye the thrall of *Margarets* Curse,
Nor Mother, Wife, nor Englands counted Queene.

Stanley. Full of wise care, is this your counsaile, Madame:
Take all the swift aduantage of the howres:
You shall haue Letters from me to my Sonne,
In your behalfe, to meet you on the way:
Be not ta'ne tardie by vnwise delay.

Duch. Yorke. O ill dispersing Winde of Miserie,
O my accursed Wombe, the Bed of Death:
A Cockatrice hast thou hatcht to the World,
Whose vnauoided Eye is murtherous.

Stanley. Come, Madame, come, I in all haste was sent.

Anne. And I with all vnwillingnesse will goe.
O would to God, that the inclusiue Verge
Of Golden Mettall, that must round my Brow,
Were red hot Steele, to seare me to the Braines,
Anoynted let me be with deadly Venome,
And dye ere men can say, God saue the Queene.

Qu. Goe, goe, poore soule, I enuie not thy glory,
To feed my humor, wish thy selfe no harme.

Anne. No: why? When he that is my Husband now,
Came to me, as I follow'd *Henries* Corse,
When scarce the blood was well washt from his hands,
Which issued from my other Angell Husband,
And that deare Saint, which then I weeping follow'd:
O, when I say I look'd on *Richards* Face,
This was my Wish: Be thou (quoth I) accurst,
For making me, so young, so old a Widow:
And when thou wed'st, let sorrow haunt thy Bed;
And be thy Wife, if any be so mad,
More miserable, by the Life of thee,
Then thou hast made me, by my deare Lords death.
Loe, ere I can repeat this Curse againe,
Within so small a time, my Womans heart
Grossely grew captiue to his honey words,
And prou'd the subiect of mine owne Soules Curse,
Which hitherto hath held mine eyes from rest:
For neuer yet one howre in his Bed
Did I enioy the golden deaw of sleepe,
But with his timorous Dreames was still awak'd.
Besides, he hates me for my Father *Warwicke*,
And will (no doubt) shortly be rid of me.

Qu. Poore heart adieu, I pittie thy complaining.

Anne. No more, then with my soule I mourne for yours.

Dors. Farewell, thou wofull welcommer of glory.

Anne. Adieu, poore soule, that tak'st thy leaue of it.

Du.Y. Go thou to *Richmond*, & good fortune guide thee,
Go thou to *Richard*, and good Angels tend thee,
Go thou to Sanctuarie, and good thoughts possesse thee,
I to my Graue, where peace and rest lye with mee.
Eightie odde yeeres of sorrow haue I seene,
And each howres ioy wrackt with a weeke of teene.

Qu. Stay, yet looke backe with me vnto the Tower.
Pitty, you ancient Stones, those tender Babes,
Whom Enuie hath immur'd within your Walls,
Rough Cradle for such little prettie ones,
Rude ragged Nurse, old sullen Play-fellow,
For tender Princes: vse my Babies well;
So foolish Sorrowes bids your Stones farewell.
Exeunt.

Scena Secunda.

Sound a Sennet. Enter Richard in pompe, Buckingham, Catesby, Ratcliffe, Louel.

Rich. Stand all apart. Cousin of Buckingham.
Buck. My gracious Soueraigne.
Rich. Giue me thy hand. *Sound.*
Thus high, by thy aduice, and thy assistance,
Is King *Richard* seated:
But shall we weare these Glories for a day?
Or shall they last, and we reioyce in them?
Buck. Still liue they, and for euer let them last.
Rich. Ah *Buckingham*, now doe I play the Touch,
To trie if thou be currant Gold indeed:
Young *Edward* liues, thinke now what I would speake.
Buck. Say on my louing Lord.
Rich. Why *Buckingham*, I say I would be King.
Buck. Why so you are, my thrice-renowned Lord.
Rich. Ha? am I King? 'tis so: but *Edward* liues.
Buck. True, Noble Prince.
Rich. O bitter consequence!
That *Edward* still should liue true Noble Prince.
Cousin, thou wast not wont to be so dull,
Shall I be plaine? I wish the Bastards dead,
And I would haue it suddenly perform'd.
What say'st thou now? speake suddenly, be briefe.
Buck. Your Grace may doe your pleasure.
Rich. Tut, tut, thou art all Ice, thy kindnesse freezes:
Say, haue I thy consent, that they shall dye?
Buc. Giue me some litle breath, some pawse, deare Lord,
Before I positiuely speake in this:
I will resolue you herein presently. *Exit Buck.*
Catesby. The King is angry, see he gnawes his Lippe.
Rich. I will conuerse with Iron-witted Fooles,
And vnrespectiue Boyes: none are for me,
That looke into me with considerate eyes,
High-reaching *Buckingham* growes circumspect.
Boy.
Page. My Lord.
Rich. Know'st thou not any, whom corrupting Gold
Will tempt vnto a close exploit of Death?
Page. I know a discontented Gentleman,
Whose humble meanes match not his haughtie spirit:
Gold were as good as twentie Orators,
And will (no doubt) tempt him to any thing.
Rich. What is his Name?
Page. His Name, my Lord, is *Tirrell.*
Rich. I partly know the man: goe call him hither,
Boy. *Exit.*
The deepe reuoluing wittie *Buckingham*,
No more shall be the neighbor to my counsailes.
Hath he so long held out with me, vntyr'd,
And stops he now for breath? Well, be it so.

Enter Stanley.

How now, Lord *Stanley*, what's the newes?
Stanley. Know my louing Lord, the Marquesse *Dorset*
As I heare, is fled to *Richmond*,
In the parts where he abides.
Rich. Come hither *Catesby*, rumor it abroad,
That *Anne* my Wife is very grieuous sicke.
I will take order for her keeping close.
Inquire me out some meane poore Gentleman,
Whom I will marry straight to *Clarence* Daughter:
The Boy is foolish, and I feare not him.
Looke how thou dream'st: I say againe, giue out,
That *Anne*, my Queene, is sicke, and like to dye.
About it, for it stands me much vpon
To stop all hopes, whose growth may dammage me,
I must be marryed to my Brothers Daughter,
Or else my Kingdome stands on brittle Glasse:
Murther her Brothers, and then marry her,
Vncertaine way of gaine. But I am in
So farre in blood, that sinne will pluck on sinne,
Teare-falling Pittie dwells not in this Eye.

Enter Tyrrel.

Is thy Name *Tyrrel*?
Tyr. *Iames Tyrrel*, and your most obedient subiect.
Rich. Art thou indeed?
Tyr. Proue me, my gracious Lord.
Rich. Dar'st thou resolue to kill a friend of mine?
Tyr. Please you:
But I had rather kill two enemies.
Rich. Why then thou hast it: two deepe enemies,
Foes to my Rest, and my sweet sleepes disturbers,
Are they that I would haue thee deale vpon:
Tyrrel, I meane those Bastards in the Tower.
Tyr. Let me haue open meanes to come to them,
And soone Ile rid you from the feare of them.
Rich. Thou sing'st sweet Musique:
Hearke, come hither *Tyrrel*,
Goe by this token: rise, and lend thine Eare, *Whispers.*
There is no more but so: say it is done,
And I will loue thee, and preferre thee for it.
Tyr. I will dispatch it straight. *Exit.*

Enter Buckingham.

Buck. My Lord, I haue consider'd in my minde,
The late request that you did sound me in.
Rich. Well, let that rest: *Dorset* is fled to *Richmond*.
Buck. I heare the newes, my Lord.
Rich. *Stanley*, hee is your Wiues Sonne: well, looke vnto it.
Buck. My Lord, I clayme the gift, my due by promise,
For which your Honor and your Faith is pawn'd,
Th'Earledome of Hertford, and the moueables,
Which you haue promised I shall possesse.
Rich. *Stanley* looke to your Wife: if she conuey
Letters to *Richmond*, you shall answer it.
Buck. What sayes your Highnesse to my iust request?
Rich. I doe remember me, *Henry* the Sixt
Did prophecie, that *Richmond* should be King,
When *Richmond* was a little peeuish Boy.
A King perhaps.
Buck. May it please you to resolue me in my suit.
Rich. Thou troublest me, I am not in the vaine. *Exit.*
Buck. And is it thus? repayes he my deepe seruice
With such contempt? made I him King for this?
O let me thinke on *Hastings*, and be gone
To Brecnock, while my fearefull Head is on. *Exit.*

Enter Tyrrel.

Tyr. The tyrannous and bloodie Act is done,
The most arch deed of pittious massacre

That

That euer yet this Land was guilty of:
Dighton and *Forrest*, who I did suborne
To do this peece of ruthfull Butchery,
Albeit they were flesht Villaines, bloody Dogges,
Melted with tendernesse, and milde compassion,
Wept like to Children, in their deaths sad Story.
O thus (quoth *Dighton*) lay the gentle Babes:
Thus, thus (quoth *Forrest*) girdling one another
Within their Alablaster innocent Armes:
Their lips were foure red Roses on a stalke,
And in their Summer Beauty kist each other.
A Booke of Prayers on their pillow lay,
Which one (quoth *Forrest*) almost chang'd my minde:
But oh the Diuell, there the Villaine stopt:
When *Dighton* thus told on, we smothered
The most replenished sweet worke of Nature,
That from the prime Creation ere she framed.
Hence both are gone with Conscience and Remorse,
They could not speake, and so I left them both,
To beare this tydings to the bloody King.

Enter Richard.

And heere he comes. All health my Soueraigne Lord.
Ric. Kinde *Tirrell*, am I happy in thy Newes.
Tir. If to haue done the thing you gaue in charge,
Beget your happinesse, be happy then,
For it is done.
Rich. But did'st thou see them dead.
Tir. I did my Lord.
Rich. And buried gentle *Tirrell*.
Tir. The Chaplaine of the Tower hath buried them,
But where (to say the truth) I do not know.
Rich. Come to me *Tirrel* soone, and after Supper,
When thou shalt tell the processe of their death.
Meane time, but thinke how I may do the good,
And be inheritor of thy desire.
Farewell till then.
Tir. I humbly take my leaue.
Rich. The Sonne of *Clarence* haue I pent vp close,
His daughter meanly haue I matcht in marriage,
The Sonnes of *Edward* sleepe in *Abrahams* bosome,
And *Anne* my wife hath bid this world good night.
Now for I know the Britaine *Richmond* aymes
At yong *Elizabeth* my brothers daughter,
And by that knot lookes proudly on the Crowne,
To her go I, a iolly thriuing wooer.

Enter Ratcliffe.

Rat. My Lord.
Rich. Good or bad newes, that thou com'st in so
bluntly?
Rat. Bad news my Lord, *Mourton* is fled to Richmond,
And Buckingham backt with the hardy Welshmen
Is in the field, and still his power encreaseth.
Rich. Ely with Richmond troubles me more neere,
Then Buckingham and his rash leuied Strength.
Come, I haue learn'd, that fearfull commenting
Is leaden seruitor to dull delay.
Delay leds impotent and Snaile-pac'd Beggery:
Then fierie expedition be my wing,
Ioues Mercury, and Herald for a King:
Go muster men: My counsaile is my Sheeld,
We must be breefe, when Traitors braue the Field.
Exeunt.

Scena Tertia.

Enter old Queene Margaret.

Mar. So now prosperity begins to mellow,
And drop into the rotten mouth of death:
Heere in these Confines slily haue I lurkt,
To watch the waining of mine enemies.
A dire induction, am I witnesse to,
And will to France, hoping the consequence
Will proue as bitter, blacke, and Tragicall.
Withdraw thee wretched *Margaret*, who comes heere?

Enter Dutchesse and Queene.

Qu. Ah my poore Princes! ah my tender Babes:
My vnblowed Flowres, new appearing sweets:
If yet your gentle soules flye in the Ayre,
And be not fixt in doome perpetuall,
Houer about me with your ayery wings,
And heare your mothers Lamentation.
Mar. Houer about her, say that right for right
Hath dim'd your Infant morne, to Aged night
Dut. So many miseries haue craz'd my voyce,
That my woe-wearied tongue is still and mute.
Edward Plantagenet, why art thou dead?
Mar. *Plantagenet* doth quit *Plantagenet*,
Edward for *Edward*, payes a dying debt.
Qu. Wilt thou, O God, flye from such gentle Lambs,
And throw them in the intrailes of the Wolfe?
When didst thou sleepe, when such a deed was done?
Mar. When holy *Harry* dyed, and my sweet Sonne.
Dut Dead life, blind sight, poore mortall liuing ghost,
Woes Scene, Worlds shame, Graues due, by life vsurpt,
Breefe abstract and record of tedious dayes,
Rest thy vnrest on Englands lawfull earth,
Vnlawfully made drunke with innocent blood.
Qu. Ah that thou would'st assoone affoord a Graue,
As thou canst yeeld a melancholly seate:
Then would I hide my bones, not rest them heere,
Ah who hath any cause to mourne but wee?
Mar. If ancient sorrow be most reuerent,
Giue mine the benefit of signeurie,
And let my greefes frowne on the vpper hand
If sorrow can admit Society.
I had an *Edward*, till a *Richard* kill'd him:
I had a Husband, till a *Richard* kill'd him:
Thou had'st an *Edward*, till a *Richard* kill'd him:
Thou had'st a *Richard*, till a *Richard* kill'd him.
Dut. I had a *Richard* too, and thou did'st kill him;
I had a *Rutland* too, thou hop'st to kill him.
Mar. Thou had'st a *Clarence* too,
And *Richard* kill'd him.
From forth the kennell of thy wombe hath crept
A Hell-hound that doth hunt vs all to death:
That Dogge, that had his teeth before his eyes,
To worry Lambes, and lap their gentle blood:
That foule defacer of Gods handy worke:
That reignes in gauled eyes of weeping soules:
That excellent grand Tyrant of the earth,
Thy wombe let loose to chase vs to our graues.
O vpright, iust, and true-disposing God,
How do I thanke thee, that this carnall Curre

Prayes

Prayes on the issue of his Mothers body,
And makes her Pue-fellow with others mone.
Dut. Oh *Harries* wife, triumph not in my woes:
God witnesse with me, I haue wept for thine.
Mar. Beare with me: I am hungry for reuenge,
And now I cloy me with beholding it.
Thy *Edward* he is dead, that kill'd my *Edward*,
The other *Edward* dead, to quit my *Edward*:
Yong Yorke, he is but boote, because both they
Matcht not the high perfection of my losse.
Thy *Clarence* he is dead, that stab'd my *Edward*,
And the beholders of this franticke play,
Th'adulterate *Hastings*, *Riuers*, *Vaughan*, *Gray*,
Vntimely smother'd in their dusky Graues.
Richard yet liues, Hels blacke Intelligencer,
Onely reseru'd their Factor, to buy soules,
And send them thither: But at hand, at hand
Insues his pittious and vnpittied end.
Earth gapes, Hell burnes, Fiends roare, Saints pray,
To haue him sodainly conuey'd from hence:
Cancell his bond of life, deere God I pray,
That I may liue and say, The Dogge is dead.
Qu. O thou did'st prophesie, the time would come,
That I should wish for thee to helpe me curse
That bottel'd Spider, that foule bunch-back'd Toad.
Mar. I call'd thee then, vaine flourish of my fortune:
I call'd thee then, poore Shadow, painted Queen,
The presentation of but what I was;
The flattering Index of a direfull Pageant;
One heau'd a high, to be hurl'd downe below:
A Mother onely mockt with two faire Babes;
A dreame of what thou wast, a garish Flagge
To be the ayme of euery dangerous Shot;
A signe of Dignity, a Breath, a Bubble;
A Queene in ieast, onely to fill the Scene.
Where is thy Husband now? Where be thy Brothers?
Where be thy two Sonnes? Wherein dost thou Ioy?
Who sues, and kneeles, and sayes, God saue the Queene?
Where be the bending Peeres that flattered thee?
Where be the thronging Troopes that followed thee?
Decline all this, and see what now thou art.
For happy Wife, a most distressed Widdow:
For ioyfull Mother, one that wailes the name:
For one being sued too, one that humbly sues:
For Queene, a very Caytiffe, crown'd with care:
For she that scorn'd at me, now scorn'd of me:
For she being feared of all, now fearing one:
For she commanding all, obey'd of none.
Thus hath the course of Iustice whirl'd about,
And left thee but a very prey to time,
Hauing no more but Thought of what thou wast.
To torture thee the more, being what thou art,
Thou didst vsurpe my place, and dost thou not
Vsurpe the iust proportion of my Sorrow?
Now thy proud Necke, beares halfe my burthen'd yoke,
From which, euen heere I slip my wearied head,
And leaue the burthen of it all, on thee.
Farwell Yorkes wife, and Queene of sad mischance,
These English woes, shall make me smile in France.
Qu. O thou well skill'd in Curses, stay a-while,
And teach me how to curse mine enemies.
Mar. Forbeare to sleepe the night, and fast the day:
Compare dead happinesse, with liuing woe:
Thinke that thy Babes were sweeter then they were,
And he that slew them fowler then he is:
Bett'ring thy losse, makes the bad causer worse,
Reuoluing this, will teach thee how to Curse.
Qu. My words are dull, O quicken them with thine.
Mar. Thy woes will make them sharpe,
And pierce like mine. *Exit Margaret.*
Dut. Why should calamity be full of words?
Qu. Windy Atturnies to their Clients Woes,
Ayery succeeders of intestine ioyes,
Poore breathing Orators of miseries,
Let them haue scope, though what they will impart,
Helpe nothing els, yet do they ease the hart.
Dut. If so then, be not Tongue-ty'd: go with me,
And in the breath of bitter words, let's smother
My damned Son, that thy two sweet Sonnes smother'd.
The Trumpet sounds, be copious in exclaimes.

Enter King Richard, and his Traine.

Rich. Who intercepts me in my Expedition?
Dut. O she, that might haue intercepted thee
By strangling thee in her accursed wombe,
From all the slaughters (Wretch) that thou hast done.
Qu. Hid'st thou that Forhead with a Golden Crowne
Where't should be branded, if that right were right?
The slaughter of the Prince that ow'd that Crowne,
And the dyre death of my poore Sonnes, and Brothers.
Tell me thou Villaine-slaue, where are my Children?
Dut. Thou Toad, thou Toade,
Where is thy Brother *Clarence*?
And little *Ned Plantagenet* his Sonne?
Qu. Where is the gentle *Riuers*, *Vaughan*, *Gray*?
Dut. Where is kinde *Hastings*?
Rich. A flourish Trumpets, strike Alarum Drummes:
Let not the Heauens heare these Tell-tale women
Raile on the Lords Annointed. Strike I say.
Flourish. Alarums.
Either be patient, and intreat me fayre,
Or with the clamorous report of Warre,
Thus will I drowne your exclamations.
Dut. Art thou my Sonne?
Rich. I, I thanke God, my Father, and your selfe.
Dut. Then patiently heare my impatience.
Rich. Madam, I haue a touch of your condition,
That cannot brooke the accent of reproofe.
Dut. O let me speake.
Rich. Do then, but Ile not heare.
Dut: I will be milde, and gentle in my words.
Rich. And breefe (good Mother) for I am in hast.
Dut. Art thou so hasty? I haue staid for thee
(God knowes) in torment and in agony.
Rich. And came I not at last to comfort you?
Dut. No by the holy Rood, thou know'st it well,
Thou cam'st on earth, to make the earth my Hell.
A greeuous burthen was thy Birth to me,
Tetchy and wayward was thy Infancie.
Thy School-daies frightfull, desp'rate, wilde, and furious,
Thy prime of Manhood, daring, bold, and venturous:
Thy Age confirm'd, proud, subtle, slye, and bloody,
More milde, but yet more harmfull; Kinde in hatred:
What comfortable houre canst thou name,
That euer grac'd me with thy company?
Rich. Faith none, but *Humfrey Hower*,
That call'd your Grace
To Breakefast once, forth of my company.
If I be so disgracious in your eye,
Let me march on, and not offend you Madam.
Strike vp the Drumme.
Dut. I prythee heare me speake.

Rich. You speake too bitterly.
Dut. Heare me a word:
For I shall neuer speake to thee againe.
Rich. So.
Dut. Either thou wilt dye, by Gods iust ordinance
Ere from this warre thou turne a Conqueror:
Or I with greefe and extreame Age shall perish,
And neuer more behold thy face againe.
Therefore take with thee my most greeuous Curse,
Which in the day of Battell tyre thee more
Then all the compleat Armour that thou wear'st.
My Prayers on the aduerse party fight,
And there the little soules of *Edwards* Children,
Whisper the Spirits of thine Enemies,
And promise them Successe and Victory:
Bloody thou art, bloody will be thy end:
Shame serues thy life, and doth thy death attend. *Exit.*
Qu. Though far more cause, yet much lesse spirit to curse
Abides in me, I say Amen to her.
Rich. Stay Madam, I must talke a word with you.
Qu. I haue no more sonnes of the Royall Blood
For thee to slaughter. For my Daughters (*Richard*)
They shall be praying Nunnes, not weeping Queenes:
And therefore leuell not to hit their liues.
Rich. You haue a daughter call'd *Elizabeth*,
Vertuous and Faire, Royall and Gracious?
Qu. And must she dye for this? O let her liue,
And Ile corrupt her Manners, staine her Beauty,
Slander my Selfe, as false to *Edwards* bed:
Throw ouer her the vaile of Infamy,
So she may liue vnscarr'd of bleeding slaughter,
I will confesse she was not *Edwards* daughter.
Rich. Wrong not her Byrth, she is a Royall Princesse.
Qu. To saue her life, Ile say she is not so.
Rich. Her life is safest onely in her byrth.
Qu. And onely in that safety, dyed her Brothers.
Rich. Loe at their Birth, good starres were opposite.
Qu. No, to their liues, ill friends were contrary.
Rich. All vnauoyded is the doome of Destiny.
Qu. True: when auoyded grace makes Destiny.
My Babes were destin'd to a fairer death,
If grace had blest thee with a fairer life.
Rich. You speake as if that I had slaine my Cosins?
Qu. Cosins indeed, and by their Vnckle couzend,
Of Comfort, Kingdome, Kindred, Freedome, Life,
Whose hand soeuer lanch'd their tender hearts,
Thy head (all indirectly) gaue direction.
No doubt the murd'rous Knife was dull and blunt,
Till it was whetted on thy stone-hard heart,
To reuell in the Intrailes of my Lambes.
But that still vse of greefe, makes wilde greefe tame,
My tongue should to thy eares not name my Boyes,
Till that my Nayles were anchor'd in thine eyes:
And I in such a desp'rate Bay of death,
Like a poore Barke, of sailes and tackling reft,
Rush all to peeces on thy Rocky bosome.
Rich. Madam, so thriue I in my enterprize
And dangerous successe of bloody warres,
As I intend more good to you and yours,
Then euer you and yours by me were harm'd.
Qu. What good is couer'd with the face of heauen,
To be discouered, that can do me good.
Rich. Th'aduancement of your children, gentle Lady
Qu. Vp to some Scaffold, there to lose their heads.
Rich. Vnto the dignity and height of Fortune,
The high Imperiall Type of this earths glory.
Qu. Flatter my sorrow with report of it:
Tell me, what State, what Dignity, what Honor,
Canst thou demise to any childe of mine.
Rich. Euen all I haue; I, and my selfe and all,
Will I withall indow a childe of thine:
So in the Lethe of thy angry soule,
Thou drowne the sad remembrance of those wrongs,
Which thou supposest I haue done to thee.
Qu. Be breefe, least that the processe of thy kindnesse
Last longer telling then thy kindnesse date.
Rich. Then know,
That from my Soule, I loue thy Daughter.
Qu. My daughters Mother thinkes it with her soule.
Rich. What do you thinke?
Qu. That thou dost loue my daughter from thy soule
So from thy Soules loue didst thou loue her Brothers,
And from my hearts loue, I do thanke thee for it.
Rich. Be not so hasty to confound my meaning:
I meane that with my Soule I loue thy daughter,
And do intend to make her Queene of England.
Qu. Well then, who dost ỹ meane shallbe her King.
Rich. Euen he that makes her Queene:
Who else should bee?
Qu. What, thou?
Rich. Euen so: How thinke you of it?
Qu. How canst thou woo her?
Rich. That I would learne of you,
As one being best acquainted with her humour.
Qu. And wilt thou learne of me?
Rich. Madam, with all my heart.
Qu. Send to her by the man that slew her Brothers,
A paire of bleeding hearts: thereon ingraue
Edward and *Yorke*, then haply will she weepe:
Therefore present to her, as sometime *Margaret*
Did to thy Father, steept in Rutlands blood,
A hand-kercheefe, which say to her did dreyne
The purple sappe from her sweet Brothers body,
And bid her wipe her weeping eyes withall.
If this inducement moue her not to loue,
Send her a Letter of thy Noble deeds:
Tell her, thou mad'st away her Vnckle *Clarence*,
Her Vnckle *Riuers*, I (and for her sake)
Mad'st quicke conueyance with her good Aunt *Anne*.
Rich. You mocke me Madam, this not the way
To win your daughter.
Qu. There is no other way,
Vnlesse thou could'st put on some other shape,
And not be *Richard*, that hath done all this.
Ric. Say that I did all this for loue of her.
Qu. Nay then indeed she cannot choose but hate thee
Hauing bought loue, with such a bloody spoyle.
Rich. Looke what is done, cannot be now amended:
Men shall deale vnaduisedly sometimes,
Which after-houres giues leysure to repent.
If I did take the Kingdome from your Sonnes,
To make amends, Ile giue it to your daughter:
If I haue kill'd the issue of your wombe,
To quicken your encrease, I will beget
Mine yssue of your blood, vpon your Daughter:
A Grandams name is little lesse in loue,
Then is the doting Title of a Mother;
They are as Children but one steppe below,
Euen of your mettall, of your very blood:
Of all one paine, saue for a night of groanes
Endur'd of her, for whom you bid like sorrow.
Your Children were vexation to your youth,

But mine shall be a comfort to your Age,
The losse you haue, is but a Sonne being King,
And by that losse, your Daughter is made Queene.
I cannot make you what amends I would,
Therefore accept such kindnesse as I can.
Dorset your Sonne, that with a fearfull soule
Leads discontented steppes in Forraine soyle,
This faire Alliance, quickly shall call home
To high Promotions, and great Dignity.
The King that calles your beauteous Daughter Wife,
Familiarly shall call thy *Dorset*, Brother:
Againe shall you be Mother to a King:
And all the Ruines of distressefull Times,
Repayr'd with double Riches of Content.
What? we haue many goodly dayes to see:
The liquid drops of Teares that you haue shed,
Shall come againe, transform'd to Orient Pearle,
Aduantaging their Loue, with interest
Often-times double gaine of happinesse.
Go then (my Mother) to thy Daughter go,
Make bold her bashfull yeares, with your experience,
Prepare her eares to heare a Woers Tale.
Put in her tender heart, th'aspiring Flame
Of Golden Soueraignty: Acquaint the Princesse
With the sweet silent houres of Marriage ioyes:
And when this Arme of mine hath chastised
The petty Rebell, dull-brain'd *Buckingham*,
Bound with Triumphant Garlands will I come,
And leade thy daughter to a Conquerors bed:
To whom I will retaile my Conquest wonne,
And she shalbe sole Victoresse, *Cæsars Cæsar*.
Qu. What were I best to say, her Fathers Brother
Would be her Lord? Or shall I say her Vnkle?
Or he that slew her Brothers, and her Vnkles?
Vnder what Title shall I woo for thee,
That God, the Law, my Honor, and her Loue,
Can make seeme pleasing to her tender yeares?
Rich. Inferre faire Englands peace by this Alliance.
Qu. Which she shall purchase with stil lasting warre.
Rich. Tell her, the King that may command, intreats.
Qu. That at her hands, which the kings King forbids.
Rich. Say she shall be a High and Mighty Queene.
Qu. To vaile the Title, as her Mother doth.
Rich. Say I will loue her euerlastingly.
Qu. But how long shall that title euer last?
Rich. Sweetly in force, vnto her faire liues end.
Qu. But how long fairely shall her sweet life last?
Rich. As long as Heauen and Nature lengthens it.
Qu. As long as Hell and *Richard* likes of it.
Rich. Say, I her Soueraigne, am her Subiect low.
Qu. But she your Subiect, lothes such Soueraignty.
Rich. Be eloquent in my behalfe to her.
Qu. An honest tale speeds best, being plainly told.
Rich. Then plainly to her, tell my louing tale.
Qu. Plaine and not honest, is too harsh a style.
Rich. Your Reasons are too shallow, and to quicke.
Qu. O no, my Reasons are too deepe and dead,
Too deepe and dead (poore Infants) in their graues,
Harpe on it still shall I, till heart-strings breake.
Rich. Harpe not on that string Madam, that is past.
Now by my George, my Garter, and my Crowne.
Qu. Prophan'd, dishonor'd, and the third vsurpt.
Rich. I sweare.
Qu. By nothing, for this is no Oath:
Thy George prophan'd, hath lost his Lordly Honor;
Thy Garter blemish'd, pawn'd his Knightly Vertue;
Thy Crowne vsurp'd, disgrac'd his Kingly Glory:
If something thou would'st sweare to be beleeu'd,
Sweare then by something, that thou hast not wrong'd.
Rich. Then by my Selfe.
Qu. Thy Selfe, is selfe-misvs'd.
Rich. Now by the World.
Qu. 'Tis full of thy foule wrongs
Rich. My Fathers death.
Qu. Thy life hath it dishonor'd.
Rich. Why then, by Heauen.
Qu. Heauens wrong is most of all:
If thou didd'st feare to breake an Oath with him,
The vnity the King my husband made,
Thou had'st not broken, nor my Brothers died.
If thou had'st fear'd to breake an oath by him,
Th'Imperiall mettall, circling now thy head,
Had grac'd the tender temples of my Child,
And both the Princes had bene breathing heere,
Which now two tender Bed-fellowes for dust,
Thy broken Faith hath made the prey for Wormes.
What can'st thou sweare by now.
Rich. The time to come.
Qu. That thou hast wronged in the time ore-past:
For I my selfe haue many teares to wash
Heereafter time, for time past, wrong'd by thee.
The Children liue, whose Fathers thou hast slaughter'd,
Vngouern'd youth, to waile it with their age:
The Parents liue, whose Children thou hast butcher'd,
Old barren Plants, to waile it with their Age.
Sweare not by time to come, for that thou hast
Misvs'd ere vs'd, by times ill-vs'd repast.
Rich. As I entend to prosper, and repent:
So thriue I in my dangerous Affayres
Of hostile Armes: My selfe, my selfe confound:
Heauen, and Fortune barre me happy houres:
Day, yeeld me not thy light; nor Night, thy rest.
Be opposite all Planets of good lucke
To my proceeding, if with deere hearts loue,
Immaculate deuotion, holy thoughts,
I tender not thy beautious Princely daughter.
In her, consists my Happinesse, and thine:
Without her, followes to my selfe, and thee;
Her selfe, the Land, and many a Christian soule,
Death, Desolation, Ruine, and Decay:
It cannot be auoyded, but by this:
It will not be auoyded, but by this.
Therefore deare Mother (I must call you so)
Be the Atturney of my loue to her:
Pleade what I will be, not what I haue beene;
Not my deserts, but what I will deserue:
Vrge the Necessity and state of times,
And be not peeuish found, in great Designes.
Qu. Shall I be tempted of the Diuel thus?
Rich. I, if the Diuell tempt you to do good.
Qu. Shall I forget my selfe, to be my selfe.
Rich. I, if your selfes remembrance wrong your selfe.
Qu. Yet thou didst kil my Children.
Rich. But in your daughters wombe I bury them.
Where in that Nest of Spicery they will breed
Selues of themselues, to your recomforture.
Qu. Shall I go win my daughter to thy will?
Rich. And be a happy Mother by the deed.
Qu. I go, write to me very shortly,
And you shal vnderstand from me her mind. *Exit Q.*
Rich. Beare her my true loues kisse, and so farewell.
Relenting Foole, and shallow-changing Woman.

How

How now, what newes ?

Enter Ratcliffe.

Rat. Most mightie Soueraigne, on the Westerne Coast
Rideth a puissant Nauie: to our Shores
Throng many doubtfull hollow-hearted friends,
Vnarm'd, and vnresolu'd to beat them backe.
'Tis thought, that *Richmond* is their Admirall:
And there they hull, expecting but the aide
Of *Buckingham*, to welcome them ashore.

Rich. Some light-foot friend post to ẏ Duke of Norfolk:
Ratcliffe thy selfe, or *Catesby*, where is hee ?

Cat. Here, my good Lord.

Rich. *Catesby*, flye to the Duke.

Cat. I will, my Lord, with all conuenient haste.

Rich. *Catesby* come hither, poste to Salisbury:
When thou com'st thither: Dull vnmindfull Villaine,
Why stay'st thou here, and go'st not to the Duke ?

Cat. First, mighty Liege, tell me your Highnesse pleasure,
What from your Grace I shall deliuer to him.

Rich. O true, good *Catesby*, bid him leuie straight
The greatest strength and power that he can make,
And meet me suddenly at Salisbury.

Cat. I goe. *Exit.*

Rat. What, may it please you, shall I doe at Salisbury ?

Rich. Why, what would'st thou doe there, before I goe ?

Rat. Your Highnesse told me I should poste before.

Rich. My minde is chang'd:

Enter Lord Stanley.

Stanley, what newes with you ?

Sta. None, good my Liege, to please you with ẏ hearing,
Nor none so bad, but well may be reported.

Rich. Hoyday, a Riddle, neither good nor bad:
What need'st thou runne so many miles about,
When thou mayest tell thy Tale the neerest way ?
Once more, what newes ?

Stan. *Richmond* is on the Seas.

Rich. There let him sinke, and be the Seas on him,
White-liuer'd Runnagate, what doth he there ?

Stan. I know not, mightie Soueraigne, but by guesse.

Rich. Well, as you guesse.

Stan. Stirr'd vp by *Dorset*, *Buckingham*, and *Morton*,
He makes for England, here to clayme the Crowne.

Rich. Is the Chayre emptie? is the Sword vnsway'd ?
Is the King dead? the Empire vnpossest?
What Heire of *Yorke* is there aliue, but wee?
And who is Englands King, but great *Yorkes* Heire?
Then tell me, what makes he vpon the Seas ?

Stan. Vnlesse for that, my Liege, I cannot guesse.

Rich. Vnlesse for that he comes to be your Liege,
You cannot guesse wherefore the Welchman comes.
Thou wilt reuolt, and flye to him, I feare.

Stan. No, my good Lord, therefore mistrust me not.

Rich. Where is thy Power then, to beat him back ?
Where be thy Tenants, and thy followers?
Are they not now vpon the Westerne Shore,
Safe-conducting the Rebels from their Shippes ?

Stan. No, my good Lord, my friends are in the North.

Rich. Cold friends to me: what do they in the North,
When they should serue their Soueraigne in the West ?

Stan. They haue not been commanded, mighty King:
Pleaseth your Maiestie to giue me leaue,
Ile muster vp my friends, and meet your Grace,
Where, and what time your Maiestie shall please.

Rich. I, thou would'st be gone, to ioyne with *Richmond:*
But Ile not trust thee.

Stan. Most mightie Soueraigne,
You haue no cause to hold my friendship doubtfull,
I neuer was, nor neuer will be false.

Rich. Goe then, and muster men: but leaue behind
Your Sonne *George Stanley*: looke your heart be firme,
Or else his Heads assurance is but fraile.

Stan. So deale with him, as I proue true to you.
Exit Stanley.

Enter a Messenger.

Mess. My gracious Soueraigne, now in Deuonshire,
As I by friends am well aduertised,
Sir *Edward Courtney*, and the haughtie Prelate,
Bishop of Exeter, his elder Brother,
With many moe Confederates, are in Armes.

Enter another Messenger.

Mess. In Kent, my Liege, the *Guilfords* are in Armes,
And euery houre more Competitors
Flocke to the Rebels, and their power growes strong.

Enter another Messenger.

Mess. My Lord, the Armie of great *Buckingham.*

Rich. Out on ye, Owles, nothing but Songs of Death,
He striketh him.
There, take thou that, till thou bring better newes.

Mess. The newes I haue to tell your Maiestie,
Is, that by sudden Floods, and fall of Waters,
Buckinghams Armie is dispers'd and scatter'd,
And he himselfe wandred away alone,
No man knowes whither.

Rich. I cry thee mercie:
There is my Purse, to cure that Blow of thine.
Hath any well-aduised friend proclaym'd
Reward to him that brings the Traytor in ?

Mess. Such Proclamation hath been made, my Lord.

Enter another Messenger.

Mess. Sir *Thomas Louell*, and Lord Marquesse *Dorset*,
'Tis said, my Liege, in Yorkeshire are in Armes:
But this good comfort bring I to your Highnesse,
The Brittaine Nauie is dispers'd by Tempest.
Richmond in Dorsetshire sent out a Boat
Vnto the shore, to aske those on the Banks,
If they were his Assistants, yea, or no ?
Who answer'd him, they came from *Buckingham*,
Vpon his partie: he mistrusting them,
Hoys'd sayle, and made his course againe for Brittaine.

Rich. March on, march on, since we are vp in Armes,
If not to fight with forraine Enemies,
Yet to beat downe these Rebels here at home.

Enter Catesby.

Cat. My Liege, the Duke of Buckingham is taken,
That is the best newes: that the Earle of Richmond

Is with a mighty power Landed at Milford,
Is colder Newes, but yet they must be told.
Rich. Away towards Salsbury, while we reason here,
A Royall batteil might be wonne and lost:
Some one take order Buckingham be brought
To Salsbury, the rest march on with me. *Florish. Exeunt*

Scena Quarta.

Enter Derby, and Sir Christopher.

Der. Sir *Christopher*, tell *Richmond* this from me,
That in the stye of the most deadly Bore,
My Sonne *George Stanley* is frankt vp in hold:
If I reuolt, off goes yong *Georges* head,
The feare of that, holds off my present ayde.
So get thee gone: commend me to thy Lord.
Withall say, that the Queene hath heartily consented
He should espouse *Elizabeth* hir daughter.
But tell me, where is Princely Richmond now?
Chri. At Penbroke, or at Hertford West in Wales.
Der. What men of Name resort to him.
Chri, Sir *Walter Herbert*, a renowned Souldier,
Sir *Gilbert Talbot*, Sir *William Stanley*,
Oxford, redoubted *Pembroke*, Sir *Iames Blunt*,
And *Rice ap Thomas*, with a valiant Crew,
And many other of great name and worth:
And towards London do they bend their power,
If by the way they be not fought withall.
Der. Well hye thee to thy Lord: I kisse his hand,
My Letter will resolue him of my minde.
Farewell. *Exeunt*

Actus Quintus. Scena Prima.

Enter Buckingham with Halberds, led to Execution.

Buc. Will not King *Richard* let me speake with him?
Sher. No my good Lord, therefore be patient.
Buc. *Hastings*, and *Edwards* children, *Gray* & *Riuers*,
Holy King *Henry*, and thy faire Sonne *Edward*,
Vaughan, and all that haue miscarried
By vnder-hand corrupted foule iniustice,
If that your moody discontented soules,
Do through the clowds behold this present houre,
Euen for reuenge mocke my destruction.
This is All-soules day (Fellow) is it not?
Sher. It is.
Buc. Why then Al-soules day, is my bodies doomsday
This is the day, which in King *Edwards* time
I wish'd might fall on me, when I was found
False to his Children, and his Wiues Allies.
This is the day, wherein I wisht to fall
By the false Faith of him whom most I trusted.
This, this All-soules day to my fearfull Soule,
Is the determin'd respit of my wrongs:
That high All-seer, which I dallied with,
Hath turn'd my fained Prayer on my head,
And giuen in earnest, what I begg'd in iest.
Thus doth he force the swords of wicked men
To turne their owne points in their Masters bosomes.
Thus *Margarets* curse falles heauy on my necke:
When he (quoth she) shall split thy heart with sorrow,
Remember *Margaret* was a Prophetesse:
Come leade me Officers to the blocke of shame,
Wrong hath but wrong, and blame the due of blame.
Exeunt Buckingham with Officers.

Scena Secunda.

Enter Richmond, Oxford, Blunt, Herbert, and others, with drum and colours.

Richm. Fellowes in Armes, and my most louing Frends
Bruis'd vnderneath the yoake of Tyranny,
Thus farre into the bowels of the Land,
Haue we marcht on without impediment;
And heere receiue we from our Father *Stanley*
Lines of faire comfort and encouragement:
The wretched, bloody, and vsurping Boare,
(That spoyl'd your Summer Fields, and fruitfull Vines)
Swilles your warm blood like wash, & makes his trough
In your embowel'd bosomes: This foule Swine
Is now euen in the Centry of this Isle,
Ne're to the Towne of Leicester, as we learne:
From Tamworth thither, is but one dayes march.
In Gods name cheerely on, couragious Friends,
To reape the Haruest of perpetuall peace,
By this one bloody tryall of sharpe Warre.
Oxf. Euery mans Conscience is a thousand men,
To fight against this guilty Homicide.
Her. I doubt not but his Friends will turne to vs.
Blunt. He hath no friends, but what are friends for fear,
Which in his deerest neede will flye from him.
Richm. All for our vantage, then in Gods name march,
True Hope is swift, and flyes with Swallowes wings,
Kings it makes Gods, and meaner creatures Kings.
Exeunt Omnes.

Enter King Richard in Armes, with Norfolke, Ratcliffe, and the Earle of Surrey.

Rich. Here pitch our Tent, euen here in Bosworth field,
My Lord of Surrey, why looke you so sad?
Sur. My heart is ten times lighter then my lookes.
Rich. My Lord of Norfolke.
Nor. Heere most gracious Liege.
Rich. Norfolke, we must haue knockes:
Ha, must we not?
Nor. We must both giue and take my louing Lord.
Rich. Vp with my Tent, heere wil I lye to night,
But where to morrow? Well, all's one for that.
Who hath descried the number of the Traitors?
Nor. Six or seuen thousand is their vtmost power.
Rich. Why our Battalia trebbles that account:
Besides, the Kings name is a Tower of strength,
Which they vpon the aduerse Faction want.
Vp with the Tent: Come Noble Gentlemen,
Let vs suruey the vantage of the ground.
Call for some men of sound direction:

Let's

Let's lacke no Discipline, make no delay,
For Lords, to morrow is a busie day. *Exeunt*

Enter Richmond, Sir William Brandon, Oxford, and Dorset.

Richm. The weary Sunne, hath made a Golden set,
And by the bright Tract of his fiery Carre,
Giues token of a goodly day to morrow.
Sir *William Brandon*, you shall beare my Standard:
Giue me some Inke and Paper in my Tent:
Ile draw the Forme and Modell of our Battaile,
Limit each Leader to his seuerall Charge,
And part in iust proportion our small Power.
My Lord of Oxford, you Sir *William Brandon*,
And your Sir *Walter Herbert* stay with me:
The Earle of Pembroke keepes his Regiment;
Good Captaine *Blunt*, beare my goodnight to him,
And by the second houre in the Morning,
Desire the Earle to see me in my Tent:
Yet one thing more (good Captaine) do for me:
Where is Lord *Stanley* quarter'd, do you know?
Blunt. Vnlesse I haue mistane his Colours much,
(Which well I am assur'd I haue not done)
His Regiment lies halfe a Mile at least
South, from the mighty Power of the King.
Richm. If without perill it be possible,
Sweet *Blunt*, make some good meanes to speak with him
And giue him from me, this most needfull Note.
Blunt. Vpon my life, my Lord, Ile vndertake it,
And so God giue you quiet rest to night.
Richm. Good night good Captaine *Blunt*:
Come Gentlemen,
Let vs consult vpon to morrowes Businesse;
Into my Tent, the Dew is rawe and cold.
They withdraw into the Tent.

Enter Richard, Ratcliffe, Norfolke, & Catesby.

Rich. What is't a Clocke?
Cat. It's Supper time my Lord, it's nine a clocke.
King. I will not sup to night,
Giue me some Inke and Paper:
What, is my Beauer easier then it was?
And all my Armour laid into my Tent?
Cat. It is my Liege: and all things are in readinesse.
Rich. Good Norfolke, hye thee to thy charge,
Vse carefull Watch, choose trusty Centinels.
Nor. I go my Lord.
Rich. Stir with the Larke to morrow, gentle Norfolk.
Nor. I warrant you my Lord. *Exit*
Rich. Ratcliffe.
Rat. My Lord.
Rich. Send out a Pursuiuant at Armes
To *Stanleys* Regiment: bid him bring his power
Before Sun-rising, least his Sonne *George* fall
Into the blinde Caue of eternall night.
Fill me a Bowle of Wine: Giue me a Watch,
Saddle white Surrey for the Field to morrow:
Look that my Staues be sound, & not too heauy. *Ratcliff.*
Rat. My Lord.
Rich. Saw'st the melancholly Lord Northumberland?
Rat. Thomas the Earle of Surrey, and himselfe,
Much about Cockshut time, from Troope to Troope
Went through the Army, chearing vp the Souldiers.
King. So, I am satisfied: Giue me a Bowle of Wine,
I haue not that Alacrity of Spirit,
Nor cheere of Minde that I was wont to haue.
Set it downe. Is Inke and Paper ready?
Rat. It is my Lord.
Rich. Bid my Guard watch. Leaue me.
Ratcliffe, about the mid of night come to my Tent
And helpe to arme me. Leaue me I say. *Exit Ratclif.*

Enter Derby to Richmond in his Tent.

Der. Fortune, and Victory sit on thy Helme.
Rich. All comfort that the darke night can affoord,
Be to thy Person, Noble Father in Law.
Tell me, how fares our Noble Mother?
Der. I by Attourney, blesse thee from thy Mother,
Who prayes continually for Richmonds good:
So much for that. The silent houres steale on,
And flakie darkenesse breakes within the East.
In breefe, for so the season bids vs be,
Prepare thy Battell early in the Morning,
And put thy Fortune to th'Arbitrement
Of bloody stroakes, and mortall staring Warre:
I, as I may, that which I would. I cannot,
With best aduantage will deceiue the time,
And ayde thee in this doubtfull shocke of Armes.
But on thy side I may not be too forward,
Least being seene, thy Brother, tender *George*
Be executed in his Fathers sight.
Farewell: the leysure, and the fearfull time
Cuts off the ceremonious Vowes of Loue,
And ample enterchange of sweet Discourse,
Which so long sundred Friends should dwell vpon:
God giue vs leysure for these rites of Loue.
Once more Adieu, be valiant, and speed well.
Richm. Good Lords conduct him to his Regiment:
Ile striue with troubled noise, to take a Nap,
Lest leaden slumber peize me downe to morrow,
When I should mount with wings of Victory:
Once more, good night kinde Lords and Gentlemen.
Exeunt. Manet Richmond.
O thou, whose Captaine I account my selfe,
Looke on my Forces with a gracious eye:
Put in their hands thy bruising Irons of wrath,
That they may crush downe with a heauy fall,
Th'vsurping Helmets of our Aduersaries:
Make vs thy ministers of Chasticement,
That we may praise thee in thy victory:
To thee I do commend my watchfull soule,
Ere I let fall the windowes of mine eyes:
Sleeping, and waking, oh defend me still. *Sleeps.*

Enter the Ghost of Prince Edward, Sonne to Henry the sixt.

Gh. to Ri. Let me sit heauy on thy soule to morrow:
Thinke how thou stab'st me in my prime of youth
At Teukesbury: Dispaire therefore, and dye.
Ghost to Richm. Be chearefull Richmond,
For the wronged Soules
Of butcher'd Princes, fight in thy behalfe:
King *Henries* issue Richmond comforts thee.

Enter the Ghost of Henry the sixt.

Ghost. When I was mortall, my Annointed body
By thee was punched full of holes;
Thinke on the Tower, and me: Dispaire, and dye,
Harry the sixt, bids thee dispaire, and dye.
To Richm. Vertuous and holy be thou Conqueror:
Harry that prophesied thou should'st be King.
Doth comfort thee in sleepe: Liue, and flourish.

Enter the Ghost of Clarence.

Ghost. Let me sit heauy in thy soule to morrow.
I that was wash'd to death with Fulsome Wine:
Poore *Clarence* by thy guile betray'd to death:
To morrow in the battell thinke on me,
And fall thy edgelesse Sword, dispaire and dye.

To Richm. Thou off-spring of the house of Lancaster
The wronged heyres of Yorke do pray for thee,
Good Angels guard thy battell, Liue and Flourish.

Enter the Ghosts of Riuers, Gray, and Vaughan.

Riu. Let me sit heauy in thy soule to morrow,
Riuers, that dy'de at Pomfret: dispaire, and dye.

Grey. Thinke vpon *Grey*, and let thy soule dispaire.

Vaugh. Thinke vpon *Vaughan*, and with guilty feare
Let fall thy Lance, dispaire and dye.

All to Richm. Awake,
And thinke our wrongs in *Richards* Bosome,
Will conquer him. Awake, and win the day.

Enter the Ghost of Lord Hastings.

Gho. Bloody and guilty: guiltily awake,
And in a bloody Battell end thy dayes.
Thinke on Lord Hastings: dispaire, and dye.

Hast. to Rich. Quiet vntroubled soule,
Awake, awake:
Arme, fight, and conquer, for faire Englands sake.

Enter the Ghosts of the two yong Princes.

Ghosts. Dreame on thy Cousins
Smothered in the Tower:
Let vs be laid within thy bosome *Richard*,
And weigh thee downe to ruine, shame, and death,
Thy Nephewes soule bids thee dispaire and dye.

Ghosts to Richm. Sleepe Richmond,
Sleepe in Peace, and wake in Ioy,
Good Angels guard thee from the Boares annoy,
Liue, and beget a happy race of Kings,
Edwards vnhappy Sonnes, do bid thee flourish.

Enter the Ghost of Anne, his Wife.

Ghost to Rich. Richard, thy Wife,
That wretched *Anne* thy Wife,
That neuer slept a quiet houre with thee,
Now filles thy sleepe with perturbations,
To morrow in the Battaile, thinke on me,
And fall thy edgelesse Sword, dispaire and dye:

Ghost to Richm. Thou quiet soule,
Sleepe thou a quiet sleepe:
Dreame of Successe, and Happy Victory,
Thy Aduersaries Wife doth pray for thee.

Enter the Ghost of Buckingham.

Ghost to Rich. The first was I
That help'd thee to the Crowne:
The last was I that felt thy Tyranny.
O, in the Battaile think on Buckingham,
And dye in terror of thy guiltinesse.
Dreame on, dreame on, of bloody deeds and death,
Fainting dispaire; dispairing yeeld thy breath.

Ghost to Richm. I dyed for hope
Ere I could lend thee Ayde;
But cheere thy heart, and be thou not dismayde:
God, and good Angels fight on Richmonds side,
And *Richard* fall in height of all his pride.

Richard starts out of his dreame.

Rich. Giue me another Horse, bind vp my Wounds:
Haue mercy Iesu. Soft, I did but dreame.
O coward Conscience! how dost thou afflict me?
The Lights burne blew. It is not dead midnight.
Cold fearefull drops stand on my trembling flesh.
What? do I feare my Selfe? There's none else by,
Richard loues *Richard*, that is, I am I.
Is there a Murtherer heere? No; Yes, I am:
Then flye; What from my Selfe? Great reason: why?
Lest I Reuenge. What? my Selfe vpon my Selfe?
Alacke, I loue my Selfe. Wherefore? For any good
That I my Selfe, haue done vnto my Selfe?
O no. Alas, I rather hate my Selfe,
For hatefull Deeds committed by my Selfe.
I am a Villaine: yet I Lye, I am not.
Foole, of thy Selfe speake well: Foole, do not flatter.
My Conscience hath a thousand seuerall Tongues,
And euery Tongue brings in a seuerall Tale,
And euerie Tale condemnes me for a Villaine;
Periurie, in the high'st Degree,
Murther, sterne murther, in the dyr'st degree,
All seuerall sinnes, all vs'd in each degree,
Throng all to'th' Barre, crying all, Guilty, Guilty.
I shall dispaire, there is no Creature loues me;
And if I die, no soule shall pittie me.
Nay, wherefore should they? Since that I my Selfe,
Finde in my Selfe, no pittie to my Selfe.
Me thought, the Soules of all that I had murther'd
Came to my Tent, and euery one did threat
To morrowes vengeance on the head of *Richard*.

Enter Ratcliffe.

Rat. My Lord.

King. Who's there?

Rat. Ratcliffe my Lord, 'tis I: the early Village Cock
Hath twice done salutation to the Morne,
Your Friends are vp, and buckle on their Armour.

King. O *Ratcliffe*, I feare, I feare.

Rat. Nay good my Lord, be not affraid of Shadows.

King. By the Apostle *Paul*, shadowes to night
Haue stroke more terror to the soule of *Richard*,
Then can the substance of ten thousand Souldiers
Armed in proofe, and led by shallow *Richmond*.
'Tis not yet neere day. Come go with me,
Vnder our Tents Ile play the Ease-dropper,
To heare if any meane to shrinke from me.

Exeunt Richard & Ratliffe.

Enter the Lords to Richmond sitting in his Tent.

Richm. Good morrow Richmond.

Rich. Cry mercy Lords, and watchfull Gentlemen,
That you haue tane a tardie sluggard heere?

Lords. How haue you slept my Lord?

Rich. The sweetest sleepe,
And fairest boading Dreames,
That euer entred in a drowsie head,
Haue I since your departure had my Lords.
Me thought their Soules, whose bodies *Rich.* murther'd,
Came to my Tent, and cried on Victory:
I promise you my Heart is very iocond,
In the remembrance of so faire a dreame,
How farre into the Morning is it Lords?

Lor. Vpon the stroke of foure.

Rich. Why then 'tis time to Arme, and giue direction.

His Oration to his Souldiers.

More then I haue said, louing Countrymen,
The leysure and inforcement of the time
Forbids to dwell vpon: yet remember this,

God

God, and our good cause, fight vpon our side,
The Prayers of holy Saints and wronged soules,
Like high rear'd Bulwarkes, stand before our Faces,
(*Richard* except) those whom we fight against,
Had rather haue vs win, then him they follow.
For, what is he they follow? Truly Gentlemen,
A bloudy Tyrant, and a Homicide:
One rais'd in blood, and one in blood establish'd;
One that made meanes to come by what he hath,
And slaughter'd those that were the meanes to help him:
A base foule Stone, made precious by the soyle
Of Englands Chaire, where he is falsely set:
One that hath euer beene Gods Enemy.
Then if you fight against Gods Enemy,
God will in iustice ward you as his Soldiers.
If you do sweare to put a Tyrant downe,
You sleepe in peace, the Tyrant being slaine:
If you do fight against your Countries Foes,
Your Countries Fat shall pay your paines the hyre.
If you do fight in safegard of your wiues,
Your wiues shall welcome home the Conquerors.
If you do free your Children from the Sword,
Your Childrens Children quits it in your Age.
Then in the name of God and all these rights,
Aduance your Standards, draw your willing Swords.
For me, the ransome of my bold attempt,
Shall be this cold Corpes on the earth's cold face.
But if I thriue, the gaine of my attempt,
The least of you shall share his part thereof.
Sound Drummes and Trumpets boldly, and cheerefully,
God, and Saint *George*, *Richmond*, and Victory.

Enter King Richard, Ratcliffe, and Catesby.

K. What said Northumberland as touching Richmond?
Rat. That he was neuer trained vp in Armes.
King. He said the truth: and what said Surrey then?
Rat. He smil'd and said, the better for our purpose.
King. He was in the right, and so indeed it is.
Tell the clocke there. *Clocke strikes.*
Giue me a Kalender: Who saw the Sunne to day?
Rat. Not I my Lord.
King. Then he disdaines to shine: for by the Booke
He should haue brau'd the East an houre ago,
A blacke day will it be to somebody. *Ratcliffe.*
Rat. My Lord.
King. The Sun will not be seene to day,
The sky doth frowne, and lowre vpon our Army.
I would these dewy teares were from the ground.
Not shine to day? Why, what is that to me
More then to Richmond? For the selfe-same Heauen
That frownes on me, lookes sadly vpon him.

Enter Norfolke.

Nor. Arme, arme, my Lord: the foe vaunts in the field.
King. Come, bustle, bustle. Caparison my horse.
Call vp Lord *Stanley*, bid him bring his power,
I will leade forth my Soldiers to the plaine,
And thus my Battell shal be ordred.
My Foreward shall be drawne in length,
Consisting equally of Horse and Foot:
Our Archers shall be placed in the mid'st;
Iohn Duke of Norfolke, *Thomas* Earle of Surrey,
Shall haue the leading of the Foot and Horse.
They thus directed, we will fllow
In the maine Battell, whose puissance on either side
Shall be well-winged with our cheefest Horse:
This, and Saint George to boote.
What think'st thou Norfolke.
Nor. A good direction warlike Soueraigne,
This found I on my Tent this Morning.
Iockey of Norfolke, be not so bold,
For Dickon thy maister is bought and sold.
King. A thing deuised by the Enemy.
Go Gentlemen, euery man to his Charge,
Let not our babling Dreames affright our soules:
For Conscience is a word that Cowards vse,
Deuis'd at first to keepe the strong in awe,
Our strong armes be our Conscience, Swords our Law.
March on, ioyne brauely, let vs too't pell mell,
If not to heauen, then hand in hand to Hell.
What shall I say more then I haue inferr'd?
Remember whom you are to cope withall,
A sort of Vagabonds, Rascals, and Run-awayes,
A scum of Brittaines, and base Lackey Pezants,
Whom their o're-cloyed Country vomits forth
To desperate Aduentures, and assur'd Destruction.
You sleeping safe, they bring you to vnrest:
You hauing Lands, and blest with beauteous wiues,
They would restraine the one, distaine the other,
And who doth leade them, but a paltry Fellow?
Long kept in Britaine at our Mothers cost,
A Milke-sop, one that neuer in his life
Felt so much cold, as ouer shooes in Snow:
Let's whip these straglers o're the Seas againe
Lash hence these ouer-weening Ragges of France,
These famish'd Beggers, weary of their liues,
Who (but for dreaming on this fond exploit)
For want of meanes (poore Rats) had hang'd themselues.
If we be conquered, let men conquer vs,
And not these bastard Britaines, whom our Fathers
Haue in their owne Land beaten, bobb'd, and thump'd,
And on Record, left them the heires of shame.
Shall these enioy our Lands? lye with our Wiues?
Rauish our daughters? *Drum afarre off*
Hearke, I heare their Drumme,
Right Gentlemen of England, fight boldly yeomen,
Draw Archers draw your Arrowes to the head,
Spurre your proud Horses hard, and ride in blood,
Amaze the welkin with your broken staues.

Enter a Messenger.

What sayes Lord *Stanley*, will he bring his power?
Mes. My Lord, he doth deny to come.
King. Off with his sonne *Georges* head.
Nor. My Lord, the Enemy is past the Marsh:
After the battaile, let *George Stanley* dye.
King. A thousand hearts are great within my bosom.
Aduance our Standards, set vpon our Foes,
Our Ancient word of Courage, faire S. *George*
Inspire vs with the spleene of fiery Dragons:
Vpon them, Victorie sits on our helpes.

Alarum, excursions. Enter Catesby.

Cat. Rescue my Lord of Norfolke,
Rescue, Rescue:
The King enacts more wonders then a man,
Daring an opposite to euery danger:
His horse is slaine, and all on foot he fights,
Seeking for Richmond in the throat of death:
Rescue faire Lord, or else the day is lost.
Alarums.

Enter Richard.

Rich. A Horse, a Horse, my Kingdome for a Horse.
Cates. Withdraw my Lord, Ile helpe you to a Horse
Rich. Slaue, I haue set my life vpon a cast,
And I will stand the hazard of the Dye:
I thinke there be sixe Richmonds in the field,
Fiue haue I slaine to day, in stead of him.
A Horse, a Horse, my Kingdome for a Horse.

Alatum, Enter Richard and Richmond, they fight, Richard is slaine.

Retreat, and Flourish. Enter Richmond, Derby bearing the Crowne, with diuers other Lords.

Richm. God, and your Armes
Be prais'd Victorious Friends;
The day is ours, the bloudy Dogge is dead.
Der. Couragious Richmond,
Well hast thou acquit thee: Loe,
Heere these long vsurped Royalties,
From the dead Temples of this bloudy Wretch,
Haue I pluck'd off, to grace thy Browes withall.
Weare it, and make much of it.
Richm. Great God of Heauen, say Amen to all.
But tell me, is yong *George Stanley* liuing?
Der. He is my Lord, and safe in Leicester Towne,
Whither (if you please) we may withdraw vs.
Richm. What men of name are slaine on either side?
Der. *Iohn* Duke of Norfolke, *Walter* Lord Ferris,
Sir *Robert Brokenbury*, and Sir *William Brandon*.
Richm. Interre their Bodies, as become their Births,
Proclaime a pardon to the Soldiers fled,
That in submission will returne to vs,
And then as we haue tane the Sacrament,
We will vnite the White Rose, and the Red.
Smile Heauen vpon this faire Coniunction,
That long haue frown'd vpon their Enmity:
What Traitor heares me, and sayes not Amen?
England hath long beene mad, and scarr'd her selfe;
The Brother blindely shed the Brothers blood;
The Father, rashly slaughtered his owne Sonne;
The Sonne compell'd, beene Butcher to the Sire;
All this diuided Yorke and Lancaster,
Diuided, in their dire Diuision.
O now, let *Richmond* and *Elizabeth*,
The true Succeeders of each Royall House,
By Gods faire ordinance, conioyne together:
And let thy Heires (God if thy will be so)
Enrich the time to come, with Smooth-fac'd Peace,
With smiling Plenty, and faire Prosperous dayes.
Abate the edge of Traitors, Gracious Lord,
That would reduce these bloudy dayes againe,
And make poore England weepe in Streames of Blood;
Let them not liue to taste this Lands increase,
That would with Treason, wound this faire Lands peace.
Now Ciuill wounds are stopp'd, Peace liues agen;
That she may long liue heere, God say, Amen. *Exeunt*

FINIS.

The Famous History of the Life of King HENRY the Eight.

THE PROLOGUE.

I Come no more to make you laugh, Things now,
That beare a Weighty, and a Serious Brow,
Sad, high, and working, full of State and Woe:
Such Noble Scœnes, as draw the Eye to flow
We now present. Those that can Pitty, heere
May (if they thinke it well) let fall a Teare,
The Subiect will deserue it.. Such as giue
Their Money out of hope they may beleeue,
May heere finde Truth too. Those that come to see
Onely a show or two, and so agree,
The Play may passe: If they be still, and willing,
Ile vndertake may see away their shilling
Richly in two short houres. Onely they
That come to heare a Merry, Bawdy Play,
A noyse of Targets: Or to see a Fellow
In a long Motley Coate, garded with Yellow,
Will be deceyu'd. For gentle Hearers, know
To ranke our chosen Truth with such a show
As Foole, and Fight is, beside forfeyting
Our owne Braines, and the Opinion that we bring
To make that onely true, we now intend,
Will leaue vs neuer an vnderstanding Friend.
Therefore, for Goodnesse sake, and as you are knowne
The First and Happiest Hearers of the Towne,
Be sad, as we would make ye. Thinke ye see
The very Persons of our Noble Story,
As they were Liuing: Thinke you see them Great,
And follow'd with the generall throng, and sweat
Of thousand Friends: Then, in a moment, see
How soone this Mightinesse, meets Misery:
And if you can be merry then, Ile say,
A Man may weepe vpon his Wedding day.

Actus Primus. Scœna Prima.

Enter the Duke of Norfolke at one doore. At the other, the Duke of Buckingham, and the Lord Aburgauenny.

Buckingham.

GOod morrow, and well met. How haue ye done
Since last we saw in France?

Norf. I thanke your Grace:
Healthfull, and euer since a fresh Admirer
Of what I saw there.

Buck. An vntimely Ague
Staid me a Prisoner in my Chamber, when
Those Sunnes of Glory, those two Lights of Men
Met in the vale of Andren.

Nor. 'Twixt Guynes and Arde,
I was then present, saw them salute on Horsebacke,
Beheld them when they lighted, how they clung
In their Embracement, as they grew together,
Which had they,
What foure Thron'd ones could haue weigh'd
Such a compounded one?

Buck. All the whole time
I was my Chambers Prisoner.

Nor. Then you lost
The view of earthly glory: Men might say
Till this time Pompe was single, but now married
To one aboue it selfe. Each following day
Became the next dayes master, till the last
Made former Wonders, it's. To day the French,
All Clinquant all in Gold, like Heathen Gods
Shone downe the English; and to morrow, they
Made Britaine, India: Euery man that stood,
Shew'd like a Mine. Their Dwarfish Pages were
As Cherubins, all gilt: the Madams too,
Not vs'd to toyle, did almost sweat to beare
The Pride vpon them, that their very labour
Was to them, as a Painting. Now this Maske
Was cry'de incompareable; and th'ensuing night
Made it a Foole, and Begger. The two Kings
Equall in lustre, were now best, now worst
As presence did present them: Him in eye,
Still him in praise, and being present both,
'Twas said they saw but one, and no Discerner
Durst wagge his Tongue in censure, when these Sunnes
(For so they phrase 'em) by their Heralds challeng'd
The Noble Spirits to Armes, they did performe

Beyond thoughts Compasse, that former fabulous Storie
Being now seene, possible enough, got credit
That *Beuis* was beleeu'd.

Buc. Oh you go farre.

Nor. As I belong to worship, and affect
In Honor, Honesty, the tract of eu'ry thing,
Would by a good Discourser loose some life,
Which Actions selfe, was tongue too.

Buc. All was Royall,
To the disposing of it nought rebell'd,
Order gaue each thing view. The Office did
Distinctly his full Function: who did guide,
I meane who set the Body, and the Limbes
Of this great Sport together?

Nor. As you guesse:
One certes, that promises no Element
In such a businesse.

Buc. I pray you who, my Lord?

Nor. All this was ordred by the good Discretion
Of the right Reuerend Cardinall of Yorke.

Buc. The diuell speed him: No mans Pye is freed
From his Ambitious finger. What had he
To do in these fierce Vanities? I wonder,
That such a Keech can with his very bulke
Take vp the Rayes o'th'beneficiall Sun,
And keepe it from the Earth.

Nor. Surely Sir,
There's in him stuffe, that put's him to these ends:
For being not propt by Auncestry, whose grace
Chalkes Successors their way; nor call'd vpon
For high feats done to'th'Crowne; neither Allied
To eminent Assistants; but Spider-like
Out of his Selfe-drawing Web. O giues vs note,
The force of his owne merit makes his way
A guift that heauen giues for him, which buyes
A place next to the King.

Abur. I cannot tell
What Heauen hath giuen him: let some Grauer eye
Pierce into that, but I can see his Pride
Peepe through each part of him: whence ha's he that,
If not from Hell? The Diuell is a Niggard,
Or ha's giuen all before, and he begins
A new Hell in himselfe.

Buc. Why the Diuell,
Vpon this French going out, tooke he vpon him
(Without the priuity o'th'King) t'appoint
Who should attend on him? He makes vp the File
Of all the Gentry; for the most part such
To whom as great a Charge, as little Honor
He meant to lay vpon: and his owne Letter
The Honourable Boord of Councell, out
Must fetch him in, he Papers.

Abur. I do know
Kinsmen of mine, three at the least, that haue
By this, so sicken'd their Estates, that neuer
They shall abound as formerly.

Buc. O many
Haue broke their backes with laying Mannors on 'em
For this great Iourney. What did this vanity
But minister communication of
A most poore issue.

Nor. Greeuingly I thinke,
The Peace betweene the French and vs, not valewes
The Cost that did conclude it.

Buc. Euery man,
After the hideous storme that follow'd, was
A thing Inspir'd, and not consulting, broke
Into a generall Prophesie; That this Tempest
Dashing the Garment of this Peace, aboaded
The sodaine breach on't.

Nor. Which is budded out,
For France hath flaw'd the League, and hath attach'd
Our Merchants goods at Burdeux.

Abur. Is it therefore
Th'Ambassador is silenc'd?

Nor. Marry is't.

Abur. A proper Title of a Peace, and purchas'd
At a superfluous rate.

Buc. Why all this Businesse
Our Reuerend Cardinall carried.

Nor. Like it your Grace,
The State takes notice of the priuate difference
Betwixt you, and the Cardinall. I aduise you
(And take it from a heart, that wishes towards you
Honor, and plenteous safety) that you reade
The Cardinals Malice, and his Potency
Together; To consider further, that
What his high Hatred would effect, wants not
A Minister in his Power. You know his Nature,
That he's Reuengefull; and I know, his Sword
Hath a sharpe edge: It's long, and't may be saide
It reaches farre, and where 'twill not extend,
Thither he darts it. Bosome vp my counsell,
You'l finde it wholesome. Loe, where comes that Rock
That I aduice your shunning.

Enter Cardinall Wolsey, the Purse borne before him, certaine of the Guard, and two Secretaries with Papers: The Cardinall in his passage, fixeth his eye on Buckham, and Buckingham on him, both full of disdaine.

Car. The Duke of *Buckinghams* Surueyor? Ha?
Where's his Examination?

Secr. Heere so please you.

Car. Is he in person, ready?

Secr. I, please your Grace.

Car. Well, we shall then know more, & *Buckingham*
Shall lessen this bigge looke.

Exeunt Cardinall, and his Traine.

Buc. This Butchers Curre is venom'd-mouth'd, and I
Haue not the power to muzzle him, therefore best
Not wake him in his slumber. A Beggers booke,
Out-worths a Nobles blood.

Nor. What are you chaff'd?
Aske God for Temp'rance, that's th'appliance onely
Which your disease requires.

Buc. I read in's looks
Matter against me, and his eye reuil'd
Me as his abiect obiect, at this instant
He bores me with some tricke; He's gone to'th'King:
Ile follow, and out-stare him.

Nor. Stay my Lord,
And let your Reason with your Choller question
What 'tis you go about: to climbe steepe hilles
Requires slow pace at first. Anger is like
A full hot Horse, who being allow'd his way
Selfe-mettle tyres him: Not a man in England
Can aduise me like you: Be to your selfe,
As you would to your Friend.

Buc. Ile to the King,
And from a mouth of Honor, quite cry downe

This

This *Ipswich* fellowes insolence; or proclaime,
There's difference in no persons.

Norf. Be aduis'd;
Heat not a Furnace for your foe so hot
That it do sindge your selfe. We may out-runne
By violent swiftnesse that which we run at;
And lose by ouer-running: know you not,
The fire that mounts the liquor til't run ore,
In seeming to augment it, wasts it: be aduis'd;
I say againe there is no English Soule
More stronger to direct you then your selfe;
If with the sap of reason you would quench,
Or but allay the fire of passion.

Buck. Sir,
I am thankfull to you, and Ile goe along
By your prescription: but this top-proud fellow,
Whom from the flow of gall I name not, but
From sincere motions, by Intelligence,
And proofes as cleere as Founts in *Iuly*, when
Wee see each graine of grauell; I doe know
To be corrupt and treasonous.

Norf. Say not treasonous.

Buck. To th'King Ile say't, & make my vouch as strong
As shore of Rocke: attend. This holy Foxe,
Or Wolfe, or both (for he is equall rau'nous
As he is subtile, and as prone to mischiefe,
As able to perform't) his minde, and place
Infecting one another, yea reciprocally,
Only to shew his pompe, as well in France,
As here at home, suggests the King our Master
To this last costly Treaty: Th'enteruiew,
That swallowed so much treasure, and like a glasse
Did breake ith'wrenching.

Norf. Faith, and so it did.

Buck. Pray giue me fauour Sir: This cunning Cardinall
The Articles o'th' Combination drew
As himselfe pleas'd; and they were ratified
As he cride thus let be, to as much end,
As giue a Crutch to th'dead. But our Count-Cardinall
Has done this, and tis well: for worthy *Wolsey*
(Who cannot erre) he did it. Now this followes,
(Which as I take it, is a kinde of Puppie
To th'old dam Treason) *Charles* the Emperour,
Vnder pretence to see the Queene his Aunt,
(For twas indeed his colour, but he came
To whisper *Wolsey*) here makes visitation,
His feares were that the Interview betwixt
England and France, might through their amity
Breed him some preiudice; for from this League,
Peep'd harmes that menac'd him. Priuily
Deales with our Cardinal, and as I troa
Which I doe well; for I am sure the Emperour
Paid ere he promis'd, whereby his Suit was granted
Ere it was ask'd. But when the way was made
And pau'd with gold: the Emperor thus desir'd,
That he would please to alter the Kings course,
And breake the foresaid peace. Let the King know
(As soone he shall by me) that thus the Cardinall
Does buy and sell his Honour as he pleases,
And for his owne aduantage.

Norf. I am sorry
To heare this of him; and could wish he were
Somthing mistaken in't.

Buck. No, not a sillable:
I doe pronounce him in that very shape
He shall appeare in proofe.

Enter Brandon, a Sergeant at Armes before him, and two or three of the Guard.

Brandon. Your Office Sergeant: execute it.

Sergeant. Sir,
My Lord the Duke of *Buckingham*, and Earle
Of *Hertford, Stafford* and *Northampton*, I
Arrest thee of High Treason, in the name
Of our most Soueraigne King.

Buck. Lo you my Lord,
The net has falne vpon me, I shall perish
Vnder deuice, and practise:

Bran. I am sorry,
To see you tane from liberty, to looke on
The busines present. Tis his Highnes pleasure
You shall to th' Tower.

Buck. It will helpe me nothing
To plead mine Innocence; for that dye is on me
Which makes my whit'st part, black. The will of Heau'n
Be done in this and all things: I obey.
O my Lord *Aburgany*: Fare you well.

Bran. Nay, he must beare you company. The King
Is pleas'd you shall to th'Tower, till you know
How he determines further.

Abur. As the Duke said,
The will of Heauen be done, and the Kings pleasure
By me obey'd.

Bran. Here is a warrant from
The King, t'attach Lord *Mountacute*, and the Bodies
Of the Dukes Confessor, *Iohn de la Car*,
One *Gilbert Pecke*, his Councellour.

Buck. So, so;
These are the limbs o'th' Plot: no more I hope.

Bra. A Monke o'th' *Chartreux*.

Buck: O *Michaell Hopkins*?

Bra. He.

Buck. My Surueyor is falce: The ore-great *Cardinall*
Hath shew'd him gold; my life is spand already:
I am the shadow of poore *Buckingham*,
Whose Figure euen this instant Clowd puts on,
By Darkning my cleere Sunne. My Lords farewell. *Exe.*

Scena Secunda.

Cornets. Enter King Henry, leaning on the Cardinals shoulder, the Nobles, and Sir Thomas Louell: the Cardinall places himselfe vnder the Kings feete on his right side.

King. My life it selfe, and the best heart of it,
Thankes you for this great care: I stood i'th' leuell
Of a full-charg'd confederacie, and giue thankes
To you that choak'd it. Let be cald before vs
That Gentleman of *Buckinghams*, in person,
Ile heare him his confessions iustifie,
And point by point the Treasons of his Maister,
He shall againe relate.

A noyse within crying roome for the Queene, vsher'd by the Duke of Norfolke. Enter the Queene, Norfolke and Suffolke: she kneels. King riseth from his State, takes her vp, kisses and placeth her by him.

Queen. Nay, we must longer kneele; I am a Suitor.

King. Arise, and take place by vs; halfe your Suit
Neuer name to vs; you haue halfe our power:

The

The other moity ere you aske is giuen,
Repeat your will, and take it.

Queen. Thanke your Maiesty
That you would loue your selfe, and in that loue
Not vnconsidered leaue your Honour, nor
The dignity of your Office; is the poynt
Of my Petition.

Kin. Lady mine proceed.

Queen. I am solicited not by a few,
And those of true condition; That your Subiects
Are in great grieuance: There haue beene Commissions
Sent downe among 'em, which hath flaw'd the heart
Of all their Loyalties; wherein, although
My good Lord Cardinall, they vent reproches
Most bitterly on you, as putter on
Of these exactions: yet the King, our Maister (not
Whose Honor Heauen shield from soile; euen he escapes
Language vnmannerly; yea, such which breakes
The sides of loyalty, and almost appeares
In lowd Rebellion.

Norf. Not almost appeares,
It doth appeare; for, vpon these Taxations,
The Clothiers all not able to maintaine
The many to them longing, haue put off
The Spinsters, Carders, Fullers, Weauers, who
Vnfit for other life, compeld by hunger
And lack of other meanes, in desperate manner
Daring th'euent too th'teeth, are all in vprore,
And danger serues among them.

Kin. Taxation?
Wherein? and what Taxation? My Lord Cardinall,
You that are blam'd for it alike with vs,
Know you of this Taxation?

Card. Please you Sir,
I know but of a single part in ought
Pertaines to th'State; and front but in that File
Where others tell steps with me.

Queen. No, my Lord?
You know no more then others? But you frame
Things that are knowne alike, which are not wholsome
To those which would not know them, and yet must
Perforce be their acquaintance. These exactions
(Whereof my Soueraigne would haue note) they are
Most pestilent to th'hearing, and to beare 'em,
The Backe is Sacrifice to th'load; They say
They are deuis'd by you, er else you suffer
Too hard an exclamation.

Kin. Still Exaction:
The nature of it, in what kinde let's know,
Is this Exaction?

Queen. I am much too venturous
In tempting of your patience; but am boldned
Vnder your promis'd pardon. The Subiects griefe
Comes through Commissions, which compels from each
The sixt part of his Substance, to be leuied
Without delay; and the pretence for this
Is nam'd, your warres in France: this makes bold mouths,
Tongues spit their duties out, and cold hearts freeze
Allegeance in them; their curses now
Liue where their prayers did: and it's come to passe,
This tractable obedience is a Slaue
To each incensed Will: I would your Highnesse
Would giue it quicke consideration; for
There is no primer basenesse.

Kin. By my life,
This is against our pleasure.

Card. And for me,
I haue no further gone in this, then by
A single voice, and that not past me, but
By learned approbation of the Iudges: If I am
Traduc'd by ignorant Tongues, which neither know
My faculties nor person, yet will be
The Chronicles of my doing: Let me say,
'Tis but the fate of Place, and the rough Brake
That Vertue must goe through: we must not stint
Our necessary actions, in the feare
To cope malicious Censurers, which euer,
As rau'nous Fishes doe a Vessell follow
That is new trim'd; but benefit no further
Then vainly longing. What we oft doe best,
By sicke Interpreters (once weake ones) is
Not ours, or not allow'd; what worst, as oft
Hitting a grosser quality, is cride vp
For our best Act: if we shall stand still,
In feare our motion will be mock'd, or carp'd at,
We should take roote here, where we sit;
Or sit State Statues onely.

Kin. Things done well,
And with a care, exempt themselues from feare:
Things done without example, in their issue
Are to be fear'd. Haue you a President
Of this Commission? I beleeue, not any.
We must not rend our Subiects from our Lawes,
And sticke them in our Will. Sixt part of each?
A trembling Contribution; why we take
From euery Tree, lop, barke, and part o'th' Timber:
And though we leaue it with a roote thus hackt,
The Ayre will drinke the Sap. To euery County
Where this is question'd, send our Letters, with
Free pardon to each man that has deny'de
The force of this Commission: pray looke too't;
I put it to your care.

Card. A word with you.
Let there be Letters writ to euery Shire,
Of the Kings grace and pardon: the greeued Commons
Hardly conceiue of me. Let it be nois'd,
That through our Intercession, this Reuokement
And pardon comes: I shall anon aduise you
Further in the proceeding. *Exit Secret.*

Enter Surueyor.

Queen. I am sorry, that the Duke of *Buckingham*
Is run in your displeasure.

Kin. It grieues many:
The Gentleman is Learn'd, and a most rare Speaker,
To Nature none more bound; his trayning such,
That he may furnish and instruct great Teachers,
And neuer seeke for ayd out of himselfe: yet see,
When these so Noble benefits shall proue
Not well dispos'd, the minde growing once corrupt,
They turne to vicious formes, ten times more vgly
Then euer they were faire. This man so compleat,
Who was enrold 'mongst wonders; and when we
Almost with rauish'd listning, could not finde
His houre of speech, a minute: He, (my Lady)
Hath into monstrous habits put the Graces
That once were his, and is become as blacke,
As if besmear'd in hell. Sit by Vs, you shall heare
(This was his Gentleman in trust) of him
Things to strike Honour sad. Bid him recount
The fore-recited practises, whereof
We cannot feele too little, heare too much.

Card.

Card. Stand forth,& with bold spirit relate what you
Most like a carefull Subiect haue collected
Out of the Duke of *Buckingham.*
Kin. Speake freely.
Sur. First,it was vsuall with him; euery day
It would infect his Speech: That if the King
Should without issue dye; hee'l carry it so
To make the Scepter his. These very words
I'ue heard him vtter to his Sonne in Law,
Lord *Aburgany*, to whom by oth he menac'd
Reuenge vpon the *Cardinall.*
Card. Please your Highnesse note
This dangerous conception in this point,
Not frended by his wish to your High person;
His will is most malignant,and it stretches
Beyond you to your friends.
Queen. My learn'd Lord *Cardinall,*
Deliuer all with Charity.
Kin. Speake on;
How grounded hee his Title to the Crowne
Vpon our faile; to this poynt hast thou heard him,
At any time speake ought?
Sur. He was brought to this,
By a vaine Prophesie of *Nicholas Henton.*
Kin. What was that *Henton?*
Sur. Sir, a *Chartreux* Fryer,
His Confessor, who fed him euery minute
With words of Soueraignty.
Kin. How know'st thou this?
Sur. Not long before your Hignesse sped to France,
The Duke being at the Rose,within the Parish
Saint *Lawrence Poultney*, did of me demand
What was the speech among the Londoners,
Concerning the French Iourney. I replide,
Men feare the French would proue perfidious
To the Kings danger: presently, the Duke
Said,'twas the feare indeed, and that he doubted
'Twould proue the verity of certaine words
Spoke by a holy Monke, that oft,sayes he,
Hath sent to me, wishing me to permit
Iohn de la Car, my Chaplaine,a choyce howre
To heare from him a matter of some moment:
Whom after vnder the Commissions Seale,
He sollemnly had sworne, that what he spoke
My Chaplaine to no Creature liuing,but
To me, should vtter, with demure Confidence,
This pausingly ensu'de; neither the King, nor's Heyres
(Tell you the Duke) shall prosper, bid him striue
To the loue o'th' Commonalty, the Duke
Shall gouerne England.
Queen. If I know you well,
You were the Dukes Surueyor,and lost your Office
On the complaint o'th' Tenants; take good heed
You charge not in your spleene a Noble person,
And spoyle your nobler Soule; I say,take heed;
Yes,heartily beseech you.
Kin. Let him on: Goe forward.
Sur. On my Soule, Ile speake but truth.
I told my Lord the Duke, by th'Diuels illusions
The Monke might be deceiu'd, and that 'twas dangerous
For this to ruminate on this so farre, vntill
It forg'd him some designe, which being beleeu'd
It was much like to doe: He answer'd,Tush,
It can doe me no damage; adding further,
That had the King in his last Sicknesse faild,
The Cardinals and Sir *Thomas Louels* heads
Should haue gone off.
Kin. Ha? What,so rancke? Ah,ha,
There's mischiefe in this man; canst thou say further?
Sur. I can my Liedge.
Kin. Proceed.
Sur. Being at *Greenwich,*
After your Highnesse had reprou'd the Duke
About Sir *William Blumer.*
Kin. I remember of such a time, being my sworn ser-(uant,
The Duke retein'd him his. But on: what hence?
Sur. If (quoth he) I for this had beene committed,
As to the Tower, I thought; I would haue plaid
The Part my Father meant to act vpon
Th'Vsurper *Richard*, who being at *Salsbury*,
Made suit to come in's presence; which if granted,
(As he made semblance of his duty) would
Haue put his knife into him.
Kin. A Gyant Traytor.
Card. Now Madam, may his Highnes liue in freedome,
And this man out of Prison.
Queen. God mend all.
Kin. Ther's somthing more would out of thee; what (say'st?
Sur. After the Duke his Father, with the knife
He stretch'd him,and with one hand on his dagger,
Another spread on's breast, mounting his eyes,
He did discharge a horrible Oath,whose tenor
Was, were he euill vs'd, he would outgoe
His Father, by as much as a performance
Do's an irresolute purpose.
Kin. There's his period,
To sheath his knife in vs: he is attach'd,
Call him to present tryall: if he may
Finde mercy in the Law, 'tis his; if none,
Let him not seek't of vs: By day and night
Hee's Traytor to th' height. *Exeunt.*

Scæna Tertia.

Enter L. Chamberlaine and L. Sandys.

L. Ch. Is't possible the spels of France should iuggle
Men into such strange mysteries?
L. San. New customes,
Though they be neuer so ridiculous,
(Nay let 'em be vnmanly) yet are follow'd.
L. Ch. As farre as I see,all the good our English
Haue got by the late Voyage, is but meerely
A fit or two o'th' face, (but they are shrewd ones)
For when they hold 'em,you would sweare directly
Their very noses had been Councellours
To *Pepin* or *Clotharius*,they keepe State so.
L. San. They haue all new legs,
And lame ones; one would take it,
That neuer see'em pace before, the Spauen
A Spring-halt rain'd among 'em.
L. Ch. Death my Lord,
Their cloathes are after such a Pagan cut too't,
That sure th'haue worne out Ch istendome: how now?
What newes, Sir *Thomas Louell?*

Enter Sir Thomas Louell.

Louell. Faith my Lord,
I heare of none but the new Proclamation,
That's clapt vpon the Court Gate.

L. Cham.

L. Cham. What is't for?
Lou. The reformation of our trauel'd Gallants,
That fill the Court with quarrels, talke, and Taylors.
L. Cham. I'm glad 'tis there;
Now I would pray our Monsieurs
To thinke an English Courtier may be wise,
And neuer see the *Louure.*
Lou: They must either
(For so run the Conditions) leaue those remnants
Of Foole and Feather, that they got in France,
With all their honourable points of ignorance
Pertaining thereunto; as Fights and Fire-workes,
Abusing better men then they can be
Out of a forreigne wisedome, renouncing cleane
The faith they haue in Tennis and tall Stockings,
Short blistred Breeches, and those types of Trauell;
And vnderstand againe like honest men,
Or pack to their old Playfellowes; there, I take it,
They may *Cum Priuilegio*, wee away
The lag end of their lewdnesse, and be laugh'd at.
L. San. Tis time to giue 'em Physicke, their diseases
Are growne so catching.
L. Cham What a losse our Ladies
Will haue of these trim vanities?
Louell. I marry,
There will be woe indeed Lords, the slye whorsons
Haue got a speeding tricke to lay downe Ladies.
A French Song, and a Fiddle, ha's no Fellow.
L. San. The Diuell fiddle 'em,
I am glad they are going,
For sure there's no conuerting of 'em: now
An honest Country Lord as I am, beaten
A long time out of play, may bring his plaine song,
And haue an houre of hearing, and by'r Lady
Held currant Musicke too.
L. Cham. Well said Lord *Sands*,
Your Colts tooth is not cast yet?
L. San. No my Lord,
Nor shall not while I haue a stumpe.
L. Cham. Sir *Thomas*,
Whither were you a going?
Lou. To the Cardinals;
Your Lordship is a guest too.
L. Cham. O, 'tis true;
This night he makes a Supper, and a great one,
To many Lords and Ladies; there will be
The Beauty of this Kingdome Ile assure you.
Lou. That Churchman
Beares a bounteous minde indeed,
A hand as fruitfull as the Land that feeds vs,
His dewes fall euery where.
L. Cham. No doubt hee's Noble;
He had a blacke mouth that said other of him.
L. San. He may my Lord,
Ha's wherewithall in him;
Sparing would shew a worse sinne, then ill Doctrine,
Men of his way, should be most liberall,
They are set heere for examples.
L. Cham. True, they are so;
But few now giue so great ones:
My Barge stayes;
Your Lordship shall along: Come, good Sir *Thomas*,
We shall be late else, which I would not be,
For I was spoke to, with Sir *Henry Guilford*
This night to be Comptrollers.
L. San. I am your Lordships. *Exeunt.*

Scena Quarta.

Hoboies. A small Table vnder a State for the Cardinall, a longer Table for the Guests. Then Enter Anne Bullen, and diuers other Ladies, & Gentlemen, as Guests at one Doore; at an other Doore enter Sir Henry Guilford.

S. Hen. Guilf. Ladyes,
A generall welcome from his Grace
Salutes ye all; This Night he dedicates
To faire content, and you: None heere he hopes
In all this Noble Beuy, has brought with her
One care abroad: hee would haue all as merry:
As first, good Company, good wine, good welcome,
Can make good people.

Enter L. Chamberlaine L. Sands, and Louell.

O my Lord, y'are tardy;
The very thought of this faire Company,
Clapt wings to me.
Cham. You are young Sir *Harry Guilford.*
San. Sir *Thomas Louell*, had the Cardinall
But halfe my Lay-thoughts in him, some of these
Should finde a running Banket, ere they rested,
I thinke would better please 'em: by my life,
They are a sweet society of faire ones.
Lou. O that your Lordship were but now Confessor,
To one or two of these.
San. I would I were,
They should finde easie pennance.
Lou. Faith how easie?
San. As easie as a downe bed would affoord it.
Cham. Sweet Ladies will it please you sit; Sir *Harry*
Place you that side, Ile take the charge of this:
His Grace is entring. Nay, you must not freeze,
Two women plac'd together, makes cold weather:
My Lord *Sands*, you are one will keepe 'em waking:
Pray sit betweene these Ladies.
San. By my faith,
And thanke your Lordship: by your leaue sweet Ladies,
If I chance to talke a little wilde, forgiue me:
I had it from my Father.
An. Bul. Was he mad Sir?
San. O, very mad, exceeding mad, in loue too;
But he would bite none, iust as I doe now,
He would Kisse you Twenty with a breath.
Cham. Well said my Lord:
So now y'are fairely seated: Gntlemen,
The pennance lyes on you; if these faire Ladies
Passe away frowning.
San. For my little Cure,
Let me alone.

Hoboyes. Enter Cardinall Wolsey, and takes his State.

Card Y'are wel ome my faire Guests; that noble Lady
Or Gentleman that is not freely merry
Is not my Friend. This to confirme my welcome,
And to you all good health.
San. Your Grace is Noble,
Let me haue such a Bowle may hold my thankes,
And saue me so much talking.
Card. My Lord *Sands*,

I am beholding to you : cheere your neighbours:
Ladies you are not merry; Gentlemen,
Whose fault is this?

San. The red wine first must rise
In their faire cheekes my Lord, then wee shall haue 'em,
Talke vs to silence.

An.B. You are a merry Gamster
My Lord *Sands*.

San. Yes, if I make my play:
Heer's to your Ladiship, and pledge it Madam:
For tis to such a thing.

An.B. You cannot shew me.

Drum and Trumpet, Chambers dischargd.

San. I told your Grace, they would talke anon.

Card. What's that?

Cham. Looke out there, some of ye.

Card. What warlike voyce,
And to what end is this? Nay, Ladies, feare not;
By all the lawes of Warre y'are priuiledg'd.

Enter a Seruant.

Cham. How now, what is't?

Seru. A noble troupe of Strangers,
For so they seeme; th'haue left their Barge and landed,
And hither make, as great Embassadors
From forraigne Princes.

Card. Good Lord Chamberlaine,
Go, giue 'em welcome; you can speake the French tongue
And pray receiue 'em Nobly, and conduct 'em
Into our presence, where this heauen of beauty
Shall shine at full vpon them. Some attend him.

All rise, and Tables remou'd.

You haue now a broken Banket, but wee'l mend it.
A good digestion to you all; and once more
I showre a welcome on yee: welcome all.

Hoboyes. Enter King and others as Maskers, habited like Shepheards, vsher'd by the Lord Chamberlaine. They passe directly before the Cardinall, and gracefully salute him.

A noble Company: what are their pleasures?

Cham. Because they speak no English, thus they praid
To tell your Grace: That hauing heard by fame
Of this so Noble and so faire assembly,
This night to meet heere they could doe no lesse,
(Out of the great respect they beare to beauty)
But leaue their Flockes, and vnder your faire Conduct
Craue leaue to view these Ladies, and entreat
An houre of Reuels with 'em.

Card. Say, Lord *Chamberlaine*,
They haue done my poore house grace:
For which I pay 'em a thousand thankes,
And pray 'em take their pleasures.

Choose Ladies, King and An Bullen.

King The fairest hand I euer touch'd: O Beauty,
Till now I neuer knew thee.

Musicke, Dance.

Card. My Lord.

Cham. Your Grace.

Card. Pray tell 'em thus much from me:
There should be one amongst 'em by his person
More worthy this place then my selfe, to whom
(If I but knew him) with my loue aud duty
I would surrender it. *Whisper.*

Cham. I will my Lord.

Card. What say they?

Cham. Such a one, they all confesse
There is indeed, which they would haue your Grace
Find out, and he will take it.

Card. Let me see then,
By all your good leaues Gentlemen; heere Ile make
My royall choyce.

Kin. Ye haue found him Cardinall,
You hold a faire Assembly; you doe well Lord:
You are a Churchman, or Ile tell you Cardinall,
I should iudge now vnhappily.

Card. I am glad
Your Grace is growne so pleasant.

Kin. My Lord Chamberlaine,
Prethee come hither, what faire Ladie's that?

Cham. An't please your Grace,
Sir *Thomas Bullens* Daughter, the Viscount *Rochford*,
One of her Highnesse women.

Kin. By Heauen she is a dainty one. Sweet heart,
I were vnmannerly to take you out,
And not to kisse you. A health Gentlemen,
Let it goe round.

Card. Sir *Thomas Louell*, is the Banket ready
I'th' Priuy Chamber?

Lou. Yes, my Lord.

Card. Your Grace
I feare, with dancing is a little heated.

Kin. I feare too much.

Card. There's fresher ayre my Lord,
In the next Chamber.

Kin. Lead in your Ladies eu'ry one: Sweet Partner,
I must not yet forsake you: Let's be merry,
Good my Lord Cardinall: I haue halfe a dozen healths,
To drinke to these faire Ladies, and a measure
To lead 'em once againe, and then let's dreame
Who's best in fauour. Let the Musicke knock it.

Exeunt with Trumpets.

Actus Secundus. Scena Prima.

Enter two Gentlemen at seuerall Doores.

1. Whether away so fast?

2. O, God saue ye:
Eu'n to the Hall, to heare what shall become
Of the great Duke of Buckingham.

1. Ile saue you
That labour Sir. All's now done but the Ceremony
Of bringing backe the Prisoner.

2. Were you there?

1. Yes indeed was I.

2 Pray speake what ha's happen'd.

1. You may guesse quickly what.

2. Is he found guilty?

1. Yes truely is he,
And condemn'd vpon't.

2. I am sorry fort.

1. So are a number more.

2. But pray how past it?

1. Ile tell you in a little. The great Duke
Came to the Bar; where, to his accusations
He pleaded still not guilty, and alleadged
Many sharpe reasons to defeat the Law.
The Kings Atturney on the contrary,
Vrg'd on the Examinations, proofes, confessions

Of

Of diuers witnesses, which the Duke desir'd
To him brought *viua voce* to his face;
At which appear'd against him, his Surueyor
Sir *Gilbert Pecke* his Chancellour, and *Iohn Car*,
Confessor to him, with that Diuell Monke,
Hopkins, that made this mischiefe.

2. That was hee
That fed him with his Prophecies.

1. The same,
All these accus'd him strongly, which he faine
Would haue flung from him; but indeed he couldnot;
And so his Peeres vpon this euidence,
Haue found him guilty of high Treason. Much
He spoke, and learnedly for life: But all
Was either pittied in him, or forgotten.

2. After all this, how did he beare himselfe?

1. When he was brought agen to th' Bar, to heare
His Knell rung out, his Iudgement, he was stir'd
With such an Agony, he sweat extreamly,
And somthing spoke in choller, ill, and hasty:
But he fell to himselfe againe, and sweetly,
In all the rest shew'd a most Noble patience.

2. I doe not thinke he feares death.

1. Sure he does not,
He neuer was so womanish, the cause
He may a little grieue at.

2. Certainly,
The Cardinall is the end of this.

1. Tis likely,
By all coniectures: First *Kildares* Attendure;
Then Deputy of Ireland, who remou'd
Earle *Surrey*, was sent thither, and in hast too,
Least he should helpe his Father.

2. That tricke of State
Was a deepe enuious one,

1. At his returne,
No doubt he will requite it; this is noted
(And generally) who euer the King fauours,
The Cardnall instantly will finde imployment,
And farre enough from Court too.

2. All the Commons
Hate him perniciously, and o' my Conscience
Wish him ten faddom deepe: This Duke as much
They loue and doate on: call him bounteous *Buckingham*,
The Mirror of all courtesie.

Enter Buckingham from his Arraignment, Tipstaues before him, the Axe with the edge towards him, Halberds on each side, accompanied with Sir Thomas Louell, Sir Nicholas Vaux, Sir Walter Sands, and common people, &c.

1. Stay there Sir,
And see the noble ruin'd man you speake of.

2. Let's stand close and behold him.

Buck. All good people,
You that thus farre haue come to pitty me;
Heare what I say, and then goe home and lose me.
I haue this day receiu'd a Traitors iudgement,
And by that name must dye; yet Heauen beare witnes,
And if I haue a Conscience, let it sincke me,
Euen as the Axe falls, if I be not faithfull.
The Law I beare no mallice for my death,
T'has done vpon the premises, but Iustice:
But those that sought it, I could wish more Christians:
(Be what they will) I heartily forgiue 'em;
Yet let 'em looke they glory not in mischiefe;
Nor build their euils on the graues of great men;
For then, my guiltlesse blood must cry against 'em.
For further life in this world I ne're hope,
Nor will I sue, although the King haue mercies
More then I dare make faults.
You few that lou'd me,
And dare be bold to weepe for *Buckingham*,
His Noble Friends and Fellowes; whom to leaue
Is only bitter to him, only dying:
Goe with me like good Angels to my end,
And as the long diuorce of Steele fals on me,
Make of your Prayers one sweet Sacrifice,
And lift my Soule to Heauen.
Lead on a Gods name.

Louell. I doe beseech your Grace, for charity
If euer any malice in your heart
Were hid against me, now to forgiue me frankly.

Buck. Sir *Thomas Louell*, I as free forgiue you
As I would be forgiuen: I forgiue all.
There cannot be those numberlesse offences
Gainst me, that I cannot take peace with:
No blacke Enuy shall make my Graue.
Commend mee to his Grace:
And if he speake of *Buckingham*; pray tell him,
You met him halfe in Heauen: my vowes and prayers
Yet are the Kings; and till my Soule forsake,
Shall cry for blessings on him. May he liue
Longer then I haue time to tell his yeares;
Euer belou'd and louing, may his Rule be;
And when old Time shall lead him to his end,
Goodnesse and he, fill vp one Monument.

Lou. To th' water side I must conduct your Grace;
Then giue my Charge vp to Sir *Nicholas Vaux*,
Who vndertakes you to your end.

Vaux. Prepare there,
The Duke is comming: See the Barge be ready;
And fit it with such furniture as suites
The Greatnesse of his Person.

Buck. Nay, Sir *Nicholas*,
Let it alone; my State now will but mocke me.
When I came hither, I was Lord High Constable,
And Duke of *Buckingham*: now, poore *Edward Bohun*;
Yet I am richer then my base Accusers,
That neuer knew what Truth meant: I now seale it;
And with that bloud will make 'em one day groane for't.
My noble Father *Henry* of *Buckingham*,
Who first rais'd head against Vsurping *Richard*,
Flying for succour to his Seruant *Banister*,
Being distrest; was by that wretch betraid,
And without Tryall, fell; Gods peace be with him.
Henry the Seauenth succeeding, truly pittying
My Fathers losse; like a most Royall Prince
Restor'd me to my Honours: and out of ruines
Made my Name once more Noble. Now his Sonne,
Henry the Eight, Life, Honour, Name and all
That made me happy; at one stroake ha's taken
For euer from the World. I had my Tryall,
And must needs say a Noble one; which makes me
A little happier then my wretched Father:
Yet thus farre we are one in Fortunes; both
Fell by our Seruants, by those Men we lou'd most:
A most vnnaturall and faithlesse Seruice.
Heauen ha's an end in all: yet, you that heare me,
This from a dying man receiue as certaine:
Where you are liberall of your loues and Councels,
Be sure you be not loose; for those you make friends,

And giue your hearts to; when they once perceiue
The least rub in your fortunes, fall away
Like water from ye, neuer found againe
But where they meane to sinke ye: all good people
Pray for me, I must now forsake ye; the last houre
Of my long weary life is come vpon me:
Farewell; and when you would say somthing that is sad,
Speake how I fell.
I haue done; and God forgiue me.

Exeunt Duke and Traine.

1. O, this is full of pitty; Sir, it cals
I feare, too many curses on their heads
That were the Authors.

2. If the Duke be guiltlesse,
'Tis full of woe: yet I can giue you inckling
Of an ensuing euill, if it fall,
Greater then this.

1. Good Angels keepe it from vs:
What may it be? you doe not doubt my faith Sir?

2. This Secret is so weighty, 'twill require
A strong faith to conceale it.

1. Let me haue it:
I doe not talke much.

2. I am confident;
You shall Sir: Did you not of late dayes heare
A buzzing of a Separation
Betweene the King and *Katherine*?

1. Yes, but it held not;
For when the King once heard it, out of anger
He sent command to the Lord Mayor straight
To stop the rumor; and allay those tongues
That durst disperse it.

2. But that slander Sir,
Is found a truth now: for it growes agen
Fresher then e're it was; and held for certaine
The King will venture at it. Either the Cardinall,
Or some about him neere, haue out of malice
To the good Queene, possest him with a scruple
That will vndoe her: To confirme this too,
Cardinall *Campeius* is arriu'd, and lately,
As all thinke for this busines.

1. Tis the Cardinall;
And meerely to reuenge him on the Emperour,
For not bestowing on him at his asking,
The Archbishopricke of *Toledo*, this is purpos'd.

2. I thinke
You haue hit the marke; but is't not cruell,
That she should feele the smart of this: the Cardinall
Will haue his will, and she must fall.

1. 'Tis wofull.
Wee are too open heere to argue this:
Let's thinke in priuate more. *Exeunt.*

Scena Secunda.

Enter Lord Chamberlaine, reading this Letter.

My Lord, the Horses your Lordship sent for, with all the care I had, I saw well chosen, ridden, and furnish'd. They were young and handsome, and of the best breed in the North. When they were ready to set out for London, a man of my Lord Cardinalls, by Commission, and maine power tooke 'em from me, with this reason: his maister would bee seru'd before a Subiect, if not before the King, which stop'd our mouthes Sir.

I feare he will indeede; well, let him haue them; hee will haue all I thinke.

Enter to the Lord Chamberlaine, the Dukes of Norfolke and Suffolke.

Norf. Well met my Lord *Chamberlaine.*

Cham. Good day to both your Graces.

Suff. How is the King imployd?

Cham. I left him priuate,
Full of sad thoughts and troubles.

Norf. What's the cause?

Cham. It seemes the Marriage with his Brothers Wife
Ha's crept too neere his Conscience.

Suff. No, his Conscience
Ha's crept too neere another Ladie.

Norf. Tis so;
This is the Cardinals doing: The King-Cardinall,
That blinde Priest, like the eldest Sonne of Fortune,
Turnes what he list. The King will know him one day.

Suff. Pray God he doe,
Hee'l neuer know himselfe else.

Norf. How holily he workes in all his businesse,
And with what zeale? For now he has crackt the League
Between vs & the Emperor (the Queens great Nephew)
He diues into the Kings Soule, and there scatters
Dangers, doubts, wringing of the Conscience,
Feares, and despaires, and all these for his Marriage.
And out of all these, to restore the King,
He counsels a Diuorce, a losse of her
That like a Iewell, ha's hung twenty yeares
About his necke, yet neuer lost her lustre;
Of her that loues him with that excellence,
That Angels loue good men with: Euen of her,
That when the greatest stroake of Fortune falls
Will blesse the King: and is not this course pious?

Cham. Heauen keep me from such councel: tis most true
These newes are euery where, euery tongue speaks 'em,
And euery true heart weepes for't. All that dare
Looke into these affaires, see this maine end,
The French Kings Sister. Heauen will one day open
The Kings eyes, that so long haue slept vpon
This bold bad man.

Suff. And free vs from his slauery.

Norf. We had need pray,
And heartily, for our deliuerance;
Or this imperious man will worke vs all
From Princes into Pages: all mens honours
Lie like one lumpe before him, to be fashion'd
Into what pitch he please.

Suff. For me, my Lords,
I loue him not, nor feare him, there's my Creede:
As I am made without him, so Ile stand,
If the King please: his Curses and his blessings
Touch me alike: th'are breath I not beleeue in.
I knew him, and I know him: so I leaue him
To him that made him proud; the Pope.

Norf. Let's in;
And with some other busines, put the King
From these sad thoughts, that work too much vpon him:
My Lord, youle beare vs company?

Cham. Excuse me,
The King ha's sent me otherwhere: Besides
You'l finde a most vnfit time to disturbe him:
Health to your Lordships.

Norfolke. Thankes my good Lord *Chamberlaine.*

Exit Lord Chamberlaine, and the King drawes the Curtaine and sits reading pensiuely.

Suff. How sad he lookes; sure he is much afflicted.

Kin. Who's there? Ha?

Norff. Pray God he be not angry.

Kin. Who's there I say? How dare you thrust your (selues
Into my priuate Meditations?
Who am I? Ha?

Norff. A gracious King, that pardons all offences
Malice ne're meant: Our breach of Duty this way,
Is businesse of Estate; in which, we come
To know your Royall pleasure.

Kin. Ye are too bold:
Go too; Ile make ye know your times of businesse:
Is this an howre for temporall affaires? Ha?

Enter Wolsey and Campeius with a Commission.

Who's there? my good Lord Cardinall? O my *Wolsey,*
The quiet of my wounded Conscience;
Thou art a cure fit for a King; you'r welcome
Most learned Reuerend Sir, into our Kingdome,
Vse vs, and it: My good Lord, haue great care,
I be not found a Talker.

Wol. Sir, you cannot;
I would your Grace would giue vs but an houre
Of priuate conference.

Kin. We are busie; goe.

Norff. This Priest ha's no pride in him?

Suff. Not to speake of:
I would not be so sicke though for his place:
But this cannot continue.

Norff. If it doe, Ile venture one; haue at him.

Suff. I another.

Exeunt Norfolke and Suffolke.

Wol. Your Grace ha's giuen a President of wisedome
Aboue all Princes, in committing freely
Your scruple to the voyce of Christendome:
Who can be angry now? What Enuy reach you?
The Spaniard tide by blood and fauour to her,
Must now confesse, if they haue any goodnesse,
The Tryall, iust and Noble. All the Clerkes,
(I meane the learned ones in Christian Kingdomes)
Haue their free voyces. Rome (the Nurse of Iudgement)
Inuited by your Noble selfe, hath sent
One generall Tongue vnto vs. This good man,
This iust and learned Priest, Cardnall *Campeius,*
Whom once more, I present vnto your Highnesse.

Kin. And once more in mine armes I bid him welcome,
And thanke the holy Conclaue for their loues,
They haue sent me such a Man, I would haue wish'd for.

Cam. Your Grace must needs deserue all strangers loues,
You are so Noble: To your Highnesse hand
I tender my Commission; by whose vertue,
The Court of Rome commanding. You my Lord
Cardinall of *Yorke,* are ioyn'd with me their Seruant,
In the vnpartiall iudging of this Businesse.

Kin. Two equall men: The Queene shall be acquain- (ted
Forthwith for what you come. Where's *Gardiner?*

Wol. I know your Maiesty, ha's alwayes lou'd her
So deare in heart, not to deny her that
A Woman of lesse Place might aske by Law;
Schollers allow'd freely to argue for her.

Kin. I, and the best she shall haue; and my fauour
To him that does best, God forbid els: Cardinall,
Prethee call *Gardiner* to me, my new Secretary.
I find him a fit fellow.

Enter Gardiner.

Wol. Giue me your hand: much ioy & fauour to you;
You are the Kings now.

Gard. But to be commanded
For euer by your Grace, whose hand ha's rais'd me.

Kin. Come hither *Gardiner.*

Walkes and whispers.

Camp. My Lord of *Yorke,* was not one Doctor *Pace*
In this mans place before him?

Wol. Yes, he was.

Camp. Was he not held a learned man?

Wol. Yes surely.

Camp. Beleeue me, there's an ill opinion spread then,
Euen of your selfe Lord Cardinall.

Wol. How? of me?

Camp They will not sticke to say, you enuide him;
And fearing he would rise (he was so vertuous)
Kept him a forraigne man still, which so greeu'd him,
That he ran mad, and dide.

Wol. Heau'ns peace be with him:
That's Christian care enough: for liuing Murmurers,
There's places of rebuke. He was a Foole;
For he would needs be vertuous. That good Fellow,
If I command him followes my appointment,
I will haue none so neere els. Learne this Brother,
We liue not to be grip'd by meaner persons.

Kin. Deliuer this with modesty to th' Queene.

Exit Gardiner.

The most conuenient place, that I can thinke of
For such receipt of Learning, is Black-Fryers:
There ye shall meete about this waighty busines.
My *Wolsey,* see it furnish'd, O my Lord,
Would it not grieue an able man to leaue
So sweet a Bedfellow? But Conscience, Conscience;
O 'tis a tender place, and I must leaue her. *Exeunt.*

Scena Tertia.

Enter Anne Bullen, and an old Lady.

An. Not for that neither; here's the pang that pinches.
His Highnesse, hauing liu'd so long with her, and she
So good a Lady, that no Tongue could euer
Pronounce dishonour of her; by my life,
She neuer knew harme-doing: Oh, now after
So many courses of the Sun enthroaned,
Still growing in a Maiesty and pompe, the which
To leaue, a thousand fold more bitter, then
'Tis sweet at first t'acquire. After this Processe.
To giue her the auaunt, it is a pitty
Would moue a Monster.

Old La. Hearts of most hard temper
Melt and lament for her.

An. Oh Gods will, much better
She ne're had knowne pompe; though't be temporall,
Yet if that quarrell. Fortune, do diuorce
It from the bearer, 'tis a sufferance, panging
As soule and bodies seuering.

Old L. Alas poore Lady,
Shee's a stranger now againe.

An. So much the more
Must pitty drop vpon her; verily
I sweare, tis better to be lowly borne,

And range with humble liuers in Content,
Then to be perk'd vp in a gliſtring grieſe,
And weare a golden ſorrow.
Old L. Our content
Is our beſt hauing.
Anne. By my troth, and Maidenhead,
I would not be a Queene.
Old. L. Beſhrew me, I would,
And venture Maidenhead for't,and ſo would you
For all this ſpice of your Hipocriſie:
You that haue ſo faire parts of Woman on you,
Haue (too) a Womans heart,which euer yet
Affected Eminence,Wealth,Soueraignty;
Which, to ſay ſooth,are Bleſſings; and which guifts
(Sauing your mincing) the capacity
Of your ſoft Chiuerell Conſcience,would receiue,
If you might pleaſe to ſtretch it.
Anne. Nay, good troth.
Old L. Yes troth,& troth;you would not be a Queen?
Anne. No, not for all the riches vnder Heauen.
Old.L. Tis ſtrange;a threepence bow'd would hire me
Old as I am, to Queene it: but I pray you,
What thinke you of a Dutcheſſe? Haue you limbs
To beare that load of Title?
An. No in truth.
Old. L. Then you are weakly made;plucke off a little,
I would not be a young Count in your way,
For more then bluſhing comes to: If your backe
Cannot vouchſafe this burthen, tis too weake
Euer to get a Boy.
An. How you doe talke;
I ſweare againe, I would not be a Queene,
For all the world:
Old. L. In faith,for little England
You'ld venture an emballing: I my ſelfe
Would for *Carnaruanſhire,* although there long'd
No more to th' Crowne but that: Lo, who comes here?

Enter Lord Chamberlaine.

L.Cham. Good morrow Ladies; what wer't worth to (know
The ſecret of your conference?
An. My good Lord,
Not your demand; it values not your asking:
Our Miſtris Sorrowes we were pittying.
Cham. It was a gentle buſineſſe,and becomming
The action of good women, there is hope
All will be well.
An. Now I pray God, *Amen.*
Cham. You beare a gentle minde,& heau'nly bleſſings
Follow ſuch Creatures That you may, faire Lady
Perceiue I ſpeake ſincerely, and high notes
Tane of your many vertues; the Kings Maieſty
Commends his good opinion of you,to you; and
Doe's purpoſe honour to you no leſſe flowing,
Then Marchioneſſe of *Pembrooke*; to which Title,
A Thouſand pound a yeare, Annuall ſupport,
Out of his Grace,he addes.
An. I doe not know
What kinde of my obedience,I ſhould tender;
More then my All,is Nothing: Nor my Prayers
Are not words duely hallowed; nor my Wiſhes
More worth,then empty vanities: yet Prayers & Wiſhes
Are all I can returne. 'Beſeech your Lordſhip,
Vouchſafe to ſpeake my thankes,and my obedience,
As from a bluſh'ng Handmaid, to his Highneſſe;
Whoſe health and Royalty I pray for.
Cham. Lady;
I ſhall not faile t'approue the faire conceit
The King hath of you. I haue perus'd her well,
Beauty and Honour in her are ſo mingled,
That they haue caught the King: and who knowes yet
But from this Lady,may proceed a Iemme,
To lighten all this Ile. I'le to the King,
And ſay I ſpoke with you.

Exit Lord Chamberlaine.

An. My honour'd Lord.
Old. L. Why this it is: See, ſee,
I haue beene begging ſixteene yeares in Court
(Am yet a Courtier beggerly) nor could
Come pat betwixt too early, and too late
For any ſuit of pounds: and you, (oh fate)
A very freſh Fiſh heere; fye,fye,fye vpon
This compel'd fortune: haue your mouth fild vp,
Before you open it.
An. This is ſtrange to me.
Old L. How taſts it? Is it bitter? Forty pence,no:
There was a Lady once (tis an old Story)
That would not be a Queene, that would ſhe not
For all the mud in Egypt; haue you heard it?
An. Come you are pleaſant.
Old. L. With your Theame,I could
O're-mount the Larke: The Marchioneſſe of *Pembrooke*?
A thouſand pounds a yeare, for pure reſpect?
No other obligation? by my Life,
That promiſes mo thouſands: Honours traine
Is longer then his fore-skirt; by this time
I know your backe will beare a Dutcheſſe. Say,
Are you not ſtronger then you were?
An. Good Lady,
Make your ſelfe mirth with your particular fancy,
And leaue me out on't. Would I had no being
If this ſalute my blood a iot; it faints me
To thinke what followes.
The Queene is comfortleſſe, and wee forgetfull
In our long abſence: pray doe not deliuer,
What heere y'haue heard to her.
Old L. What doe you thinke me —— *Exeunt.*

Scena Quarta.

Trumpets, Sennet, and Cornets.

Enter two Vergers, with ſhort ſiluer wands; next them two Scribes in the habite of Doctors; after them, the Biſhop of Canterbury alone; after him, the Biſhops of Lincolne, Ely, Rocheſter, and S. Aſaph: Next them, with ſome ſmall diſtance, followes a Gentleman bearing the Purſe, with the great Seale, and a Cardinals Hat: Then two Prieſts, bearing each a Siluer Croſſe: Then a Gentleman Vſher bareheaded, accompanyed with a Sergeant at Armes, bearing a Siluer Mace: Then two Gentlemen bearing two great Siluer Pillers: After them, ſide by ſide, the two Cardinals, two Noblemen, with the Sword and Mace. The King takes place vnder the Cloth of State. The two Cardinalls ſit vnder him as Iudges. The Queene takes place ſome diſtance from the King. The Biſhops place themſelues on each ſide the Court in manner of a Conſiſtory: Below them the Scribes. The Lords ſit next the Biſhops. The reſt of the Attendants ſtand in conuenient order about the Stage.

Car. Whil'st our Commission from Rome is read,
Let silence be commanded.
King. What's the need?
It hath already publiquely bene read,
And on all sides th'Authority allow'd,
You may then spare that time.
Car. Bee't so, proceed.
Scri. Say, *Henry* K. of England, come into the Court.
Crier. *Henry* King of England, &c.
King. Heere.
Scribe. Say, *Katherine* Queene of England,
Come into the Court.
Crier. *Katherine* Queene of England, &c.
The Queene makes no answer, rises out of her Chaire, goes about the Court, comes to the King, and kneeles at his Feete. Then speakes.
Sir, I desire you do me Right and Iustice,
And to bestow your pitty on me; for
I am a most poore Woman, and a Stranger,
Borne out of your Dominions: hauing heere
No Iudge indifferent, nor no more assurance
Of equall Friendship and Proceeding. Alas Sir:
In what haue I offended you? What cause
Hath my behauiour giuen to your displeasure,
That thus you should proceede to put me off,
And take your good Grace from me? Heauen witnesse,
I haue bene to you, a true and humble Wife,
At all times to your will conformable:
Euer in feare to kindle your Dislike,
Yea, subiect to your Countenance: Glad, or sorry,
As I saw it inclin'd? When was the houre
I euer contradicted your Desire?
Or made it not mine too? Or which of your Friends
Haue I not stroue to loue, although I knew
He were mine Enemy? What Friend of mine,
That had to him deriu'd your Anger, did I
Continue in my Liking? Nay, gaue notice
He was from thence discharg'd? Sir, call to minde,
That I haue beene your Wife, in this Obedience,
Vpward of twenty yeares, and haue bene blest
With many Children by you. If in the course
And processe of this time, you can report,
And proue it too, against mine Honor, aught;
My bond to Wedlocke, or my Loue and Dutie
Against your Sacred Person; in Gods name
Turne me away: and let the fowl'st Contempt
Shut doore vpon me, and so giue me vp
To the sharp'st kinde of Iustice. Please you, Sir,
The King your Father, was reputed for
A Prince most Prudent; of an excellent
And vnmatch'd Wit, and Iudgement. *Ferdinand*
My Father, King of Spaine, was reckon'd one
The wisest Prince, that there had reign'd, by many
A yeare before. It is not to be question'd,
That they had gather'd a wise Councell to them
Of euery Realme, that did debate this Businesse,
Who deem'd our Marriage lawful. Wherefore I humbly
Beseech you Sir, to spare me, till I may
Be by my Friends in Spaine, aduis'd; whose Counsaile
I will implore. If not, i'th'name of God
Your pleasure be fulfill'd.
Wol. You haue heere Lady,
(And of your choice) these Reuerend Fathers, men
Of singular Integrity, and Learning;
Yea, the elect o'th'Land, who are assembled
To pleade your Cause. It shall be therefore bootlesse,
That longer you desire the Court, as well
For your owne quiet, as to rectifie
What is vnsetled in the King.
Camp. His Grace
Hath spoken well, and iustly: Therefore Madam,
It's fit this Royall Session do proceed,
And that (without delay) their Arguments
Be now produc'd, and heard.
Qu. Lord Cardinall, to you I speake.
Wol. Your pleasure, Madam.
Qu. Sir, I am about to weepe; but thinking that
We are a Queene (or long haue dream'd so) certaine
The daughter of a King, my drops of teares,
Ile turne to sparkes of fire.
Wol. Be patient yet.
Qu. I will, when you are humble; Nay before,
Or God will punish me. I do beleeue
(Induc'd by potent Circumstances) that
You are mine Enemy, and make my Challenge,
You shall not be my Iudge. For it is you
Haue blowne this Coale, betwixt my Lord, and me;
(Which Gods dew quench) therefore, I say againe,
I vtterly abhorre; yea, from my Soule
Refuse you for my Iudge, whom yet once more
I hold my most malicious Foe, and thinke not
At all a Friend to truth.
Wol. I do professe
You speake not like your selfe: who euer yet
Haue stood to Charity, and displayd th'effects
Of disposition gentle, and of wisedome,
Ore topping womans powre. Madam, you do me wrong
I haue no Spleene against you, nor iniustice
For you, or any: how farre I haue proceeded,
Or how farre further (Shall) is warranted
By a Commission from the Consistorie,
Yea, the whole Consistorie of Rome. You charge me,
That I haue blowne this Coale: I do deny it,
The King is present: If it be knowne to him,
That I gainsay my Deed, how may he wound,
And worthily my Falsehood, yea, as much
As you haue done my Truth. If he know
That I am free of your Report, he knowes
I am not of your wrong. Therefore in him
It lies to cure me, and the Cure is to
Remoue these Thoughts from you. The which before
His Highnesse shall speake in, I do beseech
You (gracious Madam) to vnthinke your speaking,
And to say so no more.
Queen. My Lord, my Lord,
I am a simple woman, much too weake
T'oppose your cunning. Y'are meek, & humble-mouth'd
You signe your Place, and Calling, in full seeming,
With Meekenesse and Humilitie: but your Heart
Is cramm'd with Arrogancie, Spleene, and Pride.
You haue by Fortune, and his Highnesse fauors,
Gone slightly o're lowe steppes, and now are mounted
Where Powres are your Retainers, and your words
(Domestickes to you) serue your will, as't please
Your selfe pronounce their Office. I must tell you,
You tender more your persons Honor, then
Your high profession Spirituall. That agen
I do refuse you for my Iudge, and heere
Before you all, Appeale vnto the Pope,
To bring my whole Cause 'fore his Holinesse,
And to be iudg'd by him.
She Curtsies to the King, and offers to depart.

Camp.

Camp. The Queene is obstinate,
Stubborne to Iustice, apt to accuse it,and
Disdainfull to be tride by't; tis not well.
Shee's going away.
Kin. Call her againe.
Crier. Katherine Q. of England,come into the Court.
Gent. Vsh. Madam,you are cald backe.
Que. What need you note it?pray you keep your way,
When you are cald returne. Now the Lord helpe,
They vexe me past my patience,pray you passe on;
I will not tarry:no, nor euer more
Vpon this businesse my appearance make,
In any of their Courts.
Exit Queene, and her Attendants.
Kin. Goe thy wayes *Kate*,
That man i'th' world,who shall report he ha's
A better Wife,let him in naught be trusted,
For speaking false in that; thou art alone
(If thy rare qualities, sweet gentlenesse,
Thy meeknesse Saint-like, Wife-like Gouernment,
Obeying in commanding,and thy parts
Soueraigne and Pious els,could speake thee out)
The Queene of earthly Queenes: Shee's Noble borne;
And like her true Nobility,she ha's
Carried her selfe towards me.
Wol. Most gracious Sir,
In humblest manner I require your Highnes,
That it shall please you to declare in hearing
Of all these eares(for where I am rob'd and bound,
There must I be vnloos'd, although not there
At once,and fully satisfide) whether euer I
Did broach this busines to your Highnes,or
Laid any scruple in your way which might
Induce you to the question on't:or euer
Haue to you, but with thankes to God for such
A Royall Lady, spake one, the least word that might
Be to the preiudice of her present State,
Or touch of her good Person?
Kin. My Lord Cardinall,
I doe excuse you; yea, vpon mine Honour,
I free you from't: You are not to be taught
That you haue many enemies,that know not
Why they are so; but like to Village Curres,
Barke when their fellowes doe. By some of these
The Queene is put in anger; y'are excus'd:
But will you be more iustifi'de? You euer
Haue wish'd the sleeping of this busines,neuer desir'd
It to be stir'd; but oft haue hindred,oft
The passages made toward it; on my Honour,
I speake my good Lord Cardnall, to this point;
And thus farre cleare him.
Now, what mou'd me too't,
I will be bold with time and your attention: (too't:
Then marke th'inducement. Thus it came; giue heede
My Conscience first receiu'd a tendernes,
Scruple,and pricke,on certaine Speeches vtter'd
By th' Bishop of *Bayon*,then French Embassador,
Who had beene hither sent on the debating
And Marriage 'twixt the Duke of *Orleance*,and
Our Daughter *Mary*: I'th' Progresse of this busines,
Ere a determinate resolution, hee
(I meane the Bishop) did require a respite,
Wherein he might the King his Lord aduertise,
Whether our Daughter were legitimate,
Respecting this our Marriage with the Dowager,
Sometimes our Brothers Wife. This respite shooke
The bosome of my Conscience, enter'd me;
Yea, with a spitting power,and made to tremble
The region of my Breast, which forc'd such way,
That many maz'd considerings, did throng
And prest in with this Caution. First,me thought
I stood not in the smile of Heauen, who had
Commanded Nature, that my Ladies wombe
If it conceiu'd a male-child by me, should
Doe no more Offices of life too't; then
The Graue does to th' dead: For her Male Issue,
Or di'de where they were made, or shortly after
This world had ayr'd them. Hence I tooke a thought,
This was a Iudgement on me,that my Kingdome
(Well worthy the best Heyre o'th' World) should not
Be gladded in't by me. Then followes,that
I weigh'd the danger which my Realmes stood in
By this my Issues faile,and that gaue to me
Many a groaning throw: thus hulling in
The wild Sea of my Conscience,I did steere
Toward this remedy, whereupon we are
Now present heere together:that's to say,
I meant to rectifie my Conscience, which
I then did feele full sicke,and yet not well,
By all the Reuerend Fathers of the Land,
And Doctors learn'd. First I began in priuate,
With you my Lord of *Lincolne*; you remember
How vnder my oppression I did reeke
When I first mou'd you.
B. Lin. Very well my Liedge.
Kin. I haue spoke long, be pleas'd your selfe to say
How farre you satisfide me.
Lin. So please your Highnes,
The question did at first so stagger me,
Bearing a State of mighty moment in't,
And consequence of dread, that I committed
The daringst Counsaile which I had to doubt,
And did entreate your Highnes to this course,
Which you are running heere.
Kin. I then mou'd you,
My Lord of *Canterbury*,and got your leaue
To make this present Summons vnsolicited.
I left no Reuerend Person in this Court;
But by particular consent proceeded
Vnder your hands and Seales; therefore goe on,
For no dislike i'th' world against the person
Of the good Queene; but the sharpe thorny points
Of my alleadged reasons, driues this forward:
Proue but our Marriage lawfull, by my Life
And Kingly Dignity,we are contented
To weare our mortall State to come, with her,
(*Katherine* our Queene) before the primest Creature
That's Parragon'd o'th' World
Camp. So please your Highnes,
The Queene being absent,'tis a needfull fitnesse,
That we adiourne this Court till further day;
Meane while,must be an earnest motion
Made to the Queene to call backe her Appeale
She intends vnto his Holinesse.
Kin. I may perceiue
These Cardinals trifle with me: I abhorre
This dilatory sloth, and tricks of Rome.
My learn'd and welbeloued Seruant *Cranmer*,
Prethee returne,with thy approch: I know,
My comfort comes along: breake vp the Court;
I say, set on.
Exeunt, in manner as they enter'd.

Actus Tertius. Scena Prima.

Enter Queene and her Women as at worke.

Queen. Take thy Lute wench,
My Soule growes sad with troubles,
Sing, and disperse 'em if thou canst: leaue working:

SONG.

Orpheus with his Lute made Trees,
And the Mountaine tops that freeze,
Bow themselues when he did sing.
To his Musicke, Plants and Flowers
Euer sprung; as Sunne and Showers,
There had made a lasting Spring.
Euery thing that heard him play,
Euen the Billowes of the Sea,
Hung their heads, & then lay by.
In sweet Musicke is such Art,
Killing care, & griefe of heart,
Fall asleepe, or hearing dye.

Enter a Gentleman.

Queen. How now?

Gent. And't please your Grace, the two great Cardinals
Wait in the presence.

Queen. Would they speake with me?

Gent. They wil'd me say so Madam.

Queen. Pray their Graces
To come neere: what can be their busines
With me, a poore weake woman, falne from fauour?
I doe not like their comming; now I thinke on't,
They should bee good men, their affaires as righteous:
But all Hoods, make not Monkes.

Enter the two Cardinalls, Wolsey & Campian.

Wols. Peace to your Highnesse.

Queen. Your Graces find me heere part of a Houswife,
(I would be all) against the worst may happen:
What are your pleasures with me, reuerent Lords?

Wol. May it please you Noble Madam, to withdraw
Into your priuate Chamber; we shall giue you
The full cause of our comming.

Queen. Speake it heere.
There's nothing I haue done yet o' my Conscience
Deserues a Corner: would all other Women
Could speake this with as free a Soule as I doe.
My Lords, I care not (so much I am happy
Aboue a number) if my actions
Were tri'de by eu'ry tongue, eu'ry eye saw 'em,
Enuy and base opinion set against 'em,
I know my life so euen. If your busines
Seeke me out, and that way I am Wife in;
Out with it boldly: Truth loues open dealing.

Card. Tanta est erga te mentis integritas Regina serenissima.

Queen. O good my Lord, no Latin;
I am not such a Truant since my comming,
As not to know the Language I haue liu'd in:
A strange Tongue makes my cause more strange, suspiti-(ous:
Pray speake in English; heere are some will thanke you,
If you speake truth, for their poore Mistris sake;
Beleeue me she ha's had much wrong. Lord Cardinall,
The willing'st sinne I euer yet committed,
May be absolu'd in English.

Card. Noble Lady,
I am sorry my integrity should breed,
(And seruice to his Maiesty and you)
So deepe suspition, where all faith was meant;
We come not by the way of Accusation,
To taint that honour euery good Tongue blesses;
Nor to betray you any way to sorrow;
You haue too much good Lady: But to know
How you stand minded in the waighty difference
Betweene the King and you, and to deliuer
(Like free and honest men) our iust opinions,
And comforts to our cause.

Camp. Most honour'd Madam,
My Lord of Yorke, out of his Noble nature,
Zeale and obedience he still bore your Grace,
Forgetting (like a good man) your late Censure
Both of his truth and him (which was too farre)
Offers, as I doe, in a signe of peace,
His Seruice, and his Counsell.

Queen. To betray me.
My Lords, I thanke you both for your good wills,
Ye speake like honest men, (pray God ye proue so)
But how to make ye sodainly an Answere
In such a poynt of weight, so neere mine Honour,
(More neere my Life I feare) with my weake wit;
And to such men of grauity and learning;
In truth I know not. I was set at worke,
Among my Maids, full little (God knowes) looking
Either for such men, or such businesse;
For her sake that I haue beene, for I feele
The last fit of my Greatnesse; good your Graces
Let me haue time and Councell for my Cause:
Alas, I am a Woman frendlesse, hopelesse.

Wol. Madam,
You wrong the Kings loue with these feares,
Your hopes and friends are infinite.

Queen. In England,
But little for my profit can you thinke Lords,
That any English man dare giue me Councell?
Or be a knowne friend 'gainst his Highnes pleasure,
(Though he be growne so desperate to be honest)
And liue a Subiect? Nay forsooth, my Friends,
They that must weigh out my afflictions,
They that my trust must grow to, liue not heere,
They are (as all my other comforts) far hence
In mine owne Countrey Lords.

Camp. I would your Grace
Would leaue your greefes, and take my Counsell.

Queen. How Sir?

Camp. Put your maine cause into the Kings protection,
Hee's louing and most gracious. 'Twill be much,
Both for your Honour better, and your Cause:
For if the tryall of the Law o'retake ye,
You'l part away disgrac'd.

Wol. He tels you rightly.

Queen. Ye tell me what ye wish for both, my ruine:
Is this your Christian Councell? Out vpon ye.
Heauen is aboue all yet; there sits a Iudge,
That no King can corrupt.

Camp. Your rage mistakes vs.

Queen. The more shame for ye; holy men I thought ye,
Vpon my Soule two reuerend Cardinall Vertues:
But Cardinall Sins, and hollow hearts I feare ye:
Mend 'em for shame my Lords: Is this your comfort?
The Cordiall that ye bring a wretched Lady?
A woman lost among ye, laugh't at, scornd?
I will not wish ye halfe my miseries,

I haue more Charity. But say I warn'd ye;
Take heed, for heauens sake take heed, least at once
The burthen of my sorrowes, fall vpon ye.

Car. Madam, this is a meere distraction,
You turne the good we offer, into enuy.

Quee. Ye turne me into nothing. Woe vpon ye,
And all such false Professors. Would you haue me
(If you haue any Iustice, any Pitty,
If ye be any thing but Churchmens habits)
Put my sicke cause into his hands, that hates me?
Alas, ha's banish'd me his Bed already,
His Loue, too long ago. I am old my Lords,
And all the Fellowship I hold now with him
Is onely my Obedience. What can happen
To me, aboue this wretchednesse? All your Studies
Make me a Curse, like this.

Camp. Your feares are worse.

Qu. Haue I liu'd thus long (let me speake my selfe,
Since Vertue findes no friends) a Wife, a true one?
A Woman (I dare say without Vainglory)
Neuer yet branded with Suspition?
Haue I, with all my full Affections
Still met the King? Lou'd him next Heau'n? Obey'd him?
Bin (out of fondnesse) superstitious to him?
Almost forgot my Prayres to content him?
And am I thus rewarded? 'Tis not well Lords.
Bring me a constant woman to her Husband,
One that ne're dream'd a Ioy, beyond his pleasure;
And to that Woman (when she has done most)
Yet will I adde an Honor; a great Patience.

Car. Madam, you wander from the good
We ayme at.

Qu. My Lord,
I dare not make my selfe so guiltie,
To giue vp willingly that Noble Title
Your Master wed me to: nothing but death
Shall e're diuorce my Dignities.

Car. Pray heare me.

Qu. Would I had neuer trod this English Earth,
Or felt the Flatteries that grow vpon it:
Ye haue Angels Faces; but Heauen knowes your hearts.
What will become of me now, wretched Lady?
I am the most vnhappy Woman liuing.
Alas (poore Wenches) where are now your Fortunes?
Shipwrack'd vpon a Kingdome, where no Pitty,
No Friends, no Hope, no Kindred weepe for me?
Almost no Graue allow'd me? Like the Lilly
That once was Mistris of the Field, and flourish'd,
Ile hang my head, and perish.

Car. If your Grace
Could but be brought to know, our Ends are honest,
You'l'd feele more comfort. Why shold we (good Lady)
Vpon what cause wrong you? Alas, our Places,
The way of our Profession is against it;
We are to Cure such sorrowes, not to sowe 'em.
For Goodnesse sake, consider what you do,
How you may hurt your selfe: I, vtterly
Grow from the Kings Acquaintance, by this Carriage.
The hearts of Princes kisse Obedience,
So much they loue it. But to stubborne Spirits,
They swell and grow, as terrible as stormes.
I know you haue a Gentle, Noble temper,
A Soule as euen as a Calme; Pray thinke vs,
Those we professe, Peace-makers, Friends, and Seruants.

Camp. Madam, you'l finde it so:
You wrong your Vertues
With these weake Womens feares. A Noble Spirit
As yours was, put into you, euer casts
Such doubts as false Coine from it. The King loues you,
Beware you loose it not: For vs (if you please
To trust vs in your businesse) we are ready
To vse our vtmost Studies, in your seruice.

Qu. Do what ye will, my Lords:
And pray forgiue me;
If I haue vs'd my selfe vnmannerly,
You know I am a Woman, lacking wit
To make a seemely answer to such persons.
Pray do my seruice to his Maiestie,
He ha's my heart yet, and shall haue my Prayers
While I shall haue my life. Come reuerend Fathers,
Bestow your Councels on me. She now begges
That little thought when she set footing heere,
She should haue bought her Dignities so deere. *Exeunt*

Scena Secunda.

Enter the Duke of Norfolke, Duke of Suffolke, Lord Surrey, and Lord Chamberlaine.

Norf. If you will now vnite in your Complaints,
And force them with a Constancy, the Cardinall
Cannot stand vnder them. If you omit
The offer of this time, I cannot promise,
But that you shall sustaine moe new disgraces,
With these you beare alreadie.

Sur. I am ioyfull
To meete the least occasion, that may giue me
Remembrance of my Father-in-Law, the Duke,
To be reueng'd on him.

Suf. Which of the Peeres
Haue vncontemn'd gone by him, or at least
Strangely neglected? When did he regard
The stampe of Noblenesse in any person
Out of himselfe?

Cham. My Lords, you speake your pleasures:
What he deserues of you and me, I know:
What we can do to him (though now the time
Giues way to vs) I much feare. If you cannot
Barre his accesse to'th'King, neuer attempt
Any thing on him: for he hath a Witchcraft
Ouer the King in's Tongue.

Nor. O feare him not,
His spell in that is out: the King hath found
Matter against him, that for euer marres
The Hony of his Language. No, he's setled
(Not to come off) in his displeasure.

Sur. Sir,
I should be glad to heare such Newes as this
Once euery houre.

Nor. Beleeue it, this is true.
In the Diuorce, his contrarie proceedings
Are all vnfolded: wherein he appeares,
As I would wish mine Enemy.

Sur. How came
His practises to light?

Suf. Most strangely.

Sur. O how? how?

Suf. The Cardinals Letters to the Pope miscarried,
And

And came to th'eye o'th'King, wherein was read
How that the Cardinall did intreat his Holinesse
To stay the Iudgement o'th'Diuorce; for if
It did take place, I do (quoth he) perceiue
My King is tangled in affection, to
A Creature of the Queenes, Lady *Anne Bullen.*

Sur. Ha's the King this?

Suf. Beleeue it.

Sur. Will this worke?

Cham. The King in this perceiues him, how he coasts
And hedges his owne way. But in this point,
All his trickes founder, and he brings his Physicke
After his Patients death; the King already
Hath married the faire Lady.

Sur. Would he had.

Suf. May you be happy in your wish my Lord,
For I professe you haue it.

Sur. Now all my ioy
Trace the Coniunction.

Suf. My Amen too't.

Nor. All mens.

Suf. There's order giuen for her Coronation:
Marry this is yet but yong, and may be left
To some eares vnrecounted. But my Lords
She is a gallant Creature, and compleate
In minde and feature. I perswade me, from her
Will fall some blessing to this Land, which shall
In it be memoriz'd.

Sur. But will the King
Digest this Letter of the Cardinals?
The Lord forbid.

Nor. Marry Amen.

Suf. No, no:
There be moe Waspes that buz about his Nose,
Will make this sting the sooner. Cardinall *Campeius,*
Is stolne away to Rome, hath 'tane no leaue,
Ha's left the cause o'th'King vnhandled, and
Is posted as the Agent of our Cardinall,
To second all his plot. I do assure you,
The King cry'de Ha, at this.

Cham. Now God incense him,
And let him cry Ha, lowder.

Norf. But my Lord
When returnes *Cranmer?*

Suf. He is return'd in his Opinions, which
Haue satisfied the King for his Diuorce,
Together with all famous Colledges
Almost in Christendome: shortly (I beleeue)
His second Marriage shall be publishd, and
Her Coronation. *Katherine* no more
Shall be call'd Queene, but Princesse Dowager,
And Widdow to Prince *Arthur.*

Nor. This same *Cranmer's*
A worthy Fellow, and hath tane much paine
In the Kings businesse.

Suf. He ha's, and we shall see him
For it an Arch-byshop.

Nor. So I heare.

Suf. Tis so.

Enter Wolsey and Cromwell.

The Cardinall.

Nor. Obserue, obserue, hee's moody.

Car. The Packet Cromwell,
Gau't you the King?

Crom. To his owne hand, in's Bed-chamber.

Card. Look'd he o'th'inside of the Paper?

Crom. Presently
He did vnseale them, and the first he view'd,
He did it with a Serious minde: a heede
Was in his countenance. You he bad
Attend him heere this Morning.

Card. Is he ready to come abroad?

Crom. I thinke by this he is.

Card. Leaue me a while. *Exit Cromwell.*

It shall be to the Dutches of Alanson,
The French Kings Sister; He shall marry her.
Anne Bullen? No: Ile no *Anne Bullens* for him,
There's more in't then faire Visage. *Bullen?*
No, wee'l no *Bullens:* Speedily I wish
To heare from Rome. The Marchionesse of Penbroke?

Nor. He's discontented.

Suf. May be he heares the King
Does whet his Anger to him.

Sur. Sharpe enough,
Lord for thy Iustice.

Car. The late Queenes Gentlewoman?
A Knights Daughter
To be her Mistris Mistris? The Queenes, Queene?
This Candle burnes not cleere, 'tis I must snuffe it,
Then out it goes. What though I know her vertuous
And well deseruing? yet I know her for
A spleeny Lutheran, and not wholsome to
Our cause, that she should lye i'th'bosome of
Our hard rul'd King. Againe, there is sprung vp
An Heretique, an Arch-one; *Cranmer,* one
Hath crawl'd into the fauour of the King,
And is his Oracle.

Nor. He is vex'd at something.

Enter King, reading of a Scedule.

Sur. I would 'twer something ỳ would fret the string,
The Master-cord on's heart.

Suf. The King, the King.

King. What piles of wealth hath he accumulated
To his owne portion? And what expence by'th'houre
Seemes to flow from him? How, i'th'name of Thrift
Does he rake this together? Now my Lords,
Saw you the Cardinall?

Nor. My Lord, we haue
Stood heere obseruing him. Some strange Commotion
Is in his braine: He bites his lip, and starts,
Stops on a sodaine, lookes vpon the ground,
Then layes his finger on his Temple: straight
Springs out into fast gate, then stops againe,
Strikes his brest hard, and anon, he casts
His eye against the Moone: in most strange Postures
We haue seene him set himselfe.

King. It may well be,
There is a mutiny in's minde. This morning,
Papers of State he sent me, to peruse
As I requir'd: and wot you what I found
There (on my Conscience put vnwittingly)
Forsooth an Inuentory, thus importing
The seuerall parcels of his Plate, his Treasure,
Rich Stuffes and Ornaments of Houshold, which
I finde at such proud Rate, that it out-speakes
Possession of a Subiect.

Nor. It's Heauens will,
Some Spirit put this paper in the Packet,
To blesse your eye withall.

King. If we did thinke

His Contemplation were aboue the earth,
And fixt on Spirituall obiect, he should still
Dwell in his Musings, but I am affraid
His Thinkings are below the Moone, not worth
His serious considering.

King takes his Seat, whispers Louell, who goes to the Cardinall.

Car. Heauen forgiue me,
Euer God blesse your Highnesse.
King. Good my Lord,
You are full of Heauenly stuffe, and beare the Inuentory
Of your best Graces, in your minde; the which
You were now running o're: you haue scarse time
To steale from Spirituall leysure, a briefe span
To keepe your earthly Audit, sure in that
I deeme you an ill Husband, and am gald
To haue you therein my Companion.
Car. Sir,
For Holy Offices I haue a time; a time
To thinke vpon the part of businesse, which
I beare i'th'State: and Nature does require
Her times of preseruation, which perforce
I her fraile sonne, among'st my Brethren mortall,
Must giue my tendance to.
King. You haue said well.
Car. And euer may your Highnesse yoake together,
(As I will lend you cause) my doing well,
With my well saying.
King. 'Tis well said agen,
And 'tis a kinde of good deede to say well,
And yet words are no deeds. My Father lou'd you,
He said he did, and with his deed did Crowne
His word vpon you. Since I had my Office,
I haue kept you next my Heart, haue not alone
Imploy'd you where high Profits might come home,
But par'd my present Hauings, to bestow
My Bounties vpon you.
Car. What should this meane?
Sur. The Lord increase this businesse.
King. Haue I not made you
The prime man of the State? I pray you tell me,
If what I now pronounce, you haue found true:
And if you may confesse it, say withall
If you are bound to vs, or no. What say you?
Car. My Soueraigne, I confesse your Royall graces
Showr'd on me daily, haue bene more then could
My studied purposes requite, which went
Beyond all mans endeauors. My endeauors,
Haue euer come too short of my Desires,
Yet fill'd with my Abilities: Mine owne ends
Haue beene mine so, that euermore they pointed
To'th'good of your most Sacred Person, and
The profit of the State. For your great Graces
Heap'd vpon me (poore Vndeseruer) I
Can nothing render but Allegiant thankes,
My Prayres to heauen for you; my Loyaltie
Which euer ha's, and euer shall be growing,
Till death (that Winter) kill it.
King. Fairely answer'd:
A Loyall, and obedient Subiect is
Therein illustrated, the Honor of it
Does pay the Act of it, as i'th'contrary
The fowlenesse is the punishment. I presume,
That as my hand ha's open'd Bounty to you,
My heart drop'd Loue, my powre rain'd Honor, more
On you, then any: So your Hand, and Heart,
Your Braine, and euery Function of your power,
Should, notwithstanding that your bond of duty,
As 'twer in Loues particular, be more
To me your Friend, then any.
Car. I do professe,
That for your Highnesse good, I euer labour'd
More then mine owne: that am, haue, and will be
(Though all the world should cracke their duty to you,
And throw it from their Soule, though perils did
Abound, as thicke as thought could make 'em, and
Appeare in formes more horrid) yet my Duty,
As doth a Rocke against the chiding Flood,
Should the approach of this wilde Riuer breake,
And stand vnshaken yours.
King. 'Tis Nobly spoken:
Take notice Lords, he ha's a Loyall brest,
For you haue seene him open't. Read o're this,
And after this, and then to Breakfast with
What appetite you haue.

Exit King, frowning vpon the Cardinall, the Nobles throng after him smiling, and whispering.

Car. What should this meane?
What sodaine Anger's this? How haue I reap'd it?
He parted Frowning from me, as if Ruine
Leap'd from his Eyes. So lookes the chafed Lyon
Vpon the daring Huntsman that has gall'd him:
Then makes him nothing. I must reade this paper:
I feare the Story of his Anger. 'Tis so:
This paper ha's vndone me: 'Tis th'Accompt
Of all that world of Wealth I haue drawne together
For mine owne ends, (Indeed to gaine the Popedome,
And fee my Friends in Rome.) O Negligence!
Fit for a Foole to fall by: What crosse Diuell
Made me put this maine Secret in the Packet
I sent the King? Is there no way to cure this?
No new deuice to beate this from his Braines?
I know 'twill stirre him strongly; yet I know
A way, if it take right, in spight of Fortune
Will bring me off againe. What's this? *To th'Pope?*
The Letter (as I liue) with all the Businesse
I writ too's Holinesse. Nay then, farewell:
I haue touch'd the highest point of all my Greatnesse,
And from that full Meridian of my Glory,
I haste now to my Setting. I shall fall
Like a bright exhalation in the Euening,
And no man see me more.

Enter to Woolsey, the Dukes of Norfolke and Suffolke, the Earle of Surrey, and the Lord Chamberlaine.

Nor. Heare the Kings pleasure Cardinall,
Who commands you
To render vp the Great Seale presently
Into our hands, and to Confine your selfe
To Asher-house, my Lord of Winchesters,
Till you heare further from his Highnesse.
Car. Stay:
Where's your Commission? Lords, words cannot carrie
Authority so weighty.
Suf. Who dare crosse 'em,
Bearing the Kings will from his mouth expressely?
Car. Till I finde more then will, or words to do it,
(I meane your malice) know, Officious Lords,
I dare, and must deny it. Now I feele
Of what course Mettle ye are molded, Enuy,
How eagerly ye follow my Disgraces

As if it fed ye, and how sleeke and wanton
Ye appeare in euery thing may bring my ruine?
Follow your enuious courses, men of Malice;
You haue Christian warrant for em, and no doubt
In time will finde their fit Rewards. That Seale
You aske with such a Violence, the King
(Mine, and your Master) with his owne hand, gaue me:
Bad me enioy it, with the Place, and Honors
During my life; and to confirme his Goodnesse,
Ti'de it by Letters Patents. Now, who'll take it?
Sur. The King that gaue it.
Car. It must be himselfe then.
Sur. Thou art a proud Traitor, Priest.
Car. Proud Lord, thou lyest:
Within these fortie houres, Surrey durst better
Haue burnt that Tongue, then saide so.
Sur. Thy Ambition
(Thou Scarlet sinne) robb'd this bewailing Land
Of Noble Buckingham, my Father-in-Law,
The heads of all thy Brother-Cardinals,
(With thee, and all thy best parts bound together)
Weigh'd not a haire of his. Plague of your policie,
You sent me Deputie for Ireland,
Farre from his succour; from the King, from all
That might haue mercie on the fault, thou gau'st him:
Whil'st your great Goodnesse, out of holy pitty,
Absolu'd him with an Axe.
Wol. This, and all else
This talking Lord can lay vpon my credit,
I answer, is most false. The Duke by Law
Found his deserts. How innocent I was
From any priuate malice in his end,
His Noble Iurie, and foule Cause can witnesse.
If I lou'd many words, Lord, I should tell you,
You haue as little Honestie, as Honor,
That in the way of Loyaltie, and Truth,
Toward the King, my euer Roiall Master,
Dare mate a sounder man then Surrie can be,
And all that loue his follies.
Sur. By my Soule,
Your long Coat (Priest) protects you,
Thou should'st feele
My Sword i'th'life blood of thee else. My Lords,
Can ye endure to heare this Arrogance?
And from this Fellow? If we liue thus tamely,
To be thus Iaded by a peece of Scarlet,
Farewell Nobilitie: let his Grace go forward,
And dare vs with his Cap, like Larkes.
Card. All Goodnesse
Is poyson to thy Stomacke.
Sur. Yes, that goodnesse
Of gleaning all the Lands wealth into one,
Into your owne hands (Card'nall) by Extortion:
The goodnesse of your intercepted Packets
You writ to'th Pope, against the King: your goodnesse
Since you prouoke me, shall be most notorious.
My Lord of Norfolke, as you are truly Noble,
As you respect the common good, the State
Of our despis'd Nobilitie, our Issues,
(Whom if he liue, will scarse be Gentlemen)
Produce the grand summe of his sinnes, the Articles
Collected from his life. Ile startle you
Worse then the Sacring Bell, when the browne Wench
Lay kissing in your Armes, Lord Cardinall.
Car. How much me thinkes, I could despise this man,
But that I am bound in Charitie against it.
Nor. Those Articles, my Lord are in the Kings hand:
But thus much, they are foule ones.
Wol. So much fairer
And spotlesse, shall mine Innocence arise,
When the King knowes my Truth.
Sur. This cannot saue you:
I thanke my Memorie, I yet remember
Some of these Articles, and out they shall.
Now, if you can blush, and crie guiltie Cardinall,
You'l shew a little Honestie.
Wol. Speake on Sir,
I dare your worst Obiections: If I blush,
It is to see a Nobleman want manners.
Sur. I had rather want those, then my head;
Haue at you.
First, that without the Kings assent or knowledge,
You wrought to be a Legate, by which power
You maim'd the Iurisdiction of all Bishops.
Nor. Then, That in all you writ to Rome, or else
To Forraigne Princes, *Ego & Rex meus*
Was still inscrib'd: in which you brought the King
To be your Seruant.
Suf. Then, that without the knowledge
Either of King or Councell, when you went
Ambassador to the Emperor, you made bold
To carry into Flanders, the Great Seale.
Sur. Item, You sent a large Commission
To *Gregory de Cassado*, to conclude
Without the Kings will, or the States allowance,
A League betweene his Highnesse, and *Ferrara*.
Suf. That out of meere Ambition, you haue caus'd
Your holy-Hat to be stampt on the Kings Coine.
Sur. Then, That you haue sent inumerable substance,
(By what meanes got, I leaue to your owne conscience)
To furnish Rome, and to prepare the wayes
You haue for Dignities, to the meere vndooing
Of all the Kingdome. Many more there are,
Which since they are of you, and odious,
I will not taint my mouth with.
Cham. O my Lord,
Presse not a falling man too farre: 'tis Vertue:
His faults lye open to the Lawes, let them
(Not you) correct him. My heart weepes to see him
So little, of his great Selfe.
Sur. I forgiue him.
Suf. Lord Cardinall, the Kings further pleasure is,
Because all those things you haue done of late
By your power Legatiue within this Kingdome,
Fall into'th'compasse of a Premunire;
That therefore such a Writ be sued against you,
To forfeit all your Goods, Lands, Tenements,
Castles, and whatsoeuer, and to be
Out of the Kings protection. This is my Charge.
Nor. And so wee'l leaue you to your Meditations
How to liue better. For your stubborne answer
About the giuing backe the Great Seale to vs,
The King shall know it, and (no doubt) shal thanke you.
So fare you well, my little good Lord Cardinall.
Exeunt all but Wolsey.
Wol. So farewell, to the little good you beare me.
Farewell? A long farewell to all my Greatnesse.
This is the state of Man; to day he puts forth
The tender Leaues of hopes, to morrow Blossomes,
And beares his blushing Honors thicke vpon him:
The third day, comes a Frost; a killing Frost,
And when he thinkes, good easie man, full surely

His

His Greatnesse is a ripening, nippes his roote,
And then he fals as I do. I haue ventur'd
Like little wanton Boyes that swim on bladders:
This many Summers in a Sea of Glory,
But farre beyond my depth: my high-blowne Pride
At length broke vnder me, and now ha's left me
Weary, and old with Seruice, to the mercy
Of a rude streame, that must for euer hide me.
Vaine pompe, and glory of this World, I hate ye,
I feele my heart new open'd. Oh how wretched
Is that poore man, that hangs on Princes fauours?
There is betwixt that smile we would aspire too,
That sweet Aspect of Princes, and their ruine,
More pangs, and feares then warres, or women haue;
And when he falles, he falles like Lucifer,
Neuer to hope againe.

Enter Cromwell, standing amazed.

Why how now *Cromwell*?
Crom. I haue no power to speake Sir.
Car. What, amaz'd
At my misfortunes? Can thy Spirit wonder
A great man should decline. Nay, and you weep
I am falne indeed.
Crom. How does your Grace.
Card. Why well:
Neuer so truly happy, my good *Cromwell*,
I know my selfe now, and I feele within me,
A peace aboue all earthly Dignities,
A still, and quiet Conscience. The King ha's cur'd me,
I humbly thanke his Grace: and from these shoulders
These ruin'd Pillers, out of pitty, taken
A loade, would sinke a Nauy, (too much Honor.)
O 'tis a burden *Cromwel*, 'tis a burden
Too heauy for a man, that hopes for Heauen.
Crom. I am glad your Grace,
Ha's made that right vse of it.
Card. I hope I haue:
I am able now (me thinkes)
(Out of a Fortitude of Soule, I feele)
To endure more Miseries, and greater farre
Then my Weake-hearted Enemies, dare offer.
What Newes abroad?
Crom. The heauiest, and the worst,
Is your displeasure with the King.
Card. God blesse him.
Crom. The next is, that Sir *Thomas Moore* is chosen
Lord Chancellor, in your place.
Card. That's somewhat sodain.
But he's a Learned man. May he continue
Long in his Highnesse fauour, and do Iustice
For Truths-sake, and his Conscience; that his bones,
When he ha's run his course, and sleepes in Blessings,
May haue a Tombe of Orphants teares wept on him.
What more?
Crom. That *Cranmer* is return'd with welcome;
Install'd Lord Arch-byshop of Canterbury.
Card. That's Newes indeed.
Crom. Last, that the Lady *Anne*,
Whom the King hath in secrecie long married,
This day was view'd in open, as his Queene,
Going to Chappell: and the voyce is now
Onely about her Corronation.
Card. There was the waight that pull'd me downe.
O *Cromwell*,
The King ha's gone beyond me: All my Glories
In that one woman, I haue lost for euer.
No Sun, shall euer vsher forth mine Honors,
Or gilde againe the Noble Troopes that waighted
Vpon my smiles. Go get thee from me *Cromwel*,
I am a poore falne man, vnworthy now
To be thy Lord, and Master. Seeke the King
(That Sun, I pray may neuer set) I haue told him,
What, and how true thou art; he will aduance thee:
Some little memory of me, will stirre him
(I know his Noble Nature) not to let
Thy hopefull seruice perish too. Good *Cromwell*
Neglect him not; make vse now, and prouide
For thine owne future safety.
Crom. O my Lord,
Must I then leaue you? Must I needes forgo
So good, so Noble, and so true a Master?
Beare witnesse, all that haue not hearts of Iron,
With what a sorrow *Cromwel* leaues his Lord.
The King shall haue my seruice; but my prayres
For euer, and for euer shall be yours.
Card. *Cromwel*, I did not thinke to shed a teare
In all my Miseries: But thou hast forc'd me
(Out of thy honest truth) to play the Woman.
Let's dry our eyes: And thus farre heare me *Cromwel*,
And when I am forgotten, as I shall be,
And sleepe in dull cold Marble, where no mention
Of me, more must be heard of: Say I taught thee;
Say *Wolsey*, that once trod the wayes of Glory,
And sounded all the Depths, and Shoales of Honor,
Found thee a way (out of his wracke) to rise in:
A sure, and safe one, though thy Master mist it.
Marke but my Fall, and that that Ruin'd me:
Cromwel, I charge thee, fling away Ambition,
By that sinne fell the Angels: how can man then
(The Image of his Maker) hope to win by it?
Loue thy selfe last, cherish those hearts that hate thee;
Corruption wins not more then Honesty.
Still in thy right hand, carry gentle Peace
To silence enuious Tongues. Be iust, and feare not;
Let all the ends thou aym'st at, be thy Countries,
Thy Gods, and Truths. Then if thou fall'st (O *Cromwell*)
Thou fall'st a blessed Martyr.
Serue the King: And prythee leade me in:
There take an Inuentory of all I haue,
To the last peny, 'tis the Kings. My Robe,
And my Integrity to Heauen, is all,
I dare now call mine owne. O *Cromwel*, *Cromwel*,
Had I but seru'd my God, with halfe the Zeale
I seru'd my King: he would not in mine Age
Haue left me naked to mine Enemies.
Crom. Good Sir, haue patience.
Card. So I haue. Farewell
The Hopes of Court, my Hopes in Heauen do dwell.

Exeunt.

Actus Quartus. Scena Prima.

Enter two Gentlemen, meeting one another.

1 Y'are well met once againe.
2 So are you.
1 You come to take your stand heere, and behold
The Lady *Anne*, passe from her Corronation.

2 'Tis

2 'Tis all my businesse. At our last encounter,
The Duke of Buckingham came from his Triall.

1 'Tis very true. But that time offer'd sorrow,
This generall ioy.

2 'Tis well: The Citizens
I am sure haue shewne at full their Royall minds,
As let 'em haue their rights, they are euer forward
In Celebration of this day with Shewes,
Pageants, and Sights of Honor.

1 Neuer greater,
Nor Ile assure you better taken Sir.

2 May I be bold to aske what that containes,
That Paper in your hand.

1 Yes, 'tis the List
Of those that claime their Offices this day,
By custome of the Coronation.
The Duke of Suffolke is the first, and claimes
To be high Steward; Next the Duke of Norfolke,
He to be Earle Marshall: you may reade the rest.

1 I thanke you Sir: Had I not known those customs,
I should haue beene beholding to your Paper:
But I beseech you, what's become of *Katherine*
The Princesse Dowager? How goes her businesse?

1 That I can tell you too. The Archbishop
Of Canterbury, accompanied with other
Learned, and Reuerend Fathers of his Order,
Held a late Court at Dunstable; sixe miles off
From Ampthill, where the Princesse lay, to which
She was often cyted by them, but appear'd not:
And to be short, for not Appearance and
The Kings late Scruple, by the maine assent
Of all these Learned men, she was diuorc'd,
And the late Marriage made of none effect:
Since which, she was remou'd to Kymmalton,
Where she remaines now sicke.

2 Alas good Lady.
The Trumpets sound: Stand close,
The Queene is comming. *Ho-boyes.*

The Order of the Coronation.

1 *A liuely Flourish of Trumpets.*
2 *Then, two Iudges.*
3 *Lord* Chancellor, *with Purse and Mace before him.*
4 Quirristers *singing.* Musicke.
5 Maior of London, *bearing the Mace. Then* Garter, *in his Coate of Armes, and on his head he wore a Gilt Copper Crowne.*
6 Marquesse Dorset, *bearing a Scepter of Gold, on his head, a Demy Coronall of Gold. With him, the Earle of* Surrey, *bearing the Rod of Siluer with the Doue, Crowned with an Earles Coronet. Collars of Esses.*
7 Duke of Suffolke, *in his Robe of Estate, his Coronet on his head, bearing a long white Wand, as High Steward. With him, the Duke of* Norfolke, *with the Rod of Marshalship, a Coronet on his head. Collars of Esses.*
8 *A* Canopy, *borne by foure of the* Cinque-Ports, *vnder it the Queene in her Robe, in her haire, richly adorned with Pearle, Crowned. On each side her, the Bishops of* London, *and* Winchester.
9 *The* Olde Dutchesse of Norfolke, *in a Coronall of Gold, wrought with Flowers bearing the Queenes Traine.*
10 *Certaine* Ladies *or* Countesses, *with plaine Circlets of Gold, without Flowers.*

Exeunt, *first passing ouer the Stage in Order and State, and then, A great Flourish of Trumpets.*

2 A Royall Traine beleeue me: These I know:
Who's that that beares the Scepter?

1 Marquesse Dorset,
And that the Earle of Surrey, with the Rod.

2 A bold braue Gentleman. That should bee
The Duke of Suffolke.

1 'Tis the same: high Steward

2 And that my Lord of Norfolke?

1 Yes.

2 Heauen blesse thee,
Thou hast the sweetest face I euer look'd on.
Sir, as I haue a Soule, she is an Angell;
Our King has all the Indies in his Armes,
And more, and richer, when he straines that Lady,
I cannot blame his Conscience.

1 They that beare
The Cloath of Honour ouer her, are foure Barons
Of the Cinque Ports.

2 Those men are happy,
And so are all, are neere her.
I take it, she that carries vp the Traine,
Is that old Noble Lady, Dutchesse of Norfolke.

1 It is, and all the rest are Countesses.

2 Their Coronets say so. These are Starres indeed,
And sometimes falling ones.

2 No more of that.

Enter a third Gentleman.

1 God saue you Sir. Where haue you bin broiling?

3 Among the crow'd i'th'Abbey, where a finger
Could not be wedg'd in more: I am stifled
With the meere ranknesse of their ioy.

2 You saw the Ceremony?

3 That I did.

1 How was it?

3 Well worth the seeing.

2 Good Sir, speake it to vs?

3 As well as I am able. The rich streame
Of Lords, and Ladies, hauing brought the Queene
To a prepar'd place in the Quire, fell off
A distance from her; while her Grace sate downe
To rest a while, some halfe an houre, or so,
In a rich Chaire of State, opposing freely
The Beauty of her Person to the People.
Beleeue me Sir, she is the goodliest Woman
That euer lay by man: which when the people
Had the full view of, such a noyse arose,
As the shrowdes make at Sea, in a stiffe Tempest,
As lowd, and to as many Tunes. Hats, Cloakes,
(Doublets, I thinke) flew vp, and had their Faces
Bin loose, this day they had beene lost. Such ioy
I neuer saw before. Great belly'd women,
That had not halfe a weeke to go, like Rammes
In the old time of Warre, would shake the prease
And make 'em reele before 'em. No man liuing
Could say this is my wife there, all were wouen
So strangely in one peece.

2 But what follow'd?

3 At length, her Grace rose, and with modest paces
Came to the Altar, where she kneel'd, and Saint-like
Cast her faire eyes to Heauen, and pray'd deuoutly.
Then rose againe, and bow'd her to the people:
When by the Arch-byshop of Canterbury,
She had all the Royall makings of a Queene;
As holy Oyle, *Edward* Confessors Crowne,
The Rod, and Bird of Peace, and all such Emblemes
Laid Nobly on her: which perform'd, the Quire

With

With all the choysest Musicke of the Kingdome,
Together sung *Te Deum*. So she parted,
And with the same full State pac'd backe againe
To Yorke-Place, where the Feast is held.

1 Sir,
You must no more call it Yorke-place, that's past:
For since the Cardinall fell, that Titles lost,
'Tis now the Kings, and call'd White-Hall.

3 I know it:
But 'tis so lately alter'd, that the old name
Is fresh about me.

2 What two Reuerend Byshops
Were those that went on each side of the Queene?

3 *Stokeley* and *Gardiner*, the one of Winchester,
Newly preferr'd from the King's Secretary:
The other London.

2 He of Winchester
Is held no great good louer of the Archbishops,
The vertuous *Cranmer*.

3 All the Land knowes that:
How euer, yet there is no great breach, when it comes
Cranmer will finde a Friend will not shrinke from him.

2 Who may that be, I pray you.

3 *Thomas Cromwell*,
A man in much esteeme with th'King, and truly
A worthy Friend. The King ha's made him
Master o'th'Iewell House,
And one already of the Priuy Councell.

2 He will deserue more.

3 Yes without all doubt.
Come Gentlemen, ye shall go my way,
Which is to'th Court, and there ye shall be my Guests:
Something I can command. As I walke thither,
Ile tell ye more.

Both. You may command vs Sir. *Exeunt.*

Scena Secunda.

Enter Katherine Dowager, sicke, lead betweene Griffith, her Gentleman Vsher, and Patience her Woman.

Grif. How do's your Grace?

Kath. O *Griffith*, sicke to death:
My Legges like loaden Branches bow to'th'Earth,
Willing to leaue their burthen: Reach a Chaire,
So now (me thinkes) I feele a little ease.
Did'st thou not tell me *Griffith*, as thou lead'st mee,
That the great Childe of Honor, Cardinall *Wolsey*
Was dead?

Grif. Yes Madam: but I thanke your Grace
Out of the paine you suffer'd, gaue no eare too't.

Kath. Pre'thee good *Griffith*, tell me how he dy'de.
If well, he stept before me happily
For my example.

Grif. Well, the voyce goes Madam,
For after the stout Earle Northumberland
Arrested him at Yorke, and brought him forward
As a man sorely tainted, to his Answer,
He fell sicke sodainly, and grew so ill
He could not sit his Mule.

Kath. Alas poore man.

Grif. At last, with easie Rodes, he came to Leicester,
Lodg'd in the Abbey; where the reuerend Abbot
With all his Couent, honourably receiu'd him;
To whom he gaue these words. O Father Abbot,
An old man, broken with the stormes of State,
Is come to lay his weary bones among ye:
Giue him a little earth for Charity.
So went to bed; where eagerly his sicknesse
Pursu'd him still, and three nights after this,
About the houre of eight, which he himselfe
Foretold should be his last, full of Repentance,
Continuall Meditations, Teares, and Sorrowes,
He gaue his Honors to the world agen,
His blessed part to Heauen, and slept in peace.

Kath. So may he rest,
His Faults lye gently on him:
Yet thus farre *Griffith*, giue me leaue to speake him,
And yet with Charity. He was a man
Of an vnbounded stomacke, euer ranking
Himselfe with Princes. One that by suggestion
Ty'de all the Kingdome. Symonie, was faire play,
His owne Opinion was his Law. I'th'presence
He would say vntruths, and be euer double
Both in his words, and meaning. He was neuer
(But where he meant to Ruine) pittifull.
His Promises, were as he then was, Mighty:
But his performance, as he is now, Nothing:
Of his owne body he was ill, and gaue
The Clergy ill example.

Grif. Noble Madam:
Mens euill manners liue in Brasse, their Vertues
We write in Water. May it please your Highnesse
To heare me speake his good now?

Kath. Yes good *Griffith*,
I were malicious else.

Grif. This Cardinall,
Though from an humble Stocke, vndoubtedly
Was fashion'd to much Honor. From his Cradle
He was a Scholler, and a ripe, and good one:
Exceeding wise, faire spoken, and perswading:
Lofty, and sowre to them that lou'd him not:
But, to those men that sought him, sweet as Summer.
And though he were vnsatisfied in getting,
(Which was a sinne) yet in bestowing, Madam,
He was most Princely: Euer witnesse for him
Those twinnes of Learning, that he rais'd in you,
Ipswich and Oxford: one of which, fell with him,
Vnwilling to out-liue the good that did it.
The other (though vnfinish'd) yet so Famous,
So excellent in Art, and still so rising,
That Christendome shall euer speake his Vertue.
His Ouerthrow, heap'd Happinesse vpon him:
For then, and not till then, he felt himselfe,
And found the Blessednesse of being little.
And to adde greater Honors to his Age
Then man could giue him; he dy'de, fearing God.

Kath. After my death, I wish no other Herald,
No other speaker of my liuing Actions,
To keepe mine Honor, from Corruption,
But such an honest Chronicler as *Griffith*.
Whom I most hated Liuing, thou hast made mee
With thy Religious Truth, and Modestie,
(Now in his Ashes) Honor: Peace be with him.
Patience, be neere me still, and set me lower.
I haue not long to trouble thee. Good *Griffith*,
Cause the Musitians play me that sad note
I nam'd my Knell; whil'st I sit meditating

On that Cœlestiall Harmony I go too.

Sad and solemne Musicke.

Grif. She is asleep: Good wench, let's sit down quiet, For feare we wake her. Softly, gentle *Patience.*

The Vision.

Enter solemnely tripping one after another, sixe Personages, clad in white Robes, wearing on their heades Garlands of Bayes, and golden Vizards on their faces, Branches of Bayes or Palme in their hands. They first Conge vnto her, then Dance: and at certaine Changes, the first two hold a spare Garland ouer her Head, at which the other foure make reuerend Curtsies. Then the two that held the Garland, deliuer the same to the other next two, who obserue the same order in their Changes, and holding the Garland ouer her head. Which done, they deliuer the same Garland to the last two: who likewise obserue the same Order. At which (as it were by inspiration) she makes (in her sleepe) signes of reioycing, and holdeth vp her hands to heauen. And so, in their Dancing vanish, carrying the Garland with them. The Musicke continues.

Kath. Spirits of peace, where are ye? Are ye all gone?
And leaue me heere in wretchednesse, behinde ye?

Grif. Madam, we are heere.

Kath. It is not you I call for,
Saw ye none enter since I slept?

Grif. None Madam.

Kath. No? Saw you not euen now a blessed Troope
Inuite me to a Banquet, whose bright faces
Cast thousand beames vpon me, like the Sun?
They promis'd me eternall Happinesse,
And brought me Garlands (*Griffith*) which I feele
I am not worthy yet to weare: I shall assuredly.

Grif. I am most ioyfull Madam, such good dreames
Possesse your Fancy.

Kath. Bid the Musicke leaue,
They are harsh and heauy to me. *Musicke ceases.*

Pati. Do you note
How much her Grace is alter'd on the sodaine?
How long her face is drawne? How pale she lookes,
And of an earthy cold? Marke her eyes?

Grif. She is going Wench. Pray, pray.

Pati. Heauen comfort her.

Enter a Messenger.

Mes. And't like your Grace———

Kath. You are a sawcy Fellow,
Deserue we no more Reuerence?

Grif. You are too blame,
Knowing she will not loose her wonted Greatnesse
To vse so rude behauiour. Go too, kneele.

Mes. I humbly do entreat your Highnesse pardon,
My hast made me vnmannerly. There is staying
A Gentleman sent from the King, to see you.

Kath. Admit him entrance *Griffith.* But this Fellow
Let me ne're see againe. *Exit Messeng.*

Enter Lord Capuchius.

If my sight faile not,
You should be Lord Ambassador from the Emperor,
My Royall Nephew, and your name *Capuchius.*

Cap. Madam the same. Your Seruant.

Kath. O my Lord,
The Times and Titles now are alter'd strangely
With me, since first you knew me.
But I pray you,
What is your pleasure with me?

Cap. Noble Lady,
First mine owne seruice to your Grace, the next
The Kings request, that I would visit you,
Who greeues much for your weaknesse, and by me
Sends you his Princely Commendations,
And heartily entreats you take good comfort.

Kath. O my good Lord, that comfort comes too late,
'Tis like a Pardon after Execution;
That gentle Physicke giuen in time, had cur'd me:
But now I am past all Comforts heere, but Prayers.
How does his Highnesse?

Cap. Madam, in good health.

Kath. So may he euer do, and euer flourish,
When I shall dwell with Wormes, and my poore name
Banish'd the Kingdome. *Patience,* is that Letter
I caus'd you write, yet sent away?

Pat. No Madam.

Kath. Sir, I most humbly pray you to deliuer
This to my Lord the King.

Cap. Most willing Madam.

Kath. In which I haue commended to his goodnesse
The Modell of our chaste loues: his yong daughter,
The dewes of Heauen fall thicke in Blessings on her,
Beseeching him to giue her vertuous breeding.
She is yong, and of a Noble modest Nature,
I hope she will deserue well; and a little
To loue her for her Mothers sake, that lou'd him,
Heauen knowes how deerely.
My next poore Petition,
Is, that his Noble Grace would haue some pittie
Vpon my wretched women, that so long
Haue follow'd both my Fortunes, faithfully,
Of which there is not one, I dare auow
(And now I should not lye) but will deserue
For Vertue, and true Beautie of the Soule,
For honestie, and decent Carriage
A right good Husband (let him be a Noble)
And sure those men are happy that shall haue 'em.
The last is for my men, they are the poorest,
(But pouerty could neuer draw 'em from me)
That they may haue their wages, duly paid 'em,
And something ouer to remember me by.
If Heauen had pleas'd to haue giuen me longer life
And able meanes, we had not parted thus.
These are the whole Contents, and good my Lord,
By that you loue the deerest in this world,
As you wish Christian peace to soules departed,
Stand these poore peoples Friend, and vrge the King
To do me this last right.

Cap. By Heauen I will,
Or let me loose the fashion of a man.

Kath. I thanke you honest Lord. Remember me
In all humilitie vnto his Highnesse:
Say his long trouble now is passing
Out of this world. Tell him in death I blest him
(For so I will) mine eyes grow dimme. Farewell
My Lord. *Griffith* farewell. Nay *Patience,*
You must not leaue me yet. I must to bed,
Call in more women. When I am dead, good Wench,
Let me be vs'd with Honor; strew me ouer
With Maiden Flowers, that all the world may know
I was a chaste Wife, to my Graue: Embalme me,
Then lay me forth (although vnqueen'd) yet like
A Queene, and Daughter to a King enterre me.
I can no more.

Exeunt leading Katherine.

Actus Quintus. Scena Prima.

Enter Gardiner Bishop of Winchester, a Page with a Torch before him, met by Sir Thomas Louell.

Gard. It's one a clocke Boy, is't not.
Boy. It hath strooke.
Gard. These should be houres for necessities,
Not for delights: Times to repayre our Nature
With comforting repose, and not for vs
To waste these times. Good houre of night Sir *Thomas*:
Whether so late?
Lou. Came you from the King, my Lord?
Gar. I did Sir *Thomas*, and left him at Primero
With the Duke of Suffolke.
Lou. I must to him too
Before he go to bed. Ile take my leaue.
Gard. Not yet Sir *Thomas Louell*: what's the matter?
It seemes you are in hast: and if there be
No great offence belongs too't, giue your Friend
Some touch of your late businesse: Affaires that walke
(As they say Spirits do) at midnight, haue
In them a wilder Nature, then the businesse
That seekes dispatch by day.
Lou. My Lord, I loue you;
And durst commend a secret to your eare
Much waightier then this worke. The Queens in Labor
They say in great Extremity, and fear'd
Shee'l with the Labour, end.
Gard. The fruite she goes with
I pray for heartily, that it may finde
Good time, and liue: but for the Stocke Sir *Thomas*,
I wish it grubb'd vp now.
Lou. Methinkes I could
Cry the Amen, and yet my Conscience sayes
Shee's a good Creature, and sweet-Ladie do's
Deserue our better wishes.
Gard. But Sir, Sir,
Heare me Sir *Thomas*, y'are a Gentleman
Of mine owne way. I know you Wise, Religious,
And let me tell you, it will ne're be well,
'Twill not Sir *Thomas Louell*, tak't of me,
Till *Cranmer*, *Cromwel*, her two hands, and shee
Sleepe in their Graues.
Louell. Now Sir, you speake of two
The most remark'd i'th'Kingdome: as for *Cromwell*,
Beside that of the Iewell-House, is made Master
O'th'Rolles, and the Kings Secretary. Further Sir,
Stands in the gap and Trade of moe Preferments,
With which the Lime will loade him. Th'Archbyshop
Is the Kings hand, and tongue, and who dare speak
One syllable against him?
Gard. Yes, yes, Sir *Thomas*,
There are that Dare, and I my selfe haue ventur'd
To speake my minde of him: and indeed this day,
Sir (I may tell it you) I thinke I haue
Incenst the Lords o'th'Councell, that he is
(For so I know he is, they know he is)
A most Arch-Heretique, a Pestilence
That does infect the Land: with which, they moued
Haue broken with the King, who hath so farre
Giuen eare to our Complaint, of his great Grace,
And Princely Care, fore-seeing those fell Mischiefes,
Our Reasons layd before him, hath commanded
To morrow Morning to the Councell Boord
He be conuented. He's a ranke weed Sir *Thomas*,
And we must root him out. From your Affaires
I hinder you too long: Good night, Sir *Thomas*.
Exit Gardiner and Page.
Lou. Many good nights, my Lord, I rest your seruant.
Enter King and Suffolke.
King. *Charles*, I will play no more to night,
My mindes not on't, you are too hard for me.
Suff. Sir, I did neuer win of you before.
King. But little *Charles*,
Nor shall not when my Fancies on my play.
Now *Louel*, from the Queene what is the Newes.
Lou. I could not personally deliuer to her
What you commanded me, but by her woman,
I sent your Message, who return'd her thankes
In the great'st humblenesse, and desir'd your Highnesse
Most heartily to pray for her.
King. What say'st thou? Ha?
To pray for her? What is she crying out?
Lou. So said her woman, and that her suffrance made
Almost each pang, a death.
King. Alas good Lady.
Suf. God safely quit her of her Burthen, and
With gentle Trauaile, to the gladding of
Your Highnesse with an Heire.
King. 'Tis midnight *Charles*,
Prythee to bed, and in thy Prayres remember
Th'estate of my poore Queene. Leaue me alone,
For I must thinke of that, which company
Would not be friendly too.
Suf. I wish your Highnesse
A quiet night, and my good Mistris will
Remember in my Prayers.
King. *Charles* good night. *Exit Suffolke.*
Well Sir, what followes?
Enter Sir Anthony Denny.
Den. Sir, I haue brought my Lord the Arch-byshop,
As you commanded me.
King. Ha? Canterbury?
Den. I my good Lord.
King. 'Tis true: where is he *Denny*?
Den. He attends your Highnesse pleasure.
King. Bring him to Vs.
Lou. This is about that, which the Byshop spake,
I am happily come hither.
Enter Cranmer and Denny.
King. Auoyd the Gallery. *Louel seemes to stay.*
Ha? I haue said. Be gone.
What? *Exeunt Louell and Denny.*
Cran. I am fearefull: Wherefore frownes he thus?
'Tis his Aspect of Terror. All's not well.
King. How now my Lord?
You do desire to know wherefore
I sent for you.
Cran. It is my dutie
T'attend your Highnesse pleasure.
King. Pray you arise
My good and gracious Lord of Canterburie:
Come, you and I must walke a turne together:
I haue Newes to tell you.
Come, come, giue me your hand.
Ah my good Lord, I greeue at what I speake,
And am right sorrie to repeat what followes.
I haue, and most vnwillingly of late

Heard many greeuous. I do say my Lord
Greeuous complaints of you; which being consider'd,
Haue mou'd Vs, and our Councell, that you shall
This Morning come before vs, where I know
You cannot with such freedome purge your selfe,
But that till further Triall, in those Charges
Which will require your Answer, you must take
Your patience to you, and be well contented
To make your house our Towre: you, a Brother of vs
It fits we thus proceed, or else no witnesse
Would come against you.

Cran. I humbly thanke your Highnesse,
And am right glad to catch this good occasion
Most throughly to be winnowed, where my Chaffe
And Corne shall flye asunder. For I know
There's none stands vnder more calumnious tongues,
Then I my selfe, poore man.

King. Stand vp, good Canterbury,
Thy Truth, and thy Integrity is rooted
In vs thy Friend. Giue me thy hand, stand vp,
Prythee let's walke. Now by my Holydame,
What manner of man are you? My Lord, I look'd
You would haue giuen me your Petition, that
I should haue tane some paines, to bring together
Your selfe, and your Accusers, and to haue heard you
Without indurance further.

Cran. Most dread Liege,
The good I stand on, is my Truth and Honestie:
If they shall faile, I with mine Enemies
Will triumph o're my person, which I waigh not,
Being of those Vertues vacant. I feare nothing
What can be said against me.

King. Know you not
How your state stands i'th'world, with the whole world?
Your Enemies are many, and not small; their practises
Must beare the same proportion, and not euer
The Iustice and the Truth o'th'question carries
The dew o'th'Verdict with it; at what ease
Might corrupt mindes procure, Knaues as corrupt
To sweare against you: Such things haue bene done.
You are Potently oppos'd, and with a Malice
Of as great Size. Weene you of better lucke,
I meane in periur'd Witnesse, then your Master,
Whose Minister you are, whiles heere he liu'd
Vpon this naughty Earth? Go too, go too,
You take a Precepit for no leape of danger,
And woe your owne destruction.

Cran. God, and your Maiesty
Protect mine innocence, or I fall into
The trap is laid for me.

King. Be of good cheere,
They shall no more preuaile, then we giue way too:
Keepe comfort to you, and this Morning see
You do appeare before them. If they shall chance
In charging you with matters, to commit you:
The best perswasions to the contrary
Faile not to vse, and with what vehemencie
Th'occasion shall instruct you. If intreaties
Will render you no remedy, this Ring
Deliuer them, and your Appeale to vs
There make before them. Looke, the goodman weeps:
He's honest on mine Honor. Gods blest Mother,
I sweare he is true-hearted, and a soule
None better in my Kingdome. Get you gone,
And do as I haue bid you. *Exit Cranmer.*
He ha's strangled his Language in his teares.

Enter Olde Lady.

Gent.within. Come backe: what meane you?

Lady. Ile not come backe, the tydings that I bring
Will make my boldnesse, manners. Now good Angels
Fly o're thy Royall head, and shade thy person
Vnder their blessed wings.

King. Now by thy lookes
I gesse thy Message. Is the Queene deliuer'd?
Say I, and of a boy.

Lady. I, I my Liege,
And of a louely Boy: the God of heauen
Both now, and euer blesse her: 'Tis a Gyrle
Promises Boyes heereafter. Sir, your Queen
Desires your Visitation, and to be
Acquainted with this stranger; 'tis as like you,
As Cherry, is to Cherry.

King. *Louell.*

Lou. Sir.

King. Giue her an hundred Markes.
Ile to the Queene. *Exit King.*

Lady. An hundred Markes? By this light, Ile ha more.
An ordinary Groome is for such payment.
I will haue more, or scold it out of him.
Said I for this, the Gyrle was like to him? Ile
Haue more, or else vnsay't: and now, while 'tis hot,
Ile put it to the issue. *Exit Ladie.*

Scena Secunda.

Enter Cranmer, Archbyshop of Canterbury.

Cran. I hope I am not too late, and yet the Gentleman
That was sent to me from the Councell, pray'd me
To make great hast. All fast? What meanes this? Hoa?
Who waites there? Sure you know me?

Enter Keeper.

Keep. Yes, my Lord:
But yet I cannot helpe you.

Cran. Why?

Keep. Your Grace must waight till you be call'd for.

Enter Doctor Buts.

Cran. So.

Buts. This is a Peere of Malice: I am glad
I came this way so happily. The King
Shall vnderstand it presently. *Exit Buts*

Cran. 'Tis *Buts*.
The Kings Physitian, as he past along
How earnestly he cast his eyes vpon me:
Pray heauen he sound not my disgrace: for certaine
This is of purpose laid by some that hate me,
(God turne their hearts, I neuer sought their malice)
To quench mine Honor; they would shame to make me
Wait else at doore: a fellow Councellor
'Mong Boyes, Groomes, and Lackeyes.
But their pleasures
Must be fulfill'd, and I attend with patience.

Enter the King, and Buts, at a Windowe aboue.

Buts. Ile shew your Grace the strangest sight.

King. What's that *Buts*?

Butts. I thinke your Highnesse saw this many a day.
Kin. Body a me: where is it?
Butts. There my Lord:
The high promotion of his Grace of *Canterbury*,
Who holds his State at dore 'mongst Pursevants,
Pages, and Foot-boyes.
Kin. Ha? 'Tis he indeed.
Is this the Honour they doe one another?
'Tis well there's one aboue 'em yet; I had thought
They had parted so much honesty among 'em,
At least good manners; as not thus to suffer
A man of his Place, and so neere our fauour
To dance attendance on their Lordships pleasures,
And at the dore too, like a Post with Packets:
By holy *Mary* (*Butts*) there's knauery;
Let 'em alone, and draw the Curtaine close:
We shall heare more anon.

A Councell Table brought in with Chayres, and Stooles, and placed vnder the State. Enter Lord Chancellour, places himselfe at the vpper end of the Table, on the left hand: A Seate being left void aboue him, as for Canterburies Seate. Duke of Suffolke, Duke of Norfolke, Surrey, Lord Chamberlaine, Gardiner, seat themselues in Order on each side. Cromwell at lower end, as Secretary.

Chan. Speake to the businesse, M. Secretary;
Why are we met in Councell?
Crom. Please your Honours,
The chiefe cause concernes his Grace of *Canterbury*.
Gard. Ha's he had knowledge of it?
Crom. Yes.
Norf. Who waits there?
Keep. Without my Noble Lords?
Gard. Yes.
Keep. My Lord Archbishop:
And ha's done halfe an houre to know your pleasures.
Chan. Let him come in.
Keep. Your Grace may enter now.
Cranmer approches the Councell Table.
Chan. My good Lord Archbishop, I'm very sorry
To sit heere at this present, and behold
That Chayre stand empty: But we all are men
In our owne natures fraile, and capable
Of our flesh, few are Angels; out of which frailty
And want of wisedome, you that best should teach vs,
Haue misdemean'd your selfe, and not a little:
Toward the King first, then his Lawes, in filling
The whole Realme, by your teaching & your Chaplaines
(For so we are inform'd) with new opinions,
Diuers and dangerous; which are Heresies;
And not reform'd, may proue pernicious.
Gard. Which Reformation must be sodaine too
My Noble Lords; for those that tame wild Horses,
Pace 'em not in their hands to make 'em gentle;
But stop their mouthes with stubborn Bits & spurre 'em,
Till they obey the mannage. If we suffer
Out of our easinesse and childish pitty
To one mans Honour, this contagious sicknesse;
Farewell all Physicke: and what followes then?
Commotions, vprores, with a generall Taint
Of the whole State; as of late dayes our neighbours,
The vpper *Germany* can deerely witnesse:
Yet freshly pittied in our memories.
Cran. My good Lords; Hitherto, in all the Progresse
Both of my Life and Office, I haue labour'd,
And with no little study, that my teaching
And the strong course of my Authority,
Might goe one way, and safely; and the end
Was euer to doe well: nor is there liuing,
(I speake it with a single heart, my Lords)
A man that more detests, more stirres against,
Both in his priuate Conscience, and his place,
Defacers of a publique peace then I doe:
Pray Heauen the King may neuer find a heart
With lesse Allegeance in it. Men that make
Enuy, and crooked malice, nourishment;
Dare bite the best. I doe beseech your Lordships,
That in this case of Iustice, my Accusers,
Be what they will, may stand forth face to face,
And freely vrge against me.
Suff. Nay, my Lord,
That cannot be; you are a Counsellor,
And by that vertue no man dare accuse you.
Gard. My Lord, because we haue busines of more moment,
We will be short with you. 'Tis his Highnesse pleasure
And our consent, for better tryall of you,
From hence you be committed to the Tower,
Where being but a priuate man againe,
You shall know many dare accuse you boldly,
More then (I feare) you are prouided for.
Cran. Ah my good Lord of *Winchester*: I thanke you,
You are alwayes my good Friend, if your will passe,
I shall both finde your Lordship, Iudge and Iuror,
You are so mercifull. I see your end,
'Tis my vndoing. Loue and meekenesse, Lord
Become a Churchman, better then Ambition:
Win straying Soules with modesty againe,
Cast none away: That I shall cleere my selfe,
Lay all the weight ye can vpon my patience,
I make as little doubt as you doe conscience,
In doing dayly wrongs. I could say more,
But reuerence to your calling, makes me modest.
Gard. My Lord, my Lord, you are a Sectary,
That's the plaine truth; your painted glosse discouers
To men that vnderstand you, words and weaknesse.
Crom. My Lord of *Winchester*, y'are a little,
By your good fauour, too sharpe; Men so Noble,
How euer faulty, yet should finde respect
For what they haue beene: 'tis a cruelty,
To load a falling man.
Gard. Good M. Secretary,
I cry your Honour mercie; you may worst
Of all this Table say so.
Crom. Why my Lord?
Gard. Doe not I know you for a Fauourer
Of this new Sect? ye are not sound.
Crom. Not sound?
Gard. Not sound I say.
Crom. Would you were halfe so honest:
Mens prayers then would seeke you, not their feares.
Gard. I shall remember this bold Language.
Crom. Doe.
Remember your bold life too.
Cham. This is too much;
Forbeare for shame my Lords.
Gard. I haue done.
Crom. And I.
Cham. Then thus for you my Lord, it stands agreed
I take it, by all voyces: That forthwith,
You be conuaid to th' Tower a Prisoner;
There to remaine till the Kings further pleasure
Be knowne vnto vs: are you all agreed Lords.

All. We are.
Cran. Is there no other way of mercy,
But I must needs to th' Tower my Lords?
Gard. What other,
Would you expect? You are strangely troublesome:
Let some o'th' Guard be ready there.
Enter the Guard.
Cran. For me?
Must I goe like a Traytor thither?
Gard. Receiue him,
And see him safe i'th' Tower.
Cran. Stay good my Lords,
I haue a little yet to say. Looke there my Lords,
By vertue of that Ring, I take my cause
Out of the gripes of cruell men, and giue it
To a most Noble Iudge, the King my Maister.
Cham. This is the Kings Ring.
Sur. 'Tis no counterfeit.
Suff. 'Ts the right Ring, by Heau'n: I told ye all,
When we first put this dangerous stone a rowling,
'Twold fall vpon our selues.
Norf. Doe you thinke my Lords
The King will suffer but the little finger
Of this man to be vex'd?
Cham. Tis now too certaine;
How much more is his Life in value with him?
Would I were fairely out on't.
Crom. My mind gaue me,
In seeking tales and Informations
Against this man, whose honesty the Diuell
And his Disciples onely enuy at,
Ye blew the fire that burnes ye: now haue at ye.

Enter King frowning on them, takes his Seate.
Gard. Dread Soueraigne,
How much are, we bound to Heauen,
In dayly thankes; that gaue vs such a Prince;
Not onely good and wise, but most religious:
One that in all obedience, makes the Church
The cheefe ayme of his Honour, and to strengthen
That holy duty out of deare respect,
His Royall selfe in Iudgement comes to heare
The cause betwixt her, and this great offender.
Kin. You were euer good at sodaine Commendations,
Bishop of *Winchester*. But know I come not
To heare such flattery now, and in my presence
They are too thin, and base to hide offences,
To me you cannot reach. You play the Spaniell,
And thinke with wagging of your tongue to win me:
But whatsoere thou tak'st me for; I'm sure
Thou hast a cruell Nature and a bloody.
Good man sit downe: Now let me see the proudest
Hee, that dares most, but wag his finger at thee.
By all that's holy, he had better starue,
Then but once thinke his place becomes thee not.
Sur. May it please your Grace;——
Kin. No Sir, it doe's not please me,
I had thought, I had had men of some vnderstanding,
And wisedome of my Councell; but I finde none:
Was it discretion Lords, to let this man,
This good man (few of you deserue that Title)
This honest man, wait like a lowsie Foot-boy
At Chamber dore? and one, as great as you are?
Why, what a shame was this? Did my Commission
Bid ye so farre forget your selues? I gaue ye
Power, as he was a Counsellour to try him,
Not as a Groome: There's some of ye, I see,
More out of Malice then Integrity,
Would trye him to the vtmost, had ye meane,
Which ye shall neuer haue while I liue.
Chan. Thus farre
My most dread Soueraigne, may it like your Grace,
To let my tongue excuse all. What was purpos'd
Concerning his Imprisonment, was rather
(If there be faith in men) meant for his Tryall,
And faire purgation to the world then malice,
I'm sure in me.
Kin. Well, well my Lords respect him,
Take him, and vse him well; hee's worthy of it.
I will say thus much for him, if a Prince
May be beholding to a Subiect; I
Am for his loue and seruice, so to him.
Make me no more adoe, but all embrace him;
Be friends for shame my Lords: My Lord of *Canterbury*
I haue a Suite which you must not deny mee.
That is, a faire young Maid that yet wants Baptisme,
You must be Godfather, and answere for her.
Cran. The greatest Monarch now aliue may glory
In such an honour: how may I deserue it,
That am a poore and humble Subiect to you?
Kin. Come, come my Lord, you'd spare your spoones;
You shall haue two noble Partners with you: the old Duchesse of *Norfolke*, and Lady Marquesse *Dorset*? will these please you?
Once more my Lord of *Winchester*, I charge you
Embrace, and loue this man.
Gard. With a true heart,
And Brother; loue I doe it.
Cran. And let Heauen
Witnesse how deare, I hold this Confirmation. (hearts,
Kin. Good Man, those ioyfull teares shew thy true
The common voyce I see is verified
Of thee, which sayes thus: Doe my Lord of *Canterbury*
A shrewd turne, and hee's your friend for euer:
Come Lords, we trifle time away: I long
To haue this young one made a Christian.
As I haue made ye one Lords, one remaine:
So I grow stronger, you more Honour gaine. *Exeunt.*

Scena Tertia.

Noyse and Tumult within: Enter Porter and his man.

Port. You'l leaue your noyse anon ye Rascals: doe you take the Court for Parish Garden: ye rude Slaues, leaue your gaping:
Within. Good M. Porter I belong to th' Larder.
Port. Belong to th' Gallowes, and be hang'd ye Rogue: Is this a place to roare in? Fetch me a dozen Crab-tree staues, and strong ones; these are but switches to 'em: Ile scratch your heads; you must be seeing Christenings? Do you looke for Ale, and Cakes heere, you rude Raskalls?
Man. Pray Sir be patient; 'tis as much impossible,
Vnlesse wee sweepe 'em from the dore with Cannons,
To scatter 'em, as 'tis to make 'em sleepe
On May-day Morning, which will neuer be:
We may as well push against Powles as stirre 'em.
Por. How got they in, and be hang'd?

Man. Alas I know not, how gets the Tide in?
As much as one sound Cudgell of foure foote,
(You see the poore remainder) could distribute,
I made no spare Sir.
Port. You did nothing Sir.
Man. I am not *Sampson*, nor Sir *Guy*, nor *Colebrand*,
To mow 'em downe before me: but if I spar'd any
That had a head to hit, either young or old,
He or shee, Cuckold or Cuckold-maker:
Let me ne're hope to see a Chine againe,
And that I would not for a Cow, God saue her.
Within. Do you heare M. Porter?
Port. I shall be with you presently, good M. *Puppy*,
Keepe the dore close Sirha.
Man. What would you haue me doe?
Por. What should you doe,
But knock 'em downe by th' dozens? Is this More fields to muster in? Or haue wee some strange Indian with the great *Toole*, come to Court, the women so besiege vs? Blesse me, what a fry of Fornication is at dore? On my Christian Conscience this one Christening will beget a thousand, here will bee Father, God-father, and all together.

Man. The Spoones will be the bigger Sir: There is a fellow somewhat neere the doore, he should be a Brasier by his face, for o' my conscience twenty of the Dog-dayes now reigne in's Nose; all that stand about him are vnder the Line, they need no other pennance: that Fire-Drake did I hit three times on the head, and three times was his Nose discharged against mee; hee stands there like a Morter-piece to blow vs. There was a Habberdashers Wife of small wit, neere him, that rail'd vpon me, till her pinck'd porrenger fell off her head, for kindling such a combustion in the State. I mist the Meteor once, and hit that Woman, who cryed out Clubbes, when I might see from farre, some forty Truncheoners draw to her succour, which were the hope o'th' Strond where she was quartered; they fell on, I made good my place; at length they came to th' broome staffe to me, I defide 'em stil, when sodainly a File of Boyes behind 'em, loose shot, deliuer'd such a showre of Pibbles, that I was faine to draw mine Honour in, and let 'em win the Worke, the Diuell was amongst 'em I thinke surely.

Por. These are the youths that thunder at a Playhouse, and fight for bitten Apples, that no Audience but the tribulation of Tower Hill, or the Limbes of Limehouse, their deare Brothers are able to endure. I haue some of 'em in *Limbo Patrum*, and there they are like to dance these three dayes; besides the running Banquet of two Beadles, that is to come.

Enter Lord Chamberlaine.

Cham. Mercy o' me: what a Multitude are heere?
They grow still too; from all Parts they are comming,
As if we kept a Faire heere? Where are these Porters?
These lazy knaues? Y'haue made a fine hand fellowes?
Theres a trim rabble let in: are all these
Your faithfull friends o'th' Suburbs? We shall haue
Great store of roome no doubt, left for the Ladies,
When they passe backe from the Christening?
Por. And't please your Honour,
We are but men; and what so many may doe,
Not being torne a pieces, we haue done:
An Army cannot rule 'em.
Cham. As I liue,
If the King blame me for't; Ile lay ye all
By th' heeles, and sodainly: and on your heads
Clap round Fines for neglect: y'are lazy knaues,
And heere ye lye baiting of Bombards, when
Ye should doe Seruice. Harke the Trumpets sound,
Th'are come already from the Christening,
Go breake among the preasse, and finde away out
To let the Troope passe fairely; or Ile finde
A Marshallsey, shall hold ye play these two Monthes.
Por. Make way there, for the Princesse.
Man. You great fellow,
Stand close vp, or Ile make your head ake.
Por. You i'th' Chamblet, get vp o'th' raile,
Ile pecke you o're the pales else. *Exeunt.*

Scena Quarta.

Enter Trumpets sounding: Then two Aldermen, L. Maior, Carter, Cranmer, Duke of Norfolke with his Marshals Staffe, Duke of Suffolke, two Noblemen, bearing great standing Bowles for the Christening Guifts: Then foure Noblemen bearing a Canopy, vnder which the Dutchesse of Norfolke, Godmother, bearing the Childe richly habited in a Mantle, &c. Traine borne by a Lady: Then followes the Marchionesse Dorset, the other Godmother, and Ladies. The Troope passe once about the Stage, and Garter speakes.

Gart. Heauen
From thy endlesse goodnesse, send prosperous life,
Long and euer happie, to the high and Mighty
Princesse of England *Elizabeth*.

Flourish. Enter King and Guard.

Cran. And to your Royall Grace, & the good Queen,
My Noble Partners, and my selfe thus pray
All comfort, ioy in this most gracious Lady,
Heauen euer laid vp to make Parents happy,
May hourely fall vpon ye.
Kin. Thanke you good Lord Archbishop:
What is her Name?
Cran. *Elizabeth*.
Kin. Stand vp Lord,
With this Kisse, take my Blessing: God protect thee,
Into whose hand, I giue thy Life.
Cran. *Amen*.
Kin. My Noble Gossips, y'haue beene too Prodigall;
I thanke ye heartily: So shall this Lady,
When she ha's so much English.
Cran. Let me speake Sir,
For Heauen now bids me; and the words I vtter,
Let none thinke Flattery; for they'l finde 'em Truth.
This Royall Infant, Heauen still moue about her;
Though in her Cradle; yet now promises
Vpon this Land a thousand thousand Blessings,
Which Time shall bring to ripenesse: She shall be,
(But few now liuing can behold that goodnesse)
A Patterne to all Princes liuing with her,
And all that shall succeed: *Saba* was neuer
More couetous of Wisedome, and faire Vertue
Then this pure Soule shall be. All Princely Graces
That mould vp such a mighty Piece as this is,
With all the Vertues that attend the good,
Shall still be doubled on her. Truth shall Nurse her,

Holy and Heauenly thoughts still Counsell her:
She shall be lou'd and fear'd. Her owne shall blesse her;
Her Foes shake like a Field of beaten Corne,
And hang their heads with sorrow:
Good growes with her.
In her dayes, Euery Man shall eate in safety,
Vnder his owne Vine what he plants; and sing
The merry Songs of Peace to all his Neighbours.
God shall be truely knowne, and those about her,
From her shall read the perfect way of Honour,
And by those claime their greatnesse; not by Blood.
Nor shall this peace sleepe with her: But as when
The Bird of Wonder dyes, the Mayden Phoenix,
Her Ashes new create another Heyre,
As great in admiration as her selfe.
So shall she leaue her Blessednesse to One,
(When Heauen shal call her from this clowd of darknes)
Who, from the sacred Ashes of her Honour
Shall Star-like rise, as great in fame as she was,
And so stand fix'd. Peace, Plenty, Loue, Truth, Terror,
That were the Seruants to this chosen Infant,
Shall then be his, and like a Vine grow to him;
Where euer the bright Sunne of Heauen shall shine,
His Honour, and the greatnesse of his Name,
Shall be, and make new Nations. He shall flourish,
And like a Mountaine Cedar, reach his branches,
To all the Plaines about him: Our Childrens Children
Shall see this, and blesse Heauen.

Kin. Thou speakest wonders.

Cran. She shall be to the happinesse of England,
An aged Princesse; many dayes shall see her,
And yet no day without a deed to Crowne it.
Would I had knowne no more: But she must dye,
She must, the Saints must haue her; yet a Virgin,
A most vnspotted Lilly shall she passe
To th' ground, and all the World shall mourne her.

Kin. O Lord Archbishop
Thou hast made me now a man, neuer before
This happy Child, did I get any thing.
This Oracle of comfort, ha's so pleas'd me,
That when I am in Heauen, I shall desire
To see what this Child does, and praise my Maker.
I thanke ye all. To you my good Lord Maior,
And you good Brethren, I am much beholding:
I haue receiu'd much Honour by your presence,
And ye shall find me thankfull. Lead the way Lords,
Ye must all see the Queene, and she must thanke ye,
She will be sicke els. This day, no man thinke
'Has businesse at his house; for all shall stay:
This Little-One shall make it Holy-day. *Exeunt.*

THE EPILOGVE.

'Tis ten to one, this Play can neuer please
All that are heere: Some come to take their ease,
And sleepe an Act or two; but those we feare
W'haue frighted with our Tumpets: so 'tis cleare,
They'l say tis naught. Others to heare the City
Abus'd extreamly, and to cry that's witty,
Which wee haue not done neither; that I feare
All the expected good w'are like to heare.
For this Play at this time, is onely in
The mercifull construction of good women,
For such a one we shew'd 'em: If they smile,
And say twill doe; I know within a while,
All the best men are ours; for 'tis ill hap,
If they hold, when their Ladies bid 'em clap.

FINIS.

The Prologue.

IN Troy there lyes the Scene: From Iles of Greece
The Princes Orgillous, their high blood chaf'd
Haue to the Port of Athens sent their shippes
Fraught with the ministers and instruments
Of cruell Warre: Sixty *and nine that wore*
Their Crownets Regall, from th'Athenian bay
Put forth toward Phrygia, and their vow is made
To ransacke Troy, within whose strong emures
The rauish'd Helen, Menelaus *Queene,*
With wanton Paris *sleepes, and that's the Quarrell.*
To Tenedos *they come,*
And the deepe-drawing Barke do there disgorge
Their warlike frautage: now on Dardan Plaines
The fresh and yet vnbruised Greekes do pitch
Their braue Pauillions. Priams *six-gated City,*
Dardan *and* Timbria, Helias, Chetas, Troien,
And Antenonidus *with massie Staples*
And corresponsiue and fulfilling Bolts
Stirre vp the Sonnes of Troy.
Now Expectation tickling skittish spirits,
On one and other side, Troian and Greeke,
Sets all on hazard. And hither am I come,
A Prologue arm'd, but not in confidence
Of Authors pen, or Actors voyce; but suited
In like conditions, as our Argument;
To tell you (faire Beholders) that our Play
Leapes ore the vaunt and firstlings of those broyles,
Beginning in the middle; starting thence away,
To what may be digested in a Play:
Like, or finde fault, do as your pleasures are,
Now good, or bad, 'tis but the chance of Warre.

THE TRAGEDIE OF
Troylus and Creſsida.

Actus Primus. Scœna Prima.

Enter Pandarus and Troylus.

Troylus.

CAll here my Varlet, Ile vnarme againe.
Why ſhould I warre without the wals of Troy
That finde ſuch cruell battell here within?
Each Troian that is maſter of his heart,
Let him to field, *Troylus* alas hath none.

Pan. Will this geere nere be mended?

Troy. The Greeks are ſtrong, & skilful to their ſtrength,
Fierce to their skill, and to their fierceneſſe Valiant:
But I am weaker then a womans teare;
Tamer then ſleepe, fonder then ignorance;
Leſſe valiant then the Virgin in the night,
And skilleſſe as vnpractis'd Infancie.

Pan. Well, I haue told you enough of this: For my part, Ile not meddle nor make no farther. Hee that will haue a Cake out of the Wheate, muſt needes tarry the grinding.

Troy. Haue I not tarried?

Pan. I the grinding; but you muſt tarry the bolting.

Troy. Haue I not tarried?

Pan. I the boulting; but you muſt tarry the leau'ing.

Troy. Still haue I tarried.

Pan. I, to the leauening: but heeres yet in the word hereafter, the Kneading, the making of the Cake, the heating of the Ouen, and the Baking; nay, you muſt ſtay the cooling too, or you may chance to burne your lips.

Troy. Patience her ſelfe, what Goddeſſe ere ſhe be,
Doth leſſer blench at ſufferance, then I doe:
At *Priams* Royall Table doe I ſit;
And when faire *Creſſid* comes into my thoughts,
So (Traitor) then ſhe comes, when ſhe is thence.

Pan. Well:
She look'd yeſternight fairer, then euer I ſaw her looke,
Or any woman elſe.

Troy. I was about to tell thee, when my heart,
As wedged with a ſigh, would riue in twaine,
Leaſt *Hector*, or my Father ſhould perceiue me:
I haue (as when the Sunne doth light a-ſcorne)
Buried this ſigh, in wrinkle of a ſmile:
But ſorrow, that is couch'd in ſeeming gladneſſe,
Is like that mirth, Fate turnes to ſudden ſadneſſe.

Pan. And her haire were not ſomewhat darker then *Helens*, well go too, there were no more compariſon betweene the Women. But for my part ſhe is my Kinſwoman, I would not (as they tearme it) praiſe it, but I wold ſome-body had heard her talke yeſterday as I did: I will not diſpraiſe your ſiſter *Caſſandra's* wit, but———

Troy. Oh *Pandarus*! I tell thee *Pandarus*;
When I doe tell thee, there my hopes lye drown'd:
Reply not in how many Fadomes deepe
They lye indrench'd. I tell thee, I am mad
In *Creſſids* loue. Thou anſwer'ſt ſhe is Faire,
Powr'ſt in the open Vlcer of my heart,
Her Eyes, her Haire, her Cheeke, her Gate, her Voice,
Handleſt in thy diſcourſe. O that her Hand
(In whoſe compariſon, all whites are Inke)
Writing their owne reproach; to whoſe ſoft ſeizure,
The Cignets Downe is harſh, and ſpirit of Senſe
Hard as the palme of Plough-man. This thou tel'ſt me;
As true thou tel'ſt me, when I ſay I loue her:
But ſaying thus, inſtead of Oyle and Balme,
Thou lai'ſt in euery gaſh that loue hath giuen me,
The Knife that made it.

Pan. I ſpeake no more then truth.

Troy. Thou do'ſt not ſpeake ſo much.

Pan. Faith, Ile not meddle in't: Let her be as ſhee is, if ſhe be faire, 'tis the better for her: and ſhe be not, ſhe ha's the mends in her owne hands.

Troy. Good *Pandarus*: How now *Pandarus*?

Pan. I haue had my Labour for my trauell, ill thought on of her, and ill thought on of you: Gone betweene and betweene, but ſmall thankes for my labour.

Troy. What art thou angry *Pandarus*? what with me?

Pan. Becauſe ſhe's Kinne to me, therefore ſhee's not ſo faire as *Helen*, and ſhe were not kin to me, ſhe would be as faire on Friday, as *Helen* is on Sunday. But what care I? I care not and ſhe were a Black-a-Moore, 'tis all one to me.

Troy. Say I ſhe is not faire?

Troy. I doe not care whether you doe or no. Shee's a Foole to ſtay behinde her Father: Let her to the Greeks, and ſo Ile tell her the next time I ſee her: for my part, Ile meddle nor make no more i'th'matter.

Troy. *Pandarus*? *Pan.* Not I.

Troy. Sweete *Pandarus*.

Pan. Pray you ſpeake no more to me, I will leaue all as I found it, and there an end. *Exit Pand.*

Sound Alarum.

Tro. Peace you vngracious Clamors, peace rude ſounds,
Fooles on both ſides, *Helen* muſt needs be faire,
When with your bloud you daily paint her thus.
I cannot fight vpon this Argument:

It

It is too staru'd a subiect for my Sword,
But *Pandarus*: O Gods! How do you plague me?
I cannot come to *Cressid* but by *Pandar*,
And he's as teachy to be woo'd to woe,
As she is stubborne, chast, against all suite.
Tell me *Apollo* for thy *Daphnes* Loue
What *Cressid* is, what *Pandar*, and what we:
Her bed is *India*, there she lies, a Pearle,
Between our Ilium, and where shee recides
Let it be cald the wild and wandring flood,
Our selfe the Merchant, and this sayling *Pandar*,
Our doubtfull hope, our conuoy and our Barke.

Alarum. Enter Æneas.

Æne. How now Prince *Troylus*?
Wherefore not a field?

Troy. Because not there; this womans answer sorts.
For womanish it is to be from thence:
What newes *Æneas* from the field to day?

Æne. That *Paris* is returned home, and hurt.

Troy. By whom *Æneas*?

Æne. *Troylus* by *Menelaus*.

Troy. Let *Paris* bleed, 'tis but a scar to scorne,
Paris is gor'd with *Menelaus* horne. *Alarum.*

Æne. Harke what good sport is out of Towne to day.

Troy. Better at home, if would I might were may:
But to the sport abroad, are you bound thither?

Æne. In all swift hast.

Troy. Come goe wee then togither. *Exeunt.*

Enter Cressid and her man.

Cre. Who were those went by?

Man. Queene *Hecuba*, and *Hellen*.

Cre. And whether go they?

Man. Vp to the Easterne Tower,
Whose height commands as subiect all the vaile,
To see the battell: *Hector* whose pacience,
Is as a Vertue fixt, to day was mou'd:
He chides *Andromache* and strooke his Armorer,
And like as there were husbandry in Warre
Before the Sunne rose, hee was harnest lyte,
And to the field goe's he; where euery flower
Did as a Prophet weepe what it forsaw,
In *Hectors* wrath.

Cre. What was his cause of anger?

Man. The noise goe's this;
There is among the Greekes,
A Lord of Troian blood, Nephew to *Hector*,
They call him *Aiax*.

Cre. Good; and what of him?

Man. They say he is a very man *per se* and stands alone.

Cre. So do all men, vnlesse they are drunke, sicke, or haue no legges.

Man. This man Lady, hath rob'd many beasts of their particular additions, he is as valiant as the Lyon, churlish as the Beare, slow as the Elephant: a man into whom nature hath so crowded humors, that his valour is crusht into folly, his folly sauced with discretion: there is no man hath a vertue, that he hath not a glimpse of, nor any man an attaint, but he carries some staine of it. He is melancholy without cause, and merry against the haire, hee hath the ioynts of euery thing, but euery thing so out of ioynt, that hee is a gowtie *Briareus*, many hands and no vse; or purblinded *Argus*, all eyes and no sight.

Cre. But how should this man that makes me smile, make *Hector* angry?

Man. They say he yesterday cop'd *Hector* in the battell and stroke him downe, the disdaind & shame whereof, hath euer since kept *Hector* fasting and waking.

Enter Pandarus.

Cre. Who comes here?

Man. Madam your Vncle *Pandarus*.

Cre. *Hectors* a gallant man.

Man. As may be in the world Lady.

Pan. What's that? what's that?

Cre. Good morrow Vncle *Pandarus*.

Pan. Good morrow Cozen *Cressid*: what do you talke of? good morrow *Alexander*: how do you Cozen? when were you at Illium?

Cre. This morning Vncle.

Pan. What were you talking of when I came? Was *Hector* arm'd and gon ere yea came to Illium? *Hellen* was not vp? was she?

Cre. *Hector* was gone but *Hellen* was not vp?

Pan. E'ene so; *Hector* was stirring early.

Cre. That were we talking of, and of his anger.

Pan. Was he angry?

Cre. So he saies here.

Pan True he was so; I know the cause too, heele lay about him to day I can tell them that, and there's *Troylus* will not come farre behind him, let them take heede of *Troylus*; I can tell them that too.

Cre. What is he angry too?

Pan. Who *Troylus*?
Troylus is the better man of the two.

Cre. Oh *Iupiter*; there's no comparison.

Pan. What not betweene *Troylus* and *Hector*? do you know a man if you see him?

Cre. I, if I euer saw him before and knew him.

Pan. Well I say *Troylus* is *Troylus*.

Cre. Then you say as I say,
For I am sure he is not *Hector*.

Pan. No not *Hector* is not *Troylus* in some degrees.

Cre. 'Tis iust, to each of them he is himselfe.

Pan. Himselfe? alas poore *Troylus* I would he were.

Cre. So he is.

Pan. Condition I had gone bare-foote to India.

Cre. He is not *Hector*.

Pan. Himselfe? no? hee's not himselfe, would a were himselfe: well, the Gods are aboue, time must friend or end: well *Troylus* well, I would my heart were in her body; no, *Hector* is not a better man then *Troylus*.

Cre. Excuse me.

Pan. He is elder.

Cre. Pardon me, pardon me.

Pan. Th'others not come too't, you shall tell me another tale when th'others come too't: *Hector* shall not haue his will this yeare.

Cre. He shall not neede it if he haue his owne.

Pan. Nor his qualities.

Cre. No matter.

Pan. Nor his beautie.

Cre. 'Twould not become him, his own's better.

Pan. You haue no iudgement Neece; *Hellen* her selfe swore th'other day that *Troylus* for a browne fauour (for so 'tis I must confesse) not browne neither.

Cre. No, but browne.

Pan. Faith to say truth, browne and not browne.

Cre. To say the truth, true and not true.

Pan. She prais'd his complexion aboue *Paris*.

Cre. Why *Paris* hath colour inough.

Pan. So, he has.

Cre. Then *Troylus* should haue too much, if she prasi'd him aboue, his complexion is higher then his, he hauing colour

colour enough, and the other higher, is too flaming a praise for a good complexion, I had as lieue *Hellens* golden tongue had commended *Troylus* for a copper nose.

Pan. I sweare to you,
I thinke *Hellen* loues him better then *Paris*.

Cre. Then shee's a merry Greeke indeed.

Pan. Nay I am sure she does, she came to him th'other day into the compast window, and you know he has not past three or foure haires on his chinne.

Cres. Indeed a Tapsters Arithmetique may soone bring his particulars therein, to a totall.

Pand. Why he is very yong, and yet will he within three pound lift as much as his brother *Hector*.

Cres. Is he is so young a man, and so old a lifter?

Pan. But to prooue to you that *Hellen* loues him, she came and puts me her white hand to his clouen chin.

Cres. *Iuno* haue mercy, how came it clouen?

Pan. Why, you know 'tis dimpled,
I thinke his smyling becomes him better then any man in all Phrigia.

Cre. Oh he smiles valiantly.

Pan. Dooes hee not?

Cre. Oh yes, and 'twere a clow'd in *Autumne*.

Pan. Why go to then, but to proue to you that *Hellen* loues *Troylus*.

Cre. *Troylus* wil stand to thee
Proofe, if youle prooue it so.

Pan. *Troylus*? why he esteemes her no more then I esteeme an addle egge.

Cre. If you loue an addle egge as well as you loue an idle head, you would eate chickens i'th'shell.

Pan. I cannot chuse but laugh to thinke how she tickled his chin, indeed shee has a maruel's white hand I must needs confesse.

Cre. Without the racke.

Pan. And shee takes vpon her to spie a white haire on his chinne.

Cre. Alas poore chin? many a wart is richer.

Pand. But there was such laughing, Queene *Hecuba* laught that her eyes ran ore.

Cre. With Milstones.

Pan. And *Cassandra* laught.

Cre. But there was more temperate fire vnder the pot of her eyes: did her eyes run ore too?

Pan. And *Hector* laught.

Cre. At what was all this laughing?

Pand. Marry at the white haire that *Hellen* spied on *Troylus* chin.

Cres. And t'had beene a greene haire, I should haue laught too.

Pand. They laught not so much at the haire, as at his pretty answere.

Cre. What was his answere?

Pan. Quoth shee, heere's but two and fifty haires on your chinne; and one of them is white.

Cre. This is her question.

Pand. That's true, make no question of that, two and fiftie haires quoth hee, and one white, that white haire is my Father, and all the rest are his Sonnes. *Iupiter* quoth she, which of these haires is *Paris* my husband? The forked one quoth he, pluckt out and giue it him: but there was such laughing, and *Hellen* so blusht, and *Paris* so chaft, and all the rest so laught, that it past.

Cre. So let it now,
For is has beene a great while going by.

Pan. Well Cozen,
I told you a thing yesterday, think on't.

Cre. So I does.

Pand. Ile be sworne 'tis true, he will weepe you an'twere a man borne in Aprill. *Sound a retreate.*

Cres. And Ile spring vp in his teares, an'twere a nettle against May.

Pan. Harke they are comming from the field, shal we stand vp here and see them, as they passe toward Illium, good Neece do, sweet Neece *Cressida*.

Cre. At your pleasure.

Pan. Heere, heere, here's an excellent place, heere we may see most brauely, Ile tel you them all by their names, as they passe by, but marke *Troylus* aboue the rest.

Enter Æneas.

Cre. Speake not so low'd.

Pan. That's *Æneas*, is not that a braue man, hee's one of the flowers of Troy I can you, but merke *Troylus*, you shal see anon.

Cre. Who's that?

Enter Antenor.

Pan. That's *Antenor*, he has a shrow'd wit I can tell you, and hee's a man good inough, hee's one o'th soundest iudgement in Troy whosoeuer, and a proper man of person: when comes *Troylus*? Ile shew you *Troylus* anon, if hee see me, you shall see him him nod at me.

Cre. Will he giue you the nod?

Pan. You shall see.

Cre. If he do, the rich shall haue more.

Enter Hector.

Pan. That's *Hector*, that, that, looke you, that there's a fellow. Goe thy way *Hector*, there's a braue man Neece, O braue *Hector*! Looke how hee lookes? there's a countenance; ist not a braue man?

Cre. O braue man!

Pan. Is a not? It dooes a mans heart good, looke you what hacks are on his Helmet, looke you yonder, do you see? Looke you there? There's no iesting, laying on, tak't off, who ill as they say, there be hacks.

Cre. Be those with Swords?

Enter Paris.

Pan. Swords, any thing he cares not, and the diuell come to him, it's all one, by Gods lid it dooes ones heart good. Yonder comes *Paris*, yonder comes *Paris*: looke yee yonder Neece, ist not a gallant man to, ist not? Why this is braue now: who said he came hurt home to day? Hee's not hurt, why this will do *Hellens* heart good now, ha? Would I could see *Troylus* now, you shall *Troylus* anon.

Cre. Whose that?

Enter Hellenus.

Pan. That's *Hellenus*, I maruell where *Troylus* is, that's *Helenus*, I thinke he went not forth to day: that's *Hellenus*.

Cre. Can *Hellenus* fight Vncle?

Pan. *Hellenus* no: yes heele fight indifferent, well, I maruell where *Troylus* is; harke, do you not haere the people crie *Troylus*? *Hellenus* is a Priest.

Cre. What sneaking fellow comes yonder?

Enter Trylus.

Pan. Where? Yonder? That's *Dephobus*. 'Tis *Troylus*! Ther's a man Neece, hem? Braue *Troylus* the Prince of Chiualrie.

Cre. Peace, for shame peace.

Pand. Marke him, not him: O braue *Troylus*: looke well vpon him Neece, looke you how his Sword is bloudied, and his Helme more hackt then *Hectors*, and how he lookes,

lookes, and how he goes. O admirable youth! he ne're saw three and twenty. Go thy way *Troylus*, go thy way, had I a sister were a *Grace*, or a daughter a Goddesse, hee should take his choice. O admirable man! *Paris*? *Paris* is durt to him, and I warrant, *Helen* to change, would giue money to boot.

Enter common Souldiers.

Cres. Heere come more.

Pan. Asses, fooles, dolts, chaffe and bran, chaffe and bran; porredge after meat. I could liue and dye i'th'eyes of *Troylus*. Ne're looke, ne're looke; the Eagles are gon, Crowes and Dawes, Crowes and Dawes: I had rather be such a man as *Troylus*, then *Agamemnon*, and all Greece.

Cres. There is among the Greekes *Achilles*, a better man then *Troylus*.

Pan. *Achilles*? a Dray-man, a Porter, a very Camell.

Cres. Well, well.

Pan. Well, well? Why haue you any discretion? haue you any eyes? Do you know what a man is? Is not birth, beauty, good shape, discourse, manhood, learning, gentlenesse, vertue, youth, liberality, and so forth: the Spice, and salt that seasons a man?

Cres. I, a minc'd man and then to be bak'd with no Date in the pye, for then the mans dates out.

Pan. You are such another woman, one knowes not at what ward you lye.

Cres. Vpon my backe, to defend my belly; vpon my wit, to defend my wiles; vppon my secrecy, to defend mine honesty; my Maske, to defend my beauty, and you to defend all these: and at all these wardes I lye at, at a thousand watches.

Pan. Say one of your watches.

Cres. Nay Ile watch you for that, and that's one of the cheefest of them too: If I cannot ward what I would not haue hit, I can watch you for telling how I took the blow, vnlesse it swell past hiding, and then it's past watching.

Enter Boy.

Pan. You are such another.

Boy. Sir, my Lord would instantly speake with you.

Pan. Where?

Boy. At your owne house.

Pan. Good Boy tell him I come, I doubt he bee hurt. Fare ye well good Neece.

Cres. Adieu Vnkle.

Pan. Ile be with you Neece by and by.

Cres. To bring Vnkle.

Pan. I, a token from *Troylus*.

Cres. By the same token, you are a Bawd. *Exit Pand.*

Words, vowes, gifts, teares, & loues full sacrifice,
He offers in anothers enterprise:
But more in *Troylus* thousand fold I see,
Then in the glasse of *Pandar's* praise may be;
Yet hold I off. Women are Angels wooing,
Things won are done, ioyes soule lyes in the dooing:
That she belou'd, knowes nought, that knowes not this;
Men prize the thing vngain'd, more then it is.
That she was neuer yet, that euer knew
Loue got so sweet, as when desire did sue:
Therefore this maxime out of loue I teach;
"*Atchieuement, is command; vngain'd, beseech.*
That though my hearts Contents firme loue doth beare,
Nothing of that shall from mine eyes appeare. *Exit.*

Senet. Enter Agamemnon, Nestor, Vlysses, Diomedes, Menelaus, with others.

Agam. Princes:
What greefe hath set the Iaundies on your cheekes?
The ample proposition that hope makes
In all designes, begun on earth below
Fayles in the promist largenesse: checkes and disasters
Grow in the veines of actions highest rear'd.
As knots by the conflux of meeting sap,
Infect the sound Pine, and diuerts his Graine
Tortiue and erant from his course of growth.
Nor Princes, is it matter new to vs,
That we come short of our suppose so farre,
That after seuen yeares siege, yet Troy walles stand,
Sith euery action that hath gone before,
Whereof we haue Record, Triall did draw
Bias and thwart, not answering the ayme:
And that vnbodied figure of the thought
That gaue't surmised shape. Why then (you Princes)
Do you with cheekes abash'd, behold our workes,
And thinke them shame, which are (indeed) nought else
But the protractiue trials of great Ioue,
To finde persistiue constancie in men?
The finenesse of which Mettall is not found
In Fortunes loue: for then, the Bold and Coward,
The Wise and Foole, the Artist and vn-read,
The hard and soft, seeme all affin'd, and kin.
But in the Winde and Tempest of her frowne,
Distinction with a lowd and powrefull fan,
Puffing at all, winnowes the light away;
And what hath masse, or matter by it selfe,
Lies rich in Vertue, and vnmingled.

Nestor. With due Obseruance of thy godly seat,
Great *Agamemnon*, *Nestor* shall apply
Thy latest words.
In the reproofe of Chance,
Lies the true proofe of men: The Sea being smooth,
How many shallow bauble Boates dare saile
Vpon her patient brest, making their way
With those of Nobler bulke?
But let the Ruffian *Boreas* once enrage
The gentle *Thetis*, and anon behold
The strong ribb'd Barke through liquid Mountaines cut,
Bounding betweene the two moyst Elements
Like *Perseus* Horse. Where's then the sawcy Boate,
Whose weake vntimber'd sides but euen now
Co-riual'd Greatnesse? Either to harbour fled,
Or made a Toste for Neptune. Euen so,
Doth valours shew, and valours worth diuide
In stormes of Fortune.
For, in her ray and brightnesse,
The Heard hath more annoyance by the Brieze
Then by the Tyger: But, when the splitting winde
Makes flexible the knees of knotted Oakes,
And Flies fled vnder shade, why then
The thing of Courage,
As rowz'd with rage, with rage doth sympathize,
And with an accent tun'd in selfe-same key,
Retyres to chiding Fortune.

Vlys. *Agamemnon*:
Thou great Commander, Nerue, and Bone of Greece,
Heart of our Numbers, soule, and onely spirit,
In whom the tempers, and the mindes of all
Should be shut vp: Heare what *Vlysses* speakes,
Besides the applause and approbation
The which most mighty for thy place and sway,

And thou most reuerend for thy stretcht-out life,
I giue to both your speeches: which were such,
As *Agamemnon* and the hand of Greece
Should hold vp high in Brasse: and such againe
As venerable *Nestor* (hatch'd in Siluer)
Should with a bond of ayre, strong as the Axletree
In which the Heauens ride, knit all Greekes eares
To his experienc'd tongue: yet let it please both
(Thou Great, and Wise) to heare *Vlysses* speake.
Aga. Speak Prince of *Ithaca*, and be't of lesse expect:
That matter needlesse of importlesse burthen
Diuide thy lips; then we are confident
When ranke *Thersites* opes his Masticke iawes,
We shall heare Musicke, Wit, and Oracle.
Vlys. Troy yet vpon his basis had bene downe,
And the great *Hectors* sword had lack'd a Master
But for these instances.
The specialty of Rule hath beene neglected;
And looke how many Grecian Tents do stand
Hollow vpon this Plaine, so many hollow Factions.
When that the Generall is not like the Hiue,
To whom the Forragers shall all repaire,
What Hony is expected? Degree being vizarded,
Th'vnworthiest shewes as fairely in the Maske.
The Heauens themselues, the Planets, and this Center,
Obserue degree, priority, and place,
Insisture, course, proportion, season, forme,
Office, and custome, in all line of Order:
And therefore is the glorious Planet Sol
In noble eminence, enthron'd and sphear'd
Amid'st the other, whose med'cinable eye
Corrects the ill Aspects of Planets euill,
And postes like the Command'ment of a King,
Sans checke, to good and bad. But when the Planets
In euill mixture to disorder wander,
What Plagues, and what portents, what mutiny?
What raging of the Sea? shaking of Earth?
Commotion in the Windes? Frights, changes, horrors,
Diuert, and cracke, rend and deracinate
The vnity, and married calme of States
Quite from their fixure? O, when Degree is shak'd,
(Which is the Ladder to all high designes)
The enterprize is sicke. How could Communities,
Degrees in Schooles, and Brother-hoods in Cities,
Peacefull Commerce from diuidable shores,
The primogenitiue, and due of Byrth,
Prerogatiue of Age, Crownes, Scepters, Lawrels,
(But by Degree) stand in Authentique place?
Take but Degree away, vn-tune that string,
And hearke what Discord followes: each thing meetes
In meere oppugnancie. The bounded Waters,
Should lift their bosomes higher then the Shores,
And make a soppe of all this solid Globe:
Strength should be Lord of imbecility,
And the rude Sonne should strike his Father dead:
Force should be right, or rather, right and wrong,
(Betweene whose endlesse iarre, Iustice recides)
Should loose her names, and so should Iustice too.
Then euery thing includes it selfe in Power,
Power into Will, Will into Appetite,
And Appetite (an vniuersall Wolfe,
So doubly seconded with Will, and Power)
Must make perforce an vniuersall prey,
And last, eate vp himselfe.
Great *Agamemnon*:
This Chaos, when Degree is suffocate,
Followes the choaking:
And this neglection of Degree, is it
That by a pace goes backward in a purpose
It hath to climbe. The Generall's disdain'd
By him one step below; he, by the next,
That next, by him beneath: so euery step
Exampled by the first pace that is sicke
Of his Superiour, growes to an enuious Feauer
Of pale, and bloodlesse Emulation.
And 'tis this Feauer that keepes Troy on foote,
Not her owne sinewes. To end a tale of length,
Troy in our weaknesse liues, not in her strength.
Nest. Most wisely hath *Vlysses* heere discouer'd
The Feauer, whereof all our power is sicke.
Aga. The Nature of the sicknesse found (*Vlysses*)
What is the remedie?
Vlys The great *Achilles*, whom Opinion crownes,
The sinew, and the fore-hand of our Hoste,
Hauing his eare full of his ayery Fame,
Growes dainty of his worth, and in his Tent
Lyes mocking our designes. With him, *Patroclus*,
Vpon a lazie Bed, the liue-long day
Breakes scurrill Iests,
And with ridiculous and aukward action,
(Which Slanderer, he imitation call's)
He Pageants vs. Sometime great *Agamemnon*,
Thy toplesse deputation he puts on,
And like a strutting Player, whose conceit
Lies in his Ham-string, and doth thinke it rich
To heare the woodden Dialogue and sound
'Twixt his stretcht footing, and the Scaffolage,
Such to be pittied, and ore-rested seeming
He acts thy Greatnesse in: and when he speakes,
'Tis like a Chime a mending. With tearmes vnsquar'd,
Which from the tongue of roaring *Typhon* dropt,
Would seemes Hyperboles. At this fusty stuffe,
The large *Achilles* (on his prest-bed lolling)
From his deepe Chest, laughes out a lowd applause,
Cries excellent, 'tis *Agamemnon* iust.
Now play me *Nestor*; hum, and stroke thy Beard
As he, being drest to some Oration:
That's done, as neere as the extreamest ends
Of paralels; as like, as *Vulcan* and his wife,
Yet god *Achilles* still cries excellent,
'Tis *Nestor* right. Now play him (me) *Patroclus*,
Arming to answer in a night-Alarme,
And then (forsooth) the faint defects of Age
Must be the Scene of myrth, to cough, and spit,
And with a palsie fumbling on his Gorget,
Shake in and out the Riuet: and at this sport
Sir Valour dies; cries, O enough *Patroclus*,
Or, giue me ribs of Steele, I shall split all
In pleasure of my Spleene. And in this fashion,
All our abilities, gifts, natures, shapes,
Seuerals and generals of grace exact,
Atchieuments, plots, orders, preuentions,
Excitements to the field, or speech for truce,
Successe or losse, what is, or is not, serues
As stuffe for these two, to make paradoxes.
Nest. And in the imitation of these twaine,
Who (as *Vlysses* sayes) Opinion crownes
With an Imperiall voyce, many are infect:
Aiax is growne selfe-will'd, and beares his head
In such a reyne, in full as proud a place
As broad *Achilles*, and keepes his Tent like him;
Makes factious Feasts, railes on our state of Warre

Bold as an Oracle, and sets *Thersites*
A slaue, whose Gall coines slanders like a Mint,
To match vs in comparisons with durt,
To weaken and discredit our exposure,
How ranke soeuer rounded in with danger.
Vlyss. They taxe our policy, and call it Cowardice,
Count Wisedome as no member of the Warre,
Fore-stall prescience, and esteeme no acte
But that of hand: The still and mentall parts,
That do contriue how many hands shall strike
When fitnesse call them on, and know by measure
Of their obseruant toyle, the Enemies waight,
Why this hath not a fingers dignity:
They call this Bed-worke, Mapp'ry, Closset-Warre:
So that the Ramme that batters downe the wall,
For the great swing and rudenesse of his poize,
They place before his hand that made the Engine,
Or those that with the finenesse of their soules,
By Reason guide his execution.
Nest. Let this be granted, and *Achilles* horse
Makes many *Thetis* sonnes. *Tucket*
Aga. What Trumpet? Looke *Menelaus*.
Men. From Troy. *Enter Æneas.*
Aga. What would you 'fore our Tent?
Æne. Is this great *Agamemnons* Tent, I pray you?
Aga. Euen this.
Æne. May one that is a Herald, and a Prince,
Do a faire message to his Kingly eares?
Aga. With surety stronger then *Achilles* arme,
'Fore all the Greekish heads, which with one voyce
Call *Agamemnon* Head and Generall.
Æne. Faire leaue, and large security. How may
A stranger to those most Imperial lookes,
Know them from eyes of other Mortals?
Aga. How?
Æne. I: I aske, that I might waken reuerence,
And on the cheeke be ready with a blush
Modest as morning, when she coldly eyes
The youthfull Phoebus:
Which is that God in office guiding men?
Which is the high and mighty *Agamemnon*?
Aga. This Troyan scornes vs, or the men of Troy
Are ceremonious Courtiers.
Æne. Courtiers as free, as debonnaire; vnarm'd,
As bending Angels: that's their Fame, in peace:
But when they would seeme Souldiers, they haue galles,
Good armes, strong ioynts, true swords, & *Ioues* accord,
Nothing so full of heart. But peace *Æneas*,
Peace Troyan, lay thy finger on thy lips,
The worthinesse of praise distaines his worth:
If that he prais'd himselfe, bring the praise forth.
But what the repining enemy commends,
That breath Fame blowes, that praise sole pure transceds.
Aga. Sir, you of Troy, call you your selfe *Æneas*?
Æne. I Greeke, that is my name.
Aga. What's your affayre I pray you?
Æne. Sir pardon, 'tis for *Agamemnons* eares.
Aga. He heares nought priuatly
That comes from Troy.
Æne. Nor I from Troy come not to whisper him,
I bring a Trumpet to awake his eare,
To set his sence on the attentiue bent,
And then to speake.
Aga. Speake frankely as the winde,
It is not *Agamemnons* sleeping houre;
That thou shalt know Troyan he is awake,
He tels thee so himselfe.
Æne. Trumpet blow loud,
Send thy Brasse voyce through all these lazie Tents,
And euery Greeke of mettle, let him know,
What Troy meanes fairely, shall be spoke alowd.
The Trumpets sound.
We haue great *Agamemnon* heere in Troy,
A Prince calld *Hector*, *Priam* is his Father:
Who in this dull and long-continew'd Truce
Is rusty growne. He bad me take a Trumpet,
And to this purpose speake: Kings, Princes, Lords,
If there be one among'st the fayr'st of Greece,
That holds his Honor higher then his ease,
That seekes his praise, more then he feares his perill,
That knowes his Valour, and knowes not his feare,
That loues his Mistris more then in confession,
(With truant vowes to her owne lips he loues)
And dare avow her Beauty, and her Worth,
In other armes then hers: to him this Challenge.
Hector, in view of Troyans, and of Greekes,
Shall make it good, or do his best to do it.
He hath a Lady, wiser, fairer, truer,
Then euer Greeke did compasse in his armes,
And will to morrow with his Trumpet call,
Midway betweene your Tents, and walles of Troy,
To rowze a Grecian that is true in loue.
If any come, *Hector* shal honour him:
If none, hee'l say in Troy when he retyres,
The Grecian Dames are sun-burnt, and not worth
The splinter of a Lance: Euen so much.
Aga. This shall be told our Louers Lord *Æneas*,
If none of them haue soule in such a kinde.
We left them all at home: But we are Souldiers,
And may that Souldier a meere recreant proue,
That meanes not, hath not, or is not in loue:
If then one is, or hath, or meanes to be,
That one meets *Hector*; if none else, Ile be he.
Nest. Tell him of *Nestor*, one that was a man
When *Hectors* Grandsire suckt: he is old now,
But if there be not in our Grecian mould,
One Noble man, that hath one spark of fire
To answer for his Loue; tell him from me,
Ile hide my Siluer beard in a Gold Beauer,
And in my Vantbrace put this wither'd brawne,
And meeting him, wil tell him, that my Lady
Was fayrer then his Grandame, and as chaste
As may be in the world: his youth in flood,
Ile pawne this truth with my three drops of blood.
Æne. Now heauens forbid such scarsitie of youth.
Vlyss. Amen.
Aga. Faire Lord *Æneas*,
Let me touch your hand:
To our Pauillion shal I leade you first:
Achilles shall haue word of this intent,
So shall each Lord of Greece from Tent to Tent:
Your selfe shall Feast with vs before you goe,
And finde the welcome of a Noble Foe. *Exeunt.*
Manet Vlysses, and Nestor.
Vlys. Nestor.
Nest. What sayes *Vlysses*?
Vlys. I haue a young conception in my braine,
Be you my time to bring it to some shape.
Nest. What is't?
Vlysses. This 'tis:
Blunt wedges riue hard knots: the seeded Pride
That hath to this maturity blowne vp

In ranke *Achilles*, must or now be cropt,
Or shedding breed a Nursery of like euil
To ouer-bulke vs all.

Nest. Wel, and how?

Vlys. This challenge that the gallant *Hector* sends,
How euer it is spred in general name,
Relates in purpose onely to *Achilles*.

Nest. The purpose is perspicuous euen as substance,
Whose grossenesse little charracters summe vp,
And in the publication make no straine,
But that *Achilles*, were his braine as barren
As bankes of Lybia, though (*Apollo* knowes)
'Tis dry enough, wil with great speede of iudgement,
I, with celerity, finde *Hectors* purpose
Pointing on him.

Vlys. And wake him to the answer, thinke you?

Nest. Yes, 'tis most meet; who may you else oppose
That can from *Hector* bring his Honor off,
If not *Achilles*; though't be a sportfull Combate,
Yet in this triall, much opinion dwels.
For heere the Troyans taste our deer'st repute
With their fin'st Pallate: and trust to me *Vlysses*,
Our imputation shall be oddely poiz'd
In this wilde action. For the successe
(Although particular) shall giue a scantling
Of good or bad, vnto the Generall:
And in such Indexes, although small prickes
To their subsequent Volumes, there is seene
The baby figure of the Gyant-masse
Of things to come at large. It is suppos'd,
He that meets *Hector*, issues from our choyse;
And choise being mutuall acte of all our soules,
Makes Merit her election, and doth boyle
As 'twere, from forth vs all: a man distill'd
Out of our Vertues; who miscarrying,
What heart from hence receyues the conqu'ring part
To steele a strong opinion to themselues,
Which entertain'd, Limbes are in his instruments,
In no lesse working, then are Swords and Bowes
Directiue by the Limbes.

Vlys. Giue pardon to my speech:
Therefore 'tis meet, *Achilles* meet not *Hector*:
Let vs (like Merchants) shew our fowlest Wares,
And thinke perchance they'l sell: If not,
The luster of the better yet to shew,
Shall shew the better. Do not consent,
That euer *Hector* and *Achilles* meete:
For both our Honour, and our Shame in this,
Are dogg'd with two strange Followers.

Nest. I see them not with my old eies: what are they?

Vlys. What glory our *Achilles* shares from *Hector*,
(Were he not proud) we all should weare with him:
But he already is too insolent,
And we were better parch in Affricke Sunne,
Then in the pride and salt-scorne of his eyes
Should he scape *Hector* faire. If he were foyld,
Why then we did our maine opinion crush
In taint of our best man. No, make a Lott'ry,
And by deuice let blockish *Aiax* draw
The sort to fight with *Hector*: Among our selues,
Giue him allowance as the worthier man,
For that will physicke the great Myrmidon
Who broyles in lowd applause, and make him fall
His Crest, that prouder then blew Iris bends.
If the dull brainlesse *Aiax* come safe off,
Wee'l dresse him vp in voyces: if he faile,
Yet go we vnder our opinion still,
That we haue better men. But hit or misse,
Our proiects life this shape of sence assumes,
Aiax imploy'd, pluckes downe *Achilles* Plumes.

Nest. Now *Vlysses*, I begin to rellish thy aduice,
And I wil giue a taste of it forthwith
To *Agamemnon*, go we to him straight:
Two Curres shal tame each other, Pride alone
Must tarre the Mastiffes on, as 'twere their bone. *Exeunt*

Enter Aiax, and Thersites.

Aia. *Thersites*?

Ther. *Agamemnon*, how if he had Biles (ful) all ouer generally.

Aia. *Thersites*?

Ther. And those Byles did runne, say so; did not the General run, were not that a botchy core?

Aia. Dogge.

Ther. Then there would come some matter from him: I see none now.

Aia. Thou Bitch-Wolfes-Sonne, canst ỹ not heare? Feele then. *Strikes him.*

Ther. The plague of Greece vpon thee thou Mungrel beefe-witted Lord.

Aia. Speake then you whinid'st leauen speake, I will beate thee into handsomnesse.

Ther. I shal sooner rayle thee into wit and holinesse: but I thinke thy Horse wil sooner con an Oration, then ỹ learn a prayer without booke: Thou canst strike, canst thou? A red Murren o'th thy Iades trickes.

Aia. Toads stoole, learne me the Proclamation.

Ther. Doest thou thinke I haue no sence thou strik'st (me thus?

Aia. The Proclamation.

Ther. Thou art proclaim'd a foole, I thinke.

Aia. Do not Porpentine, do not; my fingers itch.

Ther. I would thou didst itch from head to foot, and I had the scratching of thee, I would make thee the loth-som'st scab in Greece.

Aia. I say the Proclamation.

Ther. Thou grumblest & railest euery houre on *Achilles*, and thou art as ful of enuy at his greatnes, as *Cerberus* is at *Proserpina's* beauty. I, that thou barkst at him.

Aia. Mistresse *Thersites*.

Ther. Thou should'st strike him.

Aia. Coblofe.

Ther. He would pun thee into shiuers with his fist, as a Sailor breakes a bisket.

Aia. You horson Curre. *Ther.* Do, do.

Aia. Thou stoole for a Witch.

Ther. I, do, do, thou sodden-witted Lord: thou hast no more braine then I haue in mine elbows: An Asinico may tutor thee. Thou scuruy valiant Asse, thou art heere but to thresh Troyans, and thou art bought and solde among those of any wit, like a Barbarian slaue. If thou vse to beat me, I wil begin at thy heele, and tel what thou art by inches, thou thing of no bowels thou.

Aia. You dogge.

Ther. You scuruy Lord.

Aia. You Curre.

Ther. *Mars* his Ideot: do rudenes, do Camell, do, do.

Enter Achilles, and Patroclus.

Achil. Why how now *Aiax*? wherefore do you this? How now *Thersites*? what's the matter man?

Ther. You see him there, do you?

Achil. I, what's the matter.

Ther. Nay looke vpon him.

Achil. So I do: what's the matter?

Ther. Nay but regard him well.

Achil. Well, why I do so.

Ther. But yet you looke not well vpon him: for who some euer you take him to be, he is *Aiax.*

Achil. I know that foole.

Ther. I, but that foole knowes not himselfe.

Aiax. Therefore I beate thee.

Ther. Lo, lo, lo, lo, what *modicums* of wit he vtters: his euasions haue eares thus long. I haue bobb'd his Braine more then he has beate my bones: I will buy nine Sparrowes for a peny, and his *Piamater* is not worth the ninth part of a Sparrow. This Lord (*Achilles*) *Aiax* who wears his wit in his belly, and his guttes in his head, Ile tell you what I say of him.

Achil. What?

Ther. I say this *Aiax* ——

Achil. Nay good *Aiax.*

Ther. Has not so much wit.

Achil: Nay, I must hold you.

Ther. As will stop the eye of *Helens* Needle, for whom he comes to fight.

Achil. Peace foole.

Ther. I would haue peace and quietnes, but the foole will not: he there, that he, looke you there.

Aiax. O thou damn'd Curre, I shall——

Achil. Will you set your wit to a Fooles.

Ther. No I warrant you, for a fooles will shame it.

Pat. Good words *Thersites.*

Achil. What's the quarrell?

Aiax. I bad thee vile Owle, goe learne me the tenure of the Proclamation, and he rayles vpon me.

Ther. I serue thee not.

Aiax. Well, go too, go too.

Ther. I serue heere voluntary.

Achil. Your last seruice was sufferance, 'twas not voluntary, no man is beaten voluntary: *Aiax* was heere the voluntary, and you as vnder an Impresse.

Ther. E'ne so, a great deale of your wit too lies in your sinnewes, or else there be Liars. *Hector* shall haue a great catch, if he knocke out either of your braines, he were as good cracke a fustie nut with no kernell.

Achil. What with me to *Thersites*?

Ther. There's *Vlysses*, and old *Nestor*, whose Wit was mouldy ere their Grandsires had nails on their toes, yoke you like draft-Oxen, and make you plough vp the warre.

Achil. What? what?

Ther. Yes good sooth, to *Achilles*, to *Aiax*, to——

Aiax. I shall cut out your tongue.

Ther. 'Tis no matter, I shall speake as much as thou afterwards.

Pat. No more words *Thersites.*

Ther. I will hold my peace when *Achilles* Brooch bids me, shall I?

Achil. There's for you *Patroclus.*

Ther. I wil see you hang'd like Clotpoles ere I come any more to your Tents; I will keepe where there is wit stirring, and leaue the faction of fooles. *Exit.*

Pat. A good riddance.

Achil. Marry this Sir is proclaim'd through al our host,
That *Hector* by the fift houre of the Sunne,
Will with a Trumpet, 'twixt our Tents and Troy
To morrow morning call some Knight to Armes,
That hath a stomacke, and such a one that dare
Maintaine I know not what: 'tis trash. Farewell.

Aiax. Farewell? who shall answer him?

Achil. I know not, 'tis put to Lottry: otherwise
He knew his man.

Aiax. O meaning you, I wil go learne more of it. *Exit.*

Enter Priam, Hector, Troylus, Paris and Helenus.

Pri. After so many houres, liues, speeches spent,
Thus once againe sayes *Nestor* from the Greekes,
Deliuer *Helen*, and all damage else
(As honour, losse of time, trauaile, expence,
Wounds, friends, and what els deere that is consum'd
In hot digestion of this comorant Warre)
Shall be stroke off. *Hector*, what say you too't.

Hect. Though no man lesser feares the Greeks then I,
As farre as touches my particular: yet dread *Priam*,
There is no Lady of more softer bowels,
More spungie, to sucke in the sense of Feare,
More ready to cry out, who knowes what followes
Then *Hector* is: the wound of peace is surety,
Surety secure: but modest Doubt is cal'd
The Beacon of the wise: the tent that searches
To'th'bottome of the worst. Let *Helen* go,
Since the first sword was drawne about this question,
Euery tythe soule 'mongst many thousand dismes,
Hath bin as deere as *Helen*: I meane of ours:
If we haue lost so many tenths of ours
To guard a thing not ours, nor worth to vs
(Had it our name) the valew of one ten;
What merit's in that reason which denies
The yeelding of her vp.

Troy. Fie, fie, my Brother;
Weigh you the worth and honour of a King
(So great as our dread Father) in a Scale
Of common Ounces? Wil you with Counters summe
The past proportion of his infinite,
And buckle in a waste most fathomlesse,
With spannes and inches so diminutiue,
As feares and reasons? Fie for godly shame?

Hel. No maruel though you bite so sharp at reasons,
You are so empty of them, should not our Father
Beare the great sway of his affayres with reasons,
Because your speech hath none that tels him so.

Troy. You are for dreames & slumbers brother Priest
You furre your gloues with reason: here are your reasons
You know an enemy intends you harme,
You know, a sword imploy'd is perillous,
And reason flyes the obiect of all harme.
Who maruels then when *Helenus* beholds
A Grecian and his sword, if he do set
The very wings of reason to his heeles:
Or like a Starre disorb'd. Nay, if we talke of Reason,
And flye like chidden Mercurie from Ioue,
Let's shut our gates and sleepe: Manhood and Honor
Should haue hard hearts, wold they but fat their thoghts
With this cramm'd reason: reason and respect,
Makes Liuers pale, and lustyhood deiect.

Hect. Brother, she is not worth
What she doth cost the holding.

Troy. What's aught, but as 'tis valew'd?

Hect. But value dwels not in particular will,
It holds his estimate and dignitie
As well, wherein 'tis precious of it selfe,
As in the prizer: 'Tis made Idolatrie,
To make the seruice greater then the God,
And the will dotes that is inclineable
To what infectiously it selfe affects,
Without some image of th'affected merit.

Troy. I take to day a Wife, and my election
Is led on in the conduct of my Will;

My Will enkindled by mine eyes and eares,
Two traded Pylots 'twixt the dangerous shores
Of Will, and Iudgement. How may I auoyde
(Although my will distaste what it elected)
The Wife I chose, there can be no euasion
To blench from this, and to stand firme by honour.
We turne not backe the Silkes vpon the Merchant
When we haue spoyl'd them; nor the remainder Viands
We do not throw in vnrespectiue same,
Because we now are full. It was thought meete
Paris should do some vengeance on the Greekes;
Your breath of full consent bellied his Sailes,
The Seas and Windes (old Wranglers) tooke a Truce,
And did him seruice; he touch'd the Ports desir'd,
And for an old Aunt whom the Greekes held Captiue,
He brought a Grecian Queen, whose youth & freshnesse
Wrinkles *Apolloes*, and makes stale the morning.
Why keepe we her? the Grecians keepe our Aunt:
Is she worth keeping? Why she is a Pearle,
Whose price hath launch'd aboue a thousand Ships,
And turn'd Crown'd Kings to Merchants.
If you'l auouch, 'twas wisedome *Paris* went,
(As you must needs, for you all cride, Go, go:)
If you'l confesse, he brought home Noble prize,
(As you must needs) for you all clapt your hands,
And cride inestimable; why do you now
The issue of your proper Wisedomes rate,
And do a deed that Fortune neuer did?
Begger the estimation which you priz'd,
Richer then Sea and Land? O Theft most base!
That we haue stolne what we do feare to keepe.
But Theeues vnworthy of a thing so stolne,
That in their Country did them that disgrace,
We feare to warrant in our Natiue place.

Enter Cassandra with her haire about her eares.

Cas. Cry *Troyans*, cry.
Priam. What noyse? what shreeke is this?
Troy. 'Tis our mad sister, I do know her voyce.
Cas. Cry Troyans.
Hect. It is *Cassandra.*
Cas. Cry Troyans cry; lend me ten thousand eyes,
And I will fill them with Propheticke teares.
Hect. Peace sister, peace.
Cas. Virgins, and Boyes; mid-age & wrinkled old,
Soft infancie, that nothing can but cry,
Adde to my clamour: let vs pay betimes
A moity of that masse of moane to come.
Cry Troyans cry, practise your eyes with teares,
Troy must not be, nor goodly Illion stand,
Our fire-brand Brother *Paris* burnes vs all.
Cry Troyans cry, a *Helen* and a woe;
Cry, cry, Troy burnes, or else let *Helen* goe. *Exit.*
Hect. Now youthfull *Troylus*, do not these hie strains
Of diuination in our Sister, worke
Some touches of remorse? Or is your bloud
So madly hot, that no discourse of reason,
Nor feare of bad successe in a bad cause,
Can qualifie the same?
Troy. Why Brother *Hector*,
We may not thinke the iustnesse of each acte
Such, and no other then euent doth forme it,
Nor once deiect the courage of our mindes;
Because *Cassandra's* mad, her brainsicke raptures
Cannot distaste the goodnesse of a quarrell,
Which hath our seuerall Honours all engag'd
To make it gracious. For my priuate part,
I am no more touch'd, then all *Priams* sonnes,
And Ioue forbid there should be done among'st vs
Such things as might offend the weakest spleene,
To fight for, and maintaine.
Par. Else might the world conuince of leuitie,
As well my vnder-takings as your counsels:
But I attest the gods, your full consent
Gaue wings to my propension, and cut off
All feares attending on so dire a proiect.
For what (alas) can these my single armes?
What propugnation is in one mans valour
To stand the push and enmity of those
This quarrell would excite? Yet I protest,
Were I alone to passe the difficulties,
And had as ample power, as I haue will,
Paris should ne're retract what he hath done,
Nor faint in the pursuite.
Pri. Paris, you speake
Like one be-sotted on your sweet delights;
You haue the Hony still, but these the Gall,
So to be valiant, is no praise at all.
Par. Sir, I propose not meerely to my selfe,
The pleasures such a beauty brings with it:
But I would haue the soyle of her faire Rape
Wip'd off in honourable keeping her.
What Treason were it to the ransack'd Queene,
Disgrace to your great worths, and shame to me,
Now to deliuer her possession vp
On termes of base compulsion? Can it be,
That so degenerate a straine as this,
Should once set footing in your generous bosomes?
There's not the meanest spirit on our partie,
Without a heart to dare, or sword to draw,
When *Helen* is defended: nor none so Noble,
Whose life were ill bestow'd, or death vnfam'd,
Where *Helen* is the subiect. Then (I say)
Well may we fight for her, whom we know well,
The worlds large spaces cannot paralell.
Hect. Paris and *Troylus*, you haue both said well:
And on the cause and question now in hand,
Haue gloz'd, but superficially; not much
Vnlike young men, whom *Aristotle* thought
Vnfit to heare Morall Philosophie.
The Reasons you alledge, do more conduce
To the hot passion of distemp'red blood,
Then to make vp a free determination
'Twixt right and wrong: For pleasure, and reuenge,
Haue eares more deafe then Adders, to the voyce
Of any true decision. Nature craues
All dues be rendred to their Owners: now
What neerer debt in all humanity,
Then Wife is to the Husband? If this law
Of Nature be corrupted through affection,
And that great mindes of partiall indulgence,
To their benummed wills resist the same,
There is a Law in each well-ordred Nation,
To curbe those raging appetites that are
Most disobedient and refracturie.
If *Helen* then be wife to Sparta's King
(As it is knowne she is) these Morall Lawes
Of Nature, and of Nation, speake alowd
To haue her backe return'd. Thus to persist
In doing wrong, extenuates not wrong,
But makes it much more heauie. *Hectors* opinion

Is this in way of truth: yet nere the lesse,
My spritely brethren, I propend to you
In resolution to keepe *Helen* still;
For 'tis a cause that hath no meane dependance,
Vpon our ioynt and seuerall dignities.

Tro. Why? there you toucht the life of our designe:
Were it not glory that we more affected,
Then the performance of our heauing spleenes,
I would not wish a drop of *Troian* blood,
Spent more in her defence. But worthy *Hector*,
She is a theame of honour and renowne,
A spurre to valiant and magnanimous deeds,
Whose present courage may beate downe our foes,
And fame in time to come canonize vs.
For I presume braue *Hector* would not loose
So rich aduantage of a promis'd glory,
As smiles vpon the fore-head of this action,
For the wide worlds reuenew.

Hect. I am yours,
You valiant off-spring of great *Priamus*,
I haue a roisting challenge sent among'st
The dull and factious nobles of the Greekes,
Will strike amazement to their drowsie spirits,
I was aduertiz'd, their Great generall slept,
Whil'st emulation in the armie crept:
This I presume will wake him. *Exeunt.*

Enter Thersites *solus.*

How now *Thersites*? what lost in the Labyrinth of thy furie? shall the Elephant *Aiax* carry it thus? he beates me, and I raile at him: O worthy satisfaction, would it were otherwise: that I could beate him, whil'st he rail'd at me: Sfoote, Ile learne to coniure and raise Diuels, but Ile see some issue of my spitefull execrations. Then ther's *Achilles*, a rare Enginer. If *Troy* be not taken till these two vndermine it, the wals will stand till they fall of themselues. O thou great thunder-darter of Olympus, forget that thou art *Ioue* the King of gods: and *Mercury*, loose all the Serpentine craft of thy Caduceus, if thou take not that little little lesse then little wit from them that they haue, which short-arm'd ignorance it selfe knowes, is so abundant scarse, it will not in circumuention deliuer a Flye from a Spider, without drawing the massie Irons and cutting the web: after this, the vengeance on the whole Camp, or rather the bone-ach, for that me thinkes is the curse dependant on those that warre for a placket. I haue said my prayers and diuell, enuie, say Amen: What ho? my Lord *Achilles*?

Enter Patroclus.

Patr. Who's there? *Thersites*. Good *Thersites* come in and raile.

Ther. If I could haue remembred a guilt counterfeit, thou would'st not haue slipt out of my contemplation, but it is no matter, thy selfe vpon thy selfe. The common curse of mankinde, follie and ignorance be thine in great reuenew; heauen blesse thee from a Tutor, and Discipline come not neere thee. Let thy bloud be thy direction till thy death, then if she that laies thee out sayes thou art a faire coarse, Ile be sworne and sworne vpon't she neuer shrowded any but Lazars, Amen. Wher's *Achilles*?

Patr. What art thou deuout? wast thou in a prayer?

Ther. I, the heauens heare me.

Enter Achilles.

Achil. Who's there?

Patr. *Thersites*, my Lord.

Achil. Where, where, art thou come? why my cheese, my digestion, why hast thou not seru'd thy selfe into my Table, so many meales? Come, what's *Agamemnon*?

Ther. Thy Commander *Achilles*, then tell me *Patroclus*, what's *Achilles*?

Patr. Thy Lord *Thersites*: then tell me I pray thee, what's thy selfe?

Ther. Thy knower *Patroclus*: then tell me *Patroclus*, what art thou?

Patr. Thou maist tell that know'st.

Achil. O tell, tell.

Ther. Ile declin the whole question: *Agamemnon* commands *Achilles*, *Achilles* is my Lord, I am *Patroclus* knower, and *Patroclus* is a foole.

Patro. You rascall.

Ter. Peace foole, I haue not done.

Achil. He is a priuiledg'd man, proceede *Thersites*.

Ther. *Agamemnon* is a foole, *Achilles* is a foole, *Thersites* is a foole, and as aforesaid, *Patroclus* is a foole.

Achil. Deriue this? come?

Ther. *Agamemnon* is a foole to offer to command *Achilles*, *Achilles* is a foole to be commanded of *Agamemnon*, *Thersites* is a foole to serue such a foole: and *Patroclus* is a foole positiue.

Patr. Why am I a foole?

Enter Agamemnon, Vlisses, Nestor, Diomedes, Aiax, and Chalcas.

Ther. Make that demand to the Creator, it suffises me thou art. Looke you, who comes here?

Achil. *Patroclus*, Ile speake with no body: come in with me *Thersites*. *Exit.*

Ther. Here is such patcherie, such iugling, and such knauerie: all the argument is a Cuckold and a Whore, a good quarrel to draw emulations, factions, and bleede to death vpon: Now the dry Suppeago on the Subiect, and Warre and Lecherie confound all.

Agam. Where is *Achilles*?

Patr. Within his Tent, but ill dispos'd my Lord.

Agam. Let it be knowne to him that we are here:
He sent our Messengers, and we lay by
Our appertainments, visiting of him:
Let him be told of, so perchance he thinke
We dare not moue the question of our place,
Or know not what we are.

Pat. I shall so say to him.

Vlis. We saw him at the opening of his Tent,
He is not sicke.

Aia. Yes, Lyon sicke, sicke of proud heart; you may call it Melancholly if will fauour the man, but by my head, it is pride; but why, why, let him show vs the cause? A word my Lord.

Nes. What moues *Aiax* thus to bay at him?

Vlis. *Achillis* hath inueigled his Foole from him.

Nes. Who, *Thersites*?

Vlis. He.

Nes. Then will *Aiax* lacke matter, if he haue lost his Argument.

Vlis. No, you see he is his argument that has his argument *Achilles*

Nes. All the better, their fraction is more our wish then their faction; but it was a strong counsell that a Foole could disunite.

Vlis. The amitie that wisedome knits, not folly may easily vntie. *Enter Patroclus.*

Here

Here comes *Patroclus*.

Nes. No *Achilles* with him?

Vlis. The Elephant hath ioynts, but none for curtesie:
His legge are legs for necessitie, not for flight.

Patro. *Achilles* bids me say he is much sorry:
If any thing more then your sport and pleasure,
Did moue your greatnesse, and this noble State,
To call vpon him; he hopes it is no other,
But for your health, and your digestion sake;
An after Dinners breath.

Aga. Heare you *Patroclus*:
We are too well acquainted with these answers:
But his euasion winged thus swift with scorne,
Cannot outflye our apprehensions.
Much attribute he hath, and much the reason,
Why we ascribe it to him, yet all his vertues,
Not vertuously of his owne part beheld,
Doe in our eyes, begin to loose their glosse;
Yea, and like faire Fruit in an vnholdsome dish,
Are like to rot vntasted: goe and tell him,
We came to speake with him; and you shall not sinne,
If you doe say, we thinke him ouer proud,
And vnder honest; in selfe-assumption greater
Then in the note of iudgement: & worthier then himselfe
Here tends the sauage strangenesse he puts on,
Disguise the holy strength of their command:
And vnder write in an obseruing kinde
His humorous predominance, yea watch
His pettish lines, his ebs, his flowes, as if
The passage and whole carriage of this action
Rode on his tyde. Goe tell him this, and adde,
That if he ouerhold his price so much,
Weele none of him; but let him, like an Engin
Not portable, lye vnder this report.
Bring action hither, this cannot goe to warre:
A stirring Dwarfe, we doe allowance giue,
Before a sleeping Gyant: tell him so.

Pat. I shall, and bring his answere presently.

Aga. In second voyce weele not be satisfied,
We come to speake with him, *Vlisses* enter you.

Exit Vlisses.

Aiax. What is he more then another?

Aga. No more then what he thinkes he is.

Aia. Is he so much, doe you not thinke, he thinkes himselfe a better man then I am?

Ag. No question.

Aiax. Will you subscribe his thought, and say he is?

Ag. No, Noble *Aiax*, you are as strong, as valiant, as wise, no lesse noble, much more gentle, and altogether more tractable

Aiax. Why should a man be proud? How doth pride grow? I know not what it is.

Aga. Your minde is the cleerer *Aiax*, and your vertues the fairer; he that is proud, eates vp himselfe; Pride is his owne Glasse, his owne trumpet, his owne Chronicle, and what euer praises it selfe but in the deede, deuoures the deede in the praise.

Enter Vlysses.

Aiax. I do hate a proud man, as I hate the ingendring of Toades.

Nest. Yet he loues himselfe: is't not strange?

Vlis. *Achilles* will not to the field to morrow.

Ag. What's his excuse?

Vlis. He doth relye on none,
But carries on the streame of his dispose,
Without obseruance or respect of any,
In will peculiar, and in selfe admission.

Aga. Why, will he not vpon our faire request,
Vntent his person, and share the ayre with vs?

Vlis. Things small as nothing, for requests sake onely
He makes important; possest he is with greatnesse,
And speakes not to himselfe, but with a pride
That quarrels at selfe-breath. Imagin'd wroth
Holds in his bloud such swolne and hot discourse,
That twixt his mentall and his actiue parts,
Kingdom'd *Achilles* in commotion rages,
And batters gainst it selfe; what should I say?
He is so plaguy proud, that the death tokens of it,
Cry no recouery.

Ag. Let *Aiax* goe to him.
Deare Lord, goe you and greete him in his Tent;
'Tis said he holds you well, and will be led
At your request a little from himselfe.

Vlis. O *Agamemnon*, let it not be so.
Weele consecrate the steps that *Aiax* makes,
When they goe from *Achilles*; shall the proud Lord,
That bastes his arrogance with his owne seame,
And neuer suffers matter of the world,
Enter his thoughts: saue such as doe reuolue
And ruminate himselfe. Shall he be worshipt,
Of that we hold an Idoll, more then hee?
No, this thrice worthy and right valiant Lord,
Must not so staule his Palme, nobly acquir'd,
Nor by my will assubiugate his merit,
As amply titled as *Achilles* is: by going to *Achilles*,
That were to enlard his fat already, pride,
And adde more Coles to Cancer, when he burnes
With entertaining great *Hiperion*.
This L. goe to him? *Iupiter* forbid,
And say in thunder, *Achilles* goe to him.

Nest. O this is well, he rubs the veine of him.

Dio. And how his silence drinkes vp this applause.

Aia. If I goe to him, with my armed fist, Ile pash him ore the face.

Ag. O no, you shall not goe.

Aia. And a be proud with me, ile phese his pride: let me goe to him.

Vlis. Not for the worth that hangs vpon our quarrel.

Aia. A paultry insolent fellow.

Nest. How he describes himselfe.

Aia. Can he not be sociable?

Vlis. The Rauen chides blacknesse.

Aia. Ile let his humours bloud.

Ag. He will be the Physitian that should be the patient.

Aia. And all men were a my minde.

Vlis. Wit would be out of fashion.

Aia. A should not beare it so, a should eate Swords first: shall pride carry it?

Nest. And 'twould, you'ld carry halfe.

Vlis. A would haue ten shares.

Aia. I will knede him, Ile make him supple, hee's not yet through warme.

Nest. Force him with praises, poure in, poure in: his ambition is dry.

Vlis. My L. you feede too much on this dislike.

Nest. Our noble Generall, doe not doe so.

Diom. You must prepare to fight without *Achilles*.

Vlis. Why, 'tis this naming of him doth him harme,
Here is a man, but 'tis before his face,
I will be silent.

Nest. Wherefore should you so?

He

He is not emulous, as *Achilles* is.

Vlis. 'Know the whole world, he is as valiant.

Aia. A horson dog, that shal palter thus with vs, would he were a *Troian*.

Nest. What a vice were it in *Aiax* now ——

Vlis. If he were proud.

Dio. Or couetous of praise.

Vlis. I, or surley borne.

Dio. Or strange, or selfe affected.

Vl. Thank the heauens L. thou art of sweet composure;
Praise him that got thee, she that gaue thee sucke:
Fame be thy Tutor, and thy parts of nature
Thrice fam'd beyond, beyond all erudition;
But he that disciplin'd thy armes to fight,
Let *Mars* deuide Eternity in twaine,
And giue him halfe, and for thy vigour,
Bull-bearing *Milo*: his addition yeelde
To sinnowie *Aiax*: I will not praise thy wisdome,
Which like a bourne, a pale, a shore confines
Thy spacious and dilated parts; here's *Nestor*
Instructed by the Antiquary times:
He must, he is, he cannot but be wise.
But pardon Father *Nestor*, were your dayes
As greene as *Aiax*, and your braine so temper'd,
You should not haue the eminence of him,
But be as *Aiax*.

Aia. Shall I call you Father?

Vlis. I my good Sonne.

Dio. Be rul'd by him Lord *Aiax*.

Vlis. There is no tarrying here, the Hart *Achilles*
Keepes thicket: please it our Generall,
To call together all his state of warre,
Fresh Kings are come to *Troy*; to morrow
We must with all our maine of power stand fast:
And here's a Lord, come Knights from East to West,
And cull their flowre, *Aiax* shall cope the best.

Ag. Goe we to Counsaile, let *Achilles* sleepe;
Light Botes may saile swift, though greater bulkes draw deepe. *Exeunt.* *Musicke sounds within.*

Enter Pandarus and a Seruant.

Pan. Friend, you, pray you a word: Doe not you follow the yong Lord *Paris*?

Ser. I sir, when he goes before me.

Pan. You depend vpon him I meane?

Ser. Sir, I doe depend vpon the Lord.

Pan. You depend vpon a noble Gentleman: I must needes praise him.

Ser. The Lord be praised.

Pa. You know me, doe you not?

Ser. Faith sir, superficially.

Pa. Friend know me better, I am the Lord *Pandarus*.

Ser. I hope I shall know your honour better.

Pa. I doe desire it.

Ser. You are in the state of Grace?

Pa. Grace, not so friend, honor and Lordship are my title: What Musique is this?

Ser. I doe but partly know sir: it is Musicke in parts.

Pa. Know you the Musitians.

Ser. Wholly sir.

Pa. Who play they to?

Ser. To the hearers sir.

Pa. At whose pleasur· friend?

Ser. At mine sir, and theirs that loue Musicke.

Pa. Command, I meane friend.

Ser. Who shall I command sir?

Pa. Friend, we vnderstand not one another: I am too courtly, and thou art too cunning. At whose request doe these men play?

Ser. That's too't indeede sir: marry sir, at the request of *Paris* my L. who's there in person; with him the mortall *Venus*, the heart bloud of beauty, loues inuisible soule.

Pa. Who? my Cosin *Cressida*.

Ser. No sir, *Helen*, could you not finde out that by her attributes?

Pa. It should seeme fellow, that thou hast not seen the Lady *Cressida*. I come to speake with *Paris* from the Prince *Troylus*: I will make a complementall assault vpon him, for my businesse seethes.

Ser. Sodden businesse, there's a stewed phrase indeede.

Enter Paris and Helena.

Pan. Faire be to you my Lord, and to all this faire company: faire desires in all faire measure fairely guide them, especially to you faire Queene, faire thoughts be your faire pillow.

Hel. Deere L. you are full of faire words.

Pan. You speake your faire pleasure sweete Queene: faire Prince, here is good broken Musicke.

Par. You haue broke it cozen: and by my life you shall make it whole againe, you shall peece it out with a peece of your performance. *Nel*, he is full of harmony.

Pan. Truely Lady no.

Hel. O sir.

Pan. Rude in sooth, in good sooth very rude.

Paris. Well said my Lord: well, you say so in fits.

Pan. I haue businesse to my Lord, deere Queene: my Lord will you vouchsafe me a word.

Hel. Nay, this shall not hedge vs out, weele heare you sing certainely.

Pan. Well sweete Queene you are pleasant with me, but, marry thus my Lord, my deere Lord, and most esteemed friend your brother *Troylus*.

Hel. My Lord *Pandarus*, hony sweete Lord.

Pan. Go too sweete Queene, goe to.
Commends himselfe most affectionately to you.

Hel. You shall not bob vs out of our melody:
If you doe, our melancholly vpon your head.

Pan. Sweete Queene, sweete Queene, that's a sweete Queene Ifaith ——

Hel. And to make a sweet Lady sad, is a sower offence.

Pan. Nay, that shall not serue your turne, that shall it not in truth la. Nay, I care not for such words, no, no. And my Lord he desires you, that if the King call for him at Supper, you will make his excuse.

Hel. My Lord *Pandarus*?

Pan. What saies my sweete Queene, my very, very sweete Queene?

Par. What exploit's in hand, where sups he to night?

Hel. Nay but my Lord?

Pan. What saies my sweete Queene? my cozen will fall out with you.

Hel. You must not know where he sups.

Par. With my disposer *Cressida*.

Pan. No, no; no such matter, you are wide, come your disposer is sicke.

Par. Well, Ile make excuse.

Pan. I good my Lord: why should you say *Cressida*? no, your poore disposer's sicke.

Par. I spie.

Pan. You spie, what doe you spie: come, giue me an Instrument now sweete Queene.

Hel. Why this is kindely done?

Pan. My Neece is horrible in loue with a thing you haue sweete Queene.

Hel. She shall haue it my Lord, if it be not my Lord *Paris.*

Pand. Hee? no, sheele none of him, they two are twaine.

Hel. Falling in after falling out, may make them three.

Pan. Come, come, Ile heare no more of this, Ile sing you a song now.

Hel. I, I, prethee now: by my troth sweet Lord thou hast a fine fore-head.

Pan. I you may, you may.

Hel. Let thy song be loue: this loue will vndoe vs al. Oh *Cupid, Cupid, Cupid.*

Pan. Loue? I that it shall yfaith.

Par. I, good now loue, loue, nothing but loue.

Pan. In good troth it begins so.

Loue, loue, nothing but loue, still more:
For O loues Bow,
Shootes Bucke and Doe:
The Shaft confounds not that it wounds,
But tickles still the sore:
These Louers cry, oh ho they dye;
Yet that which seemes the wound to kill,
Doth turne oh ho, to ha ha he:
So dying loue liues still,
O ho a while, but ha ha ha,
O ho grones out for ha ha ha---hey ho.

Hel. In loue yfaith to the very tip of the nose.

Par. He eates nothing but doues loue, and that breeds hot bloud, and hot bloud begets hot thoughts, and hot thoughts beget hot deedes, and hot deedes is loue.

Pan. Is this the generation of loue? Hot bloud, hot thoughts, and hot deedes, why they are Vipers, is Loue a generation of Vipers?
Sweete Lord whose a field to day?

Par. *Hector, Deiphœbus, Helenus, Anthenor,* and all the gallantry of *Troy.* I would faine haue arm'd to day, but my *Nell* would not haue it so.
How chance my brother *Troylus* went not?

Hel. He hangs the lippe at something; you know all Lord *Pandarus*?

Pan. Not I hony sweete Queene: I long to heare how they sped to day:
Youle remember your brothers excuse?

Par. To a hayre.

Pan. Farewell sweete Queene.

Hel. Commend me to your Neece.

Pan. I will sweete Queene. *Sound a retreat.*

Par. They're come from fielde: let vs to *Priams* Hall
To greete the Warriers. Sweet *Hellen*, I must woe you,
To helpe vnarme our *Hector*: his stubborne Buckles,
With these your white enchanting fingers toucht,
Shall more obey then to the edge of Steele,
Or force of Greekish sinewes: you shall doe more
Then all the Iland Kings, disarme great *Hector.*

Hel. 'Twill make vs proud to be his seruant *Paris*:
Yea what he shall receiue of vs in duetie,
Giues vs more palme in beautie then we haue:
Yea ouershines our selfe.
Sweete aboue thought I loue thee. *Exeunt.*

Enter Pandarus and Troylus Man.

Pan. How now, where's thy Maister, at my Couzen *Cressidas*?

Man. No sir, he stayes for you to conduct him thither.

Enter Troylus.

Pan. O here he comes: How now, how now?

Troy. Sirra walke off.

Pan. Haue you seene my Cousin?

Troy. No *Pandarus*: I stalke about her doore
Like a strange soule vpon the Stigian bankes
Staying for waftage. O be thou my *Charon*,
And giue me swift transportance to those fields,
Where I may wallow in the Lilly beds
Propos'd for the deseruer. O gentle *Pandarus*,
From *Cupids* shoulder plucke his painted wings,
And flye with me to *Cressid.*

Pan. Walke here ith'Orchard, Ile bring her straight. *Exit Pandarus.*

Troy. I am giddy; expectation whirles me round,
Th'imaginary relish is so sweete,
That it inchants my sence: what will't be
When that the watry pallats taste indeede
Loues thrice reputed Nectar? Death I feare me
Sounding distruction, or some ioy too fine,
Too subtile, potent, and too sharpe in sweetnesse,
For the capacitie of my ruder powers;
I feare it much, and I doe feare besides,
That I shall loose distinction in my ioyes,
As doth a battaile, when they charge on heapes
The enemy flying. *Enter Pandarus.*

Pan. Shee's making her ready, sheele come straight; you must be witty now, she does so blush, & fetches her winde so short, as if she were fraid with a sprite: Ile fetch her; it is the prettiest villaine, she fetches her breath so short as a new tane Sparrow. *Exit Pand.*

Troy. Euen such a passion doth imbrace my bosome:
My heart beates thicker then a feauorous pulse,
And all my powers doe their bestowing loose,
Like vassalage at vnawares encountring
The eye of Maiestie.

Enter Pandarus and Cressida.

Pan. Come, come, what neede you blush? Shames a babie; here she is now, sweare the oathes now to her, that you haue sworne to me. What are you gone againe, you must be watcht ere you be made tame, must you? come your wayes, come your wayes, and you draw backward weele put you i'th fils: why doe you not speak to her? Come draw this curtaine, & let's see your picture. Alasse the day, how loath you are to offend day light? and 'twere darke you'ld close sooner: So, so, rub on, and kisse the mistresse; how now, a kisse in fee-farme? build there Carpenter, the ayre is sweete. Nay, you shall fight your hearts out ere I part you. The Faulcon, as the Tercell, for all the Ducks ith Riuer: go too, go too.

Troy. You haue bereft me of all words Lady.

Pan. Words pay no debts; giue her deedes: but sheele bereaue you 'oth' deeds too, if shee call your actiuity in question: what billing againe? here's in witnesse whereof the Parties interchangeably. Come in, come in, Ile go get a fire?

Cres. Will you walke in my Lord?

Troy. O *Cressida*, how often haue I wisht me thus?

Cres. Wisht my Lord? the gods grant? O my Lord.

Troy. What should they grant? what makes this pretty abruption: what too curious dreg espies my sweete Lady in the fountaine of our loue?

Cres. More dregs then water, if my teares haue eyes.

Troy. Feares make diuels of Cherubins, they neuer see truely.

Cres. Blinde feare, that seeing reason leads, findes safe footing, then blinde reason, stumbling without feare: to feare the worst, oft cures the worse.

Troy. Oh let my Lady apprehend no feare,
In all *Cupids* Pageant there is presented no monster.

Cres. Not nothing monstrons neither?

Troy. Nothing but our vndertakings, when we vowe to weepe seas, liue in fire, eate rockes, tame Tygers; thinking it harder for our Mistresse to deuise imposition inough, then for vs to vndergoe any difficultie imposed. This is the monstruositie in loue Lady, that the will is infinite, and the execution confin'd; that the desire is boundlesse, and the act a slaue to limit.

Cres. They say all Louers sweare more performance then they are able, and yet reserue an ability that they neuer performe: vowing more then the perfection of ten; and discharging lesse then the tenth part of one. They that haue the voyce of Lyons, and the act of Hares: are they not Monsters?

Troy. Are there such? such are not we: Praise vs as we are tasted, allow vs as we proue: our head shall goe bare till merit crowne it: no perfection in reuersion shall haue a praise in present: wee will not name desert before his birth, and being borne his addition shall be humble: few words to faire faith. *Troylus* shall be such to *Cressid*, as what enuie can say worst, shall be a mocke for his truth; and what truth can speake truest, not truer then *Troylus*.

Cres. Will you walke in my Lord?

Enter Pandarus.

Pan. What blushing still? haue you not done talking yet?

Cres. Well Vnckle, what folly I commit, I dedicate to you.

Pan. I thanke you for that: if my Lord get a Boy of you, youle giue him me: be true to my Lord, if he flinch, chide me for it.

Tro. You know now your hostages: your Vnckles word and my firme faith.

Pan. Nay, Ile giue my word for her too: our kindred though they be long ere they are wooed, they are constant being wonne: they are Burres I can tell you, they'le sticke where they are throwne.

Cres. Boldnesse comes to mee now, and brings mee heart: Prince *Troylus*, I haue lou'd you night and day, for many weary moneths.

Troy. Why was my *Cressid* then so hard to win?

Cres. Hard to seeme won: but I was won my Lord
With the first glance; that euer pardon me,
If I confesse much you will play the tyrant:
I loue you now, but not till now so much
But I might maister it; infaith I lye:
My thoughts were like vnbrideled children grow
Too head-strong for their mother: see we fooles,
Why haue I blab'd: who shall be true to vs
When we are so vnsecret to our selues?
But though I lou'd you well, I woed you not,
And yet good faith I wisht my selfe a man;
Or that we women had mens priuiledge
Of speaking first. Sweet, bid me hold my tongue,
For in this rapture I shall surely speake
The thing I shall repent: see, see, your silence
Comming in dumbnesse, from my weakenesse drawes
My soule of counsell from me. Stop my mouth.

Troy. And shall, albeit sweete Musicke issues thence.

Pan. Pretty ysaith.

Cres. My Lord, I doe beseech you pardon me,
'Twas not my purpose thus to beg a kisse:
I am asham'd; O Heauens, what haue I done!
For this time will I take my leaue my Lord.

Troy. Your leaue sweete *Cressid*?

Pan. Leaue: and you take leaue till to morrow morning.

Cres. Pray you coutent you.

Troy. What offends you Lady?

Cres. Sir, mine owne company.

Troy. You cannot shun your selfe.

Cres. Let me goe and try:
I haue a kinde of selfe recides with you:
But an vnkinde selfe, that it selfe will leaue,
To be anothers foole. Where is my wit?
I would be gone: I speake I know not what.

Troy. Well know they what they speake, that speakes so wisely.

Cre. Perchance my Lord, I shew more craft then loue,
And fell so roundly to a large confession,
To Angle for your thoughts: but you are wise,
Or else you loue not: for to be wise and loue,
Exceedes mans might, that dwels with gods aboue.

Troy. O that I thought it could be in a woman:
As if it can, I will presume in you,
To feede for aye her lampe and flames of loue.
To keepe her constancie in plight and youth,
Out-liuing beauties outward, with a minde
That doth renew swifter then blood decaies:
Or that perswasion could but thus conuince me,
That my integritie and truth to you,
Might be affronted with the match and waight
Of such a winnowed puriritie in loue:
How were I then vp-lifted! but alas,
I am as true, as truths simplicitie,
And simpler then the infancie of truth.

Cres. In that Ile warre with you.

Troy. O vertuous fight,
When right with right wars who shall be most right:
True swaines in loue, shall in the world to come
Approue their truths by *Troylus*, when their rimes,
Full of protest, of oath and big compare;
Wants similes, truth tir'd with iteration,
As true as steele, as plantage to the Moone:
As Sunne to day: as Turtle to her mate:
As Iron to Adamant: as Earth to th'Center:
Yet after all comparisons of truth,
(As truths authenticke author to be cited)
As true as *Troylus*, shall crowne vp the Verse,
And sanctifie the numbers.

Cres. Prophet may you be:
If I be false, or swerue a haire from truth,
When time is old and hath forgot it selfe:
When water drops haue worne the Stones of *Troy*;
And blinde obliuion swallow'd Cities vp;
And mightie States characterlesse are grated
To dustie nothing; yet let memory,
From false to false, among false Maids in loue,
Vpbraid my falsehood, when they'aue said as false,
As Aire, as Water, as Winde, as randie earth;
As Foxe to Lambe; as Wolfe to Heifers Calfe;
Pard to the Hinde, or Stepdame to her Sonne;
Yea, let them say, to sticke the heart of falsehood,

As

As falſe as *Creſſid.*

Pand. Go too, a bargaine made: ſeale it, ſeale it, Ile be the witneſſe here I hold your hand: here my Couſins, if euer you proue falſe one to another, ſince I haue taken ſuch paines to bring you together, let all pittifull goers betweene be cal'd to the worlds end after my name: call them all Panders; let all conſtant men be *Troyluſſes*, all falſe women *Creſſids*, and all brokers betweene, Panders: ſay, Amen.

Troy. Amen.

Creſ. Amen.

Pan. Amen.

Whereupon I will ſhew you a Chamber, which bed, becauſe it ſhall not ſpeake of your prettie encounters, preſſe it to death: away.
And *Cupid* grant all tong-tide Maidens heere,
Bed, Chamber, and Pander, to prouide this geere. *Exeunt.*

Enter Vlyſſes, Diomedes, Neſtor, Agamemnon, Menelaus and Chalcas. Floriſh.

Cal. Now Princes for the ſeruice I haue done you,
Th'aduantage of the time promps me aloud,
To call for recompence: appeare it to your minde,
That through the ſight I beare in things to loue,
I haue abandon'd Troy, left my poſſeſſion,
Incur'd a Traitors name, expoſ'd my ſelfe,
From certaine and poſſeſt conueniences,
To doubtfull fortunes, ſequeſtring from me all
That time, acquaintance, cuſtome and condition,
Made tame, and moſt familiar to my nature:
And here to doe you ſeruice am become,
As new into the world, ſtrange, vnacquainted.
I doe beſeech you, as in way of taſte,
To giue me now a little benefit:
Out of thoſe many regiſtred in promiſe,
Which you ſay, liue to come in my behalfe.

Agam. What would'ſt thou of vs Troian? make demand?

Cal. You haue a Troian priſoner, cal'd *Anthenor*,
Yeſterday tooke: Troy holds him very deere.
Oft haue you (often haue you, thankes therefore)
Deſir'd my *Creſſia* in right great exchange.
Whom Troy hath ſtill deni'd: but this *Anthenor*,
I know is ſuch a wreſt in their affaires;
That their negotiations all muſt ſlacke,
Wanting his mannage: and they will almoſt,
Giue vs a Prince of blood, a Sonne of *Priam*,
In change of him. Let him be ſent great Princes,
And he ſhall buy my Daughter: and her preſence,
Shall quite ſtrike off all ſeruice I haue done,
In moſt accepted paine.

Aga. Let *Diomedes* beare him,
And bring vs *Creſſid* hither: *Calcas* ſhall haue
What he requeſts of vs: good *Diomed*
Furniſh you fairely for this enterchange;
Withall bring word, if *Hector* will to morrow
Be anſwer'd in his challenge. *Aiax* is ready.

Dio. This ſhall I vndertake, and 'tis a burthen
Which I am proud to beare. *Exit.*

Enter Achilles *and* Patroclus *in their Tent.*

Vliſ. *Achilles* ſtands i'th entrance of his Tent;
Pleaſe it our Generall to paſſe ſtrangely by him,
As if he were forgot: and Princes all,
Lay negligent and looſe regard vpon him;
I will come laſt, 'tis like heele queſtion me,
Why ſuch vnplauſiue eyes are bent? why turn'd on him?
If ſo, I haue deriſion medicinable,
To vſe betweene your ſtrangeneſſe and his pride,
Which his owne will ſhall haue deſire to drinke;
It may doe good, pride hath no other glaſſe
To ſhow it ſelfe, but pride: for ſupple knees,
Feede arrogance, and are the proud mans fees.

Agam. Weele execute your purpoſe, and put on
A forme of ſtrangeneſſe as we paſſe along,
So doe each Lord, and either greete him not,
Or elſe diſdainfully, which ſhall ſhake him more,
Then if not lookt on. I will lead the way.

Achil. What comes the Generall to ſpeake with me?
You know my minde, Ile fight no more 'gainſt Troy.

Aga. What ſaies *Achilles*, would he ought with vs?

Neſ. Would you my Lord ought with the Generall?

Achil. No.

Neſ. Nothing my Lord.

Aga. The better.

Achil. Good day, good day.

Men. How doe you? how doe you?

Achi. What, do's the Cuckold ſcorne me?

Aiax. How now *Patroclus*?

Achil. Good morrow *Aiax*?

Aiax. Ha.

Achil. Good morrow.

Aiax. I, and good next day too. *Exeunt.*

Achil. What meane theſe fellowes? know they not *Achilles*?

Patr. They paſſe by ſtrangely: they were vſ'd to bend
To ſend their ſmiles before them to *Achilles*:
To come as humbly as they vs'd to creepe to holy Altars.

Achil. What am I poore of late?
'Tis certaine, greatneſſe once falne out with fortune,
Muſt fall out with men too: what the declin'd is,
He ſhall as ſoone reade in the eyes of others,
As feele in his owne fall: for men like butter-flies,
Shew not their mealie wings, but to the Summer:
And not a man for being ſimply man,
Hath any honour; but honour'd for thoſe honours
That are without him; as place, riches, and fauour,
Prizes of accident, as oft as merit:
Which when they fall, as being ſlippery ſtanders;
The loue that leand on them as ſlippery too,
Doth one plucke downe another, and together
Dye in the fall. But 'tis not ſo with me;
Fortune and I are friends, I doe enioy
At ample point, all that I did poſſeſſe,
Saue theſe mens lookes: who do me thinkes finde out
Something not worth in me ſuch rich beholding,
As they haue often giuen. Here is *Vliſſes*,
Ile interrupt his reading: how now *Vliſſes*?

Vliſ. Now great *Thetis* Sonne.

Achil. What are you reading?

Vliſ. A ſtrange fellow here
Writes me, that man, how dearely euer parted,
How much in hauing, or without, or in,
Cannot make boaſt to haue that which he hath;
Nor feeles not what he owes, but by reflection:
As when his vertues ſhining vpon others,
Heate them, and they retort that heate againe
To the firſt giuer.

Achil. This is not ſtrange *Vliſſes*:
The beautie that is borne he in the face,
The bearer knowes not, but commends it ſelfe,
Not going from it ſelfe: but ye to eye oppos'd,

Salutes

Salutes each other with each others forme.
For speculation turnes not to it selfe,
Till it hath trauail'd, and is married there
Where it may see it selfe : this is not strange at all.
Vlis. I doe not straine it at the position,
It is familiar; but at the Authors drift,
Who in his circumstance, expresly proues
That no may is the Lord of any thing,
(Though in and of him there is much consisting,)
Till he communicate his parts to others :
Nor doth he of himselfe know them for ought,
Till he behold them formed in th'applause,
Where they are extended : who like an arch reuerb'rate
The voyce againe; or like a gate of steele,
Fronting the Sunne, receiues and renders backe
His figure, and his heate. I was much rapt in this,
And apprehended here immediately :
The vnknowne *Aiax*;
Heauens what a man is there? a very Horse, (are.
That has he knowes not what. Nature, what things there
Most abiect in regard, and deare in vse.
What things againe most deere in the esteeme,
And poore in worth : now shall we see to morrow,
An act that very chance doth throw vpon him?
Aiax renown'd? O heauens, what some men doe,
While some men leaue to doe!
How some men creepe in skittish fortunes hall,
Whiles others play the Ideots in her eyes :
How one man eates into anothers pride,
While pride is feasting in his wantonnesse
To see these Grecian Lords; why, euen already,
They clap the lubber *Aiax* on the shoulder,
As if his foote were on braue *Hectors* brest,
And great *Troy* shrinking.
Achil. I doe beleeue it :
For they past by me, as mysers doe by beggars,
Neither gaue to me good word, nor looke:
What are my deedes forgot?
Vlis. Time hath (my Lord) a wallet at his backe,
Wherein he puts almes for obliuion :
A great siz'd monster of ingratitudes :
Those scraps are good deedes past,
Which are deuour'd as fast as they are made,
Forgot as soone as done : perseuerance, deere my Lord,
Keepes honor bright, to haue done, is to hang
Quite out of fashion, like a rustie male,
In monumentall mockrie : take the instant way,
For honour trauels in a straight so narrow,
Where one but goes a breast, keepe then the paths
For emulation hath a thousand Sonnes,
That one by one pursue; if you giue way,
Or hedge aside from the direct forth right;
Like to an entred Tyde, they all rush by,
And leaue you hindmost :
Or like a gallant Horse falne in first ranke,
Lye there for pauement to the abiect, neere
Ore-run and trampled on: then what they doe in present,
Though lesse then yours in past, must ore-top yours :
For time is like a fashionable Hoste,
That slightly shakes his parting Guest by th'hand;
And with his armes out-stretcht, as he would flye,
Graspes in the commer : the welcome euer smiles,
And farewels goes out sighing : O let not vertue seeke
Remuneration for the thing it was : for beautie, wit,
High birth, vigor of bone, desert in seruice,
Loue, friendship, charity, are subiects all
To enuious and calumniating time:
One touch of nature makes the whole world kin :
That all with one consent praise new borne gaudes,
Though they are made and moulded of things past,
And goe to dust, that is a little guilt,
More laud then guilt oredusted.
The present eye praises the pres nt obiect :
Then maruell not thou great and compleat man,
That all the Greekes begin to worship *Aiax*;
Since things in motion begin to catch the eye,
Then what not stirs : the cry went out on thee,
And still it might, and yet it may againe,
If thou would'st not entombe thy selfe aliue,
And case thy reputation in thy Tent;
Whose glorious deedes, but in these fields of late,
Made emulous missions 'mongst the gods themseluer,
And draue great *Mars* to faction.
Achil. Of this my priuacie,
I haue strong reasons.
Vlis. But 'gainst your priuacie
The reasons are more potent and heroycall :
'Tis knowne *Achilles*, that you are in loue
With one of *Priams* daughters.
Achil. Ha? knowne?
Vlis. Is that a wonder?
The prouidence that's in a watchfull State,
Knowes almost euery graine of Plutoes gold;
Findes bottome in th'vncomprehensiue deepes;
Keepes place with thought; and almost like the gods,
Doe thoughts vnuaile in their dumbe cradles :
There is a mysterie (with whom relation
Durst neuer meddle) in the soule of State;
Which hath an operation more diuine,
Then breath or pen can giue expressure to :
All the commerse that you haue had with Troy,
As perfectly is ours, as yours, my Lord.
And better would it fit *Achilles* much,
To throw downe *Hector* then *Polixena*.
But it must grieue yong *Pirhus* now at home,
When fame shall in her Iland sound her trumpe;
And all the Greekish Girles shall tripping sing,
Great *Hectors* sister did *Achilles* winne;
But our great *Aiax* brauely beate downe him.
Farewell my Lord : I as your louer speake;
The foole slides ore the Ice that you should breake.
Patr. To this effect *Achilles* haue I mou'd you;
A woman impudent and mannish growne,
Is not more loth'd, then an effeminate man,
In time of action : I stand condemn'd for this;
They thinke my little stomacke to the warre,
And your great loue to me, restraines you thus :
Sweete, rouse your selfe; and the weake wanton *Cupid*
Shall from your necke vnloose his amorous fould,
And like a dew drop from the Lyons mane,
Be shooke to ayrie ayre.
Achil. Shall *Aiax* fight with *Hector*?
Patr. I, and perhaps receiue much honor by him.
Achil. I see my reputation is at stake,
My fame is shrowdly gored.
Patr. O then beware :
Those wounds heale ill, that men doe giue themselues :
Omission to doe what is necessary,
Seales a commission to a blanke of danger,
And danger like an ague subtly taints
Euen then when we sit idely in the sunne.
Achil. Goe call *Thersites* hither sweet *Patroclus*,

Ile send the foole to *Aiax*, and desire him
T'inuite the Troian Lords after the Combat
To see vs here vnarm'd: I haue a womans longing,
An appetite that I am sicke withall,
To see great *Hector* in his weedes of peace; *Enter Thersi.*
To talke with him, and to behold his visage,
Euen to my full of view. A labour sau'd.

Ther. A wonder.

Achil. What?

Ther. *Aiax* goes vp and downe the field, asking for himselfe.

Achil. How so?

Ther. Hee must fight singly to morrow with *Hector*, and is so prophetically proud of an heroicall cudgelling, that he raues in saying nothing.

Achil. How can that be?

Ther. Why he stalkes vp and downe like a Peacock, a stride and a stand: ruminates like an hostesse, that hath no Arithmatique but her braine to set downe her reckoning: bites his lip with a politique regard, as who should say, there were wit in his head and twoo'd out; and so there is: but it lyes as coldly in him, as fire in a flint, which will not shew without knocking. The mans vndone for euer; for if *Hector* breake not his necke i'th'combat, heele break't himselfe in vaine-glory. He knowes not mee: I said, good morrow *Aiax*; And he replyes, thankes *Agamemnon*. What thinke you of this man, that takes me for the Generall? Hee's growne a very land-fish, languagelesse, a monster: a plague of opinion, a man may weare it on both sides like a leather Ierkin.

Achil. Thou must be my Ambassador to him *Thersites.*

Ther. Who, I: why, heele answer no body: he professes notanswering; speaking is for beggers: he weares his tongue in's armes: I will put on his presence; let *Patroclus* make his demands to me, you shall see the Pageant of *Aiax*.

Achil. To him *Patroclus*; tell him, I humbly desire the valiant *Aiax*, to inuite the most valorous *Hector*, to come vnarm'd to my Tent, and to procure safe conduct for his person, of the magnanimious and most illustrious, sixe or seauen times honour'd Captaine, Generall of the Grecian Armie *Agamemnon*, &c. doe this.

Patro. *Ioue* blesse great *Aiax*.

Ther. Hum.

Patr. I come from the worthy *Achilles*.

Ther. Ha?

Patr. Who most humbly desires you to inuite *Hector* to his Tent.

Ther. Hum.

Patr. And to procure safe conduct from *Agamemnon*.

Ther. *Agamemnon*?

Patr. I my Lord.

Ther. Ha?

Patr. What say you too't.

Ther. God buy you with all my heart.

Patr. Your answer sir.

Ther. If to morrow be a faire day, by eleuen a clocke it will goe one way or other; howsoeuer, he shall pay for me ere he has me.

Patr. Your answer sir.

Ther. Fare you well withall my heart.

Achil. Why, but he is not in this tune, is he?

Ther. No, but he's out a tune thus: what musicke will be in him when *Hector* has knockt out his braines, I know not: but I am sure none, vnlesse the Fidler *Apollo* get his sinewes to make catlings on.

Achil. Come, thou shalt beare a Letter to him straight.

Ther. Let me carry another to his Horse; for that's the more capable creature.

Achil. My minde is troubled like a Fountaine stir'd,
And I my selfe see not the bottome of it.

Ther. Would the Fountaine of your minde were cleere againe, that I might water an Asse at it: I had rather be a Ticke in a Sheepe, then such a valiant ignorance.

Enter at one doore Æneas with a Torch, at another Paris, Diephoebus, Anthenor, Diomed the Grecian, with Torches.

Par. See hoa, who is that there?

Dieph. It is the Lord *Æneas*.

Æne. Is the Prince there in person?
Had I so good occasion to lye long
As you Prince *Paris*, nothing but heauenly businesse,
Should rob my bed-mate of my company.

Diom. That's my minde too: good morrow Lord *Æneas*.

Par. A valiant Greeke *Æneas*, take his hand,
Witnesse the processe of your speech within;
You told how *Diomed* in a whole weeke by dayes
Did haunt you in the Field.

Æne. Health to you valiant sir,
During all question of the gentle truce:
But when I meete you arm'd, as blacke defiance,
As heart can thinke, or courage execute.

Diom. The one and other *Diomed* embraces,
Our blouds are now in calme; and so long health:
But when contention, and occasion meetes,
By *Ioue*, Ile play the hunter for thy life,
With all my force, pursuite and pollicy.

Æne. And thou shalt hunt a Lyon that will flye
With his face backward, in humaine gentlenesse:
Welcome to Troy; now by *Anchises* life,
Welcome indeede: by *Venus* hand I sweare,
No man aliue can loue in such a sort,
The thing he meanes to kill, more excellently.

Diom. We simpathize. *Ioue* let *Æneas* liue
(If to my sword his fate be not the glory)
A thousand compleate courses of the Sunne,
But in mine emulous honor let him dye:
With euery ioynt a wound, and that to morrow.

Æne. We know each other well.

Dio. We doe, and long to know each other worse.

Par. This is the most, despightful'st gentle greeting;
The noblest hatefull loue, that ere I heard of.
What businesse Lord so early?

Æne. I was sent for to the King; but why, I know not.

Par. His purpose meets you; it was to bring this Greek
To *Calcha's* house; and there to render him,
For the enfreed *Anthenor*, the faire *Cressid*:
Lets haue your company; or if you please,
Haste there before vs. I constantly doe thinke
(Or rather call my thought a certaine knowledge)
My brother *Troylus* lodges there to night.
Rouse him, and giue him note of our approach,
With the whole quality whereof, I feare
We shall be much vnwelcome.

Æne. That I assure you:
Troylus had rather Troy were borne to Greece,
Then *Cressid* borne from Troy.

Par. There

Par. There is no helpe:
The bitter disposition of the time will haue it so.
On Lord, weele follow you.

Æne. Good morrow all. *Exit Æneas*

Par. And tell me noble *Diomed*; faith tell me true,
Euen in the soule of sound good fellow ship,
Who in your thoughts merits faire *Helen* most?
My selfe, or *Menelaus*?

Diom. Both alike.
He merits well to haue her, that doth seeke her,
Not making any scruple of her soylure,
With such a hell of paine, and world of charge.
And you as well to keepe her, that defend her,
Not pallating the taste of her dishonour,
With such a costly losse of wealth and friends:
He like a puling Cuckold, would drinke vp
The lees and dregs of a flat tamed peece:
You like a letcher, out of whorish loynes,
Are pleas'd to breede out your inheritors:
Both merits poyz'd, each weighs no lesse nor more,
But he as he, which heauier for a whore.

Par. You are too bitter to your country-woman.

Dio. Shee's bitter to her countrey: heare me *Paris*,
For euery false drop in her baudy veines,
A Grecians life hath sunke: for euery scruple
Of her contaminated carrion weight,
A Troian hath beene slaine. Since she could speake,
She hath not giuen so many good words breath,
As for her, Greekes and Troians suffred death.

Par. Faire *Diomed*, you doe as chapmen doe,
Dispraise the thing that you desire to buy:
But we in silence hold this vertue well;
Weele not commend, what we intend to sell.
Here lyes our way. *Exeunt.*

Enter Troylus and Cressida.

Troy. Deere trouble not your selfe: the morne is cold.

Cres. Then sweet my Lord, Ile call mine Vnckle down;
He shall vnbolt the Gates.

Troy. Trouble him not:
To bed, to bed: sleepe kill those pritty eyes,
And giue as soft attachment to thy sences,
As Infants empty of all thought.

Cres. Good morrow then.

Troy. I prithee now to bed.

Cres. Are you a weary of me?

Troy. O *Cressida*! but that the busie day
Wak't by the Larke, hath rouz'd the ribauld Crowes,
And dreaming night will hide our eyes no longer:
I would not from thee.

Cres. Night hath beene too briefe. (stayes,

Troy. Beshrew the witch! with venemous wights she
As hidiously as hell; but flies the graspes of loue,
With wings more momentary, swift then thought:
You will catch cold, and curse me.

Cres. Prithee tarry, you men will neuer tarry;
O foolish *Cressid*, I might haue still held off,
And then you would haue tarried. Harke, ther's one vp?

Pand. within. What's all the doores open here?

Troy. It is your Vnckle. *Enter Pandarus.*

Cres. A pestilence on him: now will he be mocking:
I shall haue such a life.

Pan. How now, how now? how goe maiden-heads?
Heare you Maide: wher's my cozin *Cressid*?

Cres. Go hang your self, you naughty mocking Vnckle:
You bring me to doo----and then you floute me too.

Pan. To do what? to do what? let her say what:
What haue I brought you to doe?

Cres. Come, come, beshrew your heart: youle nere be good, nor suffer others.

Pan. Ha, ha: alas poore wretch: a poore *Chipochia*, hast not slept to night? would he not (a naughty man) let it sleepe: a bug-beare take him. *One knocks*

Cres Did not I tell you? would he were knockt ith' head. Who's that at doore? good Vnckle goe and see.
My Lord, come you againe into my Chamber:
You smile and mocke me, as if I meant naughtily.

Troy. Ha, ha.

Cre. Come you are deceiu'd, I thinke of no such thing.
How earnestly they knocke: pray you come in. *Knocke.*
I would not for halfe *Troy* haue you seene here. *Exeunt*

Pan. Who's there? what's the matter? will you beate downe the doore? How now, what's the matter?

Æne. Good morrow Lord, good morrow.

Pan. Who's there my Lord *Æneas*? by my troth I knew you not: what newes with you so early?

Æne Is not Prince *Troylus* here?

Pan. Here? what should he doe here?

Æne. Come he is here, my Lord, doe not deny him:
It doth import him much to speake with me.

Pan. Is he here say you? 'tis more then I know, Ile be sworne: For my owne part I came in late: what should he doe here?

Æne. Who, nay then: Come, come, youle doe him wrong, ere y'are ware: youle be so true to him, to be false to him: Doe not you know of him, but yet goe fetch him hither, goe.

Enter Troylus.

Troy. How now, what's the matter?

Æne. My Lord, I scarce haue leisure to salute you,
My matter is so rash: there is at hand,
Paris your brother, and *Deiphœbus*,
The Grecian *Diomed*, and our *Anthenor*
Deliuer'd to vs, and for him forth-with,
Ere the first sacrifice, within this houre,
We must giue vp to *Diomeds* hand
The Lady *Cressida*.

Troy. Is it concluded so?

Æne. By *Priam*, and the generall state of *Troy*,
They are at hand, and ready to effect it.

Troy. How my achieuements mocke me;
I will goe meete them: and my Lord *Æneas*,
We met by chance; you did not finde me here.

Æn. Good, good, my Lord, the secrets of nature
Haue not more gift in taciturnitie. *Exeunt.*

Enter Pandarus and Cressid.

Pan. Is't possible? no sooner got but lost: the diuell take *Anthenor*; the yong Prince will goe mad: a plague vpon *Anthenor*; I would they had brok's necke.

Cres. How now? what's the matter? who was here?

Pan. Ah, ha!

Cres. Why sigh you so profoundly? wher's my Lord? gone? tell me sweet Vnckle, what's the matter?

Pan. Would I were as deepe vnder the earth as I am aboue.

Cres. O the gods! what's the matter?

Pan. Prythee get thee in: would thou had'st nere been borne; I knew thou would'st be his death. O poore Gentleman: a plague vpon *Anthenor*.

Cres. Good Vnckle I beseech you, on my knees, I beseech you what's the matter?

Pan. Thou must be gone wench, thou must be gone; thou art chang'd for *Anthenor*: thou must to thy Father, and be gone from *Troylus*: 'twill be his death: twill be his baine, he cannot beare it..

Cres. O you immortall gods! I will not goe.

Pan. Thou must.

Cres. I will not Vnckle: I haue forgot my Father:
I know no touch of consanguinitie:
No kin, no loue, no bloud, no soule, so neere me,
As the sweet *Troylus*: O you gods diuine!
Make *Cressids* name the very crowne of falshood
If euer she leaue *Troylus*: time, orce and death,
Do to this body what extremitie you can;
But the strong base and building of my loue,
Is as the very Center of the earth,
Drawing all things to it. I will goe in and weepe.

Pan. Doe, doe.

Cres. Teare my bright heire, and scratch my praised cheekes,
Cracke my cleere voyce with sobs, and breake my heart
With sounding *Troylus*. I will not goe from *Troy*. *Exeunt.*

Enter Paris, Troylus, Æneas, Deiphebus, Anthenor and Diomedes.

Par. It is great morning, and the houre prefixt
Of her deliuerie to this valiant Greeke
Comes fast vpon: good my brother *Troylus*,
Tell you the Lady what she is to doe,
And hast her to the purpose.

Troy. Walke into her house:
Ile bring her to the Grecian presently;
And to his hand, when I deliuer her,
Thinke it an Altar, and thy brother *Troylus*
A Priest, there offring to it his heart.

Par. I know what 'tis to loue,
And would, as I shall pittie, I could helpe.
Please you walke in, my Lords. *Exeunt.*

Enter Pandarus and Cressid.

Pan. Be moderate, be moderate.

Cres. Why tell you me of moderation?
The griefe is fine, full perfect that I taste,
And no lesse in a sense as strong
As that which causeth it. How can I moderate it?
If I could temporise with my affection,
Or brew it to a weake and colder pallat,
The like alaiment could I giue my griefe:
My loue admits no qualifying crosse; *Enter Troylus.*
No more my griefe, in such a precious losse.

Pan. Here, here, here, he comes, a sweet ducke.

Cres. O *Troylus*, *Troylus*!

Pan. What a paire of spectacles is here? let me embrace too: oh hart, as the goodly saying is; O heart, heauie heart, why sighest thou without breaking? where he answers againe; because thou canst not ease thy smart by friendship, nor by speaking: there was neuer a truer rime; let vs cast away nothing, for we may liue to haue neede of such a Verse: we see it, we see it: how now Lambs?

Troy. *Cressid*: I loue thee in so strange a puritie ·
That the blest gods, as angry with my fancie,
More bright in zeale, then the deuotion which
Gold lips blow to their Deities: take thee from me.

Cres. Haue the gods enuie?

Pan. I, I, I, I, 'tis too plaine a case.

Cres. And is it true, that I must goe from Troy?

Troy. A hatefull truth.

Cres. What, and from *Troylus* too?

Troy. From Troy, and *Troylus*.

Cres. Ist possible?

Troy. And sodainely, where iniurie of chance
Puts backe leaue-taking, iustles roughly by
All time of pause; rudely beguiles our lips
Of all reioyndure: forcibly preuents
Our lockt embrasures; strangles our deare vowes,
Euen in the birth of our owne laboring breath.
We two, that with so many thousand sighes
Did buy each other, must poorely sell our selues,
With the rude breuitie and discharge of our
Iniurious time; now with a robbers haste
Crams his rich theeuerie vp, he knowes not how.
As many farwels as be stars in heauen,
With distinct breath, and consign'd kisses to them,
He fumbles vp into a loose adiew;
And scants vs with a single famisht kisse,
Distasting with the salt of broken teares. *Enter Æneas.*

Æneas within. My Lord, is the Lady ready?

Troy. Harke, you are call'd: some say the genius so
Cries, come to him that instantly must dye.
Bid them haue patience: she shall come anon.

Pan. Where are my teares? raine, to lay this winde, or my heart will be blowne vp by the root.

Cres. I must then to the Grecians?

Troy. No remedy.

Cres. A wofull *Cressid* 'mong'st the merry Greekes.

Troy. When shall we see againe?

Troy. Here me my loue: be thou but true of heart.

Cres. I true? how now? what wicked deeme is this?

Troy. Nay, we must vse expostulation kindely,
For it is parting from vs:
I speake not, be thou true, as fearing thee:
For I will throw my Gloue to death himselfe,
That there's no maculation in thy heart:
But be thou true, say I, to fashion in
My sequent protestation: be thou true,
And I will see thee.

Cres. O you shall be expos'd, my Lord to dangers
As infinite, as imminent: but Ile be true.

Troy. And Ile grow friend with danger;
Weare this Sleeue.

Cres. And you this Gloue.
When shall I see you?

Troy. I will corrupt the Grecian Centinels,
To giue thee nightly visitation.
But yet be true.

Cres. O heauens: be true againe?

Troy. Heare why I speake it; Loue:
The Grecian youths are full of qualitie,
Their louing well compos'd, with guift of nature,
Flawing and swelling ore with Arts and exercise:
How nouelties may moue, and parts with person.
Alas, a kinde of godly iealousie;
Which I beseech you call a vertuous sinne:
Makes me affraid.

Cres. O heauens, you loue me not!

Troy. Dye I a villaine then:
In this I doe not call your faith in question
So mainely as my merit: I cannot sing,
Nor heele the high Lauolt; nor sweeten talke;
Nor play at subtill games; faire vertues all;

To which the Grecians are most prompt and pregnant:
But I can tell that in each grace of these,
There lurkes a still and dumb-discoursiue diuell,
That tempts most cunningly: but be not tempted.
Cres. Doe you thinke I will?
Troy. No, but something may be done that we wil not:
And sometimes we are diuels to our selues,
When we will tempt the frailtie of our powers,
Presuming on their changefull potencie.
Æneas within. Nay, good my Lord?
Troy. Come kisse, and let vs part.
Paris within. Brother *Troylus*?
Troy. Good brother come you hither,
And bring *Æneas* and the Grecian with you.
Cres. My Lord, will you be true? *Exit.*
Troy. Who I? alas it is my vice, my fault:
Whiles others fish with craft for great opinion,
I, with great truth, catch meere simplicitie;
Whil'st some with cunning guild their copper crownes,
With truth and plainnesse I doe weare mine bare:

Enter the Greekes.

Feare not my truth; the morrall of my wit
Is plaine and true, ther's all the reach of it.
Welcome sir *Diomed*, here is the Lady
Which for *Antenor*, we deliuer you.
At the port (Lord) Ile giue her to thy hand,
And by the way possesse thee what she is.
Entreate her faire; and by my soule, faire Greeke,
If ere thou stand at mercy of my Sword,
Name *Cressid*, and thy life shall be as safe
As *Priam* is in Illion?
Diom. Faire Lady *Cressid*,
So please you saue the thankes this Prince expects:
The lustre in your eye, heauen in your cheeke,
Pleades your faire visage, and to *Diomed*
You shall be mistresse, and command him wholly.
Troy. Grecian, thou do'st not vse me curteously,
To shame the seale of my petition towards,
I praising her. I tell thee Lord of Greece:
Shee is as farre high soaring o're thy praises,
As thou vnworthy to be cal'd her seruant:
I charge thee vse her well, euen for my charge:
For by the dreadfull *Pluto*, if thou do'st not,
(Though the great bulke *Achilles* be thy guard)
Ile cut thy throate.
Diom. Oh be not mou'd Prince *Troylus*;
Let me be priuiledg'd by my place and message,
To be a speaker free? when I am hence,
Ile answer to my lust: and know my Lord;
Ile nothing doe on charge: to her owne worth
She shall be priz'd: but that you say, be't so;
Ile speake it in my spirit and honor, no.
Troy. Come to the Port. Ile tell thee *Diomed*,
This braue, shall oft make thee to hide thy head:
Lady giue me your hand, and as we walke,
To our owne selues bend we our needefull talke.

Sound Trumpet.

Par. Harke, *Hectors* Trumpet.
Æne. How haue we spent this morning
The Prince must thinke me tardy and remisse,
That swore to ride before him in the field.
Par. 'Tis *Troylus* fault: come, come, to field with him. *Exeunt.*
Dio. Let vs make ready straight.
Æne. Yea, with a Bridegroomes fresh alacritie
Let vs addresse to tend on *Hectors* heeles:
The glory of our *Troy* doth this day lye
On his faire worth, and single Chiualrie.

Enter Aiax armed, Achilles, Patroclus, Agamemnon, Menelaus, Vlisses, Nestor, Calcas, &c.

Aga. Here art thou in appointment fresh and faire,
Anticipating time. With starting courage,
Giue with thy Trumpet a loud note to Troy
Thou dreadfull *Aiax*, that the appauled aire
May pierce the head of the great Combatant,
And hale him hither.
Aia. Thou, Trumpet, ther's my purse;
Now cracke thy lungs, and split thy brasen pipe:
Blow villaine, till thy sphered Bias cheeke
Out-swell the collicke of puft *Aquilon*:
Come, stretch thy chest, and let thy eyes spout bloud:
Thou blowest for *Hector*.
Vlis. No Trumpet answers.
Achil. 'Tis but early dayes.
Aga. Is not yong *Diomed* with *Calcas* daughter?
Vlis. 'Tis he, I ken the manner of his gate,
He rises on the toe: that spirit of his
In aspiration lifts him from the earth.
Aga. Is this the Lady *Cressid*?
Dio. Euen she.
Aga. Most deerely welcome to the Greekes, sweete Lady.
Nest. Our Generall doth salute you with a kisse.
Vlis. Yet is the kindenesse but particular; 'twere better she were kist in generall.
Nest. And very courtly counsell: Ile begin. So much for *Nestor*.
Achil. Ile take that winter from your lips faire Lady *Achilles* bids you welcome.
Mene. I had good argument for kissing once.
Patro. But that's no argument for kissing now;
For thus pop't *Paris* in his hardiment.
Vlis. Oh deadly gall, and theame of all our scornes,
For which we loose our heads, to gild his hornes.
Patro. The first was *Menelaus* kisse, this mine:
Patroclus kisses you.
Mene. Oh this is trim.
Patr. *Paris* and I kisse euermore for him.
Mene. Ile haue my kisse sir: Lady by your leaue.
Cres. In kissing doe you render, or receiue.
Patr. Both take and giue.
Cres. Ile make my match to liue,
The kisse you take is better then you giue: therefore no kisse.
Mene. Ile giue you boote, Ile giue you three for one.
Cres. You are an odde man, giue euen, or giue none.
Mene. An odde man Lady, euery man is odde.
Cres. No, *Paris* is not; for you know 'tis true,
That you are odde, and he is euen with you.
Mene. You fillip me a'th' head.
Cres. No, Ile be sworne.
Vlis. It were no match, your naile against his horne:
May I sweete Lady beg a kisse of you?
Cres. You may.
Vlis. I doe desire it.
Cres. Why begge then?
Vlis. Why then for *Venus* sake, giue me a kisse:
When *Hellen* is a maide againe, and his——
Cres. I am your debtor, claime it when 'tis due.

Vlis. Neuer's my day, and then a kisse of you.
Diom. Lady a word, Ile bring you to your Father.
Nest. A woman of quicke sence.
Vlis. Fie, fie, vpon her:
Ther's a language in her eye, her cheeke, her lip;
Nay, her foote speakes, her wanton spirites looke out
At euery ioynt, and motiue of her body:
Oh these encounterers so glib of tongue,
That giue a coasting welcome ere it comes;
And wide vnclaspe the tables of their thoughts,
To euery tickling reader: set them downe,
For sluttish spoyles of opportunitie;.
And daughters of the game. *Exeunt.*

Enter all of Troy, Hector, Paris, Æneas, Helenus and Attendants. Florish.

All. The Troians Trumpet.
Aga. Yonder comes the troope.
Æne. Haile all you state of Greece: what shalbe done
To him that victory commands? or doe you purpose,
A victor shall be knowne: will you the Knights
Shall to the edge of all extremitie
Pursue each other; or shall be diuided
By any voyce, or order of the field: *Hector* bad aske?
Aga. Which way would *Hector* haue it?
Æne. He cares not, heele obey conditions.
Aga. 'Tis done like *Hector*, but securely done,
A little proudly, and great deale disprising
The Knight oppos'd.
Æne. If not *Achilles* sir, what is your name?
Achil. If not *Achilles*, nothing.
Æne. Therefore *Achilles*: but what ere, know this,
In the extremity of great and little:
Valour and pride excell themselues in *Hector*;
The one almost as infinite as all;
The other blanke as nothing: weigh him well
And that which lookes like pride, is curtesie:
This *Aiax* is halfe made of *Hectors* bloud;
In loue whereof, halfe *Hector* staies at home:
Halfe heart, halfe hand, halfe *Hector*, comes to seeke
This blended Knight, halfe Troian, and halfe Greeke.
Achil. A maiden battaile then? O I perceiue you.
Aga. Here is sir, *Diomed*: goe gentle Knight,
Stand by our *Aiax*: as you and Lord *Æneas*
Consent vpon the order of their fight,
So be it: either to the vttermost,
Or else a breach: the Combatants being kin,
Halfe stints their strife, before their strokes begin.
Vlis. They are oppos'd already.
Aga. What Troian is that same that lookes so heauy?
Vlis. The yongest Sonne of *Priam*;
A true Knight; they call him *Troylus*;
Not yet mature, yet matchlesse, firme of word,
Speaking in deedes, and deedelesse in his tongue;
Not soone prouok't, nor being prouok't, soone calm'd;
His heart and hand both open, and both free:
For what he has, he giues; what thinkes, he shewes;
Yet giues he not till iudgement guide his bounty,
Nor dignifies an impaire thought with breath:
Manly as *Hector*, but more dangerous;
For *Hector* in his blaze of wrath subscribes
To tender obiects; but he, in heate of action,
Is more vindecatiue then iealous loue.
They call him *Troylus*; and on him erect,
A second hope, as fairely built as *Hector*.
Thus saies *Æneas*, one that knowes the youth,
Euen to his inches: and with priuate soule,
Did in great Illion thus translate him to me. *Alarum.*
Aga. They are in action.
Nest. Now *Aiax* hold thine owne.
Troy. *Hector*, thou sleep'st, awake thee.
Aga. His blowes are wel dispos'd there *Aiax.* *trũpets cease.*
Diom. You must no more.
Æne. Princes enough, so please you.
Aia. I am not warme yet, let vs fight againe.
Diom. As *Hector* pleases.
Hect. Why then will I no more:
Thou art great Lord, my Fathers sisters Sonne;
A cousen german to great *Priams* seede:
The obligation of our bloud forbids
A gorie emulation 'twixt vs twaine:
Were thy commixion, Greeke and Troian so,
That thou could'st say, this hand is Grecian all,
And this is Troian: the sinewes of this Legge,
All Greeke, and this all Troy: my Mothers bloud
Runs on the dexter cheeke, and this sinister
Bounds in my fathers: by *Ioue* multipotent,
Thou should'st not beare from me a Greekish member
Wherein my sword had not impressure made
Of our ranke feud: but the iust gods gainsay,
That any drop thou borrwd'st from thy mother,
My sacred Aunt, should by my mortall Sword
Be drained. Let me embrace thee *Aiax*:
By him that thunders, thou hast lustie Armes;
Hector would haue them fall vpon him thus.
Cozen, all honor to thee.
Aia. I thanke thee *Hector*:
Thou art too gentle, and too free a man:
I came to kill thee Cozen, and beare hence
A great addition, earned in thy death.
Hect. Not *Neoptolymus* so mirable,
On whose bright crest, fame with her lowd'st (O yes)
Cries, This is he; could'st promise to himselfe,
A thought of added honor, torne from *Hector*.
Æne. There is expectance here from both the sides,
What further you will doe?
Hect. Weele answere it:
The issue is embracement: *Aiax*, farewell.
Aia. If I might in entreaties finde successe,
As seld I haue the chance; I would desire
My famous Cousin to our Grecian Tents.
Diom. 'Tis *Agamemnons* wish, and great *Achilles*
Doth long to see vnarm'd the valiant *Hector*.
Hect. *Æneas*, call my brother *Troylus* to me:
And signifie this louing enterview
To the expecters of our Troian part:
Desire them home. Giue me thy hand, my Cousin:
I will goe eate with thee, and see your Knights.

Enter Agamemnon and the rest.

Aia. Great *Agamemnon* comes to meete vs here.
Hect. The worthiest of them, tell me name by name:
But for *Achilles*, mine owne serching eyes
Shall finde him by his large and portly size.
Aga. Worthy of Armes: as welcome as to one
That would be rid of such an enemie.
But that's no welcome: vnderstand more cleere
What's past, and what's to come, is strew'd with huskes,
And formelesse ruine of obliuion:
But in this extant moment, faith and troth,
Strain'd purely from all hollow bias drawing:
Bids thee with most diuine integritie,
From heart of very heart, great *Hector* welcome.
Hect. I thanke thee most imperious *Agamemnon*.

Aga. My

Aga. My well-fam'd Lord of Troy, no lesse to you.
Men. Let me confirme my Princely brothers greeting,
You brace of warlike Brothers, welcome hither.
Hect. Who must we answer?
Æne. The Noble *Menelaus.*
Hect. O, you my Lord, by *Mars* his gauntlet thanks,
Mocke not, that I affect th'vntraded Oath,
Your *quondam* wife sweares still by *Venus* Gloue
Shee's well, but bad me not commend her to you.
Men. Name her not now sir, she's a deadly Theame.
Hect. O pardon, I offend.
Nest. I haue (thou gallant Troyan) seene thee oft
Labouring for destiny, make cruell way
Through rankes of Greekish youth: and I haue seen thee
As hot as *Perseus*, spurre thy Phrygian Steed,
And seene thee scorning forfeits and subduments,
When thou hast hung thy aduanced sword i'th'ayre,
Not letting it decline, on the declined:
That I haue said vnto my standers by,
Loe Iupiter is yonder, dealing life.
And I haue seene thee pause, and take thy breath,
When that a ring of Greekes haue hem'd thee in,
Like an Olympian wrestling. This haue I seene,
But this thy countenance (still lockt in steele)
I neuer saw till now. I knew thy Grandsire,
And once fought with him; he was a Souldier good,
But by great Mars, the Captaine of vs all,
Neuer like thee. Let an oldman embrace thee,
And (worthy Warriour) welcome to our Tents.
Æne. 'Tis the old *Nestor.*
Hect. Let me embrace thee good old Chronicle,
That hast so long walk'd hand in hand with time:
Most reuerend *Nestor*, I am glad to claspe thee.
Ne. I would my armes could match thee in contention
As they contend with thee in courtesie.
Hect. I would they could.
Nest. Ha? by this white beard I'ld fight with thee to morrow. Well, welcom, welcome: I haue seen the time.
Vlys. I wonder now, how yonder City stands,
When we haue heere her Base and pillar by vs.
Hect. I know your fauour Lord *Vlysses* well.
Ah sir, there's many a Greeke and Troyan dead,
Since first I saw your selfe, and *Diomed*
In Illion, on your Greekish Embassie.
Vlys. Sir, I foretold you then what would ensue,
My prophesie is but halfe his iourney yet;
For yonder wals that pertly front your Towne,
Yond Towers, whose wanton tops do busse the clouds,
Must kisse their owne feet.
Hect. I must not beleeue you:
There they stand yet: and modestly I thinke,
The fall of euery Phrygian stone will cost
A drop of Grecian blood: the end crownes all,
And that old common Arbitrator, Time,
Will one day end it.
Vlys. So to him we leaue it.
Most gentle, and most valiant *Hector*, welcome;
After the Generall, I beseech you next
To Feast with me, and see me at my Tent.
Achil. I shall forestall thee Lord *Vlysses*, thou:
Now *Hector* I haue fed mine eyes on thee,
I haue with exact view perus'd thee *Hector*,
And quoted ioynt by ioynt.
Hect. Is this *Achilles*?
Achil. I am *Achilles.*
Hect. Stand faire I prythee, let me looke on thee.
Achil. Behold thy fill.
Hect. Nay, I haue done already.
Achil. Thou art to breefe, I will the second time,
As I would buy thee, view thee, limbe by limbe.
Hect. O like a Booke of sport thou'lt reade me ore:
But there's more in me then thou vnderstand'st.
Why doest thou so oppresse me with thine eye?
Achil. Tell me you Heauens, in which part of his body
Shall I destroy him? Whether there, or there, or there,
That I may giue the locall wound a name,
And make distinct the very breach, where-out
Hectors great spirit flew. Answer me heauens.
Hect. It would discredit the blest Gods, proud man,
To answer such a question: Stand againe;
Think'st thou to catch my life so pleasantly,
As to prenominate in nice coniecture
Where thou wilt hit me dead?
Achil. I tell thee yea.
Hect. Wert thou the Oracle to tell me so,
I'ld not beleeue thee: henceforth guard thee well,
For Ile not kill thee there, nor there, nor there,
But by the forge that stythied Mars his helme,
Ile kill thee euery where, yea, ore and ore.
You wisest Grecians, pardon me this bragge,
His insolence drawes folly from my lips,
But Ile endeuour deeds to match these words,
Or may I neuer——
Aiax. Do not chafe thee Cosin:
And you *Achilles*, let these threats alone
Till accident, or purpose bring you too't.
You may euery day enough of *Hector*
If you haue stomacke. The generall state I feare,
Can scarse intreat you to be odde with him.
Hect. I pray you let vs see you in the field,
We haue had pelting Warres since you refus'd
The Grecians cause.
Achil. Dost thou intreat me *Hector*?
To morrow do I meete thee fell as death,
To night, all Friends.
Hect. Thy hand vpon that match.
Aga. First, all you Peeres of Greece go to my Tent,
There in the full conuiue you: Afterwards,
As *Hectors* leysure, and your bounties shall
Concurre together, seuerally intreat him.
Beate lowd the Taborins, let the Trumpets blow,
That this great Souldier may his welcome know. *Exeunt*
Troy. My Lord *Vlysses*, tell me I beseech you,
In what place of the Field doth *Calchas* keepe?
Vlys. At *Menelaus* Tent, most Princely *Troylus*,
There *Diomed* doth feast with him to night,
Who neither lookes on heauen, nor on earth,
But giues all gaze and bent of amorous view
On the faire *Cressid.*
Troy. Shall I (sweet Lord) be bound to thee so much,
After we part from *Agamemnons* Tent,
To bring me thither?
Vlys. You shall command me sir:
As gentle tell me, of what Honour was
This *Cressida* in Troy, had she no Louer there
That wailes her absence?
Troy. O sir, to such as boasting shew their scarres,
A mocke is due: will you walke on my Lord?
She was belou'd, she lou'd; she is, and dooth;
But still sweet Loue is food for Fortunes tooth. *Exeunt.*

Enter Achilles, and Patroclus.

Achil. Ile heat his blood with Greekish wine to night,
Which

Which with my Cemitar Ile coole to morrow:
Patroclus, let vs Feast him to the hight.

Pat. Heere comes *Thersites*. *Enter Thersites.*

Achil. How now, thou core of Enuy?
Thou crusty batch of Nature, what's the newes?

Ther. Why thou picture of what thou seem'st, & Idoll of Ideot-worshippers, here's a Letter for thee.

Achil. From whence, Fragment?

Ther. Why thou full dish of Foole, from Troy.

Pat. Who keepes the Tent now?

Ther. The Surgeons box, or the Patients wound.

Patr. Well said aduersity, and what need these tricks?

Ther. Prythee be silent boy, I profit not by thy talke, thou art thought to be *Achilles* male Varlot.

Patro. Male Varlot you Rogue? What's that?

Ther. Why his masculine Whore. Now the rotten diseases of the South, guts-griping Ruptures, Catarres, Loades a grauell i'th'backe, Lethargies, cold Palsies, and the like, take and take againe, such preposterous discoueries.

Pat. Why thou damnable box of enuy thou, what mean'st thou to curse thus?

Ther. Do I curse thee?

Patr. Why no, you ruinous But, you whorson indistinguishable Curre.

Ther. No? why art thou then exasperate, thou idle, immateriall skiene of Sleyd silke; thou greene Sarcenet flap for a sore eye, thou tassell of a Prodigals purse thou: Ah how the poore world is pestred with such water-flies, diminutiues of Nature.

Pat. Out gall.

Ther. Finch Egge.

Ach. My sweet *Patroclus*, I am thwarted quite
From my great purpose in to morrowes battell:
Heere is a Letter from Queene *Hecuba*,
A token from her daughter, my faire Loue,
Both taxing me, and gaging me to keepe
An Oath that I haue sworne. I will not breake it,
Fall Greekes, faile Fame, Honor or go, or stay,
My maior vow lyes heere; this Ile obay:
Come, come *Thersites*, helpe to trim my Tent,
This night in banquetting must all be spent.
Away *Patroclus*. *Exit.*

Ther. With too much bloud, and too little Brain, these two may run mad: but if with too much braine, and too little blood, they do, Ile be a curer of madmen. Heere's *Agamemnon*, an honest fellow enough, and one that loues Quailes, but he has not so much Braine as eare-wax; and the goodly transformation of Iupiter there his Brother, the Bull, the primatiue Statue, and oblique memoriall of Cuckolds, a thrifty shooing-horne in a chaine, hanging at his Brothers legge, to what forme but that he is, shold wit larded with malice, and malice forced with wit, turne him too: to an Asse were nothing; hee is both Asse and Oxe; to an Oxe were nothing, hee is both Oxe and Asse: to be a Dogge, a Mule, a Cat, a Fitchew, a Toade, a Lizard, an Owle, a Puttocke, or a Herring without a Roe, I would not care: but to be *Menelaus*, I would conspire against Destiny. Aske me not what I would be, if I were not *Thersites*: for I care not to bee the lowse of a Lazar, so I were not *Menelaus*. Hoy-day, spirits and fires.

Enter Hector, Aiax, Agamemnon, Vlysses, Nestor, Diomed, with Lights.

Aga. We go wrong, we go wrong.

Aiax. No yonder 'tis, there where we see the light.

Hect. I trouble you.

Aiax. No, not a whit.

Enter Achilles.

Vlys. Heere comes himselfe to guide you?

Achil. Welcome braue *Hector*, welcome Princes all.

Agam. So now faire Prince of Troy, I bid goodnight, *Aiax* commands the guard to tend on you.

Hect. Thanks, and goodnight to the Greeks general.

Men. Goodnight my Lord.

Hect. Goodnight sweet Lord *Menelaus*.

Ther. Sweet draught: sweet quoth-a? sweet sinke, sweet sure.

Achil. Goodnight and welcom, both at once, to those that go, or tarry.

Aga. Goodnight.

Achil. Old *Nestor* tarries, and you too *Diomed*,
Keepe *Hector* company an houre, or two.

Dio. I cannot Lord, I haue important businesse,
The tide whereof is now, goodnight great *Hector*.

Hect. Giue me your hand.

Vlys. Follow his Torch, he goes to *Chalcas* Tent,
Ile keepe you company.

Troy. Sweet sir, you honour me.

Hect. And so good night.

Achil. Come, come, enter my Tent. *Exeunt.*

Ther. That same *Diomed's* a false-hearted Rogue, a most vniust Knaue; I will no more trust him when hee leeres, then I will a Serpent when he hisses: he will spend his mouth & promise, like Brabler the Hound; but when he performes, Astronomers foretell it, that it is prodigious, there will come some change: the Sunne borrowes of the Moone when *Diomed* keepes his word. I will rather leaue to see *Hector*, then not to dogge him: they say, he keepes a Troyan Drab, and vses the Traitour *Chalcas* his Tent. Ile after——— Nothing but Letcherie? All incontinent Varlets. *Exeunt*

Enter Diomed.

Dio. What are you vp here ho? speake?

Chal. Who cals?

Dio. *Diomed, Chalcas* (I thinke) wher's you Daughter?

Chal. She comes to you.

Enter Troylus and Vlisses.

Vlis. Stand where the Torch may not discouer vs.

Enter Cressid.

Troy. *Cressid* comes forth to him.

Dio. How now my charge?

Cres. Now my sweet gardian: harke a word with you.

Troy. Yea, so familiar?

Vlis. She will sing any man at first sight.

Ther. And any man may finde her, if he can take her life: she's noted.

Dio. Will you remember?

Cal. Remember? yes.

Dio. Nay, but doe then; and let your minde be coupled with your words.

Troy. What should she remember?

Vlis. List?

Cres. Sweete hony Greek tempt me no more to folly.

Ther. Roguery.

Dio. Nay then.

Cres. Ile tell you what.

Dio. Fo, fo, come tell a pin, you are a forsworne.-----

Cres. In faith I cannot: what would you haue me do?

Ther. A iugling tricke, to be secretly open.

Dio. What did you sweare you would bestow on me?

Cres. I prethee do not hold me to mine oath,
Bid me doe not any thing but that sweete Greeke.

Dio. Good night.
Troy. Hold, patience.
Vlis. How now Troian ?
Cres. *Diomed.*
Dio. No, no, good night: Ile be your foole no more.
Troy. Thy better must.
Cres. Harke one word in your eare.
Troy. O plague and madnesse !
Vlis. You are moued Prince, let vs depart I pray you,
Lest your displeasure should enlarge it selfe
To wrathfull tearmes: this place is dangerous;
The time right deadly: I beseech you goe.
Troy. Behold, I pray you.
Vlis. Nay, good my Lord goe off:
You flow to great distraction: come my Lord?
Troy. I pray thee stay?
Vlis. You haue not patience, come.
Troy. I pray you stay? by hell and hell torments,
I will not speake a word.
Dio. And so good night.
Cres. Nay, but you part in anger.
Troy. Doth that grieue thee? O withered truth!
Vlis. Why, how now Lord?
Troy. By *Ioue* I will be patient.
Cres. Gardian? why Greeke?
Dio. Fo, fo, adew, you palter.
Cres. In faith I doe not: come hither once againe.
Vlis. You shake my Lord at something; will you goe?
you will breake out.
Troy. She stroakes his cheeke.
Vlis. Come, come.
Troy. Nay stay, by *Ioue* I will not speake a word.
There is betweene my will, and all offences,
A guard of patience; stay a little while.
Ther. How the diuell Luxury with his fat rumpe and potato finger, tickles these together: frye lechery, frye.
Dio. But will you then?
Cres. In faith I will lo; neuer trust me else.
Dio. Giue me some token for the surety of it.
Cres. Ile fetch you one. *Exit.*
Vlis. You haue sworne patience.
Troy. Feare me not sweete Lord.
I will not be my selfe, nor haue cognition
Of what I feele: I am all patience. *Enter Cressid.*
Ther. Now the pledge, now, now, now.
Cres. Here *Diomed*, keepe this Sleeue.
Troy. O beautie! where is thy Faith?
Vlis. My Lord.
Troy. I will be patient, outwardly I will.
Cres. You looke vpon that Sleeue? behold it well:
He lou'd me: O false wench: giue't me againe.
Dio. Whose was't?
Cres. It is no matter now I haue't againe.
I will not meete with you to morrow night:
I prythee *Diomed* visite me no more.
Ther. Now she sharpens: well said Whetstone.
Dio. I shall haue it.
Cres. What, this?
Dio. I that.
Cres. O all you gods! O prettie, prettie pledge;
Thy Maister now lies thinking in his bed
Of thee and me, and sighes, and takes my Gloue,
And giues memoriall daintie kisses to it;
As I kisse thee.
Dio. Nay, doe not snatch it from me.
Cres. He that takes that, takes my heart withall.
Dio. I had your heart before, this followes it.
Troy. I did sweare patience.
Cres. You shall not haue it *Diomed*; faith you shall not:
Ile giue you something else.
Dio. I will haue this: whose was it?
Cres. It is no matter.
Dio. Come tell me whose it was?
Cres. 'Twas one that lou'd me better then you will.
But now you haue it, take it.
Dio. Whose was it?
Cres. By all *Dianas* waiting women yond:
And by her selfe, I will not tell you whose.
Dio. To morrow will I weare it on my Helme,
And grieue his spirit that dares not challenge it.
Troy. Wert thou the diuell, and wor'st it on thy horne,
It should be challeng'd.
Cres. Well, well, 'tis done, 'tis past; and yet it is not:
I will not keepe my word.
Dio. Why then farewell,
Thou neuer shalt mocke *Diomed* againe.
Cres. You shall not goe: one cannot speake a word,
But it strait starts you.
Dio. I doe not like this fooling.
Ther. Nor I by *Pluto*: but that that likes not me, pleases me best.
Dio. What shall I come? the houre.
Cres. I, come: O *Ioue*! doe, come: I shall be plagu'd.
Dio. Farewell till then. *Exit.*
Cres. Good night: I prythee come:
Troylus farewell; one eye yet lookes on thee;
But with my heart, the other eye, doth see.
Ah poore our sexe; this fault in vs I finde:
The errour of our eye, directs our minde.
What errour leads, must erre; O then conclude,
Mindes sway'd by eyes, are full of turpitude. *Exit.*
Ther. A proofe of strength she could not publish more;
Vnlesse she say, my minde is now turn'd whore.
Vlis. Al's done my Lord.
Troy. It is.
Vlis. Why stay we then?
Troy. To make a recordation to my soule
Of euery syllable that here was spoke:
But if I tell how these two did coact;
Shall I not lye, in publishing a truth?
Sith yet there is a credence in my heart:
An esperance so obstinately strong,
That doth inuert that test of eyes and eares;
As if those organs had deceptious functions,
Created onely to calumniate.
Was *Cressed* here?
Vlis. I cannot coniure Troian.
Troy. She was not sure.
Vlis. Most sure she was.
Troy. Why my negation hath no taste of madnesse?
Vlis. Nor mine my Lord: *Cressid* was here but now.
Troy. Let it not be beleeu'd for womanhood:
Thinke we had mothers; doe not giue aduantage
To stubborne Criticks, apt without a theame
For deprauation, to square the generall sex
By *Cressids* rule. Rather thinke this not *Cressid*.
Vlis. What hath she done Prince, that can soyle our mothers?
Troy. Nothing at all, vnlesse that this were she.
Ther. Will he swagger himselfe out on's owne eyes?
Troy. This she? no, this is *Diomids Cressida*:
If beautie haue a soule, this is not she:

If ſoules guide vowes; if vowes are ſanctimonie;
If ſanctimonie be the gods delight:
If there be rule in vnitie it ſelfe,
This is not ſhe: O madneſſe of diſcourſe!
That cauſe ſets vp, with, and againſt thy ſelfe
By foule authoritie: where reaſon can reuolt
Without perdition, and loſſe aſſume all reaſon,
Without reuolt. This is, and is not *Creſſid*:
Within my ſoule, there doth conduce a fight
Of this ſtrange nature, that a thing inſeperate,
Diuides more wider then the skie and earth:
And yet the ſpacious bredth of this diuiſion,
Admits no Orifex for a point as ſubtle,
As *Ariachnes* broken woofe to enter:
Inſtance, O inſtance! ſtrong as *Plutoes* gates:
Creſſid is mine, tied with the bonds of heauen;
Inſtance O inſtance, ſtrong as heauen it ſelfe:
The bonds of heauen are ſlipt, diſſolu'd, and loos'd,
And with another knot fiue finger tied,
The fractions of her faith, orts of her loue:
The fragments, ſcraps, the bits, and greazie reliques,
Of her ore-eaten faith, are bound to *Diomed*

Vliſ. May worthy *Troylus* be halfe attached
With that which here his paſſion doth expreſſe?

Troy. I Greeke: and that ſhall be divulged well
In Characters, as red as *Mars* his heart
Inflam'd with *Venus*: neuer did yong man fancy
With ſo eternall, and ſo fixt a ſoule.
Harke Greek: as much I doe *Creſſid*: loue,
So much by weight, hate I her *Diomed*,
That Sleeue is mine, that heele beare in his Helme:
Were it a Caske compos'd by *Vulcans* skill,
My Sword ſhould bite it: Not the dreadfull ſpout,
Which Shipmen doe the Hurricano call,
Conſtring'd in maſſe by the almighty Fenne,
Shall dizzie with more clamour Neptunes eare
In his diſcent; then ſhall my prompted ſword,
Falling on *Diomed*.

Ther. Heele tickle it for his concupie.

Troy. O *Creſſid*! O falſe *Creſſid*! falſe, falſe, falſe:
Let all vntruths ſtand by thy ſtained name,
And theyle ſeeme glorious.

Vliſ. O containe your ſelfe:
Your paſſion drawes eares hither.

Enter Æneas.

Æne. I haue beene ſeeking you this houre my Lord:
Hector by this is arming him in Troy.
Aiax your Guard, ſtaies to conduct you home.

Troy. Haue with you Prince: my curteous Lord adew:
Farewell reuolted faire: and *Diomed*,
Stand faſt and weare a Caſtle on thy head.

Vli. Ile bring you to the Gates.

Troy. Accept diſtracted thankes.

Exeunt Troylus Æneas, and Vliſſes.

Ther. Would I could meete that roague *Diomed*, I would croke like a Rauen: I would bode, I would bode: *Patroclus* will giue me any thing for the intelligence of his whore: The Parrot will not doe more for an Almond, then he for a commodious drab: Lechery, lechery, ſtill warres and lechery, nothing elſe holds faſhion. A burning diuell take them.

Enter Hector and Andromache.

And. When was my Lord ſo much vngently temper'd,
To ſtop his eares againſt admoniſhment?
Vnarme, vnarme, and doe not fight to day.

Hect. You traine me to offend you: get you gone.
By the euerlaſting gods, Ile goe.

And. My dreames will ſure proue ominous to the day.

Hect. No more I ſay. *Enter Caſſandra.*

Caſſa. Where is my brother *Hector*?

And Here ſiſter, arm'd, and bloudy in intent:
Conſort with me in loud and deere petition:
purſue we him on knees: for I haue dreampt
Of bloudy turbulence; and this whole night
Hath nothing beene but ſhapes, and formes of ſlaughter.

Caſſ. O, 'tis true.

Hect. Ho? bid my Trumpet ſound.

Caſſ. No notes of ſallie, for the heauens, ſweet brother.

Hect. Begon I ſay: the gods haue heard me ſweare.

Caſſ. The gods are deaſe to hot and peeuiſh vowes;
They are polluted offrings, more abhord
Then ſpotted Liuers in the ſacrifice.

And. O be perſwaded, doe not count it holy,
To hurt by being iuſt; it is as lawfull:
For we would count giue much to as violent thefts,
And rob in the behalfe of charitie.

Caſſ. It is the purpoſe that makes ſtrong the vowe;
But vowes to euery purpoſe muſt not hold:
Vnarme ſweete *Hector*.

Hect. Hold you ſtill I ſay;
Mine honour keepes the weather of my fate:
Life euery man holds deere, but the deere man
Holds honor farre more precious, deere, then life.

Enter Troylus.

How now yong man? mean'ſt thou to fight to day?

And. *Caſſandra*, call my father to perſwade.

Exit Caſſandra.

Hect. No faith yong *Troylus*; doffe thy harneſſe youth:
I am to day ith'vaine of Chiualrie:
Let grow thy Sinews till their knots be ſtrong;
And tempt not yet the bruſhes of the warre.
Vnarme thee, goe; and doubt thou not braue boy,
Ile ſtand to day, for thee, and me, and Troy.

Troy. Brother, you haue a vice of mercy in you;
Which better fits a Lyon then a man.

Hect. What vice is that? good *Troylus* chide me for it.

Troy. When many times the captiue Grecian fals,
Euen in the fanne and winde of your faire Sword:
You bid them riſe, and liue.

Hect. O 'tis faire play.

Troy. Fooles play, by heauen *Hector*.

Hect. How now? how now?

Troy. For th'loue of all the gods
Let's leaue the Hermit Pitty with our Mothers;
And when we haue our Armors buckled on,
The venom'd vengeance ride vpon our ſwords,
Spur them to ruthfull worke, reine them from ruth.

Hect. Fie ſauage, fie.

Troy. *Hector*, then 'tis warres.

Hect. *Troylus*, I would not haue you fight to day.

Troy. Who ſhould with-hold me?
Not fate, obedience, nor the hand of *Mars*,
Beckning with fierie trunchion my retire;
Not *Priamus*, and *Hecuba* on knees;
Their eyes ore-galled with recourſe of teares;
Nor you my brother, with your true ſword drawne
Oppoſ'd to hinder me, ſhould ſtop my way:
But by my ruine.

Enter Priam and Caſſandra.

Caſſ. Lay hold vpon him *Priam*, hold him faſt:
He is thy crutch; now if thou looſe thy ſtay,
Thou on him leaning, and all Troy on thee,

Fall

Fall all together.
Priam. Come *Hector*, come, goe backe:
Thy wife hath dreampt: thy mother hath had visions;
Cassandra doth foresee; and I my selfe,
Am like a Prophet suddenly enrapt,
to tell thee that this day is ominous:
Therefore come backe.
Hect *Æneas* is a field,
And I do stand engag'd to many Greekes,
Euen in the faith of valour, to appeare
This morning to them.
Priam. I, but thou shalt not goe,
Hect. I must not breake my faith:
You know me dutifull, therefore deare sir,
Let me not shame respect; but giue me leaue
To take that course by your consent and voice,
Which you doe here forbid me, Royall *Priam.*
Cass. O *Priam*, yeelde not to him.
And. Doe not deere father.
Hect. *Andromache* I am offended with you:
Vpon the loue you beare me, get you in.
Exit Andromache.
Troy. This foolish, dreaming, superstitious girle,
Makes all these bodements.
Cass. O farewell, deere *Hector*:
Looke how thou diest; looke how thy eye turnes pale:
Looke how thy wounds doth bleede at many vents:
Harke how Troy roares; how *Hecuba* cries out;
How poore *Andromache* shrils her dolour forth;
Behold distraction, frenzie, and amazement,
Like witlesse Antickes one another meete,
And all cry *Hector*, *Hectors* dead: O *Hector*!
Troy. Away, away.
Cas. Farewell: yes, soft: *Hector* I take my leaue;
Thou do'st thy selfe, and all our Troy deceiue. *Exit.*
Hect. You are amaz'd, my Liege, at her exclaime:
Goe in and cheere the Towne, weele forth and fight:
Doe deedes of praise, and tell you them at night.
Priam. Farewell: the gods with safetie stand about thee. *Alarum.*
Troy. They are at it, harke: proud *Diomed*, beleeue
I come to loose my arme, or winne my sleeue.

Enter Pandar.

Pand. Doe you heare my Lord? do you heare?
Troy. What now?
Pand. Here's a Letter come from yond poore girle.
Troy. Let me reade.
Pand. A whorson tisicke, a whorson rascally tisicke, so troubles me; and the foolish fortune of this girle, and what one thing, what another, that I shall leaue you one o'th's dayes: and I haue a rheume in mine eyes too; and such an ache in my bones; that vnlesse a man were curst, I cannot tell what to thinke on't. What sayes shee there?
Troy. Words, words, meere words, no matter from the heart;
Th'effect doth operate another way.
Goe winde to winde, there turne and change together:
My loue with words and errors still she feedes;
But edifies another with her deedes.
Pand. Why, but heare you?
Troy. Hence brother lackie; ignomie and shame
Pursue thy life, and liue aye with thy name.
A Larum. *Exeunt.*

Enter Thersites in excursion.

Ther. Now they are clapper-clawing one another, Ile goe looke on: that dissembling abhominable varlet *Diomede*, has got that same scuruie, doting, foolish yong knaues Sleeue of Troy, there in his Helme: I would faine see them meet; that, that same yong Troian asse, that loues the whore there, might send that Greekish whore-maisterly villaine, with the Sleeue, backe to the dissembling luxurious drabbe, of a sleeuelesse errant. O'th' tother side, the pollicie of those craftie swearing rascals; that stole old Mouse-eaten dry cheese, *Nestor*: and that same dog-foxe *Vlisses*' is not prou'd worth a Black-berry. They set me vp in pollicy, that mungrill curre *Aiax*, against that dogge of as bad a kinde, *Achilles.* And now is the curre *Aiax* prouder then the curre *Achilles*, and will not arme to day. Whereupon, the Grecians began to proclaime barbarisme; and pollicie growes into an ill opinion.
Enter Diomed and Troylus.
Soft, here comes Sleeue, and th'other.
Troy. Flye not: for should'st thou take the Riuer Stix,
I would swim after.
Diom. Thou do'st miscall retire:
I doe not flye; but aduantagious care
Withdrew me from the oddes of multitude:
Haue at thee?
Ther. Hold thy whore Grecian: now for thy whore Troian: Now the Sleeue, now the Sleeue.
Enter Hector.
Hect. What art thou Greek? art thou for *Hectors* match?
Art thou of bloud, and honour?
Ther. No, no: I am a rascall: a scuruie railing knaue: a very filthy roague.
Hect. I doe beleeue thee, liue.
Ther. God a mercy, that thou wilt beleeue me; but a plague breake thy necke---for frighting me: what's become of the wenching rogues? I thinke they haue swallowed one another. I would laugh at that miracle---yet in a sort, lecherie eates it selfe: Ile seeke them. *Exit.*
Enter Diomed and Seruants.
Dio. Goe, goe, my seruant, take thou *Troylus* Horse;
Present the faire Steede to my Lady *Cressid*:
Fellow, commend my seruice to her beauty;
Tell her, I haue chastis'd the amorous Troyan.
And am her Knight by proofe.
Ser. I goe my Lord. *Enter Agamemnon.*
Aga. Renew, renew, the fierce *Polidamus*
Hath beate downe *Menon*: bastard *Margarelon*
Hath *Doreus* prisoner.
And stands Colossus-wise wauing his beame,
Vpon the pashed courses of the Kings:
Epistropus and *Cedus*, *Polixines* is slaine;
Amphimacus, and *Thoas* deadly hurt;
Patroclus tane or slaine, and *Palamedes*
Sore hurt and bruised; the dreadfull Sagittary
Appauls our numbers, haste we *Diomed*
To re-enforcement, or we perish all.
Enter Nestor.
Nest. Coe beare *Patroclus* body to *Achilles*,
And bid the snaile-pac'd *Aiax* arme for shame;
There is a thousand *Hectors* in the field:
Now here he fights on *Galathe* his Horse,
And there lacks worke: anon he's there a foote,
And there they flye or dye, like scaled sculs,

Before the belching Whale; then is he yonder,
And there the straying Greekes, ripe for his edge,
Fall downe before him, like the mowers swath;
Here,there, and euery where,he leaues and takes;
Dexteritie so obaying appetite,
That what he will,he does,and does so much,
That proofe is call'd impossibility.

Enter Vlisses.

Ulis. Oh, courage,courage Princes: great *Achilles*
Is arming, weeping,cursing,vowing vengeance;
Patroclus wounds haue rouz'd his drowzie bloud,
Together with his mangled *Myrmidons*,
That noselesse,handlesse,hackt and chipt,come to him;
Crying on *Hector*. *Aiax* hath lost a friend,
And foames at mouth,and he is arm'd,and at it:
Roaring for *Troylus*; who hath done to day,
Mad and fantasticke execution;
Engaging and redeeming of himselfe,
With such a carelesse force,and forcelesse care,
As if that luck in very spight of cunning,bad him win all.

Enter Aiax.

Aia. *Troylus*,thou coward *Troylus*. *Exit.*

Dio. I,there,there.

Nest. So,so,we draw together. *Exit.*

Enter Achilles.

Achil. Where is this *Hector*?
Come,come,thou boy-queller,shew thy face:
Know what it is to meete *Achilles* angry.
Hector,wher's *Hector*? I will none but *Hector*. *Exit.*

Enter Aiax.

Aia. *Troylus*,thou coward *Troylus*,shew thy head.

Enter Diomed.

Diom. *Troylus*, I say, wher's *Troylus*?

Aia. What would'st thou?

Diom. I would correct him.

Aia. Were I the Generall,
Thou should'st haue my office,
Ere that correction: *Troylus* I say, what *Troylus*?

Enter Troylus.

Troy. Oh traitour *Diomed*!
Turne thy false face thou traytor,
And pay thy life thou owest me for my horse.

Dio. Ha,art thou there?

Aia. Ile fight with him alone,stand *Diomed*.

Dio. He is my prize, I will not looke vpon.

Troy. Come both you coging Greekes, haue at you both. *Exit Troylus.*

Enter Hector.

Hect. Yea *Troylus*? O well fought my yongest Brother.

Enter Achilles.

Achil. Now doe I see thee; haue at thee *Hector*.

Hect. Pause if thou wilt.

Achil. I doe disdaine thy curtesie,proud Troian;
Be happy that my armes are out of vse:
My rest and negligence befriends thee now,
But thou anon shalt heare of me againe:
Till when,goe seeke thy fortune. *Exit.*

Hect. Fare thee well:
I would haue beene much more a fresher man,
Had I expected thee: how now my Brother?

Enter Troylus.

Troy. *Aiax* hath tane *Æneas*; shall it be?
No,by the flame of yonder glorious heauen,
He shall not carry him: Ile be tane too,
Or bring him off: Fate heare me what I say;
I wreake not, though thou end my life to day. *Exit.*

Enter one in Armour.

Hect. Stand,stand,thou Greeke,
Thou art a goodly marke:
No? wilt thou not? I like thy armour well,
Ile frush it, and vnlocke the riuets all,
But Ile be maister of it: wilt thou not beast abide?
Why then flye on, Ile hunt thee for thy hide. *Exit.*

Enter Achilles with Myrmidons.

Achil. Come here about me you my *Myrmidons*:
Marke what I say; attend me where I wheele:
Strike not a stroake, but keepe your selues in breath;
And when I haue the bloudy *Hector* found,
Empale him with your weapons round about:
In fellest manner execute your arme.
Follow me sirs, and my proceedings eye;
It is decreed, *Hector* the great must dye. *Exit.*

Enter Thersites, Menelaus, and Paris.

Ther. The Cuckold and the Cuckold maker are at it: now bull, now dogge, lowe; *Paris* lowe; now my double hen'd sparrow; lowe *Paris*, lowe; the bull has the game: ware hornes ho?

Exit Paris and Menelaus.

Enter Bastard.

Bast. Turne slaue and fight.

Ther. What art thou?

Bast. A Bastard Sonne of *Priams*.

Ther. I am a Bastnrd too, I loue Bastards, I am a Bastard begot, Bastard instructed, Bastard in minde, Bastard in valour, in euery thing illegitimate: one Beare will not bite another, and wherefore should one Bastard? take heede, the quarrel's most ominous to vs: if the Sonne of a whore fight for a whore, he tempts iudgement: farewell Bastard.

Bast. The diuell take thee coward. *Exeunt.*

Enter Hector.

Hect. Most putrified core so faire without:
Thy goodly armour thus hath cost thy life.
Now is my daies worke done; Ile take good breath:
Rest Sword, thou hast thy fill of bloud and death.

Enter Achilles and his Myrmidons.

Achil. Looke *Hector* how the Sunne begins to set;
How vgly night comes breathing at his heeles,
Euen with the vaile and darking of the Sunne.
To close the day vp, *Hectors* life is done.

Hect. I am vnarm'd, forgoe this vantage Greeke.

Achil. Strike fellowes, strike, this is the man I seeke.
So Illion fall thou: now Troy sinke downe;
Here lyes thy heart, thy sinewes, and thy bone.
On *Myrmidons*, cry you all a maine,
Achilles hath the mighty *Hector* slaine. *Retreat.*
Harke, a retreat vpon our Grecian part.

Gree. The Troian Trumpets sounds the like my Lord.

Achi. The dragon wing of night ore-spreds the earth
And stickler-like the Armies seperates
My halfe supt Sword, that frankly would haue fed,
Pleas'd with this dainty bed; thus goes to bed.
Come, tye his body to my horses tayle;
Along the field, I will the Troian traile. *Exeunt.*

Sound Retreat. *Shout.*

Enter Agamemnon, Aiax, Menelaus, Nestor, Diomed, and the rest marching.

Aga. Harke, harke, what shout is that?

Nest. Peace Drums.

Sol. Achil

Sold. *Achilles, Achilles, Hector's* slaine, *Achilles.*
Dio. The bruite is, *Hector's* slaine, and by *Achilles.*
Aia. If it be so, yet braglesse let it be:
Great *Hector* was a man as good as he.
Agam. March patiently along; let one be sent
To pray *Achilles* see vs at our Tent.
If in his death the gods haue vs befrended,
Great Troy is ours, and our sharpe wars are ended.
Exeunt.

Enter Æneas, Paris, Anthenor and Deiphœbus.

Æne. Stand hoe, yet are we maisters of the field,
Neuer goe home; here starue we out the night.

Enter Troylus.

Troy. *Hector* is slaine.
All. *Hector*? the gods forbid.
Troy. Hee's dead: and at the murtherers Horses taile,
In beastly sort, drag'd through the shamefull Field:
Frowne on you heauens, effect your rage with speede:
Sit gods vpon your throanes, and smile at Troy
I say at once, let your briefe plagues be mercy,
And linger not our sure destructions on.
Æne. My Lord, you doe discomfort all the Hoste.
Troy. You vnderstand me not, that tell me so:
I doe not speake of flight, of feare, of death,
But dare all imminence that gods and men,
Addresse their dangers in. *Hector* is gone:
Who shall tell *Priam* so? or *Hecuba*?
Let him that will a screechoule aye be call'd,
Goe in to Troy, and say there, *Hector's* dead:
There is a word will *Priam* turne to stone;
Make wels, and *Niobes* of the maides and wiues;
Coole statues of the youth: and in a word,
Scarre Troy out of it selfe. But march away,
Hector is dead: there is no more to say.
Stay yet: you vile abhominable Tents,
Thus proudly pight vpon our Phrygian plaines:
Let Titan rise as early as he dare,
Ile through, and through you; & thou great siz'd coward:
No space of Earth shall sunder our two hates,
Ile haunt thee, like a wicked conscience still,
That mouldeth goblins swift as frensies thoughts.
Strike a free march to Troy, with comfort goe:
Hope of reuenge, shall hide our inward woe.

Enter Pandarus.

Pand. But heare you? heare you?
Troy. Hence broker, lackie, ignomy, and shame
Pursue thy life, and liue aye with thy name. *Exeunt.*

Pan. A goodly medcine for mine akingbones: oh world, world, world! thus is the poore agent dispisde: Oh traitours and bawdes; how earnestly are you set aworke, and how ill requited? why should our indeuour be so desir'd, and the performance so loath'd? What Verse for it? what instance for it? let me see.

Full merrily the humble Bee doth sing,
Till he hath lost his hony, and his sting.
And being once subdu'd in armed taile,
Sweete hony, and sweete notes together faile.
Good traders in the flesh, set this in your painted cloathes;
As many as be here of Panders hall,
Your eyes halfe out, weepe out at *Pandar's* fall:
Or if you cannot weepe, yet giue some groness;
Though not for me, yet for your akingbones:
Brethren and sisters of the hold-dore trade,
Some two months hence, my will shall here be made:
It should be now, but that my feare is this:
Some galled Goose of Winchester would hisse:
Till then, Ile sweate, and seeke about for eases;
And at that time bequeath you my diseases. *Exeunt.*

¶ ¶ ¶

FINIS.

http://stores.lulu.com/velvetelementbooks

www.ingramcontent.com/pod-product-compliance
Lightning Source LLC
LaVergne TN
LVHW061237100826
845148LV00008B/974

* 9 7 8 0 5 5 7 0 1 1 6 4 3 *